THE BABYLON PROJECT
Rise of Kronos

by Kate and Elise Fry

ISBN: 9798754980716
Imprint: Independently published

Cover design: Kate & Elise Fry

For Chris, who said to write it. For Erika, who asked to read it. And for my sister, who got on the rollercoaster as soon as I asked, without question, and went along for the ride. Surround yourself with people who help make your dreams come true.

~ Elise ~

To G - for being my soulmate. You may or may not have inspired parts of this book. And to my sister - for inviting me along on this fun and crazy ride. We're doing it!

~ Kate ~

Special thanks to our incredibly supportive and outstanding team - Colleen, Patti, Maria, Katie, and Kirsty. Your encouragement and enthusiasm have been unparalleled. We're so lucky to have you.

~ E. and K.~

CONTENTS

PREFACE

The darkest deeds often happen in plain sight;
the harshest truths sound like lies.

In the 1950s the US began highly controversial programs, developed by the CIA's Office of Scientific Intelligence, which looked into enhanced interrogation techniques, including hypnotism, forced morphine addiction, and LSD-induced amnesia. The goal was to see if a person could be *involuntarily* made to perform radical acts, such as assassination, against their fundamental personal desires, such as self preservation.

Bolstered by what they saw as early success, the USA moved on to the infamous Project MKUltra. The CIA began observing US citizens who had been dosed with biological and chemical agents, including LSD/Acid. Their goal was to study the effects of psychopharmacology on psychic functions. Drugs were used in interrogations to try to force confessions, weaken prisoners, and build a dependable means of mind control. *Unwilling and unconsenting* test subjects initially included mental patients, drug addicts, prisoners, and sex workers, but as the program grew, their experiments expanded to include military personnel, doctors, and government employees, many *completely* unaware of their participation.

The chemist who ran MKUltra had an ultimate goal of using any developed drugs in covert operations, giving them to high-ranking government officials in order to affect the course of major government decisions. As the tests expanded, adverse reactions to the dosing grew. Many subjects ended with long-term debilitation, and there were *multiple* deaths. Even so, the project continued to grow, and the government pushed their search for psychopharmaceuticals to Canada. The Montreal Experiments were mirrored in England by the British Intelligence Service, who also experimented on *unconsenting* patients.

They expanded their search in the 1970's with the Stargate Project, the new umbrella name for US investigations into the paranormal. Trying to counter the USSR's foray into mind control (and based partially off Nazi research, where Nazis studied the human psyche under extreme circumstances) the USA entered a Psychic arms race against the KGB. With reports of the enemy stopping animals' hearts using psychokinesis, the US government wanted to move quickly to develop their own psychic war room. A secret US Army unit was formed to work with the Stanford Research Institute, who had developed specific testing and criteria for remote viewing. The United States government was heavily invested in the Psychic Sciences, intent on winning the mental battleground.

And then, a sudden and unexpected turn.

The Stargate program died a very public death. Ostensibly dismantled in 1995, its demise seemingly ended the Government's involvement with the psychic world. All results were discredited; participants, willing or unwilling, were quietly paid off; and a subtle, but widespread, campaign against psychic potential for intelligence was waged by the US government. Never mind that as recently as February 2014 the Office of Naval Research held a conference for experts in neural, cognitive, and behavioral sciences to investigate sailors' "spidey sense". The US government's position was against any suggestion of psychic abilities. Publically, at least.

Privately, well, don't all the best secrets exist in the shadows?

TRIPPING IN THE NAME OF SCIENCE

Tuesday, 11 September – Maela

"... dizziness, slurred speech, shortness of breath, hives, swollen eyelids, chest pains, vomiting, and convulsions. So, if you'd just like to sign the release form here, Ms. Driscoll."

I look down at the clipboard and the list of possible side effects. Do I really want to chance blue lips and blurred vision, or, worse, bloody urine? I sigh. Yes? I mean: I do, I do. This new drug could help millions of people, and I, a young, healthy woman, am the perfect test subject. Sure, the doctors have to cover their backs, but the risks are minimal, right? And £200 is £200... Lattes add up. I scan the terms and conditions: agree not to hold the company liable... information may be shared with the relevant regulatory agencies... Yeah, yeah. I sign the form.

"Excellent." The nurse bustles over to the counter and comes back with an inhaler. The room, like all hospital rooms, is small, greyish white, and sterile. I feel a bit like a lab rat, but I guess they have better things to spend their money on than interior design. "So, all you need to do is to exhale fully, place the inhaler in your mouth, and take a deep breath while pressing down on the canister. We should start to see the effects in a few minutes, and I'll need you to make a note of them on the chart. They'll last about an hour, so make yourself comfortable."

I nod and take the inhaler. Exhale. Inhale. Easy. I hand it back and wait.

Five minutes later I feel it: a slow, dreamy goodness

spreading out from my core, like warm honey. My shoulders drop, a tension I hadn't even registered departing. Oh my.

"How're you feeling?" the nurse asks. "OK?"

I blink up at her and grin.

She smiles back and says, "Good. So, just note down the effects as they occur, and I'll be back in an hour to take stock."

I look down at the chart. Muscle relaxation? Tick. Lessening of anxiety? Tick, tick. Euphoria? Tick, tick, tick! Giddiness? Guess so.

I look around the room. There's a stack of magazines in one corner, but I'm feeling too doped to move, so I just stay perched on the examination table, swinging my legs. I haven't felt this good in ages. Who cared if I was stuck in a rut? I didn't apply for the fellowship just to *work*. Sheesh! It's supposed to be a cultural experience too, and discovering all the delights London had to offer was equally important to my... to my mental and spiritual development. I've wanted to live in England ever since reading *A Little Princess*, aged twelve, with a flashlight under the covers in my princess bed in San Francisco. And watching *Jeeves and Wooster*, *Fawlty Towers*, and *Monty Python* was my way to relax in college. In the words of John Lee Hooker: *I love the way you talk, do-dee-do-dee-do-dee-do. I likes the way you walk. Hm-hm-hm-hm-hm. An' talk that talk. La-la-la-la.* The university would understand that brilliance can't be rushed. These things take time. *This is the tiiime to remember*, I croon. Oh Billy, you're so right. *These are the daaaays to hold on to.* Holy heck I have a nice voice.

And who cared if I hadn't had sex in almost a year? Yes, I was upset when Josh Chambers decided, four dates in, to get back together with his old girlfriend. Yes, I swore off men, but I soon came to realize that that was an overreaction. There just didn't seem to be much point in dating once I'd put in the application for the fellowship. And, yes, the men

in the department are a sad crop of earnest, weedy speci-
mens, but London is a big place. There are a lot of men out
there. And I am a great, great, great person. I nod thoughtfully to myself. Great. I am smart and hard-working and
conscientious; and I love animals. I even rescue spiders
from the bathtub. Any guy would be lucky to have me.

I nibble my bottom lip and look up at the ceiling, at the
pretty, crinkly fiberglass tiles. I feel so... detached. Oh, wait.
I need to note that down. I grab the clipboard, but the letters swim before my eyes. Huh. Not to worry: I will express
myself through the medium of *art* and *draw* what I feel. A
picture is worth a thousand words anyway, so the doctors
will find it much more useful. I pick up the pen and push
it around the paper, up and down and round and round and
up and down. Finishing, I cock my head. Yes, somehow, I
have managed to capture the *essence* of floating. I lie down.

A snippet of conversation drifts in. "Now remember, Mr.
Carruthers, unwrap the suppository before inserting it, narrow end first." A murmur and "Yes, morning and evening."
I giggle and roll my head towards the door. Careless of the
nurse to leave it open. Nope, it's closed. The walls here must
be super thin. Huh.

Some time later, the door opens, and the nurse comes
back into the room. I turn my head and beam at her. She
looks at my doodles. "Hmm. You seem to be more suscep-
tible to the drug than most. We'd better give you a little
more time." I wave my hand, just like the queen, I think.

"I'll do some work on the computer here and keep an eye
on you." I yawn. OK.

Several more minutes pass, and I gradually become aware
of how uncomfortable the table is. Why am I lying on
it? First-year postdoctoral fellows at Queen's College London do not loll about in hospital rooms watching their toes
wiggle. Rapidly becoming embarrassed, I sit up, trying to
straighten out my clothes.

"Feeling better?"

My cheeks blaze. "Yes, thanks. Boy, that's strong stuff," I titter.

The nurse looks at me reassuringly, her eyes warm. "Everyone reacts differently. That's why these trials are so important, so we can calibrate the dose and make the drug safe for home use. At the moment, patients suffering from bipolar disorder, severe depression, and PTSD have to come to hospital for intravenous or intramuscular injections. We really are grateful to everyone who volunteers. Believe me, you're making a difference."

I smile weakly.

"Any palpitations? Muscle pain? Headache? No? Well, let's just check your blood pressure." I hold out my arm obediently.

"That looks fine. Now, you shouldn't experience any more unusual effects, but some people have reported feeling tired for up to twelve hours, so take the rest of the day off and don't drive or operate heavy machinery." In London? No worries there.

I put on my shoes, pick up my shoulder bag, thank the nurse, and scuttle out the door, anxious to exit stage left. Stepping out into the autumn sunshine, I groan. As per usual, I have made a complete and utter prat out of myself.

The clock on Christ Church tower chimes two as I make my way past Old Spitalfields Market. A lively and inviting place during the day, packed with stalls selling vintage and artisanal goods, at this time of night the area is weirdly foreboding. It's strange to see the streets emptied of life, and I shiver in the light breeze as a take-away cup, dropped by some careless shopper, rolls by. But what on earth am I doing here, halfway across London from my cosy little flat in Fitzrovia? I hadn't had one pint too many at the Ten Bells earlier, had I? God knows I enjoy a drink, and I certainly like the pub, with its colourful Victorian tiling and ghoulish associations (yes, I did the Jack the Ripper tour); but, I'd had a night in, hadn't I? I frown, then start as I hear voices up ahead. I look up to see two men, in the midst of what appears to be a heated argument.

"... not buying it. Perhaps you didn't understand – we supply the drugs, you sell them, and you give us the money. All of the money. Then I give you your cut. That's the way it works."

"You'll get the rest, I swear. I just need a few more days!"

The first man, not tall but solidly built, with a shaved head, gold earring, and intricate tattoo spiraling up his neck, shakes his head. "That's not the point, Benny boy. We wouldn't want other dealers to think they could do the same thing, would we? I don't do credit. There isn't an extended drugs payment plan," he sneers, sounding horribly amused.

The second man, looking scrawny and somewhat pathetic in a pale, oversized tracksuit, trembles. He has a wispy goatee, bulbous eyes, and the strung-out look of a habitual user. "Ratko, please. I had a few bills, that's all. But I'm good for the rest, I swear!"

Ratko smiles, almost gently. Then a knife flashes; and Benny gasps, whimpers, and slowly drops to his knees, hands reaching blindly for the wound. Ratko pats him on the cheek. "'The man who passes the sentence should swing the sword.' I like this. You English are so colorful."

American, I think, wildly and inappropriately. *George R.R. Martin is American. Oh God. Oh God. I have to get away and call the police. Yes, the police.*

I start to back away, and Ratko turns towards me. I freeze, my heart hammering in my chest, so hard it hurts. I feel tears welling up in my eyes, glancing at Benny's crumpled form, then back at Ratko. He has a harsh, saturnine face; thin, slashing eyebrows; a long, drooping moustache over full lips; and dead eyes. I've never seen such cold eyes, as if the person before me had been born without a conscience and didn't mind the lack. He looks at me consideringly.

My phone! Where is my phone? I fumble, searching, and then the world begins to fade. *No! No! I can't faint, not now!* But the grey fog rolls inexorably in, and I slip away into nothingness.

I come to slowly, mewling. Benny. Ratko. Ratko! I don't want to open my eyes, please no, but... my bedroom walls! I turn my head. My dresser, my beautiful plastic dresser, overflowing with books, and the little bedside clock showing 2:15am. A dream. Oh, thank Christ, it was just a dream. I sit up, shaking and tucking the duvet around me for comfort, and turn on the lamp. The warm light spills over the bed and onto the red and blue woven rug I picked up for a song in Camden Town, onto the unused exercise ball doubling as a clothes horse, and the dream catcher hanging in the corner. I huff. Clearly, it's full and needs to be emptied. I lie back down onto the pillows. "No more unusual side effects," I murmur. "Hah, bloody, hah!" My first lucid dream, and wouldn't you know, I conjured up a murder. Not ponies, or kittens, or the clichéd eating chocolate truffles while Mr. Tall, Dark, and Handsome rubs my feet. Oh no, not me! I had to think up something nice and gory, in glorious technicolor. I think back over the dream, every detail still etched in my mind: the deserted street, the fight, the – I gulp – knife, and Ratko, smiling down at a dying man. Ratko! Why had he looked so familiar? I frown. Had I met him before? He didn't seem the type to hang out at the library. Maybe at the hospital? And then my brow clears. Of course! He was the man I'd bumped into at the coffee shop, where I'd gone for a restorative macchiato after smacking myself up in the name of science. I'd still been a little, err, unsteady on my feet, and he'd been speaking on his mobile phone. He'd almost dropped his coffee, and I'd been a bit nervous, catching sight of his unusual tattoo: a snarling dragon, curling round his neck and rearing onto the back of his head. I remember thinking how much it must have hurt to get it done. But he'd been perfectly polite, and we'd exchanged apologies and each gone on our way.

I tutt to myself. *Prejudiced much, Maela? The poor man has a tattoo, so ten hours later he's starring in a drug deal gone wrong? Sheesh!*

I reach over to turn off the light, then burrow back under the duvet. *Back to sleep. And no more trips to cray cray town.*

The maddening bleep of the alarm comes far too soon. I've slept fitfully after my nocturnal foray and am not yet ready to face the day. Shuffling into my slippers, I head like a homing pigeon for the tiny kitchen. "Coffee. Must have coffee." I turn on the T.V., just to have a bit of noise, and then the kettle, reaching for the Sumatran grounds in the cupboard. Today is definitely not a day for my usual instant.

The newsreader's bubbly voice informs me that politician A had said that politician B was a right twat, and that politician B had retorted that politician A was a complete arse, blah blah blah. I take a deep sip of the elixir of life. Ahh, coffee: "pure as an angel, sweet as love." Neurons begin to fire, and I think I might manage a spot of toast. I open the fridge: raspberry jam or marmalade? Hmm.

"... police are searching for the next of kin. This marks the twentieth stabbing in London this year."

I shake my head. What was with people today? No wonder I was having violent dreams. The toast pops up, and I flick it onto a plate, trying not to burn my fingers, then slather the slices thickly with butter and coarse-cut marmalade. I take a big bite and hum contentedly. Really, is anything better than butter and sugar when you're flagging?

Quickly making short work of the toast, I gulp down the last of the coffee and pile the dishes in the sink, to be dealt with later, then head for the bathroom to shower and brush my teeth. Outside the door, I shuffle back out of my slippers and pull off my white sateen pajamas, dropping them on the floor, before stepping into the cubicle and pulling on the light cord.

The mirror over the sink shows the full horrors the night has wrought. My skin, usually a pale but healthy white, looks drained and sickly, making the freckles scattered liberally across my nose and cheeks stand out in stark relief. I tilt my head: under the fluorescent bulb and at the right angle, I could swear my skin looks a sallow green. Beneath my eyes there are deep, dark circles that no amount of concealer is going to disguise, and my normally bright blue eyes are bleary. Even my copper-red hair looks dull. I grimace. Lack of sleep does not a pretty Maela make.

The hot water helps, but I'm fighting a losing cause, so, after throwing on jeans, a white, button-down shirt, and ankle boots, I simply gather up my hair into a ponytail and slip zirconium studs into my ears. Make-up would simply draw attention to my haggard state. But that's OK, because I am going to work, and I don't need to look good to write, I remind myself sternly.

I grab my laptop and shove it into my backpack, along with my wallet, phone, and Kindle, then shrug into a black leather pea-coat and leave the flat, locking the door behind me.

Outside, the noise and bustle of Tottenham Court Road hits me like a bomb. Now, Fitzrovia is a lovely district filled with gorgeous Georgian town-houses, grand squares, and leafy green spaces, but my budget doesn't extend to a flat in one of the many quiet lanes or mews. As it is, it's only because the university provides subsidized accommodation that I can afford to live in central London at all. So my flat is above an electronics shop on one of London's busiest commercial streets, crammed with chain stores and fast-food restaurants, which bisects the otherwise Mary-Poppins-esque neighborhood.

Usually, I try to walk to the British Library, this being the only exercise I take, but today I head for the underground. A short ride in a packed carriage later, and I am walking into the imposing red-brick building, flashing my pass at the guard and heading for the reading room.

Four hours later, I've had enough. "I hate books," I mutter. "I hate reading; I hate writing; and I hate the English Romantic poets, feckity feckers the lot of them!" My work has not gone well, my tired brain struggling to come up with anything intelligent or original. I groan and turn my laptop off. There's no point in bashing my head against a brick wall; I might as well go have a coffee and try to regroup. *Sorry, Percy. You and Ozymandias are no match for a cheese scone right now.*

The cafe outside King's Library Tower is packed, with no prospect of a table opening up any time soon. Same story for the past four months. As I watch visitors and fellow researchers queuing for sandwiches, soup, and cake and consider eating standing up, my mind floats back to last night's dream. A murder at Old Spitalfields Market. Where the heck had that come from? It might have been a dodgy area in the nineteenth century, but the market had recently undergone a complete restoration, and you couldn't think of a less likely place for a murder. Lovely little independent shops, the arts market, the gourmet food stalls... Hmm, come to think about it, what about that delightful old Italian cafe I'd discovered two weeks ago? OK, it was a bit of a hike, and I *am* supposed to be working, but that *panini* had been out of this world, and the coffee, *bellissimo...* So, Spitalfields it is.

I hop onto the tube at St Pancras and half an hour later am walking into the cafe. It's just as I remember: a cheery little place – wholly unlike the characterless chain shops that now dominate town centers – with square wooden tables, polished to a shine by years of leaning elbows; a scuffed stone floor; whitewashed walls hung with black and white prints; and a long, gleaming silver counter behind which an impressive Gaggia is pouring out dainty cups of espresso. The rich scent of roasted coffee swirls in the air, beckoning me in.

I glance around the cafe. Amazingly, it isn't too busy, so I drop my bags off at a table in the corner before going up to the counter to place my order. I dutifully look over the menu on the chalkboard, just to see, but I know already that I want the classic Italian: mozzarella, prosciutto, salami, olives, roasted peppers, and tomatoes.

"And to drink?" the middle-aged woman behind the counter inquires.

It's on the tip of my tongue to order a sparkling water, 'swear. But they're offering wine by the glass at very reasonable prices, so before I know it my mouth has formed the words "a medium house red, please", and I'm sitting back at my table, drink in hand. Oh well.

I take a deep sip. It really is very good for the price. Cheap and cheerful and exactly what I need. I close my eyes and savor the feeling of treating myself "just because".

"... body discovered this morning, just a few doors down. Can you believe it?"

My eyes snap open.

"It's shocking," one of the two ladies at the next table over continues, dabbing her mouth with a red paper napkin. "Can we get two more coffees, please?" The waitress nods and turns towards the Gaggia. "You just don't expect that sort of thing here. Can you imagine turning up for work and finding that by the door?"

The first one shakes her head, heavy gold earrings sway-ing. "A stabbing. In Spitalfields. Dreadful. Oh, thank you," she says, as the waitress brings the coffee.

A stabbing. In Spitalfields. Just a few doors down. I take a sizable helping of wine and try to be rational. This is Lon-don. Knife crime is on the up. Remember the news this morning? Gosh, they must have been talking about this. I fret my napkin nervously.

"Is it true someone was stabbed nearby?" I query, as the waitress places my *panini* in front of me.

"*Si, Signora.* It's dreadful." She rolls her eyes and sighs. "I tell the police, this man is no good, sell *droga*, but do they lis-ten? No."

"Drugs?" I quaver, my napkin now in fine strips like so much confetti.

"*Si, si.* I know. I see. He hang around like a *mosca*, bzz bzz bzz, on the shit, this Bennee. *Che bastardo patetico.*"

And now I really am going to be sick. I feel hot, then cold, then hot again, and I can't seem to breathe properly. My hands shake.

"*Signora*, are you OK?" The waitress looks concerned, her dark eyes questioning. "It's terrible, *si*, but for you, for me, it's safe."

I nod like a puppet on a string. "May I," I gulp more wine. "May I have my sandwich to go, please? I... I forgot about a meeting."

She looks at me curiously but brings a box and the bill. I dump the sandwich in the box, leave a £10 note on the table, and chug the rest of my wine. I can feel the two ladies at the next table staring, but shock has literally stripped away all of my self-consciousness. Somehow, I get to the door with-out stumbling.

Outside, in the sunshine, I lean against the wall and take a deep breath, then another. I can feel a light sheen of sweat slicked across my forehead, my scalp, the back of my neck. Opening my eyes, I turn my head.

There is the scene from my dream: the red-brick buildings, the pale-blue shop-front hung with bunting, and next to it the shop selling woven wicker baskets; and there the shop with the wrought-iron lamp curling above the door, there the green awning, and the tropical-looking plants in their terra cotta pots.

OK. There's a logical explanation. I just have to find it.

Two hours and three-quarters of a bottle of wine later, thanks to an off-license conveniently located at the end of my road, I've got it. I'd last been to Old Spitalfields Market two weeks ago, but it had clearly made an impression on me. The hospital wasn't that far away –

within walking distance really – and I'd probably seen an ad for the market on the Tube or something. Yesterday, in the coffee shop near the hospital, I bumped into a scary man who, no offense to tattooed people, certainly could have posed for a drug dealer. Benny... OK. I hadn't seen him before but no doubt I've seen others just like him. And Benjamin is... I Google it... the thirty-third most popular boy's name in England and Wales. Very common. Not at all a surprise that my (legally) drug-addled mind put 3 and 3 together and came up with 26. Problem solved.

And this is why, I tell myself, *I am a post-doc. For my awesome powers of reasoning and analysis. And the next time I go off half-cocked, I will remember this.* I pour myself another glass of Barolo and lean back into my lumpy old sofa with a sigh of relief. Just like me to make a mountain out of a molehill. I yawn, glancing around the tiny lounge. The walls are a sort of dingy white, and the floor is a rank linoleum swirl, but I'd made an effort to brighten things up. On the wall to my right is a framed picture of the castle of Segovia – surely one of the most beautiful in Spain – and colorful green, blue, and purple scarves (thank you again, Camden market!) serve as curtains for the windows. The battered old table on my left has seen better days, but I've placed some dahlias in a frosted glass vase on it, which I think perks it up a bit.

I flick on the telly. Local news. Bleeurgh. I stab at the remote to change the channel, forgetting about the glass of wine in my other hand, and a few drops splash onto my pajama bottoms.

"Oh, buggery bug! Goddamn gravity!" Racing into the kitchen, I grab a cloth. Cold water! Cold water! Or is it hot? The newsreader's voice trickles in from the lounge.

"... twenty-one-year-old Benjamin Dawson."

I freeze, drop the cloth into the sink, and walk, slowly and deliberately, to the door, then turn my head to the screen.

Benny looks back at me, a little younger, dressed in a black tee-shirt with the logo of some heavy metal band on it; no goatee, but the slightly protuberant eyes are familiar, only here they're clean and bright; and he's smiling.

"Police are appealing for witnesses. An anonymous tip line has been set up."

A number scrolls across the bottom of the screen, and I go automatically, scarcely thinking, to the table for a pen and a paper to write it down. I feel numb.

Benny was real. Benny was real, and Ratko was real, and it had all happened. I'd dreamed it, but it was no dream.

I sit back down on the sofa and swallow hard, trying to clear the lump in my throat. How? How was this possible? And what should I do? I've seen a murder. A real live murder. I've seen it, but in a dream, and would the police even believe me? What would I say?

OK. OK. I can't explain this, but I have information. I need to tell the police, but I can't call them on my mobile. They'd be able to track the number, and then there would be questions, and then they'd lock me up in an insane asylum and throw away the key.

I go to the bedroom and pull my clothes and boots back on. There's a payphone outside. I can make the call from there, and this is such a busy street, the police will never know who phoned.

The temperature has dropped, and I'm chilly, but maybe

that's just shock. I walk quickly to the phone booth. Uggh. Someone, perhaps several someones, has been using it as a trash can and urinal. Trying not to gag, I put a few coins into the machine and dial.

"Metropolitan Police. How can I help you?"

"Yes, I. I have some information." I cough and clear my throat. Glancing around the fetid box, I want so badly to be back in my flat, watching a film or reading a book, and for the last twenty-four hours to have been erased.

"Yes?"

"Benny, uhh, Benjamin Dawson. The stabbing. He had an argument. With someone named Ratko. About drugs. Benny stole money, and Ratko sl-slit his throat."

"Ma'am," the operator's voice sharpens. "Can you describe this Ratko?"

I shake. "OK, he was... not too tall, just average, I guess, and had dark skin and a moustache and a gold earring. He had an accent – Eastern European, I think. Oh, and he was bald but had a dragon tattoo on the back of his head. And his neck." I shiver, remembering the look in his eyes. "Must have hurt," I add inanely.

"And you saw everything?" she queries.

Saw? Yes, I'd seen it.

"Ma'am?"

But I've said everything I can. Quickly, I hang up the phone, then scuttle back to my flat. I'm going to lock the doors and go to bed, and in the morning, I'll call the doctors and ask about any more "unusual" side effects.

I'm almost not surprised to see Ratko looming over me when I open my eyes. I cringe, but he doesn't pay me any attention, his eyes locked on the woman standing to my right.

I glance up and do a double take. The woman is gorgeous. She's tall, taller than Ratko, with choppily cut, caramel-blond hair; lightly tanned skin; wide, mocha-brown eyes set beneath thick, dark eyebrows in an oval face; high cheekbones; a long, straight nose; and so well-endowed that some part of my brain wonders how her thin frame manages to support her. No wonder Ratko's ignoring me.

"Ratko," she purrs. "You spoil me." She strokes the bracelet on her wrist, diamonds winking in the dimly lit room. "How, but how, will I ever repay you?"

Ratko's face twists into a smile at once cruel and sensual. "*Moja lepa* Magda. You are as clever as you are beautiful. But I think, this time, you will have to work very hard to pay it off."

She mock-gasps, one slender hand coming to rest lightly against plush pink lips before sliding down the column of her throat and coming to rest at the deep vee between her breasts.

A dream. I'm having another dream.

"Ratko," she murmurs throatily. "I'm disappointed. I think you underestimate me." She undoes one, two, three buttons of her blue silk shirt then quirks one perfectly arched brow at him.

Still smiling, Ratko pulls off his white tee-shirt, dropping it on the floor, and then undoes the small silver buckle on his belt.

OK. Wake up, Maela.

Magda's hands move languidly, caressing her stomach as she undoes the rest of her buttons, then lets the shirt slither to the floor.

How on earth did such large breasts stay so perky if she didn't wear a bra? Huh. Must be fake.

My attention ping-pongs back to Ratko, who is now pushing down his jeans, and oh, he likes going commando.

No, no, no. Eyes closed. Eyes closed. Time to wake up.

Magda moans.

Wake up, Maela. Seriously.

Heavy breathing. Wet, slurping kisses. A gasp, quickly

stifled.

La, la, la. I'm not listening! I put my hands over my ears and curl up into a ball.

Ratko groans, as if Magda has just taken his impressive-for-a-murderer length in hand.

Wake the "F" up, Maela! The fog – where is the fog?

Someone hisses, and I can't help myself. I peek.

Magda's head is thrown back, and Ratko's hands hold her flat waist as he feasts on her breasts. Oh. Oh my. It's rather... erotic. *No! Bad Maela! Pervy Maela!* I close my eyes again.

When the darkness finally comes, I go into it willingly.

CRUMPLED CORPSES

Thursday 13 September – Kailani

It is the season of death. Outside twisted limbs drop crumpled corpses on the ground, the air perfumed with the echoes of dust and decay. Inside the taste of rot coats my tongue. I can feel the phantom blood filling my mouth and throat, cooling and congealing slightly. My stomach twists in rebellion and I swallow convulsively, trying to clear my airways of the thick liquid. Knowing it is only a matter of time before I become violently ill, I thank the gods that I hadn't had time for a coffee before coming to the station this morning. Trying to breathe through the taste of metal, closing my eyes, I start searching for the echo of emotion we need. A wave of desire hits me so strongly I almost convulse, followed quickly by a perverse joy so deep and so oily I feel it coating my skin and sinking through to my bones. Lurching to my feet, I fly to the trash cans against the wall and start retching, praying I'll pass out before the foreign emotions have time to anchor in my body. Leaning my head forward against the cool tile on the wall, I concentrate on breathing and counting. Up to six on the inhale, hold, and out again. It's not you. It's not real. It's not you. You didn't do it. My mantra, repeated over and over again, until the taste fades from my mouth.

The man across the table from where I had been sitting, all shine and polish in an expensive, clearly custom-made suit, flashes a startlingly handsome, falsely sympathetic smile. He leans forward slightly and says in the low, sweet tones of a lover, "Are you quite alright? You're looking unwell, Officer Reed. I'm happy to help in any way I can... We can reschedule if it would suit you. I'm completely at your disposal, of course." Concern laces his tone, lines his face, and edges his posture, but none is echoed in his oleaginous feelings.

I eye him from the edge of the room, remaining quiet as I frantically try to regain my composure. He is calm, face relaxed and gentle as he looks at me in carefully crafted interest. "*Are* you alright?" he repeats, more firmly this time. "Do I need to call for someone?" He leans forward again, blue eyes radiating sympathy and worry. "You really don't look that good. I honestly think maybe we should call someone. Do you... there's water somewhere, I think? I can't do much by myself right at the moment," he says, holding up his hands with a disarming twist of his lips, "but I really think... maybe someone...?" He glances up towards the camera in the corner of the room, eyebrows furrowed, nodding towards me in a silent request.

I narrow my eyes slightly at his obsequious tone. "Oh shut the fuck *up*, you fucking insufferably dumb bag of rotted dic..."

"Ms. Reed!" a frustrated voice from the room's speaker interrupts loudly. "Focus, please!"

I shrug towards the camera in the corner of the room without responding and return shakily to my place across from him, glancing at the papers in front of me.

"Like I was saying, there are a few discrepancies in your answers that have raised some concern, including, but not limited to, information concerning Riley Beckett."

A wave of sexual longing pulses out from him so strongly my stomach twists like I have been stabbed. His face is still frozen in the guise of pleasantly befuddled school teacher, completely at odds with the twisted longings emanating out from him. Better prepared for the echo of feeling this time, I don't flinch as I wait for his answer.

"I'm sorry to disappoint you, Officer Reed, but as I indicated earlier, I can't help you in regards to Ms. Beckett. I wish I could, but the last time we had any contact was two days ago, at a press hearing, the encounter corroborated by at least three members of my staff."

"And you didn't see her after your press briefing that evening, is that correct?"

Again, a sharp, cruel wave of pleasure pours off of him.

"Correct."

I nod and smile pleasantly at him. "Odd. We have statements from two neutral parties that you were seen with Ms. Beckett yesterday at approximately 4am. Are you saying that those statements are false?"

Tennireef's face flickers briefly, like a flame, before steadying. I'm not sure if I weren't looking directly at him I would have even noticed the slight break in his persona. "That *would* be extremely surprising, considering that I have corroborated evidence that I was at my home, asleep, at that time. I'd be highly suspicious of anyone claiming otherwise."

"Ah, yeah. About that... It's definitely difficult to be suspicious of security cameras. But I'll take it into consideration. I mean, they *could* be biased I suppose. They're doing crazy things with robots right now. Have you seen that one that runs like a dog? It's insane."

"Ms. Reed..." a tired voice breaks in again, and I wave dismissively over my shoulder towards the room cam.

"Well, it's my unfortunate duty to let you know that Ms. Beckett's remains were discovered late yesterday morning by the docks. She had been restrained, and there is strong evidence of sexual assault, among other things. You were the last *confirmed* person to have been with her. Any chance you want to reconsider your statement? 'Cause *I got I got I got I got rape convictions inside that DNA...*" I sing off key. Tennireef looks at me blankly. "Kendrick Lamar? No? *I know murder, conviction...*" I shrug, letting out a deep sigh. "I guess no one really *is* perfect. 'Cause that song's a bop!"

His face tightens briefly in anger and annoyance before

he can force it back to its benign countenance.

"Charming, Officer Reed," he says tightly. Taking a deep breath, he smooths his voice and asks, "I'd like to go off record for a moment?"

I cock my head at him curiously. "I'm sorry. You know you were asked to come down here for a homicide investigation. You're literally sitting in an interrogation room. You can't go off record, Tennireef. This isn't a press conference."

He grits his teeth, politician smile darkening to a shark's bared teeth. "On record, then, Officer Reed, though it has nothing to do with this investigation. A close friend was seeing Ms. Beckett on a social basis. He contacted me early yesterday morning indicating that Ms. Beckett was behaving erratically. That she had called his apartment at approximately 3am, that he couldn't go looking for her but that he was concerned for her safety. I, along with two staff members, went to help him by searching for her. I found her at approximately 4am, called my friend with confirmation that she was safe and of seemingly sound mind, and went home. I'm sure your video will show you the exact same."

"And you didn't feel it pertinent to this investigation why..."

"My friend is a married man, unhappily married, but married nonetheless. His... business outside of our friendship isn't my concern. And he was at home with his wife the entire time, so I knew he had nothing helpful to add."

"That's super, James. But that's not the part that concerns me. What concerns me is why you wouldn't share this information with us if it's so innocent?"

He twists his lips wryly, like we're sharing some sort of secret understanding, pulling me into his sphere, leaning towards me with a rueful shake of his head. I can see how this guy has charmed so many – even knowing what I know, there's a part of me that *wants* to believe him. It's unnerving, to say the least.

"Officer Reed. I'm sure you can appreciate what it would look like in the press for a US Senator to be trolling the docks in the early morning hours. Any explanation would be wildly blown out of proportion. I promise you, when I left Ms. Beckett, she was *alive*. I had two employees with me who will also go on record that she was alive." Truth is pouring off him in nauseating waves, washing over me with a strange viscous feeling. "In light of this new information, however, I'm happy to revisit the trip in more detail to see if I can provide anything that may be of help."

I blow a tangled strand of dark-brown hair off my forehead in frustration and stare at the man in front of me. Senator James Tennireef, Seattle's favorite son and Washington's pride and joy, is currently sitting across the metal interrogation table from me, face benign, by all outward appearances ready and eager to help. Tennireef was a crafted perfection the likes of which I'd never seen. At 29, he had been Seattle's youngest councilman ever elected, and he moved quickly up the political ladder. When the Senate elections had taken place a year ago, he won the seat in a near landslide, ousting a political Methuselah. Tennireef had been charming in victory, winning the AARP crowd with his genteel speech thanking the prior senator for years served, and the younger generation with his self-deprecating humor and 33-year-old energy.

Tennireef was a media darling – smart, ambitious, and traditionally handsome in an old school Hollywood sort of way. He was every newscaster's wet dream; having grown up in a poor, single-parent household, he landed a scholarship to Danvers Academy, a boarding school in the Lake District of England. Following Danvers, he was heavily recruited by all the major Ivy league schools, settling on Harvard, which he attended on a full scholarship for rowing. He travelled back to England as a Rhodes Scholar, focusing on humanitarian issues for his postgraduate work, before returning to Seattle and interning with the Gaia Foundation, a well-known, international group which focused on homeless and displaced persons, amongst other human-welfare topics. Having worked there for several years, Tennireef then ran for his position on a platform of social justice, economic responsibility, and environmental awareness. His life was a series of carefully planned and precisely executed movements, and to the best of my knowledge, he never, *never* mis-stepped. The books were all clean on him – no Twitter rants, no salacious Instagram pics. Nothing at all. Nothing but a recently unfortunate habit of being in the wrong place at *close to* the wrong time. He was never *actually* there when things happened, but had an uncomfortable track record of being near enough – days before, days after, etc.

Tennireef is, by most accounts, hard to dislike. He has no known or obvious enemies, outside of normal school-boy jealousies. No ex-girlfriends who exposed secrets to the media, no cheating scandals, no inappropriate comments to secretaries. Widely acknowledged as a future presidential candidate, he's as close to universally loved as you can get. I *hate* him. He makes my skin crawl. Perfectly shaven, square jaw with just enough stubble to be masculine without being unkempt, light-blue eyes with long, dark lashes, cupid-bow lips, and dark-brown, "I just woke up like this" gelled hair. Most women, and a fair number of men, routinely fall at his feet. He's unfailingly kind to them all, genteel in his refusals, and is rarely seen with a date outside of necessary functions. There is *nothing* upon initial inspection which should give off such a malicious air, but it surrounds him like smog, thick and heavy. It's difficult for me to be anywhere near him.

"James," I say with a false patience. "As was explained, we asked you here because of inconsistencies in your answer regarding Ms. Beckett."

He shrugs elegantly.

"Those discrepancies aside, the video footage *also* places

you near the location where a young woman was rescued yesterday morning, restrained near Ms. Beckett, having, at first glance, been subjected to similar treatment."

"Rescued?" His eyes flare ever, *ever* so slightly, and his body stills in place, the barest hint of worry rising off him like smoke, before it disappears. I smile slightly, more a quirk of my lips than anything else.

"Unfortunately for you, all signs point to the two women having been trafficked. And with the timeframe, witness statements, and video footage, it really doesn't look great for you. So unless you're as dumb as you look, which is pretty fucking dumb, by the way, you should be at *least* fairly concerned. And the question I keep asking myself is *why* aren't you?"

I lean forward slightly over the table, gather my focus, drop my shields, and lay a net gently around him. All I can feel off him, other than echoes of the stomach-churning emotions I initially encountered, are a heavy layer of smug condescension and an almost uncontrollable desire to laugh. He's having a sincerely difficult time keeping a straight face at the moment, which makes the image he's presenting of vague concern and confusion that much more impressive.

"Hmmm... why? Why would you not be at all worried right now? Why would you be... amused? Most people would be somewhat disconcerted just being questioned in a police station, let alone sitting, locked in an interrogation room. What is so damned funny?"

He shrugs elegantly, raising one shoulder nonchalantly, before shaking his head slightly.

"Officer Reed..."

"Miss Reed."

"Miss Reed, I'm sorry to disappoint you. I'm not finding any of this funny, I assure you. I'm very concerned, of course, but I *do* have faith in the justice system. After all, this is my... fourth? Can it be? Yes, I think fourth time down here, and as I'm sure you'll see, the charges never prove fruitful. I come down, though, whenever asked, voluntarily, and comply in any way I am able." He lowers his voice as he speaks, the last line uttered in a very soft and vaguely threatening manner. "Of course, Miss Reed," (this drawn out slightly, the words savored on his tongue) "this field trip was not for nothing. It is worth meeting the infamous Seattle Psychic. And what an experience it has been. So... interesting. Eye opening, really."

If I hadn't been pissed off before his little speech, I certainly was now. The moniker "Seattle Psychic" had been laid on my unwilling shoulders a couple of months ago by some internet nut job after a story had been leaked regarding my involvement with the department. One of my *only* stipulations working with the SPD was that I remained completely anonymous. 1) Pay me per case. 2) No more than two cases a week, at the absolute most, and 3) I remain anonymous. Guess how many of my three demands had been met on a consistent basis? Not. One. Gritting my teeth, I slowly begin tightening my net around the revered senator as he continues soapboxing to the empty room.

"Miss Reed, what you need to understand is that I love Seattle. I care deeply about it and its people. I have never resisted coming in for questioning when asked; I have never hidden my tax records, license paperwork, business plans, etc., etc. My entire goal is to make this city as safe and secure as possible, economically, socially, and environmentally. I strongly support the Police Union, the Fire Department... all our first responders, really."

By this point he's given up the facade of addressing me and is speaking directly to the camera.

"I place unwavering faith in those who uphold the laws of our land. So, no. I'm not worried. But Miss Reed," he says with a small smile, "I'm curious. Are *you* at all worried? With upcoming budget restrictions, the tightening of our city's belt, so to speak, as a contract worker are you concerned? When we're done here I'd be happy to address any matters which might cause *you* anxiety."

I suddenly grin, and he flinches slightly, breaking kayfabe for the briefest moment. Seeing it, I give a short laugh as I react to his statement.

"No," I say, still smiling. "No, I'm not concerned. And I don't have anything to discuss with you. You place unwavering faith, hmmm? Unwavering?" I'm grinning like the Cheshire Cat by this point and staring straight at him as though we were sharing a joke between only the two of us. As he meets my eyes with his patented "concerned politician" look, made famous in hundreds of news conferences and briefings, I drop a slow wink and say, "I bet you do."

The tiniest whisper of worry rises from him like a phantom. Barely there, it seeps out of his tightly controlled emotions, and the moment it does, I pounce. Metaphorically speaking, of course. My net tightens at once, grabbing onto the strand of worry and pulling for all I am worth. Without taking the time to debate the wisdom of what I'm about to do, I *yank* as hard as I can, and the venerable senator's eyes roll back in his head as the blood drains from his face, and he passes out, slamming his face onto the table. Staggering slightly, I look up at the camera, nod my head slightly, and collapse.

◆ ◆ ◆

"Oops?"

"Oops? *Oops,* Reed? OOPS?" Special Investigator Tanaka paces in front of me, hands rubbing his face tiredly. "Jesus Reed. I have a *United States Senator* passed out with two black eyes and a broken nose in interrogation, a ROOM full of federal investigators next door who witnessed it and who are demanding an explanation, and a contract hire who is displaying decidedly concerning behavior at the moment. I mean, what the hell, Kai?"

Hideo Tanaka is one of my favorite people on the earth. And, considering I actively like a total of three people, that was saying something. We met when he was assigned as my mentor and then handler over two and a half years ago when I started working for the SPD. At the time the Seattle Police Department had a newly hired interim director to take over for an unbelievably corrupt captain who had previously run the force. Director Gomez was a seemingly sweet, tough, and completely unsuitable woman who had initiated several unorthodox programs during her short tenure. Besides mandatory counseling for all officers, she created a meditation room, instituted required pre-shift yoga, and had started a consultant program based upon the dubious Stargate Program, a US government baby from the 1970s that researched potential military applications of paranormal abilities. *None* of her programs were popular, but the least of all was the Stargate Initiative, which was really saying something.

I was in my probationary period as a hire in the Child Welfare Department when Gomez assigned me to Tanaka as my mentor. He was a detective at the time, and when Gomez cherry-picked me to be part of the trial unit at the SPD, she moved him with me to act as my handler, since we'd formed a kind of rapport. Despite his reluctance to participate in the program, he had always treated me with unwavering respect and courtesy and hadn't allowed any-one to haze me or obstruct my parts of the investigations. And while we were both reluctant to participate in Gomez's pet project, the unique independence it afforded us in the SPD was incredibly valuable when it came to solving cases. At least, the way *we* solve cases.

I glance over at Hideo, who is still walking around the room like a caged lion. The son of a Japanese mother and Brazilian father, Hideo is gorgeous. And not just a normal *my god look at that guy* gorgeous, but a *stop your breath Holy Jesus thank you Lord* sort of gorgeous. He has dark hair that is close cut on the sides but is just shy of rockabilly on the top, beautiful almond eyes, and cheekbones that could cut glass. He has a square jaw and sharp lips and is built like an Olympic swimmer, lean and muscular. If I had parents he would be the exact guy I would want to take home to meet them. But I've never had a shade of anything stronger than deep friendship and quiet respect from him, so that had to be enough for me. And it is, because Hideo is really the model of a man, and I count myself lucky to have him in my corner.

It's a measure of how stressed and completely worn out Hideo is that he addressed me while in the station using my first name. At boxing class? Sure. While lifting? Of course. But rarely, if ever, does he call me Kailani while on duty. The fact that he does sobers me instantly, and I try to calm down enough to continue.

"We may have him, Tanaka. I got almost everything we needed."

I'm jittery, pacing back and forth with an overflow of emotion, skin rippling in goosebumps. My right eye twitches slightly, and I have to clamp my teeth together to keep them from chattering.

"You're sure? You'll need to be *sure*, Kai. Jesus. Are you okay? I haven't seen you react like this in years."

"It's bad, Deo. It's just... so bad. I was stupid and took too much."

I can barely get out the words, closing my eyes and leaning my forehead against the wall while trying to slow my breathing. I sense him moving behind me to place a hand gently on my back.

"What can I do?"

"Get him out of my range. I can't shut off and I can't shield. Just get him somewhere far away. Please."

Having had his walls ripped out by force, James is now sitting in interrogation broadcasting so loudly I'm sure a Bleeder two states over could feel him. And he is *pissed*.

Waves of anger are rolling out like white caps, making my knees weak with their strength. Deo nods and hurries to the door, then has a hushed conversation with whatever blue suit is waiting outside. My head still pressed against the wall, I start to cramp and realize how long I've been sitting stone still, just breathing. He should have returned by now, and I turn just enough to see his back, his shoulders tensed and voice rough with a low anger. I pulse in and out of consciousness, hearing only snippets of rough conversation.

"... Say it's a gas leak all you want, Tanaka. A leak that causes only two people to pass out? Come on."

"... CO poisoning...."

"... Out of my hands. We need a reading now..."

"... it's too soon. You'll have to wait."

"Detective Tanaka?"

"Coming Reed. Give me a minute here."

"Tanaka, for real. I need to hit the tank. I can't breathe right still."

"The tank? Christ."

The other voice murmurs something from the door, and Tanaka makes a sharp motion with his hand, cutting off the sound, and walks over to me, face heavy with concern.

"Here we go, Reed," he says gently. He helps me to my feet, and I cringe. It has been months since something has hit me strongly enough that I can't stand, and much longer than that since someone has made me sick to my stomach. Loosening my long braid, I comb out my hair with my fingers, trying to ease the ache in my head. I hate being this raw and out of control but can't do anything about it at the moment. I need a soak in the tank to hopefully help balance me out, and I'll deal with everything else after. As Hideo tucks his arm under my shoulder a secondary wave of pleasure hits me, low in my gut, and I almost pass out from the feeling. I try to bite my lip to keep from crying out but am unable to push back the tears quickly enough.

"Kai, what the hell? Are you okay? What did you take that it's hitting you this hard?"

Clenching my jaw as the tears pour down my face, I drop my head. "Deo," I say quietly, almost ashamed of what I'm about to ask, "I need the tank, and... I think I need a Bleeder."

He starts, then tries to hide the movement. "Are you... Yes, of course Kai. What type? Pain? What are we looking at here?"

I duck my head further, a curtain of hair blocking my face so I can't see his reaction, and whisper, "No. A Pleasure Bleeder. I can work off the anger, but... yeah, I need a Pleasure Bleeder." He stops suddenly, and I chance a quick look at him. He's lost all color from his face and has gone a pale white under his normally golden skin. "Pleasure? Jesus. Okay Kai. I'm on it."

TROUBLE COMES IN TWOS

Thursday, September 13 – Kailani

We walk slowly out of the room and start down the hall, Hideo mumbling quietly to himself. "Tank two is shut down for repairs, but tank one is further away, maybe the meditation room for now... Can you still feel him?" The latter addressed to me. I start to shake my head, but the movement pushes a wave of dizziness over me, causing me to stumble and almost go down as we round the corner of the hallway. Hideo swears and reaches for me, but I end up crashing into a brick wall of muscle before he can grab me. Two hands curl around my biceps like vice grips and set me upright with little effort. I look up into one of the most beautiful and rugged faces I've ever seen, and the only thing I can think is, "Trouble".

He has short, close-cropped, bark-brown hair and the beginnings of a beard growing around the fullest lips imaginable, with the hint of a deep dimple showing as he smirks at me. Green eyes meet mine with more challenge than I like from someone I've never met. He instantly sets my hackles up, and I shrug off his hands with as much attitude as possible without crossing the line into complete rudeness. After all, the guy *has* just saved me from crashing headfirst into the wall. Looking at him for another second and seeing the faintest hint of a smirk pulling up his lips, I rapidly reassess. Fuck it. Hideo would most likely have caught me, so I owe this guy nothing. I step back and glare at him.

"What, no thank you?"

Of course he has to sound like fucking sex. *Of course* he

does. I glare harder, ignoring the heat from his deep voice.

"Yeah. Thanks," I return grudgingly. I *really* don't like this guy. Never mind the incredible tattoos curling out from the edges of his shirt, traveling down his biceps and forearms. Or the way his thin tee clings to the muscles on his chest and abs. *Holy shit, eyes up, Kai! Eyes UP.* I meet his knowing gaze as I jerk my head back up to meet his eyes. Already overstimulated from the morning's session, the warmth of the emotions coming off him is too much, though thankfully the lust is mixed with amusement rather than tinged with something darker. Still, it's enough that when it combines with the pool of diseased emotions from that morning, it sets me to shaking, and I step back into Hideo, darkness eating at the edges of my vision, but I'm determined not to black out again.

"What's up, Tanaka?" he addresses Hideo with something... condescending. Not openly dismissive, but not actively respectful. "I need to borrow your pet psychic for a case. I have approval from Markel and Posta."

Oh holy fuck on toast no. I move forward angrily, fueled by my own natural aggressive tendencies and a maelstrom of anger I had absorbed from our suspect and haven't had a chance to release. Hideo grabs my arm and pulls me back to him, gently but firmly.

"That's right, Tanaka, leash your Tigress."

Hideo sighs, then squeezes my arm twice, quickly, and I mutter a quiet thank you to him before flying at the newcomer. Rather than going for his face I do a fast leg sweep, and he falls like a log, unprepared, to the hard cement floor. I step on his throat firmly and glare down at him. His eyes widen slightly in surprise but don't give anything else away. His emotions, though, pour off him, surprise swirling with a reluctant respect, edged with anger that I got the jump on him. He *really* had not expected me to go after him, but Hideo and I had learned long ago that it was better for me to defend myself once than to have him defend me fifty times.

"Why in the world do you think I'd work with you?" I scoff.

"I have permission from both department heads, and a requisition form from Seattle FBI," he snarks.

I burst out laughing, and Hideo lets a small smile escape, which for him is the equivalent of a riotous laugh.

"A *requisition form?* And permission from the department heads? I'm not a tool, you fucking tool. You can't check me out from the facilities locker. Jesus Christ..." I look over at Hideo. "Who the hell is this guy?"

Hideo shakes his head. "He was in the room with the investigators watching your interview. With the Feds. Met him while you were with Tennireef. Other than that, he's not on my radar."

My foot presses more firmly into the asshole's throat. To his mild credit, he hasn't tried to move or fight back. Looking down at him, I wonder how to proceed. I desperately need to get to the tank – my body is still shaking, and I feel sick to my stomach – but walking away from people who treat you like an object never helps. Just about to give in and let him up, I hear a deep, exasperated sigh from behind me.

"Oh Christ. Really Reed? Tanaka? Why is it always in my halls? Three times last month, and we're only a week into this month. Let him up Reed."

"Negative Chief. He was disparaging to me and rude to Tanaka, and I'm owed an apology."

"You always are, Reed. Christ. Well, Donovan? What's the story?"

The guy beneath my boot grins up at me and Chief Cruise, who has appeared over my shoulder.

"Sure, Cruise. I'm deeply sorry, Tanaka. Reed," he adds, almost as an afterthought.

I lean over, placing all of my weight on my foot, which is currently wedged beneath his chin, smiling sweetly.

"No problem, Donovan," I offer, as his eyes bulge slightly. "I'm sure it was all a misunderstanding."

I remain there, staring into his face, which is rapidly turning red, until a faint tendril of concern rises unwillingly from him.

"You shouldn't play games," I whisper, "when you don't understand the rules." Pulling that thread of concern, I bundle it tightly, magnify it, stretch it, and lay it over the top of his skin like a thin layer of oil. It shimmers, covering every inch of him, and fear grows in his eyes as he fights against his body's betrayal of its emotions. Even that little bit of manipulation takes quite a lot from me, and when he sits up suddenly, fighting my hold on him, I step back, weak, but smiling cruelly. He jumps up from the ground and shakes himself all over, like a horse, trying to rid himself of the feeling that is sinking into his bones. *Be afraid*, I have woven into his concern, *be afraid, run, run, run!*

He looks behind him, as though expecting to be jumped by an assailant, hand drifting to his weapon holstered at his side. His eyes are tight, all previous amusement has fled, and he looks anxious and ready for attack.

Hideo sighs. "Reed? Remove it please."

All big eyes and feigned innocence I peer up at him through heavy lashes. Russet-brown eyes meet my almost black pair filled with all the sweetness I can muster.

"Whaaaaat? Me?" I blink at him. "Remove what?"

"Reed," he says in his *I'm rapidly losing patience* voice, "Now. We don't have time for this".

Based only on the fact that I really do feel like I am about to collapse, I pout slightly at Hideo, mutter, "Spoilsport," and pull my web off Donovan and back into myself, letting just the smallest amount remain coating his skin. Anyone walking through the hallway in the next few minutes *might* be hit with a brief moment of anxiety or concern, but nothing too troubling. Donovan relaxes his grip on his weapon and looks at me through new eyes.

"What the hell was that?" he snaps.

Chief Cruise steps between us, exhaustion lining his face.

"It never ends around here. Walker Donovan, meet Kailani Reed. Reed, Donovan is part of a task force being formed to address some troubling cases across the nation which have led them here to Seattle. Play nice."

I shake my head, still feeling dizzy with the movement and subtly leaning against Hideo to help keep me upright.

"Nope, sorry Chief. I'm done with cases for this month. I told you that. I'm not taking any more. Today's was a shit show, and it's stretching my limits. Plus, I've already consulted more than I'm comfortable with. Seven days in, seven cases? That's almost my log for the entire month. Whatever is going on, it will either have to wait until I recover, or you'll have to do it the old-fashioned way, because I'm off duty".

The chief shakes his head, clearly gearing up for a big speech about teamwork or unity or some shit, when Donovan steps all over his toes.

"Reed, I don't want to pull rank at all, but I'm afraid I may have to. All I'm asking you to do at this point is listen, and maybe talk to a couple of people for us. Your skills are apparently... difficult... to match. In regards to time saved, anyways. Traditional detective work will of course net us the same results, obviously, but I've been told you can be at least moderately helpful in developing leads. I'm not heading the taskforce on this case, so I can't offer a reprieve for you in this instance, however much I'd sincerely like to. I'm sure you're... tired or whatever from whatever you do, but I'd recommend bucking up and getting on board."

I stare at him, rolling my eyes in disdain.

"Listen Dude, I speak fluent Asshole, so I'm picking up everything you're putting down. And I'm telling you straight that there is no way I'm working with someone like you. No. Fucking. Way."

"If you just keep an open mind..."

"Are you fucking serious right now? You walk in here, doubting everything I do, doubting the people who work with me, thinking it's a waste of time and sending a shitload of misdirected anger my way, and you're asking me to keep an open mind?"

"Wha... I never said any of that. I came in here asking you in good faith to help us with a problem."

"Ruh-roh Shaggy. They obviously didn't tell you I'd do a read on you as soon as you walked in the door. And news-flash, I don't work with liars. Especially when the liar is supposed to be one of the good guys."

I grab Tanaka and try to push my way past the mountain in front of me. Even at my best it would have been hard to edge him out, but now, shaking so hard you could see me vibrating, and at my utter limit, I can't move him an inch.

"What the hell? Why is she shaking so much? And Reed, maybe you misunderstood me, but you don't have a choice here. You have been assigned to my task force, whether or not you're interested in taking more cases this month. The paperwork has gone through and doesn't need your signature. You're getting a new handler, coming to our team, and will stay there, under my direction, indefinitely. The good news for you is that I think you're a charlatan, that you're weak in general, and that you won't last two days with our group. So play nice like your Chief said, and let's get this over with." He reaches out to grab my arm from Hideo impatiently and snaps, "Now stop with the drama and the bitching and let's go."

I look up at him passively and let out a deep sigh.

"Oh Sugarplum. They obviously haven't let you in on a few very important aspects regarding how I work."

"Oh no? I'm dying with anticipation here."

"Well, first, and most importantly, you can't transfer me. I work for the department as a true contractor. A single case-by-case basis, no extended contracts, no month by month or yearly paperwork. Nothing. I don't get healthcare or benefits on purpose for this specific reason. The department isn't allowed to keep an active file or active paperwork on me as part of our deal. New paperwork is filed literally *every* time I take a case. All requests have to go through my company, for every case, and the company has to approve each one individually. The only on-file paperwork I have here is my clean background investigation, employment agreement, Academy test results, and drug test. I have no actual superior in the department, as I'm called in as a consultant. I work in the same way as a doctor who is called in to provide expert testimony in a court case. I'm hired by the department to pass along any information I can pick up with my unique skill set. So you can take your intimidation bullshit and shove it, because it won't work on me. Secondly, I don't go anywhere without Tanaka. Ever. And every single person in this department knows it. So the chances of you giving me a new handler are about equal to the chances of you not being a complete asshole. Which, by my calculations..."

I glance over at Tanaka, who shakes his head at me, but also drops a deadpan wink, which is about the cutest fucking thing I've ever seen and totally takes me off the path of my righteous anger. By this time Donovan is practically glowing with rage. Which is good, because I need to absorb a little extra for the stunt I am about to pull.

"Anything else?" he growls as I glare up at him.

"Why yes, actually," I smile. "There is one more thing..."

Hideo suddenly lurches forward. "Not a good idea, Kai!"

"Sorry, Tanaka!" I chirp, grinning.

Donovan looks at me sharply, about to say something, when I pull all of his anger from him quickly and then shove it back into him all at once. His eyes fly open briefly, like he has been electrocuted, then roll back in his head as he slumps over and falls on the ground.

I wobble precariously as Hideo reaches my side and catches me as I start to go over.

"Twice in one day, Kai?" he says with both concern and a certain level of exasperation.

"Oops?" I manage to squeak out before blackness once again takes over.

I wake up with a massive headache. Groaning slightly, I open my eyes to a dark room.

Hideo looks at me with equal measures of concern and frustration. "Honestly, Reed. Are you *trying* to cause problems at this point?"

The careful way he props me up on the couch I am currently occupying belies his fierce tone. Gently holding me upright with one arm, he reaches for a nearby glass of water for me with the other. Frowning anxiously, he whispers as quietly as possible close to my ear.

"We've *talked* about this Kai. No weaponizing in front of other people! Christ, I don't know how to mitigate this. Once I could *maybe* explain, but twice in one day? And in front of witnesses? Federal agents are here, Reed! Federal agents! No one let me know, which means they're going over my head with my own partner! I'm scrambling to keep you safe and you're blowing people's brains up."

I stare up at him, stupidly surprised by the tone of his voice. His emotions are a cool, reflective pool of calm water, totally at odds with the expression on his face and the tone of his voice. I'm not sure what to do, or what to say.

"It... I... I'm sorry, Deo. I wasn't thinking." I stumble over my words, and he curves his body around me slightly, as if hiding me from watching eyes. Looking directly at me, he speaks silently, mouthing the words slowly so I can catch them.

"No more. Not safe."

My eyes dart around the room, taking in my surroundings. I am in the waiting room for Tank 3, a room I've been in multiple times before without concern. Spotting the cameras in the upper corners, I pull my expressions back to its normal resting bitch face and roll my eyes.

"He was a complete ass, Tanaka," I snark, loud enough to be heard without seeming purposefully showy. "Sorry if he got concussed or something when I took him down, and again, sorry that I didn't think that through, but he's a complete, complete ass."

I furrow my brow slightly, questioning, and Hideo gives a minute shrug. He isn't sure yet if my explanation for Donovan's collapse is enough, and I'll have to let him explain Tennireef's, if possible. While it is widely known I can "read emotions", Tanaka and I are very careful to regulate the amount of information released regarding my abilities. We painstakingly balance the image that I am a complete waste of space and a fraud with one that I am somewhat, albeit slightly, helpful. But even the people who support me in the department don't think of me as much more than a lucky charm at worst, or a tertiary option for casework at best. They consider the cases closed with Tanaka a mix of excellent detective work on his part and unusually good observational skills on mine. Several times throughout each month I give incomplete reads on suspects, just enough to show skill without exposing myself completely. I always give Tanaka the complete read separately, which is usually enough to help on the cases. Chief Cruise is more aware than most of my abilities, having been sworn to secrecy by Director Gomez, but only Tanaka and myself know the complete scope of what I can do.

Tanaka takes a deep breath and lets it out slowly.

"How are you feeling, Reed?" he asks, concern washing over me gently.

I smile up at him shakily.

"Not my best, Bossman. Not my best for sure. How're we looking on a Bleeder for me?" The chaotic swamp of emotion I have pulled from Tennireef surges suddenly to the surface, now that I am lying in a cool, quiet space with no other distractions. I can feel my skin getting clammy, and the shaking starts again. Hideo shakes his head slightly and grabs my trembling hands in his.

"Bad news, Kai. Only two Pleasure Bleeders anywhere nearby here. A complete newbie, and I DO mean complete. JUST out of Academy training and absolutely no on-job experience. You would be his first take."

I hold my head as still as possible, trying to calm the waves of oil-slick pleasure from pulsing through me. "Fuck. I'm not a freaking guinea pig so Mr. Magic can try out his awesome skills. If he lifts even half this off me and retains some of it, he'll walk out the door and won't come back. We can't risk losing another Bleeder. We're already hurting for hires, and a trainee doesn't have the skill to do a nuanced Bleed yet. He could pull too quickly and pass out, retain, or resonate." I pick up my head quickly, wincing at the screaming of my muscles from the tension. "I won't be able to handle any resonance on this one, even the slightest amount. What's option two?"

His face tightens slightly, but that much response for him is like a full wince from anyone else. "Deo... what's option two?"

He breathes out heavily. "Dustin."

My stomach recoils sharply, and I swallow a gag reflexively. "Right. Right. I guess I'm meeting Magic Man, then."

MAGIC MAN

Thursday, 13 September – Kailani

No one really knew how Director Gomez had gotten approval for her slate of weird projects. Rumor had it that she had information on a higher up which afforded her some leeway in her overhaul of the SPD. Bets were taken as to what the information *was* precisely, because Gomez was able to rework the recruiting and hiring process from the ground up, a Herculean task, and did so in an astoundingly short period of time. The traditional path to the Academy didn't change, but the net broadened. Suddenly along with the motivated 20-year-olds wanting to save the world, or at least our city, there were 45-year-old therapists, 53-year-old chiropractors, and one completely darling grandmother. No one could quite figure out how Nana Burns arrived at the station, and while everyone was thankful for her cinnamon rolls, they felt like a laughing stock having a woman in her dotage sleeping in the break room. None of the originals lasted long, some only a matter of days. Surprisingly, Nana lasted the longest – she had been there a few months by the time I arrived. I met her just once, as I came in for my first interview. I was nervous and wired, already angry because I *knew* how the interview would go and was bracing for rejection.

They put me in a waiting room while Gomez finished up the meeting before mine. I'd gotten dressed carefully that morning and had stared at myself in the mirror for a long time, giving myself an embarrassing pep talk. Wearing an uncomfortably fitted suit and awkward nude heels instead of my usual black jeans, black tee-shirt, black leather jacket, and boots combo, I had given myself a hyper-critical once over. Dark, curly hair to my waist, a gift from my Native Hawaiian mother, was somewhat tamed in a loose bun. Almond-shaped, brown eyes, so dark they come close to being black, stared back from an angular face – high, sharp cheekbones and square chin, golden skin – all reminders of my father's Native Peruvian background. A straight nose led to unbalanced lips, my top lip ample and soft, bee stung over a smaller, only slightly less full lower lip. Meeting my eyes, I whispered, "You can do this," before I realized that talking to yourself in the mirror was complete lunacy.

While I was pacing back and forth anxiously, Nana Burns came in and sat on the couch. She pointed one gnarled and trembly finger up to the corner of the room and whispered conspiratorially, "Stop pacing, dear. They're watching, you know." I glanced up and only just kept myself from groaning. *Gods, Kailani! You've ruined it and you haven't even gotten in the Director's office yet!* Too distracted to even question who the ancient woman was, when Nana motioned to the seat beside her, I flopped down disconsolately. She smiled softly at me and patted my hand. "There there, dear," she said sweetly. "The war isn't over 'til the King loses his head. Or Queen, in this case. Deep breaths, now." Practicing my six-step breathing, I listened to Nana talk quietly beside me, not saying much of anything, just pattering on, and slowly my anger and nervousness receded. By the time Director Gomez came to call me into her office, I felt contained and focused. I turned awkwardly towards Nana as I left the room and stumbled uncomfortably over my words.

"Umm… thank you. For… just… thanks."

She nodded at me and smiled kindly. "Good luck in there. I doubt you'll need it, but good luck anyway. I'm sure you'll do well."

I followed Director Gomez into her office. Sparse was a generous word for it. Gomez had a single desk, chair, phone, and computer. *Nothing* else. No papers, no pictures, no pencils... no second chair for that matter. It felt like a spare room that you'd put a visiting officer in. Despite the lack of personalized touches, the office was actually lovely. It was on the corner of the building, with two large windows on the far walls and more space than what I had assumed an office would have. It was all painted a kind of warm, almond color – very soothing, despite being in a police department – and the light wasn't the harsh fluorescent usually found in an office. There was even room for a couch or extra chairs, though evidently Gomez didn't deal with any clutter, whatsoever.

She perched on the desk, an odd look for the older woman, and nodded towards the single chair in front of her.

"Well," she began, "I see you've met Nana. She's our best Bleeder currently, and we have no one to replace her at the end of the month. I'm hoping this interview will change that."

My eyebrows furrowed in confusion. "Was that...? I'm sorry, what? A Bleeder?"

Gomez sighed deeply, not as though she was frustrated with me, but as though she was very tired and needed a long vacation. An older woman, she reminded me of a mix of Dame Judi Dench and Angela Lansbury. Short grey hair, bright, sharp eyes, thin, wrinkled mouth - everything about her *should* have been grandmotherly, like someone who would bake you cookies or read you bedtime stories. Somehow, though, it seemed like a mask, like she'd be more likely to snap your neck than serve you sweets. She rubbed her eyes with one hand while thinking. Completely perplexed as to the direction this interview had already taken, I waited for a moment before trying again. "I'm here to apply for the opening for the Child Welfare Officer," I said unsurely. "I'm sorry if there's been some confusion? I'm happy to reschedule or come back when it's more convenient for you?" *Never mind that I had to take the ferry over on my day off, and that I've been dreaming of this for years!*

Gomez smiled wryly at me. "Oh, Kailani. There's been no confusion. Just a lot of disappointment and unmet deadlines. Tell me, how long have you been able to feel other people's emotions?"

My eyes flared open in surprise, bordering on panic, and I stood up quickly. "I'm sorry. I really think you have the wrong person here. I'm not sure what you're talking about, but this isn't..."

"Oh for heaven's sakes. Stop it and sit down," she interrupted me roughly. "Just sit. I'll explain, you listen, and we'll see what we see."

Shocked and thrown off balance, I backed up slowly towards the door.

"Reed!" she barked, pointing at the chair. "Sit. Down. Or do I need to bring Nana back in?"

Heart pounding at this point, I hovered by the door. *What the actual fuck is happening? What's a Bleeder? What the hell will Nana do? Why am I scared of a 500-year-old woman I could literally knock over with a pencil?*

Gomez rolled her eyes and called out loudly, "Nana Burns. Could you please come in here for a moment?"

The door opened instantly, and Nana walked in, shaking her head.

"Really, Elena. Less than two minutes. That's a new record." Nana reached out towards me and directed me, unresistingly, back towards the chair. "I knew after the last one you'd need me, but honestly, couldn't you at least make an attempt?"

Nana's soft manner and soothing tones calmed the chaotic swirl of emotion in me, and I looked towards Director Gomez, biting my lower lip anxiously, but able to focus through my worry to listen.

Gomez waved a hand towards Nana. "This senile old bat is our best Bleeder." Nana let out a surprisingly sharp bark of laughter.

"You *wish* you were as sharp as me!" she threw back, and

43

both old women laughed and laughed.

I am fucking loooooosing it! It's official: I have lost the plot altogether! What in seven holy hells is happening here?

"What? I mean… what?" I just managed to get out.

Gomez took a deep breath. "I'll explain, but first, how are you feeling? I don't want to make Moira stand here for longer than necessary."

"I'm not *infirm*, Elena!" she huffed, evidently offended.

"I'm…. I mean, really confused of course, but I'll listen to you before I leave," I replied cautiously.

Gomez nodded towards Nana, and Nana patted my hand once before letting go. "Just try to keep an open mind dear. And don't let this one push you around. She needs you more than you need her."

"Oh for the love of God, Moira," Gomez snapped at Nana. "Out!"

Nana smiled at me again and left the room, closing the door softly behind her.

I looked towards Director Gomez expectantly.

"Right," she began. "Right. The problem is, Reed, that the background is long and complex, and would take too long to explain. I'm on a tight leash here, and an even tighter time-line, so I'd like to start *in medias res*, as it were, and fill in any missing pieces on the back end. I *do* promise you that I will elaborate on any gaps in knowledge, but am hoping you'll just take what I'm saying as truth, for now."

I nodded, waiting.

"Have you ever met someone who instantly put you on edge? Or someone you were comfortable with almost immediately?"

I raised my eyebrows slightly, both unwilling and unable to answer.

"Forgot who I was talking to for a second," she mumbled. "Let's try a different tack. There are people with a natural ability to soothe others. Most of these individuals eventually find their way into a career involving mental health care. Therapists, clergy, counselors – all attract a certain type, correct? Someone with the ability to listen well, empathize, and help mitigate the other person's pain, or suffering."

I nodded cautiously, wondering where the conversation was headed.

"A small, almost infinitesimal number of these, have a very unique ability that pairs with their sympathetic tendencies. They are able to, for lack of a better term, absorb and dissipate energy from others."

I must have made a sound, because Gomez looked at me and held up a hand.

"I realize how this sounds. I do. But the fact is, there are people you meet in your life who make you feel uncomfortable or nervous or scared or happy within moments of being in their presence. To be honest, most people have a low-level ability to interpret energy, but it isn't part of our modern world and we learn to ignore it. Studies indicate it's attached to our more primitive plane, an instinctual reaction that we no longer think we need. But it's still there, lying in wait. Lots of names for it through history – modern ones are 'sixth sense' or 'women's intuition'. There have been rudimentary tests done – we set up two people in a closed room and have them perform an act – fight loudly or kiss or stand and stare at each other, and then they sit, not speaking, facing the wall opposite the door. A third person is then let into the room, and despite not seeing faces, or hearing voices, or witnessing any interaction, he or she is usually able to tell the relationship between the two who were there initially. 'It felt tense,' or 'I felt like I had just walked in on something' were normal responses."

Gomez rubbed her face again. "I'm trying not to fast forward here, but it's such a convoluted subject it's hard to tell where to begin and where to end. Most people interpret this as an ability to read body language well, or subconsciously processing a series of minuscule clues and having them band together to form an opinion. Probably because that's easier to understand and replicate. *Science*. Well, *modern science*." This was said with a frustrated roll of her eyes, her disdain for the word clear. "Modern science is embarrassed by the history of the psychic sciences. Largely due to the apparent inability to replicate results. It's a unique situation when the result is based upon a single person rather than the experiment in general. So tests can't be replicated unless they're replicated with that specific individual. Do you understand what I'm saying?"

By this point my head was swimming. I honestly had no idea what she was getting at and was both elated and confused that she didn't seem to be addressing my deformity specifically.

She huffed loudly, then took a steadying breath. "The best therapists have the ability to make you feel calm and peaceful as soon as you walk through their door. It is not the low lights or Enya playing, it's the actual therapist. That specific person. Because whether or not they know it, and I'd venture to guess most of them don't, they are absorbing low levels of the patient's anxiety or worry or pain, purifying it, for lack of a better word, and releasing it. They are exhausted from work at the end of the day, not because they are hearing people's problems and helping them work through serious issues, but because their bodies have been processing low levels of additional emotion all day. We affectionately refer to this type of person as a Bleeder, as they bleed emotion from a person. It's an inside baseball reference to leeches, who originally *actually* bled people to help heal them. We have about equal understanding currently of Bleeders' abilities and the effects on the psyche as medieval leeches did, which is to say, not much at all." She paused here, evidently waiting for questions or comments.

"So..." I searched for the correct words. "So these... Bleeders... can purge negative emotion?"

"Well, to the best of our knowledge at this point, they can

siphon off any *extra* emotion from the playing field. No one is ever purely happy or purely sad, but there are wild swings in that balance, and a Bleeder is able to correct those swings back to the person's neutral."

"Wait, happy *or* sad?"

"We've at this point identified three to four types of Bleeders. There's some debate currently in the classifications. No two have operated in exactly the same way, and we're still working through training programs for any future agents. How much to expose them to on any given day, how to help them access that part of themselves on purpose, how to even reach a point where they believe in their ability. Right now we at least are able to routinely identify Pleasure Bleeders and Pain Bleeders. The other two types tend to mix in with those two main categories. Pleasure Bleeders seem to be able to remove excess happiness and those emotions that identify as happiness, and Pain Bleeders can usually pull those emotions which identify *emotionally* as pain. There are so many gray areas that black and white don't even exist, but we're one of four trial programs currently in the United States working on these issues."

I shook my head, reluctant and relieved all at once. "I'm not... this. I'm sorry, but I can't be of help to you."

Gomez stood up and moved towards me. In a gentle voice, sounding much more like the grandmotherly image she presented upon first meeting her, she argued, "I'm sorry, Kailani. I understand if you're reluctant, but I have it on good authority that you *are*, in fact, someone I could use in this program."

My face tightened as I clenched my jaw. "*Whose* good authority?" I managed to grind out.

"That information, for now, is privileged. But what I'm offering here... we can *help* you! We can train you to access parts of you you didn't even know existed! You could do great things!"

"With due respect, you wouldn't be helping me at all. I'd

be helping you. As something between a test subject and a guinea pig. And I'm not interested."

"Isn't this what you want to do, Kailani? Help people? Children? You could jointly work as our Child Welfare Officer while moonlighting in our Psychic Science Division on your downtime. It's a win-win. Full benefits, a competitive salary, a community of like-minded individuals... Think about it!"

"I'm not what you're looking for, Director Gomez. I assure you."

"Kailani, this room isn't miked; the information here is private and won't leave the walls. If at the end of our conversation you don't want to join the force, which I fervently hope is not the case, but if you don't, I'll respect your decision. Until that point I'd appreciate it if you at least offered me the respect of being honest with me."

Again, I shook my head. "I don't think you're hearing me, Director. I am *positive* I'm not a Bleeder. To be clear, they can only pull a single emotion, correct? And then just let it go?"

"In 20,000 case studies, yes. They don't completely absorb the emotion, to the best of our knowledge. More just... pull it in and dissolve it?"

My eyes widened at the number of subjects. "20,000 people?" I whispered.

"Yes. This case work has been going on for decades at this point, Kailani. Decades. And not just into Bleeders. All psychic sciences – astral projection, precognition, telekinesis, ESP... All of those thrown away, laughable accounts of mind magic. It has been the underground work to separate the wheat from the chaff, those with actual abilities from the charlatans who prey on vulnerable people. And the charlatans outnumber those with real talent 1,000–1. Maybe 100,000–1. So finding someone with any ability, getting them to trust me enough to talk about it, use it, help us... It has been one dead end after another." She met my eyes with a steady gaze.

"I'm not like that," I said firmly. "I'm sorry I can't be of help."

She nodded her head like she expected my answer and held out her hand. "Well, I can't say I'm surprised, as much as I might have hoped otherwise."

I shook her hand and shrugged uncomfortably. "I'm sorry to disappoint." I gathered my things and turned towards the door.

"Oh, Kailani?" she called after me.

I paused and half turned towards her.

"You don't have enough experience to fill the Child Welfare Position. I'm sorry."

Something akin to despair filled my stomach. As much as I hadn't expected to get the job, I had still hoped, and the letdown was sickening. Keeping my face placid, I nodded.

"There's an internship opening in that department, though, and I think you'd be the perfect fit. Six months, minimum wage. But it's a foot in the door."

The unexpected offer floored me, and I had to blink back unwelcome tears, swallowing hard before trying to speak. "I'd... I'd greatly appreciate that."

Gomez waved me out the door understandingly. "Come by two weeks from Thursday with all your documents, and expect to start immediately following your paperwork submission. Ask for Hideo Tanaka when you arrive."

Straightening up and wiping my eyes surreptitiously before facing her, I met her steady gaze.

"Thank you for the opportunity, Director Gomez."

She nodded again, and I walked through the door. Just as I was about to turn down the long hallway, I heard her voice follow me, raised just enough that I could make out the quiet words.

"Oh, and Kailani? Your wording – 'only pull a *single* emotion'? We'll be speaking again at some point in the future. When you're ready."

I froze.

"Go home now, Reed. And welcome to the team."

Hideo leaves the room quickly once I've made up my
mind. I groan under my breath at the thought of being a
practice patient for the new Bleeder, then roll my eyes at
my own dramatics, and turn towards the tank. It's actually
called a Float Tank and looks like an oddly shaped clamshell. There's maybe a foot of warm water in the lower half,
which, combined with a massive amount of Epsom salt, lets
you float weightless inside. It's a modern sensory deprivation system – the room is padded to mute noise, the walls
painted a deep purple, which absorbs any ambient light. If
you're into it, you can even close the clamshell lid. There are
options for a night sky on the inside roof of the clamshell,
which makes you honest to god feel like you're floating in
the middle of a field of stars. If you're claustrophobic you
can leave the lid of the clamshell open, and a dark blue light
stays on. Gomez had three tanks put in when she was in
charge – any officers with PTSD or who have had high-anx-
iety casework have free rein to come float before or after
shift. If you don't want complete silence, you can plug in
your music or use a sound mixing machine that is in the
room. My go-to mix is Distant Thunderstorm, Train, and
Rain on Tent, all on their lowest levels of sound. It's as
close as I can get to complete peace. The tanks are in the
basement of the precinct building where people rarely have
reason to go, so there isn't a lot of emotion pressing in on
me during my time there. The rooms, all three, are in a back
corner and are buffered by three small meditation rooms,
followed by two empty workout studios used for yoga
classes and stretching in the morning, or self-defense lessons in the afternoon. Finally at the end of the long hallway,
there is a small department gym with some treadmills and

heavy weights. Everything on this floor is designed to keep emotions muted. Any time I have an exceptionally rough day at work, you can find me in one of the four areas, usually in direct correlation to how bad the case actually was.

Flipping on my regular mix, I strip out of my clothes and debate pulling on my swimsuit. My skin feels like hundreds of invisible insects are crawling over it, though, and the thought of putting anything on makes me shudder. I decide to turn out the lights completely and leave the lid of the clamshell cracked slightly, though not enough to trigger the automatic light. The Bleeder should be able to work his magic without seeing me, so my nudity won't be a problem. Mind made up, I hit the button on the edge of the tank that turns the lights in the room off and step into the warm, viscous water. It's fucking heaven. For a few minutes anyways. As my body begins to relax, the emotional overload of the day presses in on me, and my mind goes into overdrive. I'm completely used to this – meditation takes practice and patience, and I begin my breathing and body check, trying to get my mind to comply, but I can't rid myself of the oily pleasure sitting at my sternum. I start getting jittery and can feel my chest getting tight as I force it to expand and contract normally.

Fucking panic attacks! My eyes well up with frustration. I've had them since I was a kid – my body's protective response to excess emotions. Like I didn't already realize things were completely shit, my body evidently felt the need to drive the point home, making me feel like I was about to have a heart attack. Panic attacks were the bane of my existence. Completely out of my control, other than vain attempts at tamping them down with my breathing, when I had an attack it was hard to pull myself back to rational, and I had, embarrassingly, passed out from having them, though not for years at this point, thank god. Deciding to give Hideo and the new Bleeder another thirty seconds before I give up completely, I begin counting slowly backwards. Around fifteen I hear the door open, and before I can open my mouth, a wave of such warm, sweet energy washes over me that I feel like I'm drowning in chocolate. It's extraordinary, and delicious, and I can feel myself begin to *pull* before I come back to my senses. *Well shit! Maybe this new Bleeder won't be so bad after all!*

I lie in the tank, yearning to reach out again and absorb all that goodness, but manners matter, and I wait patiently for him to approach. I figure he'll sit near the tank, and I'm almost humming in anticipation of ridding myself of that morning's emotion cull. Still relaxing under the weight of the new Bleeder's unique energy, I'm not paying close attention to the goings-on around me, and a small scream is startled from my throat when I feel two very large, very warm male hands settle lightly on my head.

"Whoa! Whoa! I'm sorry! I didn't mean to scare you!" The smooth, smoky tone of the Bleeder's voice does nothing to calm me down.

"What the actual fuck? Why are you touching me? Did you not *just* graduate from the freaking academy? Holy hell, man!" Feeling at a distinct disadvantage, what with being naked in a freaking tank of water in a dark room with a man I've never met, I take a brief second to reevaluate my life choices to this point. The Bleeder, who I can't make out in the dark of the room, starts stammering,

"I'm so sorry. I really am. That guy who got me was like, super intense, and I'm pretty sure he threatened me, like, several times. He was incredibly specific regarding my value relative to your worth, and he mentioned some really inventive options should I 'fail at my given task'."

I settle down slowly, still pressed against the far wall of the tank, but more relaxed now that the Bleeder has started talking. His voice is so soothing, a deep baritone, not quite a bass, and somehow sweet. Still confused, I blurt out, "But dude! Why were you *touching me?*"

He sighs deeply. "I grew up with this... thing, Bleeding or

whatever. It's different in my culture; we call it balancing. I can control the results best when I'm touching someone, but I haven't practiced a lot using it more remotely. That guy just got in my head and I got worried I'd pull too much too quickly or something, and I just reverted to what was comfortable. I really am so sorry. I'm tremendously embarrassed that I've made you uncomfortable. I can try from back here, or, if you'd prefer, I can leave."

He pauses, giving me time to think, not pressuring me for an answer. The minutes drag on as I try to calm my racing heart and work through my options, and he just waits silently and patiently. "Okay," I finally decide, albeit reluctantly. "Okay, we'll... you can try this."

I sense, rather than see, him nod, and I cautiously shift towards the front of the tank. By this point I'm shaking and feel like I'm close to exploding. Literally. I can feel pressure in every part of me, even my teeth, and I wait, anxious, to see if things are about to get better or a whole hell of a lot worse.

His voice enters my consciousness, hesitant but soothing. "Can I touch you? It will make things a lot easier for me... I'll just be more confident in my balancing. If not, it's okay. It may just take longer."

"Just my head?"

"Just your head," he confirms.

"Fine. Just get to it," I grind out, clenching my jaw to keep from screaming at this point.

Two large, warm hands are placed gently on my head, by my temples. He inhales audibly, then lets it out with a long and uncomfortably loud groaning sound. He does the same thing again, and by the third time I'm having trouble stifling laughter. *This cannot be real. Holy geez. I mean, at this point I'm feeling really bad for his girlfriend, having to hear that sound every night!* There's a long pause, and then he repeats the process. I can't help it, and I audibly snort trying to keep the laughter contained. He pauses again and asks me quietly, "Are you... are you *laughing* at me?" I try every-thing in my power to think of a work-around, but can't, and finally give up. Laughter pours from me as my eyes water, and it feels so good and pure it helps to dilute some of the tainted pleasure swirling inside me.

"I'm so-so-sorry!" I try to say, helplessly through the gig-gles. "Do you... do you have to... I mean... the *groaning!*" I dissolve again thinking of the painful sounds he was mak-ing, and my laughter reverberates off the walls, laced with a sort of hysterical chaos.

"Good!" comes the unexpected answer. "I was wondering how long it would take. You were so tense I was worried about hurting you or something. Now you've got some real joy in you, it'll make the whole thing easier."

"You were doing that on purpose?"

"Of course!" he answers cheerfully. "Could you imagine having to sit through that for an entire Bleed?" He groans again, like a dying cow, and I gurgle with laughter.

And with that he quickly and *quietly* lays his hands on my head again and *pulls*. Bleeding is the oddest sensation, if someone is doing it rapidly and on purpose. It's totally different in a social setting. You may feel worn out at the end of the night, inexplicably tired, manically happy, un-usually depressed... all for no reason. You chalk it up to coming down with a cold, or the alcohol, or a conversation, but really, someone near you was probably intentionally or unintentionally messing with your emotions. Most do it unintentionally – that friend who is always a bit of a downer and you can't figure out why, because they're usu-ally so nice, but just draining to spend time around. The one who is always the life of the party, and who makes you feel like the sun is shining directly on you every time you're with him or her, but as soon as they leave it's cold and empty. Those people are usually just low-level Bleeders. But when you sit through a purposeful Bleeding, it's like going down an incredibly steep roller coaster. You feel this slow build of pressure, and then all at once, your stomach drops out, and you're shooting downhill, leaving all of the emotion behind you. It's a really unique and almost addictive feeling, having all of that excess removed cleanly from you, leaving you feeling completely balanced. Well, as balanced as your personal neutral, which for most people isn't really neutral at all.

I lose myself in the moment, feeling the sick pleasure drain from me bit by bit. The Bleeder's hands gently rub my temples as he works, and, despite my best efforts, between the darkness of the room, the soft sounds of my mix in the background, and the gentle, positive energy pouring off the Bleeder, I slowly fall asleep.

The quiet beeping of the tank's alarm wakes me up, as does the gradually lightening room. They're built to start wakeup procedures after an hour, using a natural light system and an increasingly loud alarm meant to wake you slowly should you fall asleep. I smile softly as I wake up, feeling better than I have in weeks. I reach to push up the lid of the clamshell when I realize that there are still two unknown hands resting lightly on my head. And the room is getting lighter. And I'm buck naked. Brief panic flares, and then I reach up and tap one of the hands firmly.

"Um... hey... guy. I'm cool here, so you can just skedaddle, yeah?"

He makes a surprised sound, clearly having fallen asleep himself, then leaps to his feet, knocking over the stool he was resting on in the process.

"Towel! Towel!" he says as he races around the small room, looking in the limited cupboards before finding one. "My eyes are closed!" he calls, voice moving towards me. Not two seconds later I hear him connect with the stool and faceplant into the top of the clamshell, forcing the lid to snap shut. I hear a muffled sound of frustration, or possibly embarrassment, before the lid cracks open slightly, and he whispers, "towels just here, cool? I'm gonna step out."

Before I can thank him, the door to the room opens and shuts, and I'm left alone.

A CLUSTERF*CK OF AWFUL

Thursday, 13 September – Kailani

After drying off and getting dressed, I feel a million times better. All mellow jello, I walk into the hall where Tanaka is waiting, looking anxious. The tension drains from him as he sees me, and he smiles tightly. "All good?" he asks briskly, and I nod once. "Okay, so. In short. They're asking you to do a reading on a victim of human trafficking."

My eyes widen slightly. "The Feds?" I ask.

He nods in reply. "I know."

The Feds are notoriously squeamish when it comes to asking for outside help, so I'm a bit doubtful. Frowning at Tanaka, I check my watch. "It's already 6:00. This can't wait until tomorrow? I'm beat."

He looks me over carefully and sighs. "Not really my choice on this one, Reed. If it helps, it's meant to be a quick one. The victim is non-verbal, close to comatose. The only reason they're coming to us at all is because she was discovered by our guys and brought in under our protection." His face creases slightly with worry, which means he's seriously concerned about what is happening, but I don't know why. Other than it being unusual for the Feds to ask for help, reading victims is pretty straightforward. I'm guessing she's really been through something and that's why he's so on edge.

Reaching out a hand, I lay it on his arm gently. "I'm okay, Tanaka. Honestly. I can handle it. The Bleeder ended up being fine. *I'm* fine."

Tanaka grumbles under his breath, and I give him a little

nudge. "Come on now, Bossman. Let's go help some Feds."
Flexing a little, I start singing, "Tanaka and Reed, suuuper
crime fighting team!" He winces and covers his ears.

"Stop! Jesus Christ, no theme songs. Let's go, Trouble."

Grinning at him I motion for him to lead the way
and sing quietly behind him, following him up the stairs.
"Crime fighting beeeeeesties, we're going to kick some ass!"

"Reed!"

"Going to kiiiiiick sooooome assssss!"

The woman in front of me is a skeleton, all skin and
bones and hollow eyes. She's lying down in bed, closed eyes
staring at the ceiling of the hospital with a dead, empty
face, gaunt lips pulled back into a Munch-like expression.
Nothing on her is moving but a paper thin in-out of her
chest. The only reason I'm sure she's alive is the steady
beep-beep-beep of the machine next to her bed, and the concerned, apple-cheeked nurse hovering over her anxiously.
She keeps fussing with the silent woman's blankets and pillow, like it's going to make a difference.

Deo flashes his badge, and the nurse frowns at him, quite
matronly in attitude despite her young age, saying, "What
exactly are you planning on asking, Detective?" She motions towards the supine victim again. "First those other
men and now you. She's comatose." Huffing slightly, she
starts messing with the tubes leading to the victim's arm,
adjusting them and retaping one while I ask Deo quietly,
"Other men?"

He nods. "The Fed team came in first to see what they
could get."

Nurse Hatchet audibly scoffs, flashing brown eyes our
way. "Honestly. Do any of you understand what the word
'comatose' means?"

Deo asks me under his breath, "Can you just do it now?"

I shake my head firmly. "I'm already tired, and you know hospitals beat me up as soon as I drop shields, so I'd rather wait and have as few people as possible."

The nurse finishes her ministrations and exits, not bothering to hide her unhappiness at our presence. Which I get, honestly. I feel like a vulture hovering over carrion, picking the bones clean of flesh, and my stomach turns slightly.

"Okay," I sigh, unintentionally letting some of my feelings seep out in my tone. Deo moves behind me and lays a comforting hand on my shoulder.

"I know, Kai," he says quietly. "Greater good, right?"

I shrug half-heartedly. It's something I've grappled with for years – the intrusive nature of my so-called gift. Despite what others may think, I don't actually enjoy knowing what everyone is feeling. What's more, human beings are so mercurial, so volatile – one moment they're overcome with love, the next hatred... it's hard telling the *true* from the *true to the moment* emotions. The only thing I can say is that they taste different to me – long held or deep emotions feel different... thicker or richer – it's difficult to describe. Sometimes hatred skitters across my tongue like the bitterness of a pill, there until I swallow, then disappearing, leaving just a faint aftertaste. Sometimes hatred is acid, corroding my tongue, spreading down my throat, like eating a Carolina Reaper whole.

But whatever the emotion, people should be allowed to feel it, privately, unjudged, without having someone burst in and riffle through their thoughts uninvited. I don't mind reading criminals, or suspects, or doing what I can do to ease the suffering of a child, but I worry at times like this that I'm walking perilously close to a moral line I've set in stone for myself. As long as my shields are strong and I'm able to hold them in place, I try my hardest not to read people accidentally, beyond the scattered emotion they throw off naturally. It's kind of the difference between smoking a cigarette yourself and walking by someone else who's smoking. You can smell and kind of taste the smoke in the air when you walk by someone who's smoking – that's the way I feel emotions that just ebb off people naturally. When I read someone it's like taking a monster pull off the cigarette, turning the entire stick to ash in one enormous gulping breath.

I glance at her chart for her name, then sit beside the woman, taking her hand gently. "Okay, Becca," I start, trying to keep my voice low and soothing, "I'm Kailani Reed, an agent with the Seattle Police Department. I'm here to help." There's a low murmur of sound from the door but I don't turn, trusting Deo to handle things. I feel him squeeze my shoulder briefly, then tune out the low hum of sound behind me. "If there's anything, anything at all that you think could help us find who did this to you, I need you to focus on it as much as possible for me. Okay, here we go. 3… 2… 1…"

I drop my shields, and a scream of emotion pours off Becca so strongly I instinctively let go of her and clap my hands over my ears, fingers flexing white against my head, bowing forward so my forehead is against her arm.

"Shit. *Shit!* Tanaka!" I cry out, trying to hear myself above the high-pitched din of emotion slamming into me. Immediately I feel his hand on my back, rubbing slowly in circles, and I focus on the physical touch to help steady me.

"Okay, Becca. Okay, girl. I gotcha. I gotcha." Breathing deeply, I sink back into her emotional maelstrom, more slowly this time, better prepared for what's to come. She's all darkness, with flashes of horrific, painful light. Not the comforting type, the gentle night-light glow or firework burst, but a 1,000-watt searchlight flashing straight in your eyes as you wake from a long sleep, or the crackle of fire outside your bedroom door when there's no escape. Grabbing a tiny sliver of sanity, I pull slightly, trying to untangle it from the knotted strings of pain, of agony, that is webbed through her entire being.

Becca's eyes fly open, and her mouth gapes, dry and cracked, a faint rot of death already corroding the air around her. She flails wildly, with what little strength she has, and there's a burst of movement behind me, nurses running in and pressing buttons, paging doctors over loudspeakers in the hallway. A deep, masculine voice is swearing from outside the door, arguing with an orderly who is barring anyone but hospital staff entry, and the same brunette nurse from before is trying to physically remove me from Becca's side.

"Ma'am! Ma'am!" she's saying, as Becca's bony fingers scrabble at my hand, trying to find purchase. "Ma'am, you have to move. We need to get to the patient."

I pull against her, leaning towards Becca, whose lips are soundlessly moving, repeating the same motion over and over again.

"Ma'am!" The nurse is grabbing me now, pulling me back, and I can feel Deo remove her hands, and I'm finally able to put my head next to Becca's. She stares at me with desperate eyes, focusing intently on me, using every bit of strength she has in her, and so quietly I almost don't hear her beneath the noise of the nurses and machines and arguments around me, she whispers, "Kronos."

"I'm telling you she's not a fucking skeleton, she's a fucking mummy!" Frustration knocks my tone from anxious into angry as the hospital staff around me question me for the third time regarding the patient and what happened. "She's fucking starving, she can hear everything, she's scared out of her mind, and she's trapped in her body! What the hell? What's happening here?"

Throwing my hands up, I turn as Hideo takes over, always the more diplomatic of the two of us. It's been that way since we started working together. Sometimes the high of emotions makes me... slightly less reasonable than he is, and we have to "good cop–bad cop" situations quite often. Well, we do if good cop–bad cop actually means sane cop–crazy cop.

Deo's smooth baritone is a calming presence in the room as he speaks. "Doctors. I appreciate the admittedly strange nature of the case, but I have little room to maneuver here. The case involving this woman has been passed to Federal–"

The lead doctor, a silver haired man with heavily lined skin interrupts. "I don't give a rat's ass about your case, Detective. What I'd like to know is what this woman did to my patient!" He motions towards me dismissively, and I'm about to burst again, when Deo's face tightens, and he turns towards the doctor. "*This woman*, as you so elegantly put it, is my partner, Ms. Reed, and I suggest, should you wish to maintain any level of civility, you address her as such. May I remind you that we don't *have* to answer your questions, but are doing so out of professional courtesy, and nothing else."

Ooooo. Go Hideo! I take a break from my crazy pacing to watch him. Most people underestimate him at first. He's good at projecting a gentle, understanding facade, but when he wants to be, he's lethal in word and manner. His face tightens and darkens, sharp jaw tense in a cut-glass face. Something about how he moves – quiet, almost graceful – gives the impression of an assassin, and I love every minute of it. He stalks soundlessly towards the table of doctors in front of us, their protests dying away as he draws closer to them, and the room is still as he stops, consideringly, in front of them.

"As a matter of fact..." Hideo locks eyes with each doctor at the table before continuing. "... I think we need to discuss the negligence in care regarding your patient."

It's the equivalent of a bomb going off. All three men jump to their feet, protesting loudly about the quality of care, her state when she was brought to the hospital, the efforts they'd gone through.

"And yet, despite all that, Becca is quite literally dying of thirst and is trapped in her own body!" I say angrily, breaking through the noise around me.

They all look at me, confused, and I slam my hands down on the table. "*Becca!* The woman currently dying in Room 210!"

Ol' Silver shakes his head disdainfully. "You're mistaken, *Ms. Reed*," he snaps out. "She's getting plenty of saline, and has a drip of nutrients running that... actually, I don't need to explain *anything* to you."

A quiet knock sounds on the door, and Nurse Appleface comes in, reluctance heavy in her step.

"Um... Dr. Corrian? I'm afraid Becca Abernathy just coded. The Resident tried to bring her back for almost ten minutes. I... I'm sorry."

She backs out of the room, leaving the doctors staring across their table at us.

"Ah," says Hideo, almost pleasantly. "Well now. As it turns out, you *do* need to explain *everything* to us."

The doctors are still protesting when we leave. There's no known next of kin – apparently, she was brought in with no possessions other than a scuffed-up wallet with a student ID in it and a few dollars cash. When contacted, her school indicated she was an exchange student from a little town in England, in the States on a university visa. Calls to her hometown overseas proved useless – she'd lost both parents in an accident while a freshman in college and had no siblings. She'd been enrolled at Georgetown, but they hadn't received tuition for the fall semester, and she hadn't signed up for any classes. How she got to the West Coast is a mystery, as are her whereabouts for the last several months. The only lead at all was a roommate from the previous semester who told police that Becca said she was taking some time off school after her parents' deaths. Her body is being taken to the morgue for an autopsy, and Deo and I leave a scrambling, discomforted Director of Hospital with strict instructions to call us as soon as the results are in.

Afterwards, we have to sit through a wrap-up session with Chief Cruise, whose face looks fifteen years older than it did this morning. He rubs one hand over his face tiredly, looking through the photos in front of him with worn-out eyes.

"This girl was my daughter's age," he says quietly. "19 years old. Sophomore in college." He shakes his head. "The doctors found thirteen injection sites on her. Between her toes, her fingers, on her arms. Two broken ribs. Broken shin bone. Severely malnourished." He sighs heavily, then pushes one folder towards me and a second towards Hideo. "You two need to read up. I know it's late, but this is relevant to a meeting happening tomorrow morning. Your presence is required."

I raise an eyebrow at Cruise, who shakes his head. "Not tonight, Reed. Okay? Can you just show up to the fucking meeting without arguing for once?"

Seeing how truly beat down he is, I nod, not arguing, and he looks almost surprised. "Okay then," he says. "See you both tomorrow."

By the time everything's wrapped up it's almost 10:30, and I groan softly to myself, thinking of my commute back home. There are times that living on an island, away from the chaos of Seattle, is wonderful. This is *not* one of them. Hideo smiles at me sympathetically.

"You okay, Reed?" he asks gently. "Rough day. You need a ride home?" I laugh, albeit tiredly, rubbing my eyes.

"No, you know I'm taking my bike. Thanks though."

"It's a death trap," he says, rehashing an old argument we'd been having for years at this point. I echo the next line, mockingly, along with him. "Statistics prove…"

Shaking my head, I reach out suddenly and pull him into a hug, surprising him into silence. I don't often initiate physical contact, and I think I've worried Hideo a little. My face is buried in his chest, breathing in the soothing smell of him – a kind of clean laundry scent, with a warm ginger and cinnamon faint behind it. I can feel his hands hesitate over my back before wrapping around me, muscles flexing against me, and I hear his voice soft in the shell of my ear, close enough that his breath curves around the edge.

"Kailani? You okay?" Concern is heavy in his voice, and I don't move, drugged by the darkness, his warmth, and the feeling of having him to myself, even for a moment. "Kai?" An edge of something sneaks into his voice, and I pull back, shaking my head a little.

"Just tired, Deo. Just tired. Today was a clusterfuck of awful."

He nods, still looking me over carefully, but lets it go for now. "You know tomorrow's going to be rough, right? Debriefing Tennireef's interview, whatever this meeting is... you up for it?"

Forcing a smile, I smack him lightly. "Think I can't handle this shit, Tanaka? I'm on this like white on rice!"

He's still watching through attentive eyes, and my smile falls away under his gaze.

"You can handle it, Kai. I just wish you don't have to." We stare at each other for too long a moment, and I see something new in his eyes as he looks at me. He glances around quickly, nods once, like he's made up his mind, and moves towards me. "Kai, I.... something.... I have a bad feeling about what's coming. And I wanted to ask you... to tell you–" the blare of an ambulance shatters the darkness separating us from the world, and he startles back, before his face shuts like a book, pages unreadable.

"Anyway. Tomorrow looms, right Reed? Get home safe. Text me so I know you got in okay." And, giving a half wave, Hideo turns and is swallowed up by the night.

ON HER MAJESTY'S SECRET SERVICE

Thursday, 13 September – Maela

O ddly enough, I wake up in the morning feeling pretty well rested. Sex, even vicarious sex with a vicious murderer, clearly agrees with me, sicko that I am. I scratch my head and scramble out of bed, then have a nice, deep, pretzel-y sort of stretch. Today is going to be better. I can feel it.

The weather agrees with me – I won't even need a coat. I put on a pale-blue, long-sleeved tee decorated with tiny white flowers around the neck, jeans, and my ankle boots, secure part of my hair into a loose topknot, and slip on dangly gold earrings. I even manage a slick of lip gloss.

Right. Time to call the doctors. I take a sip of instant coffee. Aaah: "The morning cup of coffee has an exhilaration about it which the cheering influence of the afternoon or evening cup of tea cannot be expected to reproduce." How true, how true. I dial the number.

"St Cosmas's Hospital, clinical trials unit. How may I help you?"

"Good morning. My name's Maela Driscoll. I volunteered the other day as a test subject."

"Yes, Ms. Driscoll. What can I do for you?"

"Well, I didn't see it on the list of possible side effects, but since the test I've had a couple of really, umm, odd dreams. I wondered: is that normal?"

"Hmm. Let me check. Can I put you on hold?"

The line goes to some anodyne, tinkly instrumental

music, and while I wait, I think about last night's dream. Wow. Ratko and Magda had gone at it hot and heavy, and, judging by his response, I'd say she more than earned that bracelet. I mean, when she...

"Ms. Driscoll? Thank you for holding. I've checked the records, and no one else, in any of the trials, has reported having unusual dreams. I'd say they were likely caused by something totally unrelated. It could be stress, a scary movie, even something you ate. I wouldn't worry about it."

"Oh. OK. Right, well, thanks."

"You're welcome. And thank you again for volunteering."

Hanging up the phone, I sigh. So, no help there. Well, with any luck, the drug was out of my system, and there wouldn't be any more dreams. I've done my civic duty, and there's no point in phoning the police about Magda. They'd definitely lock me up if I started reporting that people were having sex.

I pack up my stuff and head out the door. Today, I will make progress and earn the stipend the university has so generously granted me.

"Season of mists and mellow fruitfulness, / Close bosom-friend of the maturing sun; / Conspiring with him how to load and bless / With fruit the vines that round the thatch-eves run," I declaim as I make my way home from the library. As predicted, it's been a good day. I've even managed to write a whole thousand words, and they're good words, too. "Hah! Go me!" I do a little jig as I open the door to my flat.

There's an envelope lying on the floor. Uggh. Junk mail. Right, what is it? Window glazing? A new car dealership? A request for a donation? I snort. I'm one step up from a student. They'd come to the wrong shop.

I pick it up and close the door behind me, dropping my

keys, along with my bag, onto the small table beside the door, then go to the fridge to grab a glass of chilled water before flopping onto the couch. OK, what is someone trying to sell me? And is it sad that I'm taking the trouble to open up junk mail?

I blow a strand of hair out of my face as I slit open the envelope and pull out the piece of paper.

Huh? The Home Office? The Home fecking Office of the United fecking Kingdom? What? What!

I scan the letter. It's an "invitation" to a meeting tomorrow at Thames House to discuss my status in the United Kingdom. Oh. My. God. I'm going to have a heart attack.

I race into the bedroom. My passport. Where is my buggery bugger of a passport? Oh, top drawer of the dresser, with my jewelry and underwear. I pull it out, practically hyperventilating.

But, but, my visa is in order. I double-check the date. Yup. Good for another two and a half years, and as long as I don't try to access public funds, I'm legit. Slowly, my heart goes from a crazy gallop to a steady canter. A mistake. It's clearly a mistake. Perhaps the letter's meant for one of my neighbors?

I walk back into the lounge and pick up the letter. No, it's addressed to "Ms. Maela Driscoll". I bite my bottom lip and twirl my finger around a strand of hair. Right. Well, maybe this is just a meeting to check up on me, see that I'm complying, that I'm carrying out my research, that I'm obeying all the rules and regulations? Yeah, that's probably it. Heck, maybe this is standard procedure, and I just didn't notice it in the paperwork for the visa.

Feeling marginally calmer, I pull off my boots and go to the kitchen to pour myself a large glass of wine – this is no time to worry about adhering to the recommended fourteen units a week. Besides, it's medicinal. I take a deep draught of the healing nectar, sit back down on the couch, and stare at my socks, a bright-blue pair gaily decorated with puffins.

This is not a problem, Maela. You will simply go to this meeting tomorrow, with your passport, and a copy of the letter from the university, and your laptop, to show that you've been working. And here I blench, guiltily. I *have* been working, but I've also gone to an awful lot of exhibitions and art galleries and second-hand book shops and parks and cafes. I begin to bite my nails. Will it be enough? OK. Mental slap. *Everything is fine*, I tell myself sternly. I gulp another sip of wine. *Fine. This is routine.*

◆ ◆ ◆

Needless to say, I sleep badly. On the plus side, I don't dream of Ratko.

Coffee. Shower. Dress. In keeping with the occasion, I'm going to wear an "I'm a law-abiding, no-trouble-here-sir" outfit. I pull on a pair of black trousers and a green, silk shirt; slip into a pair of conservative black heels; pull my hair into a loose knot; add a pair of gold studs and a plain gold necklace; and spritz on some perfume. I then go to the bathroom to do my make-up. Today, I need to make an effort, so I do the works, mascara and all. It takes me twenty minutes, as I'm so nervous that I give myself panda eyes the first attempt.

I look in the mirror. A worried, haggard face stares back at me, all mouth, wide eyes, and round-tipped nose.

Time for a pep talk.

You haven't done anything wrong, Maela. They're just checking up. It's all perfectly fine. Riiight.

I don't want to be late, so I put my passport, wallet, paperwork, phone, and laptop into a large leather hold-all and leave the flat with an hour to spare.

Outside, the weather matches my mood: flat and grey. No one is smiling today, and the underground is packed with cross, tetchy commuters. According to the map, the nearest station to Thames House is Pimlico, so I walk to Oxford Circus, along with half of London, it seems, for the Victoria Line.

All too soon for my nerves, we arrive. Despite the crowds, I'm really, really hoping for a delay, but the god of transport isn't with me. Oxford Circus is the city's third busiest station, so even before I've got on the train, I'm battered by people pushing and rushing to get to work. It doesn't do anything for my composure, and by the time I get to Thames House, I am hot, frazzled, and a bit sweaty.

Thames House, as the name implies, sits on the bank of the river and is a large, appropriately imposing building in the Imperial Neoclassical style, which means a white, stone facade; columns; a massive entrance archway; and twiddly bits over the windows. I feel suitably cowed and very, very nervous as I walk up the steps and towards the middle door under the arch. Of course, it turns out that those three doors are just for show or reserved for terribly important people, and a guard has to flag me down and gesture me towards one of the side doors.

Inside, I stumble as I make my way to the entrance desk, but the receptionist is professional enough to pretend not to notice.

"Hello. I'm Maela Driscoll. I have an appointment at 9:00?" I pull out the letter, along with my passport, and shove them at her.

"Ah yes, Ms. Driscoll. Your appointment is with Mr. Ryder. First floor, second office on the left. I'll let him know you've arrived."

"Thank you," I squeak, as the silver-haired lady, who could have played an older Miss Moneypenny, reaches for the phone.

Upstairs, I pause outside the indicated office and take a deep breath before rapping on the heavy oak door.

"Come in," a polished voice calls out.

I open the door and walk into a small but nicely appointed room. Jeepers, but the Home Office must pay their staff well. The carpet is a light cafe au lait, deep and plush, and the walls are painted a rich cream. On one wall is a framed, black-and-white print of a London street scene in the 1920s, and on the other, a traditional Japanese sword or *katana*.

Opposite the door and behind a mahogany desk sits a man in a midnight-blue suit, frowning down at some papers.

Hesitantly, I clear my throat and stammer, "Good morning?"

He looks up, and "Starlight, wafting him out of it; and / Glow, glory in thunder", he is the stuff of my every fevered adolescent dream. A rectangular face; long, straight nose; piercing pale-grey eyes under thick brows; light-brown hair, short at the sides and slightly longer on the top, with one errant piece falling over his forehead; and slightly thin, stern lips. Classically English aristocratic good looks, in short.

I quickly put on my "I do not find you attractive and am not in the least affected by you" face.

"Hello, I'm Maela Driscoll," I say, pleased that my voice is steady, while all the while my inner slut is shrieking, "Ravish me! Oh God, please ravish me! RAVISH! ME! Please. Thank you."

He stands, gesturing toward the dark-green armchair in front of his desk. "Emlyn Ryder. Please, have a seat."

Shades of Downton Abbey and Merchant Ivory rolled into one. His voice! And that accent! Cool and wonderfully, terribly manful. I have always been a sucker for a good accent, and his makes my knees go weak. Feeling rather warm, I sit down before I can fall down, clutching my shoulder bag in my lap and hooking one foot around the chair leg, a sure sign that I am nervous.

He sits back down himself and picks up a piece of paper. "Maela Driscoll," he reads. "An unusual name. Welsh?"

"Close, Breton. My dad's American, but my mom's French.

She chose it," I babble.

"Aged 26. From San Francisco." He pauses. "Funny, you don't look Californian."

Why did everyone imagine that all California girls were tall, tanned, and blonde? What's wrong with 5'3" and freckled?

He continues, "Currently a first-year post-doc at Queen's College London. Not a bad school. Studying English Romantic poetry. Hmm. 'Poetry is the breath and finer spirit of all knowledge,' is it?"

"Something like that," I bleat.

"Now Ms. Driscoll," he says, abruptly dropping the mask of pleasant interest. "Would you care to tell me what led to your calling the Metropolitan Police about the Benjamin Dawson murder?"

"That was an anonymous number! You can't know it was me," I blurt out, thereby confirming that, yes, it was of course me.

"You gave a very specific description of the murder and the murderer." He looks back at the paper in his hand. "Dark skin, a moustache, a dragon tattoo on his head and neck, and an Eastern European accent. I take it you saw the murder?"

"Umm," I squirm in my chair.

"Ms. Driscoll, the man you've described has been under surveillance for some time now. We suspect him of running a nationwide drug and sex trafficking ring, among other things, although we have no useable evidence which would stand up in court. He has a reputation for extreme violence, and yet here you sit, safe and sound after witnessing him commit a murder."

"Oh," I say, weakly.

"Oh indeed. And I'm curious to know, Ms. Driscoll, just what your involvement in this is. And why, if you were close enough to Ratko Kurgan to watch him kill Benny Dawson, you have chosen to turn him in. Lovers' quarrel, was it?"

"What!" I shriek, this time out loud. "No!" I bite my bottom lip, my nails digging into my leather bag while my spine locks up and my stomach threatens to heave. "No, I don't know him!"

"Ratko and Benny had an argument about money. About drugs, wasn't it?" he prods remorselessly. "Ratko slit Benny's throat. That detail wasn't released to the public, and yet you knew it. Which means that you were there. So why don't you make a clean breast of things and tell me everything you know? It will go much easier for you if you do." He leans forward intently, those eyes boring into me as if he would divine all of my secrets.

I begin to tremble. I am so royally, unutterably screwed.

"You wouldn't believe me," I say in a very small voice. I look away from him, down at the gleaming mahogany desk, then up to the sword on the wall, then down again at the carpet.

"Try me."

And out it pours. The drug trial, the strange dream – the first, not the second, God no – the news report, my anonymous call from the phone booth. And here I do look up, accusingly, before dropping my eyes to my lap again. "And that's that," I conclude. I stare at my nails. I really must stop biting them. It's a disgusting habit, slovenly and unladylike.

"I see."

I look up, some mad spark of hope wondering if he could possibly believe what even to my ears sounds far-fetched.

His face is inscrutable. "Very well, Ms. Driscoll. Thank you. You may go now, but I'll need you to come back here this afternoon, about 2:00."

I get up out of the chair, clutching my bag, and stumble to the door. "This afternoon, 2:00," I whisper.

Well that's that, then. I'm going to prison. I wonder what the British equivalent of a supermax is like. I'm going to end up in solitary confinement, chained to a pillar by the neck and slowly wearing a groove in the floor as I pace, year after year, round and round, aren't I? Or maybe they'll just dump me in a hole in the ground and let me starve slowly to death, locked away from sunlight and all mortal kindness. With luck, and if I play my cards right, I'll merely end up some-one's bitch.

Surprise, surprise, I spend the next few hours in a daze, wandering aimlessly around the streets and trying and fail-ing to keep my imagination in tow. This is going to kill my father, isn't it? My mother will think it's all very ex-citing, and might even brag about it, but my poor father's going to have a heart-attack. Back at Thames House, Miss Moneypenny waves me through. I go up the steps like a con-demned man going to his execution and, steeling myself, knock on the door.

That same beautifully modulated voice calls out, "Come in."

I enter without smiling. It might be pathetic, but I don't see why I have to be nice to the man who is going to im-prison me for *doing my civic duty.*

"Ah, Ms. Driscoll. Thank you for coming back." A wave of the hand at the chair.

Hah. As if I had a choice. And why did he keep calling me Ms. Driscoll, as if I were a spinster or an old maid? It was really getting on my nerves. Bastard.

I plonk myself down in the seat and begin to fiddle with the straps of my bag, my beautiful, soft-green leather bag. I flash forward twenty years: me, being let out early for good behavior, listening as the warden catalogues my meagre possessions and solemnly intones, "one bag, green". I swal-low, hard.

Emlyn Ryder doesn't seem to notice anything amiss. "Now, Ms. Driscoll," he smiles. Ooh, he has a dimple in his chin. "This morning, you told me a rather unusual tale."

"It was the truth," I mutter.

"Indeed. Well, as I mentioned, MI5..."

MI5. MI5. That doesn't sound like a branch of the Home Office. More like...

"... has had Ratko Kurgan..."

"James Bond!" I blurt out, then blush, my cheeks no doubt going as red as my hair. He looks at me, one eyebrow elegantly raised.

"Close, he's MI6. MI5 deals with national security. Now, normally, the National Crime Agency would handle someone like Ratko Kurgan – drugs, human trafficking, prostitution. Oh yes, he's been a busy chap, our Ratko. However, we've taken a special interest in his case. Mr. Kurgan, it appears, has also been dabbling in terrorism, supplying arms to Northern Irish dissidents."

Dabbling? How did one "dabble" in terrorism? Was this Brit-speak for "This man is up to his neck in it?" And, oh God. Oh God! I'm never going to be let out, am I? Being an accomplice to murder is surely a minor misdemeanor compared to being a terrorist's moll. I'm going to die in prison. I've only had a handful of partners, and the first time wasn't even that good, and I was rat-arsed for the second, so... I want to cry.

"... need to get him, even if it's on a lesser charge. Take him in, and there's a chance we can break him. And that is where you come in."

Huh? I look up, blinking.

"Ms. Driscoll, have you been listening?" His expression becomes, if possible, even more austere. "Up until now, we've had no usable evidence. But with you, we might be able to get it."

My eyes bug. "Ah," I clear my throat. "But–"

"MI5 needs your assistance, Ms. Driscoll."

I want to cry again, but this time I don't know whether it's from shock or the complete unreality of the situation. Me – a secret agent?

"No, Ms. Driscoll. Not a secret agent." *Oh, I'd said that out loud, had I?*

"Um, Mr. Ryder?" I quaver. "I don't see how. And, uh, you mean, I'm not going to jail?"

"No, Ms. Driscoll, not quite yet." He looks amused.

I really don't see what's so funny. And "not quite yet" isn't in the clear, is it? I try to pull myself together.

"Mr. Ryder," I say, with what I hope is a cool, not sickly, smile, sitting up straighter in my chair. "I don't see how I can help. I mean, I've only had a couple of dreams, so." I shrug.

"A couple?" He leans forward, tapping his *Montblanc* pen on the desk.

Oh, feck.

"Describe the second dream, Ms. Driscoll."

Ugh, would he please stop calling me that? I mean, sure, it was my name, but no need to wear it out.

"It wasn't about anything important," I assert quickly. Describe the second dream in front of him? Pass.

"I'll be the judge of that. Get on with it, please."

Feeling like I want to die of embarrassment, I stutter, "Well, uh, Ratko and this woman, Magda, uh, they, uh..."

"Yes?" He raises his eyebrow again.

"Well, they," furiously, I try to think of a genteel way of putting it, "were having intimate, umm, intimate relations." I'm so mortified even my scalp feels hot. And God knows what my face looks like.

"I see," he says impassively. "Monday morning, after our session, you can meet with a sketch artist. We might be able to get an ID from surveillance footage."

After our? After our session? "After our session? I don't understand."

"Ms. Driscoll, have you ever heard of telesthesia?" He steeples his fingers on the desk.

"Tele-what?" My brain can't take this many changes of direction.

"Telesthesia is a subset of clairvoyance, somewhat akin to what the *hoi polloi* might call astral projection. It means the ability to see distant events as they happen. And it appears you have it. This makes you of great interest to us."

"Astral projection?" I scoff, seizing on the one thing that sounds familiar. "That's just a load of *da da da-da, do do do-do*," I sing tunelessly. "It's bollocks," I snap rudely, crossing my arms under my chest. It has to be.

"Is it? And yet, you have twice now accurately dreamed of Ratko, including, I believe, his bollocks."

That quells my little outburst of bravado.

"Back in the 1970s, your government funded a project on what they called remote viewing at the Stanford Research Institute. Most people think that it failed. The transcripts that were released certainly gave that impression."

"It didn't?"

"Far from it. But for reasons of national security, it was decided to let out that the research was flawed, and the tests, unsound. It was also decided to keep the British government's involvement a secret. Wouldn't do to advertise such a potent weapon to the criminals, now, would it?"

"It wouldn't?" My right foot hooks around the chair leg.

"Not at all. Best to work quietly and not reveal our methods. Nor just how close the international and inter-agency links really are. Let the spies think we're territorial and only a step up from incompetent. Besides," he grimaces, "we wouldn't want to be deluged with job applications from every crackpot who fancies himself a psychic. No, Ms. Driscoll, we prefer to be more discreet and to vet our viewers before approaching them."

"Your... viewers?" I'm having a hard time taking it all in. I look at him and frown. He can't be serious, can he? Those pewter-grey eyes look calmly back at me. It really isn't fair, a man having such thick lashes. I have to use mascara to achieve the same effect.

"That's what we call people like you. People who can observe events remotely. We're not entirely sure how it works, but in your case, I'd guess that the drug trial triggered a latent genetic ability. With training, you can learn to control it and direct what you want to see, seven times out of ten. Right now, it's coming out in bits and spurts, when your mind relaxes in sleep. We'll help you to focus, so that you can see while awake."

"I don't want to see when I'm asleep!" I object.

"I'd say you have a rare natural ability, Ms. Driscoll," he continues, ignoring me. "Most viewers need years of training to see the level of detail you did. And even then, they can only see a few seconds at a time. With a monitor and daily sessions, you could become a real asset."

"A monitor!" I've been reduced to a parrot. "Who'd be my monitor?"

"I will." He sits back in his chair and smiles. "Congratulations, Ms. Driscoll. You're now working for MI5."

"No, I'm not," I say stupidly. "I'm doing a post-doc at Queen's."

"That can wait." He glances down at some papers on his desk. "It's all sorted."

"But, but," I splutter. "You can't just decide I'm working for you. I've got a contract! I'm writing a book!"

"We've already spoken to the provost at Queen's. He's delighted that your research on Romantic poets may prove useful in helping us to decipher a complex code and thinks that an internship with MI5 will look very good on your resume."

"He bought that? Wait – what? I'm not doing an internship with you!" I say hotly. I glance around the room, as if seeking reassurance that this bizarre conversation is actually happening.

"Aren't you?" His soft voice probes. "You did get a letter from the Home Office, didn't you? Something about your status? We wouldn't want to see you deported for refusing to cooperate with the authorities, Ms. Driscoll, would we? I think England agrees with you and you with England."

"Why you...!" I stick a finger in my mouth to chow down on a nail and glare.

"Now, now, Ms. Driscoll. *Regnum defende.* As your CIA says, *the work of a nation.* I know that you're delighted at this opportunity to bolster the special relationship between our two great countries. We'll start Monday morning at 9:00am." Dismissing me, he turns to his computer.

I get up, trying to gather the shreds of my dignity about me as I hike my bag over my shoulder and go to see myself out.

"Oh, and Ms. Driscoll?" That sigh-worthy voice follows lightly after me.

"Yes," I say, turning.

"If you tell anyone what you're really doing without my sanction, we *will* be sending you to prison. The Official Secrets Act, you know."

I charge down the polished stone steps like a bat out of hell and pace besides the wrought-iron street lamps. *That absolute Fuck*, I fume. *That absolute tossing, wanking, sodding...* "That fully rigged, rate A-1, ocean-going Fuck!" I spit. A passing pensioner in a tweed coat and walking a Corgi starts. "Steady on, old girl."

"Sorry," I mumble and turn left to march up Millbank. I need to walk off my anger. The grey day matches my mood, and as I trudge, I fantasize about all the ways I'd like to torture one Emlyn Ryder, government agent and world-class fuck, to death. He might be a member of MI5, but I am a humanities major with years of extensive, varied, and generally useless – until now – reading. Iron Maiden? No, too quick. The rack? I consider it as I gaze out over the sludgy water, me slowly turning the screws as Emlyn's tall, powerful body, with those broad, muscular shoulders arrowing down to that lean waist, slowly stretched, joints popping... I shake myself. Locked into Little Ease? Hah, that's better. His height wouldn't be such an asset then. Oooh, and the Spanish Donkey. Emlyn, those long legs hanging astride a triangular wooden beam, as I loaded his ankles with weights, crushing his testicles to smithereens and... Oh. Oh that would be bad. I shudder. And undoubtedly a terrible waste, not to say a crime, as I bet he was well-endowed and beautifully made and... Sheesh! What is this? Stockholm Syndrome? I kick a pebble, and my shoulders slump. Who am I kidding? I'm going to have to cooperate, aren't I? Well, at least MI5's going to pay me more than the university, I console myself. Wait – they are, aren't they? I mean, if I'm going to be working for the government on a top-secret project and all? I fret at my lip.

I pass the Victoria Tower gardens. Blah blah. And here's Westminster Abbey. Ho Hum. A few minutes later, "Hey look, kids. There's Big Ben, and there's Parliament... again." The scene from *European Vacation* brings a reluctant smile to my lips, and I stop. *Hey look, Maela. There's Big Ben, you know, way station for Peter Pan? And there's Parliament. Parliament! You're in the heart of a thousand years of history and the center of British government, and you're moping? Come on, girl: you can fly, you can fly, you can fly!* I straighten my spine. OK, so I'm now a secret agent – and I *am* despite whatever Mr. "I'm so superior" Ryder might say. In that case, I will be the best damn secret agent I can. My mind flashes ahead: me, being knighted – or was it "dame-d"? – by the Queen, in thanks for my *single-handedly* bringing down Ratko and his criminal enterprise. I'd be dressed in a long, flowing, black gown, which would look wonderfully dramatic against the white and gold furnishings and red carpets of Buckingham Palace. Curtsying demurely and murmuring, "It was nothing, your Majesty. Mr. Ryder would have done the same, had he been able, I'm sure." I wonder what my title would be? Dame Driscoll? Lady Driscoll? Dame Maela of Fitzrovia?

That would show him! My lips curve happily as I head towards St James's Park. In honor of my new vocation, I'm going to treat myself to a cup of tea and watch the pelicans.

I'm too late to see the pelicans get fed – Emlyn the wanker saw to that – but one comes to sit beside me on the bench. He looks at me, one gleaming, dark eye fixed on the flapjack I'm holding in one hand. Delighted, I stare back at him, hardly daring to breathe. *Sorry, sweetie*, I think, *I'm pretty sure toasted oats smothered with Golden Syrup aren't good for you.* After a moment, he hops off, waddling towards the lake on webbed feet, brown and white wings held out stiffly behind him. At one point, he stops and turns towards me, giving a rasp like a wooden guiro, before hopping into the water. "Thank you," I call out quietly.

The brief encounter feels like a sign, like nature is giving me an encouraging pat on the back, reassuring me that things are proceeding as they should. So much has happened in the last few days that I don't know whether I'm coming or going. Everything seems surreal, as if I'm looking at the world through water, or an old-fashioned pane of glass, rippling and bubbled, blurring the view. All of a sudden, I give a little half-sob, half-laugh, feeling slightly manic. Am I really sitting here, in London, sipping tea, having just been "hired" by MI5? I'm nobody. Coming to London is the biggest thing I've ever done. Sure, getting my degree was hard work, but hunkering down with my nose in a book is my default setting. It's where I'm comfortable. I'm the shy girl, the nerd, the kook, who struggles to make friends. The quiet one who looks on from the side-lines, clutching her computer bag, watching the beautiful people mingle. The one who'd love to say "hi" to you at a party but is sick with nerves and who stands instead in a corner, by the table with the drinks, smiling inanely. And now I'm supposed to work with a government agent to take down a criminal? I'm just... me.

A flapping of wings interrupts my pensive meditation. I look up to see the pelican, brown-tipped plumes extended, standing on a rock. For all his ungainliness, in that moment he's magnificent, head held proudly high, backlit by the autumnal sun. "Alright," I call out, smiling faintly. "Message received. Faint heart and all that. Enough of the collywobbles." A titter sounds behind me, and I turn round to see a young girl, maybe eight or nine, staring at me. She's adorable, dressed in jeans and a warm, woolly sweater, her hair done up in blonde pigtails, and has clearly wandered away from her parents to come see the birds. I smile again and make a funny face: "No more collywobbles!" She giggles and scampers away to her parents, who are now calling for her. "Yeah," I say to myself, "no more collywobbles." I stand, gathering my things together: "Come on, Dame Maela. You've got a murderer to catch."

GIDDYUP

Friday, 14 September – Kailani

Work the next day is tense, to say the least. I had barely made it home in one piece the night before, I was so drained. Stumbling through the door at midnight, I had walked straight to my room and collapsed. When the alarm went off this morning, I had almost shattered a perfectly good phone in frustration. Up and out by 5:00am to beat the rest of the Vashon commuters, and not stopping for coffee, I made it into the station by quarter to six in the hopes of having a couple of hours to myself before everything went to hell. That idea goes out the door when I walk in to see Tanaka sitting in my office. All the lights on the floor are still in energy saving mode, and all I can see is his silhouette outlined in front of the window, shoulders tense and tight. I roll my eyes as his head snaps up to watch my approach.

"So," he says flatly. "The Feds want to meet. They've assembled some kind of task force, and they want you to brief them on what happened yesterday."

"Jeeeeesus," I groan. "Tanaka, it's too early for this shit."

He waves a coffee slowly through the air, and my eyes track it like a starving man. "There's a price to this. You have to listen before you say no."

I shake my head. "No."

"Reed." He says my name warningly, edged with frustration. Clearly, I wasn't the only one who didn't get enough sleep last night.

"No. I'm heading to the break room and by the time I get back I want you out of my space. I'm cleaning up the loose ends today, attending whatever requisite meeting Cruise set up, and then I'm off for the weekend. I barely made it in today as it is, and my shields are blown to pieces." I turn to leave the room and hear him rise to his feet behind me. The smell of coffee approaches quickly, and I stop unintentionally as my brain and stomach engage in warfare. Tanaka, not expecting my sudden halt, bumps into me gently from behind. His voice when he next speaks is unexpectedly close to my ear, and I can feel the breath of it caress my skin as a shiver rolls down my back. *Shit. Get it together Kai.* Despite my warning to myself, I lean back slightly into the warmth of Tanaka, and his breath hitches as we pause in the empty office, barely touching each other in the low lights of the early morning.

"Reed," he begins softly, before clearing his throat and trying again, "Reed..."

He pauses and takes a deep breath, letting it out slowly, and it skitters over my bare shoulder, sending my senses haywire. On the exhale, I can feel him lean forward slightly and rest his forehead against my shoulder. We stay like this for what feels like forever, just breathing together, caught in an inbetween. He inhales deeply again and rubs his forehead softly against my bare skin, before exhaling sharply, and I can tell this moment, whatever it was, is over. As he straightens up, one of his arms wraps around me briefly, and everything inside me flares to life before dying back down as he pushes my coffee into my hand and then steps away.

"Reed," he begins again formally. "We really need to talk. And we don't have a lot of time before the team gets here."

I turn to face him, confused and oddly desperate. I feel like that moment *meant* something, and if I don't grasp it now, it will slip away forever.

"Deo..." I whisper softly, looking at him with wide eyes.

He shakes his head slightly, before closing his eyes, looking oddly pained. "Reed," he says again, stiffly this time, and it's like an unexpected knife in my stomach. "We can't... I don't want..."

Shivering slightly, I *reach*, searching his senses, only to feel regret, regret, regret. It swirls around me, mixed with a vague sense of admiration, a deep feeling of friendship and camaraderie, but nothing else, nothing more. It washes over me, and I feel sick to my stomach. Slamming my walls back up, I gulp my coffee and move towards my desk swiftly. I perch on the edge, rigid, feeling tremendously awkward and perilously close to tears. Hideo stares out the window, kindly giving me a moment, before beginning. He clears his throat and looks casually around my office.

"Pretty empty in here still. Are you ever going to put anything up?"

I pull myself together, answering the question I know he's really asking. "Totally empty, Tanaka, and it will stay that way. Though it was locked when I left last night." I look at him pointedly. I do daily sweeps of my small area, cautious of any attempts to infiltrate my space. About six months ago fourteen bugs had been found at key points throughout the Department. Every few weeks since then, like clockwork, someone would discover another bug. No one knew who planted them, and nothing came to light after they had been discovered. The investigation was ongoing, but everyone was on edge, and morale had plummeted. Someone in our midst was information mining, and not knowing who it was was creating an uneasy working environment. Tanaka wanders my office, seemingly aimlessly, looking around him.

"It was locked this morning. I used my key to get in and wait for you."

I shake my head, smiling slightly for the first time that morning. "The audacity!"

He hears the teasing tone in my voice and flashes a quick, blinding grin my way before continuing his careful perusal. Longing slams into me as my heart stutters. Real smiles from Hideo were rare and valuable things, and it was harder to box my emotions when he looked at me like that. Hiding my flaming face behind my coffee, I do some six-step breathing to calm my racing heart, tuning Hideo out until I hear a sharp note enter his voice. I jerk my head up to meet his angry gaze, and I furrow my brow, confused for a moment, until I notice where his hand is resting.

"Reed, I need you to pay attention. We have to discuss what happened yesterday." He's shaking his head slightly as the anger in his voice wars with the concern on his face. His right hand is resting on top of my sun lamp, and I make a face as I groan internally. *Shit. I love that freaking lamp. Well that's what happens, Kai, when you have no pictures to bug, or knick-knacks or some shit.* I reluctantly walk towards Tanaka, purposefully kicking over my trash can loudly on the way, and scream, "Ow! God da…" before knocking the lamp to the floor and dumping my coffee on it. It sparks briefly and dies. Tanaka looks at me wryly and unplugs the lamp before leaning over and picking off a small black dot. I shake my head wordlessly. It hadn't been there yesterday, and he nods in understanding. He reaches for my coffee and drops the tiny bug into the remains.

"You owe me another coffee. And a lamp."

His eyebrows fly up. "The lamp wasn't my…"

"AND A LAMP!" I interrupt loudly, already at my limit for the day, and he concedes with a shrug of his shoulders and an amused shake of his head.

"So, onto more important things."

"Like… coffee."

Having made a new pot of bitter goodness, we refilled our mugs and headed back to my now clean workspace, and are now sitting on opposite sides of my small desk staring at each other. Tanaka is clearly frustrated with me, his jaw tight and tense as I hold both middle fingers up in front of my face, with my chin resting on the heels of my hands.

"I need you to consider this offer, Reed," he says, just short of patiently.

I shake my head slightly. "The amount I'm not interested in doing this is equal only to my love of coffee." I'm being obstinate, and I know it, but it feels like a waste of time to engage in any discussions of the almighty task force when I have zero interest in changing the way things are.

"Reed!" he all but growls at me. "This ties directly to our current caseload! The Feds are here, apparently, because of our last *fifteen* cases! Fifteen! If you don't brief them, they'll be set back months trying to dig through storage and familiarize themselves with our cases and the major players. Which means they'll be *here* for months. *Months*, Reed. Months of observing you and watching how you work."

I shake my head again. "I'll write a brief."

He all but snorts in frustration. "A written brief will do no good. They need this to be a fast-paced operation. They've lost the lead on this four times already."

My eyebrows shot up. "*Four* times? Sounds like they need more help than we can give."

He grimaces and looks around before dropping his voice. "We need to assist on this, Kai. We need to be amenable, and brief them as thoroughly and quickly as possible so they *leave*. Because if they stay, they ask for help. If they ask for help, they see what you can do. And if they see what you can do..."

He trails off, and we exchange a long look. We both know how the government operates, and neither of us is interested in their methods. I sigh reluctantly and lean back in my chair, staring at the ceiling.

"Sooooo. If I do this, what's the plan? How are we going into this?"

He frowns at me. "Did you not read *any*thing that was given to you? You assist for the next two, three weeks at the most. Brief them on the cases they're interested in. Try to lay low." His frown deepens, and he hesitates briefly before plowing on. "You'll need to do a couple of reads for them *if* and *only* if they press on it. But let's hope it doesn't get to that."

I shake my head. "I'm sorry, Tanaka, but I am. Not. Interested. I *like* my life now. I like my routine. This is so outside my comfort zone it's not even funny. And what are the rules? I doubt they'll let me stay on as a contractor, or that I'll be able to call off if I'm feeling drained. Four times means they're grasping at straws at this point, and we're the straw they're grabbing. I'm so strongly against this I can't even tell you." Pausing, I think through the last twenty-four hours, and my heart starts pounding. "Why are they even *here*?"

"The last six drug-running cases, the four human-trafficking cases, Tennireef..."

"Then give them our files. Everything is in there. Start to finish."

"They want in-person reviews, Reed."

"Then you can handle it. I'm getting a really bad feeling about this."

He shakes his head reluctantly. "They, uh... they have asked for you specifically. So that's not an option."

Trying not to panic now, I fight the steel band tightening around my chest. "What if they make me travel? There'll be no tanks, no Bleeders if we hit a bad situation. Gemms wouldn't be there. How much do they even know about me? How did they even *find* me? Why am I even on their radar?" My voice gets higher and higher as I begin to spiral.

"The cases..." he replies, unconvincingly.

I shake my head sharply. "Bullshit. You know it's not the cases, at least, not completely. If it were they could just have us brief them. Something isn't right here, and you know it. It doesn't matter anyways. They asked; I said no. It's that simple."

"Reed!" He rolls his eyes, clearly at the end of his rope. "It's *clearly* not that simple. They came here *for you*, specifically. They watched that entire interview with Tennireef, watched you weaponize... I didn't even know they'd be here. I found out *during* the interrogation. As I was watching you."

I shake my head stubbornly. "I'm being strong-armed here. I don't like being pushed into situations when I'm uncomfortable, without time to think or consider what I'm agreeing to. This is all too fast."

"Kailani," he begins softly, clearly trying a new tack. "As your friend, I..."

"So we're friends now, Hideo?" I interrupt. "You need to give me advanced warning, because I'm getting whiplash. You set the rules, Bossman. In office, colleagues only. You can't change the rules of the game while it's being played."

"Christ, Kai!" He explodes upwards suddenly and begins to pace the room. I startle backwards – Hideo losing his temper is so rare as to be non-existent. The fact that he's lashing out makes me pause. He shakes his head and turns his back on me to look out the window.

"Kailani. There *are* no rules to this game. Why aren't you understanding that? This is a joint task force between the CIA and FBI, and if I'm not very much mistaken, there are international ties as well. At the moment they are *asking* you to assist on this. I'm not sure when that will change. I'm getting exactly zero information from *any*one as to what is happening, and I've been told by four different people at this point that I'm out as your handler. And you're acting like you can just walk away from this now that they know about you, and I'm trying to impress upon you that *you can't*. That ship has sailed, Kai. You're on their radar and you will have to cooperate, one way or another."

I stutter something unintelligible, then stop. He walks over to me quickly and crouches down in front of where I'm sitting, resting his elbows on my knees and grabbing my hands.

"I'm not even part of this at the moment, Kailani. They haven't asked me to move to the task force. You're walking into this situation alone, and I have no way to protect you, or assist you. I'm on the outside on this one, and I'm doing the best I can to help blind. It's my *hunch*, nothing more, that it will go better for you if you *seemingly* cooperate at the beginning to buy some good grace. I have no idea what to do from there. I'm checking with all my sources, but I need to do so carefully and quietly, which is unfortunate because in this instance, time is of the essence."

He stands up and walks to the window again, pacing like a restless tiger. "They gave me only enough information to convince you, Kai. And that's my job at the moment. To convince you to willingly be a part of this. I want to make that clear – I am cognizant that what I'm doing is exactly what they want. But I can't see a play around this at the moment."

"You're not coming with me?" I ask tremulously.

"I can't." His reply is angry, concerned, and frustrated all rolled up into two tight words. "Trust me that I've asked. But I've been shut down by the team lead and the second. The lead is an agent by the name of Maddox Smith. By all accounts he's a decent guy, he's just so by the books it makes me look like a cowboy from the wild west."

I grin up at him, despite the situation, picturing him in a ten gallon and some wranglers. *Oh my... Deo all dusty and riding a horse?* My mind wanders for a second until Hideo's repetition of my name pulls me back towards reality.

"Really, Kailani?" he asks wryly. "What could possibly be so important at this moment that you can't focus on the topic at hand?"

"You as a cowboy..." I reply dreamily, eyes flaring briefly as I realize what I've said.

Hideo starts, taking a sharp intake of breath at my tone, then recovers quickly. "And that image... amuses you, I'm assuming?"

I nod my head indecisively without replying. He comes back and sits in front of me again, exhaling slowly, and rests his head in his hands tiredly. "Well, I'll do what I can for as long as I can, but pretty soon here you'll be on your own, and I'm going to be honest, Kai. That worries me. Not because you can't handle yourself...," he holds up a hand placatingly, "but because you'll be safer with someone who cares about you watching your back."

He reaches out a hand and grabs one of mine, just holding it, and we sit in silence together until the lights come on in the office.

TASK FORCE, MEET THE HBIC

Friday, 14 September – Kailani

I make it my goal this morning to read the entire information packet that was given to me last night. It's a pointless endeavor, as the sparse bundle covers no real information. It is clear that Hideo isn't included in the temporary move to the task force – he had gotten a similar packet, but solely for the purpose of getting me up to speed, nothing more. It's also very clear that the "invitation" to join them was more of a requisition. My temper flares at the implication that I'm government property that can be passed from unit to unit without my explicit agreement. These fuckers. This wording is bullshit. "Voluntary compliance" my ass. "Mandatory temporary reassignment"... You can't fucking reassign me! I don't work for you!

Having reached my boiling point by the last page of the bundle, I throw it into my shredder (as assigned), completely overwhelmed with helplessness. It's very clear that I'm going to have to attend the meeting this morning, if nothing else. Rapidly stacking information in my brain, I realize that I'm not getting paid for the last seven cases until the following week, and I have to give two weeks' notice to the department or I forfeit my training fee, as detailed in the hiring agreement. I'm a consultant on a case-by-case basis, yes, but I still had to have mandatory department training, which I was unable to fund at the time I joined. It was a real workaround, I came to realize later, because I had already interned there for almost six months, and if I had made it the full six months, that would have counted as the mandatory training time. Gomez, however, had pulled me three weeks before my internship ended, and while my agreement with the department was fairly cut and dry, it became clear to me later that she had tied me to the unit in some clever ways. The hitch in her plan was that I got to choose cases, so while I had to give two weeks, I didn't *have* to accept any cases during that time. I did, however, have to show up to the office daily should I not take any cases during my separation period.

A thought hits me out of nowhere, and I dig through my desk to find the agreement. *Voluntary case assignment... consultant basis.... mandatory two weeks' notice... oh you fucking pig riding cat wrangler!* I groan loudly, slamming my head on my desk. *Agrees to attend two TBD exit meetings of the department's choice. Sweet grandmother my ass.* Well, this could count as one of my exit meetings. The other could be me holding two fingers up in the air screaming obscenities at the ex-station chief. Gomez had started as a real mentor, but it didn't take long for me to see the steel bitch hiding behind that gentle exterior, squeezing stones for every drop of blood she could get. Frowning now, I take a deep breath. Right. I can handle this. Step one is getting Hideo back on my side, because no one and nothing can make me do a *thing* without him as my handler.

As I'm plotting and planning, the man himself knocks on my door. "Time to go, Kailani."

My brain isn't moving fast enough today. Too many things have been thrown at me, and I'm too tired. Our caseload the past few weeks had been intense, and I was due for a few days away. Putting away my papers, I stand and walk over to him, grabbing his hand tightly. "Let's go." He shakes his head, and I hold on to him more insistently. "If I'm going, you're coming with me. We'll figure it out as we go, but we're going together or not at all." A horrible thought hits me, and I stare at him, worried. "Unless..." I say hesitantly. "Unless... you don't want to? That's your choice, Deo. You may not want to stay my handler...."

He stares down at our hands for a long moment, making me nervous. Running his thumb gently over the back of my hand, he sighs softly, and says so quietly I can barely hear him, "Oh Kai. Don't you know by now that where you go, I will always follow?" Without lifting his eyes to meet mine, he pulls away gently and opens the door for me, letting me lead the way.

The walk to the meeting room is like a funeral march, and a heavy, nervous feeling bubbles over, making me jittery. I walk into the room reluctantly, looking over my shoulder at Tanaka with a worried grimace. Tanaka meets my glare with an almost apologetic look, opening his mouth to say something, when a sarcastic drawl interrupts our wordless communication.

"Well isn't this a pleasant surprise. Useless One and Useless Two, reporting for duty." Facing forward I meet Donovan's green eyes, bright and contemptuous as he looks at me.

"Walker..." a slightly deeper voice says warningly, and I follow its bass rumble to meet the steady gaze of... *dear sweet baby Jesus. A fucking Viking. An honest to god, tear my clothes off and ravish me Viking.* Before me stands a beast of a man. His biceps are the size of small children, for Christ's sake. A long, complex tattoo winds itself down his right arm, all black, and his shirt stretches tight across an insanely muscled chest. He has a strong face – sharp cheekbones and a slightly crooked nose with a small scar on its bridge. Icy blue eyes stare at me, unblinking as he completes his own, slow perusal of me. His blond-brown hair is short on the sides and longer on the top, swept to one side, and his rough face is framed by a neatly kept beard. I'm guessing he stands about 6'5 or 6'6 to my suddenly diminutive 5'8. I finish running my eyes over him and meet his in a long stare, which rapidly changes from contemplative to challenging. My shoulders tense up the longer we look at each other, and the atmosphere in the room charges with an unknown emotion. Hideo lays a hand lightly on my shoulder, and I glance back at him, thankful for the respite from the tension in the air. He squeezes it lightly before removing his hand and ushers me forward, pulling out a chair at the sparse table.

The Viking changes his appraising gaze to Hideo, for a much shorter time, then walks to the front of the room. He motions vaguely towards the chairs, and Hideo and I sit, waiting for him to speak.

"Maddox Smith, CIA." He gestures towards Donovan, whose feet are now up casually on the table and who reluctantly formally introduces himself.

"The Wonder Twins and I have already met, but Walker Donovan, FBI."

Hideo leans forward slightly so he can take in the whole room before he says coolly, "Hideo Tanaka, SPD."

I shake my head at the male antics and chirp, "Kailani Reed, HBIC."

I startle a barked laugh from Hideo, and I grin over my shoulder at him as he shakes his head at me. Smith quirks his head at me and opens his mouth to speak when the door to the meeting room opens again, and Director Fucking Gomez walks calmly in.

"Oh Kailani, I think you'll find, in this instance, I'm the HBIC." I startle, whipping around to face a now very tense Hideo, and then look back to Gomez.

"What, and I cannot stress this enough, the fuck is happening here?"

"Calm down, dear. You're so prone to histrionics. We're just all going to have a little chat. Good heavens."

I shake my head and stand. "Nope. No. Just... so much Nope the nope is overflowing from the Nope River and flooding the land of Nope with all of its nopeness. This..." I gesture wildly with my hands, "this is *not... YOU!*" I point accusingly towards Gomez. "We had an agreement, and you fucking fucked me to Fuckville!"

She shakes her grandmotherly head gently, clearly disappointed in my response to her presence. "Oh Kailani, for heaven's sake. Sit down. We just don't have time for this today."

I remain standing and edge towards the door slowly. "I am beyond uninterested in anything you have to say to me. Promises were made that have *never* been kept, but I've carried through on my end of the deal. You'd have to pay me the GDP of a small country to sit here and listen to your bullshit again. I'm out."

"You walk out that door, dear, and I think you'll find that you *are* very much *out* indeed."

The odd threat hangs heavy in the air, as Director Gomez sits elegantly in her chair at the head of the table, and turns to Smith. "Tea, dear, please. Two sugar and milk," she requests gently. *This fucking woman....*

"Okay, I'll bite. What do you mean by that obvious but super fucking vague threat, you old bat?"

Smith and Donovan suck in their breaths quickly and look, startled, towards Director Gomez. Hideo just groans quietly behind me, and I reevaluate her position based on the big men's reactions.

"Kailani. I think you'll find life very... unpleasant... shall we say, if you refuse to even listen to me. I have it on the best authority that you've withheld vital information on cases in the past. Information that could have closed cases more quickly, or could have, at the least, provided valuable leads for our detectives, hmmm? Tampering with an investigation is an imprisonable offense, as is obstruction of justice. I'd hate to have to incarcerate you for any length of time should a full investigation be needed. I think we can agree that any time in a prison environment would be... detrimental to you, to say the least."

My stomach twists sharply as the blood drains from my face. Prison would be a death sentence for me. My shields wouldn't be able to block the amount of emotion in a place like that, and I'd go insane. Like Azkaban. And this freaking grandmotherly bitch sitting in front of me is my own, personal Dolores Umbridge. *God damnit! God fucking damnit to fucking hell!* My breathing increases and becomes shallow, and the world in front of me narrows to a pinprick. I hover between the table and the door, swaying slightly on my feet as panic crashes over me.

Gomez's calm voice echoes through the room: "Mr. Tanaka? I wasn't aware that you'd be joining us today?" She gestures vaguely towards the door as she focuses on the papers in front of her. "Close it on your way out, if you would, dear."

Oh holy fuck on toast no.

Hideo moves towards me, shrugging helplessly as I look to him pleadingly, like a trapped animal. He pauses as my hand shoots out and grabs him like a vice grip. *Think, think, think Kailani. THINK!*

Gomez clears her throat and motions towards the door again, a hint of ice entering her voice. "Mr. Tanaka, I won't ask again." She looks up and locks eyes with me. The woman has incredibly strong mental shields, having practiced for years, but isn't accounting for my desperation. Holding Hideo's arm so tightly my nails make perfect half-moon indents on his skin, I focus completely on the woman in front of me and *grab*, with brute force, any emotion I can. It's like trying to find a handhold in a granite wall, but at the last second I feel an unknown emotion and yank it towards me. Her eyes flare open briefly, and she says in a slightly choked voice, tense with warning, "Ms. Reed...."

I frown at her and hold tight as her shields begin to weaken. Donovan looks at her, concerned and confused, as Hideo stands frozen beside me. Gomez and I stare at each other, locked in a battle of wills. I can see her trying to shore up her barricades, and I start stripping them brutally. I know from experience it feels like knives peeling away layers of your brain, and I see her eyes flare with the realization of what I'm doing. She presses her lips together into a tight line. Meeting my glare with calm, though slightly pained, eyes, she grinds out, "I won't ask you again, Tanaka. Ms. Reed, this is your final warning."

This antique bitch is underestimating what I'm able to do when fueled by panic. As she waves her hand dismissively, used to being obeyed without question, I use everything in me to drive a thin needle of pain straight into a small hole in her mental walls. Her jaw flexes, and she swallows audibly as she stares at the papers in front of her. There is a long silence, then she finally says, in a voice tight with pain, "Upon further consideration, Mr. Tanaka, you're welcome to stay. For the moment. While Ms. Reed settles in."

I wrap her emotion around me more closely, pulling harder as her face begins to redden slightly. There's no other sign of her discomfort, and we stare at each other. She's clearly determined to win this conflict, but between determination and desperation, there's no contest. As I pull tighter on the single emotion I have, her shields start to crumble and I'm able to grab more and more. Her defenses are more like a weakening dam now, cracks appearing all over. Gritting my teeth and without breaking the eye lock, I begin to slowly gather from her. As she feels herself losing the battle her eyes widen and then narrow to slits. *Ahhh, the snake behind the sparrow makes its appearance.*

Her voice taut and angry, she concedes. "Detective Tanaka, I'm of course happy to have your expertise consulting the task force as well. While you don't have proper clearance, I am prepared to make an exception in this case, given how much you clearly mean to Ms. Reed." There's an unknown threat in her words, but I'm too focused to process it. She gestures towards the table. "I assume you'll accept the position of Ms. Reed's handler for the length of time she works with the task force?" Donovan starts upright from his reclined position, storm clouds racing over his face, but Gomez makes a short, sharp hand gesture to him, and he remains silent.

Tanaka looks around the room, taking in the occupants, and looks back towards Gomez. "Of course. It would be an honor." She waits for him to sit, raising a single brow when he makes no move towards the table. "An honor I would need to see in writing, prior to committing."

"Of course," she replies tightly, making a note on the papers in front of her and showing it to him. He nods and initials it. "We'll have copies made for you."

He moves to pull out my chair and then sits beside me. She looks to me and says shortly, "Kailani, if you would?"

I stare at her, confused, until I realize I'm still pulling her emotion, like a boa constrictor wrapped around her chest, tightening. Being petty, I shove everything I've pulled back into her all at once, and she chokes for a moment before taking a deep breath and frowning at me. "I see," she grinds out. "Be careful, Ms. Reed. My patience isn't what it once was."

I shrug back, seemingly careless. "My blind acceptance isn't what it once was."

The uncomfortable stalemate is broken by Smith returning with her tea. He takes his seat again as Gomez shuffles the papers in front of her once more.

"We're just waiting on one more… Ah. Here he is."

A familiar, soothing, warm wave of energy washes over me, and I turn like a sunflower to meet the slight smile and sweet face of the Pleasure Bleeder from yesterday. Seeing him for the first time is surprising, to say the least. From his accent and diction, I had thought he'd be a surfer dude, all blond-haired, blue-eyed Californian boy, not Native American, all bronze skin and black eyed. The man in front of me is a 180 from the image I had crafted in my head. Full, full lips and a square jaw with high, sharp cheekbones are framed by long, tousled black hair. It has streaks of lighter brown in it from where the sun has bleached it slightly and, from what I can see, goes at least halfway down his back, if not longer. He has a dimpled face even when he isn't full-out smiling, skirting between adorable and dangerous. I'm guessing he's maybe 26 or 27, still boyish in his energy. He has the body of a surfer, though, well-muscled arms, broad shoulders that trace to a sharp V at his hips, and long, powerful-looking legs. He has leather bands wrapped around one of his wrists, and a tattoo peeks out from under the sleeve of his tee-shirt as he moves forward.

"Jonah Shotridge", he says, voice smoky and warm. I smile slightly, unintentionally, the edges of my lips barely curving up. Despite the fact that he's a pleasure bleeder, he brings such a joyful energy with him into a room that it's hard to resist. He looks around the room and takes in the seating arrangement. Gomez is at the head of the oval table, clearly the Queen in this domain. Smith is immediately next to her on one side, and Tanaka and I are close together at the other end. Donovan is on the opposite side of the table, again, close to Gomez, with an empty seat beside him. Shotridge walks around the table calmly, grabs the chair from beside Donovan, and moves it to my other side, putting me between him and Tanaka, and putting himself between me and Smith. The arrangement is awkward, with a huge space in the middle of the table on both sides between the two groups.

Gomez raises a single eyebrow curiously, watching the proceedings with a hawklike focus. Shotridge smiles back at her and says, "Clearly battle lines are being drawn here for some reason. I feel like I've missed something important, but, given my limited knowledge of the situation, I'll just sit here with Kailani and Hideo."

Smith and Donovan grumble under their breaths as Gomez grits her teeth slightly, trying to maintain her composure.

Shotridge turns to me, still smiling, and moves to fist-bump me. Still tense from the past few moments, I don't respond, and he carefully picks up my hand, closes it into a fist for me, and bumps it gently with his own. "Go team!" he whispers dramatically, and I snort unexpectedly at his ridiculousness. He leans around me and looks at Hideo, holding out his hand again: "Hey man! I'm Jonah."

Hideo stares at him for a minute, flummoxed, then shakes his hand firmly. "Hideo Tanaka."

"Oh dude. Yeah. I know. Nice to meet you." Jonah nudges me gently and wags his eyebrows at me dramatically. "Top secret, right girl? What's happened? Fill me in." The juxtaposition between his look and his surfer-boy lingo finally cracks me, and I burst into slightly manic laughter. Jonah's sweet smile deepens to a grin, and he laughs with me, and Hideo rolls his eyes at the two of us.

Gomez shakes her head, clearly frustrated, and knocks her hand on the table to get our attention.

"Well, look around you and get comfortable please, because the five people around this table will be your team for the foreseeable future."

That sobers me up quickly, and I lean forward to listen.

"Brief introductions, before I get into the meat of why we are all here. On my right is your task force leader, Maddox Smith. Maddox is an active CIA operative whom I have personally requested take control of this... unique situation. He has worked previously with a similar task force in Britain, and maintains contacts in MI5 and MI6. Should this transition into an international case, *which we expect* it will, Maddox will run point between our two units. Walker Donovan, on my left, is second in command. He is FBI and has worked closely with Maddox since they graduated from their respective academies. I believe they are approaching six years as partners. Each is effectively peerless within his agency, and is uniquely suited for this particular casework."

Donovan flexes slightly at her words, a smug, condescending look settling on his face. "Damn right..." he smirks.

Gomez frowns at him briefly, before continuing, while passing out what look to be briefing sheets. "Donovan is here because, despite his attitude, he's very, *very* good at blending in places and not being noticed."

I grumble under my breath, "I don't see how anybody could *fail* to notice him..."

A brief flare of purely male satisfaction pushes its way into my senses. I groan slightly under its weight and frown at Donovan. *"Not* how I meant it, Asshole."

He shoots me a confused look, raising his eyebrows slightly, and I shake my head tiredly.

Gomez sighs deeply. "Now, now, Reed. Let's continue please."

Tanaka leans towards me under the auspices of passing me the briefing sheets and brushes his hand comfortingly against mine. A thin tendril of worry weaves its way across his skin and skitters over mine before it disappears. *Jesus, my shields are weak. I've been working too much.* The prospect of sitting in this room for the next few hours, being weighed down with other people's emotions, suddenly triggers the beginnings of a panic attack. My breath grows short and my heart feels like it is skipping beats. I try to lengthen the space between breaths and calm myself down, but it just makes me inhale and exhale in weird, staccato rhythms, like you do when you're about to cry. Tanaka inches closer to me, pressing his leg against the length of mine, as I frantically try to get control of my emotions. I stare at the table ferociously, blinking back tears and counting my breaths. Suddenly a small piece of paper enters my view, with a little drawing of a T-Rex trying to do push-ups. At the top it says, "T-Rex *hates* push-ups" with a frowny face, and it's so unexpected and incongruous in the moment that it jolts me out of my spiral, and I glance up at Jonah with watery eyes. He meets my gaze with an incredibly serious expression and whispers sadly, "He really does."

I grin unexpectedly, and he shakes his head in disappointment at my expression. "Poor guy. So sad and you're laughing at him. What kind of person *are* you?"

Gomez's sharp voice interrupts our whispered conversation. "Am I *boring* the two of you?"

Without looking back at her, still holding my gaze, Jonah says, "Yes, actually," before dropping a quick wink at me. We both start giggling like school kids who have gotten called out by their teacher and refocus our attention on Director Gomez, who is fast losing her patience. *Too fucking bad*, I think rebelliously. *I didn't ask to be here.*

"Well," she huffs. "Perhaps we'll skip introductions for the time being and move into the purpose of this task force. A little background first. *Please* try to concentrate. Kailani, I'm talking to you here."

Jonah echoes her quietly under his breath, saying with mock outrage, "Yes, for the love of god, Kailani! The rest of us are trying to focus." He glares at me with an exaggerated frown, and I start giggling again as Hideo groans beside us. He glares for real at Jonah and nudges me, trying to get me to focus on the front of the room. Smith and Donovan are watching the interaction between Jonah and me with barely concealed interest, and Director Gomez is openly frustrated as she clears her throat for attention. She gestures to the white screen behind her on the wall, which displays a black slide with a single white star in the center. "You have all been briefed on the Stargate Project, to a point. Am I correct?"

Jonah, Hideo, and I nod. Donovan rolls his eyes dramatically, mumbling under his breath.

"Something you'd like to add, Donovan?" Gomez says coolly.

"You know how I feel about this bullshit already. No disrespect, Director Gomez." She frowns and makes a quick motion towards Smith, who raps sharply on the table once. Donovan sits up from his slouched position and says, "Apologies, Director Gomez."

She nods and continues. "You're all aware of the public dissolution of the Project in the 1990s, correct? For all intents and purposes, the US government had publicly disavowed its research on the psychic sciences. Privately, however, it had had a major breakthrough. Unwilling to expose any of its results to public scrutiny, or risk any of its agents being turned, they chose to push the development of any psychic assets into a newly created clandestine agency. Operating under the unassuming moniker "Center for Developing Sciences", the CDS was completely black ops." The slide behind her changes and displays a bland, nondescript government logo – CDS written in black letters superimposed on the image of two descending triangles within a larger circle. The triangles have what looks like sun rays extending out from them, and in the center of the smaller, thicker triangle is a stylized eye. It is incredibly similar to the eye on top of the pyramid on the dollar bill.

She continues, "No known paper trail existed for it beyond a small, low-staffed building in Washington D.C. Located several streets away from the White House on a small side street, the CDS headquarters was a converted private residence, with five offices, a kitchenette, and one tiny meeting room. Its miniscule budget wasn't enough to argue about while the US was busy waging wars on multiple fronts, and the unknown professors who trudged in and out every day were unexceptional in every way. Rarely, if ever, questioned, the small office ran like clockwork for years, until its existence faded completely from the minds of those in Washington."

The slide changes again and is now a complex, layered map. The top layer shows multiple buildings, beneath which are a series of colored lines stretching from location to location.

"Miles away, in Northern Virginia, the real minds of the CDS resided on the bottom floors of Langley. The George Bush Center for Intelligence, commonly referred to as Langley, was the known headquarters for the CIA. The buildings comprising the HQ rise six visible stories above ground, and are situated on 258 open acres. Wikipedia lists the known floor area as 2,500,000 square feet, and aerial images show an impressive conglomeration of architecture spread in the middle of a fairly dense forest."

She pauses, and the slide behind her changes to a massive map, seemingly of subway lines or something similar. "Nothing revealed the existence of a massive, subterranean web of floors, tunnels, and roads running from Langley the full 10.6 miles to the Pentagon, and then a further 3.6 miles to the FBI headquarters in downtown D.C. The planning committee was limited to four highly trained architects who studied subterranean living before drawing up the blueprints. The Maginot Line in France. Cappadocia in Turkey. Pilsen in the Czech Republic. Wieliczka Salt Mine in Poland."

"The construction of the Interagency Underground was surprisingly easy to achieve. Anyone who has ever lived in Washington would tell you about the never-ending and soul-crushing roadwork, often existing for years at a time in any given area. Orange barrels were just as common a sight as broken-down cars or potholes. Seeing it every day rendered the constant building invisible to the local populace. No one even looked at the construction projects anymore. Thus, deep within the bowels of the Virginia water table, surrounded by reinforced steel and double-thick concrete, the unknown and shadow government operates, often unencumbered by the bureaucratic red tape which holds the rest of Washington DC together. Housing offshoots of the CIA, FBI, DIA, NSA, and NSAC, the lower levels also host lesser known agencies such as the Office of Intelligence and Counterintelligence, The National Geospatial Intelligence Agency, and The National Reconnaissance Office. And, on sublevel 6, office block A, ring 2, corridor C, The CDS."

The slide changes for a fourth time, showing a series of subterranean tunnels, with a large section highlighted.

"The CDS is a joke, even amongst the lesser intelligence agencies. The US government waged such an effective war against the validity of the psychic sciences that the disdain trickled down through the various offices, and the CDS retained little to no credibility. An entire history of verifiable psychic events was erased in order to gain ground in a quiet war. Despite the fact that every nation in the world has documented cases of psychic activity – from second sight in Ireland to Nostradamus, from Jeane Dixon to Baba Vanga, from the Oracle at Delphi to the Nechung Oracle – belief and support of the psychic sciences fell out of vogue. Other agencies avoided the CDS like the plague, and over time, the CDS was left completely to their own devices, not required to participate in any interagency regulations, or really, any regulations at all. They were seen as harmless, brainless, and toothless.

The quiet and unassuming agency stumbled along at first, with between 1,000-5,000 agents at any one time. Operating under the premise that consistency would determine respect, the officers of the CDS worked determinedly to develop indisputable tests, screening procedures, and provable data points. A screening of over 20,000 potential agents had occurred just prior to the Stargate debacle, and of those a measly 200 had proven to have any measure of psychic powers on the metric. Observing those agents and putting them through rigorous testing, the CDS began classifying psychic categories and identifying fields which naturally attracted those with psychic potential."

She pauses, looking around at us. I can't hide my interest, which has always been my problem with Gomez, and I'm leaning forward, drinking in her words. Hideo is leaning back, eyes narrowed as he listens to her spiel. Shotridge isn't looking at her at all but is glancing between me and the notes in front of him. Smith is nodding along at specific points, like he knows the speech by heart and is silently agreeing. But Donovan, well, Donovan is openly rolling his eyes and scoffing. Gomez raises a single brow as she takes in his disbelief and sighs deeply.

"Alright, children," she says condescendingly. "Clearly we have some different takes on the CDS and its methods of gathering intelligence."

Donovan shakes his head slightly, snorting derisively. "Intelligence is clearly being used loosely here."

Gomez takes a steadying breath and looks towards Smith.

"Agent Smith, I thought I made myself *very* clear when asking for your input on this task force. I was extremely forthcoming regarding my opinion of Donovan's position on this team, and I believe you'll remember giving your word that his personal shortcomings would not impact the work we need to complete."

Daaaaamn, Gomez! Old girl is laying down the law! I smirk slightly in Donovan's direction, thoroughly enjoying his being read the riot act.

Gomez continues, calmly but firmly. "I'm afraid that, at this point, I don't have the time or inclination to deal with people whose capacity for information is so limited." She looks pointedly at Donovan, who is shifting slightly under her glare. "Agent Donovan, Agent Smith. We no longer need your services. Please remove yourselves from the room. Perhaps Detective Tanaka would be kind enough to walk you out."

Smith and Donovan both rise to their feet in protest, talking over each other.

"Director Gomez, this situation is being blown out of..."

"You won't find someone to replace us and you know it..."

"Enough!" Director Gomez snaps. "To be clear, everyone on this task force is completely and totally replaceable, other than Ms. Reed and, to a lesser degree, Mr. Shotridge."

The room falls silent immediately, and Jonah looks carefully at Gomez before turning to me with his adorably dimpled smile. "Well, dayam girl! We should write a list of demands now, before we get pulled too far in. Ice cream! I vote ice cream!"

"Coffee," I reply grinning. "ALL the coffee. Ever."

He shakes his head ruefully. "Augh! How could I forget coffee? I'll add it to the list."

We grin at each other, while Donovan glares at me across the table, and Smith gives me a long, assessing look. Hideo shifts his body slightly to cut me off from their eyes as much as possible, and Jonah, watching him, makes the same adjustment, so I'm hidden between the two men.

Gomez points at the two agents still on their feet. "Consider yourself on probation, gentlemen. If you desire to be a part of this unit, you will fall in line immediately, or find yourself sitting in a field office in Nebraska counting cows until retirement. Do I make myself clear?"

Both men nod, chastised, and sit quietly.

Gomez rubs her face tiredly, and for the first time since she arrived in the room I take a moment to look at her. Her eyes are sunken and grey, the smoky circles of purple surrounding them indicating a serious lack of sleep. Her round, grandmotherly face has lost some of its fullness and looks sallow, and the lines on her forehead have deepened since I last saw her. Clearly whatever this is has been weighing on her heavily. I sigh deeply.

"Alright you old dragon," I huff, Hideo groaning beside me. "I'm listening."

Gomez frowns elegantly. "Really, Kailani. Would it cause you irreparable damage to behave for a moment?"

I look at her thoughtfully. "It might. It really might."

She grimaces and mutters to herself, "Of all the people I could end up having to depend on..." then continues in a more normal tone of voice, "Well. Back to it. The CDS... oh for the love of *God* Kailani. What now?"

My hand half-raised in the air, I look to my empty cup of coffee plaintively. She all but growls and says tightly, "You will have a break in an hour, Ms. Reed. Until that point I suggest you don't push me any further. Please believe me when

I say that I am at my breaking point with you."

Donovan smirks from across the table as I look at my mug sadly. Tanaka wordlessly passes me the last of his coffee, which I drink happily, smiling at him and squeezing his hand as a thank you. As I look back to the front of the room where Gomez has begun speaking again, I see Jonah quietly pouring half of his coffee into my mug. My eyebrows shoot up in surprise, and he holds out his hand. Tentatively I squeeze his hand as I had moments before with Tanaka, and Jonah grins at me happily before turning to face the Director. She begins recapping what we've discussed to that point, including a run-down of all of the US intelligence agencies and their purposes, and I settle in for a long morning.

SHOW ME YOURS, I'LL...

Friday, 14 September – Kailani

An hour and a half later the promised break has yet to emerge, and Gomez is wrapping up on a history of interagency cooperation on international casework, which, yawn, and I'm needing out of the room so badly that my eyelids are twitching. No reasonable person should be expected to sit through a briefing this boring without a caffeinated support line. I swear to god, I never thought someone could make psychic sciences and spy school this dull if they tried, but this is like watching grass grow. Except not as exciting. I'm going to die. I'm going to slowly calcify into a stone Kailani, and people ages on will come and stare at the... oh shit!

"MS. REED!" Director Gomez barks sharply as I suddenly rocket to attention. My head jerks up as I realize she must have said my name several times before I heard her.

"Um, yeah? Yes? I mean... yes?"

She presses her face into her hands briefly and takes a deep breath before focusing on me again.

"I was saying that, at this point, it would behoove us to introduce ourselves to the team. We need to know each other's strengths and weaknesses in order to function properly as a unit."

I look at her warily, processing her statement. "What exactly do you mean by that, Director Gomez?"

"We need to know what everyone is able to do, Ms. Reed. Yourself included. I'm sure that Smith, Donovan, and Shotridge would like to know *why* exactly you're so valuable at the moment."

Jonah shakes his head from beside me. "Naw, I'm cool. Kailani can let me know in her own time."

Gomez dismisses him with a casual wave. "No, Kailani can let us know on my time. Which is now."

I edge back from the table, trying to think, and press inconspicuously against Tanaka. His hand rests gently against my back underneath the table, and he rubs it softly, trying to soothe me. He speaks up unexpectedly,

"I'll go first, I suppose. Hideo Tanaka, SPD."

"Oh Mr. Tanaka," Gomez interjects icily. "We all already *know* your ability – you can rein in and handle Ms. Reed. Lord knows how you do it, but don't give away all your secrets, or you won't have a place here anymore. The moment she begins to listen to anyone but you, your usefulness here will have expired."

Donovan chuffs loudly as both Hideo's and Jonah's faces turn thunderous. I'm used to Gomez's treatment of me – she sees everyone and everything as a commodity, their worth based on their ability and attitude. In her opinion I wasted my ability and had a bad attitude, so I was little more than a dancing bear to her. There for a purpose, but not encouraged to think on my own. But to say it so openly and disparagingly, that was new. She was usually more politic with her opinions.

Deo takes a deep breath and continues like she hadn't spoken. "I've worked on the force for several years now as a detective. Kailani and I have been partners for two years, give or take, with a higher than average close rate on cases." He pauses, and Gomez stares at him, clearly waiting for him to continue.

"We're currently the top ranked team in the department."

Smith and Donovan look up at that consideringly. Gomez makes a small sound of protest, and Hideo turns to me, mouth curling up at one edge.

"We're actually the top ranked team in the entire state." Smith's and Donovan's brows go up at that, and I rest my face in one hand and scrunch up my face, knowing what's coming as Gomez stares at Hideo pointedly.

"And we have been, for over the past year."

Aaaaaand there it is. While we try very hard to fly under the radar, it's incredibly difficult for Hideo and me to not help if we're able to. So although I don't usually incorporate *everything* I discover into our reports, and while Hideo tries very hard to downplay my involvement, we haven't been able to do it at the expense of any of the victims. Especially since a lot of our caseload involves women and children. I didn't realize how long our run at the top had gone, however, and I kicked myself for being so careless.

Smith startles slightly, asking, "Surely not that entire time?"

Flipping through a stack of papers in front of her, Gomez murmurs, "98% solve rate. Impressive. And closer to two years, Tanaka. Almost since the start."

Donovan grunts. "They taking the easy stuff to pad their numbers?"

She shakes her head. "No. Rather the opposite in fact. They're usually given cold cases no one else wants to or is willing to touch."

Both of the agency men stare at us, and I bristle under their watchful eyes. The air in the room grows heavy as the two groups look challengingly at each other, a tension Jonah breaks in his easy, laid-back style.

"So yeah, I'll go next I guess. I'm Jonah Shotridge. Pleasure Bleeder. New to the force as of just a couple weeks ago. This is my first case."

Donovan groans in protest. "You have *got* to be kidding me. This is a multi-bureau, federal task force, and we've got a complete greenhorn? What the fu... hell?"

Gomez replies casually. "For some reason we have trouble keeping Bleeders in our trial programs. I can't *possibly* think of why, when so many of the officers are every bit as welcoming as you've been."

There's a pause, and Donovan shrugs dismissively. "You can't tell me that there isn't someone more seasoned than this guy."

"There is. He's not an option at this time."

I look quickly to Hideo who shakes his head minutely. Gomez looks over to me and starts to speak when Smith interrupts.

"Maddox Smith," he rumbles. *Oh god, how bad is it that I want to curl up on his chest naked and listen to him purr?* I stare at him wide-eyed, trying to focus through the insane rush of hormones.

"Director Gomez has already given you my background with the agency, I believe. CIA, prior special forces. JSOC, Task Force Green. As Director Gomez indicated, I'll run point for any interagency work with our British counterparts, should the need arise. I've also been through CDS training, and am familiar with their guidelines and operations as well."

Donovan scoffs, and Smith turns to him with a dark face. A constrained wave of anger pulses off him, sending shivers up my spine, and Deo raises a brow at me, seeing the goosebumps on my skin. I shrug a little, dismissing it.

"*As* Director Gomez was saying," Smith pushes on, Donovan having cowered slightly under his noticeable anger, "CDS has several trial programs currently running, and–"

I raise my hand, interrupting him.

"Yes, Reed?"

"Sorry, I must have missed that part. Where are the programs?"

He looks at me, befuddled. "She just... I mean.... She literally *just* went through all this."

I look up at him with plaintive eyes, saying sadly, "I *did* say I needed a break."

"She did," Jonah concedes beside me. "You can't say she didn't warn you."

Smith looks almost disbelievingly towards Gomez, who

motions for him to continue. "Oookay. Are you focused now, Reed, so we won't have to do this a third time?"

"Sir, yes sir!" I snap out, saluting sharply, and his eye twitches a little, so I'm pretty sure he's going to kill me here soon.

"Programs in Austin, Seattle, New York, and DC." He levels a steady glance at me, and I nod at him. *Active listening!* I think, proud of myself. *Nod to show you're participating in the discussion.* I nod impressively, and he sighs audibly before continuing. "I've been floating between the other three for the last six months, watching their procedures while chasing leads. They all have units experimenting with Bleeders and Pushers, though the efficacy of..."

I lean forward slightly, interest peaked, and Hideo and I look at each other, puzzled.

"Sorry, what? That's a new term to us," Hideo interrupts respectfully, and Smith clarifies.

"A Pusher? It's a new category at the CDS, classified differently than Bleeders. Bleeders drain emotion from the subject. Pushers, for lack of a better term, inject emotion into the subject."

God knows I'd let him inject something into me! Damn, that man's arms! Shit! Stop it, Kailani!

Donovan glares up at Smith. Clearly this is news to him, and he's unhappy about having been kept out of the loop.

"What the hell, man! I've been with you on those trips. Where was I when this was happening?"

Smith shrugs, somewhat uncomfortably. "It's new, Walker," he replies quietly. "It's only something they've just recently classified." Smith looks to Gomez, who motions for him to continue. He rubs the back of his neck, the movement looking odd for such a confident man.

"There have been some, *very limited*, trials run on people, testing whether Pushing is a variation on Bleeding or its own thing."

Donovan links his hands over his head and leans back,

eyes narrowed. He's clearly pissed off, though the anger isn't rolling out of him like it did from Smith moments before. It's more a haze surrounding him, and he stares up at his friend.

"And?" he says combatively.

"And?" Smith asks, feigning confusion.

"*And?*" Donovan spits back, obviously seeing something we don't. Deo, Jonah, and I exchange confused looks, watching the battle play out before us.

"And... I've had some training in it. I clearly have no talent for Bleeding, but have shown some, very mixed, very limited, mostly unproven, results on Pushing."

Donovan's face is a thundercloud now, as Smith continues. "Really, take it with a grain of salt," he says, downplaying it. "The results are really scattered, and there's no clear evidence that there's anything happening at all."

Gomez says his name, once, from where she's sitting, and it's laden with meaning. "Smith."

He looks to her and nods. "I can try to show you, but..."

Donovan jerks his head up, eyes lit with scorn and anger, as Smith straightens and an odd look comes over his face, something between embarrassment and concentration. Moments later, he flexes slightly and rolls his neck a little. Waiting for the emotion to push out from him, I watch him consideringly. *Jesus his arms are like tree trunks. He's a fucking mountain. I'd climb that like a monkey. I bet he's a freaking Boss in the bedroom...* Lost in my perusal of him, imagination running wild, images of him taking *charge* fill my brain. Suddenly a feeling of domination washes over me, a bone-deep intimidation with an edge of fear running through it. I shiver, eyes widening as a thrill runs from my head to my toes, with a long, lascivious pause right in the middle. *Oooooooo! Oh seven holy hells!!!*

I shoot to my feet, disrupting whatever sex wave Smith is putting out, and say in a strangled voice, "*That's* what you can Push?"

He looks at me startled, and I notice the rest of the group has expressions mirroring him. "Uh... *what's* what I can Push?"

I wave my hands wildly around, panting slightly. "That... that... mojo or whatever! Jesus! Warn a girl next time! It's... it's *impolite* for the love of god!"

Hideo shifts next to me. "Kailani?" he asks quietly. "What exactly did you feel?"

I pause, looking around the room again, more cautiously this time. "I mean... the uh... the..." I gesture vaguely towards my chest and then my nether regions. "And the... uhhhh... the sex punch thing," I finish hurriedly.

Everyone is staring at me with varying degrees of emotion. Donovan looks confused, Hideo looks thoughtful, Gomez looks somewhat disgusted, and sweet Jonah looks amused and intrigued. "What... what is happening here?" I say, feeling oddly embarrassed. "I mean, everyone else... what did everyone else feel?"

The answers overlap as each of the men speaks.

"Not a single fucking thing."

"*Maybe* a little fearful?"

"Kind of a vague sense of dread or something."

Eyes wide, I bite my lip in consternation. "Oh... uh... yeah. For sure. Me too. But, ah, kind of with a whole... sensual edge?" I end on a questioning note, my voice trailing off as I see Jonah and Hideo shake their heads in disagreement.

Smith walks around the table towards me, moving like a panther cautiously approaching its prey. He stares at me with his icy eyes, focused completely on me, and his jaw tightens as he pauses in front of me. Taking a deep breath I see his face set again, and the same feeling of edgy danger races over me, titillating, sending a thrill of fright down my spine. Every single bit of me sits up to take notice, and I have to forcibly stop myself from licking him.

"WOULD YOU STOP FUCKING SEX PUNCHING ME!" I

scream in a strangled voice.

He starts, growling, "Stop saying sex punch! I'm not.... I'm not doing... that!"

"Oooooo you *definitely* are," I purr before getting a hold of myself. Giving myself a mental slap I step back into Hideo's body, which, if I'm being completely honest, doesn't diffuse my hormones like it should.

Donovan's voice cuts through the room, darkly amused. "Well, it looks like we've learned something about Kailani today. Clearly she doesn't have a problem with danger. Rather the opposite, I'd guess."

Face flushed and horribly embarrassed, I stare at my feet, feeling confused and incredibly exposed. As the silence lengthens uncomfortably, embarrassment starts to morph into anger until it bursts out of me.

"Fuck this noise," I mutter furiously, shaking off Hideo's soothing touch. "I didn't agree to sit through anything like this. I'm not a guinea pig."

Smith makes a kind of rumbling sound in his throat, as though he's about to talk, but Gomez raps her hand on the table loudly, and he turns to face her.

"I think," she says acerbically, "that now might be a good time for that break."

Having stormed out of the room, I wander down an empty hallway and sit in an empty office, head buried in my hands

"Hey girl, hey!" calls a happy, but tired voice. I scrunch up my face in a frown, determined to remain miserable. I am angry and frustrated and altogether upset, and I don't want to be teased out of my bad mood by the dimpled grin of Shotridge. "Oooooh, man." He nods, suddenly serious. Knowing I am being beyond ridiculous but refusing to give up my mood, I furrow my eyebrows further and glare in his general direction. Even in my pissed-off state I can't imagine glaring directly at him. It would be like shooting daggers at a baby bunny, for Christ' sake. I settle on the door behind him. *Fucking smug ass door.*

Shotridge moves beside me and follows the direction of my eyes. "Oh fuck yeah!" he growls unexpectedly. "That door's been giving me attitude since I started here. Let's mess it up!" He leans forward aggressively, flexing his arms by his sides a little, and says angrily, "Don't hold me back, Reed. That fucking door deserves what's coming to it."

My lips twitch. I can't help it. He turns to me, eyes twinkling, but face still faux-angry. "What's the plan, Boss? Are we flanking it? Good cop, bad cop? Do we threaten its family?" I press my lips in a firm line, fighting the smile. Still making every effort to glare, I shake my head slightly.

"Right. Well. I'm sorry to have to bother you, Reed. But you have a new case that needs our attention immediately."

"What? Tanaka didn't say anything!"

"Yeah, it just crossed his desk, and I knew I was coming this way, so I said I'd brief you."

"What happened?"

"It's crazy. Active missing person case. Multiple witnesses. No suspect."

My eyebrows go up sharply. "Multiple witnesses and no suspect? What are the details?"

"It was at El Ranchero Restaurant over near the Airport. They had a magician in for the night. Apparently he was doing a trick. All the witness statements were the same. The guy was in front of the room, says he's going to vanish on the count of three. He counts *'uno, dos…'* and then disappears without a *tres*."

Shotridge stares at me unblinking as my mind catches up to what he says. I try desperately, I really do, but the giggles burst out of me despite my best effort. He looks at me with a shocked face and says, "Geez! You're heartless, girl! That poor man. The worst of it is that later that same day a man matching his description was found dead in a nearby Falafel Truck."

I shake my head, laughing so hard I'm wheezing at this point. "Don't you fucking say it..."

"Say what Reed? Your response is awful! Be serious for a minute please! The police are treating it as a Hummuscide!"

I groan and roll my eyes, but now that I've caught the giggles they won't go away. Shotridge grins at me, dropping the faux-serious look, and starts apologizing. "Sorry Reed. I know you wanted to be mad, for real, actually. But I didn't want to let that sit in you for too long if I could help it. I also didn't want to take it away from you if you needed it though. Anger can be a useful tool."

I nod at him in appreciation. "Naw, thanks Shotridge. I was getting all up in my feels. I'm actually glad you ran into me. Bad things happen if you let temporary emotions make permanent decisions." I hold out my hand in a fist, and his dimples deepen to criminal hotness as he reaches up to gently bump my hand.

"Want to grab some coffee? We aren't due back in for another twenty minutes. That's enough time to make a quick run..."

I smile at him. "I'd like that. I could use the boost to get through the rest of today."

He moves to my side, and we start walking down the hall together.

"Hey Shotridge, you mind if I ask you a kind of personal question?"

Stiffening imperceptibly, he nods and replies in that same, sweet, smoky voice, "Sure. But could you drop the whole Shotridge thing? It's not... I just prefer Jonah. If it's us."

I smile up at him in agreement. "Okay. And I'll just be Kai. If it's us."

He smiles back, and our walking slows slightly as we look at each other. Giving myself a little shake and facing front

again, I ask cautiously, "I don't mean to pry, it's just that…
and god, this sounds so stupid, but you're so happy all the
time. Not that there's anything wrong with that, but it's *all*
the time. And I mean, I've done a quick read on your energy,
and it's just so warm and positive… what's… how do you…
I'm not even sure what I'm asking."

"You're asking why I'm so happy all the time. Are you
wondering if it's a side effect of the Bleeding?"

"Not really. Well, kind of, but also not at the same time. I
know you can't hold any energy. Is it a kind of resonance?
I've just never met anyone who was just so genuinely…
nice?"

He gives a wry twist of his lips and shrugs self-deprecat-
ingly. "You're hanging around the wrong people, then. But
you wouldn't be wrong, actually. That it's a side effect. Just
in a different way." He pauses as we reach the coffee cart,
clearly searching for the right words. Ordering quickly, we
move to the ground under a tree in the small courtyard. He
nods towards a table, asking a question with his eyes, and I
shake my head in reply.

"If you don't mind, I'd rather just sit here. I like being
outside and kind of away from things, even if it's just the
difference between sitting at a table and leaning against a
tree ten feet away."

He looks thoughtful, then says, "Yeah. I get that."

Taking a deep breath, he pauses, and I hurry to fill in the
gap. "Hey Shot… Jonah. I didn't mean to make you uncomfortable or anything. You definitely don't have to answer…"

He shakes his head slightly. "No, I really don't mind
Kailani. I'm just trying to think my way through how to answer. I don't want people exposed who don't want to be exposed, and…"

I interrupt. "This will stay between us. You have my
word. I'm not interested in getting anyone else mixed up
in this…" I say, waving my hands in the general direction of
the precinct.

"So," he begins, "I'm not really that unusual where I come from. I mean, yes, I'm unusual, but we're not as far away from it as most people. Probably because instinct is still very much a part of our lives. We don't have the same technology dependence, and we just are more attuned to what we call 'the old ways'."

I notice as Jonah speaks of his home, a solemnity settles over his normally smiling face, and his voice deepens and lengthens slightly. Even the low hum of his energy signal settles into something more serious, dark around the edges. He runs a hand over his face tiredly, and when he pulls it away the surfer boy has disappeared completely, replaced by the face of a man burdened by the weight of unknown responsibility.

He continues: "When I was a child, my *Léelk'w*, my grandmother, she was the only one in the village who could Balance. Sorry, Bleed. She could Bleed pain. And the Bleeder before her, one from memory only, could balance pain. And then again, the last known only of story, he could balance pain. So we grew up knowing about Bleeding, but other than old stories from other tribes, we thought that someone could only Bleed pain, and it was looked at as a great gift. It is a great gift, the ability to take away someone's sorrow, or anguish, or alleviate their suffering."

His face tightens. "I couldn't balance pain. When I started showing traits of a Bleeder, the village was extremely happy. To have two in the same tribe who could balance, that was an unheard-of thing. But as I grew older, we came to realize that I balanced in a different way. I balanced happiness... joy. And people didn't look at it so much as a blessing. No one wants pleasure taken from them. So for many years, when I was a small child, things were not... there needed to be some growth. My parents and grandmother wanted to protect me, and sent me to live with my *Ananaksaq*, my Innuit grandmother, every summer, to give me space from my mother's clan. Those summers were wonderful. She made a space for me in the world, and taught me that everything needs balance, that both light and dark have a place in the order of things. She used to have me watch the chaos of the other children in the village, watch their games as they jumped higher and higher or played harder and harder, until the chaos swirled the happiness to anger or pain. And she'd rock me and remind me in her way that too much laughter turns to tears. That they were truly twin emotions. And that my gift *was* a gift."

"One winter, when I was eight, so still very young, one of our hunters was hurt. In the same accident, he lost his son, and it broke something in him. He started terrorizing people in our village and the neighboring tribes. He hid it well at first, and no one realized. People went missing and were later discovered in the hills, mutilated and left to the wild. The neighboring clans came together and realized we had a killer in our midst, and asked my grandmother to search for the culprit. She went from tribe to tribe and found no one. Even within our own, she couldn't feel him. Everyone despaired. And then a child went missing, and the village erupted in chaos. A meeting was called and all were required to attend. The child's parents pleaded for anyone to come forward, and in the height of their pain, I felt a surge of pleasure like I had never experienced."

My hand lifts up to cover my mouth in horror. "Oh Jonah. You don't have to..."

He shakes his head gently, reaches out to grab my hand, and continues. "The hunter was at the back of the meeting house. He looked the right way – angry, frustrated, supportive of the parents. But inside it felt like he was smiling and screaming at the same time. It rolled off him in thick waves of ugly happiness. At some point his pain had morphed to joy in causing pain for others. I told my grandmother, and she told the leaders." Jonah stops to swallow audibly, and I squeeze his hand softly. He starts, stops, then starts again. "It was... not good. They wanted me to balance him, and I tried, Kailani. I really tried. But I hadn't been trained, and I was scared, and... I took all of his happiness. All of it. I couldn't figure out how to stop, because all of it was tainted at that point. There was nothing left, even in the heart of him, that was pure. And they told me to take away everything that had been edged in darkness."

Jonah stares at the tree branches above him, jaw clenched, and eyes staring wide and unblinking. "I killed him," he whispers, barely audible. "At eight years old. I pulled and pulled, and I took away all of his joy. And an hour later, he went to the edge of the cliffs and jumped, because he had nothing left in him but pain. I left nothing. And the village looked at it as a gift, as a blessing, and from then on things became easier... and harder. All at once."

I sit, stunned, and murmur, "Jonah. I'm so sorry. I am so, so sorry... How did you... I thought Bleeders couldn't take that much...."

Looking over at me with dark eyes, he responds softly, "Well, we all have secrets, don't we Kai?"

We sit in a heavy silence for a moment, then he shakes his head sharply, coming back to himself. His words smooth out, losing the unfamiliar low, long tones, and return to his normal cadence. "So, yeah. I decided that I'd learn to meditate, to focus on happiness. And once I learned to focus myself on happiness, on joy, I spent my time learning how to spread that to others. As a balance for my gift, you see? If I take happiness, joy, pleasure, from this world, then in balance I must also create it. Or I get lost in the taking, and I lose part of myself."

He stands abruptly, reaching down to pull me up. "Jonah," I begin, in almost a whisper.

He smiles at me ruefully and shakes his head. "No Kailani. I know. I know it wasn't my fault, and that it's not my responsibility. But I realized that day that, just like pain is a learned thing, so is joy. And you can cause happiness, in the same manner that you can cause pain. And I had to make a decision. To cause happiness. Now, your cup is empty, no? And I don't know about you, but I can't survive the rest of this day without support."

I silently hold my cup out to him, and he takes it and goes to get us refills as I reevaluate the man before me.

TATTOOED UNDERGROUND

Friday, 14 September – Kailani

We begin our walk back to the conference room in comfortable silence, both of us lost in our thoughts, but lost together. Out of nowhere, and with no conscious decision, I blurt, "I'll tell you my story. Next time, when I'm able. I'll tell you."

He shakes his head, not hesitating. "No Kai. I didn't tell you to get something from you. You can tell me when you're ready. But you don't need to ever be ready, not if you don't want to be."

Flexing my jaw stubbornly, I say, "No. A gift for a gift, Jonah. If you want to hear it, I'll tell you."

He looks at me with a strange expression, and there is a long pause that has me feeling like I've made a drastic mistake, then he says very softly, "I will take any gift you choose to give me, and gladly, Kai."

I exhale sharply and nod. "Right. It's a promise," I say, and we fall back to silence as we turn down the last long hall before the meeting room. In the hall are two uniformed officers I know well, and I grit my teeth. 90% of the men and women who work here are good people, people who want to make a difference and try hard to do the best they can. Maybe 8% aren't great people but aren't *actively* horrible human beings. They'll take advantage of loopholes, yes. But they won't do things to hurt people, more taking advantage to help themselves. Like giving speeding tickets for doing 3 over the speed limit to boost their numbers. Or making an arrest when a kid steals a pack of gum. Real asshole moves in general terms, but by the book they're in the right. Power Trippers, we call them. PTs are jerks, but rule-following jerks.

The other 2% are Predators. People who hide behind their badges to hurt, or harm, but are clever enough to not get caught. Tanaka and I made it our mission about a year ago to start weeding these officers out of the department. Just keeping our eyes open, watching jobs carefully, and bringing any concerns or evidence to the chief when we could. They gave all of us a bad name, and Tanaka particularly was disgusted by their representation of justice. About six months ago we were given credible information which led to the arrest of three officers in the department for drug dealing and human trafficking. Those three officers – Poe, Jameson, and Rivera – were friends with the two unit heads who are currently in the hallway before me.

Markel and Posta are complete scum, and how they've kept their jobs this long is astounding. The chief knows they're assholes, but they haven't done anything stupid enough yet to be caught or ousted. Tanaka and I are gunning for them though, and it's only a matter of time before they screw up. I had actually initially been assigned to Markel's unit, but a major and ongoing personality clash had caused my transfer to Posta's. I lasted slightly longer there before Director Gomez had given up and let Tanaka and I operate as an independent entity, with no general unit overseeing us. We answer solely to the Chief now. Markel and Posta had been censured for their treatment of me at the time and hadn't forgotten. They were a terrible combination of cruelty with just enough intelligence to make them dangerous, and I wouldn't have wanted to be alone in a back alley with them.

I pick up my pace unintentionally, silently cursing myself for showing any weakness in front of them. Jonah, distracted by our conversation, is several steps behind me when Markel's voice echoes in the empty hallway, brash, but not so loud it carries beyond the immediate vicinity.

"Posta, you hear fuckin' Pocahontas there was picked to help the Feds?"

Posta's braying laugh grates on my nerves as I clench my fists 'til my knuckles turn white. "I'd poke that hot ass." Both men chortle as Posta makes an obscene grunting sound.

Oh Jesus take the wheel. Are you kidding me with this? An image of Posta touching me pushes into my mind and makes me gag. Flexing my shields a little, it takes me a moment to realize that I'm not the only one gagging. Hearing a strangled sort of sound behind me I turn to see Jonah's forearm pressed to Posta's neck and Posta's feet kicking feebly in the air. Markel moves to take Jonah down, and Jonah straight up elbows him in the face with a resounding crack that has me wincing. Markel falls to the floor moaning, blood spurting everywhere as he cradles his *clearly* broken nose, and Posta's face is fast turning purple from the pressure of Jonah's arm.

Jonah stands in front of Posta, seemingly exerting *no* energy while keeping the large man suspended against the wall in front of him. Locking eyes with Posta, I can see Jonah's face tighten and an unfamiliar chill fall over him. "*No*," he says simply, still staring in Posta's face. "*NO.*" Posta's eyes are brimming with tears at this point, either from pain or fear, I can't really tell. Markel makes an effort to sit up, and Jonah kicks out his heel, catching Markel in the cheekbone, who collapses back, howling in pain.

Holy shit! He's a fucking ninja! Look at his arms! I take a second to appreciate the flexed biceps in front of me, shivering slightly. *Is it wrong that this is so freaking hot? Focus Kai!*

"Jonah!" I call sharply, trying to maintain a serious tone, but failing miserably. "Oh shit! This is bad! You can't beat up officers!" Despite the severity of the situation, I lose the plot altogether and start laughing my ass off. "Jonah!" I try again, having trouble getting the words out. "You've got to put him *down*!"

"The fuck I do!" he replies darkly. "This racist asshole can think about his choices for a couple of minutes." Jonah looks at me consideringly. "Are you even Native American?"

I grin at him helplessly. "Native Hawaiian and Native Peruvian."

Johan presses his forearm harder against Posta's throat and growls, "Hawaiian and Peruvian, asshole! Pocahontas was Powhatan!"

I touch his arm gently. "I cannot tell you how incredibly sweet this is," I start, Markel staring at me incredulously from the floor and Posta pleading with me as he gasps for air. "I mean, sincerely, this is so, so freaking sweet of you. But you *may* get arrested. And I'd really like you to *not* be arrested, you know?"

He looks at me for a moment, then blinds me with an adorable grin, shaking his head incredulously. "*This* is sweet? I mean, damn, girl. How do I follow this up? Flowers obviously aren't going to cut it."

I dissolve into laughter again. *I swear, I've laughed more with this guy in two days than any time in the past five years. Minus that time with Gemma and the fake Jamaican waiter.*

Jonah finally lets Posta down, who crumbles to the floor gasping for air, leaning against Markel. "You fucking... you're fucked, you asshole!" screams Markel. Posta can't talk and settles for glaring.

"Oh I don't think so," I say sweetly. "Because if you bring a complaint to HR of any sort, you know they'll do a due diligence investigation. And who knows what sorts of things will surface if someone were to do some digging."

They both stare daggers at me but can't deny the truth of my words. The problem with dealing in the darkness is that if you ever need the light, a whole lot more shit gets exposed than you may plan on. They have no room to move and they know it. Both mutter obscene threats and curses but make no move to stand. Jonah steps over their supine bodies and extends an elbow gallantly to me. "Milady?" he asks sweetly. I take his arm, and he escorts me back to the conference room without a backwards glance.

◆ ◆ ◆

The rest of the team is already gathered around the conference table by the time Jonah and I get back. All eyes are on us as Jonah escorts me in, arms linked, both smiling. Hideo's face darkens somewhat, and Donovan rolls his eyes. Smith just glances up briefly, then returns to his paperwork. Gomez looks at the two of us appraisingly, tapping her pencil lightly against her mouth, before speaking. "Alright now, as we are all *finally* ready to continue, let's take our seats please." The last was clearly directed at Jonah and myself, as the only two standing.

While we were gone, someone had moved the chairs so they were more evenly spaced around the table, rather than clustered together in the little groups from this morning. In unison, with no discussion, Jonah and I grab our chairs and move them back to the far end of the table, away from Gomez and her crew. Hideo's already at the far end, so our little group forms right back up. As we pull our chairs together, Hideo stands and moves to the side, putting me between him and Jonah again, and he quirks the edge of his lip up when I look at him questioningly. Gomez's exasperated voice breaks into our silent communication, "Are you *quite* finished?"

Jonah looks up consideringly, then stands up, screeching his chair backwards as he moves to gather our papers and supplies from before the break. I'm surprised Gomez doesn't break her teeth with how tightly she's clenching her jaw, and I wonder briefly if we're pushing her to her breaking point but think mutinously *You pushed me here first!* Before Jonah sits down, he stacks my handouts neatly in front of me and sets up my pencils beside them, then adjusts my coffee. Giggles start bubbling up inside me as he sees how long he can delay the inevitable, and he grins down at me like he can feel the laughter well up inside me. Just before it bursts out, he nods like he's satisfied and goes to sit quietly. "I think we're all good down here. You?"

Gomez is practically purple by this point and opens her mouth to say something when Hideo interrupts.

"Kai…" he says quietly, a clear reminder in his voice of what's at stake, and I sigh, slumping back in my chair. Gomez is nothing but ice.

"Well now, Ms. Reed," she begins coldly, "on to you now."

I shake my head stubbornly, narrowing my eyes slightly. Jerking my head towards Donovan, I question, "what about that guy?"

Gomez shrugs dismissively. "He's nothing."

Donovan's face tightens slightly, and in any other man I would say her words had hurt him in some way, but I doubt the hot idiot in front of me could feel anything beyond the basics. I'm having too much trouble keeping my shields up to do a deep dive into his emotions, though, and decide to ignore his response for the moment.

"Reed," says Gomez firmly, "brief. Now."

I look to Tanaka, trying to get some kind of read from him before I begin speaking, and can read a sort of warning in his eyes, but don't have time to process it before Gomez's voice commands my attention. "Eyes front, Reed. Eyes front, and report. Now."

Uncomfortable with the focus on me, I shift restlessly in my seat. Suddenly so tired I can barely move, I rest my head in my hands, trying to think. The past few days have been draining. I've barely been at home and haven't had time to recharge or recover from the onslaught of information and emotion from the week prior. I'm missing something and can't think of what. Slowly I run through the morning's proceedings in my head. "I don't think," I begin softly, but steadily, "I don't think I ever *agreed* to be a *part* of this task force. I was under the impression that I'm here to bring you up to speed on several cases, and that's it. And despite your threats, Director, you've given me no reason to *voluntarily* comply with this. You've actually given very little information at all, beyond the outline of *what* the CDS is. So you'll have to excuse me, because I don't believe I'm going to participate in your little gang of misfits." I grimace apologetically at Jonah, who smiles back understandingly. I wait for the explosion from Gomez and am taken aback when she smiles at me, suddenly worried what the rapid change in her will mean for me.

"That *is* a valid concern, Ms. Reed, and one I'm happy to address." I get the unnerving feeling that I'm playing straight into her hands, but can't figure out how or why. Gomez turns slightly to face the screen behind her and clicks something in her hand. A woman's face, gaunt and hollowed out, skin gray and taut, appears behind her. The woman's eyes are wide and empty, lips cracked and dry. There appears to be bruising on her face and the vague impression of fingerprints at her neck. I barely have time to take in the entire image before a second, similar photo flashes. Then a third, fourth, and fifth, leading to a seemingly never-ending line of these corpse-like faces, staring blankly at the camera from hospital beds, or waiting rooms, or booking rooms. My stomach clenches as I watch the morbid parade before my eyes, but when a child's tear-stained face fills the screen, I finally fold, holding up my hand and choking out, "Stop!"

A brief smug look flashes across Gomez's complexion, and I think, in that moment, I could happily kill her for whatever she has done, and whatever she is about to do, to get me to commit to this. Because I know in my heart if I have the ability to help any of those poor souls and choose not to, I'll never be able to be alone in my thoughts again. Gomez makes the screen go black behind her and sits down at the table. She passes out a second set of folders, this one marked "Eyes Only" on the front, and for a split second, before I open it, I meet her eyes. I must be off my game today, though, because I swear that, for a moment, they look like they are full of pity. Not for the horrors she's about to unleash from the folders, but for me, and my shoulders tense in anticipation.

"These folders contain what little information we possess on three suspected criminal syndicates that have, for all intents and purposes, taken over the major crime rings in the United States."

"In what geographic areas?" Jonah asks.

Gomez raises her eyebrows and shakes her head slightly. "No areas, Mr. Shotridge. They have taken control of the Underground covering the *entirety* of the US. Human trafficking, drug production and distribution, and arms running. Possible, though unconfirmed, medical experimentation. Definite instigation of gang warfare. And that's just to name a few."

"Mafia ties?" Hideo asks, flipping through the papers.

Gomez shakes her head. "None. No family ties whatsoever. No Russian ties, no Italian, no Irish. No connections between the three organizations, no leaders known of the operations..." Frustration enters her voice, and her hands curl on the papers in front of her. "We're not even entirely sure there are only three organizations. They seem to be run by independent unit heads who operate fully autonomous enterprises, with no obvious ties to each other. We're not talking about a snake with many heads, here. We're talking about many, many nests of snakes existing all over the world."

"We've been unable to trace most of the human trafficking victims – the ones we've found have been the same as, or worse off than, Ms. Abernathy from last night. *None* have been conscious, *none* have been able to talk, and *none* survived much beyond their initial discovery. To be blunt, we are operating blind, gentlemen. And lady," she adds as an afterthought. "The FBI has been working in conjunction with ATF, the CIA has been operating independently, the DEA doing whatever it is they do... All chasing down leads for the last three years that time and again turn into dead ends. No one, not one person, has flipped. No informants have been discovered. All efforts to infiltrate have been a complete bust. All indications are that the organizations are being protected by someone, or many someones, who have a massive amount of clout."

"How do you even know there *are* specific syndicates?" I ask, interested despite my better judgement. "If you don't know any operatives, parameters of the groups, heads of the organizations... what makes you think there are any actual entities? 'Cause it sounds a bit conspiracy theorist at the moment."

Gomez sighs but doesn't argue with me. "I realize how it sounds, Reed. While we don't have much, we *do* have multiple victims of the organization. Unfortunately all have such scrambled brains by the time we get to them that they are worse than useless." Gomez motions vaguely toward the screen behind her, continuing, "Nothing is left of them by the time we find them."

She clicks the controller in her hand again, and an image of charred flesh appears behind her – an arm buried in rubble, darkened around the edges. I swallow convulsively, staring at the gruesome photo. Gomez stands, dispassionately pointing at a tattoo barely visible on the burnt remains. It looks like a snake of some sort eating its tail. "But here," she begins with relish, "Now here is something." She clicks again, and a second, almost identical tattoo fills the screen. "And here." A third, smaller picture of the snake is shown. "And here."

"These were found on three different people, on three different continents, who worked for three seemingly different criminal organizations. We thought nothing of it until one of our victims showed up with the snake marked behind her ear. Not permanently tattooed, mind you.

Marked in henna, made to wash off or disappear within weeks. Then a second and a third victim, different countries, same snake."

"Then this–" A distance shot of someone's arm with an ornate hourglass shows on the screen behind her, followed by a washed-out henna tattoo of the same hourglass on an indeterminate body part, and finally a small plastic bag with the same detailed hourglass flashes on the screen. "Not long after, a local gang began testing the market with an unknown drug, sold in dime bags with the hourglass on it. We were closing in on the gang, when an apparent turf war broke out in the area and the entire gang was wiped out, as well as their supply. They were all put in an abandoned home and the thing was torched. Nothing was left by the time we got there except the first charming image. No rival gang was found; it just initially had the hallmarks of typical gang conflict."

"However, when going through the rubble, we found a few, very minor things, which piqued our interest. The first was that the fire was set from the inside, in a very methodical fashion. It was started in an inner ring, then caught to a second, then a third, so the entire building would burn evenly and there would be no accidental clear pockets where for whatever reason, the fire would skip. Secondly, the gang members were all handcuffed to pipe fixtures on the outermost ring. It appears, in that manner, to have been something between a punishment and a warning. They were left alive to wait for the fire to consume them."

"This," and here she returns to the first image of the charred arm with the snake tattoo, "person appeared to have gotten their pipe free from the wall, but succumbed anyway, as the doors and windows were barricaded from the outside. He made it to the edge of the burn circle though, which is why we're left with this image. And finally, there was word on the street that the drug they were selling was being cut with lesser ingredients – we found a baggie in a known drug house that was 90% rat poison – which leads us to believe that this wasn't gang warfare at all, but retribution. We believe the suppliers of the drug found out this small offshoot was skimming off the top, and they took care of the betrayal in spectacular fashion."

"We're unsure whether we're looking at rival syndicates, or possibly a drug deal gone wrong? But here is where things get interesting," she says with relish, eyes gleaming a bit. "Your Ms. Abernathy showed up to the hospital with *this* on her..." Gomez shows a close-up of a kind of curved knife with a short handle.

"A sickle?" I ask, confused. "Russian ties maybe? Hammer and sickle and all that?"

She nods, leaning forward. "It's entirely possible. Human trafficking in Russian is a gold mine. And we were lucky to get this photo – it was an accident. The officer who accompanied the ambulance was trying to send a picture of her ID to see if he could get a hit. He put the ID by her face so the depot would have some reference, and it caught the tattoo under her ear."

Jonah is listening intently and points to the tattoo. "Why lucky?" he asks, frowning slightly.

"Lucky because by the time she had been admitted to the hospital and put on an IV, that tattoo was gone. There was just a smear of henna or ink in its place. The sickle was no longer visible."

I shake my head. "This seems like a stretch, Director. Three tattoos and some new drugs, and suddenly we have three organizations with previously unheard-of power?"

She nods understandingly. "I know, Reed. I can see where you're coming from, but please believe that *years* of effort have gone into this, and the best investigative minds in several countries have been piecing together this puzzle for a long time now."

"Three units independently taking over the criminal underground at the same time?" I murmur. "With no connection to each other? That seems highly unlikely."

Gomez nods in agreement. "No *known* connection, Ms. Reed. There have been no crossovers between the three units other than the drug bust. Then, a few days ago, a young, female victim was recovered during a trafficking raid in Toledo, OH. She had overdosed. Normally this wouldn't spark any interest, as drugs and prostitution in this specific ring have gone hand in hand. But this woman was subjected to some kind of drug experimentation program – she was locked up, and obviously trafficked. She was marked with an identifier on the back of her neck that we hadn't seen before: OT-1-S-1. No other markings – no henna, nothing that would indicate she has any place in our investigation. Just typical street trafficking. Your Ms. Abernathy, though, also had a combination – OT-2-S-1. So now we have two bodies, with similar alphanumeric identifiers, plus a new, previously unseen symbol."

Opening the folder, I glance through the information before me. Photos of victims, with scant information. I scan the pages, and the room is silent for a few minutes as we all flip through the papers.

"So what's Kronos?" I ask finally, not seeing reference to the name before me.

"Excuse me?" Gomez replies, confused.

"Kronos?" I repeat, somewhat hesitantly. Her end of the table is looking at me like I'm speaking in tongues, and I try again. "Becca said it to me before the nurse pulled me away. Quietly, so I'm not sure who heard it–" I look to Hideo, and he shakes his head.

"Too much was going on in there," he says. "It was way too loud with all of the commotion."

Gomez straightens, shoulders tight suddenly, and turns to Smith and Donovan, saying, "Anything?" Both shake their heads, and she directs her attention back to me.

"What did she say about Kronos?" she asks intently. "Specifics, Ms. Reed. This is the first victim who has said *any-*

thing."

"Uh, literally nothing. She looked at me, said 'Kronos', and that was it."

Donovan interrupts. "I thought that girl was comatose? Non-verbal?"

"Yes, well." Gomez smirks slightly. "Our Ms. Reed has some hidden talents. Smith – you'll reach out to your contacts?'

Smith nods. "Affirmative. I'll see what the Brits know, but I haven't heard it mentioned before. Any ideas? A weapons system? A new drug strain maybe?"

"A front company?" Donovan is scrolling through his phone. "An app? Or a developer?"

"A Titan?" I say under my breath, and they all stare at me. "What?" I ask defensively. "Greek mythology...."

Gomez sighs and presses the heels of her hands against her eyes. "Really, Kailani," she says, sounding exasperated. "Gentlemen? Can we start running down those leads? You can push out what you need to your respective agencies. So for today we'll break from this, and Monday we'll have Reed and Tanaka give us a full synopsis of James Tennireef."

ACROSS THE SOUND

Friday, 14 September – Kailani

The door to the cabin bursts open, and a tiny, purple-haired pixie of a girl falls through, like an over-stuffed closet giving way. Her arms are laden down with sketchbooks and magazines, she has a large satchel that gets caught on the door knob and upends its contents all over the floor as she pushes in, her oversized, knee-length sweater is covered in paint and charcoal, and there are at least two paint-brushes holding her vibrant hair in a messy bun. Inexplicably she is only wearing one of her heavy, black boots, and her large, owl-eye glasses are crooked on the bridge of her nose.

"SHIT! Fucking... god damn.... ow! Are you on lockdown?" she yells, trying to unhook her bag without looking up at me. "Seriously? Are you locked tight? Because woman, I have had a FUCKING day that will drown you if you're not barricaded like fucking Fort Kno... what the fuuuuuuuuuck?" The end of her sentence is drawn out in a long, surprised question, and she drops everything from her arms with a sudden bang as she finally looks up and makes eye contact with me.

"Are you fucking... are you baking? Shiiiiiiit." She breathes out heavily, pushes up her long sleeves, and joins me in the small kitchen, leaving the door open and all of her things sprawled on the floor in front of it. Grabbing a bowl, she looks around like a confused and very concerned bird. "Right, what are we doing here?"

Gemma, my roomie and best (well, only) friend, and I had met five, almost six, years ago. I was a few months away from graduating with an online degree with a major in criminal psychology and was looking for a job. I knew I couldn't work in a traditional environment and was beginning to lose hope. I thought about applying for the night shift at a local AM/PM, because money was fast running out, and waitressing was proving too emotionally draining. Late night diners were filled with battering rams of emotion. You'd think the day shifts would be the most tiring, but in general, people who roam during the day aren't as aggressive with their emotions in public settings. There's a lot of quiet seething, restrained anger, and under-the-surface tension, but there's also a lot of joyful meetings for cups of coffee, laid-back lunches between friends, and calm, quiet times away from the office. I took the night shift hoping that I'd run into less people, and I did, but the people I usually met at 2am were up and out for a reason, emotional powder-kegs with stories miles deep and short, ready fuses. Or drunks with dropped walls who projected with unrestrained force. Or the depressed, lonely, nefarious, or sad outliers who didn't moderate their moods at night, where only shadows judged them. It was easier for emotions to be released at night, and easier for emotions to become magnified through alcohol, or sleep deprivation, or just loosed from the constraints of day. And every morning I'd fall through the door feeling like I'd been punched repeatedly in the gut, or feeling so locked down that my skin was cold and my head hurt, and I'd collapse into bed until the buzzing in my head and stomach cleared.

I was having a particularly bad night the first time I saw Gemm. Christmas had just passed, and the diner was still sparsely decorated with strings of lights which occasionally flicked on and off. The tables had small fake trees on them, and our cook insisted upon playing holiday music until the new year, so I was on my third rotation of "Now That's What I Call Christmas!". The diner was oddly busy for a late-night Thursday, with more than half of our tables being claimed.

Some bar down the street had had a pipe burst mid-quiz night and had closed unexpectedly. They had relocated the quiz to our small restaurant, and I had been flying until almost midnight, dealing with the unexpected influx. It would have been fun – the quiz was an "Office" based game, and I knew almost all of the answers. I was yelling them out in my head as the questions were asked. *Bears, Beets, Battlestar Galactica! BJ Novak! Niagara Falls!* But the clientele was drunk, rowdy, and getting more and more adventurous with their hands when I dropped off food and drinks. Between the physical and mental assaults, I knew I wouldn't make it through the night. I could feel a migraine pushing out my eyes, and my temples were throbbing. But I needed this job desperately, and the owner didn't take calling off lightly. I was just about to throw in the towel when Gemma walked in. At the time her hair was pink, like, PINK pink, but the rest of her was the same. Black gauges in her ears, giant, black-rimmed owl glasses, clothes that hung off her tiny frame, snake-bite lip hoops, and a general sense of dishevelment and distraction that hovered over her like clouds. She glanced around the diner like she was unsure of how she had gotten there and absently wiped at a smear of paint on her face. It just resulted in the paint smudging further across her cheek, and even though it was "seat yourself", I took pity on her.

"Can I help you?" I offered.

"What? A table?" she said, still looking around as though confused.

"Yeah, okay", I almost laughed, and then drew in a sharp breath. I realized that, even with being as beat down as I was that night, the only thing I could pick up from this stranger was kind of a misty coolness. Not just coolness in the sense of emotion, but a literal coolness. I didn't understand it, and couldn't explain it, but standing next to her felt like a cold cloth had been put on my forehead, and the unceasing noise in my head quieted slightly, as though a door had shut and the noise of the party had been muffled. The only excuse I can make for what happened next was that I was worn out, and sad, and just plain tired from the reality of my life. No friends, limited human contact, constant isolation... I leaned forward, just slightly, really just swayed a bit, and I dropped all my shields. Her emotional presence drifted into me, like a heavy fog, cool and dense, and it numbed almost everything. I could feel, of course I could feel, but it was how I imagined a normal person went through the day. For the first, and maybe only, time I could remember, I could only feel myself. The silence was overwhelming, and intoxicating, and it was like a flash of lighting in the sky. Just a moment, an instant, of complete clarity in the vast, endless darkness.

I reached out and touched her hand, and the world came rushing back with the force of a sledgehammer as she suddenly focused on my face with a startled clarity.

"What? I'm so sorry. I was drifting. I tend to do that. What were you asking? Do I need a table? Yes, only, do you know, is it going to be like this all night? I was hoping for something more quiet."

I felt like I was going to throw up from the punch of the emotions that hit me while my barriers were down, and I could barely respond.

"No, it's not. I mean, it's not normally like this. It's normally quiet. But tonight it's this." I had no idea if I was making any sense, and was struggling to put my blocks up so I wouldn't pass out.

"Oh. Right. Well, okay", she kind of mumbled, then turned around and walked out of the door. I didn't see her again for six months.

She was an anomaly I couldn't stop thinking about. I looked for her for weeks. It sounds crazy to think of it now, but at the time I was desperate. I was beyond lonely, almost broke, and barely surviving as a human being. I avoided people as much as humanly possible, my shields weak and unsustainable for long periods of time. And that moment of quiet I had had in her presence was like a drug. To taste that, even briefly, was too much to give up. I frequented art supply stores, took a few random classes at the local paint and pottery shop, walked vaguely by the neighborhood's two tattoo parlors, and then, finally, realized I was acting like an insane person, and stopped. Beyond the sheer magnitude of finding a single person in the metropolis of Seattle, I didn't really even know what I'd say to her if and when I found her. "You calm my brain down, please be my friend?" Just... no. So I refocused on my studies, sent feelers out for jobs after graduation, and worked on my shields – even started dating. If this was going to be my life, I was going to move through it with purpose. I'd had years of feeling sorry for myself, of letting myself be pushed from event to event without ever actually participating in my own life. For some reason, meeting Gemma that first time was the catalyst to my ambition. Knowing that it was possible to be in the same room with another person and not be washed away from myself by the strength of their emotions gave me hope, and hope, while a fragile thing, is also strangely and disconcertingly powerful.

I graduated in June, with no fanfare and no foreseeable future outside of waitressing. The letters I'd sent out across the state to various police and government agencies had gone mostly unanswered. I'd received a few "we'll be in touch" responses, a couple of outright rejections, and one very kind letter which almost made me cry, suggesting I intern somewhere for a bit while working on my Masters. The letter was handwritten, and obviously worded carefully, but the gist was that a waitress with no experience in the criminal justice field outside of an online degree from a no-name university was going to have a hard time finding work. I hadn't given up, though, and was looking at applying to Master's programs. One Saturday I arrived early for my shift so I could eat some dinner and look through another stack of student-loan forms, Masters brochures, and job applications. The entire process was a snake eating its tail. I couldn't get a new job without an advanced degree. I couldn't get my degree without a loan. I couldn't get a loan without a better job. I was struggling to find my way out of the maze of moving forward. I'd just begun considering the idea of picking up a second job for a year, saving as much as humanly possible, and then readdressing the issue. I'd thought of it before – usually the nights were so draining that I needed a full day to recuperate before going back to work – but I'd been steadily increasing my shields and was reaching the point where a second, part-time job, might be feasible.

I was so lost in the minutia of student-loan language that I didn't even notice the change in the air until Gemma sat down opposite me at the small booth. I looked up in exasperation, ready to snap at whoever had pushed their way into my space, when I saw her. My entire body froze in confusion as I watched her lay out a large sketchbook in front of her and organize a set of oil pastels in careful chaos. She looked up at me distractedly and said, "You're right. It's much quieter today," before opening her sketchbook and starting to draw. I sat, just staring at her, completely bewildered by her sudden appearance.

"I have a project?" she mumbled.

"Ooooooookay?" I managed, thinking to myself *it figures that she's batshit crazy. Then again, who am I to talk?*

Hearing the hesitancy in my voice, she put down her book, took a deep breath, and looked at me, eyes focusing on my face.

"I know, right? I get it. Cards on the table. I have a final project due for my MFA. I'm terrible at portraits. It's not my thing. And I have to turn in a series of portraits in different mediums. I have seven other pieces to the final project, all complete. But the actual charcoal drawing has been driving me crazy. Insane. I have looked for faces for months to finish the project, and I haven't found anyone. Then I remembered you for some reason, and knew I had to use your face. So here I am. I can pay you. I just need your face."

Somehow she had managed to say everything in one single breath and in one long, continuous sentence. I didn't even know how to begin to respond, and evidently, she didn't need me to. Nodding like something had been solved, she said, "Okay," picked up her pencil again, and started drawing. Opening my mouth to protest, I was just about to speak when she started humming absentmindedly under her breath, singing quietly to herself about shadows and shading. And as she did, that same wave of numbing coolness washed over me, and I felt like crying it felt so good. So I just sat, and she drew, and occasionally she would look up for a second, focus, and say something like "angles, *angles!*" like that was supposed to mean something or I was supposed to do something, and then she'd go back to drawing. Ten minutes later my boss called me to the kitchen for work, and she grabbed her things.

"Right. Well, I'm Gemma. I need maybe another week. Okay? So I'll just come again tomorrow."

She pulled a twenty from her satchel, handed it to me, and left.

Over a week of popping in at the weirdest times while I was working, Gemma and I had gotten to talking. She'd forget what she was talking about halfway through her sentences, stare out the window for half an hour dreaming of a new project, and would spill her paints, or charcoal, or pastels every single time she was in. She was also fearless for such a tiny person. Once while she was sketching me, she heard a table of guys giving me a hard time, just being typical frat-holes. Eyes sharpening from her usual dazed expression, she stormed over while one of them was loudly talking about my ass, grabbed his ear, honest to god, and yanked his face down to hers. The verbal beatdown she gave him would have made sailors blush, and not only did they shut up, they left my best tip of the night. She was surprisingly funny, irreverent, and tough, but most importantly, every time she worked and dazed out, that blissful silence drifted out and over me. It was literally the best week of my life. My shields were stronger because I got more breaks. I slept better, worked better, flirted with customers for the first time... just lived like a normal human being.

The rest, as they say, is history. We started hanging out outside of work because she needed the light in her studio to finish her sketch, celebrated the finished product (which made me look significantly more badass than I was) with a bottle of wine, and decided that we were meant to be friends. "Old Souls," Gemma called us. "We've known each other for a lifetime, Kai. A lifetime," she said once to me, very seriously. "So rather than starting new, we're just picking up where we left off. We must have been sisters or some epic shit before. And now, we're us again and just continuing." Gemma was like that. Very deep into meditation, spiritual connections, reincarnation. She smudged our cabin when we first moved in together, and planted protective herbs around our front door and windows. After what felt like an eternity of being on my own, she decided that we'd be family and made it happen, dragging me along for the ride. I joked with her that she bulldozed her way into my life, and she nodded in agreement.

"You needed me to. And I needed a real friend. Not those pretentious art assholes who judge me for watching The Bachelor or liking vanilla ice cream. I mean, honestly! At the last Class Showcase they served Pear and Blue-Cheese Ice Cream! What the fuck? What's wrong with the classics? Vanilla! Chocolate! Strawberry!" She raised her jaw and clenched her teeth together, affecting a bored air, "Too *plebeian*, darling! SO unoriginal!" She shook her head, throwing up her arms. "I'd go crazy in that life without someone real."

When Gemma's lease expired five months later, she was

left scrambling because, in typical Gemma fashion, she'd started a sketch on the back of the renewal paperwork, then put it in her sketch journal and forgot about it. I was living in a shed at the time – literally, my room was a converted shed out back someone's house. We decided to try to find a place together, far enough away from everyday life that I could relax and she could paint, and when the cabin out back of Lachy's fell into our laps we jumped on it. For the last four years we'd been housemates, which meant that when Gemma came home and saw me baking, she knew instinctively that some shit had gone down. So, holding the mixing bowl she had grabbed when she came in, she looked at me for directions, not pushing for information, just wanting to support me in whatever it was that I was working though.

"Are we... I mean, what are we looking at here? Brownies? Double fudge brownies? Christ, double fudge with chocolate chips? Just give me a clue." She looked at me very seriously, with glasses still askew, paint all over, chocolate somehow already on her cheek, and I burst into laughter, the stress of the day draining away in her presence.

"Oh Gemma. Just wait. It's insane. But first, what the hell happened to your other boot?"

"So *then* he says, 'I need that boot to complete this sculpture!'"

"And you *gave* it to him?!?! Gemma!" I roll my eyes. "Again?"

"He was so *convincing*, Kai. You should *see* his art! It's..." she makes a noise like an explosion, along with the universal hand movement for mind blowing. "I mean, it's intense and moving and surreal! He's incredible! A revolutionary!"

"*Gemma!*" I groan, exasperated. "He let you take the ferry

home with *no shoe!* I cannot stress that enough!"

She stares off into the distance, through the large bay window overlooking the water. "He's just... and his *eyes*, Kai! And there were like fifteen people around and he stared straight through them to me and just, *bam!* And then whoosh! And the sculpture! It's like, all these found pieces combined to make one whole. And it's just..."

I shake my head. "Gemms," I say gently. "Remember last month? With the Italian guest lecturer? Or four months ago? With *Derek*? You can't just keep going around giving guys your shoes, or jackets, or *Keurig Machines!*"

Gemma frowns grumpily. "He said he hadn't had a decent cup of coffee since he'd been here, and one thing led to another and *blam!* How was I supposed to know he wouldn't return it! It won't even work in Italy for fucks sake." She pauses and then says seriously to me, "Kai, I'm just thinking that maybe he *wasn't* actually Italian! Anyway, forget about me. Why in the seven holy hells are you baking? Did someone die? Did you get fired? Is Lachy kicking us out?" The last is said with an edge of panic. We have been in the cabin for so long at this point that we view it as ours and couldn't imagine living elsewhere. She looks at me with concern and then freezes.

"Kailani." Gemma stares at my face. "Kailani Yanaymi Reed. Did you... did you *MEET SOMEONE?*" Her voice gets progressively louder and higher until the last few words are squeaked out at painful decibels. "Wine, Jesus, wine. Ack. You don't drink. Sparkling water and brownies and then you tell me everything. This instant."

"Gemma, it's not that..."

"*THIS. INSTANT!*" she commands, sitting me down and fixing me with her *don't fuck with me* gaze. 99% of the time Gemma lives in the clouds, but that 1% of the time she focuses on something you couldn't shake her loose if you tried. I sigh, knowing I'd have to relay what I could about the day.

Who was I kidding? If I hadn't wanted to talk it out with her, I could have hid in my room. The minute I picked up a spatula I knew what I was getting myself into.

IT'S THE LITTLE THINGS

Saturday, 15 September – Kailani

I decide to run into the city with Gemma the next day. She's working at her gallery – "Blank Walls". It's a quirky, funky gallery specializing in amazing, one of a kind art. I love it there. There are two huge gallery rooms with twisting walls like waves, so you keep turning round and arriving somewhere new without knowing how you got there, and there are little side rooms with specialized lighting so you can view individual works on their own. It's really an amazing space, and Gemma really comes into herself when she's there. The flighty, dreamy artist somehow transforms into a serious, focused, well-versed gallery docent. She actually started showing there before she started working there, and they liked her enough they brought her on full time, with on-site painting benefits.

When we get there I take a wander, pretending to look around, but really heading towards my favorite piece in the gallery, as always. Gemma looks over at me knowingly, and without asking, moves the giant painting to the private room farthest to the back. It's my favorite space, smaller than the others, the walls painted a muted black. There is a beautiful loveseat in the room, deep and soft, so when you sit in it to look at the painting, you feel like you're being hugged. There is a line of three lights on the ceiling, perfectly aligned to keep the room dark and highlight whatever piece of art is being showcased. The lights are on a dimmer, so you can make the room as bright as you'd like, but I always prefer the spotlight look, with just my painting lit, and everything else darkness.

The painting is a one off, like everything else in the gallery, and has been hanging on the wall for almost a year. I come visit it when I can, like a secret lover. It's hard to describe – when I first saw it, I sat in front of it half an hour, lost in it. It's of a cliff, a golden field, a wild ocean, and a storm approaching. It's so vivid you can feel the electricity in the air when you look at it, smell the waves, feel the sudden drop in temperature as the winds approach. It's dark and ominous, and I don't know what it says about me that when I look at it, I feel peace like nothing else in the world. I've tried to buy it, but the artist won't sell. It's a showpiece to draw people in to his other works, and no matter how desperate I've been to own it, he's turned down all inquiries. Gemma isn't even really supposed to take it off the walls, but we do strange things for the people we love. She can't put her laundry in the hamper to save her life, but risking losing her job to do something that calms my soul isn't a problem at all.

I don't really know how long I'm in there, zoned out in the painting, but it's long enough that Gemma comes in quietly and says apologetically, "I have to put it back, Kai."

"I know. Thanks though. Can you –"

"Ask him again? I always do. You'll wear him down eventually, I'm sure. But even then it's going to be a really, *really* expensive painting."

"I know. I know. It just… It's not that it makes me happy, exactly. It just makes me feel… I don't know. Something…"

She gives me a quick squeeze in understanding and puts the painting back on the main wall, before heading to help a couple who just walked in. I give a quick wave goodbye and walk out, feeling oddly sad and a little lost. *I need to shake off this feeling. It was just a long week.* Pausing in front of the gallery, I make my mind up and head a few streets over to Hideo's and my favorite cafe. It's owned by an old French woman and serves typical French country foods and pastries. I have a longing for good coffee and a *pain au chocolat,* and need some time to think through the events of the past few days.

As I approach the cafe, situated on a small green park with willowy trees and a view of the Bay, I feel a million miles away from everywhere. It's fairly empty, with only two tables occupied, but I groan as I realize one of them is the table Hideo and I consider "ours". I had really hoped that one would be free. It faces away from the rest of the cafe, almost tucked in an outside corner, and it feels immensely private. I'm about to reconsider even staying, when the man at the table turns slightly, and a smile breaks through as I realize it's Hideo.

"Deo!" I call, happiness bubbling in me like champagne.

He turns and grins his adorable, unrestrained, boyish grin I so rarely get to see. We stare at each other for a moment, both smiling like fools, before I move over to him.

"Can I sit?"

He grabs my hand and pulls me down. "Ridiculous," he teases, looking me over carefully. "Hmmmm. Be right back."

As he walks away, I watch him the entire way. I love seeing him like this – out of the office, out of his work clothes. He looks younger and lighter this way. Today he's in a heather-gray Henley that clings to every single muscle on his body and some darker, well-worn jeans. He was a collegiate swimmer and still trains daily as part of his workout regime, so he has that lean, muscular swimmer's body with the deep V from shoulders to hips. There's not an ounce of fat on him, no softness anywhere, from his sharp cheekbones and squared chin to his lickable biceps and six-pack.

I stare a little too long today and get caught as he turns to me suddenly. His dimple deepens as he calls out, "Checking out my ass, Reed?"

Usually I'd reply with something sarky, but I can't form the words as my face suddenly burns from my blush. *Oh fuckity fucking fucks! I'm not thirteen! Why am I blushing for*

Christ's sake?

Hideo's eyes narrow slightly as he gauges my response, then his smile breaks free again before he turns away. I try to busy myself with straightening napkins and shit at the table until he returns. Putting a *pain au chocolat*, cappuccino, latte, almond scone, and fruit bowl on the table, we silently go about our usual routine before speaking. Hideo scoops the foam off his latte and adds it to my cappuccino, then opens two sugars in the raw, sprinkling half of one on top of my foam and stirring the other packet and a half into his latte. Meanwhile I cut the food in half and give each of us a portion of each sweet. He passes me a spoon to eat my sugar foam, and I divide the fruit into two portions – grapes and cantaloupe for me, melon and kiwi for him, strawberries and blueberries divided down the middle. Once everything is sorted, we both look up at the same time and start laughing.

"Oh you two! You're so sweet together. I remember when my husband and I were just like you. Young love!" An older woman's voice interrupts the moment, as an elegantly dressed lady walks past us on the sidewalk. She pauses for a moment, watching us, and her face softens slightly as she says, "Enjoy every moment together. Sometimes it's over before you know it." Her eyes growing misty, she turns somewhat abruptly and walks away, leaving Hideo and me sitting awkwardly in silence 'til she's out of earshot.

"Soooo...," he draws out with a half laugh. "What's new, pussycat?"

I raise a brow at him, and his half laugh turns into a full grin. Something has Hideo in a good mood today.

"What's up with you?" I ask suspiciously. "I'm not used to this version of Hideo. Oh god, it's drugs isn't it. Is it drugs? It's drugs." I lean forward mock seriously and grab his hands. "We'll get through this together. We'll climb the mountain of sobriety hand in hand."

He wrinkles his face at me and says, "Weeeeirdo!" under

his breath, but as I try to pull back from him to grab my coffee, he keeps my hands gripped firmly in his. I make a grumpy face at him and he relents slightly, letting one of my hands go so I can grab my cup, but holding the other, lightly stroking it with his thumbs. It's not normal for us, but I don't fight it, the feeling of him running up my arms, skittering along my skin. We sit like that in silence for several minutes, the sound of boats on the water and distant birds filling the space where no words are being spoken. I let myself relax into the peace that is Hideo, watching his absentminded movements as he stares out across the water, letting my gaze linger longer and longer until I'm sure he can feel the weight of it, and he turns to me, suddenly serious, like he has made a decision.

"KaiKai," he begins, quiet, but confident. I can suddenly hear my heart beating, it's thudding against my chest so loud. It feels like a panic attack coming on – my breathing shallows, my vision narrows – but it's something new. Something different, as different as Deo calling me by my childhood nickname, the name only Gemma uses now. My hand is shaking as I lift my coffee to take a sip, shaking with nerves or hope or something beyond my knowledge. He notes it, and a strange twist of a smile crosses his expressions.

"Kai," he tries again. "I've been thinking a lot lately."

"Making lists?" I quip, trying to lighten the tension slightly.

"Making lists," he confirms, staying focused entirely on me and my responses. "I've been... dreaming, a little. And I wanted to ask you about something. Get your opinion. It would be a big change between us. For us."

Oh my gods. Oh my gods. I can barely breathe for looking at Deo, a face I know so well I could draw it in my sleep. I know every angle, every line, every scar on that face. The stories that make up the map of him are all held in my heart, and a sudden and unexpected hope breaks free from its little cage inside me, flooding my body with feelings I've tried desperately to shove into dark corners and closed closets inside of me. I'm reminded of that moment in my office a couple of days ago and look away from him for a moment, trying to compose myself, but know as I turn back to him that I haven't done a good enough job, that some burning emotion is written across my face, because he startles back slightly and loosens his grip on my hand.

With an almost frantic pace, I try to reinforce my walls, not the ones that keep others' feelings out, but the ones that lock my feelings in. Only now they are like a weakened dam, overflowing now that this nameless longing has been given hope, and it has torn free inside me and has imprinted itself in my eyes. Hideo looks at me for a long, long moment, drinking in the look on my face, and I have just enough time to think, *This is it*, with so much happiness I can't breathe, before he sits back and continues.

"I want to leave the force with you and open our own private detective business." His voice is not as confident as before; I have shaken him with my unexpected response.

My face flares red. I am mortified. He continues hurriedly, looking away and giving me time to compose myself. "It would be perfect. It's the right time, well, almost the right time. I've been thinking about it for ages. But now with all of this going on... you're not happy with the idea of the task force, and I've been thinking about everything we talked over Thursday. They want you, obviously, and have seen too much to let you go right now. We won't be able to resign right away – Gomez would never let that happen. But I think if we're careful, and we downplay your abilities, we can convince her that you're not as strong as you are. We'd have to plan it down to the minutia – we really should have done this months ago, but I wanted to be in a better position... well, never mind. But if we don't go soon, she'll have her hooks into you deeper than she already does. I'd have to stay on for a little bit longer, just so we don't raise suspicion."

Everything's moving in slow motion, like I'm swimming through sand, but I try to rally. "I thought... you said in the office..."

His face tightens with anger, though obviously not directed towards me. "I know. It was a knee-jerk reaction to the situation." He leans forwards to me and drops his voice so low that it becomes difficult to hear him. "It's a giant chess game, Kai. One giant chess game. And you make the moves you think best in the moment, but sometimes the obvious move is the wrong one, and you find yourself in check before you know it. I think... I think we're in check right now, and if we don't move very, *very* carefully, we'll be in checkmate before we can blink. We need to play six, ten moves ahead, against pieces we don't even know are on the board. If you *want* to be part of this task force long term, if you *want* to be part of CDS, then I'm with you all the way. But I'm trying to say, if you're going to want to get out, Kai, then we need to plan our exit strategy *now*, not later."

"Our?"

He looks at me with something near frustration and waits for a second, like he's searching for words, or some different response from me. Then he shrugs, almost in disappointment, though I can't tell if it's with himself or with me.

"Always our, Kai. Always our."

Just then a guy we train with at our gym calls out to us, and by the time he leaves the moment is gone, and I'm late meeting Gemma, so we leave in a rush of things unsaid and not understood.

CHANNELING CHAKA KHAN

Monday, 17 September – Maela

I'm in a good mood Monday morning, after a generally pleasant long weekend of reading novels, window shopping and giving myself pep talks. Normally, I'd have spent the time trying to do research, but I am now a secret agent and the country's needs must come first. Regnum defende and all that. Going out the door, I check myself in the hall mirror and, yup: Looking fine, Agent Driscoll! At the local Costa Coffee, Chaka Khan urges me on as I order a large Vanilla Latte. I'm every woman, it's all in meeeeee. I can read your thoughts right now, tum te tum te tum ta tum, whoa, whoa, whoa, whoooaaaa. Miraculously, there is a free table, and I settle on the hard, varnished chair, sipping my coffee and wondering what my training will be like. Emlyn Ryder. He of the perfect sneer and sooty grey eyes. Hmm, should I have bought green tea with a touch of matcha and hibiscus blossom instead? Did seers drink coffee? And am I dressed appropriately? This didn't seem like a business-suit type of occasion, so I've thrown on dark-chestnut moleskin trousers and a soft cream top. But maybe I should have bought a Kaftan or something colorful and spangled? How did one prepare for this astral-projection thingy anyway? In spite of myself, I begin to feel nervous. I close my eyes and give myself a stern talking-to: Maela, you're good enough, you're smart enough, and gosh darn it, people like you. Now go kick ass!

Kick ass, kick ass, kick ass, I chant as I walk up the steps to Emlyn Ryder's office just under an hour later.

"Ah, Maela, you're early. That's good." Those cut-glass

tones seem to mock me as he nods and gestures towards the familiar green armchair. Damn it! Is nothing about the horrid man unattractive?

And, *Maela?* Was this a coffee klatch now? Were we mates all of a sudden? I thought not.

"*Mr.* Ryder," I answer, with all of the affronted gravity I can muster, which seems to bypass him entirely – for a spy, he isn't very observant – as he simply says, "Ready? Excellent. Let's get started."

"Now, it's very simple. We'll start with some relaxation exercises to help you to clear your mind of all noise and mental clutter. Then, I'm going to show you a photo of Ratko Kurgan. You concentrate on him and tell me anything you see, even if it's just a fleeting impression."

"That's it?" I feel a bit disappointed. After all the build-up, surely there's something more advanced, more super-duper secret, hush hush-y?

"That's it," he smiles briefly. "It's really quite simple." Subtext: so simple, even a ditzy Yank like you can do it.

"Alright," I mutter doubtfully.

Emlyn rises and turns off the overhead lights, leaving just a small, green-shaded lamp on his desk lit. Matching colored curtains have already been pulled across the high window behind his desk, and the room softens to a cozy intimacy. The back of my neck tingles, as if a light breath has whispered over it. I'm very aware all of a sudden that we two are alone in the room, and the rest of the world shut out.

"Alright, Maela." Emlyn perches gracefully on the edge of his desk. "We want you relaxed but alert. Make sure both of your feet are flat on the floor."

I unhook my left foot.

"And we'll need you to sit up a little straighter. No, not that straight. OK, that's better. Now, place your hands loosely in your lap."

I feel like the young Victoria in an etiquette lesson. Is he going to place a book on my head next to check my posture?

"You don't need to stare straight ahead. In fact, why don't you try closing your eyes? It might help you to relax."

I feel a mad giggle try to escape and press my lips together but obediently close my eyes.

"OK, Maela," that beautiful voice rolls over me. "We're going to tense and then loosen each of your muscles in turn. This will calm your body which will in turn calm your mind. Let's start with your feet."

I scrunch up my feet inside my boots. Ow! Foot cramp.

"And, relax. Now your calves... and relax. Now your quads..."

Huh? Quads? Oh right, my thighs.

"Now your stomach..."

I suck in for all I'm worth. In this, I am experienced.

"And relax. Now your chest..."

Oh my God, he did not just say that. Was he really expecting me to squeeze and release my breasts? Could I use my upper arms to help?

"And relax. Now your hands... and relax. Now your forearms."

I lock my elbows, and, feck, that hurts.

"Now your upper arms... and relax. Now your head..."

How in the love of all that is good and holy am I supposed to tense my head? I squeeze my eyes tighter and grimace, my shoulders shooting up to my ears.

"And... relax." There is a long pause, then, in that same slow and soft cadence, "Excellent, Maela. I trust you're feeling more relaxed?"

No. No, Agent Ryder. I am not more relaxed. In fact, I could not be more tense.

"Errr."

"Now, I'd like you to take a few deep breaths. OK?"

I nod and suck in a deep breath.

"Using your diaphragm."

Using my? I start to snort, then try to cover it up and give a weird "heep".

"A few more deep breaths, in and out, contracting and expanding your diaphragm."

Oh God. This needs to stop. OK, in and out.

"Now, try to empty your mind," that crisp voice coaxes.

Empty my mind. Empty my mind. Empty mind. Empty, empty, empty. Why did I have a vanilla latte? It's not sitting well, what with all this squeezing and releasing. Should have had pure, green, cleansing tea. I wonder what Emlyn drinks in the morning. Black coffee? Yeah, that sounded more kick-ass spy-y. Emlyn. Disdainful, devastating, let-me-give-you-what-for, you-saucy-little-minx Emlyn. Wonder what he looks like with his shirt off. Bet he has beautiful pecs. A smooth expanse of warm skin and rock-hard abs. And toned arms, for fighting bad guys, but not too bulgy. Wonder if he has jodhpurs. If he's an aristocrat, he'll have a country estate. And if he has a country estate, he'll have a horse. And if he has a horse, he'll have jodhpurs. It would stand to reason, right? God, Emlyn in nothing but riding boots and skin-tight trousers molding what I just know is a beautiful ass. And, ooh, does he have a crop? I shiver.

"Maela? Are you alright?"

My eyes snap open. Emlyn is frowning at me. He's nearer than I remembered. Great. Just great. Front-row seats to the Maela-is-a-moron show, part the second.

"Do you have a stomach ache? You look like you're in pain."

Oh, so that's what I look like in the throes. Like I have trapped wind. My cheeks blare red.

"Fine, just, trying to concentrate!" I squeak.

"OK. I'm now going to show you a photo of Ratko, and you can either close your eyes or look at a blank surface, like the wall. And then just let the impressions come, alright?"

I nod, wishing myself a million miles away. He looks searchingly at me, then reaches across his desk and turns back, holding up a photo.

Ratko's black eyes, cold as a shark's, stare at me.

I swallow and close my own eyes.

◆ ◆ ◆

I try, I really do. But nothing comes except flashbacks of Ratko and Benny, or Ratko and Magda, interspersed with ideas for my interrupted book. Ratko, smiling as Benny's blood spurted out, dark under the street lamps. "The hound all o'er was smeared with gore, / His lips, his fangs, ran blood." Arterial spray, wasn't it? Blood propelled from a severed vessel by a heart that doesn't know it's dead. I shudder, feeling sick. "Ratko, you spoil me." Diamonds sparkling in a darkened room. Death and Sex. Sex and Death. Round and round and round.

After an hour and a half, we give up. I am exhausted, and Emlyn looks disappointed, though, as he tries to mask it, only mildly.

"It's just the first day, Maela. We can't expect it all to come at once. You did your best."

Strangely, his being nice only makes me feel worse. Stupid, stupid Maela. I feel like I did the first year at school, when no one had figured out I was dyslexic, and the teacher spoke to me slowly and carefully, like I was a complete thicko. You'd never think that I would become an English major, but I wanted to prove everyone wrong. Scrappy, my dad calls me. It's why my *maman* named me Maela. "I zought my bébé would be a angel, but zere you were, wiz ze rrred fuzzy 'ead and screaming and wanting to be fed all ze time; and I zought, zis one, she is a demanding leetle cheftain." My father was kinder: "You were my fearless princess." I sigh and nod at Emlyn. "I'll work on it."

My session with the sketch artist doesn't go much better. Supermodel with caramel hair and a rack you could nestle a pint in doesn't exactly narrow things down. And her face is becoming fuzzy, her features indistinct. It takes over an hour to come up with a sketch of someone vaguely approximately Magda, and I know it won't be of much use.

I spend the rest of the day slumped on the couch, trying and failing to stave off feelings of inadequacy. *Can't write my stupid book, so aren't going to get a job as a university lecturer. Can't do this telesthesia thing, so aren't going to make it as a spy. I'll be lucky if I get a job screwing caps on toothpaste tubes, the rate I'm going. Why am I so crap?* I wiggle my toes in my socks, a yellow and blue plaid, and think about my life up to now. I had a good childhood, growing up in the heart of the "Hashbury" neighborhood of San Fran. My parents had bought one of the old, nineteenth-century houses there when they were cheap and spent years doing it up. If she'd had her way, my mother would have painted it a flamboyant peacock blue, but my father had prevailed, and it was a sedately lovely pale olive green with burgundy accents. They'd intended on having more children, but something had gone wrong during my birth, and my mother had had her tubes tied as a precaution. Still, we were a happy family. Every so often, as a treat, we'd go for a ride on one of the cable cars, to Fisherman's Wharf or Chinatown, where I'd gorge myself on Singapore Noodles. And once a year, we'd go to Kauai to visit my father's family. They were Anglos who'd gone over as sugar planters in the nineteenth century, but my father liked to boast that his great-grandmother was native Hawaiian. If so, the genes didn't get passed on to me. He is brown-haired and brown-eyed, whereas I take after my mother, except her hair is more of a fire-engine red. In personality, though, I must be a throwback to some unknown ancestor. I've inherited neither my father's calm self-confidence nor my mother's wild self-belief. I'm basically a jelly who refuses to admit it's a jelly. I slurp my hot chocolate and let my head fall back on the cushion. I'm going to end up living with my parents, aren't I? I can see it now: me, twenty years in the future, in a tatty old bathrobe and unwashed hair, bickering with my mother over the remote control, while my dad makes everyone a microwave dinner and tells me that he has a friend at the bowling club whose son, Norman, is newly divorced and quite a catch. Aaargh. I have to get this right. I just have to. But how? Deep down, I worry that I won't be able.

Yet that night I dream again of Ratko.

Emlyn takes one look at my face when I come in the next morning and knows.

"Well?" he demands, his voice sharp. "What did you see?"

"Lemme sit down first," I mumble. It hadn't been a scary dream, but I'd woken up drained.

I stumble to the chair and collapse, sinking into the soft leather. God, what a night. I had bags under the bags under my eyes. "Ratko was meeting someone."

"Who?"

"I don't know! A man, small, thin, wearing jeans and a leather jacket. He looked a bit like a rat. Pale skin; dark, lank hair that hadn't been washed in a while."

"Where?" Emlyn's fingers tap away on a keyboard.

"A big space, industrial, maybe for storage?"

"Any identifying details?"

I think back to the dream, nibbling on a nail. "No really. It was just a big, dark space."

"Any sounds?"

"Err..."

"Think, Maela!"

"Maybe water? By the Thames? Oh! And I heard something go 'clang'."

Emlyn pinches the bridge of his fine, straight noise and closes his eyes. "Water. Thames. Clang. What did they say?"

"Well, the smaller man just said that the shipment would be leaving tomorrow, uh, today, and Ratko," I shiver, "said, 'good'. And then they left."

"And did you follow them?"

"Well, I tried to, but I woke up when they reached the door."

"Anything about the door?"

"It said 'exit'."

"It. Said. Exit. So, an exit sign in a big dark space. Maybe by the water. Ratko was last seen in Spitalfields, so on this side of the Thames. If it's a warehouse, it's probably in the Docklands."

I stare at him. "Wow, you're good. How big are the Docklands? Does that narrow it down?" I ask excitedly.

"About nine square miles."

"Oh," I say, deflated. I probably should have known that, but I haven't really had any reason to venture that far east.

"Alright, anything else about the man Ratko was meeting?

I frown, wrinkling my nose. The dream had started off so peacefully. I'd come to in a warm, dark place and heard the sound of voices, speaking quietly, so had followed them. It had sounded like a normal conversation, the kind you might overhear on the underground, so I hadn't been afraid. But then I'd rounded the corner of a packing crate and seen Ratko, the dragon tattoo unmistakable even in the dim glow of the single, overhead bulb. I'd gasped and shrunk back against the crate, the hard, wooden edge digging into my back, trying to become invisible. The man he'd been talking to was much shorter, and, really, "rat" was the best description. He had small, dark eyes that darted about and yellow, nicotine-stained teeth and... "A scar!" I exclaim, sitting up. "He had a short, thick scar running from the side of his nose down through his bottom lip!"

Emlyn taps a bit more. "Got him!" he says, sounding satisfied. "Maela, come have a look at this photo and let me know if it's the same man."

I get up and walk round the desk, leaning down to peer at the computer. The man from my dream is on the screen, but I am too distracted by the smell of Emlyn's cologne. A spicy lime scent mixed with something indefinably clean and cool that I know is Emlyn. I breathe in deeply.

"Well?"

"Yes," I sigh breathily, sounding like a bad Marilyn Monroe impersonator. I cough. "Yes, that's him." I peer at the scar.

"Ratko gave it to him."

"What?"

"That scar, so rumor says." Emlyn nods at the screen. "Word is that Vlado there was thinking of leaving the fold, so Ratko cut him."

I gulp: "Why didn't he kill him?"

"They're both from the same village in Serbia, apparently. Some tiny place just outside Belgrade, where everyone knows everyone and their mothers bake *Gibanica* together. It's ironic, really. Did you know that 'Vlado' means 'born to rule'?" I shake my head. "And yet he's Ratko's lackey. Followed him over here and, from what you've seen, continues to do his bidding. Unfortunately, we don't have anything usable on him. But I'll send a man out to his usual haunts and see if we can get a tail." He picks up the phone and has a brief, low-voiced conversation with his own lackey, while I play with the strap of my bag. "In the meantime, we'll see what we can do here."

"Huh?" I look up.

Those grey eyes darken. "You do remember why you're here, Maela, yes?"

I color: "Of course!" Sheesh, it's not like I could forget. A week ago, I was in the library, chewing on the end of a pencil, and now here I was with James Bond. Only not as nice. Weren't secret agents supposed to be charming?

Emlyn slowly nods his head, as if unconvinced. "Hmm. Well then, let's begin. If there's any chance you might be able to see what Ratko or Vlado are doing right now, we need to take it. Who knows? We might even be able to intercept the shipment."

Holy shite, we were going to do this! I was going to use my super-duper spy powers and see Ratko. Yes! I was going to track him, and we'd nab him in the act, and he'd be like "Whaa?" I was going to...

"Relax." Emlyn's crystalline tones shiver over me. Oh, right. I squeeze and release a few times and try to let my mind go blank. To be honest, I really want a nap, as my double espresso that morning doesn't seem to have kicked in. And, spy-y or not, black coffee is rank. It smells nice, but the taste! There's a reason why flavored syrups were invented. Emlyn smells nice: fresh and with a hint of bite. It really works with the whole intense "I'm going to save the planet" vibe he has going. I bet his cologne is Italian, made with limes from Sorrento or something. I shiver. What would it be like to go on holiday there with the masterful Emlyn Ryder? Would we lie in soft white sand in a secluded cove, with only the azure waves to bear witness as he poured champagne over my naked body and licked it off my sun-warmed skin?

"Maela?"

"Yes?" I whisper.

"Are you relaxed?"

"Mmm." I smile.

"Excellent. Now, I'd like you to concentrate on Ratko."

Just like that, the daydream shatters, and we're back in MI5 headquarters, and I have to remember that I am more brownie than bombshell. Right, Ratko.

The next two hours are painful. Painfully boring. I do try to think of Ratko. And Vlado. And even Magda of the perfect breasts. But nothing comes. It's like looking at flashcards. *Math* flashcards. I don't know how Emlyn stands it, waiting for me to make a breakthrough. You'd think he'd want to pass the time reading reports, but whenever I sneak a peek, there he is, watching me. I might have felt flattered, if I hadn't suspected that he viewed me as something akin to a lab experiment.

The session finally comes to a halt when the phone rings. I'm pathetically grateful when Emlyn answers it and I can stop the pretense of trying to concentrate. "Ryder here. Ah, Seef. How's it going?" He looks over at me, catching me mid-yawn. "Early days. Tendency to woolgather."

Hang on – is he talking about me? He is, isn't he? "Woolgather" indeed – try coming up with a better method, Mr. James Darcy Bond!

"What've you heard from Maddox? She finally agree? Not yet? Provisionally? Better than nothing, I suppose... Yes, I'll keep you posted."

I'm bracing myself for another go when he hangs up, torn between wanting to prove myself and fearing I'll go catatonic; but he says that he has a lunch appointment and that we can stop for the day, suggesting that I take a walk around the Isle of Dogs neighborhood that afternoon, on the off chance that I might recognize something. I decide I'm glad to go. I'm not sure I like how I'm responding to Agent Emlyn Ryder and need to pull myself together.

As I leave his office, I pass a tall, statuesque blond in the corridor and hear him say behind me, "Ah, Clarissa. Come in. Won't be a moment." Clarissa, eh? Yeah, that sounds about right. Clearly one of those double-barreled, home-counties trust-fund types, who "worked" in an art gallery to pass the time in between long lunches at the Ritz and shopping on Bond Street. I loathe her on sight, and it has nothing to do with her clearly expensive, pale-grey linen suit, paired with matching heels and handbag. Nor her porcelain skin and silver-blonde hair, perfectly coiffed in an up-do. I mean, what is wrong with TK Maxx? You can get designer gear there too. Well, if that's what Emlyn likes, he's welcome to her. It's nothing to do with me, thank God. And if that wanker thought I was going to march all over the East End without sustenance first, he had another think coming. I'm going to treat myself to a proper coffee, with milk and vanilla syrup, and a scone. And maybe go shoe shopping at the Clarks I passed on my way here. Come to think of it, my flats are looking a bit scruffy.

The next two days are a bust. I don't recognize anything in the Isle of Dogs, or Canning Town, or the Royal Docks. Notwithstanding Canary Wharf, it's all pretty industrial, and I think Emlyn is grasping at straws, hoping that my brain will somehow "prime" itself for a vision. Or perhaps he's looking to get revenge for my failure to see anything? I try, I really do, but nothing comes during our sessions. Outside, yes, I have the odd waking flash – once of Magda "entertaining" Ratko, when I got so engrossed that I burnt the spaghetti sauce. But during the sessions? I just freeze up and go blank. Emlyn, man of titanium that he is, doesn't betray any impatience, but I can't help but wonder if the dreams are just a fluke, something that will level off the farther from the drug trial we get. And I'm not convinced that the government's method is all that hotsie totsie, to be honest. Show me a photo and expect me to have a vision on command? Puh-lease. I don't know what I'm doing, and I don't think *he* knows what he's doing, and my life has been turned upside down. And for what? I don't know any more. I don't know anything except that everything is *entirely his fault.* So when my parents call Thursday evening, I'm not in the best of moods.

My dad manages to get in a "Hello, princess" before my mother grabs the phone.

"Daaaahling, ow are you?" she trills. I swear, thirty years in the States, and my mother becomes more French with every passing day. It's like her accent is growing apace with her quest to stay a young and seductive femme fatale, false eyelashes and all. She's a nightmare to go shopping with, flirting madly with the male assistants and giving the females unsolicited advice.

"So, any news? Ow is work? Any lovaires?"

"Simone!" I can hear my father exclaim in the background.

"*Quoi?* Daahling, your fazaire, ee is a imbecile. Men! Pfff. But I tell you, *moi*, you are not getting any youngaire. Ow old you are? Twenty-seex? And no lovaire? And no *petit-enfant* for me. My friend, Suzanne, she as two grand-children and anozaire on ze way."

"*Maman!*" I protest. "Have a heart."

"You know, Maela, *ma chère*, when I was your age, I was already pregnant wiz you. And your fazaire and I, we always wanted more children, but, of course..." and she drones on and on. About how I apparently kicked my way out of the womb, and she would so love a granddaughter, and how a regular sex-life was important not only for physical but for mental health, and how she and my father apparently went at it like rabbits, twice a week, new positions and all.

"*Maman!*" I hiss. "TMI." I so do not want to think of my school-teacher father and Zsa Zsa Gabor of a mother in the bedroom. "Anyway, I have met someone," I blurt out, narrowly resisting the urge to stick my tongue out and add "so there."

"Oh yes? Oo? Oo?" she asks eagerly.

Oh bugger. Must learn to engage brain before opening mouth. "Just, someone. Early days, you know," I laugh, in a "no big deal" sort of a way. Yeah, I've met someone alright. Devastatingly good looking but, sadly, also a dictatorial prick. But she doesn't need to know that, because I don't fancy him.

"Mmmm?"

"So, how are things at the shop? Anything new come in?" And blessedly, she takes the bait and is off. My mother has a little boutique selling, what else, imported French clothing and accessories. She loves talking fashion. I don't, but it's a small price to pay to get off the subject of my love-life.

After hearing about silk scarves, and the importance of owning at least one perfectly fitted white blouse, and how this season's colors are violet, teal, and burgundy, because unexpected combinations are in, I finally get off the phone. Outside, pigeons are cooing as the dusk draws in, but I am not feeling chirpy. And this, too, is Emlyn's fault. The one attractive man I've met in London, and he prefers tall, beautifully dressed blondes. Well, sod him. I grab a bottle of wine and drink and brood until I fall asleep on the couch.

When I wake up, it's pitch-black outside. I roll over and sit up, yawning, then do a double take to see Magda sitting on the couch next to me. I take a moment to assess her. She really does have the most impressive cleavage, and I gaze down at my own chest wistfully. My breasts are nicely shaped, I think, but Magda's are in a league of their own, full and firm and showcased beautifully in a tight, black sweater. I bet Emlyn would fancy her. I bet most men do. Like the one she's video-calling. If I crane my neck, I can just see the screen. Naturally, the man on it is model-esque good-looking: dark-brown hair, soft-blue eyes, cupid-bow lips, and a square jaw. He could be a Hollywood actor on the strength of his looks alone. And he's got that slick, groomed, poses-with-orphans-and-puppies politician's vibe going on. I wonder if there's a Stepford Wife somewhere in the picture. I'm sure there's a mistress or three. Not my type, though, nor, I slowly realize, Magda's. Her whole being practically drips with disdain. Bad breakup?

"So, you took care of it?" Her tone is flat, and she taps her burgundy-polished nails impatiently.

The man on the screen smirks: "Of course." Ugh. Insufferable, oleaginous twat. Stupidly good-looking, yes, but clearly full of himself and so a personality-vacuum, as far as I'm concerned.

"I trust there won't be any blowback? That next time you won't be tempted to stick your hand in the cookie jar?"

His eyes narrow: "Careful. You're not my boss."

"But I am your supplier," she hisses. "And the new shipment's on its way. We can't afford for you to indulge your little perversions. You draw any more attention, and there's a chance it could blow back on to me."

"And we mustn't have that, must we. Calm down. I know what I'm doing. But do you?" A look of faux concern comes over his handsome features, and I'm not surprised to see Magda's jaw tighten. I'd want to punch him myself.

"And just what is that supposed to mean?" Her voice is sharp, and the man on screen smirks again. Twat.

"Just that, from what I hear, you're indulging yourself. And is that really clever?" He shakes his head and sighs. "We wouldn't want you to lose control, would we?"

If looks could kill, he'd be dead. "Worry about yourself," Magda bites out. "I'm not the one under suspicion. I'm not the *idiot* who's compromising the operation."

"No," he shoots back. "You're just the one fucking the muscle." Ooh, yes, this must have been a bad break-up. And now they still have to work together. But who dumped whom? "How many are you servicing now, *hora?*" he sneers. Ah, OK. Magda was the dumpor, and screen-man was the dumpee. Otherwise he wouldn't be calling her what I'm pretty sure sounds like "whore".

Magda's lips whiten. "Don't help yourself to the supply. I won't tell you again." She slams the screen shut before he can reply, then turns toward me, glaring and reaching out. Alarmed, I try to jump out of the way and feel myself slipping into the void as her hand passes through me. It makes me shiver.

Emlyn's fired up by the news when I tell him the next day. A second, previously unknown player counts as a significant breakthrough. He takes me through the dream step by step, recording every detail, and is particularly intrigued by my description of screen-man. The fact that I can recall his features, while Magda's are fuzzy, is curious, but neither of us can think of a reasonable explanation. Deep down, I wonder if it's because I'm jealous, but I'm not going to share *that* theory. I'm mainly relieved that I haven't lost my mojo. I like the idea of being a secret agent, although I do worry that I apparently have to get blotto to trigger the visions. Ah well, if needs must. After our session, Emlyn has me work with a sketch artist, and we come up with a reasonable photofit.

Screen-man doesn't have a distinctive accent; he sounds "middle of the Atlantic" and the product of an expensive education, so who knows where he's from; but I would guess he's well-heeled. From the conversation, he and Magda are working together, and he's been helping himself to the product. The vision changes the dynamics. We'd assumed that Magda was Ratko's plus one, but it seems that she's a player in her own right, although whether she or Ratko is in charge isn't clear. He could be the "muscle", but screen-man's jibe could be just that. And Magda hasn't shown up before on MI5's radar, whereas Ratko has, so we have to keep an open mind. Matching up this vision with the previous, though, it seems reasonable to assume that the shipment Ratko and Vlado were talking about on Monday night is the same that's arriving somewhere in North America soon. Drugs most likely. Emlyn's going to circulate the photofit to his colleagues, but the chances of getting a hit are slim.

His smile of approbation, when we finish up, should warm me, but Magda's bad mood must have turbocharged my own, because all I can think is that he's a prize idiot and distinctly annoying. I sweep huffily out of the office, passing Clarissa in the hallway, and spend the weekend grousing in my flat. Men!

BABYLON

Monday, 17 September – Kailani

Deo and I get to the meeting a little early, laughing together as we walk through the door. Or rather, I'm laughing at him as he grumbles under his breath at his early morning wake-up call today. It had been a while, too long really, since we'd run together, and things had been so awkward after our lunch on Saturday, that I decided to go into the city before dawn and let myself into his small apartment quietly. I'd had keys since the year before when he'd come down with a hideous case of the flu and needed me to play Florence Nightingale. Even the memory made me grin – he'd been a terrible patient, grumpy and totally at odds with his normally calm and cool demeanor. I took leave from work, and we spent four days curled up on his couch watching Kung Fu movies for me, and romantic comedies for him, which to this day he swears was a fever delusion. I went home every night except the last, when we fell asleep next to each other during a particularly bad Hallmark movie, and I woke in the morning with a painful crick in my neck and Hideo's head nestled in my lap. A passing truck woke him, and he sat straight up, confused and startled, 'til he focused on my face, and a smile of such singular sweetness softened his sharp lips that I couldn't breathe. We sat still, staring at each other, until the smile fell from his face, and something more serious settled in its place. I had jumped up on the pretense of making tea, and the moment wasn't repeated.

This morning, though, I had gone in with a bike horn and had woken him loudly and rudely, no smile for me. His crazy hair and completely bewildered expression had me in hysterics, and he had stormed over where I had collapsed in laughter on the floor and grabbed his key back in a fit of mock anger. About two miles in on our three-mile circuit though, he wordlessly grabbed my hand and had passed it back. After the run we decided to come straight to the office to have a pre-game meeting.

As we walk through the door I'm giggling at Deo's sour expression. "Weak Sauce, Tanaka. Weak Sauce. Those legs for running or just for looking pretty?"

Without skipping a beat he takes his rolled-up meeting notes from last Friday's meeting and smacks me in the nose. "No! Bad puppy."

Oh, it's ON! I think, leaping at him. He blocks me quickly, dropping his paperwork to throw a punch at my face. I grab his wrist as I move, using his force to pull him off balance, and we're straight into fight mode, despite the relatively tight conference room. Chairs get knocked out of the way, books shoved off the table... it's full out Mr. and Mrs. Smith up in here. One thing I love about Hideo is he never pulls punches with me because I'm a woman. When we train, we train hard. When we spar, or even playfight, we don't hold back. I launch a beautiful, tight kick at him, which he blocks, pushing me back into the table, and I use my momentum to roll smoothly backwards over the table. Both of us are full out laughing right now, like kids playing – it's nothing but sheer fun. He moves to leap over the table after me just as the door opens again, and I see a brief flash of surprise on Jonah's face as he takes in the scene before him. I don't have time to process it though because Deo's right in front of me, having grabbed my shirt tight in his fists.

"Concede?" he asks in his smooth voice, its normal coolness replaced with barely controlled glee.

I get right in his face and whisper back, "Never!" as I twist out of his grip, and we start a series of rapid, hand-to-hand combat jabs and blocks. He grabs a pen off the table and drops low, like it's a knife fight, and says in a truly horrible accent, "That's not a knife. *This* is a knife!" I try, I try *so* hard, but a fit of laughter overwhelms me, and I fall into the chair behind me, wheezing. "Crocodile Tanaka?" He grins, pushing his hair out of his face, and he looks so happy it's like sunshine. The sound of Jonah's laughter startles him for a minute, and he shrugs ruefully, meeting Shotridge's eyes.

"That. Was. *Awesome!*" Jonah crows. "You guys are like music when you fight. You must train together non-stop! Do you ever let anyone join you?"

Hideo shrugs a little uncomfortably but shoots a wicked, wicked look my way and blandly replies, "You can train with me anytime, but you notice Kai gets too easily distracted, so you probably won't learn much from her."

Completely affronted, I grab my own pen and attack, and we go straight back into it, with Jonah watching through shining eyes. We're seconds from a stalemate when Smith walks in, talking on the phone. His brows shoot up in surprise, and an inscrutable look crosses his face. Deo immediately sobers, dropping his weapon, and straightening, and you can *see* him putting on his responsibility. I glower briefly at Smith, who hasn't actually done anything wrong, but who ruined the light atmosphere, and he returns my look with a strange, sad expression. The unexpected exchange throws me, and I walk over to my seat, slightly off balance from the entire encounter.

Smith, still talking, holds up a finger to indicate he'll be done in a minute, and as Jonah, Deo, and I set up for the meeting, I overhear bits and pieces of his conversation.

"I'll see what I can do. What's Emlyn say...? Oh Jesus... we're tracking here, but have only discussed CDS, no Babylon... what...? Ours?" He glances at me quickly, almost like he can't help it, and his lips twitch slightly like he's fighting back a smile. "Too soon to tell really. Recalcitrant. Trouble with authority. Kind of obstinate." My eyes narrow as I take him in, and he meets my stare with an amazingly innocent expression, then looks away, voice dropping too low to hear.

Letting my guard down a little, I pick up on a vague unease coming off Deo, and I siphon it, watching his shoulders relax slightly. Pushing it out towards Smith's back, I can see the moment it hits. His head picks up and glances around like he's looking for something, and he moves so he can see the door, his back to the wall. His back straightens, and I can see his muscles tighten, and I can't help but smirk. Smith sees the expression out of the corner of his eye and shakes himself a little, like he's trying to shrug off the feeling, but I double down, still messing with the papers in front of me, not meeting his now heavy stare.

Without skipping a beat, he raises his voice so I can hear him and says into the phone, "Reassessment. Definitely obstinate. And trouble. Reed, if you please?" He gestures at himself, and I roll my eyes before pulling back the emotion I had sent his way. He shoots an unexpected wink my way, and since giant Viking-esque men shouldn't look fucking adorable, I forgive myself for the sudden rush of bow-chick-a-wow-wow that lights me up.

Gomez sweeps into the room about fifteen minutes later, breaking up the quiet, friendly chatter between Jonah, Deo, and myself. Somehow they got to talking about Survivalist training, and hearing their back and forth about scavenging in the wild and medicinal plants was surprisingly interesting. Smith and Donovan had been sitting silently at the far end of the table doing paperwork, but I saw each pick up his head to listen to certain parts. Smith's eyes narrowed slightly as Deo described a moss used to stop bleeding, and cocked his head slightly when Jonah knew its name and specific properties. I rolled my eyes a little – Smith clearly didn't know that Jonah grew up learning the information as part of his daily life, or that Deo was a survivalist junkie who had been to multiple survivalist camps for *amusement.* He had even dragged me along on two, which, despite the lack of coffee, were shockingly fun. Donovan actually looked over at us almost longingly a couple of times, like he wanted to join the conversation, but as soon as he caught me looking at him his face shut down and he leaned back over his work.

We're debating a group campout on Vashon, and lord only knows how we had gotten to that point, when Gomez enters. She sends a cold look over the group and waits until we're completely quiet before she begins speaking.

"To be *very* clear, from this moment on, all information in this room is rated TS-SCI, with initial and secondary background checks having been completed on you all over the weekend. Initial checks were done by OPM to grant you the appropriate public clearances. I took the liberty of compiling and populating all information needed on your SF-86 forms. Secondary clearances were completed by an outside group, and are being reviewed by a small panel of a multinational group. We are waiting on their board's approval. They have dossiers on each of you, including, but not limited to, all pertinent information over the past ten years of your lives. So–"

I raise my hand, waving it wildly when Gomez tries to ignore me. Heaving a deep sigh and pinching the bridge of her nose, she calls on me without looking at me.

"Yes, Reed?" she says in a voice tight with annoyance.

"Uh, question, Director. What the *fuck?*"

I watch her take calming breaths, inhaling deeply and holding it before exhaling. I'm beyond furious with the unasked-for invasion of my privacy. Jonah shoots me a look I can't interpret and raises his hand. She catches the movement out of the corner of her eye and calls on him, clearly relieved to be dealing with someone other than me.

"Shotridge?"

"Um, yeah, follow-up question. What the *actual* fuck?"

Gomez audibly groans, and I, despite my best efforts to the contrary, completely lose it. I'm not a giggler at the best of times, but something about the tone of Jonah's indignant question sets me off, and I start making these weird, high-pitched noises, my mind fighting my body on the laughter, so it turns into something between. It's a truly terrible sound and for some reason sets Jonah off, not his normal, smooth, smoky, rolling laugh, but also a higher-pitched freaking adorable giggle, totally unexpected and surprising. His giggle feeds mine, and before long tears are rolling down both of our faces, but we can't get control, either of us. We're caught in some sort of horrible giggle-loop, where as soon as one of us calms down, the other starts up again, and even though it's awful and inappropriate, we can... Not... Stop.

I shoot a look at Hideo, whose jaw is clenched tightly, but whose lips are pressed into a thin, tight line that I recognize as him being seconds from breaking. I'm about to poke him and make him join in, when I'm distracted by a strange choking cough from the head of the table. Smith is bright red and staring at the far wall, face on complete lockdown, other than the small twitch to his lips and that strange, seal cough. Gomez focuses on him with laser eyes, looking betrayed, and I realize that Smith is fighting laughter. Seeing it makes me grin in my big, stupid way that I try to hide from most people. My normal smile is nice, pretty even. But when I'm really happy, or if I really get going and can't control my laughter, I have this awful, scrunched nose, ear-to-ear grin that squinches up my eyes and makes me look like a demented Cheshire Cat. It doesn't happen often, except with Gemma, because I'm usually so self-conscious about it, but seeing the giant Viking fight so hard breaks me for some reason.

Gomez is now shooting daggers at Deo, and I see his face buried in his hands and his shoulders shaking. Even though he's not making noise, I can tell he's lost his grip. He must have seen me Cheshire – it never fails to make him lose the plot.

Gomez's sharp voice cuts through the hilarity. "Are you *quite* finished?"

The three of us, chastised, try to calm down and do a fairly admirable job of it, only occasional laughter breaking through. We're all staring directly at the table, so I don't see Gomez start up again.

"*As* I was saying," she begins, clearly at the end of her patience.

"Sorry, Director," Donovan's slow, sardonic voice interrupts her, "what, just to circle back around, the *fuck*?"

A peculiar, shrill sound bursts out of my mouth before I can capture it, and I slap my hands over my face trying to muffle it, but it just succeeds in making me snort. I give up, looking at Gomez almost apologetically at this point, shaking my head helplessly.

Gomez is fuming and slams her hands down on the table. The sudden sound is like a slap and knocks the laughter out of me. She glares down at us, and gives a smug little nod at our silence, and says, "You're children. All of you. *As* I was saying–"

I surge to my feet, surprising her and Jonah, who startles back next to me.

"Don't you *dare!*" I seethe, the strange hilarity from moments before completely gone. "Don't you fucking dare. You can't stand up there getting pissed at us when you've run our lives through the meat grinder and passed pieces out to who the fuck knows. You don't get to stand there and act affronted and like *we're* the ones being unreasonable!"

"You *are* being unreasonable."

"Are you out of your fucking mind? You didn't ask us for permission to dig into our private lives. You sure as hell didn't get my signature on any paperwork, so I'm assuming you forged any necessary documents. You think you can come in and shove your personal agenda so far down our throats that we'll choke on it and not have any energy left to fight you on this shit, right? Except you forget that I've been through this with you before. You and I are old friends, aren't we, Gomez?"

She glares at me, distaste and disappointment warring on her face. "What a waste. What a complete and utter waste you are, Kailani. So much ability in such a useless package. You are, and I say this with complete conviction, essentially worthless."

Jonah furrows his brow. "Aren't you supposed to be a good guy?" he asks seriously.

Gomez rolls her eyes in exasperation. "Aren't *you* almost 30, Mr. Shotridge? How you got through life being this naive I'll never know. If Reed would restrain her violent nature for long enough to let Daniels on this task force, I'd have you out of here in a moment. A word of advice for you, Shotridge. Grow up. More quickly than slowly, if at *all* possible. Your innocence is exhausting."

Jonah startles back, looking ridiculously hurt, and anger flares inside me. "Jonah," I turn and address him gently. "What you're missing here is the fact that that withered old hag up front is the devil incarnate, only this devil plays for our team instead of theirs. She's not a good guy. She's just a bad guy who passes under the authority of the US government."

Jonah frowns at me, and I reach out and squeeze his hand. "She'd bury you in a minute if she could. There's nothing but poison running through those veins."

Gomez sighs audibly. "Oh for heaven's sake, Reed. Enough with the dramatics. Mr. Shotridge, I *am*, as you so succinctly put it, a good guy. I just don't have the luxury of indulging in the small fits of passion Ms. Reed seems to enjoy, and while it may seem distasteful to some, I need to make hard decisions in order to preserve the greater good. Your Ms. Reed there has too much difficulty seeing beyond the rigid structure of her moral compass to realize that there are many paths one can take towards True North. And while some travel straight and on solid ground, others necessitate swimming in murkier waters. She's never had to wear any mantle of responsibility, so she couldn't possibly fathom the weight it bears. But we must let our talented children throw their tantrums, I'm afraid. After all, the prima donna carries the chorus, no matter how her director may feel towards her personally."

We lock eyes over Jonah's head, tension rippling off us through the room. I'm vibrating with anger at this point, and Gomez has a death grip on the folders in her hands, knuckles purple-white on clenched fists. Smith is half standing, looking concerned, and Donovan has suddenly perked up, like he's a spectator at Wimbledon.

"You," I begin slowly, muscles tight at my neck, "you are a Power Whore dressed in a debutant's clothing. And you can tell yourself all you want while you're gutter-sucking some politician's dick that you're doing it for the greater good, but you and I both know you're a Collector and that you're banking all your odds and ends for your own purposes. 'Little lost souls looking for direction', right Grandma? Cup those balls and swallow deep, because we *both* know who you are on the inside."

Instantly I can tell I've pushed her too far. Her eyes narrow to slits and she hisses out, "So sad, Reed. Such a chip on your shoulder, hmmm?" all soft and sibilant. "Honestly, I can't blame you though, can I? Given your upbringing?"

I tense, Hideo mimicking my movements, shoulders tight as he presses the side of his leg against mine.

"I'm sure it's hard knowing who to trust, dear, when all your life you've been left behind. Who to believe will finally be the one to stay, hmmm? I know you have a hard time feeling like you have value." Her voice drops and smooths out, infused with false sadness and sympathy, sounding, to any casual observer, like a truly concerned and loving mentor. "I have to remember that," she says softly, as though to herself. "I have to remember what your life has been to this point. Friendless, filling voids with inappropriate relationships with work colleagues. Abandoned, left to suffer through the foster system on your own. Returned even... Unwanted by anyone..." she trails off thoughtfully and looks at me through gentle eyes. "Oh Kailani. I just need to remind myself every now and again that I can't expect so much from you. I forget. I just forget. And it's my fault, I know. You're so talented, but so broken, Dear. And I think, from my experience, that some broken things can never be put back together."

I stare at her, unmoving, mesmerized by the soothing tone of her voice, by the cold truths she's laying bare before me, by the secrets she is pulling from my soul. Hideo is pressing against me, trying to pull me back into myself, but Gomez is letting her truth spill from her lips and swirl around me so that all I can feel in the moment is the marrow-deep belief she holds in her next words.

"You are broken, Kailani. And I, as you say, have made a career of broken things. Things that don't fit anywhere else, things that have been cast aside or left adrift. And I have collected them. I have. And I have fixed them and given them purpose and made them new again. But you..." her voice drops so low that I unintentionally lean forward to hear the rest, a moment mimicked by the men around the table, "... you cannot be fixed. I am telling you, with everything in me, I know you cannot be fixed. And someday you will realize that your partner is just a detective trying to solve cases with the tools available, and your landlord is just a man who you've provoked to pity you, and your roommate is just a girl who protects the needy. And you will be alone, again, and again, and again. You're too broken to be any other way..."

Deo shoots to his feet, chest heaving as though he's run a race, eyes wild. She stops speaking, and raises her snake's stare to meet his eyes, and half laughs to herself.

"Careful now, Mr. Tanaka. I'd be very careful now, if I were you."

I can't look away from her, brain bombarded with everything she's said, freezing me in place, and Hideo is still vibrating on his feet next to me, when, to my surprise, Donovan's low drawl interrupts the moment.

"I need a fucking break. I'm getting a drink. Anyone else?"

The men shoot to their feet, almost comically, grasping at the straw offered to them. Gomez's phone rings, and she shoots me a self-satisfied look before leaving the room to answer it. And I am left alone, staring blankly at the table before me, her final words pressing in against me with suffocating heaviness... "And you will be alone again, and again, and again. You're too broken to be any other way..."

Eyes wide and unseeing, the words sink into me, wrapping their cold tentacles around my heart and fragmenting into tiny shards into my blood, tiny messages delivered to every vein within me, pumped through me with conviction and cold, painful clarity. *I am too broken to be any other way.*

By the time the men return, I have rebuilt my shields and am sitting in a carefully casual pose when they walk in. Flashing a quick grin towards Hideo and Jonah, which leaves them looking more concerned than reassured, I then look to Smith with a question.

"So what's this all about, then? I'm getting confused with the whole you, Donovan, Gomez, international committee thing."

Smith looks at me carefully, nods as though to himself, then begins speaking in that rough, almost hoarse voice of his, sending pleasant shivers down my spine.

"You know Donovan and I are FBI and CIA. Gomez is the

CDS liaison, and was tasked with forming this unit, largely because up until recently..." he pauses thoughtfully before continuing, "... actually, even at this point, CDS is considered a joke. CDS, IDM, which is the Institute of Developmental Medicines... there are actually a whole host of them. Low-funded government agencies that most agents feel suck necessary funding from those departments that do actual work." Here he has the grace to look slightly abashed, but forges on. "The problem was, when this task force was first brought up by Babylon, no one knew how to find CDS field agents."

"Babylon?" I query.

"I'm getting there. But let me get through this first," he replies, not unkindly. "Babylon doesn't have the hesitation regarding paranormal or parapsychic activity that the US government agencies have. So when they initiated a task force to address growing concern over these syndicates and their many international tentacles, their first request was a unit fully staffed with CDS agents. All of the sudden the other agencies realized that, not only did they not really know *what* CDS did, they had little to no idea of *who* com-prised CDS. We'd shoved them into the shadows for so long, embarrassed by their presence at the table, that they ceased to operate under the normal constraints of other agencies. And that left them with an unmitigated amount of nego-tiating power. Honestly, if Gomez had played her cards right, she could have had the entire task force. But she got too ballsy, and was demanding some unprecedented things. Babylon doesn't play like that, so they cut her people down, and added representation from the CIA and FBI. There was talk of someone from ATF as well, but it didn't pan out."

"What about the DEA?" I ask, fascinated. "They seem like the natural go-to for drug runners."

Donovan cracks a grin at this, and it's a sign of how un-fair the Universe is in general that this ass-monkey's smile would turn an Angel into a Devil for a night. I find myself smiling back in spite of myself, and for a moment our eyes meet and it seems like the sun is shining directly in the space between us. Then his face flips to a frown, like a light-switch, and he grinds out, "Why are *you* smiling?"

I catch myself, flushing deeply. "I... I don't..." I mutter, but thankfully Smith starts talking again and saves me from deeper embarrassment.

"The DEA," he begins, the edge of laughter in his voice. "The DEA? They're a single mission agency. Literally their only job is enforcing drug regulations. Tell me how well *that* seems to be going for them."

I smile again at his tone, and he continues. "In all serious-ness, the DEA is not aware of these operations. Were any of their agents to be included in this, any and all illicit medi-cation would need to be reported, by law, to the DEA and be turned in."

"And we...?" I ask, trailing off at the end.

"We, uh. We aren't constrained by those same guidelines. Historically the CIA, FBI, definitely the CDS, we are more... lenient... with some level of experimentation. In addition, we believe it's in no one's best interests to make any level of this public, and the DEA has a bad habit of flooding the marketplace with information regarding new drugs. Which often results in people seeking those drugs out, ra-ther than avoiding and reporting. So, yeah. No DEA."

"So, the real question, after all of this, is who or what is Babylon." Smith looks at me though a careful, considering gaze. His eyes are so pale that the inner circle is almost white, and they're ringed with a thin, darker blue. It's al-most impossible to look away from his when he's focused on you, and he's definitely focused on me now. I can feel the weight of him pressing around me, making my breath pause, freezing me like prey caught in the eyes of the hunter. I don't know how long we stay like that, but Jonah's inquisi-tive voice breaks into the moment.

"Who or what *is* Babylon?" he asks softly.

Rather than jerking his gaze away from me, as I assume he would, Smith very deliberately holds my eyes for another moment before curling up the very corner of his lips. "Babylon," he says quietly, before looking at Jonah. "Babylon, or rather, the Babylon Project, is a multinational, government-funded organization set up to investigate the paranormal for military and law-enforcement purposes, among other things. Its reach is... impressive, to say the least. The organization was formed following the public disavowal of the Stargate Project. Britain and the US both had enough success in their unique programs that their leaders at the time held a summit, at which point it was decided to scrap the public programs and link the shadow programs. In Britain, it includes members of MI5 and MI6; in America, the FBI and CIA. Usually, MI6 and the CIA act as the liaisons. Until now, the US has operated slightly underhandedly, I'm ashamed to admit, by downplaying the work of the CDS and funneling information through the CIA and FBI instead. Britain has operated under the impression that the CIA and FBI have been running test programs, rather than the CDS."

"Why? And also, is it just the UK and the US? And also..."

Smith holds up a hand, smiling to soften his request for quiet. "Why? I can't answer that completely, largely because I wasn't there. You have to remember, in the 80's we were deep in the Cold War. For all that Thatcher and Reagan got along, I'm sure there was a desire on each part to maintain some edge, however small. The ability to control the information funneled was just a political move. And in regards to the countries participating in Babylon, to my knowledge, of the 193 countries in the UN, a quarter participate in some capacity." He looks at Donovan for confirmation, and Donovan nods, sitting up slightly and suddenly looking more professional.

"Yeah," Donovan confirms. "The biggest of course are Australia, New Zealand, US, Britain, Canada..."

"Egypt, South Africa..." Smith adds thoughtfully, almost

under his breath. "What else...?"

"France, Ireland, Italy, Spain..."

"Switzerland," Smith growls.

"Fuuuucking Switzerland!" they say together, and it's ridiculously adorable for no apparent reason. Clearly there's a story there, and it's nice to see their friendship break through their professional exteriors and humanize them. At least, it is until they make faces at each other and put on accents, like the Chef from the Muppets. Then things get real strange, real quick.

"*All* the fon-*DUE!*" Donovan suddenly bellows, wobbling his head back and forth.

"ALL the fondue!" Smith agrees, making the same face and wobbling his head in the same way. I'm completely perplexed and enchanted. It's like watching an odd mating ritual between two insane albatrosses.

"DuFOUR DuFOUR and SONNENBURG TUUUUUUUN-NEL!" they chant together, half singing and flapping their arms like wings.

I sidle over surreptitiously towards Jonah and mutter under my breath, "What the fuuuuuck is happening?"

"They've cracked," he replies seriously. "If they make any sudden moves, I want you to make a run for it. I'll try to give you enough time to get out."

We flash grins at each other, then turn to look at Smith and Donovan again.

They're still doing the crazy chicken dance, now yelling back and forth, "*Wo ist das BADEZIMMER?!?!*" and "*WO IST DIE bibliothek?*"

Honestly, I don't know what to make of it. Hideo and I exchange stunned glances, which Smith must catch out of the corner of his eye, because he suddenly straightens up and nudges Donovan, who does the same.

"Ummm..." I begin. "First, and most importantly, thank you for that. Seriously. It's a gift that we can never repay. Also, and I'm not sure how to phrase this... what in gods' green earth just happened? Like, are you okay? Do we need to call someone?"

Smith and Donovan are torn between looking embarrassed, angry, and, for some reason, still head wobbly. I literally cannot begin to contemplate what may have happened in Switzerland.

Smith opens his mouth to reply when his cell rings. He glances at it, then flips it open quickly, barking his name: "Smith."

The person on the other end responds, and Smith checks his phone again in surprise. "Seef! What the hell? Whose number is...?" He nods thoughtfully, then says, "We're briefing the CDS operatives now. Filling them in on Babylon..."

I must make a small sound of surprise, because he waves his phone at me. "Government issue, untraceable – the long-term equivalent of a burner phone."

Someone's deep voice is resonating out through the tiny speaker, and Smith rolls his eyes at me. "See... SEEF! I'm just... I'm paying attention. What? No, we were talking about Switzerland." A flurry of angry sounds loud enough to be heard in the room blares out from the phone, and Smith nods, saying very seriously but in what I assume is meant to be a Swiss accent, "*Villicht, villicht.* Tick tock says the clock, yes?"

Donovan's head jerks up and he yells out, "TICK FUCKING TOCK SEEF!" and I'm seriously wondering if I've entered the Twilight Zone at this point. Smith clearly sees some version of terror on my face because he mutters, "I'll call you back later," before snapping the phone shut again and staring at Hideo, Jonah, and me.

"So... Babylon. When the countries joined forces, so to speak, they created a unique initiative, unlike anything that's existed before. Half scientific research, half shadow police, it's similar to the UN in many ways. It was named Babylon based on the legend of the Tower of Babel – rediscovering lost languages and ways of learning…"

"I'm sorry, I am so, so sorry, and I am trying so hard to focus, but are we just going to pretend that whole thing never happened?" I interject.

Smith and Donovan exchange glances, and Smith continues without acknowledging my question. "So since the 80's various task forces have been formed and disbanded. There are no permanent teams that I'm aware of, but like I said, I'm newer to this project and just getting caught up. I've been aware of their existence for several years now, but was only recently recruited to Babylon." He looks briefly discomforted, then says, "To my knowledge, usually they are careful to only recruit people who are open to the possibility of parapsychic sciences existing."

"How did *he* make the cut, then?" Jonah asks, surprisingly acerbic in tone.

Donovan's eyes narrow as he takes Jonah in, and Jonah's jaw flexes slightly as his face hardens. Smith knocks once on the table, breaking the tension heavy in the air.

"I asked for him," he replies simply. "I asked for him. I trust him with my life, and as your team lead, with yours. And I understand that we're not starting off in the most positive way right now, but I promise you that Walker is solid."

There's a long pause, and Smith lets out a deep sigh. "So that, in the world's shortest and messiest explanation, is the Babylon Project. It is *not*, despite Gomez's overwhelming presence, run by or overseen by the CDS. Also, despite what you may think, we're not in bed with Gomez. So with all of that on the table, can you explain *you* to us? In layman's terms?" He stares directly at me, and there's no doubt he's asking about my ability.

"In theory, yes," I respond seriously. "I could. But this has snowballed so rapidly I think you all are forgetting that I am not *part* of this task force. I don't *work* for CDS, I don't *work* for Babylon, and, to be clear, because I think there has been some massive misunderstanding, I don't even work directly for the SPD."

Smith's eyes flare open in surprise, and he turns to Donovan who shakes his head slightly.

"So," I continue, "I'm happy to brief you on whatever cases you require. I'll help in any way I'm able to for the next few weeks. But I'm under no obligation to expose any of my skillset to you, as I'm not one of your operatives."

Smith looks at me carefully and nods once. "I hear what you're saying. But we may have to revisit this at some point in the future."

I shrug, but am about to reply, when Gomez breezes in the room like the earlier inferno hadn't occurred, and she stands at the head of the table with an air of forced calm. Smith shakes his head minutely at me, and I quirk an eyebrow but close my mouth as Gomez sits down.

"Alright, Team. Let's dive into some cases. Gentlemen, if you'd grab the file marked February 26, 2018? Nicolo Bogdan? Good. Reed, Tanaka, if you please?"

And flipping open the file, Hideo begins. "Serbian drug runner...."

AN ARTIST IN WET WORK

Monday, 24 September – Maela

I'm still cross with life in general when I wake up Monday morning to see that rain is sheeting down. By the time I arrive at Thames House, I'm damp, cold, and thoroughly out of sorts. We've only just got started when Emlyn's phone buzzes.

"Maela, I've got to meet with the director for a few minutes. You stay here and practice your relaxation techniques. I'm hoping we might make some progress today."

"Yes, sir, Agent Emlyn, sir," I mutter under my breath. I slump in the armchair as soon as the door closes. "Pillock. Stupid, blind pillock." I'm not bad-looking! I'm also pretty smart, even if I can't get the hang of this bloody telesthesia. But what the *feck* do I care? *No good can come of this, Maela. Yes, he has beautiful grey eyes, and a floppy fringe you want to run your fingers through, and a voice that makes you go all tingly; however, he's also aloof, domineering, and undoubtedly thinks of you as an underperforming half-wit.*

I put on my best British accent. "Ms. Driscoll. You must concentrate. It's really very simple. So simple, even a lowly colonial like yourself can figure it out, surely." I get up and strike a pose, hands on hips and nose in the air, all la-de-da. "If *only* you would concentrate and tell me what Ratko Kurgan is doing right at this moment, I, the masterful agent Emlyn Ryder," I strike my chest, "with my big strong hands and hard body, could go and arrest him, and it would all be *tickety boo!*"

"Just so," comes a crisp voice behind me.

I practically jump out of my skin, as Emlyn stalks by; and

then I wish I had jumped out of my skin because that would have killed me, and it would have been less painful than looking up to meet Emlyn's stormy grey eyes. He glares at me, his lips thinned.

"Ms. Driscoll" – oh, God, we were back to Ms. Driscoll – "do you think that all of this is a game?"

I shiver under the lash of his voice, so arctic it's practically dripping icicles, and mutely shake my head. I've gone beyond embarrassment straight through to mortification, cycling between cold and clammy and hot and flushed. I can feel two damp patches under my arms.

"Yes, I do wish you would concentrate. Ratko may be out there killing or mutilating someone right now, and if we could develop your abilities, we could stop him. He's been very clever never to leave any evidence which could be traced directly back to him, and the victims he's left alive have been too scared to testify against him."

"I," I stutter. But my throat is too dry. I glance away and bite my lip.

"You know," he says conversationally, "smuggling – drugs, weapons, young women – is just a day job for Ratko, something to keep the money rolling in. He really prefers the wet work. Bit of an artist in human flesh. A month and a half ago, we thought we had a lead: one of his henchmen had agreed to share details of Ratko's next shipment, so we could catch him in the act, and then testify against him. An officer with the National Crime Agency had worked for months to turn Emil. One day, the officer didn't show up for work, so his colleagues went looking. Do you know what they found?"

I can't speak, can only look down at my hands.

"The officer was lucky. He only had his throat slit. But Emil, ah Emil, he didn't fare as well. We think Ratko must have cut out his tongue first, to muffle the screaming, though the gag would have served just as well. Still, Ratko's thorough. We don't know whether Ratko then turned his attention to Emil's fingers or his toes; but we do know that he was alive when Ratko carved a dragon into his forehead. Would you like to see?"

I whimper, my eyes glassy with unshed tears. I can hear Emlyn reach into his desk and then the sound of a photo falling on the desk.

"Benny, you know, of course." Another photo falling, and then another. "And here are his parents. They raised an idiot son, but they didn't deserve to die." Another photo. "And here's Emil." Another. "And the NCA officer." Emlyn's voice catches on the last. "Have a look."

I shake my head.

"Look at them!"

I look. Dead people, with pale, waxy skin, eyes closed, a neat line across their throats where the morticians had stitched them up. No blood, but I feel sick. Dead people, all in a row. Benny's stupid goatee; he didn't look anything like his parents, their faces slack and plump. Emil, a crude design etched into his forehead. Dead people, dead, dead, dead, murdered by Ratko. The last one, the officer, had light brown hair.

The tears pool, spill over, run down my cheeks. I look up at Emlyn. He is staring down at the photos, so remote he might have been carved from granite.

My nose begins to run, as the tears fall fast and thick, and I can feel my lips begin to wobble. I sniff and reach blindly in my pocket for a tissue.

Emlyn starts, as if coming to, then looks at me; and his face hardens.

"That was unforgivable of me," he says quietly. He gathers up the photos and turns his back, his head bowed. "Go home, Maela. Go home and get some rest, and we'll try again tomorrow." His voice is toneless.

I nod, though he can't see, and wipe my eyes. The tears won't stop, so I put on my sunglasses, then shrug on my leather coat and pick up my bag. I can hear a desk drawer opening. At the door, I turn back to say – I don't know what. Emlyn is staring down at one of the photos, his jaw clenched. Slowly, he lifts a finger and traces the outline of a face. I open the door and go out.

I don't go home. I'm too upset. I just get on the underground in a daze and get off at a random station, then wander aimlessly, until I look up to see that I am standing outside one of the saddest places in London: the Battersea Dogs and Cats Home. Housed in an unlovely building by railway lines and a power station, the Home is probably the most famous animal shelter in the country. I stare at the blue and white logo – a dog and cat curled around each other – and blub. Recently, I read that 7,000 animals pass through the charity's doors every year. 7,000! Some lost, but most abandoned and unwanted. Old, sick, disabled. I think of them and think of the photos Emlyn showed me, and I cry, the tears dripping down from under my sunglasses and by the side of my nose to hang off my chin. Thankfully, there aren't many people out and about, and those that pass are too engrossed in their mobile phones to notice me quietly going to pieces. I suspect a lot of people cry around here. It's a sad place. After several minutes, I begin to feel marginally calmer, so I shuffle along, thinking I might go for a walk in nearby Battersea Park and try to pull myself together. My nose is still running, and I have to stop to search for a tissue in my bag. On the wall ahead is a photo of a little cat, next to the words "Ready to be loved". I take one look and start bawling again. Poor thing! I wish I could help. But I'm useless. I can't help that fluffy little tabby with the whiskers and the big brown eyes, and I can't help the people Ratko will surely murder, because I am too useless to learn remote viewing. An elderly woman in a dark-blue coat and hat pats my arm.

"Now, now, dearie. Don't take it to heart. All of the animals are very well looked after here. They don't put them down, you know, not unless they're so sick that it's really a mercy. Most of the animals are fixed up and rehomed. This is where I got my little Tilly and Olly."

I follow the leads in her hand to the two Mastiffs sitting at her feet. Standing, they would have easily come up to her waist, and they must have weighed 150 pounds each. One is fawn-colored and missing an ear; the other is a brindle and missing a leg. She reaches down and scratches them under the chin. Tilly barks and wags her tail; Olly rubs his head against her knee.

She continues, "I don't know what I'd do without them. I look after them, and they look after me. It's a second life for all three of us."

I manage a smile and a nod, and she gives me another pat and walks on. Giving my eyes a wipe and my nose another blow, I head towards the park. The encounter has done me good. I'd been wrong: this isn't a place of sadness; it's one of hope. And if "little" Tilly and Olly could make a fresh start, then surely I could too.

The plane trees along Carriage Drive are a fiery orange and gold, their catkins hanging ready for hungry squirrels. I amble along the Boating Lake, trying to let the peace of the place sink into me. While I'm not weepy any more, I'm still subdued. I will have to try again and keep on trying until I get the hang of far-seeing; and I honestly have no idea how to make it happen. I bite my lip and shake my head. A little tea-house up ahead beckons invitingly. Tea, according to the English, cures all ills; and heaven knows I could use a cuppa.

Thankfully, the rain has stopped, and the sun is making a valiant effort to come out from behind the clouds, so I'm glad to find they have outdoor tables and chairs. I order a pot of Earl Grey and breathe in the scented steam with something akin to gratitude. "Give me, give here my tea; /

Ladies' nectar! Give it me." The hot liquid slides down my throat and unknots my stomach. Aah. "Tea 't is makes the spirits flow, / Tickles up the heart of wo." I stare into the cup pensively. How would I magic up visions of Ratko? Or Magda? How? Emlyn said I have a rare natural ability, but the evidence seems to me to be pretty thin. Let's face it: I haven't exactly done a stellar job so far. I sigh and swirl my tea, brooding.

A shadow falls across my table. *"Permíteme?"*

I look up, and my mouth falls open. Before me stands the most sensually beautiful man I have ever seen. His skin is a rich tan with undertones of old gold, and bright hazel eyes smile at me out of an oval face. Like Emlyn, he has thick, sooty brows that I want to trace and a long, straight nose, but his is slightly broader and just a touch more rounded. I suddenly want to reach up and tweak it. Choppily cut brown hair, the color of the finest dark chocolate, brushes his shoulders, and a short moustache and stubble frame a soft, sensitive mouth. He is wearing a black leather jacket over a light-grey tee-shirt and black jeans and has a pendant in the shape of a shark's tooth around his neck.

My mouth is still open. He smiles, as if he can sense what I'm feeling, and repeats, *"Permíteme?"* gesturing at the empty chair. I nod dumbly and take a big sip of tea to cover my confusion. He sits down gracefully and extends his hand.

"Jorge Alfaro Giménez." The liquid syllables roll off his tongue and trail down my spine, making me feel all wriggly. His voice is smooth and deep, like the finest brandy.

I take his hand. It's warm and strong. "Mae," I splutter, forgetting that I still have tea in my mouth, which promptly goes up my nose. I sneeze. "Excuse me, touch of hay-fever." At times like this, a girl has no choice but to resort to subterfuge. I dab at my nose with a tissue, hoping I'm doing it prettily.

"Mae?" he prompts, cocking his head at me.

"Maela," I try again. "Maela Driscoll."

"Maela." I like the way he pronounces it: Ma-ay-la. It makes me sound so exotic. "American or Canadian?"

"American, from San Francisco. It's not obvious?"

"I've been in London for a year and have learned it's safer not to assume. That way, I don't annoy the Canadians, and the Americans are charmed."

I smile. "That makes sense." There's something about him that's making me more comfortable by the minute, when normally someone of his singular good looks would have me scooting deep inside my shell, too awestruck to do more than peep out.

"So, Maela Driscoll from San Francisco, what brings you to London?"

"Oh, I," I stop. What could I say? I came over to do post-doctoral research in English Romantic poetry at Queen's College, and I'm now working for MI5? He'd leave me to the pigeons. "I'm doing an internship," I say brightly. "What about you? What brought you to London? You've been here a year? Are you from Spain?" When cornered, ask questions. OK, that was advice given to me for my first date, ten years ago, but I figure it's adaptable. *Get him talking about himself.*

He starts to laugh, and my heart does a funny little pitter patter. He has a beautiful smile: it lights up his whole face, and I can't help but notice how soft and kissable his lips are. I kind of want to lick and nibble and taste.

"*Sí*, I am from Spain." I like the way he says it, with a slight catch: "Eh-Spain". "From a little village called Zamarramala." *Thamarrramala.* Mellifluous, I think, entranced; his voice is mellifluous. "Just outside Segovia."

I sit up. "Segovia! That's my favorite castle!"

"You have been?"

"No, but I've seen pictures; and I'd love to go. Did you know that it helped inspire Disney's Cinderella Castle?"

"*Sí?* There are many beautiful things to see in Segovia:

the castle, the cathedral, the aqueduct, the gardens. I am glad London has so many parks. I like to walk in them and clear my head."

"Tough job?" I take another sip of tea.

"Sometimes. I work as a counsellor at an addiction center. When things get too heavy, it helps to get outside and get some fresh air. And sometimes," he grins, "a nice American girl from San Francisco takes pity on me and lets me join her for tea."

Mercy. I want to fan myself. "Eh, no problem," I say nonchalantly. "Least I can do." Huh? "Think nothing of it," with a wave of my hand. Oh God, I'm rapidly descending into Georgian-romance-babble. Next thing you know, I'll be asking if he wants to take a refreshing stroll round the grounds. "Tea! You don't have tea! Would you like a cup? My treat."

He smiles: "But it is I who should be treating you." He stands up. "One," he glances at my tea bag, "Earl Grey, coming up. Don't go anywhere."

I gulp, suddenly feeling rather warm. "Wouldn't dream of it." As soon as he is inside the café, I dive for the compact in my bag. I've never, not once in the five years I've owned it, used it to powder my nose, my cheeks, or any other part of my face; but it's something every girl carries, right? And, it has a mirror, smudged, but it will do. I rapidly scan my reflection. Is my nose red? I am not an attractive crier. My skin does not remain a luminous alabaster while my eyes pool with limpid tears. My whole face joins in, going red and blotchy while my nose produces copious amounts of snot. Thankfully, it's not too bad. I give a swift dab, dab to my nose and think I might chance taking off the glasses.

Just in time. Jorge comes back carrying a tray with two pots of tea and, joy! a slab of chocolate cake *with whipped cream*. "I thought you might like something sweet."

"You thought correctly." If I hadn't found him perfect before, I would have now. It might be a cliché, but chocolate really is the way to a girl's heart. If that basic fact isn't taught at boyfriend school, it should be. Just saying.

We pour out our tea, and Jorge clinks his cup against mine. "To new friends."

And, just like that, all my self-consciousness melts away, and the conversation flows freely. At times, I'm even chattering like a monkey. He tells me about his time so far in London. He's renting a small studio flat in Brixton, just off Electric Avenue. It's noisy, but he loves being so close to the covered markets. Did I know that you could get food from all over the world there: West Indian, South American, Ethiopian, Keralan, Pakistani, Japanese? And the best tapas outside of Spain. The best tapas, *naturalmente*, are to be found in a little hole-in-the-wall bar in Zamarramala; but there is a place in Brixton that is almost as good. And if you want a woven wicker basket, vintage clothes, or Chinese medicine, Brixton is the place to go. He likes going swimming in the Lido, which is open year-round, and he's thinking about having a go at bouldering at a nearby climbing center. At night he likes to try a microbrew in one of the craft beer pubs (although Spanish wine is better) or see an arts film, or listen to reggae, but he has not, he solemnly assures me, visited the world's largest fetish club – yet.

His enthusiasm is infectious, and I find myself telling him about Fitzrovia. "Posh," he whistles, but there are some good Spanish bars there too. How I like wandering through the quiet backstreets and spotting the blue plaques marking the homes of famous former residents. Did he know that Dylan Thomas, George Bernard Shaw, and Virginia Woolf had all at one time or another lived there? "No. *Sí?*" He has not read, but he knows of them. Bedford Square Garden is beautiful, but the one in Fitzroy Square is at least open to the public, so I like to go there with a picnic lunch sometimes. He, Jorge, likes to sun himself on Clapham Common when the weather is fine; and my mind zigs to images of him lying shirtless and strokable in the sun. That caramel skin and coffee hair would be warm to the touch, and I could nuzzle his neck and breathe in his bergamot, black pepper, and mahogany cologne. I blush and quickly remember that the British Museum is within walking distance from my flat. My favorite gallery is the Assyrian: the winged lions are really cool. Jorge prefers the Egyptian.

We finish our tea, and Jorge suggests a stroll up to the Pagoda. I would have been happy to stroll round a car park with him by then but have just enough presence of mind not to say "Oooh, really? Do you mean it? Yes, please. Thanks!" I simply smile and feel giddy yet at the same time peaceful walking beside him under the trees. There's just something about him that invites self-acceptance, and my worries of the morning whisper away along with the clouds. By the time we reach the Pagoda, a lovely, two-tiered building perched incongruously on the edge of the Thames, the sun is shining brightly. Jorge points out the statues telling the story of the Buddha's life, and I look at the gilt-bronze figures and the beautiful man standing next to me and feel happier than I have in weeks.

All too soon, Jorge glances at his watch and says he has a meeting back at the clinic. "Administration," he grimaces, but he asks if we can exchange numbers and meet up again. I manage to keep my cool and enter my number in his cell, all the while feeling fizzy. I want to laugh, and I want to jump up and down, but I can't because then he would think I was mental. I think he guesses, though, as his eyes dance at me when he gives me back my phone. Jorge says he'll walk me to the station, to make sure I get there safely, aw, and will then continue on foot to the clinic, as it is between stops. At the door, he leans down and kisses me on each cheek. "It's been a pleasure, Miss Maela Driscoll from San Francisco. Speak to you soon." I nod like an obedient puppy and squeak, "Mmm-hmm," and then float into the station. I'm still floating half an hour later when I get off at Tottenham Court station. But I don't go home – I'm too excited. I go to the British Museum and spend the rest of the afternoon in the Egyptian galleries.

The evening passes in a blissful haze. I just can't stop thinking about Jorge. Jorge, with his luminous hazel eyes and whose lips felt so soft and warm on my skin. I lift my hand to my cheek and giggle to myself: just like a teenager, I am seriously considering never washing it again. The Divinyls come on the radio while I'm getting into my pajamas, and I fall back onto the bed and sing along. "I love myself. I want you to love me. When I feel down, I want you above me." My hands are on my bare stomach, and I look down. Not too bad. Ok, from this angle my breasts look a little small, but my stomach is pretty trim, maybe from all of the recent walking. "I don't want anybody else. When I think about you I touch myself." And I do, running my hands up over my breasts and shivering. "Ooh I don't want anybody else, oh no, oh no, oh no!" My hand slips under my pajama bottoms and through my curls to my center. I rub lightly, dipping my finger down to my folds and then back up again. "You're the one who makes me come runnin'." I rub harder, imagining hot male skin gleaming in the sun. "I close my eyes and see you before me." Jorge's long brown hair would feel like strands of silk trailing over my breasts as he kissed his way down to my navel. "I'd get down on my knees. I'd do anything for you." My body is taught with anticipation. I imagine taking him in my mouth, and I explode. "I don't want anybody else. When I think about you I touch myself." I quiver with little aftershocks, and, just like that, roll over and fall asleep.

O' LORD EMLYN

Tuesday, 25 September – Maela

I suppose it's no surprise that I dream of Magda that night, what with all the hormones whooshing around my system: thankfully, not with Ratko, although I recognize that silk shirt. She's in a large, stylish penthouse, decorated in Scandi style, all white, beechwood, and chrome. She herself provides the color "pop", lounging on one of the leather couches as she talks on the phone. The couches form a "U" around a glass coffee-table and face a floor-to-ceiling window-wall. I can see the lights of London twinkling beyond it. A far cry from my homely little flat. Whatever she did, it paid well. The cow.

"Yes, it's all going well," she drawls. "Ladon doesn't suspect a thing, and he's proving a nice little earner."

Lay-dun? Weird name. But maybe it's common wherever Magda is from? She has an accent I can't place.

"Yes, it's disappointing about the latest matrix. It doesn't look like it's yielded any candidates. And it seemed so promising. We'll have to tweak the recipe."

Huh? Is she a cook, a biologist, or a head-hunter?

"I'll keep you informed. When will you be in London next? You must have a fund-raiser coming up soon. We should do lunch." She yawns and reaches for her wine glass.

"Well, let me know. In the meantime, I'll keep channeling money to the armamentarium. Poor Ladon. If he only knew – do you think he'd still want in?"

This conversation is beyond weird. I look around the room, knowing Emlyn will want the details. Beyond "open plan" and "very, very expensive", I can't see anything identifying. The

room is clean and devoid of personal details: no photos, no help-
ful mail, not even a magazine. And I can't recognize any of the
buildings in the distance. Thinking back to the last vision, when
Magda seemed to reach for me, I windmill my arms a bit, but
she doesn't notice. Why would she? I'm not technically here,
right? Or am I? Is this how ghosts are born? Maybe I could make
myself corporeal. On second thought, bad idea. But maybe it
could be done. If I could manage it, could I pick up evidence?
Or scare people? If I appeared before Ratko, going "woo woo",
would he be afraid? Hah! I could channel him right into the
arms of MI5, and then Emlyn wouldn't think I was so wet. And
Jorge would think I was this fantastic über-woman, although I
couldn't tell him, not without going to jail, so. Hmm.

"Alright, Rhea. I'll give you another update in a month.
Unemi ái." She hangs up the phone and takes another sip of
wine, staring thoughtfully into the distance.

Ray-Enemi-Whoey? What was going on? And who was the
poor mug, Lay-dun?

Whoever he was, Magda was taking him for a ride. But, re-
membering her perky breasts, maybe he didn't mind too much.
I wish any of this made sense.

Magda stretches, displaying those fantastic assets, then
gets up off the couch, leaving her empty glass on the table.
Tsk tsk, I think hypocritically but glad to find out she isn't
so perfect after all. She comes right toward me, and for a
moment I think I'll faint, but she simply walks by and down
an adjoining hallway. She has a "not-nice" smile on her face,
and I wonder what she's thinking about. I try to follow but
can't move, and when I look down, I can see that my legs are
disappearing, and I am fading, fading, fading.

When I wake up, the sun is shining and my bedside clock
reads 8:00am. Shiiiiiiite! I scramble out from under the
duvet and race into the shower. I am going to be late, and

I really don't think either Emlyn or I can take that. As it is, I am only fifteen minutes late, and Emlyn doesn't seem to mind. He simply looks up when I knock and open the door and says, "Good morning, Maela. Come in and have a seat."

Is it just me, or does he have a faint flush to his cheeks? Normally, I'm the one who'd be feeling hideously embarrassed, but my cathartic blubbing in Battersea and then Jorge – Jorge! – had cleansed and cheered me. OK, yesterday, it had all gotten a bit tense, but we agents of the Crown had to go with the flow. And chasing criminals was bound to get stressful once in a while.

"I'd like to apologize for my outburst, Maela." Yes, he is definitely blushing. Aww, how cute.

"It was deeply unprofessional and won't happen again. You have my word. My only excuse is that sometimes the job gets the better of me. And this mission? Well, let's just say it's personal."

"Oh, uh, thank you. And no problem. I understand." I try to convey a "we're all in this together and mistakes happen" demeanor.

He smiles, a touch sadly, at me and nods. "I appreciate that. Well then, shall we get started?"

"Of course." I wish I could maintain this calm, grown-up persona – although, to be honest, it's kind of freaking me out – but I have a feeling I will soon regress. "But, before we do, I had another dream."

He looks at me sharply. "A dream? Describe it. Please."

"Well, Magda was in her apartment – and, wow, super nice – talking on the phone to someone named," I frown, wrinkling my nose, and shake my head, trying to concentrate. "Uh, Ree, Rah – Ray-ah! That was it. Ray-uh." I nod.

Emlyn listens, frowning himself now, but writes it down. "OK. What did they talk about?"

I twirl a strand of hair about my finger. "Honestly? It made no sense. Sounded like they were milking someone for money, and he didn't suspect a thing. Didn't sound English, though. Lay-dun? Is that a British name? Lay-den? Lay-down?" Oh God, here came the babble. Why was it that, whenever I spent more than two seconds with a gorgeous man, I suffered an episode of foot-in-mouth disease? And Emlyn had just changed the rules of engagement. I could just about cope when he was being haughty and treating me like a bug – the annoyance kept the lid on the attraction – but he had *apologized* and said *please*. He wasn't just a sadistic task-master with a bad taste in girlfriends. He had feelings and depth, and he *cared* about his job.

"Nnn-oo, don't think so," Emlyn says slowly. "Anything else?"

I look at his hand, at those long, elegant fingers clutching the pen, then to the window behind his desk. The sun is shining, a tiny ray streaming through to gild that oak-brown hair.

"Just something about a matrix, and candidates, and then needing to change the recipe. And channeling money to the armamentarium, which, come to think of it, must have something to do with arms, because, you know, '*Arma virumque cano*' and all that." I nod, trying to look wise, although I can't really remember the exact translation. Latin 101 was a long time ago, and I had only taken it as a course requirement. It's not like I really needed it for nineteenth-century English lit.

"Yes. Virgil. 'I sing of arms and the man.' Did she now?" he asks softly. "Well, well."

I think back to the dream, to that "not nice" smile on Magda's face. *Matrix, recipe, arms.* I sit bolt upright. "Oh my God, do you think she's trying to create a biological weapon?"

Emlyn continues to jot down notes, but, did his lip twitch? I peer suspiciously at him. Hmm.

"We won't rule anything out, but it's unlikely," he assures me gravely. "That all?"

"Just something about an enema, which, if you ask me,

is a really weird way to end a conversation." I feel horribly flustered now, and my brain-to-mouth coordination is suffering.

"An enema?"

"Yes," I say defensively. "It sounded like she said 'enema', or, at least, something like it, and then hung up the phone."

Not a muscle moves on that impassive face, but I could swear Emlyn is amused and trying not to laugh. I look closely at him. Yup, there is a hint of a dimple. And now there's a corresponding little flutter in my pulse. And, dear Lord, what does that say about me? Only yesterday I was lusting after Jorge... I blush, remembering. His beautiful face comes back to me, with that exquisite mouth, and his strokeable skin, and toned arms. I'd gawked surreptitiously at them when he'd taken off his coat by the river. But here is Emlyn looking all manful and coolly intelligent yet approachable, those grey eyes almost twinkling; and I can't help but feel *un petit frisson* in certain places. Is it wrong that I am attracted to them both? Lime and mahogany. Sharp and smooth. Emlyn, with his cut-glass voice, and Jorge, with his musical rolled "r"s that, really, just make me want to jump him. God, what would it be like to be with them both? My nipples perk up, and I imagine the three of us in my little flat, slowly undressing. My bedroom is too small, so it would have to be in the lounge. Me, leaning back against Jorge's warm, bare chest, while Emlyn wraps those strong, capable hands about my waist and draws me to him, his eyes glowing as he lowers his head and...

"We have to assume you're dreaming about Magda because of her connection to Ratko."

I snap to attention. "Yes? Uh, yes. Right. Yes." My breasts are almost painful, and I cross my arms and surreptitiously try to assuage the ache. I am a *salope*, aren't I? A scarlet harlot with throbbing knickers. Or am I? Surely, in this liberated day and age, if a woman wants to shag two men, even simultaneously, that is her prerogative?

"Yes," Emlyn muses, "this has something to do with Ratko. I suspect they're using code. I'll do some research." He looks at me and, yeah, there's that twitch again. "I think we can take it as a given that 'enema' doesn't mean 'good-bye'."

My cheeks heat. "No," I say faintly. "Of course not. No." He is never going to be able to look at me without thinking "enema", is he? Any chance he might see me as a sexy, desirable woman has been shot to bits. Damn that stupid Magda and her stupid code. It's bad enough that my brain automatically melts in the presence of an attractive man. Emlyn's probably thinking that I forged my Ph.D. I open my mouth to say, what I don't know, just something to try to recover the situation, when the phone rings.

"Ah, Seef. Good morning. How's it going?" He listens for a moment and frowns. "Kronos? No, nothing yet. We'll keep looking... Did you get the photofit...? She says he sounded mid-Atlantic, so he's obviously spent significant time on both sides of the pond. Any hits here...? What about in Canada or the States? Can you ask your contacts? It's clearly trans-Atlantic and bigger than we assumed..."

I shamelessly eavesdrop, wondering idly about this Seef person – interesting name, that, "Sayf", where's he from? – and criminals and their codes. If I didn't know better, I'd think they were a group of undergrads playing Dungeons and Dragons. *For I am Lord Lay-dun. And I am the Lady Magda. All hail Ray-uh. And you, Lord Kronos... Hang on. Kronos. Ray-uh. Rhea! Kronos and Rhea!* By the time Emlyn hangs up, I'm practically bouncing with excitement.

"Sorry about that, Maela–"

"Emlyn, I've figured it out." He looks at me quizzically, and I charge ahead: "Kronos. Kronos and Rhea. The Titans? According to Greek mythology, Rhea was the wife of Kronos, the king of the gods, and mother of the Olympians. 'Zeus himself, the son of Kronos, makes way, and all the other immortal gods likewise make way for the dread goddess,' as the poets say. Her name's thought to be Minoan, which would make sense, of course, as she was originally worshipped on Crete. She and Kronos ruled the world during the Golden Age, a time of peace, harmony, and prosperity. Kronos, however, is best known for devouring his own children – there are some marvelous although disturbing paintings by Rubens and Goya – which is interesting, as he's frequently associated with time, time being cyclical." I'm in full lecture flow, any hint of nervousness banished. I may not have retained my Latin, but I loved Greek mythology growing up, devouring any book about it I could get my hands on; and although I eventually went into English literature, all those wonderful fables have stayed with me. If I hadn't been distracted by "enemas", I might have figured out Rhea sooner, although, to be fair, it's equally possible that I might have thought of the giant bird. But Kronos clinches it.

Emlyn's staring at me, as if he's only really seeing me for the first time. "Of course. Of course, Maela. I'm embarrassed I didn't figure it out for myself. So much for my expensive Eton and Oxbridge education." He smiles ruefully.

I smile back: "Glad I can help."

"But this is excellent, Maela. We're really getting somewhere!" And gosh, there is that dimple again in all its full glory.

"I'd like to keep chipping away at this, Maela, so do you mind if we curtail our session? You deserve a break."

And, weirdly, for the first time ever, I don't want to leave. I want to stay and have Emlyn praise me some more.

"Sure, no problem." I get to my feet and pick up my bag and coat. "I'll see you tomorrow."

Emlyn nods and smiles again. As I reach the door, the phone rings again, and I hear "Clarissa! Hello! Sorry. Can't talk now, but I'll see you later. About 7:00?"

I shut the door behind me feeling very conflicted.

If I were a truly dedicated scholar, I'd take the unexpectedly free day as a wonderful opportunity to get some work done on my book. Somehow, though, theorizing about Romantic poetry doesn't seem all that important right now. Deep down, I'm not sure whether or not I've ever really had anything new and original to say; I just jumped at the chance to live in London for three years. And, being here and with a day off, I'm going to enjoy it. Where should I go? I could go to Electric Avenue on the off chance that I would bump "unexpectedly" into Jorge? No, that would be too sad. Besides, he's undoubtedly at work. What I really want to do is just pootle about looking at pretty things, maybe pick up something cheap and cheerful for the flat or browse through a few second-hand book stores. And then I have it: Portobello Road! OK, it would be a bit of a faff getting there, but I could get off at Notting Hill and see how the other half lives on Kensington Park Road before cutting over to Portobello. And Portobello has just about everything.

An hour later, having stopped for a coffee on the way, I'm happily strolling down the famous street with its pastel-colored buildings, nosing through stalls, and drifting in and out of twee little boutiques crammed with bric-a-brac. Did I have a use for a vintage tin? Or an old leather trunk? For a moment, I imagine myself, dressed in fluttery clothing, getting onto a steamship bound for the Far East. But, oh, here is the very definition of a second-hand book store, the windows in its small, bright-blue facade crammed with haphazard stacks. I push open the door and take a moment to breathe in the unique scent of old paper and crumbling bindings before starting leafing through the shelves.

A green paperback titled *Guide to the Peerage* catches my eye, and I pull it out and flip it open. And there is Emlyn. Or rather, not Emlyn, but Emlyn in another thirty years or so, standing next to a small, fair-haired woman with Emlyn's eyes. I look at the caption: "Major General Peter Ryder with his wife, the honourable Mary Grey, daughter of Viscount and Lady Lisle." It can't be. But when I look at the family tree, yes, there it is: "sons, Emlyn (b. 1992) and Eadric (b. 1994)." Well good heavens. Agent Ryder is a member of the peerage. I'd never met an actual lord before. Should I curtsy the next time I see him?

I can't stop thinking about it, not over the delicious lamb *shawarma* I grab for lunch, nor while browsing through the pre-loved clothing racks (I really want a chic little sundress à la French 1950), nor on the Tube journey back to my flat. Emlyn a lord. Feck me. I'm still thinking about it that night, watching the telly and eating mint-chocolate-chip ice cream, when my phone pings, announcing the arrival of a text.

Querida, some friends and I are getting together for a drink tomorrow night. 7:00 at The Marquis, Covent Garden. Join us? Jorge

I squeal. A date! Jorge wants a date! I do a little horizontal victory dance, forgetting the bowl in my lap, which promptly tips over, its cold contents spilling over my pajama bottoms and sliding onto the couch. Gaaah! I grab the rapidly melting balls and chuck them back into the bowl, then race to the kitchen to get some paper towel. Uhh. Was there no end to my klutziness? But, ha ha ha, Jorge wants a date! With me! I do another little dance and flop back onto the couch to re-read his text.

Querida. Ooh. I have just enough Spanish to know that this means "darling". Tee hee! *Some friends and I.* I stop. Hmm. Date or mate? Mate or date? Date masquerading as mate, or mate masquerading as date? Maybe date as mate in case things go pear-shaped? Or mate as date as a test-run? My head is spinning.

OK. I need to respond. Friendly but not gushy. Breezy, obviously, but not cool. I nibble on a fingernail.

"Hey there!" No, God no.

"Hi!" Better. But then, he's written *querida*.

"Darling!" No, no, no, no. Too intimate. Maybe the Spanish use "querida" like the Americans use "pal" or the British, well, "mate"?

"*Chéri!*" No, I couldn't pull it off. I wasn't my mother. OK, no greeting. I'll just get straight to the message.

"Sounds good! See you then." Meh, too lackluster. But the second half is spot on.

"Love to! See you then." Hmm, maybe? Yes? No? Oh for feck's sake. I hit send.

God, I'm exhausted now. Is 8:00pm too early to go to bed? After all, I did need my beauty sleep, seeing as how I had a maybe-date tomorrow. I feel a little few butterflies flutter in my stomach then settle lazily back down. A maybe-date. With Jorge the Spanish sex-god. Bags under the eyes would be baaaad. But, oh, Bake-Off is starting! Maybe just one more bowl of ice-cream, to stave off hunger pangs while I watch the contestants create luscious-looking cakes, and then straight to bed. I run to the freezer, pull out the carton, and look inside. Sod it – I'll finish it off. Not worth washing another bowl. I get back in time to hear Paul and Prue announce that this week is chocolate week. Chocolate, I think dreamily, like Jorge's hair. I pull the spoon slowly through my lips, letting the dark chips melt and blend with the fresh tartness of the mint on my tongue. This ice-cream is like a blend of Jorge and Emlyn, I reason. Aaand, once again, my mind flashes to a fantasy of me with the two of them. I moan, letting my eyes close. Emlyn would be masterful in bed, I suspect, all take charge and have his wicked way with you. I squirm. But professional pride would mean that he'd give a lover at least three orgasms before even thinking of coming himself. What would it take to make him lose it and just go Bonobo-monkey crazy off his head with lust? I pant at the image. And Jorge? Jorge would be slow and gentle but intense. He'd want to kiss that sensitive spot between neck and shoulder until you went weak at the knees, lick the shell of your ear, and lock eyes as he rocked home inside you. I quiver. And together? I groan, goose-bumps breaking out on my skin. Dear God, together! Someone's *génoise* collapsing brings me back to the present, and I open my eyes, feeling tingly and flustered. I do try to concentrate on the program, but I really couldn't say who won star baker and who was sent home that night.

DOUBLE CREAM WITH A DASH OF CHAMPAGNE

Wednesday, 26 September – Maela

I'm still feeling giddy and almost completely out of it when I sit down in the familiar green chair the next day. Frankly, I'm surprised I've managed to dress myself. Matching my mood, I've gone for a cashmere, lavender top, cream trousers (winter white so acceptable), and suede boots. Emlyn, looking divine in a pinstripe suit paired with a crisply ironed shirt of a pale, pale grey, looks curiously at me.

"Everything alright?"

"Fine, fine," I smile at him. "Oh! Should that be 'fine, fine, my lord'?" remembering the book I had found the day before.

He sighs and pinches the bridge of his nose. "No, 'Emlyn' will do just fine."

"Well, I want to do things correctly. Are you sure?"

"Quite sure. My mother's a member of the peerage, not me."

"So I don't need to curtsy?"

He gives a short bark of laughter. "No, Maela. No curtsying."

"OK. Because, you know, I'm not a ditzy colonial. Well, I am a colonial, but I'm not a ditz. My parents brought me up properly."

"I never thought otherwise," he assures me, his grey eyes dancing.

"You kind of did," I protest. "When we met. Didn't you?"

"I didn't. Viscount's grandson's honor."

"Oh, OK. That's good." I smile at him again. He really is a lovely man.

"Well, now that that's settled, shall we begin?"

"Yup. Let's do this!" I settle back in the chair, closing my eyes, but not before seeing Emlyn bite his lip, as if to stop himself from laughing. We go through the usual relaxation exercises, which I'm afraid to say are useless, as my mind is darting about like a hummingbird. Not even the picture of Ratko punctures my happy bubble. Fifteen minutes later, peering at the wall behind Emlyn's shoulder, with my eyes half-closed, waiting for any flash of sight, I ask him, "Emlyn?"

"Yes, Maela? Have you seen anything?" He sounds excited. This is the first time I've interrupted our viewing sessions.

"If your dad's a major general, and your mom's an honorable, why aren't you a lord?" For all my Anglophilia, I'm not really sure how the peerage works. Watching Downton Abbey doesn't count as an education.

"Maela!" he groans. "Please concentrate! I'm not a lord because my father is not a member of the peerage."

"I'm just curious. OK, I'm concentrating." I go back to staring at the wall, trying to let my mind go blank and usher in visions of Ratko. But fifteen minutes later, after wondering what I should wear for my maybe-date that night and then what I wanted for lunch and then why Emlyn was dating such an obvious gold-digger like Clarissa, I pipe up again.

"Emlyn?"

"Yes?" he says warily.

"Where did you grow up? In a country house?"

"Maela! Concentrate!"

"Alright, sheesh! Just making conversation."

"You are supposed to be working on bringing the visions to order." He pinches the bridge of his nose again, his fine features wreathed in exasperation.

"Well, this is pretty boring. And I don't think it's the ideal method."

"I'm beginning to see that," he says dryly.

"Took you long enough. Don't you find this boring, too, just watching me?"

"No," he says softly. My cheeks pink, and suddenly my mind goes blank. My mouth drops slightly open, but I manage to cover it up with an inane "good-o" and close my eyes again. I just need to get into the zone. I will Ratko to mind: the dead eyes; the blue, red, and gold dragon tattoo; the gold earring; the full, surprisingly sensual lips; the bare chest, hard muscles roped and corded, and just a scattering of hair. And his penis, my mind supplies helpfully. Don't forget his penis. Remember how shocked you were that a man on the slightly shorter side was a bit on the slightly longer side? And, not that I had a great deal of experience or anything, but it seemed fairly thick and full too. I give myself a hard mental slap and try to concentrate, but it's no good.

"Emlyn?" I hear a sigh and open my eyes. "Did you find anything interesting during your research yesterday?"

"Maela, I really, really need you to concentrate. I know that this is frustrating, but it's a tried and tested method. The ability to see is there; we just have to get you to tap into it." He looks at me earnestly, those beautiful, black-fringed eyes calm and steady. Today, his eyes were a pale grey, almost matching his shirt. I'd noticed that they changed depending on his mood, not in color but in tone.

"And staring at the wall, or going cross-eyed from boredom, is the way to do it?" I sit up straighter in the chair. "Look, Emlyn, I know that you think I'm a complete flake." He makes a gesture of denial, which I ignore. "But you haven't seen me in my best light. I mean, two weeks ago, I was sitting in the library thinking about Tennyson's poetic technique, and the next day I'm pulled into MI5 and told I'm psychic and that I need to learn to remote-see to order. It's been a bit much to take in, and I'll admit I'm struggling, but I do have a brain, you know. Not everybody can get a PhD, or a fellowship, and, OK, it's just in English poetry, but..."

"I read poetry for my degree. I don't think it's useless," he interrupts.

"There's a reason my undergraduate students nicknamed me 'Driscoll the Demon'. I have a mind like a steel trap, and I don't put up with nonsense, and, wait, what?"

"I read poetry for my degree," he repeats.

"What kind?" I ask suspiciously.

"French, although I also studied Russian and English."

Of course he did. "You speak French and Russian?"

"*Oui* and *Da*. French, yes; Russian, up to a point." He now looks amused, as if he's thinking *bet you never imagined that.*

"You went from French poetry to MI5?" I say stupidly.

"*Oui* and *Da*. Now, can we get back to work?"

"*Non* and *Nyet*," I reply calmly. Hah! Two can play at that game, although, beyond "yes", "no", and "vodka", I'm lost. "This method isn't working for me. It's been over a week now, and I haven't had any visions."

"You have," he says. "You've dreamed of Ratko and Magda both."

"Well, yes, when I'm sleeping, but not here. Do you know what I do after our "relaxation exercises", which, by the way, aren't all that relaxing? Eventually, despite trying to order up a vision for you, I inevitably lapse into just trying to pass the time. The other day, I tried to work out the exact shade of paint on your walls. Double cream? Single cream? Jersey cream? Cream with a dash of champagne?" I blow out strongly through my lips and slump back down into the chair.

"I... see. I thought you were finally getting into it. You had such an intent look on your face." He looks so disappointed that my heart gives a funny little twist.

"Sorry. I am, truly. But isn't there another method? Surely you've developed other techniques. And do I really

have to traipse around the east end of London every afternoon? Maybe Ratko has a softer side and likes to wander around Kensington or Belgravia," I say hopefully, even
though I know I'm grasping at non-existent straws. Still, I
did see him by the hospital, so he can't spend all of his time
in the Docklands. I just really, really could do with a change
of scenery.

"Or Mayfair?" His lips twitch, and I'm relieved to see he's
looking amused again.

"Ugh, shopping? No way." I shudder. Maybe I'd like it
if I had the budget, but most of the time it was an exercise in trying to match my aesthetic aspirations to my bank
balance.

"Really? In my experience, most women love shopping,
and the more exclusive the store, the better." He taps his
Mont Blanc pen on the desk, and I think, *Yeah, I bet you've
only dated a succession of Clarissas, and they all loved Bond
Street and the Burlington Arcade, and you, being the gallant
lord chump that you are, probably paid whenever you went out.*
Still, I hold my tongue and simply observe, "Although, that
bracelet he gave Magda didn't come from a corner store.
Any reports of a break-in at high-end jewelers recently?"

He looks sharply at me. "Unpretentious and, as was
made abundantly clear yesterday, intelligent. That's a good
thought, Maela. I'll check on it."

I flush with pleasure and smile: "See, not just a ditzy
colonial."

"For the record, I never said you were. Now, I know you
don't think the current method is working, so I'll look into
it; but, for today, can we give it another go?"

I haven't the heart to deny him. "Fine," I sigh and close
my eyes.

When the time's up, Emlyn looks at me: "What color are
my walls, then?"

I snort: "Double cream with a dash of champagne."

"Ah," he nods solemnly. "Enjoy the Docklands."

Damn it, I think, as I gather up my things.

Outside the Marquis pub, I wipe my hands nervously on my skirt. I feel like I'm about to take a physics exam, but at the same time I'm so excited that I'm in danger of lurching through the doors and bounding up to Jorge like an exuberant puppy, jumping up and down and begging for a pat. Thank God the nerves freeze me into place, because if I embarrass myself tonight, I will check into the nearest nunnery and throw away the key. I take a deep breath and look at the pub, which is absolutely lovely and just what a pub should be. The upper floors are a pale ochre brick with white framed windows and flower boxes, while the ground floor is a gleaming ebony with gold consoles and more baskets of pink flowers hanging between wide panes of glass. I only hope I'm dressed appropriately, because the people inside seem pretty stylish.

I did not, of course, go for a walk around the Docklands. I had more important things to do, like get ready for my maybe-date. Preparations were extensive. I put hot coconut oil on my hair and wrapped it in a towel, to condition it; and read *An Intimate Guide to Erotic Pleasure*, to brush up on my techniques, just in case. After half an hour, I slathered on a mud mask and then gave myself a good hard scrub with a body brush before smearing depilatory cream on my legs and, yes, around my bits because, well, because. I'm tidy like that. Several awkward minutes followed, with me standing X-legged in the bathroom, trying not to smear the cream while continuing to source sex tips. Washing everything off with shea-butter and vanilla shower gel and almond-milk shampoo, I hoped I might smell good enough to eat – hint, hint to Jorge. And then it was time to choose an outfit, and here I almost went to pieces, because I had nothing to wear that wasn't dowdy. I'd never before realized what terrible taste I had and could have wept, because there was no time, of course, to nip out to the shops and pick up something delectable. Why, oh why, hadn't I listened to my mother any one of the many times she had droned on about fashion? She might be a certifiable nutter, but there was no denying she was chic. After trying and rejecting several combinations, I finally settled on a bright-blue top with a floaty white skirt, weather be damned. I decided I would wear a simple gold bangle on my wrists and my favorite gold, flower-shaped earrings, for luck, and because my brain was on the verge of imploding and I couldn't deal with making any more choices.

And now here I am, outside the pub, and I do and don't want to go in.

I go in. The place is full but not packed and just as charming on the inside as it is on the outside. The walls are a pale yellow, and a long, black bar, with scrolling white writing on the front, draws the eye. Above, sparkling glasses are hanging from a silver rack, and behind are row upon row of spirits and wine. I glance around the room, biting my lip, too late remembering that I'm wearing lipstick. And then I spot him, and my insides start to fizz and I go all tingly.

Jorge sees me at the same time, and his face breaks into a smile, making me feel as if I've got champagne dancing through my veins, and he comes over.

"Mah-ay-la!" He leans down and kisses me on both cheeks. "Hi! I'm so glad you could make it. Come. Meet the others."

He takes my hand and draws me with him towards a group standing by the bar. Sofía, a dark-haired stunner, is thankfully with her boyfriend, Eduardo. Mike is a cheerful, sandy-haired Aussie. And then there is Charlotte, a porcelain-skinned English rose with chestnut hair, deep-blue eyes, an overflowing bosom, and a pert bottom. She and Mike do not seem to be together. *Feck.*

I stammer hello to them all, and Jorge goes to get me a

white wine.

"So, Maela. How do you know Jorge?" Charlotte asks. Her tone seems to be friendly, but I know there and then that she doesn't like me.

I tell them that we met on Monday in Battersea Park.

"Oh, Battersea Park!" Charlotte breaks in. "Jorge and I met in Green Park, by St James's Palace, you know," in a tone that implied she'd won the park competition. "I work at a broker's nearby. I was on my way for drinks with friends and stopped to ask him the time, and we just got to talking. He's such a sweetie."

I smile politely and agree, and Mike asks me what brings me to London. I say that I'm doing an internship and quickly ask about him. He's doing a traditional gap year and is bartending in Brixton. "How I met my mate Jorge," he says. "He doesn't yet fully appreciate the value of a pint, but I'm working on it."

Sofía has just finished telling me that she and Eduardo work as teachers and that they met Jorge at the Spanish film festival, on Regent Street, when he returns with my wine.

"We should all go this year," he says, handing me the glass. "The films are subtitled, so even an *ignorante* like Mike can follow them." Jorge grins and slaps Mike on the back.

"Rack off, ya bastard," Mike replies amiably. It's clear they're good friends. "Why learn Spanish when everybody speaks English anyway? Maela, back me up here."

I giggle and shake my head, while Sofía exclaims and calls him an *idiota*. She, Eduardo, and Mike start chatting about the perks of learning a foreign language, and even Charlotte gets stuck in. Jorge turns to me. "I'm really glad you could come," he says softly. "You look lovely."

I color: "Oh. Thanks. So, good day? Take any walks? How'd you find this place? It's great. Do you come here often?"

Jorge laughs, a rich deep chuckle that rolls over me and

makes me feel warm and a little giddy. I know I'm babbling, but somehow I don't mind, and I start to laugh too.

"Yes, a good day, but we were busy, so I worked through lunch and didn't have time for a walk. We discovered this place by accident, me and Sofía and Eduardo, after seeing a show in Leicester Square. It's a little farther for me and Mike, but we only have to change once on the Tube, and it's easier for the others. And," he adds solemnly but with a twinkle in his eye, "With your love of blue plaques, I thought you'd like it. It's very historic."

"It is?"

"*Sí*. You see the bar?" I glance over: "The writing?"

"*Sí*. It tells the story of the pub. This building dates back to the seventeenth century, and many, many *bandidos* came. And later, your Mr. Charles Dickens liked to drink here."

"He did, really? Charles Dickens?" I don't believe it: I'm hanging out at Charles Dickens' pub! I crane my neck for another look around the bar.

"And," Jorge concludes with a flourish, "they say that Brydges Place, outside, inspired Diagon Alley."

I squeal. "It did? Can we go look? Right now? Have a look? Just a quick peek?" I can't help it: I know I'm acting all of twelve, but *Charles Dickens and J.K. Rowling*, together in one pub? And *highwaymen*? This is just too cool.

Jorge takes my hand. "Come." He murmurs to the others that we'll be back in a minute and draws me with him. Charlotte's eyes narrow, but, thankfully, she doesn't try to tag along. It turns out that the pub backs directly onto the alley, so in a minute we're standing there, along with a few other punters. I peer around eagerly. On the wall, there are pictures of highwayman Claude Duval being seized while drinking in the pub, and there are more baskets of ivy and flowers and old-fashioned, gas-style lamps. It's not very wide, perhaps enough space for four people standing shoulder to shoulder, and Jorge tells me that it's only fifteen inches at the other end. I, of course, want to go explore, but

Jorge tells me I'll be disappointed, as it's nothing but slabs of stone and graffiti. "This is where the magic is."

I look up at him and smile. He's right about that. He's looking just as gorgeous as he did on Monday. He's wearing a simple, brown tee-shirt that matches his eyes, dark blue jeans, and brown boots. His hair is mussed, as if he didn't bother to dry it after getting out of the shower, and his stubble's a little longer today. I lean a little closer and catch a hint of bergamot and black pepper. As I'm taking a deep breath, I notice a woven bracelet around his wrist. It's a twist of black and brown leather and has a silver clasp.

I gesture at it: "That's nice."

Jorge glances down and smiles. "Ah, *sí*. Thanks. My sister made it for me. She says she is glad to get rid of me, but this is her way of saying she misses me. That and that *mantecados* she sent. Very typical. A little like your shortbread. I taste them and I am home." He takes a sip of his red wine.

"She's very talented. I take it she's your older sister?"

He nods. "Only by three years, but she thinks it gives her the right to boss me around. She says I have the *cabeza* in the clouds and need looking after. I am patient because she loves me. But I wish," he continues, swirling the wine in his glass, "she would remember that I am not six like my nephew but twenty-six." He takes another sip, looking pained.

I giggle and raise my own glass. "I never thought there were advantages to being an only child, but maybe I should be grateful. And your mother? Does she boss you around too?"

He smiles gently. "She did. Always telling me, '*chiquito*, clean up your toys;' '*chiquito*, do your homework;' '*chiquito*, turn off the *televisión* and go outside;' '*chiquiiiiito*, come inside and set the table.' My sister takes after her." He shakes his head in mock disapproval, clicking his tongue. "This is not a good thing."

I laugh a little awkwardly. It sounds like his mother died

when he was a kid, and I feel like I've stumbled into a blunder, but Jorge looks down at me, eyes warm. "Of course, I was also spoiled most badly by my grandparents and all of my aunts and uncles."

This time I laugh for real. I notice he hasn't mentioned his father but follow his lead and keep the mood light. "Were you a brat?"

"*Un mocoso*? *Sí*, I think I was." He laughs out loud and starts to tell me about some of his escapades, his eyes shining. There was the time he brought a slug to school and left it on the teacher's desk, though, sadly, the teacher did not scream; and the time he hid his sister's favorite shoes before a big date (but the boy was no good, so it was OK). He's just in the middle of telling me about eating an entire caramel flan that his grandmother had made for Sunday dinner, because he was so hungry and it looked so good, when Charlotte appears.

"Jorge, darling, don't be antisocial. Come back in. Mike's getting another round." She trails her finger down his arm and pouts.

Jorge looks a little startled but says, "Oh, of course. Maela, shall we go back inside?"

I would prefer to stay where we are, and I think Jorge would too; but I don't want to be impolite, so I agree, and we follow Charlotte back to the group. While we've been outside, the place has filled up, and the atmosphere is lively. It looks like there'll be a band on later. Mike's at the bar and takes our orders: a small white wine for me, a medium red wine for Jorge, and a large white wine for Charlotte. I thought I was a drinker, but she's outpacing the men, and I can't help but feel smugly virtuous. Sofía asks me about growing up in San Francisco, and Jorge, Mike, and Eduardo start talking about an indoor ice-climbing center. Charlotte stands close to Jorge, occasionally joining in but mostly taking big swigs out of her glass. She's done before anyone else is halfway through and goes to get herself another. Jorge looks worried but resigned at the same time, just glancing occasionally over at her as if to check that she's still on her feet. Charlotte keeps patting his arm, and it's getting on my nerves; but I'm having a nice chat with Sofía so try not to fret about it. I really like Sofía and think that maybe we could become friends; she's shy, like me, but sweet and has a surprisingly wicked sense of humor.

Eduardo gets another round in. I try to volunteer, but the men are having none of it. It's their treat. Sofía's telling me about a New Year's Eve tradition in Spain – eating twelve grapes, one for every stroke of midnight, for good luck – when Mike sees a group of new arrivals and exclaims, "Strewth, that's a handsome woman. I'm getting a stiffy just looking at her." We all groan, except for Sofía, who seems confused.

"Aaargh. TMI, Mike!" I say.

Jorge looks at him solemnly: "You are truly disgusting, my friend." Eduardo shakes his head, and Charlotte punches his arm.

"Catch you later, mates. I'm on the pull." Mike winks and heads off towards the busty blonde and her friends. Eduardo puts his arm around Sofía, telling her he will explain later; and I think Jorge is turning to join us, when Charlotte pulls him aside. I grit my teeth and smile at Eduardo and Sofía. He's just as nice as she is but more outgoing, so the conversation doesn't lag. I'm enjoying hearing about their life in Madrid and how it compares to London but can't help looking over at Jorge and Charlotte from time to time. They seem to be in a little world of their own, Jorge bending down to listen to her as Charlotte chatters, her eyes bright. At one point, it seems as if he makes to rejoin us, but Charlotte hangs back; and they continue talking privately. After another fifteen minutes, I'm quietly seething and wondering how I can break up their cozy tête à tête, but I don't want to be rude to Sofía and Eduardo so do nothing and try to concentrate on having a nice time.

Finally, Jorge comes over, Charlotte's arm wrapped through his. My eyes snap to it, and I feel a little sick. He says something in Spanish to Eduardo and Sofía, who nod, then turns to me. "Maela, I'm so sorry. I need to take Charlotte home, but Eduardo and Sofía will look after you."

My fingers clench my wine glass so hard I'm in danger of snapping the stem. *What the ever-loving fuck!* I'm speechless, but I quickly plaster on a smile and nod. It's either that or burst into tears. Jorge is going home with Charlotte. With Charlotte: not me. So I'm the mate, and she's the date. Was this an audition? A try before you buy? Did he want to see how I measured up? I feel confused and utterly crushed. Strike two for Maela! One more and I'll be out. I take a big, miserable swallow of wine. Jorge's eyes darken, and I think he's about to say something, but Charlotte tugs on his arm. "Jorge, darling, I'm feeling a little faint," she slurs. "It's so warm in here. Can we leave now?" She sways prettily on her heels.

Eduardo mutters something in Spanish, and Jorge looks alarmed. "Of course. Eduardo, Sofía, *hasta luego*. Maela–"

Charlotte hiccups. "Oops. Jorge, I really need some fresh air. There're so many people here." She sways again, clutching his arm tighter.

"*Sí, sí.* OK." He throws a distracted smile of good-bye at us and turns, shepherding her out of the pub. I feel very cold as the door shuts behind them.

"Another drink, Maela?" Eduardo asks me.

"Thanks, but I think I've reached my limit." All of a sudden, the pub is too loud, the lights are too bright, and I just want to be safely snuggled under the covers in bed. I smile brightly at them: "Actually, I should be getting home myself. Long week, you know." I give a brittle little laugh.

"Of course! We should be going ourselves. Come. Sofía and I will see you to the station." He drains his glass.

"Really, there's no need. It's just a short walk." I don't want to ruin their evening – it's only nine o'clock – and I'd rather be alone.

Sofía looks concerned, and Eduardo protests, but I insist. "It was lovely meeting you both. I hope I'll see you around some time."

"But of course," Eduardo says. "It was a pleasure." Sofía asks if we can exchange numbers, which I'm happy to do, and then, mercifully, I can escape the pub and into the anonymity of the evening streets.

KRONOS

Wednesday, 26 September – Kailani

Sitting staring at my coffee, I wonder how much longer I need to put up with this shit before I can call it a day. The last week and a half has been, to put it mildly, a complete and utter mess. I'd love to say we tucked right in with abandon and immediately got along as a crack unit of crime-solving awesomeness, but, and there's really no better way to say it, we were a cluster fuck of epic proportions. Deo and I spent the week catching the rest of the group up on our cases over the last few months. Smith and Donovan picked apart every decision we made along the way, questioning our procedures and methods. Smith was respectful and approached it from a learning perspective, so, while it was frustrating, it was understandable. Donovan, though, scoffed and rolled his eyes so much I thought he'd injure himself. Nothing was done correctly in his opinion. Methodology aside, he didn't even like the way Deo and I split up work or how much leniency Deo appeared to give me, and seemed personally offended that Hideo and I had what amounted to a secret language from the length of our time working together.

Jonah, bless him, was a problem of an entirely different nature. Having never worked on the force before he was hopelessly lost. His role was as a Bleeder, who weren't active agents or detectives, but rather were a kind of outside option to pull in on specific cases. The real problem though was, as much as he tried, he had a hard time being serious. He took specific things seriously, for sure, but he'd always be trying to make me laugh or smile rather than concentrating on the task at hand, and while it came from a good place, it was frustrating. He'd get upset at the way the guys spoke to me, and I think he was trying to alleviate some of the tension and possible upset he imagined I must be feeling. I'm pretty sure he was trying to protect me in some way, which grated on my nerves. I had worked hard to get where I was, and to earn my position, and the fact that he thought I'd crack under the weight of a little rough office talk was disappointing.

Gomez watched over it all like a queen with her subjects, listening carefully and remaining fairly silent, thankfully. She looked over our casework with hawk-like eyes, though, shooting Deo and me long, considering glances from time to time, making notes in her tiny journal. Every time she'd ask us to go back over a series of events or decisions made, Deo's shoulders would tighten and his jaw would flex. He was exhausted from dancing between telling the truth and glossing over details that would expose too much. At the end of every day his face was heavy, worn with concern and worry.

Today we were *finally* briefing the Tennireef case, then Thursday and Friday we were due for a recap Q&A series now that the guys had had an overview of the players in the Seattle area. We'd done kind of a brief run-through of everything we'd thought pertinent, but tomorrow and the next day the plan was for Smith and Donovan just to study the cases more in depth and look for things that maybe Tanaka and I had missed.

Sighing, I close my eyes for a minute, just concentrating on my breathing and the warmth of the cup in my hand. Today's going to be a shitshow. I have no desire to revisit the details of Tennireef's interrogation and am feeling run down, which isn't a great combination. The door opens, and, feeling Donovan's energy signature, I groan softly to myself. He pauses, and there's a pulse of what feels like hurt, but it's hard to tell because I have my walls so tightly drawn. Hurt and anger have a lot of the same flavor some-times, as do hurt and sadness, so I'm not sure I'm reading him correctly.

"Reed," he says shortly, before going to sit down. "Working hard?" he adds snarkily, and I shake my head a little.

"Hardly working," I reply in a faux jocular voice, before dropping my face into my hands. "Actually, can we just not today, Donovan? Gotta be honest, I'm not looking forward to this morning."

I wait for the acerbic reply, but there's a long pause, and then he says, "Sure, Reed." He sits across from me, surprising me, and looks at me consideringly. "Bad case today?"

I half laugh, devoid of mirth. "Aren't they all bad cases?"

"Yeah," he nods, "but this is the first one I've seen on your face. The rest you've handled like a champ."

Pretending to gasp, I hold a hand to my chest. "Why, Donovan, that can't be... was that a compliment?"

He frowns. "Everyone has one or two that get under their skin, Reed. No shame in that. What's on the docket today?" He glances at the folder in front of him and lets out a slow whistle through his teeth. "Ah. Today's Tennireef?" Shaking his head, he says, almost under his breath, "I don't like that guy. I know he's everyone's Golden Child, but he hits me the wrong way. Guy seems like a prick."

Flashing the first real smile I've ever directed at him, I say, "Donovan, that's literally the nicest thing you've ever said to me."

He lets out a surprised bark of laughter, dimple flashing, and I think for a minute how *nice* he seems when he's not a complete asshole, before the door opens and the rest of the team pour in, along with Cruella DeVille. Jonah walks to grab his usual chair, eyes narrowing when he sees Donovan sitting there.

"He bothering you, Kai?" Jonah asks under his breath.

Donovan, who looked like he'd been about to stand, now settles back deeper in the chair and locks eyes with Jonah challengingly.

"Jesus Christ," I say, rubbing my eyes, before I hear the chair push back and see Donovan rise to his feet.

"Forgot, Reed. Today's your hall pass." Waving a hand mockingly over the seat, he smirks at Jonah, before going back to his normal position at the table. Jonah raises an eyebrow at me but wisely keeps silent, pulling his chair to sit by me. Hideo sits beside me as well and surprises me by reaching over to grab my hand and give it a squeeze, despite the presence of the other guys and the Wicked Witch of the West.

Looking around and seeing everyone settled, I dive straight into it. "Today's Tennireef. You'll notice three case files on him. One is from his time as a councilman, one is from his time as a senator, one is the private file Tanaka and I have put together."

There are a few surprised looks around the table at that, and I explain. "Tanaka and I noticed that information was being very, *very* subtly altered in his official file. Nothing major – in some instances the time was only off by minutes. 3:43 changed to 3:48, that sort of thing. As all case notes and recordings are required to be submitted with official paperwork on his cases, it has been hard to prove."

Tanaka flashes me a quick smile, which I return. "The only reason we even realized it," he says quietly, "is because Reed is OCD about her paperwork. Annoyingly, frustratingly OCD."

"Weird flex, but okay," I say jokingly, and he laughs a little.

"The number of times she's gone back into files to triple check things..." He shakes his head.

"Hey!" I say, mock affronted. "You *know* that..."

"Good police work is..." he begins jokingly.

"Ruined by bad paperwork!" We finish together. Smiling at him, I poke him in the side. "What," I say, "am I supposed to be like you? A filthy kitchen sink of paperwork?"

He rolls his eyes, catches a strange look from Gomez, and schools his face back to seriousness.

"Anyway," he says abruptly. "She went back into the file a couple of days after the last interrogation, which happened in March, was closed. Our best guess is, whoever changed the info thought it was safe because we'd been pressured, fairly strongly, by the mayor's office to cease and desist. It was 'verging on harassment', in his words, of our much-loved senator, that he kept getting pulled in for question-ing. So the inquiry was closed, and put away. Reed wasn't happy with the way we had wrapped up a section, and went back to check it. She found a time discrepancy – only by ten minutes – which she never would have noticed months down the line, but that close she still had a time-stamped receipt on her Starbucks app..."

"Coffee!" I crow, waving my cup. "Helping police since 19something or other."

He shoots me a long-suffering look and continues. "She remembered that trip in particular because we had spotted Tennireef across the street at the same time, and had com-mented on the coincidence."

"I checked my handwritten notes, and the time had been altered there too, pretty expertly, I have to say. I wouldn't have noticed it unless I was looking for it. Since the source material had been corrupted, there was no way to prove the case was off at all. A Starbucks receipt and our memories won't hold up in court against an obviously well-connected US senator. So we decided to keep copies of all the original casework from that point on."

"Which is why you have the separate file in front of you. That contains all information on our investigation since March. The other is the official file kept by the department." Here he looks slightly discomforted. "Ah, the uh... Chief Cruise is unaware of our backup, as are all other officers. It's an off-the-books sort of arrangement until we can figure out who is altering our material."

The faces around the table, even Donovan's, are heavy with concentration. Hideo motions to me.

"So," I begin. "His interview. Well, he was definitely there when Beckett was tortured. Close enough to be covered in quite a bit of the arterial blood spray."

It was like a bomb had gone off at the table. Smith, Donovan, even Gomez, started talking a mile a minute, unintelligible noise creating a din, until Smith's bass voice barked a quick, "Quiet!", startling the others into silence.

"Explain," he says simply and waits.

"Here, here, here…" I say, touching my face, neck, and arm. "But most of all…" I tap my mouth, then clear my throat, the memory of the iron tang strong. "He could taste it, so I'm fairly sure a decent amount got in his mouth? It definitely didn't bother him." Shivering slightly, I continue resolutely. "He got off on it anyways. That and the rape."

"He *raped* her?" Donovan explodes. "How is there not physical evidence pointing towards him?"

I shake my head. "No. Sorry. He didn't rape her personally. He witnessed it. Possibly directed it, organized it? Definitely enjoyed it."

"That's the feeling I got," Jonah murmurs beside me, and I turn to him in surprise.

"What?" I say, shocked.

"Yeah, it wasn't a really clean pull," he replies, face pale. "I got some residual from that, for sure. Nothing that stayed with me, and not even a quarter as much as you got, but I got a taste of it."

"Why wasn't that reported?" snaps Gomez, and Jonah just looks at her with flat eyes and shrugs.

I watch him for a long moment, then turn back to the table to continue. "I'm about 99% certain that he didn't actually witness her die. There were a lot of variations on lust…"

Smith interrupts with a raised finger, and I nod at him. "Variations on lust?"

"Oh. Yeah. So, like, blood lust carries a certain feel to it. Sometimes sexual, sometimes not. But a killer who is hunting for death and gets high off that... that's a lot different than a rapist. And usually a rapist isn't a sexual lust, well, not completely. It's a power lust? Like a perverted variation of domination lust? But Tennireef's definitely had strong sexual overtones with a ton of pleasure attached, so the feel wasn't the same as a rapist. He enjoyed watching. There were some other tones to it though, spikes of pleasure when he thought of it. So I'm guessing some torture did it for him too."

Hideo taps my foot sharply, and I look up to see Gomez's gleaming eyes fixated on me.

"Well *done*, Kailani," she says softly, and I shiver again, this time from the feral glint in her gaze. Looking back to my papers, I continue, nervous now, though I'm not certain why.

"In any case, he was definitely there. His story isn't accurate, not the way he's telling it anyways. My guess is there's enough truth there that he'd beat a lie detector if necessary. You know. 'Did you kill Riley Beckett' – 'No'. Truth. Right? 'Were you there when she died?' 'No' would be the probable truth. I'm betting he left prior to her actual passing, so he would be clean. 'Did you harm her'... you know, that's different than 'did you cause her to *be* harmed'... again, 'no' would be the literal truth, I'm guessing. So the basic questions he could definitely beat. And since his team has approval over the questions he answers *unless* he's *actually* arrested, he'll never pop. And it makes chasing him down very difficult, as he can release to the public the fact that he's come in, multiple times, voluntarily. That there's been no physical evidence, only circumstantial evidence. No DNA ties. That he's taken multiple lie detector tests and passed with flying colors – he can even release the questions he's been asked, and answered willingly. So he's clean. It's possible that he can even get around other questions," I say, now lost in thought. "Like, did you *order* Beckett's murder?"

"Ah," says Hideo from beside me, picking up my train of thought. "Possibly no, correct?"

I nod, beginning to feel the excitement of the chase. "Or, did you *personally* cause harm to Beckett."

"Were you involved with the murder or rape of Beckett?" replies Hideo thoughtfully.

"Son of a bitch…" I breathe out. "Son. Of. A. Bitch."

The others look at us, confused. "The interpretation of the questioning is important. He doesn't have to lie at all. Not once. Not if we don't get the questions exactly correct. It's a dangerous work-around, but it *is* a work-around. If you can answer honestly, Reed won't pick up on guilt."

"So there's another fish somewhere," Donovan states somewhat disbelievingly. "You think he's being paid to look the other way?"

I shake my head slowly. "Noooo…" I draw out thoughtfully. "I don't think he's being paid off. There was a satisfaction – the feeling of a problem being solved, so I'm not sure. But I don't think he'd have been personally involved if he were being paid to ignore it. I don't think he'd risk it."

I blow a strand of hair out of my face in frustration. "I'd pick up on guilt if we asked the right questions. I didn't get any, so I'm thinking we weren't looking at it correctly. I *did* pick up a shit-ton of amusement, like I was entertaining him." Looking back through the papers, I wonder what I'm missing, before replaying what Donovan said. "What if," I begin slowly, "what if it's not *another* fish, what if it's a *bigger* fish? If he's not being paid off, but is on the payroll?"

"You think he's taking orders," says Smith flatly.

"Possibly," I reply, still unsure but gaining confidence.

"The question is," Gomez interjects thoughtfully, "*who* has enough power to seek out and sway a man who will, almost undoubtedly, be President of the United States within the next decade, barring any unforeseen complications?"

Smith's phone beeps, and he picks it up, reading the message with a frown. Turning to the computer in the corner, he pulls up a screen and begins keying in a username and password.

"Seef just sent a message. Wants help identifying a suspect their Viewer hit on. They haven't had hits in their system, and she heard a mid-Atlantic kind of accent."

Seeing my questioning look, he waves me off with a mumbled, "Later, Reed," before turning back to the computer. The screen takes a moment to load, and then, in near exact pen and ink detail, James Tennireef's face is staring back at us.

"Pick up, pick up...", Smith mutters under his breath. "Seef!" he almost shouts, "Jesus, man! Wait 'til you... Oh!" His voice changes from a warm, familiar tone to a cooler, though not unfriendly, more professional tone. "Sorry Emlyn... Mmmm... yeah, I'd assumed he'd be at his office at this ti... yes, of course. We got a hit on your Viewer's info... Didn't even need to run it. Recognized him right away. She got the details perfect – it's like a photo... James Tennireef. And he's a US senator. I'll send a file over."

He frowns a little, then his face darkens into something viciously gleeful. "Yeeees," he almost hissed. "Nice, Emlyn. Putting that fancy education to good use... Oh!" He sounds surprised, with a hint of a smile in his voice. "*She* did, did she? Rhea and Kronos? Smart girl. No... we haven't been pushed info on Rhea, so pass along... yeah. So what, we're looking for a man, code Kronos, and a woman, code Rhea?" He falls silent, clearly listening.

Running through the bits of conversation I'm overhearing in my head, something bothers me. Flipping through the stack of papers in front of me, I wait for it to jump out at me, ignoring the hum of conversation between Hideo, Jonah, and Donovan.

I'll start with Becca and go from there, I decide. Grabbing her file, I open to a stack of photos that have been added since last week. Wincing slightly, I hurriedly turn them over. *Poor girl. Jesus Christ. She was emaciated at the end. How long did they have her? Any amount of time would be too long... Time... time... shit!*

Turning the stack back over hurriedly, I find the photo I'm looking for, then rustle through the rest of the files Gomez had given me, and run to Smith.

"Smith!" I say urgently, but he waves me off, still concentrating on the phone call. "Smith!" I try again, and he turns to me, frowning slightly, motioning in exasperation to the phone. I shove the photos in his face, and he looks at me in confusion.

"Hang on Emlyn. *What*, Reed?"

"Time!" I say triumphantly, pointing to the hourglass, the odd snake, and the sickle in the photos. He raises an eyebrow and shakes his head slightly. "Kronos – he was the god of time. The hourglass, time. Right? The snake eating its tail – it's an ouroboros! Life, death, and rebirth!"

He looks down at the table, at the photos scattered over it, slow realization dawning on his face.

"Kronos, Smith," I say, waving my hands over the photos, "Kronos!", and he sits down heavily, his voice dark as he speaks into the phone again. "Emlyn..." he begins softly, "we've got a problem..."

ALL MEN ARE BASTARDS

Thursday, 27 September – Maela

I am, naturally, cross and out of sorts all night. I don't
know what to think. On the one hand, Jorge chose the
pub for me, which is a good sign; on the other, he left with
Charlotte, even if, replaying the evening in slow motion,
he did seem a bit reluctant. But maybe that's just my imagination, trying to soften the humiliation of having been
rejected on the first date. Or wasn't it a date? While I'm
brushing my teeth, Kate Bush's Wuthering Heights comes
on the radio, and I leap about the room, shout-singing "Oh,
Jorge! I'm so cold. Let me in through your window – oh –
oh –oh – oh!" By the time I've got into bed, I've moved on
to Denis Leary's "He's an asshole. He's an asshole. What an
asshole. He's the world's biggest assho – oh – ole."

I'm in a fine fit of a mood when I plonk myself down in
the green armchair the next afternoon. Emlyn had to move
our session back, so I've had all morning to brood. What is
wrong with me? Am I just a terminally dull person? I know
I'm no supermodel, but I thought I made up for cup-size
with character. Clearly not. Why choose a sparrow when
you can have a scarlet macaw? There should be a law that
men have to spell out exactly what they mean: "Dear average but moderately interesting person. Some friends and I
are getting together tomorrow night. I had an OK time with
you the other day, so I thought you might like to join us.
Just as friends. I repeat, for the avoidance of all doubt: Just
as friends. Yours in friendship, Jorge."

Emlyn raises an elegant eyebrow. "Let me guess. All men
are bastards." He, bastard in chief, is looking as handsome

as ever but a little tired, like he's spent all night schtumphing a certain leggy blonde. Hah!

"What, are you psychic now?" I ask nastily. There's a thread loose in my cotton sweater – green, subconsciously chosen, no doubt, to reflect my seething jealousy – and I pick at it.

He sighs and stands up. "Come on, get your coat. We're going out for tea."

"I don't want tea," I mutter. Sheesh! Contrary to what the British think, tea doesn't solve all ills. I narrowly resist the urge to cross my arms, settling instead for sagging even further into the chair.

"Well I do. Come on, don't be an imp." He comes round from behind his desk and stands by my chair, waiting.

I'm outraged and sit bolt upright. "Why you! That's hardly professional!" I glare at him, angrily pushing a piece of hair out of my face.

"Neither is your attitude, *Agent* Driscoll. But I'm willing to overlook it." He looks at me challengingly and holds out his hand.

I chunter, "Thought you said I wasn't an agent. Fine. Fine! We'll have tea." I take his hand, those long musician's fingers wrapping round mine, and allow him to pull me to my feet.

"I said you weren't a *secret* agent," he counters, a slight smile playing about his lips. "Come on, there's a nice place round the corner, and you can tell uncle Emlyn all about what's eating at you."

I blow out strongly through my nose but grab my coat and follow him obediently out the door.

To his credit, I admit to myself, begrudgingly, the café is indeed nice. There's a cheerful red awning and, inside, a long glass case filled with luscious-looking cakes. My spirits rise. Emlyn gestures me towards a table. "What would you like? Earl Grey?"

"No," I say quickly, "I don't like Earl Grey." I mean, I do, but the associations are too painful right now. "I'll have, umm, Lapsang Souchong." That sounds sophisticated, right? And I'm feeling a little out of my depth.

Emlyn looks a bit surprised. "Really, I wouldn't have had you down as a Lapsang-Souchong sort of girl."

I bristle: "And why not?" Does he think I'm simple? Too much the boorish colonial?

"No reason," he says mildly. "I just see you as liking more perfumed, delicate teas." Well, that's true, and now I want to change my order, but I simply state, "Lapsang Souchong, please. No milk."

He shortly comes back with two pots of tea, Earl Grey for him – blast – and Lapsang Souchong for me, along with a plate of *madeleines* dusted with icing sugar. Joy! Little, buttery, lemon-zesty morsels of goodness. "Ooh, thanks!" I pick one up and inhale it, my spirits rising further.

"I thought, being half-French, you'd like them." He swirls the tea around in his pot and pours out a cup. "Now, tell me. What's got up your nose?" Emlyn takes a sip and looks at me expectantly.

Aaand, just like that, I choke on the cake and want to kill him. "Agent Ryder," I say frostily, "your manners leave much to be desired." I pour myself a cup of tea and gag: the aroma is not promising.

"I expect they do. Mummy and Pater would be disappointed if they knew. So I won't tell them. Now, 'fess up." He takes a bite of *madeleine* and smiles sweetly at me, dimple and all.

I drum my fingers on the table. "Well, seeing that you can't keep your snout out of my business, it's like you said. All men are bastards, and you, may I say, take pride of place." I take a sip of tea. Ugh, no, no, no. It's awful – all smoky and piney. And I've got a whole pot to get through. I look forlornly at Emlyn's cup.

"Ouch! And to what, may I ask, do I owe this distinction?" He brings his own cup to his lips and inhales beatifically, half closing his eyes. Drat! He noticed me looking at it, didn't he? Did he?

"Your charming personality," I answer sarcastically. "No doubt you too think it's acceptable to invite a girl out and then leave her high and dry. Well, that may be acceptable behavior in *London*," I hiss, "but it's not where I come from." And out it flows, the whole sorry saga. "And," I conclude with a flourish, "he hasn't even had the decency to call or text!" OK, it's been less than a day, but still. I slump a bit in my chair and take a large sip of tea, trying not to grimace.

"Well," Emlyn answers reasonably, "why don't you contact him?"

He takes another cake, and I stare at him. Is he mental?

"Me, contact him?"

"Yes. More tea?"

"Ugh, um, I mean, no. No thanks. Me? Get in touch with him? No. Yeah, that's attractive. Not happening." Thank God I've reached the end of the cup.

"Maela, weren't you the one reading me the riot act yesterday that you're a strong, confident, intelligent woman? If you want to know what's up, ask him."

He's serious. Only someone who's never been turned down could be so stupid.

"Let's drop it, shall we? He's made his feelings known, and I accept that. Now, can we get back to work?"

Emlyn rolls his eyes at the ceiling. "Women! Alright, have it your way. But before we go–" he pauses and pours me a cup of Earl Grey, "have a cup of my tea. It goes much better with the *madeleines*."

Drat! He did notice me looking after all.

Back in the office, I settle myself in my chair, feeling more magnanimous now that I've had tea and cake. Emlyn, on the other hand, grows grave when he fires up his computer and reviews whatever file he was reading when I came in. We've had our little time out, and now it's back to work.

"There's been a disturbing development in the case. I've been working on it since last night with Seef and the Americans. Maela, in your visions, have you ever seen a tattoo on Magda or Ratko, apart, of course, from the dragon?"

"A tattoo? No, I don't think so," I say slowly. Where is he going with this?

"Think, Maela! It's important." Emlyn's voice is sharp, and I look at him in surprise, tinged with a little indignation: I thought we'd gotten over the "Maela is a halfwit" attitude.

But I see that his face is tense, and he's clenching his jaw slightly, perhaps even unconsciously, so I don't bristle. I mentally review my visions.

"No, no tattoos." I shake my head and shrug. "But I've only seen them from a couple angles. Magda likes to be on top," I say dryly. "Why? What's happened?"

Emlyn pauses for a moment, as if considering how much to share, then gives a slight nod to himself. "The man you saw talking to Magda? We've got a hit. He's a US senator by the name of James Tennireef."

What the fuuuuh? A US senator? I probably should have known that. But I've been so wrapped up in my ivory tower that I've only spared a passing thought for politics over the past few years. Let's be honest: it's usually a bunch of old, white men jawing at each other. I vote, of course, but he's not a California politician. I know that much. And what on earth is a US senator doing with Magda?

Emlyn reads the question on my face. "Exactly. A Washington senator, working with a woman who's clearly involved in a criminal enterprise. And there's more. Your deduction about Kronos and Rhea was spot on and has led to a troubling breakthrough. Over the past few years, we've become aware of several new crime syndicates. Well, that's not surprising: there's always one, and allegiances are fluid.

There's no honor among thieves, despite what Cicero says. What *is* surprising is that we haven't been able to infiltrate the organizations. We've very little idea about how they operate or how far their tentacles stretch, though we suspect them of the usual: drug running, gang violence, murder, forced prostitution. The only thing we do have are logos, for want of a better word. Here, we've had reports of drugs stamped with an hourglass. Once, we found the dead body of a pimp inked with a sickle and then that same image, on the body of a prostitute, but in another part of the country. The hourglass and sickle have also turned up in other countries, along with an image of a snake eating its own tail, the *ouroboros*. In the States, they've had all three, so we know that these syndicates are operating internationally. Two weeks ago, an English trafficking victim was found in Seattle. Before she died, she whispered "Kronos". You had a vision this week of Magda, on the phone with, we assume, a woman, codenamed "Rhea", whom you correctly identified as a reference to the Greek goddess. Yesterday, the Americans were able to put all the pieces together. The sickle, the hourglass, the *ouroboros*: these are all symbols identified with the god Kronos, which means it is likely that we are dealing not with three separate organizations but one. One, very well-organized, multinational crime syndicate."

I'm silent for a moment, taking it all in, then stir in my chair: "So the fact that Magda is connected to Rhea, who must be pretty high up in the organization or maybe even in charge, if she's the wife of Kronos, and, oh flip, to Tennireef–"

Emlyn nods: "Kronos, if that's the name of the organization and not a code-name for another player, seems to have a US senator in its pocket, or maybe even on the books." He taps his pen against the desk while I mull through the implications.

"Emlyn, how does Ratko fit in? Is his network part of Kronos? I haven't seen any of the images you've described, but drug-running, human trafficking... It would make sense, wouldn't it? And is Ratko in charge or Magda? Are they running the gang together? Or is Magda some sort of, I don't know, recruiter or liaison for Rhea?"

"It's possible. Likely even. This may be how Kronos operates: subcontracting out the work, so to speak. We just don't have enough information yet. Which is why we urgently need to figure out how to refine your visions. You could be our ticket in, Maela. You might be able to crack Kronos wide open."

His excitement is catching. *Holy hell*, I think. *Me, the key to the whole thing. The secret weapon. The agent extraordinaire.* It's an awesome responsibility.

"But not today," Emlyn continues. "Today we need to go back over things, see if we've missed anything, take stock."

We spend the rest of the afternoon reviewing my visions, speculating, trying to tease out any details, no matter how small, which may give us a better sense of what we are dealing with. It's exhausting but exhilarating.

Despite my resolve, I'm flagging when I get home the next day. Emlyn has me trying a new technique. After the obligatory body-loosening exercise, I have to try to quiet my mind and visualize pulling myself out of my body using an imaginary rope. The idea is that this will "free" me from my physical constraints and open my consciousness to visions of Ratko, Magda, or Tennireef. When I do manage to shush my mind for five minutes, I keep imagining accidentally hanging my spirit body with the rope, which is freaking me out.

I throw my keys on the table and kick off my shoes before padding to the kitchen to see what I can make for dinner. This week I'm exploring back-of-the-cupboard cookery. I'm eying up a tin of chickpeas and a pack of linguine when my phone pings. There's a text: "*Querida*, I'm sorry about Wednesday night. Are you free tomorrow for lunch? Currently in Spain. Jorge."

I sit down on one of the chairs, horrible plasticky things that came with the flat, and stare at the phone. I don't know what to think. Part of me is hopping gleefully about, while another part is angry, and another part just plain sad. And what is he doing in Spain? I twirl a piece of hair absentmindedly about my finger as I try to think what to do. Do I want to see him? Do I *not* want to see him? The phone rings, and I jump. My mother's number is on the screen.

"Daaaahling, ow are you?" Her familiar throaty tones burble out, and suddenly I'm homesick.

"Hi, *Maman*," I quaver.

"Maela?" her voice sharpens. "What is wrong? Is it zis man? It is, yes?"

Too late I remember boasting on our last phone call that I'd met someone, only that someone, of course, was Emlyn, and I was sort of, maybe, kind of, lying. "Ummm."

"Now, Maela. Men, zey do not know what is best. You must tell zem. Look at your fazaire."

"Uhhh."

"Is true! So, zis man, what? Ee is dull, no good in bed? Zen you must say: 'You are not *intéressant*. You must do bettaire. You bore me.' And if ee does not, or if ee cannot, zen you dump im, and you find anozaire lovaire."

"Errr." Honestly, first Emlyn, now my mom. As if eligible men were queuing up to meet me, and all I had to do was go down the line saying *you, you, no, not you, you, you, and you.*

"Now, let me tell you about some lovely sings zat came into ze boutique." And she's off, and I can just sit and listen to her comforting trilling. By the end of the call, I know what I'm going to do. I'm going to be the strong, confident woman Emlyn said I was and have lunch with Jorge. And go French on his ass.

I send off a casual text, and a reply comes almost immediately back. We're going to meet at a little Spanish bar on Hanway Street, just down the road from me. I go to bed that night feeling gleefully smug.

Jorge is waiting for me outside the bar, and my heart skips a beat when I see him. I can't help it: he's just so mouth-wateringly sexy. He's wearing jeans and a white tee-shirt under his leather jacket, with the shark-tooth pendant round his neck, and carrying a scuffed, leather duffle bag. I'm suddenly glad I took care with my appearance this morning, defying the inner voice that said I shouldn't make an effort for *him*. It's a warm-ish day so I've got a navy blue and white, short-sleeved, polka-dot dress on; and my hair is in a loose French braid.

Jorge's face lights up when he sees me, which I have to say puts a little extra spring in my step. "*Querida!* You look lovely." He bends down and kisses me on both cheeks. I breathe in his scent and tremble, just a little.

"Hi, Jorge." I'm pleased that my tone is cordial and even. "Did you just come from the airport?" I gesture at the bag.

"*Sí*, I didn't want to wait to see you." The dusky gold of his cheeks colors slightly, and he grins, ducking his head. I feel absurdly pleased, but I'm also confused. Why didn't he call me earlier, then?

Jorge motions towards the door, which is propped open. "Shall we go in? I've reserved a table."

I step into a little piece of Spain. The walls are rough-plastered ochre, and the bar is lined with red tiles. On top, behind a glass case, are a tray of yummy-looking *tapas*, and wooden tables and chairs are scattered throughout the room. Jorge greets the waitress in Spanish, and she shows us to a table tucked in the corner, out of the way of the foot traffic. There's a pleasant hum of conversation, but the place isn't overly crowded.

We order two red wines and a selection of *tapas*, and when she brings them, Jorge looks at me seriously. "So," he murmurs. I'm unaccountably nervous all of a sudden and surreptitiously wipe my hands on my dress. "So," I reply, plastering on a smile.

"Sorry about the other night."

"Oh. Ah. Oh no. Umm. Fine. No, it's all good," I babble, casting my face into what I trust is an insouciant look. Jorge leans across the table and, taking my hands in his, looks into my eyes. His hands are broad and warm, and I melt a little.

"The evening did not go as I'd planned. I wanted you to meet my friends. I didn't know that Charlotte would be there."

"Sooo, Charlotte's not your friend? You two seemed pretty close." I get cross, remembering, and try to tug my hands away. His grip tightens.

"No, not really. I met her a few weeks ago. She saw me in the pub on Wednesday and came up to us."

"But," I stop, wondering how direct I want to be, then think, *to hell with it*. "If that's the case, why did you leave with her?"

Jorge grimaces: "She was drunk. I wanted to make sure she got home safely. She said she didn't feel well, and I was worried she was going to be sick in the pub."

I think back to how quickly Charlotte had put away her wine. She must have had over a bottle. And I remember how Eduardo had said something in Spanish and how worried Jorge looked. "Why was she drinking so much? Do you know? Even Mike couldn't keep up with her."

"In confidence?" I nod. "Her boyfriend broke up with her earlier that day – that's what we were talking about. She needed a shoulder to cry on." *And a replacement shag*, I think but bite my tongue.

"So, when you got to her house?"

"I helped her to the door. And then went back to help the cab driver clean up the vomit. He was not happy." Jorge shudders, and my mouth twitches.

"She was sick?"

He nods. "We were in traffic, and he couldn't pull over in time."

I'm feeling more cheerful by the minute. "Why didn't you call me?"

"It was too late when I got home, and I didn't want to disturb you. And then, the next morning, my sister phoned to say that my grandmother had had a bad fall and was in hospital. I got on the next available plane."

I gasp: "Is she OK?"

"*Sí*. We thought at first she had broken something, but it was only a bad sprain. But I wanted to stay until she was settled. And then," he says, looking down and rubbing his thumbs lightly over the backs of my fingers, "I wanted to see you and explain."

My insides are fizzing again, and my cheeks blaze up. This time, he lets my hands go, and I take a large sip of wine, hoping it will steady me. *Mercy!*

"Forgiven?" he asks softly.

I take another sip. "I suppose I could give you another chance," I say solemnly.

Jorge grins, and I notice again how sensual and, well, lickable his lips are. "I am on probation, then?"

I nod: "Yes, one misstep, and your butt is back in the slammer." I'm finding it hard to keep a straight face.

"Ouch!" He mock-winces. "Well, then," he says softly, looking straight into my eyes, "I had better not make any mistakes." He picks up a *tapa* and, holding my gaze, lifts it to my mouth.

My eyes widen, and I have a moment of panic. How shall I play this? Am I blushing? I'm blushing, aren't I? Here, with this beautiful man wanting to hand-feed me, as if I too were desirable, and I don't know how to respond. I'm on the verge of making a joke and royally bolloxing up the moment, when thankfully, my greed or my inner French goddess, not sure which, impels me forward, and I take a bite. The meat is tender and just a touch spicy, and I close my eyes in pleasure. When I open them, Jorge is smiling at me: "Good?"

I sigh: "Very."

"Then, *buen provecho*." He lifts up a glass and toasts me. "So, now, Miss Maela from San Francisco, tell me what you've been up to these past few days."

"Oh, err, this and that." I take another *tapa*. I'm still not sure how to handle work questions. I mean, what can I say? *Well Jorge, I've developed psychic powers, which means that I can see events from afar. My visions at the moment seem to be fixated on a Serbian criminal, who is suspected of running a drugs and prostitution ring, among other things, and his busty girlfriend, who might be a recruiter for an international crime syndicate. I spend my mornings trying to empty and calm my mind in front of a rather gorgeous, but arrogant, MI5 agent, in the hopes that I will have a glimpse of what the criminals are up to, and my afternoons walking around the most industrial parts of London, on the off-chance that something I see will prime my mind for a vision. It's getting a bit boring, and I would never admit it, but after half an hour's failed meditation, I tend to lapse into fantasies of having sex with the agent in exotic locations. But don't feel left out: in the evenings, I fantasize about having a threesome with you and the agent. You're both very good.*

He quirks an eyebrow. "This and that? But you are an intern, *sí*? Where do you work? At a school? For your literature?"

I circle my finger round the rim of the glass. "Weell," I say slowly, "actually, it's at MI5."

He whistles. "On Her Majesty's secret service?" He looks intrigued and cocks his head at me, like an adorable puppy.

"Ahh, heh heh, not really." What to say? Emlyn's cover story, that I'm working as a code-breaker, is absolute pants. "Uuh, actually, I'm just doing a research project on, uuh, well, non-traditional research methods." I take a big sip of wine so that I can stop talking.

He looks curious, which is hardly surprising, and slowly shakes his head. "No."

"No?" I warble, biting my lip. Feck. I'm trying not to lie, but options are limited. There's the threat of jail and all that.

"No," he says definitively and leans forward. "I think that you, Miss Maela, are a spy. You are very clever, but I have found you out. Oh yes, I have read your Sherlock Holmes, and I know how to ask the questions *muy difíciles*. But what are you doing here?" He lowers his voice. "I have it! You are on the trail of an infamous con *artista*! He worked his way across California, then fled to London when San Francisco became too hot to handle. You have followed him across the ocean and now pretend to be a humble intern while you seek to corner him in his lair!"

I giggle.

"And I, Jorge Alfaro Giménez, am part of your plans. I was walking innocently across the park when you saw me and thought that I could help your cover. So you lured me to your table with your big, big eyes–" I snort and grab a *tapa*, smiling broadly. "And the next thing I know, I am sitting in a restaurant, while you scope out the joint. But who is our suspect? The young man in the corner? The old *hombre* by the bar?" He raises his lovely, thick eyebrows and looks around dramatically.

I laugh out loud at his antics and a little bit of relief. "All right, all right. You've got me! But I must swear you to secrecy. My life depends on it!"

He leans forward again and taps me on the nose. "You, Miss Maela, may always depend on me. Now, let us finish our *tapas* and then I will take you on a stroll."

I sip my wine with a little burble of happiness. "Well, if you insist ..."

IN FOR A DIME

Monday, 1 October – Kailani

In the pale, cold light of early morning in a near empty office, Smith looks exhausted. He's sitting at the table quietly reviewing photos in front of him, making neat stacks, then flipping through the stacks again, frowning. Occasionally he'll rest his head on his hand, pinching the bridge of his nose, eyes closed, then mix the stacks back up and start over. I stand silently at the door, taking a long moment to really look at him. He clearly spent most of the weekend at the precinct, having replaced his normal button-down with a plain black tee-shirt that wraps tightly around his muscles. More of his tattoo is on display today, incredibly detailed, swirling and twisting down his arm in a complex Polynesian pattern done in deep blacks and greys. It's magnificent and must have taken hours upon hours of work. It flows out from under the sleeve of his shirt, clearly a massive piece, and continues in brilliant and fine-lined detail to his mid forearm, where it ends in the image of a splintered shield.

His phone vibrates on the table, and he picks it up without looking at it.

"Smith," he barks, before letting out a bone-deep sigh, face still in his hand. "Seef." He says, and the relief in his voice is stark. "My brother." There's a long pause and Smith lets out a short, exhausted laugh. "Just a long weekend, friend. Just a long weekend... No, *Mom*. I had trouble sleeping so I thought I'd get some work done... Mmm. Yeah. Somalia." He's silent, listening for a moment, and shakes his head slowly. "They're always the same, man. Always the same. Two steps too late. Two fucking steps." His voice catches for a moment, then he continues. "Of course I tried meditating, asshole... fuckall help, but I did. Yeah." His deep voice sounds lost under a layer of self-deprecation, and all of a sudden, I feel like I'm intruding, like I'm witnessing something private that isn't my business. I leave as quietly as I arrived, Smith still listening intently to the person on the other end of the line, his entire body curved to the small cell in his hand.

Deo and Jonah are in the room when I return, Donovan just behind me. Smith is back to his usual work attire, all traces of the tired man from earlier replaced by a calm, focused leader. Walking over to him I place a black coffee in front of him, and he looks at me curiously. Not knowing quite what to say, I shrug in reply and make my way back towards Deo and Jonah, who greet me with smiles.

"How was the weekend, Reed?" Deo asks quietly. "Missed you at the gym Saturday."

A grin breaks out on my face. "Lachy *finally* got back from his camping trip. We spent the weekend catching up." Pure happiness explodes inside me for a moment, a small, brilliant ball of light in my chest as I think of my weekend, and I can't keep my face from scrunching into its Cheshire Cat. Jonah looks over at me sharply, something catching his attention, and he asks carefully, "Who's Lucky?"

"*Lachy,*" I reply, before Deo interrupts me shortly.

"Lachlainn is her landlord. He's been on a month-long camping trip."

"Oooookay, Grumpus!" I laugh, poking him in the side. "I have room in my life for more than one friend." Turning to Jonah, I say, "Lachy is one of my best friends. He's *also* my landlord. But everything *sucks* when he's gone."

"He's a real mountain man," Deo interjects flatly, "apparently goes primitive camping for a month every year, leaving the girls alone out in who knows where. Like Paul Fucking Bunyon."

Turning to him, a little surprised, I tilt my head curiously. "What crawled up your butt and died? And it's not 'who knows where', you idiot. It's Vashon Island, for Christ's sake. It's completely safe, which you'd know if you ever actually took the ferry out to visit."

He harrumphs for a minute, then shakes his head. "Eh. I'm just having a strange morning."

Giving him another careful look, I decide to leave it. Mostly. I do say softly, trying not to get too upset or overreact, "Don't take shots at Lachy, Deo. He's my friend. And he takes care of me and Gemms."

Hideo nods once and reaches out a hand to squeeze mine. "I know, Kai. Sorry. I think," he adds carefully, "I'm probably just jealous of him. Living out there, not dealing with all this..." he waves his hands around at the room.

"You... want to live off the land? Like, for real? Not just at camps?" I say cautiously, trying to hold back laughter. "Like... Lachy? You know that means no monthly massage package, no Martini Bars, no pedicures..."

He sits fully at attention, looking affronted. "I do *not* get pedicures, Kailani!"

Staring at the ceiling, I hold back a grin and whisper, "Tokyo..." under my breath, and he smacks my arm.

"One time. *ONE TIME.* Jesus Christ, Reed."

Finally breaking, I start laughing, and he growls at me. Jonah's making a valiant effort not to laugh with me, and Donovan and Smith are at the other end of the room speaking to each other in low tones, ignoring our chatter.

We talk for a few more minutes, Jonah asking questions about our training regime and if he can join us, then making plans for lunch, before Smith checks his watch, looking annoyed.

"Okay, Team," he begins brusquely, sighing at my raised

hand but inclining his head towards me with a humorous glint in his eye that belies his tone, "Team *and* adjacent consultants who have *no obligation* to this task force other than as outside, temporary help."

Pretending to think for a moment, I wave my hand magnanimously for him to continue, and finally get a little twitch of a smile on his lips.

"Tanaka, you're a saint," he says, shaking his head before continuing. "I've been going back and forth with the team in England all weekend. Realizing the situation is drastically different than we first anticipated, *should* our hypothesis prove correct, we sent over the *entire* file to Emlyn and company. They, in turn, sent theirs." He motions to the papers in front of him. "They've had similar hits, but there was no connection previously. Our job now is to comb through mountains of case files, trying to connect details. This is, for lack of a better term, a complete clusterfuck. We were in the weeds when there were suspicions that we were looking at three distinct criminal syndicates. Even the possibility that it could be a single entity should frighten the fuck out of you. We've had hits on this from the Guam team, the Indo-Asian team, the Oceanic team, and the goddamned motherfucking Swiss. We're so far behind, *if* this is true, that we've been blind for years while Kronos has built up the equivalent of an underground empire."

Well shit. Talk about dropping a bomb. I look at Tanaka, his face tense.

"Who is running the mission?" he asks tightly.

Smith watches him with an appraising look, then taps the paperwork in front of him. "Babylon," Smith replies softly. "And Reed," he adds gently, "we're going to need an actual commitment from you on this."

I start to shake my head, but he interrupts me, voice now commanding and urgent. "Reed. Come on. Enough. I see the way you look at the photos of the victims. Christ, everyone here can see it written on your face. It's probably why

Gomez printed them 8x10 in color. You're in this. I know it. You know it. And while I truly appreciate your recalcitrance, you're wasting time that we don't have now. We *don't have time.* So please, just get on board, let us know your skillset so we can plan appropriately considering all our assets."

Letting out a deep breath, I stare again at the photos in front of me and think of the terror in Becca's eyes when she grabbed my hands, the effort she put into saying a single word. An effort that cost her her life. Deo and I exchange a look of complete agreement, and, shifting uncomfortably, I do my best to answer. If we're a team, at least temporarily, things will go to shit fast if I don't even attempt some level of professional trust. Deo lines his foot up alongside mine, pressing lightly into it, and I know he'll tell me if he thinks I should answer a question or not.

Choosing my words carefully, I begin, "I can, *at times,* and in the right circumstances, pick up some emotions from people in close proximity to me."

There. That should be enough of an... what the hell?

Smith is smiling at me, but not a nice smile exactly. More of a disappointed smile, like he expected the answer I gave him but was hoping for something different.

"That's it?"

"I mean... that's what I can do... so... yeah?"

He levels a hard stare at me. "That's *it?*"

"Yes." I return his stare belligerently.

He walks over to me quietly, pulling up a chair next to Jonah and sitting down. Jonah's a built guy – his forearms are lickable, and he's taller than me at about 6'1, but Smith is a fucking massive wall, and he towers over Jonah at 6'6 or so. Even sitting down Smith is huge, in a totally different way than Lachy. Smith is all muscle and looks like he could twist someone's head completely off with very little effort. There's no softness, nothing comforting or comfortable about Smith. Just violence and gunpowder, constantly coiled and ready to explode outward at the slightest spark. It makes his rigid control all that much more impressive. He smiles at me as he sits down, and leans forward into our little group, ignoring Deo and Jonah, and leaving Donovan completely out of the quiet conversation.

"Reed," he says softly. "I get that your introduction to our unit hasn't been conducive to building trust. You have a history with Gomez of which I was unaware – I was only told that you had worked together. This..." he hunts for the correct word, then finding it, continues, "manipulation of the situation isn't how I operate. So you need to let me know what *you* need in order for us to build a bond here. The work we're going to be doing is too important for mistrust and suspicion. Okay?"

I nod shortly and look to Deo, who cocks his head consideringly, and I frown. Smith watches us carefully, noting our wordless conversation, and sighs. "That's what I'm talking about. This is what we need to build as a whole. It can't just be you depending on Tanaka."

I smirk slightly at him. "First off, it *isn't* just me depending on Tanaka, although I trust him with my life. He depends on me equally."

Tanaka confirms my words. "True."

"And secondly," I continue, taking a moment to shoot a smile at Deo, who turns up the corner of his mouth at me, "it's not just me and Tanaka. Shotridge and I can do it too."

Smith raises a dubious eyebrow at my statement, so I look to Jonah with pleading eyes, hoping he picks up on my cue.

"Yes, of course my Queen," he responds instantly, grabbing my empty coffee cup and pouring half of his into it, similar to our first day.

I grin at Jonah, who flashes his dimples back at me, and Smith rolls his eyes.

"Okay, I'll bite. How did you know she wanted coffee?"

"It's a mystery!" Jonah says happily. "But top-secret tip. If Kailani is pleading with you for any reason, it's a safe bet that coffee tops the list."

Deo frowns at Jonah, but I don't have time to dwell on it. I grab Jonah's hand, giving it a quick squeeze. "Awwww... you know me so well."

He squeezes back, and we grin at each other. Smith looks at us consideringly, then addresses Jonah and Deo.

"Okay, then. What would the two of you recommend to build some trust?"

"That's probably a good first step," Hideo says. "Reed doesn't like when you try to cut her partners out of discussions." He motions towards Smith's body placement, where he's leaned forward, giving Jonah his back and pushing Deo to the side.

Smith immediately sits back and adjusts and murmurs a quiet apology to both men, which earns him points in my book. To his credit, I don't *think* he meant to cut them out – he just seems like someone who is laser focused on his task. But whether or not he meant to, if he wants to build a team, he needs to equally appreciate all members.

The door opens, and a pinched-looking Gomez enters the room, in the process of hanging up her phone.

"Also, just a guess, but I'd have the Evil Grandmother leave," Jonah says under his breath.

Smith's jaw clenches, and he gives a tight nod, before standing and addressing Gomez. "Director Gomez. While we've appreciated and benefited from your presence to this point, I've been instructed to take full command of the task force from this point forward," he says firmly.

"I don't *think* so," she begins, but he interrupts her almost immediately.

"With all due respect, Director. You are here as a liaison and a representative of CDS. Once we all received our proper clearances, oversight and direction of this task force passed immediately to The Babylon Project. Their committee finished the approval process on our paperwork this past weekend, as I'm sure you know. And while you were tasked with the creation of the team, now that the unit has been formed, your jurisdiction is limited to any operations linked directly to the CDS. But the *actual* task force... you don't need to be here for any of that."

Gomez is puce with anger by the end of his speech. "If *you think* you can speak to me in *that tone* without repercussions, you'd best check your facts. As I told you previously, the only two I need on this team are–"

She and Smith are locked in a staring contest, but after a moment he shrugs carelessly and says almost dismissively, "Well, at that point our clearances and approvals hadn't gone through. And, as you so helpfully stated, you expedited the process. And as soon as our dossiers were approved by the committee, we transferred out of your hands. So if you'd please, close the door behind you as you leave. We'll of course call you should we need your assistance in any way."

Awwww shit man! Smith is hardcore!

Gomez and Smith are like flint and steel, and we're all sitting, breaths held, to see where the sparks fly. Gomez is not a woman to be intimidated by a large man, I'll give her that, and she stares him down with an iron strength. "Let me remind you, Agent Smith, that I am the Head Liaison with the CDS. As Tanaka, Reed, and Shotridge now fall under the CDS, just over half of this team falls under my jurisdiction."

I clear my throat awkwardly. "Not really," I interject. "I never agreed to be an agent of CDS. I'm still considered an independent contractor, and Tanaka and Shotridge get their pay cheques from SPD, if I'm not mistaken."

Gomez narrows her eyes at me menacingly. "Reed, I believe we talked about the wisdom behind your joining CDS when we first brought you to this team."

"No, *you* talked about it, but no decisions were ever made, and no paperwork was signed. Now, if I'm not mistaken, Smith is indicating that this task force is part of a separate entity, so I guess I'll need to take up my employment status with them."

Gomez's nostrils are flaring, face mottled by the time I finish speaking. She leans forward over the table, resting her hands in front of me, disgust heavy on her face.

"You think you're outmaneuvering me?" she asks softly, in her sweet grandma voice. "You're jumping blindly into a pit of snakes and hoping you don't get bitten." She shakes her head in mock disappointment and drops her voice so she's barely audible. "Call me when you need help, dear. And you *will* need help."

She's so self-assured and smug it makes my teeth hurt. "I won't be calling. Thanks for the offer though. I'm pretty sure we're done. Permanently," I respond dismissively.

Suddenly Gomez laughs, a bright, truly amused sound that shakes me deeper than I'd like to admit. "Oh Kailani," she chortles, amusement pouring off her in disconcerting waves. "You have no idea. You truly have no idea. I wasn't sure, not completely. How utterly charming."

She pats my hand and smiles at me, shaking her head slightly, voice now sincerely kind and gentle, like you would address a small child, an edge of true pity lacing her words. "And here I thought you were just being obstinate. Well, I'll be going for now and let you firecrackers get to know each other. We'll be seeing each other again. Smith. Donovan. Mr. Shotridge. Mr. Tanaka." She addresses each, then turns to me last. "And Ms. Reed. Should you feel the need for some outside guidance, please don't hesitate to call."

And with that, Gomez walked out the room to the sound of complete silence.

◆ ◆ ◆

"So," Smith begins, looking at me consideringly, "let's try again. What is it, *exactly*, that you can do?"

Donovan watches me through narrowed, thoughtful eyes, and Jonah and Deo move minutely closer to me so I can feel their protective warmth on either side.

I sigh. *In for a dime, in for a fucking dollar.* I look once to Deo, briefly, and he shrugs very slightly. He's leaving this one up to me.

"I can read people's emotions," I say blandly, trying to make it seem like an everyday occurrence.

"Brief us on it. Please," Smith demands, but gently. It's clear he's trying to be patient with me. I think he can tell how uncomfortable I am with the entire situation and is trying to make it easier for me, but he needs the end result, gentle or not.

"I'm what's called an Empath," I begin, only to be interrupted by Donovan.

"Aren't those like Woo-woo hippie people who think they have the ability to feel someone's pain?" he asks disparagingly.

Surprisingly, Smith answers for me before I can speak. "Shut it down, Donovan. A foundation of any functional team is respect and trust. How's Reed going to fit in if you're constantly belittling her and pushing back at her?"

Donovan raises his hands slightly in the universal "my bad" signal and sits back. Smith nods at me to continue.

"Soooo, yeah. It actually kind of *is* like that. I don't really... I can feel someone's emotions, and kind of pull them into me. Like a Bleeder. But I can't just let them dissipate, as a Bleeder would. I just hold it... I pull it into me, rather than just out of someone else, and if I hold it too long without creating balance in some way, it makes me sick. Like migraines, nausea... ummm... what else?"

"You can pass out, go blind briefly..." Deo mutters beside me.

"Oh, yeah. I can pass out for sure. I *have* gone temporarily blind, but that's a side effect of the migraines, more than a symptom by itself."

"So what do you do with it?" Smith asks, fascinated.

"Usually it just balances itself, like when you're really sad but you rest or watch a show or meditate. It just does it naturally if I haven't taken in too much. Otherwise I'll do a forced meditation, like go to the meditation room downstairs where it's completely quiet, or go for a float in the Tanks. If it's *really* bad, like, *really, really* bad, I'll call in a Bleeder to help pull some off me."

"She's done that maybe six times," Hideo interjects. "She's not a fan of Bleeders in general –" he smiles almost apologetically at Jonah, who looks at me carefully, like he's cataloging what Hideo is saying. "– as she's had some... trouble... with the department Bleeders in the past."

Smith furrows his brow in a silent question, and I press my lips together tightly. Deo sighs and says carefully, "They're not always trustworthy with the way they take emotion, and most have very, *very* poor control. Kai doesn't..." He pauses, obviously searching for the right words. "*We* don't go to the precinct Bleeders. Traditionally. Having said that, at the moment there are only two, anyway, so I don't think it will be an issue. The only Pain Bleeder tapped out a couple of months ago, and the other Bleeder is not an option. And Smith – *that* you *can* write down. Reed is never to be taken to Daniels for any reason."

We exchange a look, and I shoot a small smile at Jonah.

"*You*, however, can bleed me anytime," I say, trying for a compliment but coming off vaguely and oddly creepy, a fact which is solidified by Donovan choking slightly on his coffee. I try to stammer out an explanation but give up, and Jonah is full scale grinning at me as Hideo keeps going.

"... then there's what you all call 'Pushing', which we thought of as just a side effect of her Empathy," Hideo says, prompting me to continue.

"Oh, yeah. So I can Bleed, kind of, but since I hold that, I can push it back out into someone else."

"But, forgive me for saying this so baldly, what good is it? How does it help you so much more than pure Bleeding, for example?" Smith asks. "Because I have to say, to be completely honest, my experiences with Pushing have been lackluster, to say the least. I don't really see that it has any effect at all."

I nod. "Right. I'm sorry, I've never just had to sit down and catalogue things for someone. Deo, sorry, Tanaka knows because we've worked together for so long, and since I've never had actual training in it, it's kind of hard to know what's important, or what makes a difference."

"You never fully briefed Gomez?" Smith says, surprise in his voice.

Deo and I exchange a long look before I answer. "Noooo... not really," I say tightly. "She isn't entirely trustworthy in my eyes."

"So who *does* know the full list?"

"Tanaka. Gemma, my roommate. Lachy, my friend. That's it."

He nods. "Continue please."

"Okay. So, in short. I can read and pull in emotions. I can hold them without them affecting me if it's not too much for too long. I can push them out into other people."

Donovan leans forward slightly. "So many questions," he says sarcastically. "But to start, what do you mean, *reading* emotions? How is it helpful just to know someone is sad? Like, they could be sad about anything. How do you know it's attached to a specific thing, in a specific case or something?"

Jonah looks at me almost apologetically. "Same question," he says softly. "I can't do that. I can just *feel* pleasure, and kind of the type of it, but it dissipates so quickly that it's like trying to tell the notes of wine when you sip it. I can get a brief flash of the flavor of the emotion, but that's it."

I smile at Jonah. "It's okay, Shotridge. Ask all the questions you want. I'll answer whatever I'm able to. Reading emotions is... Jesus. How do I explain it? Emotions are images. And depending on the strength of the image, I can sense those."

"You're claiming you can *read* someone's *mind?*" Donovan

scoffs disbelievingly.

"No," I respond sharply. "I can't read someone's mind. Think of it this way – emotions are all sensory input. Everything attached to the senses is usually an emotional response. Everything attached to words or pure thought is a logical response. So if you stay in pure logical thought, I get nothing. Mathematics, some sciences depending, military strategy, grocery lists... I mean, if it's just random, logical thought, there's nothing I can get. And a lot of times I can't get clear reads on emotion either. There's a low-level hum of emotion that exists in everyone, all day, every day. Because most of your day isn't spent in a heightened emotional state, right? And that low-level hum is like eating mass-produced white bread. There's a taste there... I mean, mostly. Or kind of. But it's hard to know what that flavor is, right? You eat it, but without anything on it, it's hard to describe. That's what most emotion is, on a daily basis. Just Wonderbread. Or filtered water. It's there, it has some kind of faint taste, but it's not really anything I can work out. *In general*. And there's secondary emotion too, which isn't as strong, or as purposeful. It doesn't linger in the same way. Like seeing a sad movie or reading a sad book. It hits you, and if it's really good it can stay with you, but you didn't experience the pain first hand, so it's more of a referred emotion, and you emote it differently. So..." I huff, blowing my hair from my forehead.

"Fascinating," Smith responds sincerely. "What impacts your responses? What makes it stronger? Or weaker? Does anything cause it to shut off?"

Deo's foot taps mine, but I don't need his warning to be on guard. I narrow my eyes, studying Smith carefully. "Why?"

He holds up his hands placatingly. "Not to attack you, Reed. Any good team lead would want to know what situations help their team members, and what would harm them in some way."

I continue to stare at him through hard eyes, and he sighs

deeply, before mumbling under his breath, "Your code name should be Hellcat. Fine. I stay away from tight, dark spaces. That's my main weakness. And noises like firecrackers, unless I'm prepared. Holdover from my time in service."

I nod once and purse my lips thoughtfully. "Fine. If I'm really tired, or sick, it's incredibly difficult to keep my shields up. Meaning I can read you really well, but I can't keep you out, and I can pass out if there's too much emotion pushing at me. Crowds, in general, aren't great, unless they're a specific type. Like weddings are usually okay, for example. Birthdays sometimes. Anything where the overriding feeling is happy rather than sad, angry, or confused. So positive crowds can actually be really energizing, but things have a tendency to flip quickly. Um... let's see. If I've had enough sleep, and exercise and time to meditate, I'm usually pretty strong. Meaning I can read you but *also* keep you out, for at least a short time. Pain can cause physical pain in me, so that can be distracting. Like if you've broken your arm, I can feel that in a way. Not the physical part of the broken arm, but the emotions attached to it make me sick."

I look to Hideo. "What else?"

"Grounding. If she's really affected, it helps to touch her. Physical contact helps settle down any emotional surge, in general. Black coffee, though she doesn't like it. The kind of bitter punch it gives can clear her head enough that she can get her shields up if they've been knocked out or weakened. Sounds crazy, but a vapor stick – like those ones they sell when you're sick? That you wave beneath your nose and they smell like Vapor Rub? Wave that under her nose and that can help."

Smith looks like it's physically painful for him not to be taking notes right now. "How does it work? Can we see an example?"

"I guess so? Jonah, do you mind if I use you as a guinea pig?"

He responds immediately. "Whatever would help, Kai."

Donovan leans forward. "Aw hell no. If you need to prove something, it won't help to use your buddy there. You can use me or Smith, Ms. Cleo."

I smirk at Donovan. "Happy to, Ass-clown."

Smith just sighs, looking back and forth between the two of us.

"Teamwork."

I shrug. "Fine. Donovan, think about something you truly love. Think of it in words, nothing else. Just the facts of it, listed in order. Start with a basic list of things you love about it. That's all."

Donovan frowns at me but plays ball. I watch him carefully, about to drop my shields slightly, when he snaps, "Done. You got nothing?"

Sighing, I say, "Seriously, man. Can you work with me here? Think of each piece of whatever it is, and break it apart, word by word, in a non-emotional description."

He nods shortly and closes his eyes as I lower my shields. As always, the noise of emotion in the room pushes in until I can focus on Donovan, letting the others fade away for the time being. When I'm able to narrow my focus, it helps drown out the rest of the chaos around me. As Donovan concentrates, his face smooths out slightly, and I begin to pick up on the growing emotion. Neat trick – it's almost impossible to think logically about something you love. You start with the basic list, but as soon as you get into it, your emotions wrap around your thoughts and consume them whole. You may think "Bright yellow Ford Mustang" at first. But then emotions rush in like a Bore Tide, unexpected and out of nowhere, and they hit you ten times harder because you weren't expecting them. And that "bright yellow Ford Mustang" turns into "the first car I owned, and I worked so hard that summer, and I remember the way the light glinted off it, and how proud I was, my first kiss..." and everything else that went along with it. Emotions don't exist in a vacuum – that's all logical thought. Emotions are the opposite – they spread into everything and everywhere, a giant spider web of chaos, linking together strange memories, making bedfellows of the oddest events.

I wait, and wait, until Donovan opens his eyes and stares at me, almost accusingly. And I know why. I look at him apologetically with soft eyes, trying not to let pity show its face.

"Ah…" I clear my throat and start again, closing my own eyes to concentrate. "Apple pie is what I got. Really, really sharp bursts of cinnamon, really tangy apples that hit you back here…" I touch the back of my jaw lightly. "Somewhere that feels safe, that smells like mountains, cold, thin air. Pine. Couldn't get the house much, so no strong emotional attachment to the actual structure. An older woman, though not a relative I think – too much gratitude attached to the emotion. Confusing, kind of. Mixed with longing. Love, with longing and gratitude… I don't know. I have trouble with that sometimes…"

Hideo's foot taps mine sharply, and I cut off my wandering words, tapping him back a quick thank you.

"Right. Yeah. A fire, something smoky and sweet. Reminds me of a peat fire. And some pain attached? Like, I don't know. A stomach ache? An almost crippling sadness. But it's from now, not then? Actually, lots of pain. Some now, lots then. And an incredible amount of regret." I frown, reaching deeper and pulling on memories beyond what he's giving me. "Oh. Donovan. I'm sorry…" He stands abruptly, and I can tell he knows I followed the little trail of his thoughts down into the darkness, into a closet that felt like a cave filled with corpses in the dark, into a sharp stinging of leather and metal on his skin. "I'm sorry," I say again quietly. "Are you okay?" I open my eyes and meet Donovan's hard stare. His jaw is clenched tight, and I feel like I've just revealed something about him that was intensely private, without his permission.

"Is that all you got?" he asks, angry and accusing.

"Uh... mostly." I have trouble meeting his eyes, and he grips his hands into tight, white-knuckled fists.

"Can we take a break?" he murmurs to Smith, who puts a gentle hand on his shoulder.

"Sure man. Let's meet back here in fifteen."

When we return fifteen minutes later, Donovan and Smith are already at the table, Donovan's face hard and closed off. I breathe out heavily and decide it's time for a small show of peace. Walking in, I move down to the middle of the table, as far as I'm willing to go, literally meeting them halfway. Jonah and Deo flank me, and, after careful consideration, Smith and Donovan move to the other side. For the first time we're sitting as a group rather than two warring camps.

"So," Smith says. "Let's continue where we left off. You can't read minds, but you come pretty damn close, hmmm? So you could feasibly see a killer's victim?"

I shake my head immediately. "I mean, it's definitely possible, and I have done in the past, but it's not a for sure thing."

"Clarify?" Smith says shortly, raising an eyebrow. Donovan is still sitting silently, glaring at me, but I give him a small, sympathetic smile. My shields are down slightly so I can read the room, and I can tell that the hurt and anger pulsing off him aren't directed at me specifically: I'm just the reminder of his emotion. It's a "don't kill the messenger" sort of situation, and the level of feeling directed at me is muted, despite how he appears.

"It depends on how the killer feels, right? So... did you guys watch the interrogation with Tennireef?" I ask. They both nod in the affirmative, so I continue. "I could read every *second* of that. He was so–" I choke a little on the words, a vague echo of the day washing over me. Jonah reaches out immediately and grabs my hand, and I feel a gentle pull before the remembered pleasure dissipates. I smile at Jonah gratefully as Smith and Donovan look on through narrowed eyes. "Anyways, I could definitely get all of that. If it's someone completing a hit, and they're not linked emotionally to the victim, then no. If it's coldly calculated, really well planned out – well, sometimes yes and sometimes no. Usually people who plan things out well are doing it methodically, logically, very organized. They may feel bits and pieces of pleasure or something along the way, but they're very task oriented, so other than a sort of satisfaction, I may not get vivid images."

Smith nods and opens a notebook to write something down.

"No!" Deo snaps from beside me. Smith jumps slightly, surprised by Hideo's voice after he's been quiet for so long. "No notes. Nothing written. No computer entries. No emails. No physical log of any of this."

"Tanaka, surely you can see that we'll need–"

"*No.* As a condition of Reed working with you. Her contract with SPD is the only written agreement you have to her willing participation, and part of that contract stipulates that there is no existing paperwork on her."

Smith answers almost sympathetically. "You have to know that Gomez has a file on Reed, right? She has a ton of information already."

"I know," replies Deo, voice tight with anger and agitation. "But not as much as you'll have. Not most of what we're discussing. So no."

Smith hesitates, then nods once, sharply. "Agreed."

Jonah raises a hesitant hand beside me, his normally placid face uneasy.

"Yes?"

"Yeah, none on me either please."

Smith throws his hands up in the air and answers in an

exasperated voice. "Fine. Jesus. Reed, is that it then?"

It's not it, not nearly. I don't detail how I can choke some-one with their feelings, inducing panic so strongly they can't breathe. How I can make someone think they're going crazy. It's not it, but it's enough. More than enough until I'm sure I can trust them. I nod.

"Okay," Smith says. "Opening the table for questions. My first is, how do you protect yourself?"

"My first is, why are we all listening to this bullshit? And follow-up, why can't we just get real fucking agents instead of this mess?"

I lock eyes with Donovan, my previous sympathy fast being worn thin. "You deal with this every day, man. I get it. It's weird. But you deal with people like me *every day*. People who are easier to talk to, who feel easy to trust. Or people you're instinctively cautious of – that inner voice that tells you to be wary of someone. You could walk down the street and pass six people, and you won't notice five of them. But that sixth one doesn't sit well with you, right? There's something off about him. Something that makes you pay attention, even before you can see him clearly."

"It's instinct," he replies shortly.

"What's instinct?"

"Instinct is how you respond to a situation on a gut level."

"Wrong. The definition of instinct is an innate or fixed pattern of behavior in response to certain stimuli. In *response* to *stimuli...* What're the stimuli that are different between the first five people on the street and the sixth guy? What's different?"

He stares at me, perplexed but defiant. "You tell me, since you fucking seem to know everything."

"There's a stimulus that you're responding to at a base level. He's either pushing fear towards you, usually subcon-sciously, or pulling happiness or something. It's not some-thing that most people are in contact with, and that's fine. But to say it doesn't exist at all is foolish. It's like people who said man couldn't run a four-minute mile, because no one had ever done it. That yes, man can run, that there have been fast men in the past, that everything exists in order for man to run at that speed, but that it's not possible. Well, the fastest recorded mile is 3:43. Everyone else in the world thinks that a five-minute mile is fucking jet fuel, but to this one man on earth, Hicham El Guerrouj, 5:00 is an easy mile. Now, I'm not saying that I'm the one person on earth who can run a 3:43, right? But I can fucking run a 4:00, and that's still pretty damn fast. Do you get what I'm saying?"

He nods, face still a thundercloud, but silent for now.

"Ah... back to mine, maybe?" Smith offers, trying to smooth out the tensions between Donovan and myself.

"What? Oh. Yeah. Ummm... shields is the short answer."

"Shields?" Jonah asks gently. "What do you mean?"

"You already have some, innately. The Id, the ego, the superego? Those are just variations of shields. What you tell to the world, what you keep from the world. They protect you on a daily basis from the pressure of the chaos around you. Otherwise the emotion of the world would cripple you."

"I work on two different layers of shielding. One keeps emotion out, and one keeps emotion in. Let's see. It's like a poker face kind of? So a poker face hides your emotions, right? The best poker face hides your tells, all those little movements you make to indicate you're happy or worried or whatever. So for me, I practiced the external poker face for a long time, just working on that. I practiced not letting my emotions through at all. No tells, no ticks. After I mastered that, I moved on to internalizing the poker face. Meditation helps a lot with that, and yoga. Six-stage breathing. Oddly, really boring lectures."

A quick smile flies across Hideo's face, and he nudges me slightly. I know he's thinking of a weekend we spent together on a team-building retreat up in the mountains, hunting down the most boring college lectures we could find. We had a chart set up, and all sorts of criteria for judging. Drone of the voice, pitch, length of the words... it all went on a truly magnificent color-coded chart. First one to fall asleep listening to the lectures owed the other a month of Starbucks. It was one of the first times we really bonded. I smile back at him, thinking of how we'd both fallen asleep, me right after him, listening to an hour and a half explanation of Microsoft, and how, when I'd woken up, a hot cup of coffee was waiting in front of me, with a note saying "You win".

Jonah clears his throat from beside me, and I startle, realizing I'm sitting staring at Hideo instead of talking. *Jesus Kai, be more obvious. Get your shit together.*

"Ah, yeah. So as I was saying, that is more to keep my emotions from pouring out and influencing people around me, though admittedly it's easier to do that than keep emotions from flooding me. It takes effort for me to push emotion into people. It takes effort to *stop* emotions from coming into me."

"So how do you do *that* part?" Smith asks, fascinated.

"Kind of the same. Meditation helps. Visualization. I picture building a wall, reinforced with steel, etc. I use grounding techniques, name the feeling... it helps to have someone who knows you near you, so you can lock onto them if you feel like you're taking in too much and losing yourself. Positive emotions like love, kindness, happiness – those just strengthen me. They don't influence me as much, don't wash me away from myself. Negative emotions are like a bomb, though, or a tidal wave. I drown in those. Deo and I once thought maybe I could help in a children's hospital. I... I..." Here I stutter to a stop, unable to continue. Deo squeezes my hand softly and speaks for me.

"She wanted to help ease some of their fear or worry if she could. I agreed to try to help in our off time. We went to take a tour of the hospital one Saturday, and it was too much, all at once. Her shields can hold out limited amounts of emotion, but we weren't counting on the levels there. She made it through maybe a floor, and wanted to try for more. I should have stopped her," he says bitterly. "I could tell something was wrong, but she kept saying she was fine. All of a sudden her eyes went really wide and rolled back in her head, and she fell to the ground shaking. I thought she was having a seizure, til I realized she had overloaded. It was a mess. They kept trying to keep her in the hospital to get her help." His face tightens, and he looks so, so angry, and I take back over.

"It was a lesson, I guess. I couldn't help the way I wanted to. So, we just work it another way."

"You take mainly cases revolving around children?" Donovan asks softly, speaking to me without an edge for the first time since I read his emotions.

I nod. "Children... well, women and children, anyways. We try."

Hideo looks at me, his face unusually soft for work. "We try," he agrees quietly.

A smooth, feminine voice comes from the doorway. "Fascinating."

The entire room erupts at once. Smith is on his feet before the word finishes coming out of the woman's mouth, with Donovan close behind him. I turn a panicked look to Hideo, who looks incredibly tense. Jonah, face creased with worry beside me, moves to block me from direct view of the newcomer. I feel sick, wondering how much she overheard and how she got by me, undetected. I run a quick check on her, feeling nothing but cold marble.

Peering around Jonah cautiously, I meet the cool, grey eyes of Elizabeth Cole. Alabaster skin is tight over her high, sharp cheekbones, and her pale face is framed with short, wavy, dark hair. She's of medium height and breakably thin, with a sharp, pristine elegance. Her lips are two narrow slashes of color on her face and are smiling in a brittle way, trying to convey warmth but failing. She's in no way pretty, but all the parts come together to form a striking woman whom you won't easily forget.

Cole is well known as a philanthropist. Not much is known about her family – her father was a low-level scientist, and her mother a professor who taught science. Cole herself had attended Duke University and had gotten a "Mrs." degree, having married a significantly older and incredibly successful businessman named Sam Cole. She doted on him and was by his side at all functions. Over time she became well known for her volunteer efforts. By all counts remarkably smart, Cole didn't settle for small-scale projects. She once famously talked the major oil companies in Houston into a giving war, which resulted in a $55 million overhaul of the homeless shelters there, providing training and childcare for abused women and single-family homes for struggling families. It was a massive undertaking and made national news.

Cole became a regular on the donation circuit and was found as often with Hollywood players and politicians as she was in soup kitchens and at Habitat for Humanity. It was a worldwide story when Cole and her husband were in a horrific car wreck weeks before opening a massive charity organization together – the Gaia Foundation. They'd just arrived home from an overseas trip. Cole's husband, Sam, had been sitting in the front seat with their long-time driver, and Elizabeth had been in the back, sleeping. A truck had crossed the median, the driver high on some illegal substance, and had completely taken out the front of the car. Elizabeth had suffered internal bleeding and a broken arm, but her husband and both drivers died on impact. She showed up at the opening of Gaia weeks later, still bruised, now gaunt with dark circles beneath her eyes, and declared that the organization would focus on running outpatient clinics for the indigent and homeless, while researching new medications to help addicts conquer their demons. Gaia also focused on providing treatment and recovery services for trafficked women and youth and was the largest recovery organization in the country.

After two years, Gaia became known internationally – Cole travelled relentlessly to countries where trafficking was prominent. She spoke with politicians, debated multi-millionaires, exposed previously protected people with little care for their wealth or money. She was single minded, incredibly focused, and loved and feared in equal measures. The Gaia Foundation, by my last count, had hubs in sixteen different countries and was still expanding. Her goal was to completely end human trafficking in any way possible, and the foundation was funded in large part by the wealth left to her by her husband. She had never remarried, was never seen with another man, and famously wore his wedding ring around her neck still. I tracked her obsessively when I was in school – Gaia was the epitome of what I wanted to do with my life, before I was recruited to SPD.

And now, here she is standing in front of me, having overheard god knows what of our private conversation, and I couldn't get a fucking read on her if she was covered in Times New Roman with a fucking spotlight on her face.

"I'm sorry," she says sincerely in a cool, surprisingly low voice. "I truly didn't mean to interrupt. I do apologize." Her accent is unusual – tight and short, almost mid-Atlantic sounding, caught between upper-crust East-Coast American and British. "I was invited to attend a meeting here by a Ms. Gomez. I'm–" she checks a thin, elegant gold watch on her equally thin, elegant wrist, "rather early, I'm afraid. I haven't been to this area before and wanted to make sure I was on time."

Torn between excitement and something akin to fear, I stay silent while the guys introduce themselves, first to Elizabeth, and then to a petite and plain brunette behind her, holding a tablet and a phone. I assume she's Cole's assistant. Elizabeth's eyes constantly flick back to me between shaking the guys' hands, laced with some internal amusement, her lips quirking slightly up at the sharp corners. She rolls her eyes ever-so-slightly at me, as though we share some inside joke, when Smith starts talking about proper procedures and asking her firmly, albeit politely, who had let her into the station and led her to our conference room.

Interrupting him mid-sentence, she moves towards me, saying in her strange accent, "Yes, well, perhaps this delightful woman would show me where to get some coffee while you all figure out your heads from your asses here. If you'd be so kind...?"

I get slowly to my feet, watching that glimmer of amusement hide just beneath the surface, and reach out once more to see if I can read anything on her. For a second time I meet nothing but cool marble, and I frown slightly.

As I consider her, she holds out her hand to meet mine in a surprisingly firm grip. "Hello. I'm Elizabeth Cole. I'm quite serious regarding the coffee, if you wouldn't mind? I'm not sure what is happening here, but I'm fairly certain they'll be able to work it out in the next few minutes or so, giving us enough time to grab a latte. And I'd really prefer not to be stuck with that one, if I'm being honest." She inclines her head towards Donovan, who is arguing thunderously under his breath with Smith and Tanaka in the corner. Jonah is still sitting near me, unobtrusively listening to the exchange. I'm amazed at how still and small he can make himself appear when desiring not to be noticed.

I nod, shortly but politely, and introduce myself. "Kailani Reed. Of course I'd be happy to show you the way, Ms. Cole."

"Elizabeth, Kailani, please."

Inclining my head in agreement, we leave the room as Smith, Donovan, and Tanaka all start making calls. Tanaka watches me leave through narrowed eyes and gives a quick jerk of his head towards Jonah, who immediately stands and is moving towards the door as Elizabeth and I walk out.

"So, that was a fascinating bit of information on which to walk in," she says conversationally.

My stomach drops, and I push out a third time, trying to figure this strange woman out. She stops walking and turns to me, locking eyes with me seriously. "I feel I should let you know that Ms. Gomez has told me all about your abilities, and, hearing the end of your explanation in the room, want to let you know that I'm afraid you'll have a difficult time getting a read on me."

Turning back to continue walking, she asks over her shoulder, "Is the coffee cart this way?"

I catch up to her in a few strides. "I don't know what you think you heard back there, but–"

"Kailani. Working together will be significantly easier if we come to an understanding. Let me be frank. My father was a lead scientist with the original Stargate Project."

My eyes widen in surprise, and Elizabeth continues, "My mother was also a scientist on the project. Their public profiles were a farce. When they passed, they left their private research in my possession, and part of Gaia's more, shall we say, quiet endeavors, is the continuation of that research. On a much more theoretical level, of course."

I nod, still stunned at her revelations. "While the original purpose of the organization was to continue their research full-time, following the accident where I lost my Sam," her hand moves, almost unintentionally, to her throat, where a thin, gold necklace drops behind her high collared shirt, "I decided to alter our aims to a more altruistic purpose. I've continued my parents' legacy on a smaller scale, however, thus am uniquely suited to assist your endeavors."

"That doesn't explain…" I start, trying to find the correct words. I've never met someone who just *knows* all about me, and am feeling very thrown off balance.

"... Why you can't read me?" she says wryly. I nod. "Well, Kailani, I'm afraid I'm all science and logic."

"But your foundation!" I protest.

"Yes, well. It wouldn't function if someone who was all heart was in charge. No offense intended, but I often find those who let emotion run their daily life are less successful in achieving their purposeful goals. My daily life is dealing with women who have been trafficked, beaten, abused. Children who have been left behind, who were born into chaos, or addicted to drugs. You have to understand, it would bury me, quite literally I think, if I went in with my heart exposed every day."

I nod slowly. "I do understand that."

Smiling warmly at me now, she responds, "I rather thought you would. We're two sides of the same coin, you and I, I suspect. You, all feeling, and me all thought. Should we decide to team up at some point, I think we would be close to unstoppable, hmmm? I'm rather bullish in my approach sometimes, I'm afraid. I see a problem, I see a solution, and I can't understand why I would deviate from that course of action." She frowns slightly, shaking her head. "It's maybe the same way for you, no? You feel the problem, and therefore all of the emotions surrounding each possible deviation from the plan." Shrugging slightly, she touches her neck again. "That's what Sam was for, to me." Raising a single brow, she cocks her head. "You know of Sam, I assume?"

"Yes," I reply softly. "I'm sorry for your loss."

"Yes, well. Thank you." Waving behind her at the little mouse of a woman scuttling in her wake, she says, "That's what I have my assistant for now. All heart. No head," she murmurs, somewhat dismissively. Looking consideringly at me, she continues, "Perhaps someone with a little more backbone would be more useful. Ah, here we are!"

Arriving at the coffee cart, I inhale deeply, the strong,

sweet smell of the grounds curling up the corner of my lips. "Well, at least you like coffee," I say, smiling slightly. "I never trust anyone who doesn't."

"Oh dear," she replies, laughing for the first time in a way that registers through my shields. The amusement races along my barrier like tiny bubbles of champagne, pure and honest, and it makes me feel slightly more at ease with her. "I do hope you'll reconsider. I'm more of a tea girl myself."

Laughing together, we order – a mocha for me, and a matcha tea latte for her – and then walk back to the conference room.

By the time we return, the room is tense with an uneasy silence. Gomez has returned, mouth pursed in a sort of smug smirk. Smith sits beside her at the head of the table, face a thundercloud of anger. Donovan has, surprisingly, moved down to what I now consider "our end" of the table, shoulder to shoulder with Hideo. Jonah's nowhere to be seen. Elizabeth and I exchange glances as we enter, and she quirks her lips in that funny way of hers that's meant to convey amusement.

"Well," she drawls in a slow, sardonic way. "Lovely."

I flash a quick grin at her. As we take our seats, Jonah slips into the room and settles down beside me with a coffee.

"So," Gomez begins imperiously. "Now that we're all here, let's begin. Ms. Cole is here on the recommendation of the CDS in an effort to help our task force track human trafficking and drug-cartel movement in the area. I am her direct liaison, and am required to be here as part of the agreement between the CDS and task-force management." Her smug tone is so insufferable I *almost* miss the fact that she does not refer to the Babylon Project by name. *Interesting. I wonder if that's an oversight or a purposeful move.*

Gomez continues, "She is here in an advisory capacity,

and will be providing us with information gathered from her United States bases of operations. She has trusted members of Gaia listening for any mention of Kronos, and looking for any identifying marks on victims' bodies. Her database is something we cannot replicate on our own, as it's a far-reaching, previously existing structure, and we're fortunate to have her assistance in this matter."

Cole raises one elegant finger, like a patron signaling a waiter, and Gomez flushes at the slight but remains courteous. "Yes, Ms. Cole?"

Elizabeth folds her hands calmly in front of her and leans forwards slightly, pinning Gomez with a cold stare. "Perhaps you've already reviewed this information, but just to be clear. You have come to us multiple times before seeking access to private medical and personal records, and were refused. The sole reason I agreed to help at this point in any capacity is because you offered unfettered access to Ms. Reed, and full read in on her abilities, for the length of this endeavor, in order to help continue my parents' research. Am I to understand that this was discussed and agreed to already, as it was a condition of my cooperation?"

I surge to my feet before Cole has finished speaking and whiplash a chain of anger at Gomez that I've gathered from Jonah and Hideo and, surprisingly, Smith and Donovan as well. Gomez flinches, then stands her ground. "Ms. Reed," she bites out. "You would do well to remember that as an employee of this precinct, you go where and do what you are assigned to do."

"Oh *fuck you!*" I snap back. "I'm not your fucking circus monkey, and I don't know HOW many more times I need to say this. *I don't work for you.* I *don't* need to be a part of this, and as of..." I make a show of checking my watch, "5pm today, I no longer work as a consultant for the SPD. So... have fun with that."

Gomez clenches her teeth together so tightly I can hear it from across the room, and I can see her hands shaking with anger.

"Reed," she grinds out. "I believe we discussed the matter of your co-operation in our first meeting. I would *hate* for things to be unpleasant for you from here on out. It's so much easier for all concerned if we can maintain a cordial relationship."

"I take it you have *not* had a conversation with Kailani, as promised?"

"Reed, as you'll come to find, is talented, but difficult. Some would call her head-strong, or obstinate," Gomez begins but is interrupted.

"Oh no," Elizabeth says coolly. "I find you to be quite incorrect in that matter. Kailani and I have become fast friends, you see. I have some reservations regarding your judgement of character in light of your opinions regarding her."

Gomez turns purple, and for a moment, I honestly think she's going to have a heart attack.

"Elizabeth, if you please," begins Gomez placatingly.

"Ms. Cole, if *you* please," responds Elizabeth, tightly but pleasantly. "You have asked me to feed you information, which I have agreed to, although it goes against my moral and ethical code. I realize it is for a greater good, and will help the mission of Gaia in the long run. But I need to be comfortable and confident with my liaison, which I'm sure you understand. I am quite happy if Kailani is my point of contact. I shall relay all information to her, and will depend upon her to share any necessary updates with me. To be frank, Ms. Gomez," here she levels a flat stare at the Director, "I find you deeply unpleasant and don't relish working alongside you. I'm sure you understand."

With that, she smiles at me, again with the light, champagne amusement that bubbles along my shields, and motions to the woman behind her. "Fallon will be in touch with my personal information. But for now," she passes me a business card that has a single number on it, "this is the fastest way to reach me."

She stands and glances around her. "You should take care," she says in a pleasant voice, but one tinged with warning. "Someone who sees the true value in people may try to lure Ms. Reed away from you."

Gomez can barely speak through her anger but replies tightly, "We know how to use our people."

Shaking her head ever so slightly, Elizabeth says, "Just because a carpenter knows how to use a tool doesn't mean he's a knowledgeable craftsman who recognizes its value." Turning to meet my eyes, she continues quietly, "And recognizing someone's true value and import happens to be a specialty of mine. Good day, everyone. Kailani, I'll be in touch soon."

With that, she motions to her assistant and leaves.

JUST SEE HIM

Tuesday, 2 October – Maela

The rest of that Saturday afternoon was wonderful. Jorge and I wandered around Fitzrovia and ended up in Regent's Park, where he rented a boat and rowed me around the lake while I trailed my hand in the water. I saw any number of ducks and geese and Sandpipers and even Grey Herons. He had to get back to his flat in the evening, to unpack and check in on his grandmother, whom he had promised to call promptly at 7:00pm. She'd practically raised him, so I couldn't complain. In Spanish families, Jorge explained, when your abuela said "jump", you said "how high?". I kind of envied him that: my mother's parents had died years ago, and my father's parents lived far enough away that we didn't get to see them that often. Jorge had been busy since then trying to help his sister sort out a temporary carer for his grandmother, but we were texting. Everything, in fact, would have been peachy had the new technique been working out. Instead it was same torture, different method.

"Emlyn, I don't think this is working out." I've spent all morning trying to relax and visualize pulling myself out of my body with a rope. I now have a pounding headache, and I'm pretty sure that the only sightings I've had of Ratko and Magda were simply flashbacks. I no longer know.

"Give it time. The Americans have had a good success rate with this technique."

I'm momentarily diverted. "The Americans have a psychic division? Really? Where?"

He nods: "Yes, yes, and in the United States."

Grrr. Why does he live to aggravate me? Why? Why!
"Gee, thanks for the helpful answer," I respond sarcastically. "You're a font of information."

"Maela, you caught a glimpse of Ratko yesterday morning, didn't you?" He looks up from his computer at me.

"Dunno," I mumble. "Maybe?"

"It's only been three days. You just have to keep working at it and be patient."

"Seriously, Emlyn, what happens if I strangle my spirit body trying to pull it out? Have you thought of that? What then? And what if I get out and then *can't return*?" I'm feeling tetchy and more than a little tired.

I can see he's biting the inside of his cheek trying not to smile. "Then your work here will be done. Now Maela, what's up? More problems with the boyfriend?"

I'm going to have a brain aneurysm, and it will be all his fault. "For your information, Mr Peter Perfect Pants, everything is going swimmingly."

He smiles benignly at me. "Let's leave my undergarments out of this, shall we?"

I'll kill him. I'll kill him, and no jury in the world will convict me. "What!" I squawk. I literally don't know where to begin. "I know you think you're God's gift to women, but your, your–"

"Knickers?" he interjects helpfully.

"*Those* are of seriously no concern to me." And when I die, I'm going straight to hell for telling massive whoppers, but he doesn't need to know that.

"So, did you talk to the boyfriend?" He steeples his hands under his chin, elbows resting on the desk.

"If you must know," I say airily, "*he* talked to *me*. And he's not my boyfriend."

"Didn't think so.

"And I really don't see how – wait, what? What do you mean *you didn't think so*?"

"Really, Maela. If a man's interested in a woman, he

doesn't invite her on a group date. What is he? Fourteen?"

I open my mouth, then close it again.

"Now, can we get back to work?" He smiles at me again, looking innocent as a cherub.

"No, we bloody well cannot! In the first place, we're taking things slowly. In the second place, it's none of your business. And I'll have you know that men actually do find me attractive, strange a concept as that may seem to your aristocratically inbred brain." I'm so angry I'm sputtering.

"I didn't say you weren't attractive," he counters. His grey eyes are alight, and he leans across the desk.

"You did! What?" My head's going to implode. And then I see it, a tell-tale little chink. "Hah! You're *jealous*, aren't you?"

I swear I can see a rosy tint skim his cheeks. "Maela, you *have* met Clarissa, haven't you?"

"And?" I say challengingly.

"Well then. There you go. Not to mention, it would be completely unprofessional–" The phone rings, and he picks it up. "Ryder speaking."

"Saved by the be–ell," I sing under my breath.

He looks steadily at me, reverting to his calm, imperturbable self, and says "Yes, sir" before hanging up. "Maela, I'll be back in about twenty minutes. In the meantime, you stay here and read up on the technique. The file's open on the computer."

"Anything you say, sweetcakes." I flutter my eyelashes at him.

He sighs, looking up at the ceiling and shaking his head, and walks out of the room. I'm feeling pretty punchy, because I got one over on Agent Emlyn. Tee-hee-hee! I perch myself on his chair and start reading. It's actually pretty interesting. Apparently, I have a physical body, an energetic body, an emotional body, and a body of ideas, and they all come together to make up little ole' me. The idea is to relax to the point where I enter a vibrational state, whatever the heck that is, then pull myself out and go roaming. I wonder which of the bodies goes roaming. Is it my energetic body, my emotional body, or my ideas body? Is my soul composed of all three – ideas, emotions, and energy? I read on. Other ways of triggering an out of body experience are through trauma, illness, or water and food deprivation. I shudder: no thanks. Vibrations it is. I lean back in the chair and think about how weird everything is and how much my life has changed in a few short weeks. Then, I was a slightly awkward introvert, who felt overawed but enchanted with her exciting new life, and who hadn't really clicked with any of her colleagues. Now, I'm a slightly awkward... mediocrivert, who feels terrified but elated by her exciting newest new life, and who has a... relationship of sorts with her... boss and her... not-yet-boyfriend. A good several minutes pass, and when I look up, there's a screen saver up. It's a photo of Emlyn and a younger man dressed in some sort of police uniform. They're both grinning at the camera, and I don't think I've ever seen Emlyn looking so carefree. Even when he's teasing, you can tell that there's always a slight shadow behind his eyes and a certain weight on his shoulders. I peer closely at the photo. The young man looks familiar, and I wonder where I've seen him before. Light-brown hair. Grey eyes, just like Emlyn's. And then I stop. It's the murdered officer from the set of photos. Here, his skin is glowing with health, but when I last saw him, he was pale and waxy and had a neat little line across his throat. And he has Emlyn's eyes, and, now that I look closely at the photo, the same rectangular face and long, straight nose. I feel sick. His name? What was his brother's name? Frantically, I think back to the guide to the peerage. Eadric, that was it. Unusual name, but so is Maela, so I can't throw stones. I click on to the web, and, sure enough, up comes an obituary. Eadric Ryder, fallen in the line of duty, 10 August 2018.

I clear the search history for the past hour – thank God

Emlyn hadn't been using the internet – and stumble to my green chair. It all makes sense. No wonder Emlyn's so driven. He's actually been fairly patient with me, considering, when all the time he must have been willing thoughts of Ratko into my head and bitterly disappointed with my progress. Here was I, getting bored and letting my mind wander, whining about having to walk around the East End, and there was he, desperately trying to catch his brother's murderer. It's not just about trying to catch criminals or infiltrate Kronos; it's personal. I feel terrible and huddle into the chair, trying to get warm. The door opens behind me.

"Sorry about that, Maela. Took a bit longer than expected." He strides past me and sits down. "Are you alright?" he asks, catching sight of my no doubt chalk-white face, freckles scattered like drops of blood.

I smile wanly. "Actually, Emlyn, I've got a bit of a stomach ache. Do you mind if we finish for the day?"

"That's fine. It's almost lunch-time. And you look like you could use some fresh air. Tell you what, why don't you go home for the rest of the afternoon? No sense going to Barking if you're feeling peaky."

His being nice only makes me feel worse, but I manage to whisper out an "OK, thanks" before shuffling out of the room, his concerned face looking after me. This week, I vow, I am going to get my shit together so I can help him take the murdering assholes down.

Our next two sessions are a disaster. I'm desperate to have a vision, but I'm wound up tighter than a drum, my body tense and my nerves stretched taut. I squeeze my eyes shut and try with every fiber of my being to *see* Ratko, right there, just *see him. See him, see Ratko*, I chant silently, over and over. *What is he doing? Where is he? See him.* But all I can see is Eadric's waxy face, floating in front of me. I wonder what he felt, seeing Ratko come at him with a knife. Was he afraid, or did he think he might be able to disarm the bastard? Or was he somehow knocked out, then woke to sense Ratko standing behind him. And then the sharp bite of the blade, slicing across his throat, hot blood spurting as the cold darkness enveloped him? Would the same thing happen to Emlyn? Would I one day see a photo of Emlyn, those grey eyes closed forever, mouth never again giving me that teasing hint of a smile, a neatly stitched line across the Grecian column of his throat? I feel sick.

Emlyn wraps up our session on Thursday early, and I can tell he's worried. "Don't push yourself so hard, Maela. It'll come. Look, we'll try another method." He brings a hand, loosely clenched, to his mouth and leans on it, brow furrowed. "I'll ask Seef to speak to Maddox," he says to himself. "See what other techniques have worked for them."

My eyes fill with tears, and if I don't get out of there immediately, I'll break down in front of him. And I've already done that once. *All your fault, of course*, the demon on my shoulder taunts me. "'Kay," I venture, not trusting myself to say anything further. I gather up my coat and bag and walk tiredly to the door.

"Maela," Emlyn calls behind me, but I give a slight shake of my head, with a pasted-on smile, to let him know "Hey, no worries" and quickly let myself out.

On the street, I manage to forestall a breakdown by swallowing hard several times and digging my nails into the palms of my hands so hard I leave crescent-shaped marks. And then I go to Barking and spend the rest of the day wandering up and down the streets, past row after row of red-brick buildings and tower blocks and run-down shops. To me, it looks soulless and a bit grim, though, to be fair, in my condition, so would Blenheim Palace. I'm exhausted when I get home, and my feet are killing me. My spirits are somewhere down at the level of my shoes, so I suppose it's fitting. Jorge and I have arranged to get together at a pub in

Waterloo – I insisted on at least being on his side of the river – and I think seriously about cancelling, but I can't think of an excuse that wouldn't sound like a brush-off, and, besides, I really, really want to see him. He makes me feel better just by being around. So I slap on the war paint and head to The Tankard. It's a friendly-looking place, like an old-time music hall, and Charlie Chaplin used to drink here, so I should be feeling excited; but I just can't shake the sense of despair. I get there early, grab a small table, and plaster myself to it. The place is filling up, and a group of four gives me pointed looks, but I don't think I can face standing all evening. When Jorge comes through the door and spots me, his face lights up. I try to dredge up an answering smile, but I must not be very successful, as Jorge is looking grave by the time he reaches me.

"*Querida*," he leans down and kisses me on both cheeks, and it's a measure of my distress that I just feel numb.

"Hi, Jorge. Everything good? How's your grandmother?"

"*Querida*, what's wrong?" He sits down and takes both my hands in his, looking searchingly at me.

"I'm fine, just a bit tired. Long day at work, you know? So, what do you want to drink? I'll get it. Red wine?" I jump up, but Jorge pulls me back down. "Sit," he says, almost sternly. "I'll get the drinks, and then you can tell me what's happened." He stands up and strides to the bar, where he manages to catch the attention of the female bartender in about two seconds flat.

When he comes back, I'm nervously chewing on a nail. Maybe this wasn't such a good idea. I'm in no fit state for company. I should be at home, having a good cry under the duvet.

"Now," Jorge continues, putting a large glass of wine in my hand. "Take a big sip and then tell me what's upset you." I start to protest, but he trains his eyes on me: "Drink." So I take a big gulp and – wow, he's clearly splashed out on something much more expensive than the house white. I feel the liquid swirl down to my stomach, and my tension dissipates a bit. Enough that I feel I can try to bluff this one out.

"Thanks. That's lovely. Chardonnay? Is it Chardonnay? It is, isn't it? Do they grow Chardonnay in Spain? Yup, that's the cure for all ills. Sometimes research can just get to you, you know? And you think 'oh, this is such a huge problem', but it isn't, not really. So, Spain. How's your grandmother? Is your sister well? Has she sent more *mante, mante*?" I fumble, trying to remember the name.

"Maela," Jorge cuts in, "stop stalling." There's a little stroke of amusement brushing his voice, but his eyes are worried.

My shoulders slump. "I'm terrible at my job," I say dejectedly.

"That's it?"

I look up, feeling slightly wounded. "Isn't that enough?"

"*Y yo soy el Papa de Roma.* No you're not. Come on, Maela. What aren't you telling me?" The hazel of his eyes has darkened almost to amber, and the rich wood and walnut tones of his voice deepen.

I bury my face in my hands. "I can't tell you," I mumble through my fingers.

"Sure?" he questions, taking my hands again.

I nod. "Can't. Really. Jail. Bad."

"You can't tell me because you'll get in trouble at work, maybe even go to jail?"

I nod again. "I'm not joking." I look worriedly at him in case he thinks I'm being melodramatic.

"I don't think you are, *querida.* You do work for MI5. It is to be expected." His warm brown eyes reassure me, and I feel a little better. "Can you tell me anything else? Perhaps I can help you, even without knowing the details."

"I don't think so. But it's really important I do a good job, Jorge. It really, really, really is." I want to cry again, and his fingers tighten on mine.

"Then, we will figure something out. Now, you're worried about doing a good job, and you're stressing, and the more you stress, the more difficult your job becomes, *sí*?"

"Uh huh." My voice is very small, and my eyes dart about, the jangling in my stomach starting up again.

"So, *querida*, have you ever tried meditation?"

I want to gag. "Yes," I blurt out, a little bit petulantly. "A lot." I shudder. *That's* his solution? Make me stare at walls until I go blind? Brain of Spain, there.

This time the smile reaches his eyes. "Maela, there are many different ways to meditate. I think you need a proper teacher."

"You?" I ask. I'm not sure that's such a great idea, seeing as how I masturbated to thoughts of him and all.

"No, not me. I've got a good friend who works as a yoga teacher and meditation instructor. We can go see him tomorrow, if you like."

"Umm."

"What time can you get off work?"

I think quickly. "Four?"

He nods. "OK, I'll pick you up from work at four."

I twist a lock of hair about my finger. "Well, I'm not always at MI5 headquarters. In the afternoons, I, uhh, do field research."

"So, where will you be at four o'clock tomorrow afternoon?"

I wrinkle my nose as I try to figure out where Emlyn might send me. "Err, not sure, to be honest. It depends."

Jorge nods again. "OK, then let's meet at your office. Where is headquarters?"

I'm not one-hundred percent sure that I'm down with this plan, but I can't see any way out of it, so I sigh, "Thames House. The nearest stops are Pimlico and Westminster."

"Then I will pick you up in front of Thames House at four o'clock and take you to meet my friend."

"Yaaay," I sing off-tune, just a tiny bit sarcastically.

Jorge simply smiles in response. "It will help. You will

288

see."

"Hmmm." I'm not convinced; and now, tomorrow is going to consist of meditating and failing at far-seeing, walking around some grotty bit of London, and then more meditation. Great. But maybe Jorge will take me out for dinner afterwards? That would be worth being bored for another hour. And then I remember what Emlyn said, about a man not being interested in a woman if he invites her on a group date. I fiddle with the stem of my glass.

"Jorge," I begin, tentatively.

"*Sí*, Maela?"

"Well, uhh, the other night. Wednesday, you know."

"*Sí*?" There's a curl of amusement in his voice again.

"Well, it was great meeting Sofía and Eduardo. They're really nice. I liked them." I peer up at him earnestly and blink, as if to emphasize my sincerity.

"I am glad you think so. I wanted you to know my friends."

"And that was a nice thought; I appreciate it; and they were super and all. Charlotte, not so much. But them, yeah. Totally. But." I stop, wondering how to continue.

"But?" he prompts, tipping his head to one side and giving an encouraging smile. He looks so adorable, and so kissable, with that wide mouth and those even, white teeth, that my brain gets a little scrambled.

"Well, uhh. You know what? Forget it. It's no big deal. I mean: I obviously got my wires crossed. Yes. Mmm hmm. Good. And thanks. I think maybe Sofía and I could become friends. And friends are so important. Don't you agree?" I take a large sip of wine before my mouth can run away with me further.

His smile deepens. "Maela, would I be correct in thinking that you want to know why I invited you to meet me first with friends, rather than on a proper date?"

I choke on my wine, and some of it goes up my nose. Super. First tea, now wine. To Emlyn, I'm Enema Girl; to

Jorge, I'm Señorita Snots-a-Lot. There is no hope for me. I'm doomed. Blushing, I think to myself: how much worse could it really get? So I say, in what I hope is an offhand tone of voice, "Well, uhh, now that you *mention* it..."

"A strange man comes up to you in a park, in London, and invites himself for tea. I wanted to show you that I was normal. And," he hesitates, for the first time looking a little unsure of himself.

"And?" This time, I am the one prompting, intrigued.

He looks down at his glass, swirls the wine, and sighs. "And I sensed that you were very vulnerable and lonely. I thought, maybe, you would feel more comfortable meeting me again in a neutral setting, so, if you wanted, you could leave without feeling embarrassed."

The hot flush starts at my toes and sweeps up over my body to the crown of my head, so that every bit of me is prickling with mortification. I will never, ever be able to live this down. "You did?" I croak. "It was that obvious?" How soon can I leave England? Will Emlyn let me go? No, I can't leave. I have a killer to catch.

"No," he says quickly. "No, Maela, there's something that you need to know about me, and I'll understand if you don't want anything further to do with me after hearing it."

The biggies like death and plague aside, what could possibly be worse than being exposed as a complete loser in front of someone you fancied? I am eighteen-years-old again, standing awkwardly in front of Markus Manning, two days after gifting him with my virginity, while his friends nudge themselves and laugh.

He takes a deep breath. "I can't have you feeling bad about yourself, Maela. *Vale. OK.* Maela, do you know what an empath is?"

"You mean, as in empathy? Being able to identify with someone else's emotions, step into their shoes, so to speak?" I'm confused. Where is this going?

He nods. "That, but more than that. I can sense what

other people are feeling. *Literalmente.* In here." He taps his chest. "My gift is weak – the strongest empaths can control emotions. I think, maybe, it is only women who have that skill. But I have just enough that I can read people. It is why I became a social worker." He shrugs and takes a sip of wine and looks away, as if to give me time to make my excuses and leave.

A month ago, I might have thought he was weird, the sort of man who eats vegan burgers, consults tarot cards, and dresses up as a druid on the weekends. Either that, or he was spinning me a line. Now? I'm dying to tell him about my own "gift". But I can't without getting both of us sent to prison, so I merely say, "That's incredible. Jorge, have you always had the ability?"

He glances at me, and I can see the relief in his eyes. "I do not think so, no. Or maybe it was there, but, *latente*, not active. But when *mi madre* died, when she died, my father became sick again. One day, he'd be miserable; the next, too happy, too excited. I think she had the gift too, and she helped him. And without her, he couldn't control his moods. I too began to feel the same way. Then, six months after she died, on a day when things felt very dark, he killed the man who had killed her."

I gasp out loud: "Oh, Jorge!"

"The man was drunk. He said it was an accident, that he'd swerved to miss an animal, but everybody knew. He didn't go to prison. The *policía* just took his license away. So my father killed him. And then my father went to prison. He died there."

I'm stunned and feel wretched for him. "Oh, Jorge," I say again, softly. "How old were you?"

"Twelve. And for a long time, I was angry. And sad. Bitter. Guilty. Worried. All of these feelings, coming from me, from my sister, from all of the adults around us, and pressing in on me. I couldn't breathe properly, couldn't think. When a friend from school found his brother's marijuana, I tried it. He thought he was cool. I just felt better.

"Twelve. What happened?"

"My grandmother happened. At first, she was angry, but when I began to shout at her, she knew. And she took me in her arms and said, 'It will be alright, *mi tesoro*. It will be alright.' And she helped me, as she had helped my mother. Why the gift came to me and not to my sister, I do not know."

"Jorge," I breathe. "I don't know what to say."

"That you want to stay for another drink?" He gives me a crooked smile.

I give a half-laugh, half-sob. "Can't you tell?"

"When I am feeling so nervous myself? No." He traces a pattern on the table, following the grain of the wood. I look at him and marvel that a man so beautiful could ever feel insecure.

"Well I do. So, same again?" I reach for my bag, but Jorge stands up quickly: "I will get them, Maela."

While he goes to the bar, I sit quietly, chin on hand, trying to absorb everything. Mostly, I think about Jorge, how he seems so confident, so cheerful, and yet underneath, he's known loss and fear. I guess everyone wants to seem a swan, gliding serenely over life's waters, but underneath, we're all paddling madly away.

When he comes back, he raises his glass and clinks it against mine. "So," he says softly.

"So," I reply, just as quietly.

He bites that luscious bottom lip. "Do you come here often?"

I burst out laughing, and he grins: "Wait, I've got another. Was your father a thief? Because he stole the stars from the sky and put them in your eyes. No? OK, how about–"

"Stop!" I giggle. "Enough! Mercy!"

"Really? But those are my best chat-up lines."

I feel smugly pleased. "You're trying to chat me up, huh? So tell me: what do you like best about me?" Does he think

I'm cute? Maybe even pretty? Or sexy?

"You have a beautiful soul."

I feel like I've just swallowed a bowling ball, and it's shot through my stomach to land on the ground, ricochet back up, and drop again with a great big *thud*. "Oh! Oh. That's good." I take another gulp of wine. So he doesn't see me as a sex kitten. Big deal. I am not disappointed. Nope, not me. We're friends. Mates. Mates are great. "So, you're not... I mean, you don't..."

His eyes flare with sudden heat, and he leans across the table. Tenderly, his mouth brushes against mine, soft as mist on the morning dew. Then he takes my bottom lip between his teeth and flicks out his tongue. "Yes, I do." He leans back in his chair. "But not yet, not while you're feeling so uncertain and confused. You don't need any more pressure right now."

I've stopped breathing and can only stare at him, mesmerized. Then my brain catches up with his words. "Actually," I exhale, "actually–"

He gives me a level look. "Maela, don't tempt me. I am not a saint, and my *abuela* raised me to show respect."

Respect is overrated, I think wildly. It's one of those things women say they want, but they don't, not really. We want cave-men and the hornier the better. I try again. "But–"

He taps me on the nose. I think it's becoming our thing. "Be good, *dinamita*."

HOT YOGA

Friday, 5 October – Maela

I'm feeling pretty chipper the next day. Lust-addled, yes, but chirpy. When I float into Emlyn's office, I can see the eyebrow go up, but he's also relieved. I can tell from the tone of his voice as he takes me through the exercises. He sounds warmer, more relaxed himself. And I manage to have a flash of a vision: weirdly, Tennireef, laughing, in some sort of nightclub, I think. I don't know what that's about, maybe nothing, but both Emlyn and I are encouraged. I'm even sanguine about the prospect of yet more meditation when Jorge deposits me in front of the Naya Jeevan center in Clapham that afternoon. I thought he would go in with me, but he tells me that he has a last-minute appointment and needs to head back to work right away. He worked through lunch so that he could pick me up and take me to the center, so I can't be too upset. "Ask for Kavi," he says. "I called him last night and told him you'd be coming instead."

"I took your spot? Jorge, I can't do that!"

"You can," he replies calmly. "I'd have had to reschedule anyway. This way, Kavi will actually have to work to earn his fee." He grins, looking slightly devilish, and my whole body stands to attention, excitement shivering through my veins. In my stomach an otter flips over and over, rolling playfully and waving a flipper at me.

"Friend of yours?" I ask dryly, fiddling with the straps of my bag and trying to regain my composure. Knowing Jorge can sense what I'm feeling is going to take a bit of getting used to. I can't allow myself to go around in a permanent state of arousal: it'll go to his head.

"*Sí*," he nods, still looking gleeful. "The best. Text me later to let me know how it goes."

He heads off, and I turn and walk into the center. From the outside it's not much, but inside it's bright and airy. The ash-wood flooring and eggshell walls give it a contemporary feel, as do the globe lamps suspended from the ceiling; but the effect is softened by the hanging baskets, trailing ivy, overhead. Windows in the far wall, beyond the reception desk, give onto a small enclosed garden. The girl at the desk looks ridiculously fit and trendy – sharp-cut, pink-tinged hair, a diamond nose-stud, and skin-tight workout clothes, the top slightly cropped to show off an enviably flat stomach – and I begin to get a little nervous. I'm in good shape, what with all the walking, but this place looks a little out of my league. I consider it a success that I did the laundry this weekend so have a clean pair of yoga pants and a soft, oversized sweatshirt to wear. Hesitantly, I ask for Kavi, and the girl, who's perfectly pleasant, tells me he'll be right down.

I wander over to the windows to look out at the garden. Brilliant-red Virginia creeper is growing over brick walls, and in the center there's a small sundial. It looks like a nice place to rest and gather your thoughts.

"Maela?" a deep voice, resonant as a brass bell, inquires behind me.

I turn and all of the breath goes out of me. *Hot men are like busses*, I can only think inanely. *You wait and wait and wait, and then three come along all at once.* He's tall, taller than Emlyn or Jorge, and solid, but without an ounce of fat on him. Ink-black hair feathers round an oval face, dominated by an aquiline nose and dark eyebrows. He has a short, thick beard and moustache and white, even teeth in a smiling, full-lipped mouth. Most remarkable are his eyes, a pale jade-green, striking against the warm cinnamon of his skin. They're clear as a tide pool under the summer sun. Through his loose, open-necked shirt, I can see smooth, well-defined pecs, and his arms are heavily muscled. He gives the impression of strength held in check, a hard-won calm.

"You are Maela, aren't you?" He has the sort of open, friendly face that makes you want to smile just by seeing it and incongruously cute, shell-like ears. And his accent! His voice is even posher than Emlyn's. He looks like he stepped out of the pages of the *Kama Sutra* but sounds like he just came from taking tea with the queen.

I realize I'm still gasping like a puffer fish and hold out my hand. "Yes!" I squeak. He has a strong, firm grip, and my hand feels almost delicate in his.

"Excellent. I'm Kavi, Kavi Sharma. Jorge told me that you wanted to learn meditation, to calm your mind and help with your stressful job?"

"Yes!" I can't help gawping, which is not a good look, but damn! Quickly I try again. "Yes, I err, would like to do you. I mean, do that with you." I nod my head like a bobble doll, and, oh shite, I can feel myself start to perspire. What is up with me? I think the onslaught of hot men in the past few weeks is breaking down my defenses. OK, when I met Emlyn, I was struck dumb and collapsed in a chair, but I'm pretty sure he didn't notice anything. Then I met Jorge, but fortunately I was already sitting down and – oh feck, come to think of it, he probably knew exactly what my reaction to him was. And now here's Kavi, and my brain really, really can't process this much stimulation. I hope meditation will involve me lying flat on my back, with a cold compress over my face. *And then Kavi can stretch that long, heavy body of his over yours and* – gaah! I slap the devil on my shoulder silly and thank Christ I am wearing a sports bra. You can't see pearled nipples through that, can you? Please no.

"If you'd like to come with me, we can get started." He gestures towards a corridor, turning, and I follow along behind me. He's not wearing shoes, and I notice his feet. They're strong and broad, like his hands, with a few dark hairs on his toes. I pad after him into a small, white-painted room, with a few dragon trees by a glass-cubed wall and a small table and chairs. There's a kettle on the table, a tea caddy, and two mugs.

"This is the break room," he says. "I thought we could begin by you telling me a bit more about what you hope to get out of our sessions, and then I could tell you more about what's involved. Care for some tea?"

"Uh, OK. But, I'm, I'm not sure how many sessions I can do. I'm on a grant, and, you see..." I'm feeling a bit embarrassed, because I thought this would be a one-off and I hadn't even thought about the cost. Not after Jorge nibbled on my lip.

"There's no charge." He smiles at me, and I beam at him. I can't help it. "Jorge did me a big favor a while back, and I'm happy to return it." He opens the tea caddy. "Chai OK?"

"Sure." I think? I don't know. I haven't tried it before. "But really, Kavi. You can't. I mean, I have to–"

He holds up a hand. "I insist. Now, please, have a seat and tell me what's brought you here."

I give up and subside into the chair, taking the mug Kavi holds out. It smells wonderful, so I take a sip, and the flavors of India dance on my tongue. Ginger, clove, cardamom, and cinnamon, swirled with sugar, and the hot, sweet liquid slips soothingly down my throat. I feel relaxed enough to open up a bit, and I tell him what I told Jorge: that I'm having trouble concentrating at work and that it's really important that I get a handle on things so I can do a good job. Like Jorge, he whistles when he hears I'm "interning" at MI5. "Shaken, not stirred, eh? Well, let's see what we can do."

Kavi then tells me I'm not just going to be meditating but practicing yoga as well, that there's a whole program we can do, with breathing exercises and poses, that will reduce stress and anxiety and help me to relax. Kundalini yoga will help to unblock the divine energy coiled within me and allow it to flow unhindered throughout my body, creating balance, firing my creativity, awakening my consciousness, and attuning me to my inner self. It sounds a bit "woo woo", but then, so did far-seeing. And Jorge can sense emotions, so I'm beginning to see that *There are more things in heaven and earth, Maela, than are dreamt of in your philosophy*". I'm just glad I thought to wear work-out clothes. And, really, Kavi could tell me that he wanted me to do head-stands for an hour while chanting, and I'd gladly, happily do it, although I sincerely hope that's not involved. So I just nod and say, "OK. I'm in your hands." *Like putty*, the angel on my other shoulder sighs.

We go to another room, with yoga mats, and Kavi asks me to sit cross-legged on one. So far so good, I think. Nothing's creaking, so, go me! Kavi then flows easily into a lotus pose on the mat opposite me, and I begin to feel a little self-conscious. He's so close! And he's facing me, *looking* at me, concentrating on me.

"OK, Maela. We're going to start by doing a basic chant to tune in."

Chant? Chant? That's really a thing?

"Repeat after me: *Ong Namo Guru Dev Namo*." The bell-like tones ring out, slowly, sonorously. "*Ong Namo Guru Dev Namo*."

"*Ong Namo Guru Dev Namo*." I whisper the words, stumbling over them. I think only dogs could hear me.

Kavi opens his eyes and smiles encouragingly at me. "Maela, are you embarrassed?"

"Errr." I'm blushing and bite my lip.

"Do you think I'm silly when I chant?"

"No! Oh no! It's just that–"

"Just that?" Kindness radiates off him.

"Well, you're you, and I'm me," I say, as if that explained everything.

"Ahh. And you think, because you're you, that you cannot chant without looking silly?"

"Well," I trail off and shrug.

"Would it make you feel better if I chant very loud, so that I cannot hear you?" He puts his hands over his ears and booms out, "*Ong! NAmo! GURu! DEV! NAMO!*"

I burst out laughing, and he winks at me and says, "OK! Let's try again."

It takes me a couple of goes, but I get there. On the fourth try, I'm even hoping that he notices what a nice voice I have. Kavi then has me warm up my spine, which involves raising my arms over my head and shaking and swaying. He's doing it too, so I can't feel self-conscious.

"Now, we are going to learn some breathing techniques," he announces. *Hah!* I think. *I've got this.* Breathing comes easily to me, except when I'm with hot men, of course. But no. Apparently, there's breathing and then there's breathing. Kavi has me practice deep breathing, which is tougher than it sounds. I concentrate so hard my stomach starts to ache. But this will, eventually, help me to calm myself in stressful situations, or so he says. Breath of Fire is worse. I have to pant, through my nose, and I think this will cleanse my toxins, or something; but I'm pretty sure I'm just going to hyperventilate and pass out.

"And now for our *kriyas*." I groan. Kavi has explained that these are poses, paired with a breath or meditation; and I think I've done enough for one day.

"Up, up, up, Maela," Kavi sings. He, of course, is looking limber and refreshed.

I give it a go. "So, I think what we've learned today is really useful, so, perhaps I should let it solidify, you know? Don't want to do too much and then forget things, right?" The pub is beckoning, calling out to me.

Kavi doesn't answer, just picks me up under the arms and pulls me to my feet. "Come on, *ladki*." Ooh! If he wanted, he could just sling me over his shoulder and carry me away. And from that position, I could get my hands on his ass, which, as the fine cotton trousers have revealed, is particularly delectable. Yoga has many benefits I'm beginning to see.

"The sun salutation is a good way to start the day," Kavi informs me. "I'd like you to try practicing it every day." He takes me through the sequence, which, to me, looks awfully complicated. I like saluting the sun with a cup of coffee and some toast, but Kavi is adamant. He, of course, glides through the movements. I am rather less graceful, more like a baby duck trying to walk on land for the first time. But I get through it.

"Is that it, then?" I ask hopefully. I could really use a long, cooling drink. With alcohol. Lots. But Kavi waggles his eyebrows at me, his eyes dancing, and tells me that we need to finish by meditating.

"Oh." I flop down on the ground and throw my hand over my eyes. "No," I mumble. "Nu-uh." I know he's my teacher and I should show respect, but I'm done. I really thought what with all this breathing and posing, we could skip over the meditation part.

I can feel him grinning down at me, and then his hands are grabbing mine and he's pulling me up to a seated position. "Gah," I say. "Isn't there a law against woman-handling your students?"

"Not when they're not paying, there isn't."

I glare at him, but he's unrepentant.

"You insisted!"

"So I did," he responds, equitably. "And now, please get into a comfortable position and place your hands on your knees, like so." He's formed a circle with his thumb and forefinger, with the other fingers stretching out. "This is the *gyan mudra*. It will stimulate wisdom and a calm and receptive mind." God knows I could use a little of that, so I emulate him.

"Meditation is not so difficult," Kavi continues.

"Says you," I mutter.

He ignores me, but his mouth curls up a little at the edges.

"You cannot do it wrong. Just pick something to focus on, your breathing, a sound, or an object and observe it. Be aware, and be in the moment. If you find your attention wandering, don't berate yourself. Just bring it back to your focal point and try again." His voice is steady and soothing, and I close my eyes. I'm going to count my breaths, in and out. One, two, three, four ... all of a sudden, I'm hyper aware that I'm alone in a room with an attractive man not three feet away from me. I can sense the heat of him and smell sandalwood and spice. I don't know if that's him or maybe there's an incense-burner somewhere, and I want to lean in and nuzzle the base of his throat to check. I can feel my cheeks beginning to flame red again.

"Breathing is really difficult. Am I doing it right?"

"Yes," I hear. "Now focus. In and out." He begins to speak, low and soft, in Hindi, I think; and I go back to counting my breaths. One, two. *Poor Emlyn. You'd think an MI5 agent would know everything, even how to teach meditation, but clearly not.* Oh, breathing. Five, six. *And Jorge. He's so sweet. And what a sod it must be, knowing what everyone's feeling all of the time. He and Emlyn are each troubled in their own way, aren't they?* Nine, ten. *And Kavi. He's like a gentle giant. There's a sense of humor there. And a damn fine body. I'd pant for that any time. But does he too have a secret sorrow? I'd like to be the woman who fixes it, for all of them.* Ahh, one, two.

"OK, Maela. You can open your eyes."

I blink and yawn. I'm feeling incredibly refreshed.

"Now, repeat after me: *Sat Nam.*"

"*Sat Nam,*" I chant dutifully. "Are we done?"

"Yes," he smiles at me. "Are you going to come back?"

"Do you know?" I grin, "I think I will." We make an appointment for next week – happily, he's had a cancellation – and then he takes my hand in a firm, alpha-male sort of grip, and I want to swoon, but I manage not to make too much of an ass out of myself. On the way home, I can't help but muse on the irony that, after years of waiting and hoping, I am now circling the orbit of three staggeringly good-looking men, none of whom I can currently date. Emlyn is my monitor and is seeing a beautiful but no doubt cruel blonde; Jorge can literally read me like a book and, very sadly and mistakenly, thinks I need time to find my footing; and Kavi is my teacher, and I'm pretty sure that there's some rule against fraternizing with students. I sigh. I must either have been very good or very bad in a former life.

Monday morning, I'm hovering outside Emlyn's just-open door, about to knock, when I hear him exclaim, slightly irritatedly, "No, sorry, Clarissa. I've told you: I can't. Nothing's changed."

Oh ho! Trouble in paradise? My ears perk up.

"I thought you understood. I can't just take time off."

Now I feel a little bad. I shouldn't really be listening in, should I? It's impolite. But what if I back away and he hears? There's a squeaky floorboard somewhere behind me, as I recall.

"I'm sorry you feel that way. But you know how important my work is."

Clark Gable was wrong: eavesdroppers do *not* often hear highly entertaining and instructive things. This is embarrassing.

"Well, if that's what you want... In that case, I hope you'll be very happy." There's a sudden silence, and I can almost sense Emlyn pinching the bridge of his nose. It's what he does, I've noticed, when he's at the end of his tether. He's been doing it a lot lately. Right, I'm going to chance the squeaky board. Cautiously, I stretch out one foot and–

"You can come in, Maela." His voice, calm and crystalline as ever, slivers through me. Taken off guard, I wobble slightly but catch my balance and poke my head around the door. "Hello?"

He's sitting at his desk, in his customary midnight suit, hair a little mussed, as if he's just run his fingers through it, and his eyes are stormy. My first thought is that Clarissa must off her rocker, because, why would you ever let go of someone that gorgeous if you weren't clinically insane? Yes, Emlyn could be curt, and arrogant at times, and, OK, a lot of the time; and he was driven, perhaps dauntingly so, but he had good reason, hadn't he? He wanted to catch his brother's killer. And he could also be kind and sometimes even approaching supportive.

I walk to the green chair and perch gingerly on the edge. "Soooo. Hello!" I try.

"You heard that, I take it?" He picks up the *Mont blanc* and flips it between his fingers, looking broody.

"Ahhh." For someone with a decent education, I'm not doing well, but this situation is more than a little awkward.

Emlyn glances up at me, lips thinned. "Why can't women—" He shakes his head and returns to staring at the pen.

"Be more like men?" I venture. Emlyn starts, and his brows draw together quizzically.

"Because men are so decent, such regular chaps?" A little glint sparks in those slate-grey eyes, and I warm to my theme.

"Ready to help you, through any mishaps." I let my voice go sing-song. "Ready to buck you up whenever you are glum. Why can't a woman be a chum?"

His mouth twitches, and I can see the smoke softening to silver.

"Why is thinking something women never do?" He gives a short, surprised bark of laughter.

"Why is logic never even tried?" I can see him bite the inside of his cheek, and then he holds up his hand. "Touché! *Gigi*?"

"Close, *My Fair Lady*." I'm feeling smugly pleased with myself and emboldened enough to ask, "So, Clarissa?"

"Has given me to understand that my work is a problem. We've agreed that she needs a more emotionally available man. One who can take her to Scotland for Daddy's shooting party."

I wince. "That's a bit shallow. But then–" and now it's my turn to catch myself.

"Then what?" I can tell Emlyn's feeling more in control of himself as one elegant eyebrow slides up.

Oh well. In for a penny, in for a pound, as I heard someone say at the pub. "Well, honestly, Emlyn. Men! Couldn't you tell?" I realize I'm indulging in the stereotyping I was recently mocking, but it's for his own good. He needs to understand that ice blondes named Clarissa are bad news and should be avoided in future. Even if they do dress beautifully and look the sort of girl you'd want to introduce to your major-general father and honorable mother.

"Evidently not," he replies dryly. "Well, now that we've established that I'm selfish, emotionally immature, and obtuse, shall we get started?"

And then I remember what I was going to say before I came in. "Emlyn?"

"You've had another dream." He leans forward, utterly focused now, all thoughts of his lost relationship cast aside. I envy that: I can't compartmentalize. If one area of my life blows up, the fallout bleeds into all the others. But maybe that's part of his training.

I nod soberly, my good mood draining away. "Just a flash. It was Ratko again. He was on the phone with Magda. I don't know what time it was; I didn't wake up after. He was saying he'd take care of it, whatever 'it' is." I shudder. "Ratko's eyes – they were so cold yet so excited. Just like when he killed Benny." And it was terrifying.

Emlyn looks searchingly at me. "Maela, do you feel up for a try? If we could get a lead, well, it could be a game changer."

I nod again. I want to do this. How many baby brothers

has Ratko murdered? How many sons? How many families will he leave grieving if he's not stopped? Emlyn takes me through the exercises, and this time, I really concentrate. I breathe in as I tense up my muscles and breathe out as I relax them. When Emlyn asks me to focus, I do. I remember Kavi's instructions and count my breaths, slowly, steadily. I visualize the rope, hanging above me, silver-threaded and shining. I imagine climbing it, hand over hand, pulling myself up and out. My body tingles, and I step forward into the soft blackness. It swirls around me, susurrating, urging me on, and I turn my head. I can see a flickering light up ahead. It's a lightbulb. I look around and see that I am back in the warehouse. There's a voice, and Ratko comes around the corner, so I duck back quickly into the shadow of a packing crate. "I'm doing it now," he laughs. "Be patient." Hanging up the phone, he flicks a lighter and sets it to the neck of a bottle on the floor, then another, and another. They flare up, but he bends calmly, picks up one at a time and throws them at packing crates, one of them right next to me. There's a whoosh and a roar, and then the crates are alight. Has he doused them in petrol? They shouldn't burn that quickly, should they? Ratko smiles and turns on his heel. He doesn't seem to care that the warehouse is going up in flames and that he could get caught in the blaze. I do. I watch the fire flick out its tongue, like a lizard, tasting the crate beside me, and I start to breathe faster and faster. This is it. Oh God.

"Maela," a voice calls faintly. "Maela!" I look around, trying to see who is there, and hands grasp my shoulders, pulling me back, away from the flames. "Maela!" I faint.

When I come to, Emlyn's hands are cupping my face, eyes radiating worry. "Maela, come back to me. Come on, copperhead. That's it. You're safe. Take a deep breath."

I'm shaking, and half of me is still in that warehouse. Everything's a bit fuzzy. "Name's not copperhead," I mumble. My tongue feels thick, and my throat raspy, as if I really had been breathing in smoke. I scrub at my eyes.

Emlyn rubs his hands up and down my arms. "Isn't it? When you spit and hiss at me like a viper all the time?" He tries to smile.

"Hah, hah, hah," I say weakly. "Can I have some water?"

"Coming right up." He stands and goes to a corner of the room and comes back with a glass. I gulp at it. It's warm, but soothing all the same. Slowly, I can feel my heart rate begin to subside.

"Are you OK to talk now, Maela? What happened?"

"Ratko set fire to it, to the warehouse. He told her to be patient and then threw Molotov cocktails round the place. It went up so fast, and I couldn't... I couldn't get out! And then you came."

"Jesus," he breathes. "I knew you were having a vision. Your breathing changed. But it was slower, steadier. Then all of a sudden, it sped up, and you looked terrified. I was shaking you and calling your name, trying to snap you out of it. You didn't respond. You were rigid. I thought you were having a fit." He passes a hand over his face, and I can see that he's just as shaken up as I am. Then he squares his shoulders and goes to the phone. "Ryder here. You need to check for fires, somewhere in the Docklands... No, I can't be more precise. It's a warehouse, and it's going up fast. Molotov cocktails... Fine."

He puts the phone down and comes back to me. "I'm sorry, Maela. This. This level of vision. Nothing like this has ever happened before. We knew you had potential, but we weren't prepared for this. There's nothing in the manuals. We're in uncharted territory, and I think we need to stop. You've given us a good lead, and we can take things from here."

"No!" The protestation bursts out of me before I'm aware of it. "No! Emlyn, we can't stop! *I* can't stop!" I don't want to stop. *Let Ratko get away with murdering Eadric? What if he goes after Emlyn? And what about Kronos and everything they're up to?* "These visions are happening, and they'll keep on happening. With or without you. I'd rather they were with you. You need to help me learn to control them."

"But Maela," he looks troubled.

"You can help me. Speak to the Americans. Maybe they know something. At the very least you can pull me out if something like this happens again." I'm desperate for him to agree. I need to learn to get a handle on my "gift", just like Jorge's done.

Emlyn gazes at me, for a long time, it seems. "Alright," he finally says, quietly. "We'll give it a try."

My shoulders slump in relief. "Thank you."

"But you're going home now. You're going home and you're going to rest. I'm putting you in a taxi myself. I'd go with you, but I'm expected to join the Docklands search. And you're taking tomorrow off."

I open my mouth but shut it again at his look. "Sir, yes, sir." I give him a jaunty salute.

He shakes his head at me. "The things that come out of your mouth."

ROOT CHAKRAS

Tuesday, 9 October – Maela

I know I was supposed to rest, and I did this morning, drinking "flat whites", or, as I like to call them, home-made lattés, and reading a romance novel; but this after-noon I nipped out for a quick visit to Oxford Street, just one Tube stop away so not tiring and not breaking the rules. I really couldn't go back for another yoga lesson with Kavi in my manky old gear. It would distract me from learn-ing, which would impede my work for MI5; and no, I didn't really believe that, but I grabbed at the excuse anyway. I found some black leggings, which looked exactly like my old pair except less moth-eaten, and a cute grey tee-shirt, not skin-tight but with the merest hint of a crop.

When I walk into the center, I feel pretty good. Kavi comes out, looking sigh-worthy in a pair of loose, wide-legged, Thai-style trousers and a thin cotton tee. We go into a practice room and sit while Kavi tells me more about Kundalini. It's associated with Shakti, the divine femin-ine principle and creative life-force. Apparently, medita-tion, breathing, and exercises awaken Kundalini, allowing it to rise up through the *chakras*. *Chakras*, Kavi explains, are energy centers or focal points in the subtle body which lie along the spine and the vagus nerve. Yoga coaxes the Kundalini up to the thousand-petalled crown at the top of the head, where it can unite with Shiva, consciousness, the masculine principle, leading to self-awareness. I nod as if I understand, and Kavi smiles and tells me that it will all be-come clear in time.

I'm actually excited when we get to the meditation part,

as the breathing and *kriyas* have gone a bit better today. I assume we're going to count breaths, but Kavi wants me to concentrate on my root chakra. When I look blank, he smiles again and tells me it's located by the base of my spine. I'm scrunching up my nose and trying to work out where *precisely* he means – my lower back in general? my tailbone? my butt? – when he adds, "Between the perineum and the tailbone." Oh feck. I didn't realize that this would be a biology lesson too. OK. The peri– Oh. Ohhh. The area in question gives a little throb, as if to say "Here I am!" Kavi explains to me that the root chakra is particularly associated with the color red, which is good, because my whole body is now that shade. Thinking about my perineum while sitting a foot away from a big, warm, muscled man who is beautifully limber and could bend me like a pretzel is not good for my composure. Thankfully, he seems not to notice, as he goes on to say that this *chakra* represents support and stability. It is where Kundalini resides, and we're going to shake that girl awake.

The meditation for today involves focusing on my root chakra, pulling deep breaths down into my body and imagining a red glow there, while intoning *"lam"*. I still feel a bit silly about chanting, but I don't think an easier meditation could have been chosen, as all of my attention is completely focused there already. Poor root chakra. So neglected this past year. No wonder you're blocked. What you need is some good old-fashioned TLC. But, I reflect, I could think of a more direct way of stimulating my chakra. Visualization is all well and good, but *stroking* my Kundalini awake might be better. Kavi, with his strong fingers. And I've never had a man with a beard go down on me before. Wonder what the sensation would be like? Would it tickle? A damp heat flares between my legs, and my root chakra gives another little throb to let me know that it is *down* with that plan. When Kavi calls time, the red glow is more of a furnace and is burning merrily away.

We've arranged to meet up with Jorge at a nearby pub afterwards. It's a short walk, and on the way, I ask Kavi how long he's been in London. Judging by his accent, I'd say he went to boarding school at Eton or something; but he tells me that he attended a private school in Lucknow, "The City of the Nawabs", in Uttar Pradesh. I'm floundering to place it, when he continues that Uttar Pradesh is just south of the Himalayas, right up on the border with Nepal. Kavi, though, was not born in Lucknow but in nearby Ayodhya, an old, old city on the banks of the Ghaghara, said to be the birthplace of the god Rama and a place where the Buddha came to preach. I listen, fascinated, as he describes pink bridges, intricately carved buildings, blue and green temples, and golden shrines; and I wonder why he left and how he ended up as a yoga teacher in London. But I don't want to pry, so I merely suggest, naively, that Ayodhya sounds a little like Haight Ashbury; and he laughs and tells me it could be so. When we reach the pub, he holds open the door and gestures, "After you."

Jorge is waiting for us, and my heart leaps in my chest when I see him. "Jorge!" I squeal and run towards him.

"*Querida!*" He bends down to kiss me on both cheeks, and I breathe in mahogany and black pepper. Then he and Kavi clasp hands and slap each other on the back, the way that men do.

"Drinks?" Kavi asks. "First round's on me." I order a Pinot Grigio, and Jorge wants a Shiraz. We head to a nearby table while Kavi goes to the bar. Thankfully, the place isn't crowded, and he's soon back with our order, taking a seat on my other side so that I'm sandwiched between them.

"*Salud!*" Jorge toasts us, then turns to me. "So, how did it go? Do you still hate meditation?" His eyes twinkle as he takes a sip of red wine.

"Jorge!" I hiss. "I never said I hated meditation! I just needed a good teacher." I can't believe he's landed me in it like that, wind-up or no.

Jorge's eyes widen. *"Dinamita*, I am so sorry! You are right, and I sent you to this *imbécil!* What have I done?" He manages to look both mortified and playful all at once, and I consider kicking him in the shins.

"Well," says Kavi placidly. "It takes a *murkh* to know a *murkh*." He raises his pint of IPA. "Cheers." I can see that I'm going to be picking up a lot of interesting vocabulary around these two.

"Too true, too true." Jorge looks rueful, then flashes me a grin. "So, it's going well?"

"Very," I say primly, taking a dainty sip of wine.

"In truth, my friend, I think she's a natural," Kavi adds. "We need to work on her dislike of *kriyas*," and here he sends me a warm, slightly apologetic smile, "but I think meditation will come easily to her."

I almost spit out my wine to hear that – I'm pretty sure Emlyn wouldn't agree – but I'm not going to turn down a compliment. "See," I crow to Jorge. "I'm a natural. My teacher says so." I studiously try to avoid remembering that I spent both meditations sessions thinking about sex. It doesn't matter what I focus on, does it? Kavi said so. And if mentally undressing him and Jorge and Emlyn works, so be it.

"I never doubted it," Jorge replies, looking affectionately at me, and all of a sudden, I feel flustered, like a little bird is trapped in my chest.

"Now Jorge here," Kavi continues, "was not so proficient. It took him many, many weeks just to get where you are after two lessons."

"Hey!" Jorge protests. "I wasn't that bad."

Kavi ignores him. "And his *kriyas*?" Kavi shudders. "He was like a baby elephant on skates."

"Kavi!" Jorge growls warningly. "I'll have you know, Maela, that I did everything perfectly. I amazed even myself with my natural ability."

"Say what you like, my friend," Kavi shakes his head, "but

you pulled a muscle the first time you tried the sun salutation."

At that, Jorge mock-punches him in the arm, and Kavi
bursts out laughing. I'm grinning too, and Jorge's ears go a
little pink. "On the video I'd seen, the man jumped into the
plank position."

"Yes," agrees Kavi. "But he'd had years of training."

The two of them start to talk about yoga and soon are in
a complicated discussion about advanced techniques. The
names sound colorful – Firefly Pose, King Pigeon Pose, Peacock Pose – and I'm content to sit quietly and listen. At one
point, Kavi throws back his head in laughter, and a bolt of
lust sizzles through me at the sight of the strong muscles of
his throat and his face alight with joy. I can't help it: I want
to wrap myself up in that strapping, powerful body and feel
it move in mine. Then I catch a glimpse of Jorge's face, and
the craving falters. He looks like he's been gut-punched,
and I see a resigned sadness steal across his features. I feel
wretched and look worriedly at him. He must sense my
change in mood, as he conjures up a lopsided smile for me
and gives a little shrug as if to say he understands. He and
Kavi keep chatting, and all I can think of now is how to
put things right. The best I can come up with is to try to
let Jorge know that I still fancy the pants off him. Yes, I'm
pretty sure I'm a slut for being attracted to two men – *three*,
the little devil on my shoulder pipes up, *own your libido, you
naughty minx* – at the same time, but there's nothing I can
do to change that. So I begin to think about Jorge and everything I'd like him to do to me, trying to "aim" the feelings in
his direction.

I imagine him coming up behind me, wrapping his arms
around my waist as he bends his head to kiss my neck where
it meets the shoulder. *His breath is warm as it feathers across
to my collarbone, and his lips, oh so soft, as they touch my skin
in homage. I sigh, leaning back into him, and he takes the invitation to run his hands lightly up to cup my breasts. He gives*

a gentle squeeze, thumbs strumming the sides, and I shudder, my head falling back. Jorge sips at my lips, coaxing, nibbling, tempting, and I give a soft, almost mewling cry, mouth blindly seeking his. I move restlessly against him and feel him smile against my mouth as his hands move to my waistband. He's undoing the button of my jeans, pulling down the zipper, as his mouth continues to dance against mine, his lips warm and sure. He tastes of wine and summer suns, white stone baking in the noonday heat, shadowed where the bougainvillea blooms. His body is a furnace, burning away my reserve. I can feel him, thick and pulsing against the small of my back, and I rub against him in reckless abandon. Jorge makes a sound deep in his throat and pushes my jeans down roughly, along with my panties, baring me to him. "Maela," he whispers. He bends me over, placing my hands against the wall, dropping a kiss to the nape of my neck, and kneads my ass. I hear the sounds of his trousers dropping to the floor, and I tremble, flushed and waiting.

"She messing with you, my friend?" Kavi's amused voice breaks in.

I come to, choking on my wine, and a little goes up my nose. *For fuck's sake! Is Kavi "gifted" too?* I shoot a quick glance over at Jorge, my cheeks aflame, to see him staring at me, eyes heavy lidded.

"Only in the best of ways," Jorge replies a little hoarsely. "OK, Maela. Message received. Can you think about paint drying now, so that I can get up to get us another round?"

My mouth is open, and I look from him to Kavi in wordless question.

"No, I'm not empathic like Jorge," Kavi chuckles. "But when I see him get a glazed look in his eye, and he doesn't respond when I tell him he's a muppet, and he's sitting by a pretty girl, and the girl in question keeps shooting him little glances, well." He lifts those broad shoulders. "It's not too difficult to figure out. That and the fact that his tongue was hanging out of his mouth, and he was looking at you the way I look at a plate of *gulab jamun*." Jorge slaps the back of his head, but Kavi only grins. "Sterling work. Don Juan here needs to be kept on his toes. Though I should tell you, Maela, that you can seriously do better." He leans across the table and looks solemnly into my eyes. "Like me, for instance. I know tantric sex," he whispers dramatically. He waggles his thick, dark brows at me, and I giggle. I don't quite know why, but I don't feel self-conscious any more. Neither of them seems bothered by my wayward hormones, and I can feel myself relaxing, the cherry red of my cheeks fading to hollyhock pink. *Hey*, I think. *I'm a strong, confident, modern woman. I have needs. I have desires. So sue me.*

I lean closer to Kavi. "That so?" I make my voice breathy, and an answering spark lights in those imperial-jade eyes.

"Oh yes," he promises, his tone equally intimate. "I can last for hours and bring you to the heights of ecstasy. Time will slow; our souls will connect; you will see the sun and stars and know the wonders of the cosmos."

"Ooooh," I sigh, only half in jest. "Well, when you put it like that, I think I'll–"

"Have another drink and have pity on me," Jorge interjects. He's trying unsuccessfully to scowl and settles for looking half-disapprovingly at us. "Don't fall for his 'I know the Kama Sutra' line while I'm at the bar," he admonishes me.

The rest of the evening is wonderful. Kavi and Jorge are clearly good friends, and at times their banter has my sides aching with laughter. When I finally get into bed, I'm glowing.

Emlyn has news when I get to the office the next morning. A warehouse in Beckton, between the sewage works and London City Airport, has burned down. The police are still going through the site, but there's evidence of arson.

Thanks to Emlyn's warning, the firefighters were able to get there before the warehouse was totally consumed and the conflagration could spread to the neighboring buildings.

I'm stunned. I mean, I know my vision of Benny turned out to be true and that Emlyn and his colleagues believed me when I told them about Tennireef – God, he's probably under surveillance now – but I'm not sure that *I* believed me. Deep down, I think I've been telling myself that the dreams were just a bad reaction to the drug and that telesthesia was some new age, mystic guff. Now, I can't pretend that this isn't happening. I feel a little shaky.

There's more, Emlyn tells me, his face grim. They found evidence of human occupation – multiple. The working theory is that the site was used for human trafficking, but whether into or out of the country they can't be sure. Probably the former, they think, but who knows?

"Evidence? You mean–" I whisper, now feeling sick.

"No," Emlyn interjects quickly. "No bodies." Thank God. It was bad enough feeling the flames race towards me in my vision. If someone had actually been caught in them – I shudder.

"A pretty dramatic way to get rid of evidence. Or was this a diversion? Maybe to mask a flight? Or moving a large group of people by lorry? Or, hell, just to confuse us, keep us running round in circles." He seems tired, his face drawn. "Petrol bombs, more petrol on the crates, piles of trash, even a few car tires… If we hadn't gotten there when we did, it could have taken out a whole block." I gulp. This is very, very real. Drug-dealing and murder seem almost prosaic, the stuff of TV crime dramas: horrible, but par for the course in a major city, right? But human trafficking, and trying to burn down buildings as a diversion?

"We've had other incidents over the past few months, in London and other major cities. But no motives that we could see, beyond the usual gang warfare. Who would deliberately draw the attention of the authorities? Now we know that the incidents must be connected somehow." Emlyn shakes his head, one oak-brown lock sliding over his forehead. "Which brings us back to that interesting phone call." I blink at him. *Which* phone call? There have been a few.

"'Laydon', the matrix, the armamentarium, and–"

"Rhea," I breathe. He nods his head. "Rhea. She and Magda speak in code. They know something 'Laydon' doesn't. And they're using him. Knowing what we now know, I did a little digging last night and this morning." I'm hooked but also wondering if he ever sleeps. But he's got more reason to be motivated than most, I remind myself. "It turns out that 'Laydon' is a Scottish name, meaning 'muscular' or 'strong'. A good name for a henchman. Better than 'lay down'." He grins at me, that dimple appearing in his chin, and I simultaneously feel a little abashed and aching to jump his bones. "But," he stops and looks exultant.

"But?" I feel like we're on the verge of a great discovery, and he's drawing it out just to torment me. Sheesh – get on with it already! He's milking the moment, and I'm practically bouncing in my chair.

"*Ladon* was the dragon in the Garden of the Hesperides. It guarded the Golden Apples."

My eyes bulge. "Ratko has a tattoo of a dragon," I blurt out.

"Yes," Emlyn agrees, his grey eyes alight. "Ratko has a tattoo of a dragon. And now we know. He's a bit player, a 'nice little earner' for Magda, who's channeling money to an armamentarium, some sort of war-chest, if I had to guess. And Magda reports to 'Rhea', who may be in charge of Kronos."

Emlyn strokes his chin, deep in thought, and I can practically see the gears whirling in his head. "Ladon, who became the constellation *Draco*, the Greek version of *Lotan*, forerunner of the Leviathan, servant of the sea god. Could be a Scottish name, but it all fits."

I bob my head; it certainly does. I mean, I thought I knew my mythology, but...

"So, Maela?"

I glance up at him. "Hmmm?"

"Are you up for another session? I don't want to take any chances, not after last time, but if we could see what Magda is doing now..." He trails off, and I nod. There's no way I'm going to pass on this chance.

"On it." I get comfortable in my chair and begin to count my breaths. It takes me a lot longer this time to feel the vibrations; my mind is too busy pondering what everything means: Ratko, who is Ladon; Rhea, whoever she is; Tennireef. I wonder what his code name is. Is there a god of wankers? As to that, what is Magda's code name? Aphrodite? Would stand to reason. Eventually, though, my body "hums", and I step out into the same, soft blackness as before. I look around. There's nothing: no light, no location coming into view, no Magda. I wait. And wait. And then wait some more. Dear Lord, this is boring. I sink to my knees, gazing into the darkness, trying and mostly failing to stay alert. Every so often, I think I see a flash of color, as if in a dream, but nothing materializes. I yawn, and then I feel myself sliding down the rope and back into my body. When I open my eyes, Emlyn is gazing at me, tense, expectant.

"Well?" he asks.

I lift my hands in a helpless gesture. "Nothing."

"Nothing?"

"It was really weird. I definitely went somewhere else. But there was nothing to see. Maybe she was asleep?" It's the only explanation I can come up with.

He's disappointed, I can tell, though he tries to hide it; but he just nods and says that we can't expect a vision every time, and we're already making great progress. He asks me to take another walk this afternoon but not to push myself. Aww. This new, improved, solicitous Emlyn is making it hard for me to remember boundaries. If I'm not careful, he'll soon have me eating out of the palm of his hand. I nod and say "No problem." He needs to follow up on the warehouse tomorrow, so I tell him I'll see him on Friday.

I decide I'll take a scout around Beckton, near the scene of the crime. I half do and half don't want to go there, remembering the terror I felt in the warehouse, but I pull up my big girl socks. I've got a job to do, and cowering away in some other corner of London isn't going to get us anywhere. The architecture's pretty modern, lots of housing and industrial buildings, so nothing much historic to distract me. I never thought, when I came to London, that I'd be spending quite so much time away from the center, and I wonder wistfully why Ratko couldn't have set up headquarters in Kensington, cunningly hiding in plain sight. I turn down another street. Convenience store. Trudge, trudge. Garage. Trudge. Fish and chips takeaway. Trudge. A clinic for, judging by the people loitering by the door, those down on their luck. I recognize the logo in the window. The Gaia Foundation. They help the homeless, I think, and won some award or other a couple of months ago. Trudge, trudge. A coffee shop. Here, I stop. My feet are getting sore, and I could really use a break. It's a chain, and there's a short line at the counter when I go in. I'm scanning the board and trying to decide between a millionaire's shortbread and a banoffee slice when I hear a familiar voice behind me.

"Why Ms. Driscoll!"

I turn, and there, behind me, is the Dean of the English Faculty at Queen's. He's short and rotund, with tufts of grey hair sprouting above rather large ears, and looks like he stepped straight out of the nineteenth century. I wouldn't be surprised if he owned a monocle.

"Dean Fernsby! What are you doing here?" We're a rather long way, figuratively speaking, from the rarified atmosphere of the senior common room, with its chandelier, silk-hung walls, and marble fireplace.

"University's thinking about setting up a satellite. Expanding. New student accommodation. I'm on the committee, y'know." I nod politely. "But you, m'dear! MI5, eh? How's it going?" He beams at me, his faded blue eyes twinkling, like a kindly old cherub. "I couldn't believe it when Mr. Ryder asked for you especially! Who would have thought? Codes! But then, people always dismiss the humanities, don't they?"

"Oh, err. It's not actually that exciting." I give a little laugh, but mentally I'm cursing Emlyn. Who would have thought a government agent would come up with such a bollocks cover story? It's not like it was spur of the moment. He had time to think about it.

"Nonsense! It just goes to prove what I always tell my students: a humanities degree prepares you for anything! Look at you! Interning at MI5 with Agent Ryder!" This last practically booms out, Dean Fernsby having had plenty of practice over the years at speaking over recalcitrant students. A couple of people look at us curiously.

"Honestly, it's not important." I think furiously. "It's really just archival work. You know, sorting through files. I think they're writing a history."

He winks at me, then taps his nose. He couldn't have been more obvious if he had just come out and said, "That will be our little secret." To get him off the subject, I ask about the proposed satellite, and he thankfully takes the bait.

Half an hour later, he's off to an appointment nearby, and, promising to keep in touch, I can escape. I'm not ecstatic to be pounding the pavement again, but, fortified by sugar and coffee, I decide I'll keep going for another hour or so. While I walk, my mind goes back to the conversation with Emlyn that morning. Jesus, human trafficking. Somehow, that hits me harder than Benny's murder. Is it because Benny was a drug dealer and so "guilty"? Or maybe, because the murder, horrible as it was, was at first nothing but a bad dream, as if my mind was remembering something seen in the movies. Gory, but unreal. The warehouse going up in flames, though, that was very real. Jesus. Well, we know who 'Ladon' is, but who the hell are Magda and Rhea? I'm deep in thought, not really watching where I'm going, when a cold sense of foreboding suddenly slicks over my skin. I look around. This isn't the best area, and I wonder if some-one's watching me, waiting to pounce. But there's nothing out of the ordinary. It's a sunny day; cars are passing; and people are going about their business. I shake my head. Is this what life is like for secret agents? Always on alert? Re-garding people with suspicion? Shadows? Cloaks and dag-gers? No wonder Emlyn ended up with Clarissa. Her very superficiality must have been appealing: no hidden depths, no challenge. I take a few steps forward, and my stomach roils. Maybe the banoffee slice was a mistake. It looked so good: biscuit, caramel, cream, banana. What's not to like? But it was awfully sweet, and I'm now starting to feel a bit queasy, so I turn on my heel and head for the nearest Tube station. Should have gone for the millionaire's shortbread.

The next day, I'm feeling much better and at a bit of a loose end. Who would have thought I'd get so many days off working for the government? I go through my sun sa-lutation, badly, and think about calling up Jorge or Kavi to see if they want to play hooky but resist the impulse. They won't thank me for disturbing their work. So I have a bit of a wander round Russell Square, then go to the Cartoon Mu-seum, which is brilliant. In the evening, Kavi, Jorge, and I have a three-way text, and we arrange for them to come by this weekend. I go to bed fairly early and wake up shattered.

Emlyn looks alarmed when I stagger into his office Friday

morning. He actually leaps up and helps me into the arm-chair before ringing for a pot of tea. He doesn't say anything until it arrives, then presses my fingers gently around the mug, admonishing me to take a sip. I clutch the mug, let-ting its warmth seep into me, and do as he says. One minute and several sips later, I lean back into the armchair and sigh. It's not the tea, though, that's soothing me: it's just being here with Emlyn, knowing that he will handle what I'm about to share.

"Do you want to tell me?" he asks now, quietly, eyes fixed on my face.

I nod, then share what woke me up weeping sometime in the early hours. The dream had started out mildly enough. It was night-time, and Tennireef was walking down a dimly lit hallway. He'd stopped in front of a door, given a brief rap and pushed it open. And then the perspective had changed, and I was suddenly seeing things through *his* eyes. There was another man there, and I? Tennireef? smiled coldly at him and said "do go ahead" and nodded towards a corner of the room, where a bed suddenly came into view. And on the bed was a naked woman, bound and gagged, with wide, pleading eyes, and she shook her head, but we leered down at her. And then I was back in my body and looking on horrified as Tennireef stretched out in a chair, as if he were about to watch a film, and the other man grinned and then proceeded to rape the woman. She screamed and cried, and I cried along with her and tried to pull him off, but my hands went right through him. And then, worse to come. Tennireef stood up and moved to stand beside them. And my perspective shifted again, and I? Tennireef? hoarsely ordered, "Finish it." And the other man took out a knife and began to cut her, and blood sprayed and we could taste it and shivered with pleasure. And then I was back in my body, as Tennireef turned on his heel and walked out of the room, with a curt "now take out the trash". And Tennireef was back in his bed, and I was watching as he masturbated, eyes closed in obscene ecstasy. And then the darkness took me, and I'd mercifully woken up.

Emlyn listens to me, his face grim. "I'm sorry, Maela. Sorry you had to see that. That poor woman. Christ! How bloody awful."

"Maybe, maybe this time it was just a nightmare?" I look up at him hopefully, hands tightening on the armchair.

He sighs: "I doubt it. Let me ring Seef, see if he's heard anything. I'm afraid there's nothing else we can do for the moment," he says bitterly. He has a quick conversation, sharing the details I give of the woman – young, blonde, blue-eyed – and the location – a nondescript room – then hangs up and turns back to me. "You, OK?"

"I don't want to see any more today," I whisper. I feel exhausted and wish I could wipe my brain. I half-wish I could wipe away my ability, but deep down, I know I wouldn't, not really. Someone has to bear witness, to help find justice for the victims, and if my visions can do that, then they're worth the pain.

"No, of course not. But I don't think you should go home just yet. Look, why don't you stay here and finish your tea, maybe try to take a little nap. I'll get some paperwork done."

I consider it for a moment, then nod. "OK." And so I sit, sipping at my tea and watching Emlyn, who occasionally looks up to give me a quick, reassuring smile. I don't think I'll be able to sleep, but my eyelids soon grow heavy, and I lean back into the chair, and before I know it, I'm not thinking any more.

The ringing of the phone, cut off abruptly, wakes me up. I resist, snuggling deeper into the cushion, chasing the elusive threads of sleep. I yawn, swiping my hand across my face before tucking it under my chin. I lie boneless a moment, before remembering that I'm not in my bed. Blinking, I open my eyes to see Emlyn gazing tenderly at me. He colors slightly and clears his throat. "Sorry. I dismissed the call as quickly as I could."

"'S OK. I hope it wasn't important?" I sit up, covering another yawn with my hand and feeling relaxed and content.

"Just Clarissa. I can call her back later. So, feeling better?"

My warm glow abruptly dissipates, but I nod mechanically. "Better. But I wouldn't mind if we had to track down a corrupt banker next time. Visions of fraudulent spreadsheets sound pretty good right about now."

He smiles, dimple showing, "I'll see what I can do."

"Well," I stand up, gathering my coat and bag. "'I'll let you get on with things." *Like call the gold-digger back*, I think sourly.

"Have a good weekend, Maela, and take it easy. I'll see you Monday."

As I walk to the door, I don't know whether to be annoyed that Clarissa and Emlyn are apparently an item again or amazed that I'm already thinking about our next case.

ME TARZAN, YOU JANE

Tuesday, 9 October – Kailani

The past week has been a complete mess of us trying to set up tactical options and plans. Smith wants to lead, and was tasked to lead, but doesn't know Seattle specifically, which makes it more difficult. Hideo keeps stepping in to correct information or offer suggestions, albeit politely, but it causes Donovan to bristle and defend Smith as a leader, then Jonah makes jokes about hedgehogs and porcupines or something to relieve the tension. The days are too long and don't give me enough time to go home and recover from the epic levels of warring testosterone in the room, which I would have needed to do even without my ability. A girl can only stand so much flexed muscle and "Me Tarzan You Jane" attitude before she wants to punch a wall. I get home at ten or eleven at night and fall, face first, onto our couch, often not even making it to my bedroom most nights. In the morning I'm up and out by 5:30. Bless Gemma, who wakes up every morning while I shower and dress and makes me a bagel and coffee to go, before crawling back in her bed.

I usually arrive at the station by 6:30, and our day starts by 7:00. Because Deo and I have a long history of letting him talk and present information while downplaying my involvement, it's an incredibly difficult habit to break and results in the other three guys, Jonah included, thinking that I was more of a passive bystander on most cases than an active participant. It's not Deo's fault – we'd agreed upon this tactic and had perfected it over the years – but when I *do* try to interject or make a comment, I'm ignored, talked over, or looked at with something akin to a tired tolerance.

By Tuesday, I've stopped trying completely, and when the fourth hour goes by without anyone directly addressing me or asking my opinion, I slip out of the room silently and go to get a coffee.

While the men are arguing over routes and reasons, I spend a blissful half hour, eyes closed, under a shady tree drinking a mocha in complete silence, until my phone rings. Not recognizing the number, I answer cautiously. "Hello?"

"Kailani! It's Elizabeth Cole," she replies in that tight, succinct way of hers. "I thought it time we had a little meeting, no?"

"Sounds good, Ms. Cole. When and where are you thinking?"

"Elizabeth, please, Kailani. And perhaps this coming Thursday? You can come tour the Gaia facility here in Seattle, if you'd like."

"That's fine. I'm happy to do it sooner..."

"I'm afraid I'm out of the States at the moment, and won't return 'til tomorrow night."

"No problem," I agree. "I'll see you then."

By the time I get home, my frustration with the team has reached epic levels but doesn't even begin to compete with the growing excitement of actually getting to visit the Gaia headquarters. No longer tired from the day's battles, I grab an old dream journal off my shelf and flip through the pages, looking at wish lists I'd made of places I wanted to work, all of them topped by Gaia. Beyond their stated mission, Gaia, and Cole, have a reputation for being a female-friendly company, banking heavily on the fairly untapped resources of female scientists, managers, and workforce. They have an inhouse day care, a generous parental leave policy, and good health care. No one can say that Cole doesn't take care of her people.

Suddenly a bit worried about what I'm going to wear Thursday, and wanting to make a good impression, I riffle through my closet, looking for the right outfit. I find an old pantsuit combo that makes me look vaguely like a middle-aged HOA board member and hold it up to me.

"Gemma?" I call out loudly, making sure she's not in hearing distance. *No response. Thank god.* I look myself over carefully in the mirror, angling my face this way and that.

"Okay, Kai. You look good. You're fine. You definitely don't look like you're about to complain to the manager," I murmur to myself, trying to pump myself up. "One cup of coffee and you'll conquer the day. You've got this. You are a bad-ass bitch."

A soft, serious voice starts narrating from the doorway behind me. *"Reader, she does NOT have this. She is not, in fact, a bad-ass bitch. She cries during the Olympics and inspirational sports movies..."*

Flying around I grab my hairbrush and fling it at Gemma. "Jesus, Gemma!" Flushing to the roots of my hair, I start braiding a crown braid to wrap around my head. "You're obnoxious, you know that? Did you not hear me calling you?"

Gemma laughs, ducking the flying brush, and keeps speaking in that same voice. *"She loves rainstorms and Hallmark movies...."*

Flying at her, I tackle her and pin her, yelling, "Too far! Too far! I do *NOT* love Hallmark movies!"

Gemma goes limp, like a puppy flipped on its back, grins up at my face, and whispers, *"Reader, the Hallmark Christmas channel is in fact, her favorite."*

Growling at her, I push off indignantly and straighten up imperiously, brushing off my clothes. "Can I *help* you in some way?"

Still lying on the floor, she laughs at me. "Yeah. Some guy named Walker is on the phone for you. Sounds like a sexy, angry gnome."

I stare at her. "Gemms. I don't... I mean... a what?"

"You know, like those Garden Gnomes?"

"Yeah, I know Garden Gnomes, Gemm. But in what universe are they sexy?"

"They guard your house and scare things away, but are really marshmallows because they take care of your gardening and flower beds. Get it? *Flower beds?*" She waggles her eyebrows at me like Groucho Marx, and I press my face into my hands.

"I don't even... I can't address this right now. But we're signing you up for some form of therapy, like, as soon as possible. You understand?"

She nods, laughing. "I'll tell him you're on your way."

Finishing my braid quickly, I hear her down the hall saying, "She'll be right here. She's sorting her teddy bear collection."

Groaning to myself, I rush down the hall. "I've got it. I've *got* it, Gemma. Hello?" I say questioningly. Despite what Gemma said, I doubt it can be Walker.

"Reed," his chocolatey voice snaps through the phone, and I sigh.

"Donovan," I reply flatly. "You know it's like 10:30 at night, right?"

He scoffs audibly, and I frown. "*You* know Smith and I are both at the station still working, right?" he replies snarkily. "We've decided to come with you Thursday."

I shake my head slowly, even though he can't see it. "You weren't invited, Donovan. That's not how it—"

"Direct from Smith. We don't need you tomorrow. Tanaka says you need a break." The judgement in his voice sets my teeth on edge. "So go ahead and nap while the rest of us are working. *If* you think you can manage, Smith is sending you some unclassified files to look over. And let Cole know we'll be there Thursday with you." The line clicks, and I'm left staring at the phone in disbelief. Gemma comes up behind me and puts her head on my shoulder thoughtfully.

"Oooo..." she says. "He's an *angry* Gnome."

Grinning at her, I shake my head and head off to bed.

ALL THE ROADS LEAD HOME

Wednesday, 10 October – Kailani

I would have argued harder with him, but the truth is, I do need a break. Still, the next day, after an admittedly late start, I head over to Lachy's because our internet connection has dropped out, and I want to check on the info Smith sent me. At the edge of the tree line between our homes, I zone out slightly, watching Lachy chop wood. He's shirtless in the cool afternoon sun, thick, corded arm muscles straining as he swings the ax in a careful rhythm. He hasn't noticed me yet, half hidden behind the pines on the walk to his house, and I give myself a few moments to just take him in. Lachy doesn't have a gym-bro body – it's not rippling muscle the entire way down from head to foot. He's strong from the woodworking and mountaineering, but it's a strength built from a lifetime of work, not from lifting weights. That's not to say he isn't toned – he is, defined pecs and strong legs – but he's also softer in a way. There's a slight cushion to him that I've always loved. He looks warm and comfortable and inviting, and there are times like right now all I want to do is curl up in his arms and feel safe and secure and like nothing and no one could ever hurt me. Lachy had to have been some kind of Grizzly Bear or something in a former life – cuddly and dangerous all at once.

A quiet, amused rumble edges into my consciousness. "And what are you doing here, Kai?" he asks in his deep, slow voice.

"Perving on you," I begin absentmindedly, still staring at the sweat running down his arms, before I startle to full awareness. "What? I – I mean I was looking for you."

He grins, teeth flashing straight and white. I love Lachy's smile – he's generous with it, flashing it any time he's around me. I never have to earn it – it's like me being with him is enough to bring it out full force every time we're together.

"Well, you looked plenty, and found me," he replies teasingly.

Face slightly flushed from watching him and getting caught, I mumble back in a mutinous tone, "I was just thinking you look like a Grizzly Bear."

He raises an eyebrow consideringly. "Hmmm… not sure how to take that." Patting his belly gently, he addresses it in a serious tone, "Seems you and I have some work to do old friend. May be time to part ways."

"No!" I burst out before I can help it. His grin lights up again, all mischievous and happy.

"No?" he says, still staring down thoughtfully, poking at his stomach. "Are you sure?"

"Jesus," I say under my breath, half-prayer half-exasperation. "I, uh. I think you look cuddly." The words are forced out in a strangled tone, and I desperately look for a way out of this somehow suddenly awkward conversation. He looks very dubious at the word "cuddly". "Like in a good way. Not bad cuddly. Sexy cuddly. Like Sexy Dangerous cuddly." *Christ, Kai, abort, ABORT!* "Some women like that. The muscles with the uh…" I wave my hand around, motioning towards his body, "the uh… this whole thing is… I mean *I* wouldn't change it… the… there's like a thing… even Jason Momoa… kind of a softer… it's nice when you're naked…" *Oh holy fuck on toast! Shut up, Kai, shut UP!*

Lachy's openly laughing now, his deep, thunder-rumble laugh, a low bass sound you feel in your stomach. I can't help but smile back at him as he tosses his head back, now gasping for air.

"Oh Christ, Suge. I swear. Your face right now." He roars

in amusement, and I press my hands to my cheeks, hiding behind them.

"Oh shut it." I reply helplessly. "Can we please just forget the last three minutes happened?"

Trying valiantly to stop laughing, he motions me over to him. "Sure, Suge. What's up?"

"Our internet is down again, and I need to do some work. Can I come up to the cabin and hop on yours?"

He looks at me with a half-frustrated, half-amused face and shakes his head slightly. "Kailani. Do you or do you not have a key to my place?"

I nod sheepishly.

"And have we, or have we not, had this conversation about five million times?"

I nod again. "But..."

"No buts, Kai. Just come up and come in when you need anything. The fridge, the washer-dryer, the tv. Come up if you're lonely, or bored, or want to hang, or if Gemma's gone and you want to eat proper food."

I glare at him over the last one. "I can make proper food!" I say rebelliously.

"You *can*, but you forget to until you're too hungry and then you eat crap, which is terrible for you."

I shrug, and he frowns at me. "Don't shrug at me. You know you do better here and here–" he reaches out a massive hand and gently taps over my heart, then my head, "when you eat healthy food."

It's annoying but true. My shields are better and I'm better able to handle things if I fuel my body correctly. If I do too much junk food, those sugar highs can really fuck with me.

"But what if you're... I don't know... entertaining the laaa-aaadies or something," I tease him gently.

"Well, just don't come upstairs then. The house is pretty well soundproof," he answers pragmatically. A strange, uncomfortable flare of emotion rockets through me and pushes out of me before I can catch it, and I see Lachy's eyes widen briefly in confusion before I can grab the emotion and pull it back. The edges of his soft lips quirk up at the corners, and he reaches out to grab my hand.

"Come on, then, Suge. Let's head in."

After we go inside, Lachy makes me a snack plate and a coffee, then leaves me in his office so I can work. I ask him if there's anything I shouldn't look at while I'm in there, and he laughs and shakes his head at me like I'm crazy.

"What's mine is yours, Kai," he says, before heading to the door. "If you need me, I'm outside in the shed."

Lachy's "shed" is actually a full barn where he does most of his carpentry and woodworking, but we all call it a shed because, strictly speaking, he doesn't have *exactly* the necessary permits to have a building that size on his property. When he first moved in, the property had a single small cabin on it, plus a small shed. Gemms and I live in the updated cabin now, and Lachy got permission to build a larger cabin towards the front of his property, which became his home. Over the years he'd built the "shed" out too, so someone *could* actually live there if they needed to. All of his tools and wood are downstairs, and then on a small second floor is a small bedroom, bathroom, and kitchenette. He used to get so engrossed in a project that he'd end up passing out on a couch out there, which is when he decided to build it out a little. We joke all the time that this is fast becoming a compound – the two bedrooms in Gemma's and my cabin, the living space in the shed, the five rooms in Lachy's massive cabin… and he's working currently on a giant in-ground firepit surrounded by natural stone seating. He's creating our own little slice of utopia.

Flipping on his computer, I wander his office while I wait for it to boot up. Lachy's office is a dream spot for me. I love it here so much. There are floor-to-ceiling, arched windows that look out over the water and the distant mountains. His place is just high enough above ours that everything at our cabin is hidden by trees, and you can only really see the edge of the roof. The walls here are a pale, pale grey, like mist on the water in the dawn, and the trim is a crisp white. Two walls are lined with white, built-in bookshelves, and in the far corner of the room, right by the window, there is an incredibly squishy, white, overstuffed chair and a half, with huge pillows that you sink into like a cloud. Lachy bought it for me right after Gemms and I moved in. I frown slightly as I realize how long it's been since I've been over to his house to hang out.

Walking over to the chair, I look out across the grey water. It's a cool day for October, and a stormfront is just beginning to creep across the sound. Behind me the computer chimes, and as I turn towards the desk, a photo tucked onto one of the shelves catches my eye. It's a picture of me and Lachy, from a couple of months after Gemma and I moved into the cabin. I'm curled up on an old couch he used to have in his office, passed out completely. My face is tight even in sleep, lines between my brows, mouth downturned, and I flex my jaw looking at how sad I seem even asleep. Lachy is standing over me in the photo, unaware of the camera, and is laying a blanket over me with a strange look on his face that manages to be both hard and soft at the same time. I pick the photo up, examining it. I've never seen it, but I remember the day it was taken.

Gemma and I had decided to move in together maybe three months before the photo was taken. She had, in typical Gemma style, let her lease lapse accidently and was really and truly stuck. I helped her out for a couple of weeks, letting her sleep on the couch in my tiny studio apartment, but I was due to re-sign soon, and the current living situation wasn't tenable. Once we decided to move in together, we had to find a place quickly, and we were getting increasingly desperate after viewing the seventh property in as many days. Studio apartments were going for $1800 a month at less than 500 square feet, and our combined requirements meant that almost nothing worked for us. I couldn't live in an apartment building – the press of emotions was too much and invaded my psyche even in my sleep. Gemma needed some natural light for her art but also needed to be close enough to downtown that she could get to class and work. It was impossible.

"Oh. My. God!" she whispered frantically under her breath, all the while maintaining a frenetic smile as a landlord showed us a dilapidated converted garage which had been listed as an "adorable fixer-upper with gorgeous natural light in a charming garden". The landlord motioned towards the hole in the crumbling ceiling, which had a skylight kind of placed *over* the hole, and grunted something about a small leak. Gemma grabbed my hand and, eyes wide, muttered, "This is where we're going to die. This guy has skin suits in his basement, Kai! Call the police! He's never letting us go!"

I wanted to tell her she was overreacting, but the pulse of dirty emotions coming from him were as stained and dank as his wife-beater. He showed us the two minute bedrooms, lust flaring as he pointed out the recessed lighting in the rooms, and I elbowed Gemma as I looked more carefully at the ones directly over the bed frames. "Cameras, *cameras!*"

Gemma frowned and looked more carefully around her. "So what would my commute to the *Police Station* be?" she stressed loudly as she leveled the creep with a stare.

Needless to say, our tour was cut short, and Gemma sent off a frantic text reporting him as we left.

Sighing deeply, she frowned, and I felt a touch of concern wash over me before she fuzzed out. "I'm not gonna lie to you, Kai. I'm getting a little worried."

I nodded, agreeing with her. "I know. I *know.* Look at this shit!" I waved a worn newspaper in front of her. "Charming, unique bungalow..." we both shook our heads at that one – the charming, unique bungalow had been a condemned dumpster fire, "small, quaint studio... quirky, lively house-share... the list is terrible!" We stood, heads together, pouring over the paper desperately looking for something, anything, that could work for us. Gemma pointed to a short ad near the bottom of the page.

"Small, two-bedroom cabin on the Sound. Kitchen, separate dining, great room, sunroom. Two and a half bath, wood floors, wood-burning fireplace? Small porch?!?!" Her voice got higher and higher as she read the listing, until nearby dogs were wincing at the tone. Then everything plummeted as she read the last line. "Oh. Vashon Island. Inquire re price."

We both deflated. Vashon was nowhere near our price range, and an "inquire about price" never boded well. Still, we were really at the end of our ropes and called to arrange a tour that same afternoon. Gemma handled the phone call and looked worried as she hung up. "How'd they sound?" I asked anxiously, and she replied, "Brusque" with a wince.

The ferry ride over was stunning. The sound stretched out flat and smooth before us, mountains high and bright in the distance. The salt air was cool and sharp even for November, and it felt like we were leaving real life behind us as we stepped off the boat. A mammoth man was waiting for us, leaning against a beat-up old truck. Maybe 6'3 or 6'4 with auburn, wind-tousled hair and a well-kept, matching beard, the guy had on a tight flannel shirt with sleeves rolled up, exposing strong, corded forearms and rough, calloused hands. He had on dark, muddy jeans and beat-up boots and looked at us through cool, though not unfriendly, whiskey-colored eyes that were catching the edge of what little sunlight was showing that day.

We stood looking at each other awkwardly until he said in the deepest voice I had *ever* heard in my life, with just the hint of a Cajun accent, "Lachlainn Baird. Well. Hop in the truck."

Gemma raised a brow at me, and I shrugged in return. Noticing our exchange, a warm sort of amusement floated off the man, though his expression didn't change. He raised his voice slightly and called out over our heads, "Hey! Jordan!" Gemma and I turned to look at a uniformed man who was walking toward us. Lachlainn motioned towards us and said, "I'm taking these two up to look at the cabin for rent. Ladies, your names for Deputy Jordan?"

"Gemma Doll and Kailani Reed," Gemma stammered slightly.

"Well, Ms. Doll and Ms. Reed are planning on returning to Seattle on the 6:00. If you don't see them, you know I've done something nefarious, so come arrest me."

I tried not to smile, and so did Gemma, but the thought of the tiny, wiry policeman trying to arrest the bear of a man beside us was amusing. Evidently Jordan thought so as well, as he rolled his eyes and said, "Ladies, you're safe with Mr. Baird here. He may bore you to death talking about woodwork and carpentry, but otherwise you couldn't be in better company."

The drive to the cabin wasn't too long, and Gemma and I were too busy quietly exchanging longing glances with each other as we noticed the beauty of the island to talk much. Coming around a particularly empty bend with nothing but trees and thick vegetation as far as the eye could see, Lachlainn turned down a rough dirt path that had been hidden in the undergrowth. We drove through open gates, then briefly passed a turn to a stunning, modern wooden house with enormous windows and a deck, before driving down through a thick growth of trees and suddenly emerged in a clearing. In front of us was a gorgeous, *gorgeous* cabin made of wood, glass, and concrete, with the Sound immediately beyond it. Gemma and I looked at each other in complete despair. It was, without a doubt, the most perfect place we could have asked for, and by the time Lachlainn finished showing us silently around, we both could have cried.

"Could we... could we just look at it one more time?" Gemma asked sadly as Lachlainn watched through careful eyes. He nodded, and Gemma and I drifted different ways as we both tried to think of any way to make this cabin ours forever. Gemma went back to the small sunroom off the side of the home, no doubt dreaming of canvas and paint, and I went back to the porch leading down to the water. Staring out, feeling exhausted suddenly, I imagined how *nice* it would be, just to be here, in this peace, and call this place home. A warm presence lit up beside me, and I turned to face the landlord.

"Well?" he asked.

"I mean..." I waved my hands around helplessly.

"I know. It's a bit isolated."

"It's *perfect!*" I replied fiercely, and desperately. "It's perfect," I said once more, more calmly, but hopelessly.

He watched the emotions flash over my face and furrowed his brow. "Well. What's the problem then?"

"I'm inquiring about the price, I guess," I replied.

He shrugged. "How much do you pay now?"

I named the figure, which had previously seemed enormous for one person to pay for a studio apartment in the city but now seemed unbelievably tiny standing on the deck of this paradise. "That's just what I pay on my own..." He frowned thoughtfully. "I know," I said sadly. "I know. I appreciate you showing us the place though."

"There are two of you?"

I nodded miserably.

"And you both work in the city?"

Again, I nodded. He hummed quietly under his breath, the sound unexpectedly soothing, like a cat's purr. "I think we'd have to double it, then subtract maybe a quarter of that to account for your commute, no? And then just work something into the contract about upkeep or something."

I stared up at him, completely confused, and he flashed a stunning smile at me.

"Welcome home, Kailani."

From there it was a rapid series of events. It started with moving our tiny scraps of furniture and having Lachy looking at them, disgusted with the craftsmanship, before replacing them with solid, raw-wood bedroom sets "to fit the aesthetic of the cabin", and ended, somehow, with weekly Sunday dinners at Lachy's place. He'd cook for us while Gemma would entertain us with wild, exuberant stories of her work, or school, or friends, and I would sit quietly in the corner, taking it all in, cautiously, waiting for the other shoe to drop. Lachy would watch me carefully, nudging a bit more food my way, or trying to draw me out with conversation, but in those days I was more of a scared cat than a tiger.

Early one morning after a particularly rough night at the diner, I'd spent hours baking cupcakes and 7-layer bars and small lemon tartlets. Gemma stumbled into the kitchen, rubbing her eyes, and looked around, confused.

"What... ah... what is this?" she said.

I shrugged anxiously, waiting for her to get upset at the mess or decide that it was just too much dealing with me. Her face softened, and she walked over to sit on a bar stool. "Well, whatever this is, I have never been happier to have you as a roommate than right now!" and she stuffed a lemon tart into her mouth, moaning slightly at the taste. "Oh my gods, Kai. Marry me. Make an honest woman of me. If you can give me orgasms from food, why do I need a man?"

Startled, I laughed, and we decided to put together a plate to take up to Lachy's. He'd answered the door all rumpled and tired but smiled when he saw us and the food. Gemma motioned to me and said, "Kai's been baking!"

He took the plate reverently. "Are you trying to bribe me to do something with all this sugar? I mean, it would work, but what do you need fixed?"

I shook my head silently, and, still smiling, he leaned over to look me in the eye. "You still have sugar all over you," and he wiped off my cheek with one calloused thumb, before saying thoughtfully, "Hmmm. Alright. While you're here, I want to let you know about some work I'm going to do on the property."

He'd taken us into his office, and while he and Gemma talked, I'd fallen asleep on his couch, exhausted from the night before, and the weeks before, and the months before. There was something so comforting about his home, and so comforting about him, it was almost impossible not to relax in his presence. I'd drifted on the edge of sleep for a long time and heard him ask her, concerned, "How's she doing?"

Gemma answered, "I think she's healing from something, Lachy. I don't know what, but…"

Sleep had grabbed me then, and I'd missed out on the rest of the conversation. I woke up covered with a blanket, the late afternoon light casting shadows in the office. Lachy was at his desk and smiled over at me as I blinked blearily, stretching like a child waking from a deep sleep.

"Oh my gosh!" I whispered frantically. "I'm so sorry!"

"Well now," he rumbled. "We can't have that now, can we? My supplier of baked goods needs to be well rested." He frowned at the couch I was on. "There's no way that's comfortable…" he added thoughtfully.

I grabbed my things up in a flurry, folding the blanket and moving towards the door. "I'm so sorry," I repeated. "I was just tired… Why didn't Gemma… Oh my gosh…"

Lachy moved towards me slowly and reached out to grab my hands. Holding them, he ran his thumbs over my skin gently and said quietly, "Kailani, that corner is your corner. It's your spot now, okay? I like you here. It's okay. Okay?"

I calmed down as he held my hands still, and whispered,

"Okay" softly. Lachy looked up and smiled at me with the full force of his happiness, and I could feel it radiating off of him, letting me know he meant every word.

"So now, Suge, I'm putting in a request for next time. Can you do beignets?" I nodded carefully, and he said softly, "I'm glad you're here now."

I smiled slowly back up at him until his happiness washed over me and mixed with my own, and my face crinkled up into my squashed, Cheshire-Cat smile, and his look changed as his eyes widened and his breath skipped, and he repeated even more quietly, "Extra glad you're here."

Returning to the present, I stare at the photo. Gemma must have taken it during the quiet moment, and I wonder, with some unnamed feeling accelerating my heartbeat, why Lachy has it here, where he can see it every day from his desk.

IN THE DNA

Thursday, 11 October – Kailani

Arriving at the Gaia Headquarters located on the waterfront in Downtown Seattle, I stare at the complex in front of me. The building, commissioned by Cole and designed by Frank Gehry, is a massive, modern, twisting sculpture which reflects the water both in form as well as literally on its silver sides. It has an open, meticulously clean plaza in front of it, all white-grey stone, and the entire thing reminds me of Cole herself. Modern and functional, but with a surprising heart in the middle of the cold, somewhat sterile, though beautiful, landscape.

The guys had insisted upon coming with me, despite not being expressly invited and against my vigorous protests, and I'm flanked on all sides by stern, somewhat sour-looking men. We'd had an incredible row over coming here as a unit – I'd wanted to ride my bike, Deo wanted to take a car, and Smith and Donovan had some other plans. Smith ended up pulling rank, and we had to fall in a very reluctant line. I'm pretty sure they're *all* having second thoughts about working together. I know I am.

There's no visible security, but as soon as we step into the square in front of the building, a harried-looking woman comes scurrying out of nowhere to meet us, holding a clipboard and speaking briskly into a walkie-talkie which is clenched in her hand.

"I *am* sorry!" she calls out in a crisp British accent as soon as she's within polite earshot. "I wasn't expecting you for another–" checking her watch, she frowns briefly, "half an hour! I was just about to send a car!" She looks at us questioningly, though not accusingly. I'm about to step forward when Smith moves from beside me to address the flustered woman.

"I'm so sorry to have intruded," he begins in a deep, thunder-rumble of a voice that has me curling my toes unintentionally. "It's my fault, you see. Ms. Reed indicated she was invited, and curiosity got the better of me. I do hope that's alright, Ms...." he smiles at her with what is, I'm sure, meant to be a gentle, coaxing smile, but looks more like a feral, dangerous sort of flashing of his teeth. I wouldn't have blamed her for stripping naked and jumping him in that moment, and from the way her clipboard shakes in her hand, I'm sure she's having a thought or two about how quickly she could get her buttons undone.

"Agnew. Fallon Agnew," she says, honest to god almost panting.

"Nice to meet you, Fallon," he murmurs. "I'm sure Ms. Cole won't have a problem with our presence if *you* explain it to her."

Rolling my eyes, I push past Donovan, who tries to stop me, and move forward, Deo glued to my side. "My god, Smith," I gripe. "You met Fallon when Elizabeth came to the station. Hi, Fallon. Can you let Elizabeth know we're here, and apologize for us being so early?"

She blinks up at Smith like she's having a hard time looking away from him but responds softly, "Of course, Ms. Reed." She reluctantly walks a few feet away and says something quietly into her walkie-talkie, before leading us into the cavernous foyer of the building. Cole is descending from a twisting staircase to our left as we enter and has an amused look on her face, which she smooths out rapidly as she walks straight to Smith.

"Agent Smith, I'm delighted you could join us."

He shoots me a look saying, *see? It's fine*, and I grit my teeth in frustration. Cole has taken Smith's arm and is leading him forward through the entrance hall to a long corridor in the back. She waves off security as they approach with badges for us and leads us into a large meeting room. "Please, everyone, sit. I'm so glad you could all be here. I thought it would just be Ms. Reed," she shoots me her signature half smile, "but of course I'm thrilled to have the entire team."

Smith and Donovan start mumbling half explanations when an older, white-haired gentleman in a crisp lab coat enters the room, along with a nondescript, though well-built man. Cole motions to them with a smile.

"Agent Smith, Agent Donovan, Agent Tanaka, Mr. Shotridge, may I introduce our head scientist, Dr. Phos, as well as our head of security, Mr. Nikos. I've asked them to come and brief you thoroughly on where we are with our little project." She moves towards me, still smiling, and takes my arm in hers. "Gentlemen," she says, giving a little nod, "I'm sure you won't mind if Ms. Reed and I go have a coffee. I've gotten in a new sculpture which I'm dying to get her opinion on, and I'd love to show her my office. I've just redecorated, you see, and want to peacock a bit, if you will."

Smith flashes her a tolerant smile and waves vaguely at her. "Of course, Ms. Cole. I'm sure Reed would be more than happy to keep you company while we run through the information here."

Tanaka hovers between the table and Cole and myself, a frown marring his face. "We really should have Reed with us..." he begins, only to be interrupted by Cole.

"Oh come now, Agent Tanaka. I'll return Ms. Reed to you in one piece, I promise. I'm sure you can brief her later on the proceedings." He looks at me, uneasy, and I give him a miniscule nod, which he returns, before turning to the table. Jonah stays by my side, silent, but radiating a happy, puppylike energy.

Donovan motions towards the door. "Let her go, Tanaka. We've got enough brain power here. We'll call if we need to have a talk about our feelings," he says dismissively. Tanaka looks angry and opens his mouth to argue, I think, when Jonah interrupts.

"I'll just come with you, if that's alright," he says cheerfully. "I'm absolutely no help here, and god knows I could use a coffee. I'll be silent, like the grave, yeah? But cooooooffeeee..."

Even Elizabeth can't resist the overwhelming happiness that is Jonah, and her practiced smile relaxes into something more genuine. "All right," she concedes. Jonah flashes me a small smile of triumph, which quickly changes into an adorably bewildered face as we leave the room and Cole motions to one of three waiting secretaries standing outside the room.

"Ms. Jentru, if you'd please be so kind as to take Mr. Shotridge to the lounge and show him where our coffee shop is, I'd greatly appreciate it. He's in rather desperate need, I'm afraid."

Jentru hops to it, and Jonah is taken away quickly, looking back at me as though he's trying to figure out why I'm not coming. Cole takes me the opposite way towards a hidden staircase and rolls her eyes, which is the most human look I've seen on her face.

"Oh lord," she sighs. "Honestly, how do you put up with that every day?"

Startling a laugh out of me, I search for a response, glancing towards Fallon as we reach the top of the stairs. Something is different about her, and it takes me a moment before I realize she's walking with a purpose, no scuttling or simpering, all traces of the mousy, harried personal assistant gone. She hands Cole a stack of papers, which Cole looks through quickly while saying, "So. We had some unexpected guests this morning, hmmm?"

Fallon grins at Cole, shaking her head. "It was fine. He laid on what I assume was supposed to be heavy flirtation, and I batted my eyes at him. Voila."

My eyes widen in surprise. "You mean Smith? This

morning?"

Both women laugh real, ringing peals of laughter. "Yes, Kailani. Smith."

Fallon rolls her eyes, before saying mockingly in a good imitation of her earlier, panting voice, "Oh yes, Agent Smith. Right away!"

Cole shakes her head with amused disapproval. "Oh Fallon, not really that bad." Both turn to me and laugh again at the apparent shock on my face. "Did she sound like that, Kailani?"

I nod, starting to smile. "She did. She really, really did. I thought she was about to climb him like a tree."

"Oh no," Fallon almost purrs. "I'd be much more likely to scale something slightly smaller." She gives me a wicked look which has me blushing to my toes, and Cole rolls her eyes again. "Come now, Fallon. No flirting with the guests please."

Fallon gives me a sort of "oh well" shrug, which also seems to be a bit of a "we'll see about that" shrug, and leads us through a complex series of hallways and staircases until we reach a nondescript door. Cole turns to her assistant with quietly murmured instructions, then opens the door to reveal an enormous, glass-walled office which looks out over the waterfront in Seattle. It's a stupendous view, with floor-to-ceiling windows. There is a clear desk and a low, clear coffee table, and the floors are a dark, burnished wood. There are two small, white couches, as well as a coffee station and drinks bar. In the near corner there is an elaborate silk screen, which Fallon quickly disappears behind. Otherwise, the office is completely empty.

"Well, Kailani," says Cole in an amused, simpering voice. "Do you like what I've done with the place?"

I look around, unsure, and she laughs. "I haven't spent a day in my life decorating. It's just an easy excuse men tend to buy – decorating, makeup, shoes... all these things I have little to no interest in, but are good ways to guarantee *some* level of privacy, hmmm? We'll go shoe shopping next time I'd like to see you. That should make sure we have no hangers-on."

Although I'm smiling, I do feel the need to defend my team. "We are a unit, Elizabeth," I begin. "It's natural…"

"Are you?" she says cryptically. "Because if they were here, you'd have two of them talking over you, one reminding you at every step to guard your words, and one… well, I'm not sure what Mr. Shotridge would do, actually."

"He'd be distracting me," I reply, somewhat reluctantly.

"Exactly," she says. "Now. I realized after our last meeting that, while I know quite a lot about you, I didn't give you a chance to ask any questions of me. I'd like you to feel comfortable with us working together, Kailani, and I do feel I should say up front that my goal at the end of this is to hijack you and bring you to our team."

My brows shoot up in surprise, and Elizabeth does a short half-laugh. "Yes, yes. I understand. It's surprising for me to admit it so openly, hmmm? I work a bit differently than your Ms. Gomez. I find I have much better luck if I'm direct from the beginning. I told you it's a talent of mine to recognize value, and you, Ms. Reed, are woefully undervalued where you are currently. It's nothing to talk about now, of course, but let me be frank. We have a diverse, exciting environment that is light-years ahead of CDS in regards to research. And, not to be gauche, but your pay would be *significantly* more substantial. For now, however, let's begin with any questions you may have of me."

She walks over to the coffee area, giving me a moment to collect my thoughts.

"Sugar? Cream?" she calls over her shoulder.

"Just cream please," I reply. "Elizabeth… I guess my main question is – why do you believe all this? You're so scientifically minded, why is this so easy for you to accept?"

She smiles and indicates I should sit, as she passes me my coffee.

"I suppose, for me, it's *because* science, not in spite of science, that extrasensory abilities are not only possible, but plausible."

I look at her questioningly, and she continues. "Why are there different blood types, Kailani?"

Shaking my head, I respond, "I don't know. Something about disease and immunity, I think?"

She nods but says, "That's more what the different blood types do – they process sugar differently, have different responses to viruses, etc. But *why* do they exist? Why are we genetically so similar, yet so different? Why did our DNA mutate to create these different types of something which is so essential to all human life? And what does it mean for human survival? What does it mean for the future? Are there further mutations coming which will alter blood types and provide a new grouping? For example – what blood type are most Olympic athletes, and why? If a blood type is eradicated, what impact does that have on human development? What does it mean, in a broader sense, that certain blood types clash so badly that you would perish from receiving a wrongly categorized infusion? We are all humans, are we not? The same basic building blocks create us all? And yet there are people who feel no pain, who remember every moment that has ever happened, who can play any piece of music they have ever heard, who have no capacity to forget. Super endurance – there is a man who ran for 350 miles without stopping once, even to sleep... men whose lungs hold up to 50% more oxygen than the average person... hyper photographic memory... echolocation abilities..."

I sit, staring at her, confused but fascinated. She leans forward towards me and grabs my hand, flipping it over so we're both staring at the veins in my wrist.

"Kailani, I don't believe in magic. I believe there are answers to questions that have been asked throughout history, and I believe..." she traces my vein lightly with a single finger, "I believe... that the answers lie in these tiny molecules." Letting go of my hand, she watches as I pull it back to me, cradling it slightly in my lap, cautious, slightly afraid, but captivated.

"There's no need to be afraid, Kailani." She stands up and goes to stare out the windows. "My single mindedness can be intimidating, I know. It's something about myself that I can't change, much like you. The world is a tangled ball of mystery, and there's something within me day and night, driving me to unknot it and discover what it all means. It is built into *my* DNA, Kailani, as your sensing of emotions is, I believe, built into yours. It is the heart beating within me, finding the answer to the question my parents were looking for... the why."

I move to stand near her, and I look down to the ground, far below me. "For now, Elizabeth, I just want to help the people I can."

"Then we are not as different as we seem, hmmm? I just want to help the people I can as well."

Walking back to the couches, we sit, and for the rest of the afternoon we talk about the things we can do to help, and how we can work together to save the people who can't save themselves.

By the time we rejoin the rest of the team, several hours have passed. Elizabeth and I had a surprisingly easy discussion, despite our differences. I suppose we're two sides of the same coin – emotion and logic. Fallon sat silently in the background taking notes, though her private persona with Elizabeth was much different than her public persona. Elizabeth noted my surreptitious looks at one point, and smirked. "We find it much easier if Fallon scuttles around behind me most of the time. People take less notice of her, you see, when she makes herself small, and they speak more freely in front of her when I have to excuse myself. We've avoided several disasters that way... people wanting to contribute to Gaia for tax loopholes, or to launder money, etc. She may not have your backbone, but she's my right-hand woman." Fallon flushed with pleasure at the compliment, and I realized that Elizabeth must not give out praise lightly. "I'm somewhat surprised, actually, that with your steel spine you weren't able to convince your team to stay back."

I shrugged uncomfortably, unwilling to say anything bad about my unit, despite their recent behavior. "It's a new team. We're still finding our voices and our places."

Leveling me with a stern look, she responded, "Well, the rest were content to let your place be looking at a remodeled office, and your voice be heard only commenting on my new artwork. I admire your loyalty, Kailani, but I admire your fighting spirit more, and I'm not seeing that at the moment."

Feeling vaguely like I'd disappointed my school principal, I changed the topic, but the uneasiness remained, leaden in my stomach.

When we walk into the conference room, still debating some finer points of a plan we had roughly concocted, we're met with a wall of silence. The men are all sitting around the table, staring at us. Smith looks thoughtful, Donovan annoyed, Hideo concerned, but it's sweet Jonah who catches my attention. His normally placid face is lit up with anger, and he flies to his feet as soon as he sees me.

"Four HOURS! FOUR HOURS, KAI!!! *Where* have you *been?*"

I stutter to a halt, completely confused. "I've been with Elizabeth. You knew that."

"We've been trying to reach you via your mobile," Hideo interjects calmly. "You haven't been answering."

I glance down at my phone, then wave it in front of them. "No signal. Why didn't you just send someone to get me if there was an emergency?"

"I'm afraid that's my fault, in some ways," Elizabeth says coolly. "We track all cell traffic anywhere beyond the entrance hall and this first conference room, but my office is completely blocked in order to maintain strict privacy. And the staff knows not to interrupt me, barring emergency situations." She looks around, face laced with a sort of disdainful amusement. "*Has* there been an emergency of some sort?"

Following her gaze, I notice the leftovers of a large lunch littering the table, plus fresh cups of coffee, and several small plates full of deserts. There are white boards with lists in various handwriting, and stacks of files and papers scattered around. I raise an eyebrow. "You seem to have been really concerned. Distraught even..." I motion towards Donovan, who freezes, a bite of cake halfway to his mouth. "Drowning your sorrows in cheesecake, hmmm?"

Smith responds, light irritation and frustration lacing his tone. "That's not the point, Reed. We're a team, and we need to know the movements of our team to be effective. You running off for hours at a time doesn't help anyone. Yes, we were able to get some work done, but this was meant to be a brief meeting. Not an entire afternoon."

"*This* wasn't meant to be a group activity at all!" Elizabeth interjects, real annoyance heavy in her voice for the first time. "If you'll recall, gentlemen, *only* Kailani was invited to my premises. I let you stay in a show of goodwill, but you forced your presence on us. If we *must* tolerate you, we will, but please do not be the barnacle on the whale and demand the whale follow your directions."

I meet her eyes, embarrassed by the guys' behavior and by my tolerance of it.

"Ms. Cole, I'm sorry for imposing upon you, but we were under the impression that this meeting would be beneficial to the movements of our team as a whole, which is why we–"

Elizabeth laughs in a short, sharp way, scoffing slightly.

"What team?" she says, echoing her earlier thoughts. "Who is on this supposed team? Whose voices matter and are heard, hmmm? You were perfectly happy to let Kailani come with me and skip the bulk of the meeting, yes? It was only when you were inconvenienced by the lack of her presence that you noticed her absence. Why? Did she drive? Do you have the keys?" she says, turning to me. I shake my head mutely. "You're all free to leave at any time." Elizabeth motions towards the door. "I believe you were offered company cars back when you started whinging about your presence here. Several times, in fact."

Jonah, still standing, holds out his hands placatingly, but frustration still creases his features. "That's not entirely fair," he says firmly. "I wanted to come with you. It was important to me to have someone stay with Kai."

Elizabeth's face softens slightly as she looks at him. "That is true," she responds. "But you weren't invited."

Fallon clears her throat softly from the doorway, and Elizabeth starts slightly, then raises a hand to rub her brow lightly. "Yes. Well. Kailani, I hope you know how much I've enjoyed our time together today. The front desk staff have your pass ready, and my assistant has organized an office on the first floor for you. My head of security is under instructions to make himself available at your discretion. Let me know how the plan is received, and thank you for a lovely afternoon. Gentlemen? You will not be welcome back."

With that, she sweeps out of the room, leaving the rest of us in silence. After a disappointed look at the rest of them, I follow, walking out of the room and the building, and heading straight home.

MILQUETOAST AND TEAMWORK

Friday, 12 October – Kailani

I get to the office earlier than usual the next day, having been unable to sleep the night before after the meeting with Elizabeth. Thinking through the night, I recognize that I've been lacking in the "self-care" department, and as much as I hate new-age speak and buzz words, as an empath, if I don't give myself time to fully rest and recover daily, I'll get worn down or worn out, and then bad, bad things happen.

Heading down to the basement, I make a beeline toward the meditation room and am surprised when I see it's occupied by Smith. The lights are always kept low, and the room is divided into small, open sections delineated by pale fabric curtains. There's an open view of every section from the doorway, and from each section you can see the door, but once you're in your little area you're cut off from the others in the room. Smith is almost immediately in front of the door, and his eyes fly open the second the air pressure changes. I hesitate for a moment, but I *really* need this time, and I let my eyes slide politely away from his without really connecting.

Settling down in the section furthest from the door, I sink into Lotus Pose and relax into my six-stage breathing. The world outside hammers at me as I chase silence, and it isn't until I hear the door softly open and close that I'm able to wrap my mind in a soft blanket of blankness. Losing all track of time, I stay there, blank and empty in perfect peace, only surfacing when I hear another person enter the quiet room. I look up quickly, but it's only one of our social workers, who gives me a soft, apologetic smile, which I return, before stretching and gathering my things. Exiting as quietly as possible, I take a moment to let my eyes adjust to the harsh light of the hallway, and startle to see Smith sitting on the floor in front of me, leaning tiredly against the wall. He opens heavy eyes and looks up at me.

"Hey, Reed," he says softly. "I think we need to talk."

We go to our conference room, my stomach clenched in nervous anticipation of what's to come. No good ever came from the phrase "we need to talk". It's funny how anxious it can make you even when there's nothing to be worried about. Smith and I have no history, no relationship of which to speak. I don't even really want to be part of the task force, except to burn Tennireef, so I honestly have no concerns. Even still. "We need to talk." Ugh.

We sit in neutral territory, opposite sides of the table, but in the middle, between where he and Donovan and Deo, Jonah, and I normally sit. He audibly exhales and looks at me.

"Okay, Reed. What are we going to do?"

I meet his eyes, frowning slightly in confusion. "What do you mean?"

He motions in the air between the two of us. "This isn't working. And we need it to work. I owe you an apology. I took what you and Tanaka presented at face value, because, to be honest, it was easier. But I read through the cases again last night. Spent the entire night looking through the last sixteen months of your work as partners. And I dismissed your part in this too quickly. I'm sorry."

I breathe out slowly, thinking through his words. "I owe you one as well. Deo and I are used to having to present our information in a certain way in order for people to feel that it's valid, and we fell into that habit when presenting to the team."

He shakes his head and holds up a massive hand to stop me. "No. We're working as a team, and however you lead us through your cases, whatever part you play or Tanaka plays, you're still partners and had vital parts solving those cases. We, Donovan and I, overlooked that. I mean, you left mid-meeting one day and I didn't even stop you." He clenches his jaw in frustration, though with himself rather than with me. "I'm a better team lead than that. I know better than that. But I had blinders on. This is new for me, Reed. The use of CDS as an asset is, to put it mildly, unheard of. Our part in this started almost two years ago, chasing down drug runners. It was a joint task force between the FBI, CIA, and DEA... the things we saw... it took a long time to move past some of it. And then the higher ups decided to try a new direction with CDS. To be frank, none of us were on board with it. We had two guys retire from the agency in protest. It was a–"

A sharp knock sounds at the door, and then it's opened slowly. One of the officers who mans the front desk opens the door slowly and smiles when he sees me.

"Sorry for interrupting, Reed, but you have a special visitor I thought you'd like to see."

Opening the door a little farther, the officer reveals a young girl, hair in two bunches on the top of her head. A huge smile lights up her face and is echoed on mine.

"Lani!" she shrieks; we both squeal happily as she runs to my waiting arms. I pull her up into an enormous hug.

"Mikaela! What in the world? What are you doing here?"

"Mama Cass brought me! I'm on my way to school, and I told her you worked here and I haven't seen you in *weeks!*" The last was said very accusingly, as only a seven-year-old can.

"I told you, girl! I've been busy, but I promised to come

by next week and you know I keep my promises. Now then, where's Mama Cass?"

An older woman peeks her head around the door, a sheepish look on her face. "Mikaela! You know I can't move as fast as you! I told you we could only see if Ms. Kailani was available, not bum rush her meeting!" Affection wars with exasperation in her tone as the little girl on my lap turns her gap-toothed grin to the newcomer.

"Lani, I got my forever Mama! That's why I had to come tell you!"

I stand up immediately, taking Mikaela with me in my arms. Turning to face the older woman, I make a face of mock despair. "You didn't! You should have talked to me first! She'll eat all the ice cream! She snores! She sings off tune!"

Mikaela swats me and giggles. "Laaaaani!"

I kiss her cheek and hug her close to me. "I'm just teasing, kiddo. I'm so happy for you both. The paperwork finally went through?"

Cass nods at me with relief clear on her face. "Once you and Mr. Hideo sent in your letters of recommendation. And I hear someone made a phone call or two?" She raises an eyebrow at me with a faux-stern look.

I shake my head at her. "Come on now, Cass. You know Mom-looks don't work on me. You need to grow up with one for them to have any effect."

Cass's face softens, and she reaches out a hand to cup my face. "Now, now, Ms. Kailani. I'll take you too if you're not careful."

I smile at her and squeeze the wriggly girl in my arms again. "Can I come celebrate with you soon, K? Cupcakes all around!"

She nods and wraps her small arms around my neck. "Thank you for my Mama, Lani."

Eyes welling up a little, I put her down and kiss her head. "Sorry I can't visit longer today, but next time for sure.

Thanks for coming to tell me, buddy. I'm so happy for you."

They wave and are escorted out, and I take a moment to wipe my eyes before sitting down again across from Smith. He looks at me curiously, silently asking for an explanation.

"Oh. Yeah. Before I worked in investigations, I was in Child Protective Services. Mikaela was... it wasn't a great situation. I got her out, but the courts sent her back after six months in foster. Things got worse, not better, and by that time I was on Investigations. Deo and I kind of – hmmm – used the tools we had available to us to expose what was going on in her house. And went through some back channels to get her placed in a stable environment. They were dragging their feet a little on the adoption paperwork, so I made some calls and called in some favors." I beam, mostly to myself, at the thought of her face moments ago when she told me she had a forever mama, then try to school my face into something more serious, but the damned smile keeps breaking through.

Smith sighs. "I'd really like it if we could start over, Reed."

"We're not on bad terms, Smith," I reply.

"We're not really on good terms either though, are we? I'd like to see some of that–" he motions behind me towards the door, "in here. Some of that happiness. You're defensive, and I get that. We've put you in that position. But this task force is together for as long as it takes to infiltrate and bring down Kronos, and I've been at that for two years already at this point. I don't want two more years of distrust and defensiveness. I want us to be a team. I don't want you to be miserable the whole time."

I look at him thoughtfully. "I'm all for being a team, Smith, but it takes time to find that balance. We can start over, start at the beginning, but we can't jump straight to full trust."

He nods. "Starting over is all I'm asking for at this point. I–" His phone rings, and he glances at it, then to me. "I have to take this. I'm sorry. Smith here," he says brusquely as he answers. His voice changes slightly as he continues, from short and annoyed to friendly but annoyed, like you'd speak to a sibling almost. "Seef? What's up?"

He doesn't drop his voice and locks eyes with me briefly before grabbing a sheet of paper and taking some notes. "We haven't had a Viewer here in ages, but I can send it back to CDS and see what they can pull… What have you tried?… Mmmhmm, so you think a… well have you even met her yet? Oh Jesus. *Ryder?* How's that going?" Smith barks out a short, amused laugh. "Seef, no guarantees, right? But I can try to have something to you tomorrow, maybe Monday at the latest. What's she like?… Oh Christ on a cracker, that's not promising… It's a saying, Seef… Lots of people say… Well, I *am* American." He rolls his eyes at me, and I flash a quick smile back at him. It's nice seeing him funny and frustrated, instead of composed and serious. "Okay. What else have you heard?… Mmmm… I *am* writing it down, Seef. Magda? Draco? Oh, sorry. Ratko?" He shakes his head, frowning now. "Nothing here… Yeah. Keep me updated. I'll check for you on the other thing. Right. Later."

Hanging up, he frowns at the paper briefly and makes a quick note in his phone, before looking up at me. "Right, it's time we get the entire team on the same page. As soon as the others get here, we'll begin." He stands and flashes a bone-melting smile at me. "I'm heading to grab a coffee. You want one? Cream only, right?" I nod, somewhat surprised, and he leaves.

The room is still empty when he returns, though, looking at the clock, I know Deo should be here shortly. Smith sits directly across from me again and pushes my drink towards me. I flash a small smile of thanks, and we sit in companionable silence for a moment, before he leans forward and pins me down with a stare.

"Alright Reed. The rest are going to be here shortly, but I'd like to have an idea of what would make this a more companionable working environment for you."

My lips twitch slightly. I can tell he's trying, but it's so *Smith* to use a phrase like "companionable working environment" rather than "less hellmouth, more puppies" or something. He catches my almost smile but soldiers on. "You have a good professional relationship with Tanaka, and seem to get along well with Shotridge, so I'm thinking it's just me and Donovan."

My face wrinkles in a dubious expression before I can stop it, and I quickly try to smooth it, but this time Smith doesn't let it slide. "You *don't* have a good relationship with Tanaka?" He watches me carefully, then nods as if to himself. "Not Tanaka. Shotridge then. What's the problem there? I thought you guys got along well?"

I shrug slightly, fighting with myself. The problem is that I like Jonah *so much* as a person, so I don't want to throw him under the bus at all, but he doesn't seem to have much faith in me as an agent. He's always trying to protect me from all angles, but he's a baby officer, and it ends up seeming disrespectful because he doesn't seem to understand my seniority and experience. Deo and I may butt heads sometimes, but there's no doubt in my mind that he thinks I'm fully as capable as he is. Smith is watching and waiting, clearly seeing the struggle play out on my face, and doesn't pressure me, letting me work through things on my own, which I appreciate.

"Eh..." I begin, quite elegantly. "I really like Shotridge. He's *great*. He is."

"Uh-oh!" laughs Smith. "Never a good start."

"I just... he's not a problem to work with. I enjoy his presence, and he makes things easier. He makes me laugh, and that helps me so much. It's just... sometimes he makes things *too* easy, does that make sense? He wants to protect me, I think, but it comes across as not thinking I can handle myself, or take care of myself. But it's all from a good place. It's not easy to be a Bleeder on the SPD. You're never sure where you fit in – always a little outside. No matter how good you are as an officer, you're also something else, and it makes everyone uncomfortable, if not downright hostile. He just sees us as the same, I think, and wants to shield me from the shit he's taking. Donovan just needs to dial the hostility down a notch. I don't care if he doesn't like me or has a bad attitude, to be honest. Just maybe go from Volcanic hostility to like, regular hostility?"

"And me?" says Smith, clearly making notes in his head.

"You?" I pause, looking at him carefully. "You... nothing."

He looks confused. "Me, nothing?"

I shrug. "I don't know anything about you. We don't clash; we just don't gel either, right? You're the boss. I get that. And you seem... fine? So I guess just time on that one?"

He looks almost hurt, which can't be right, and slightly affronted, which I completely understand. "Let me just make sure I'm understanding you correctly. Tanaka is your trusted partner, Shotridge is your friend, Donovan is a volcano, but I'm... milquetoast?"

I wince slightly. Put like that it *does* sound kind of offensive. Calling a giant Viking "fine" could ruffle some feathers, I guess.

"No!" I say soothingly. "*Not* milquetoast. Of course not." I scrabble to find the right words as his jaw drops open slightly.

"Are you... are you trying to *placate* me?"

"Placate you?" I squeak. "No! Of course not! You're... you're... *inscrutable.* Or... enigmatic?" I question unconvincingly.

He groans and rubs his hands over his face. "Four years Special Forces, six years CIA dark ops, countless hours of kill training and somehow I'm *boring*."

"Not *boring!*" I say helplessly, beginning to laugh a little, which doesn't help matters at all. "You're very... tall?"

He looks at me incredulously and sighs. "How Tanaka has dealt with you for all these years I'll never know."

His teasing tone pulls a full smile from me, which widens even further as I hear a long-suffering voice from behind me agreeing with Smith. "She's impossible. Utterly impossible."

I grin over my shoulder as Hideo walks in the room and chirp, "Aw, come on now, Tanaka. You know you love me."

He rolls his eyes dramatically. "If that's your take-away from our relationship..."

"You know you loooove me, you think I'm preeeeeetty..." I sing off key, thinking back to a weekend we had binge watched romantic comedies together. Deo had a *thing* for Sandra Bullock.

He mock-frowns at me and growls, "Watch it, Reed. Short leash."

MAGNOLIA LANE

Sunday, 14 October – Maela

It's been a quiet weekend. Jorge and Kavi both had to work yesterday, so I took the time to catch up on my chick-lit reading, not that I'd really fallen behind, and determinedly to *not* think about Ratko, Magda, Tennireef, or Rhea. This morning, though, I cleaned the flat. Jorge and Kavi are coming over this afternoon to watch a movie. We were texting, just catching up really; and Kavi found out I've never seen a Bollywood film, and before I knew it, he decided he would bring over *Lagaan*, to introduce me, as he says, to one of India's best exports. Jorge's bringing *jamón serrano* and is going to make *pan con tomate*. I'm bringing: me. It's all going to be very cosmopolitan.

I've cleaned myself up too and am now waiting impatiently for their arrival. They're not due for almost an hour – yeah, I may have been a bit overexcited. I'm lying on the couch with my Kindle in my lap, but I'm not really reading it. I'm wondering what my mother would say if she knew I had not one but two ridiculously good-looking men coming over. I grin: once she'd stopped shrieking with joy and calmed herself down, she'd most likely give me sex tips. My dad, on the other hand, would worry and ask if I knew what I was doing. Parents! Can't live with them: wouldn't want to be without them. There's a beam of sunlight coming in through the window, and I watch the dust motes dancing idly. I'm warm and comfortable, and I let my eyelids slide shut. It was really weird the other day, when I tried to see Magda. Must have caught her in a deep sleep. Everything looks the same now: the soft, swirling blackness punctuated by occasional flecks of color. I yawn and look up. The street in Beckton's deserted today. What was its name? Something inappropriate, dreamt up by a developer to try to over-egg the pudding. Like naming a collection of dreary suburban prefabs "Castle Estates". Magnolia Lane, that was it, for a street that barely had weeds. I hear a high-pitched noise, like a dog yowling, that abruptly cuts off, and I swing my head towards the building that, I now notice, I'm standing right beside. It looks run-down and abandoned, as do the two on either side. It's set a little way back from the road, as if it's a garage or a car showroom. Has a stray dog or cat got trapped inside? There's a whimper, and I start to walk towards the door. I've got to check it out. I can't just leave an animal in pain.

Surprisingly, or maybe not surprisingly, if an animal got in, the door opens; and I slip inside. There's only a dim light, coming through cracks in the boarded-up windows, but enough to see by, and I walk towards the noise. There's another whimper, and I think: *It's OK, sweetie. I'm here. I'll help you.* The noise seems to be coming from a room at the back of the building. I walk towards a door in the far wall, past a desk that maybe once served as reception, but otherwise the room is empty. There's another howl as I reach the door, and I tremble slightly. I hope the animal won't attack me out of pain or fear. But I brace myself and push open the door.

At first, I don't understand what I'm seeing. There are three men: one sitting in a chair, facing me, and two standing next to him. They're half turned away, and I can't quite see their faces. "Should have known better," one of them says. I know that voice, and my breathing starts to speed up. The dragon on the back of his head snarls at me as he turns more fully towards the man in the chair. There's a moan and a shriek, and then Ratko throws something behind him. It lands at my feet, and I look down.

It's a finger. I can see the nail and, and blood on a white

flash of bone where the skin has retracted. I gag. There's another howl, and then another finger flying towards me. A pinky. My stomach revolts, and I press a trembling hand against my mouth. Another cry, another finger. My knees give out, and I cower against the door.

Ratko smiles: "Get me a beer." The other man, small, rat-like, with a scarred face, turns and bends, plucking a bottle out of a cooler. I know him, I think fuzzily. It's ironic, really, because he's born to rule. Emlyn said so. But Ratko cut him. Cut him. Cut him, because their mothers baked cakes together. He looks pale, and his eyes are darting nervously about.

"Šefe," he asks. "should we be doing this here? The neighbors–"

"Won't say a thing." Ratko laughs: "Besides, they're all in church or having Sunday lunch. Right, Altan?"

The man in the chair moans again, and I look up. Emlyn was right, I think. Ratko cut out Altan's tongue before starting on his fingers. Blood drips from the corners of his mouth, staining his chin, splatters on his shirt, and his eyes are dull. I bend over and retch, feeling weak and sick and clammy. I retch and retch until my stomach hurts, but nothing comes out.

Ratko tosses his beer bottle. "So, Altan, shall we get started on the other hand?" The man in the chair quakes and moans. Ratko bends down. "So sorry. I don't understand what you're saying. Vlado, a fresh pair of shears, please."

No! I think. *No!* But the howls start up again.

"You see, Altan," Ratko says conversationally, "bad things happen to greedy people. You should have been content with your corner of North London and the very reasonable payment I wanted. It seems I must remind people of that." Altan shrieks, and I huddle up into a ball, my arms crossed protectively over my head. This can't be happening. Can't. Just. Can't. I will stay very still and very quiet, and when I raise my head again, all will be well. I take a peek: Ratko has the sheers around Altan's thumb, and as I watch, the handles close. I pass out.

When I come to, Altan's head is lolling forward. His shirt is now soaked in red, and rivulets of blood are running down his face. There's a crude design etched into his forehead. Ratko is standing near the body, a look of – peace – on his own face. He seems relaxed and satisfied, as if he's just orgasmed, and is smoking a hand-rolled cigarette. Vlado is packing tools into the cooler.

"Dump the body in Haringey. I want it found quickly," Ratko says. Vlado murmurs assent. Ratko tosses the cigarette to the floor and grinds it under his heel. He turns towards the door, then stills, and smiles. I whimper as Ratko comes closer and closer. He stops, looking down at me with a smirk, then bends over, hand outstretched. I break. I scream and scream as his hand reaches out for me.

"*Querida!*" a voice calls through the fog. "*Querida!*" I don't want to open my eyes, to look at my hands and see bloody stumps where my fingers used to be. I moan and burrow in closer to the warm chest. It smells of bergamot, and I clutch at the soft material I'm lying against.

"She's terrified. I can't get through to her. Kavi, do you think you can help?"

"I can try," another voice rumbles. "Here, give her to me." I feel myself lifted. Are they taking my body away? To dump it? I start to cry, and then I'm enveloped in the scent of sandalwood and spice, and a hand is rubbing slow circles on my back. A hand. Still with its fingers. I cry harder.

"Come on, Maela, *ladki*. Come back to us. You're safe," the voice hums.

"You're safe, *querida*. Come on, open up those pretty blue eyes for us," the first voice coaxes.

But I can't. If I open my eyes, I'll see. And I don't want to. "Gone," I gasp to my rescuers. I can sense their puzzlement.

"What's gone, Maela?"

"F-fingers. Chopped off. Ratko." I sob. "Tell Emlyn."

There's a sharp intake of breath, and then a hand is grasping mine, fingers intertwining. "No, Maela, no. Your fingers are here." The hand rubbing my back never stops its slow circles.

"Not gone?" I quaver.

"No, *querida*." I collapse against the broad chest holding me, quaking, and I can feel a bearded cheek laying itself tenderly over the top of my head as arms tighten around me. It takes a long time, but eventually, I calm and fall asleep.

When I wake up, I'm lying on the couch, with a blanket tucked around me. There's the low murmur of male voices, and blearily I open my eyes and peer at the room. Jorge, Kavi, and Emlyn are sitting round the table, talking quietly. I blink. What are they doing here? And then I remember. Quickly I glance down and could almost weep when I see both hands, whole and unharmed. At that instant, Jorge turns his head and sees that I'm awake.

"Maela! How are you feeling, *querida?*" He, like the other two, looks worried; but while Jorge and Kavi also appear puzzled, Emlyn's mouth is set in a grim line. He knows. I feel a little flutter in my stomach, because I know an explanation is coming, and whisper, "OK. Thirsty." My throat hurts, and my voice is scratchy, as if I've been screaming, but that was just in my vision, right? I'm having trouble distinguishing between what's real and what isn't. Kavi stands and heads to the kitchen, while Jorge comes over and helps me to sit up and then settles beside me. Emlyn leans forward, bracing his arms on his thighs, his eyes searching mine. Some part of my mind registers that he's looking good in jeans and a forest-green sweater. I've never seen him out of his suits before. Kavi hands me a glass of water and sits on my other side; we're a bit squashed now, but their warmth and closeness are comforting. Three pairs of eyes watch me as I gulp down the water.

"So, Maela, do you feel up to talking?" Emlyn asks softly.

I shake my head and wince; even that slight movement hurts, as if my whole body's been battered. "No?" I try. I haven't forgotten prison and don't want to be responsible for Jorge and Kavi getting sent down. Emlyn can clearly read the direction of my thoughts, as he sighs and says, "Don't worry. There won't be any repercussions. I think we're beyond that."

So, haltingly, I tell them about the vision, about Ratko mutilating and murdering Altan and then reaching for me to do the same. At some point, I realize that tears are rolling down my face, but I'm too drained to care. The men sit quietly, listening in silence. When I reach the end, I stare down into my lap, fingers fretting the blanket. I feel terribly exposed.

Jorge is the first to speak. "What a terrible nightmare, *querida!* No wonder you screamed."

Kavi concurs, his deep voice soft and soothing, "I would have too."

I don't say anything, just look up at Emlyn as he takes out his phone. He keeps his eyes on mine during the brief conversation. "Abandoned building... Magnolia Lane... Body... Somewhere in Haringey." I can feel Jorge and Kavi stiffen beside me. "Maela?" Jorge queries. My eyes plead with Emlyn: I don't want to explain. He gives a brief nod.

"Maela is a clairvoyant." His voice is brisk and matter-of-fact. "Specifically, she has the gift, or ability, let's say, of telesthesia. She can witness distant events in real time."

Kavi stirs: "So, this dream–"

"Was no dream," Emlyn responds. "It was a vision. Maela saw a real murder, as it happened. She's the strongest clairvoyant we've ever come across. Most only see in flashes, a few seconds at most. Maela can see for several minutes and in full detail, as if she's watching a movie. Almost as if she's *in* the movie."

"Maela, *querida*," Jorge breathes. "Why didn't you say something? When you know that I... I, of all people–"

I glance up at him, shamefaced, then concentrate on the blanket again.

Emlyn continues: "It was a condition of Maela's... recruitment that she tell no one. Knowledge of the program is strictly controlled, and the penalty for breaking confidentiality is severe."

Kavi stares at him, anger darkening his features. "Recruitment? You mean, when you found out what she could do, you bullied her into working for you and threatened her with – what? Deportation? Prison?"

"Yes," Emlyn says levelly. "She's a valuable asset. We needed her, and we couldn't risk word getting out."

Kavi's arms flex, as if he's just clenched his fists, and his jaw tightens. I put out a hand and pat his thigh. This is all getting very tense. "I want to help, Kavi." I shrug. "I *need* to help." He looks over at me, jadeite eyes incandescent, then places one broad hand over mine.

"Why are you telling us?" Jorge demands, his voice hard. His face is stormy, as if he's a heartbeat away from launching himself at Emlyn.

"What's happened today means that I have no choice. But the same conditions apply. You tell anyone, and you go to prison. The program is too important to compromise. And that's a decision that's far above my paygrade." Emlyn's voice is impassive, and he hasn't moved a muscle, but I can see a single, slight tic at the corner of his eye.

Jorge's own eyes narrow, the color deepening almost to amber. "*Cabrón*," he bites out.

"Yes, I'm a bastard," Emlyn concedes. "But that is the situation."

I feel that I need to stand up for Emlyn. "Jorge," I say hesitantly. "He tried to get me to stop. I wouldn't."

Jorge's gaze swings to me. "Maela, you need to think, really think about this. About the toll it will take." He runs his hands through that fall of luscious chocolate hair. "Do you know how we found you? We were coming up the hall when we heard you cry out. We thought you were being attacked. I've never heard anything like it. We called out your name, and when you didn't respond, just continued to scream, we broke down the door." Surprised, I look at the door, and, oh heck, the lock's come away from the frame.

Kavi continues, speaking softly. "We rushed into the room and saw you lying on the couch. Your body was rigid, and you kept jerking and crying. It took a long time to calm you down."

My cheeks pink. I feel horribly embarrassed. That they saw me like that! I bite my bottom lip and go back to playing with the blanket. It seems the safest place to look.

Emlyn's voice is toneless: "You said 'Tell Emlyn'. Jorge found my number on your phone and called me over. When I got here, you were asleep, and they told me what had happened. They're right, Maela. This is dangerous."

I peek up at him shyly. "But Emlyn–"

"No," he interjects, shaking his head. "The fact is, Maela, there's no manual for someone like you. This is getting out of hand. First Monday, then Friday, and now this. It's becoming cumulative. If we stop our sessions, if we stop priming your mind, maybe the visions will stop."

I stick out my lip mulishly. "You don't know that, Emlyn! I told you! I need you to help me learn to control them!"

"I can't!" he shoots back. His eyes are blazing, and he punches his hands on his knees. "I don't know what I'm doing!"

"You can! And I'm not going to stop! I'm going to keep trying to see Ratko, and Magda, and Tennireef and Rhea, whoever she is. I'm going to do it with or without your approval. Do you think I'm going to let you end up like Eadric!"

At that, Emlyn goes preternaturally still, and Jorge grunts, as if he's just gotten hit with a burst of an unexpectedly strong emotion. Kavi is silent, watchful. Oh Christ. I didn't mean to let that last slip out.

"Emlyn," I try. He shakes his head again, violently, and spins out of his chair to stalk to the window. He's taking deep breaths, and his shoulders are shaking. I look at Jorge, then at Kavi, who says, "Who is Eadric, Maela?"

I open my mouth to say – I don't know what – when a voice from the window beats me to it: "Eadric was my brother. He was an officer with the National Crime Agency. Ratko murdered him two months ago."

Jorge sucks in a breath, and Emlyn turns to look at me. His face is ravaged, but his eyes are dry. "How did you find out?"

I shrug my shoulders shyly. "I saw a photo of the two of you on your computer one day, when you'd been called out of the office. And then I remembered the other photos you showed me and what you told me about Ratko and all the murders."

Emlyn's mouth tightens: "Jorge's right. I am a bastard." He walks over and squats down in front of me, taking my hands in his. "That's why," he says quietly. "That's why you started to push yourself, isn't it?"

I nod. "But it's not your fault," I add quickly. "I want to do this, Emlyn. I *need* to do this. But not just for Eadric, for all the people Ratko and the rest of them have hurt and will continue to hurt if they're not stopped. I don't know why I have this ability or how the drug unlocked it, but it's happened, and I need to control it. It's not just going to go away."

Emlyn looks searchingly at me, then turns away, running a hand down his face. "Fuck!" he snaps out. I can't help it then; I giggle. To hear the elegant Agent Emlyn Ryder swear somehow unlocks all of the tension inside me. The giggle seems to be a signal to the room to relax. Kavi reaches out and pulls me to him, my back against his chest, and Jorge picks up my feet and places them on his lap, tucking the blanket around them again. Today, I'm wearing thin, pale-blue socks, which match my sweater, as I wanted to look put together; and Jorge must have thought my feet might be cold.

"I think," Kavi says, "that you'd better fill us in."

Emlyn drops back in his chair with a tired smile. "You might want a drink for this."

"White wine," I pipe up. "In the fridge."

Emlyn comes back with the bottle and four glasses, and over the next hour we fill Jorge and Kavi in, Emlyn adding details of the program that he previously hadn't shared. Today, MI5 specializes in counter-terrorism, counter-espionage, and cyber threats but it also worked on serious and organized crime until 2006, when the Serious Organized Crime Agency, now the NCA, was created. The two agencies still worked cases together under the radar, though; and, while Ratko and his gang would normally be handled by the NCA, the suspected arms trafficking and continental links had drawn the attention of MI5. Eadric was handling the brief for the NCA, and Emlyn for MI5. It would normally be a breach of protocol, but they were the best in their fields and worked well together, and the infraction was let quietly slide. Then Eadric was murdered, and Emlyn was pulled from the case, the conflict of interest too great. Until I had had my vision. I was Emlyn's ticket back in as well as the only lead the agencies had. Because Emlyn was also point on a very exclusive unit within MI5. A unit formed in the 1970s as part of the Stargate Project, now, along with representatives from MI6, part of the Babylon Project, a multinational, government-funded organization set up to continue research into the paranormal for military and law-enforcement purposes.

In the States, the project was run by the FBI and CIA, and the links with their British counterparts were close. They shared research methods, analysis, and intelligence, trying to build up databases, training, and assets. When I'd shown up and Emlyn had become my handler, he'd briefed his counterpart in MI6, who in turn had briefed *his* counterpart in the CIA. However far Ratko's associations went, I was a potential asset who, with training, could be used in other cases in the future. My status as a US citizen made me of even greater interest to the CIA: when I returned to California, I might be willing to join them.

"But for now," Emlyn concludes, "Maela is still our only lead on Ratko, Magda, and potentially Rhea, unless the US team can get something on her through Tennireef. They're monitoring him, but he's slippery. Here, anyone who knows anything won't talk. Ratko is vicious, as we've seen, and Kronos, as in the States, may have friends in high places."

We all sit quietly. It's a lot to take in: MI5, MI6, the FBI and CIA, the Babylon Project, Kronos, drugs, arms running, and human trafficking. And in the middle: me.

"So," Jorge says after a minute or two. "What can we do to help?" A starburst of happiness flares to life inside me, and Jorge looks over and smiles. Kavi squeezes my shoulder. Emlyn notices both their actions, and a hint of what looks like sadness flickers across his face. Then he squares his shoulders and nods.

"As you've seen, the visions can come upon Maela at any time. You can help me to look out for her, check up on her. We need to get her to the point where she can enter and leave the visions at will. The only tools we have are relaxation and meditation, so that she can learn to focus. Kavi, you said you've been giving Maela lessons. She'll need them every day. MI5 will cover the cost."

"That won't be necessary," Kavi interjects.

"And Jorge," Emlyn continues. "You're a counsellor? Maela's likely to see a lot worse than Altan before this is over. She'll need to talk things out, have someone keep an emotional eye on her."

"*Sí*. I will make sure that we catch any fear, any pain, before even Maela knows." My eyes pop, and I open my mouth to speak, because, really, I'm starting to feel like a racehorse in training for the Grand National, with feeding, exercise, and vet schedules; but Jorge beats me to it. "*Compórtate!* Behave, Maela."

Emlyn raises a quizzical eyebrow, and Jorge says simply, "I am an empath. We will know exactly what she is feeling and if she is in trouble."

"Interesting," Emlyn replies. "The US team has a woman with incredible abilities. She's already helped to close a number of cases for the local police."

Jorge shrugs. "As to that, my gift is not very strong. But it will be enough."

"Just as well for you," Emlyn's mouth twists in a wry smile, "else I'd have to try to recruit you."

"We'll make sure she has what she needs," Kavi adds, his deep voice reverberating in his chest. I give a little shiver. I'm not quite sure how this has happened or where it's going, but for now I'm going to bask in the testosterone. They're all so manful.

"Good. I'll continue to work with Maela on visualization while chasing up intel on Magda and Rhea. Judging by past patterns, it won't be long before there's another incident. They seem to be accelerating. Either something big is in the works, or Ratko's starting to kick at his traces. We know, thanks to Maela, that he's not in charge. Could be he's trying to reassert control."

The three men begin a discussion of my schedule, and I close my eyes. I'm warm and comfy, and there doesn't seem to be much point in joining in. I have a feeling I'd get overridden anyway. But I jolt to full awareness when I hear them start talking about night-time rotations.

"No! Nuh-uh. No one's sleeping over!" What am I: two?

If any of them is going to spend the night, it's not going to be to monitor me. Have one of them see me in my jammies with bed-head in the morning? Not happening. Not unless it follows a night of passion and I have kiss-swollen lips.

"Maela," Emlyn says reasonably, "several of your visions have been at night. What if you have another violent one and can't pull yourself out? Someone needs to be here."

"Not just no, but hell no!" I widen my eyes and stare meaningfully at him, to let him know that I mean business.

"Alright," he agrees. "We'll install surveillance devices instead."

"What!" I squawk.

"Your choice, Maela. We need to respond if you're in trouble."

I look from him, to Jorge, to Kavi. Emlyn is impassive; Jorge cants his head with a brief, apologetic smile; and Kavi raises his palms in the air. I'm not going to win this one, am I?

"There won't be cameras, will there?" I ask querulously.

"No, just audio." Great, just great. No more singing in the shower.

"And who'd be listening?"

"Just me, and we'll agree on a schedule. You agree not to take any naps, and I'll only turn on the monitor at night, just while you're sleeping."

I huff. "I suppose I need to wear a tag too, so you can keep track of me *all day*?" I really want to cross my arms over my chest, but I can't because I'm still draped over Kavi and Jorge, and it wouldn't have the same effect.

Emlyn smiles: "No. If you have a vision when you're out and about, someone is sure to notice and call the police. And then I'll come pick you up."

I settle for nibbling on a fingernail. "Fine!" I say grumpily.

"It's just until we know you can pull yourself out of a bad vision. We're operating blind here, Maela, and we need to take precautions."

"Hphmm," I chunter. "Yes. Well." I nibble on another fingernail, and, forgetting where I am momentarily, squirrel my foot around Jorge's crotch, tucking it under his leg. Jorge freezes, a slight blush staining his bronze cheeks. Kavi and Emlyn don't seem to notice anything amiss, but I'm horrified. Should I try to pull my foot back out? What if Kavi or Emlyn see? But I can't just leave it there, can I? Feck, feck, feck.

"That's settled then," Emlyn continues. "So, we just need to fix your door, so that it will hold until a locksmith can come out – send the bill to me – and then we'd better let you have a quiet night. We're all going to be very busy these next few weeks. Do you have a screwdriver?"

Seizing the excuse, I withdraw my legs and sit up. "Yup! Under the sink. I'll get it!" I practically leap off the coach in my haste and scurry into the kitchen, not daring to look at any of them. I shudder to think how red my face must be.

While Emlyn and Jorge attend to the door, Kavi gets me another glass of wine and makes me a serrano ham, cheese, and tomato sandwich. He's going to leave me the movie. "You'll like it," he promises, that big grin of his lighting his face. "And I guarantee you'll be hooked, so we'll watch the next one together."

Soon, they're ready to leave. I'm tempted to tell them to stay, but they're right: I'm feeling tired and just want to snuggle up on the couch. Emlyn nods at me and tells me he'll see me tomorrow. Kavi wraps me in a big bear hug: "Until tomorrow, Maela *ladki*." Jorge leans in, a warm, virile, and intense presence, and kisses me on the cheek: *Hasta luego*." He turns as they're filing out and gives me a smoldering look. "*Dinamita*," he whispers. I color, and he shakes his head and smiles at me, and then I'm alone in the flat.

I flop down on the couch and spend a long time thinking, mostly about the day's revelations but more about the feel of Jorge's erection, thickening and hardening against my stockinged foot. And I may not have that much experience, but I can tell he'd fill me up oh so good, and I get a little thrill, knowing that I make him respond.

CAGE FIGHTING

Monday, 15 October – Kailani

"Oof!" I stare at the ceiling, trying to remember my name, my age, how to breathe... and a smirking Donovan appears over me, face twisted into a smug fucking smile. I'd give anything in my power to be able to remember how to kick my leg and connect with his groin, but at the moment all I can do is focus on trying to inhale and exhale.

"Again!" shouts Smith, watching from the side of the ring and taking notes. I roll my eyes towards him, unable to move my head, and the bastard laughs at the expression he sees on my face. "On your feet, Reed. You're fine."

Easy for you to say. You didn't just have your ribcage forced into your spine, I think mutinously. There's a small scuffle at the side, and I see Smith barring Jonah from entering the ring, presumably to come help me. That more than anything forces me to stand, wheezing through aching lungs.

"Kai! Jesus. Smith, let me in. You okay?" Jonah sounds incredibly worried, and I wave him off as I concentrate on standing without falling over.

"She's fine, Shotridge." Hideo's smooth voice is laced with laughter, and I shoot him a betrayed look. He raises a single brow at me and says, "I've *told* you to watch your right side, Kai. You're just too used to sparring with me and can get away with it."

Still glaring at him, I shrug slightly, the only acknowledgement I'll give him that he might be right. *Damnit. He is right. I've gotten lazy.*

We've been training together for almost an hour now, trying different combinations of partners under Smith's watchful eye. It was his idea to try this "team-building exercise" – close to no holds barred fighting. I had a blast against Deo, well-practiced combinations flowing like music, our hands and feet moving like a dance. He got off a couple of clean hits that I *know* are going to bruise tomorrow, and I landed a kick that knocked him on his ass, but otherwise it was like play, ending in laughter between the two of us, with Jonah watching almost longingly and Smith rolling his eyes.

"That's not going to work," he said. "You both need to change it up a little."

Smith hopped into the ring with Deo, nodding towards Donovan, who took the role of trainer, and I settled back beside Jonah to watch the two men fight. It was like watching a lion and a panther square off. Deo's body stilled, light on the balls of his feet, eyes intent on Smith's massive form. Smith wasn't heavy on his feet by any means, but I knew he was going to move in swinging, just based on his stance. The moment Donovan barked out the start command, it was like a masterclass in MMA. The men in the ring were serious, focused, professional. It was odd to watch Deo fight from the outside, and I found myself catching my breath as he wove in and out of Smith's reach.

Watching Smith fight was a revelation. For being so massive, he had a lethal grace to his movement, and I found myself entranced. You could literally see his muscles ripple under his skin, flexing and releasing as he and Deo sparred. They were incredibly different fighters, balanced but contrasting in nature – fire and ice – and it was truly fascinating to watch. I found myself blushing at points and pressed a cold water bottle to my face.

Jesus, Kai. Get yourself under control. Just two fucking gorgeous men sweating and wrestling half naked in front... no. NO! Christ. Distract yourself. Do your times tables.

Thankfully their match wasn't long and ended in a draw, with Smith and Hideo doing some kind of one-armed bro-hug at the end, laughing with each other. It was... surprising, to say the least, but really nice to see. Usually it was just me and Deo. I wasn't used to seeing him relaxed and happy with anyone else, and it was really nice to see him have a little *fun*.

Smith and Donovan fought under Hideo's guard, and it was explosive, undeniable entertainment. They were as well matched as Deo and me, years of partnership resulting in a roughshod melee between two gladiators. They'd shouted insults at each other, had gone in swinging like tree trunks, and were, all in all, like watching boulders collide. I found myself laughing along with them, with Jonah and Deo shouting encouragement and narrating the match. It was the first time I'd really felt a part of the team, got a glimpse into what we could all be if we tried. So when Smith called me into the ring to fight Donovan, I was excited, almost happy.

But now, Donovan's smirking at me, body loose, feet flat – it's an insult to a fighter. He doesn't think I can recover from his throw. All of the fun from the earlier fights has drained away, and he looks at me with a condescending gaze.

"Done, Reed?" he snarks.

"No," snaps Smith, answering for me. "Back at it, Reed."

My lips twitch before I can get them under control. They think *that* throw was going to cause me to go home and cry into my pillow? He may have flipped me like Sunday pancakes, but he left his side open while he did it. Feigning a little more weakness than I feel, I move towards him, and he laughs in my face.

"Again, Reed? When will you learn?" He moves into me, grabbing me again to take me to the ground, when I twist suddenly and connect with his ribs in a massive, completely unguarded hit. His eyes widen as all the air in his body leaves, and I swing around, flinging my entire body weight against his arm, one leg against his throat, the other helping propel me into a back breakfall. We land hard, his face going red immediately as he struggles against the arm bar, but he can't move without breaking his elbow.

I can tell he's not willing to tap out and know that unless Smith intercedes, he's either going to pass out or get his arm broken, but I refuse to break my hold on him. The playful, laughing air of a few minutes ago drains out of the room, and anger skitters across his skin like biting teeth. He tries arching his body up to buck me off, but his low groan of pain shows he's paid for the move. Gritting my teeth, I think *come on, Smith. Come ON.* Despite my personal feelings about Donovan, I don't want to choke out a member of my own team if I don't have to. I know instinctively though that if I don't finish this, we'll keep battling, Jonah will keep being a mother hen, Smith will wonder if I have what it takes... Donovan's eyes are flaring and falling, a sign that he's right on the edge, and I growl at him.

"Tap out, Asshole. Just fucking tap out!"

He shakes his head slightly, gets dizzy eyes, and oops, he's taking a nap. I let the pressure go immediately and jump to my feet, hovering over him.

"Deo!" I snap, and he throws me a water bottle, which I spray in Donovan's face. His eyes pop open, and he sputters slightly, before settling and staring at me with an inscrutable expression. I hold my hand out to him, and he hesitates for a moment, then grabs it as I help him sit up.

"Just sit for a second, you freaking idiot. Are you okay? Why the hell didn't you tap? Do you need water?" Sitting beside him, I prop him up and hold the water for him to drink, before I turn to glare at Smith. "What the hell, man? What in the actual, ever-loving hell? Why didn't you call that?"

Smith gets in the ring and squats in front of us, speaking softly. "Reed. Donovan needs to learn that you can beat him and that you're as capable as the rest of us. Shotridge over there needs to learn that he doesn't have to protect you."

Shooting a glance at Jonah, I see him gaping like a fish,

expression surprised and befuddled.

"I needed to see that you could finish it, if you had to–" Smith continues calmly.

"Well what the fuck did *I* need to learn?" I snarl. "Did it ever occur to you that I may not *like* choking out a teammate? We don't train like that."

Deo shakes his head, confirming my words. "We don't. We take it to tap. There's no need to endanger anyone. And choke outs are never completely safe."

Donovan's finally able to speak and narrows his eyes at me. "You're saying you didn't get *any* satisfaction from taking me out?"

I shake my head angrily. "Dude. Despite your attitude, we're on the same side. That wasn't fun for any of us."

"Then why didn't you let the hold go?" Smith asks curiously, and I stare at him through flat eyes.

"Because I trusted you as my team lead and as our grappling instructor to call it when you thought best. I won't make that same mistake again."

Smith flinches slightly, face still blank, but I can feel my anger pushing out and slicing him like knives before I get it pulled in and under control.

"Deo?" I snap, and he appears like magic beside me with a second water bottle and towel.

"We won't be training together again until this is resolved," Deo says calmly, passing me the towel and staring down at Smith and Donovan. "Come on, Kai."

I shake my head as I turn away.

"Wait." Donovan's reluctant voice stops me, and I look over my shoulder at him. "Reed. That was my fault. I'm sorry." Sighing deeply, his voice changes slightly, and I hear real contrition lace his words. "That was on me. I fucked up. I... I just didn't want to fucking tap to you. It was my mistake."

Looking at Hideo, we have a silent conversation before I turn fully to face Donovan. "Thank you. But I'm not training with either of you again unless I can trust you. And I don't."

Both Smith and Donovan frown, and Smith says, "You've got to trust *someone*, Reed."

I point at Hideo. "Someone."

Jonah makes a small sound, and I look at him with a soft smile. "Jonah. Seriously? You were going to jump in the ring and try to save me. During a training exercise. Where no one is *supposed* to be able to be hurt." Frowning a little, I look at him more consideringly. "Though maybe you read the room a little better than I did, in this case."

He shakes his head, albeit reluctantly. "Ah... no. I just... I wasn't thinking."

Shrugging, I look at Smith. "You keep saying you want us to work, that you want us to be a team, and then you pull shit like this. At least Donovan doesn't try to fake it. He doesn't like me or respect me for shit, but at least he's open about it."

Donovan's eyes widen in surprise, then narrow into a thoughtful look, and he opens his mouth to speak when the training timer dings.

"Saved by the bell?" I say, then jerk my head at Hideo, and we walk out of the room, leaving three troubled faces behind us.

The light streaming in my room jolts me awake, and I look at my clock in panic, then relief. I have a late start today at the office because I have to be at court midmorning for a custody hearing. I don't have many open cases left on my books, having switched over completely to assisting the task force, but there are a few, and I have to testify at one today.

Groaning, I turn over and cover my head with a pillow. I feel sick with unhappiness and worry. The entire day ahead is weighing heavy on my shoulders, and I would give almost anything to stay in bed and ignore the chaos my life has become for a little while. Unfortunately, my stomach didn't get the message that I don't have to be awake yet, and the smells of cinnamon and vanilla mix with coffee and lure me to the kitchen.

Stumbling down the hall, hair wild and yawning wide enough to crack my jaw, I come to a sudden halt when I see Lachy in the kitchen, laughing quietly with Gemma. They haven't noticed me yet, despite my elephant-like trodding in the hallway, and I smile to myself watching two of my favorite people. The smile fades slightly when Gemma leans into Lachy's arms, and he rubs her back comfortingly, tucking her tiny head against his massive chest.

"Come on now, Tiny," he says softly. "It's not as bad as all that."

She mumbles something unintelligible against him, and I frown, strange feelings warring inside me. Concern for whatever is bothering Gemms, jealousy that she told Lachy and not me, and something... some other type of something I don't want to examine too closely. Ignoring the feeling that I'm intruding, I walk into the room cautiously.

"Gemms?" I ask quietly, and she turns to me with a rueful face, disappointment heavy on her features.

"Sorry, KaiKai. Did we wake you?"

Lachy stretches one arm out to me, keeping the other one wrapped around Gemma.

"Group hug this morning, Kai," he says. Something inside me loosens at being pulled into them with no hesitation, and I wriggle in against them, wrapping my arms carefully around both of them.

"What's up, guys?" I ask concernedly.

"I didn't get the gallery spot. Just found out." Gemma's sad voice is stifled against my shoulder, and I sigh. She'd worked so hard the past few months, creating an amazing series of paintings and drawings of hidden spots in Seattle.

The gallery where she works has a bi-annual new artist showcase, and spots were highly coveted. A blind submission and judging guaranteed that there was no favoritism for friends, family, or employees, and Gemma had desperately poured her heart into her work, devoting every spare minute to creating incredible, detailed pieces of art. I'm stunned and heartbroken for her all at once. Her artwork is amazing, and I'm at a loss as to why she wasn't chosen.

We're still in a huddle when the phone rings, and Gemma walks away to answer it. She's speaking softly so we can't hear her, but her face creases in confusion before it lights up in disbelief. It's like a switch has been flipped, and I move to pull away from Lachy to go see what's happening, but his massive arms tighten around me and keep me against his chest.

"Not yet, Suge," he rumbles softly, so as not to disturb Gemma. "This is nice."

It is, and I smile against him, but as the moments tick by, I'm realizing the simple hug has lengthened into something different. Unsure what to do, I give him the universal "squeeze and release", and I feel more than hear his thunder rumble of laughter in my ear. He's curled around me, head resting on my shoulder, face turned into my neck, and his warm breath skitters across my skin, causing it to ripple, and my own breath to catch.

"I like this, first thing in the morning," Lachy whispers against my skin. "Having a place here with you... making something for you to eat other than a power bar or a bagel."

I want to pull back and protest, to turn the suddenly serious moment into something more lighthearted... I don't know how to process what's happening right now. It's like the world has narrowed to the space between our heartbeats, the edges faded away, my eyes closed, curled up in his safety and warmth. All of my fears and doubts about the day have drifted away, and I feel delicate happiness lace my skin, spreading from the feel of his lips, whisper light against my collarbone, moving as he talks to me.

"I made coffee and apple-cider donuts," he begins, and I smile.

"That's right baby, talk dirty to me," I try to say jokingly, but his arms flex around me at the words, and his entire body stills, pressing me against him.

Turning my head slightly to look at him, our faces are millimeters apart, his eyes blown and heavy lidded, neither of us breathing. If I say a single word, move at all, our lips will touch, and we sit, caught in the in-between, breaths shaky and stuttered.

"Kai!" Gemma's voice squeals happily, shattering the moment, and I jerk back so suddenly I fall over the chair behind me, crashing to the floor. Gemma rushes to me to help me up, but Lachy stands frozen, staring down at me with an expression of such desperation and hopelessness, edged in such hurt, I surge to my feet towards him. By the time I stand though, and shake off Gemma's ministrations, the expression has disappeared, and he's plating up breakfast for me. I'm shaking, almost vibrating really, but he keeps his back resolutely turned, and Gemma demands my attention.

"Giiiirl! Oh my god! You'll never guess…"

It turned out that the reason Gemma hadn't been chosen for the temporary exhibit is because they wanted to offer her a two-month chance to earn a permanent spot on the wall. She was beyond excited – sure, her location in the gallery was a far corner, limited to three paintings – but knowing how talented she is, I assured her that she'd be on the front wall in no time. The three of us talked for a bit over breakfast about which of her paintings to highlight, and by the time breakfast was over, things appeared to have returned to normal.

Gemma had to run to make the next ferry for work, so

Lachy shooed me out of the kitchen and started on the dishes while I got ready for my court appearance. When I'd reappeared in the kitchen, make-up on and ready to go, we'd exchanged a long look before Lachy pushed me gently out the door, assuring me he'd lock up and wishing me luck at the trial.

Nothing went right from that point on. The judge granted 50–50 custody, which was a miscarriage in justice. The kids' father was demonstrably the better parent... their mother was negligent, but despite the evidence and testimony, the judge wouldn't be swayed. The kids were in hysterics at the thought of having to go with their mom, and I was scrambling to try to figure out *some* way to help. It was chaos. The mom was supposed to take the kids after the court hearing, but not five minutes after the verdict, the court deputy witnessed her shooting up in the bathroom, and an emergency order had to be issued to keep the kids with their dad.

There were literally *hours* of paperwork and processing following the fiasco, and while, thank the gods, it all worked out in the end, by the time I get to work it is almost four, and I'm exhausted and at the end of my rope, emotionally speaking.

Walking into the room, I see the men grouped around a set of what appears to be blueprints, speaking in low voices.

"Hey all," I say tiredly, dropping my bag onto my chair and making my way over to them. "What'd I miss?"

Hideo looks up at me, initially smiling slightly, but face creasing in concern as he takes in my expression and appearance. He raises a single brow at me, asking how it went silently, and I do a half-shrug, half-shake of my head in response. Sighing, he says quietly, "The Mom?"

"Not in the long run," I reply, "but long enough to do damage." We exchange a long, knowing look. This case has been a monster from the beginning, and those poor kids are going to need a shitload of therapy when all is said and done. That's how most of our cases are, actually, and for a brief moment, I'm almost glad I'm getting a respite from the heartbreaking work.

Well, a *very* brief moment. Because then Donovan had to go and open his fucking mouth. His full lips twist into something ugly, somewhere between a smirk and a snarl, as he gives me a dismissive once over. "What's this all about, Reed?" he says, motioning to my outfit. You got a hot date or something? Someone drunk or brave enough to hit that?"

Deo and I start laughing, clearly startling Donovan, and Smith looks at us sharply as we exchange glances. "Reed doesn't date," said Deo disdainfully. "And if she did, she wouldn't wear *that* on one. Christ, Donovan. Not that you don't look nice," he hurried to add.

I look down at my modest dress and small heels and roll my eyes. "I had a court date, you fucking idiot," I snark back. "I had to testify at a trial. Not get drinks with some Neanderthal."

Donovan bristles at my tone. "Aw, poor Reed can't find a dick to ride?"

Deo stops laughing abruptly and shoots to his feet, growling at Donovan. "Watch your mouth, Walker. That's your fucking teammate, and in case you don't remember, only one of you is disposable. So keep making this uncomfortable for Reed and my boot will be so far up your ass on your way out the door that you'll choke on it."

I can't help grinning up at Hideo, who's lit up with fury. "Deeeeeo! You are the fucking *sweetest!*" Hopping up to hug him, I frown down at Donovan, who is sputtering, face red with anger. "And no, Donovan. I can't find a dick to ride. That make you feel better about yourself now? I can't keep my shield up while I'm intimate, and so my partner's emotions overwhelm and flood me, and cause me to either resonate *their* feelings, or occasionally just pass out. So I've had a total of... hmmm, let me think..." I pretend to count sarcastically, "*one* boyfriend. One. Who ended up being an anthropomorphic bag of pus, so I'm sorry to say all your slut shaming and dick waving is pointless."

I motion to myself vaguely. "All of which means, long and short, that this is out of commission. Permanently. Relationships aren't made for people like me."

Leaning forward, placing my hands on the table, I meet Donovan's eyes with a hard stare. "So you can keep making fun of me for not being able to '*find a dick to ride*', as you charmingly put it. It's fine: it's true." I shrug bitterly. "I hope it makes you feel better to know that. Not sure what mark you were aiming for, but if it was 'make Kailani feel like shit on an already terrible day', you got it in one. Great job."

Donovan flushes and frowns. "Why court?" he asks belligerently, like he has some right to know.

Ignoring him, I look at the blueprints, trying to figure out what they've been planning. Deo answers for me. "Custody hearing. A really nasty case that Kai ran point on. She sometimes goes in as a character witness if things aren't going right."

Donovan waves his hands around like a cheap lounge magician. "You make them change their minds with your thing?" He sounds interested, angry, and disdainful all at once, and I can't for the life of me figure this guy out. Things would be a hell of a lot easier if he weren't on this task force.

Sighing, I look up at him. "*No*, Donovan," I say, faux patiently. "I don't 'change their minds with my thing', as you so eloquently put it." Now Smith and Jonah are looking at me in interest, so I grit my teeth and continue. "I can't. And won't. For several reasons. I *won't* because despite my personal beliefs and desires, I don't have the right to alter the court's ruling. If I start down that road, there's no turning back. I adjust one thing on a case because I don't think things have gone right, it means I don't believe in our justice system. It means I believe I'm above or beyond the law.

And then what do I do? It's vigilante justice at that point. And beyond that, I *can't*, not really, even if I wanted to. The brain isn't a traffic light. Red doesn't mean stop in there. It's a spider-web, and you don't always know what strands are connected to each other. So let's say a father is angry about losing custody, but has fought so hard for so long that he's thinking of giving up, right? And I want him to fight, because I know the kids will be better off with him. So I push a little fire into him. But I misjudge how much, or the type, or he has some unknown factors in his background that are triggered, and instead of fighting the system, he grabs a gun and shoots his wife. And that would be my fault. I don't mess with people's emotions much, not if I can help it. You pull one strand of the web and it all falls down."

Deo looks at me with a slightly dubious expression, and it's so adorable and funny that I suddenly Cheshire-cat grin in response, and the fucker boops my nose. A stunned expression flashes across his face as he flicks his eyes down to his hand, like it acted of its own accord, before his face returns to its neutral, professional expression.

"You don't mess with people's emotions?" he asks, looking pointedly at Donovan before looking back at me.

Still grinning enough that my cheeks hurt, I say combatively, "I said I don't mess with them *much*."

He gives up and flashes a quick smile at me, and we turn back to the others. Donovan's looking mutinous and growls, "So you let a kid go into a bad situation rather than help them? Jesus Christ, Reed. How do you live with yourself?"

Rearing back like I've been hit, I clench my jaw to force down the wave of emotion threatening to overtake me. It's a sickening pit of guilt I wrestle with daily, the idea that I've let kids be put into precarious situations, that maybe, *maybe*, I could have done something more. Deo rests a comforting hand on my shoulder and speaks in a low, level voice directed at Donovan.

"Kailani has never let a child return to or remain in a bad situation if she can do anything about it. She helps parents file paperwork, assists them in getting financial aid, find affordable childcare, legal representation... She walks them through the system as many times as they need until they know how to navigate the red tape. She advises them on which judges are more lenient, which are fair, speaks to lawyers to donate pro bono time. She volunteers extra hours to check on children in bad situations, often enough and at random enough times that their guardians get nervous to do anything, which buys us time to get the kids out. But she is one person, and can only do so much, and she tries her damnedest every day to help. So until and unless *you* do something more than armchair quarterback the decisions that we've been forced to make, you can shut the fuck up."

The silence in the room is heavy. Turning to Smith, I point at the blueprints, willing him silently to move on with the conversation.

"What's all this about?" I ask, trying to keep my voice level.

"Interesting developments," Smith begins, clearly picking up my plea and refocusing on the work in front of us. He flips on the projector, and an image appears behind him. A zoomed-in shot, obviously taken surreptitiously, is on the screen. A naked back is barely visible through a thick curtain of foliage: really more of a sliver of skin than anything else. Smith clicks again, and the photo comes into sharp focus – in the center of the back, between the shoulder blades, is a clear image of a snake eating its tail, with an hourglass in the center.. One moment later, and the image is obscured by a shirt. It has obviously only been visible for a split second before being covered up. I look to Smith, confused, and he bares his teeth at me in a kind of victorious, vicious smile. Looking back to the screen, he continues clicking through the series of images, 'til finally just the edge of a face is seen. More an impression of a face than anything else, but I start sharply, leaning forward and breathing out softly, "James Fucking Tennireef."

Smith nods. "James. Fucking. Tennireef."

The camera pulls back, and though the mysterious photographer is trying, there are no other photos of Tennireef. I stare at the last image, nothing more than a screen of trees, thoughtfully. "Where did you get these? No one would know that's him. It would never hold up in a court of law. The only reason I recognize his smug mug is because I spend so much time staring at it in the interrogation room. But it's definitely him. *How* did you get these?"

"They were taken on his private estate, just outside the city."

My eyes flare in surprise. "*What?* Jesus! That's next to impossible! He's notorious for his security measures! He lives in freaking Fort Knox! Plus the entire thing is cut off from view by a forest that goes fully to the home, from what I've heard. Completely gated. You can't even get a decent view from overhead – that photog tried a few weeks ago with a drone and nothing! Wherever these came from, you should pay them more."

A snort from the other end of the table has me looking down from the photo on the screen. Donovan looks at me challengingly. "Thanks," he says dryly. "Nice to know my talents are appreciated."

I stare at him briefly, look back up at the screen, then back down to him. "That was you?"

He shrugs like it was no big deal that he had somehow infiltrated Tennireef's compound unseen.

"Wow." I sit back, somewhat stunned that the MMA fighter in front of me must be better than I had initially thought. "That is some impressive skill, man," I say sincerely. "Don't know how you did it, but that's amazing."

Donovan narrows his eyes at me suspiciously, like he's looking for the sarcasm in my words, but credit where credit is due. I may not like the guy, but he's obviously good at his job. I jerk my head slightly toward the screen. "How did you catch that?"

He replies reluctantly, like he's looking for a trap. "The guy has a pool out back his house. It's completely covered, so you can't get any overhead shots, but one side has glass that opens onto an outside patio. It's shielded really well by trees and planting, so it took me over a week to find a place I could see anything. I wasn't trying to get a shot of his tattoo – obviously we didn't even know he had one. But we've been casing his place for a while now, and I was just trying to get some sight lines. To be honest, I was just shooting to give an idea of holes in his cover, and got lucky."

I shrug slightly. "A lot of luck is just persistence and talent combined. You may have gotten lucky on the shot, but getting into his place in the first place and not being caught for over a week – that's not luck."

Donovan looks from me to Hideo, who responds to his inquisitive look. "Reed may not like you," he begins quietly, "but she's honest about people's skills, in spite of any personal opinions."

Smith taps the blueprints again and takes back over. "So these are the layouts of Tennireef's compound," he begins. "We can't go in without a warrant, and to be completely honest, we have no idea what we're looking for anyways. A tattoo isn't enough reason. But I want us to know it, entrances and egresses, in order to be prepared to move when and if we need to. And we need an in with Tennireef. Somehow."

So we spend the rest of the afternoon plotting and planning, but getting little done.

GET OUT OF YOUR HEAD

Wednesday, 17 October – Kailani

"Oh, you fucking fucker!" I growl, kicking the wheel of my bike. "God damnit! *GEMMA!*" I yell. "Help!"

Gemma races from the house, still blinking sleep from her eyes, purple hair sticking up in every direction, fumbling with putting her glasses on with one hand and wielding a... spatula? with the other. "What? Who? What? Back the fuck off!" she yells, brandishing the spatula like a sword and waving it wildly around.

I burst out laughing. "I'm so sorry!" I say, trying to breathe.

She frowns at me angrily. "What the hell, Kai? I thought you were being attacked or something!"

I wince sheepishly and point at the flat on my bike. "Can I have a ride in today? I have an early meeting."

"Aw, sorry, girl. I can't. I have a virtual tour in an hour." Concern lines her face. "Maybe Lachy?"

I shake my head thoughtfully. "Maybe to the landing. But not into town. It'll be okay. It's still early."

Gemma's face crinkles into worried lines. "But that means public transport..."

"I know," I reply, falsely cheerful. "I'm sure it'll be fine."

We walk back into the house together, her shooting me nervous little glances, until I poke her side and say gently, "Also, and side note, what's with the spatula?"

Growling, she says, "Girl! You're on my last nerve! All I heard was 'help!' and I grabbed the nearest weapon to me and..."

Trying to hide a grin as I listen to my friend describe her

plan of action, I'm able to forget for a minute what the next hour and a half holds.

By the time I get into the office, my head is throbbing and my skin is crawling with the feeling of hundreds of ants running over it. I shiver like a horse when flies land on it, skin rippling uncomfortably. Early morning public transport is never good to me. If I'm tired, it takes a while for my shields to harden enough to withstand the press of bodies, and the morning work rush is always heavy with worry, thick enough that it feels like I'm breathing it in, flooding my veins with a dark, tar-like substance. Worry is one of those emotions that overtakes you before you know it. I'll think my shields are fine, but one little strand will make its way through and attach itself to the deep pit of anxiety that lives permanently in my stomach, and then it's off to the races. Occasionally I'll get lucky and sit next to someone who loves their job, and that peace is a gift to me, but more often, it's a desperate scramble of emotion that coats me and stays with me for hours.

This morning I sit next to a frantic woman with a stoic face, panic seeping from her in suffocating waves. She offers me a gentle smile when I get on the bus and moves over apologetically, as if she's sorry for the little space she's taking up. Her wild swell of anxiety combines with a combative anger from the small, unassuming man in front of me, reading "7 Ways to Be at Peace." Every flip of the page hits me like a punch in the gut with rage, belied by his careful smoothing of the paper with every turn. Someone on the bus is so unbelievably sad that the emotion sounds like a song, and two, sitting next to each other holding hands, have the feel of "goodbye" so strongly I can taste its ash in my mouth.

Shit, I think to myself. *Shit shit shit. This was a terrible idea. Learn your freaking lesson, Kai! You can't handle the early morning commute.*

I hold my shields as tightly as I can, but then a young boy, maybe eleven or twelve, boards the bus, shoulders tight around his ears, eyes darting around him and books held protectively against his chest. The swell of emotion from him has tears filling my eyes before I can block him. Dark, bruised-looking eyes sit in a slightly too-thin face, already creased with worry for the day to come. Looking at him, I can taste dirt and stale air, and I know that he is desperate and at the end. He glances up, feeling the weight of my eyes on him, and folds further into himself, watching me with a wary gaze. I offer a small smile at him, which he regards suspiciously, and I begin *pulling* from him slowly. I grab some of the dark, moldy, rotting emotions and siphon them off bit by bit. As his shoulders drop minutely, I lean across the aisle to him quietly.

"Hey – how's that book? I've been thinking about taking it out from the library."

His eyes widen slightly in response to being addressed, but he answers in a small, clear voice, "It's good. Not as good as the first in the series, but good."

I roll my eyes dramatically. "Damn. Ain't that always the way?"

A harsh, tired voice snipes from behind us: "Shut up! No one cares about your reading habits."

Before the kid has a chance to fold in again, I raise an eyebrow and call over my shoulder, "Aw, now, tough guy. Don't be like that! No need to be jealous that the kid and I can read. You'll get there eventually."

The kid squeaks out a surprised laugh, which lightens me briefly, but the rest of the people around us laugh in a darker, mirthless way, and I feel nauseous. The kid looks about 50% better, at least, and my mouth doesn't taste like the grave when I look at him, so that helps.

I'm in a lousy mood by the time I get to the conference

room. The rest of the team is sitting, talking quietly over coffee, and I try very hard to just slip, unnoticed, into my seat. Only Jonah and Hideo look up, Deo's small welcoming smile quickly turning into a frown.

Gods. He's probably regretting agreeing to be my handler. I can't even keep my shit together long enough to get to work in one piece.

My hands flex, knuckles white against my mug of coffee, skin burning from the heat, but I refuse to move or look up. I can feel, more than see, his unhappiness, and I clench my jaw tightly, willing myself not to cry.

When he tells you he's done, that this is all too much trouble, you need to be a fucking rock, Kai. Christ, my shields are shit today. Breathe. Breathe. Stone by stone, build them up. He can fucking leave if he wants to. Probably has been planning this for a while. Who would want to work with me? I'm a fucking mess. Shields first. Shields first and then everything...

A sharp flick of a finger in the center of my forehead has me look up, startled.

Hideo is staring straight in my eyes, concern and... something else... lacing his tight expression.

"Get out of your head," he commands gently.

I open my mouth to speak, stammer out some response, but my eyes flood and I jut my jaw forward to maintain my composure.

"Get out of your head," he repeats softly, taking my hands. I look down at where our hands meet, his long, elegant, piano-player fingers softly rubbing the back of my clenched fists. "It's okay. Hmmm?" He reaches one hand out to my face and lifts it to meet his eyes. "What happened today? You take public? Why didn't you call me? Lachy or Gemma couldn't drive you?"

The rest of the team is now watching our interaction carefully.

"What's this about?" Smith asks quietly and respectfully. "Is everything okay?"

Deo sighs and tilts his head at me, the question heavy in his eyes, and I shrug miserably. *Might as well, I guess. They'll kick me off the team for sure. Weak link.* I feel myself curl into a ball on the inside, though I don't physically move. *I don't even want to be a part of this. This is a good thing. Fuck them! I don't need this.*

Deo is still gazing at me steadily with soft eyes, and despite my best efforts, my lower lip begins to wobble precariously. I feel a strong stinging across the bridge of my nose, and I bite my cheek to keep the tears at bay. Jonah's next to me, his emotions frantic butterfly wings of concern, but he just takes one of my hands quietly, without speaking.

"Oh, Kai," Hideo begins softly, sighing deeply. "Bad one today? It's okay. Let's get you grounded."

Worry and panic gnaw a little hole in my solar plexus, and it fills with sadness. Logically I *know* that these aren't my feelings, not really, but it's impossible to separate them from my own, especially when they find cousins in my psyche.

Hideo would be better off without you, the dark corners inside me whisper. *You're holding him back. It's why nothing has ever happened between you. He's being kind. It's pity. Smith doesn't respect you; Donovan thinks you're a fraud; Jonah thinks you can't handle yourself. You're too weak. You're a liability, unstable. He's right. They're right. They'll leave.*

"Seriously, what is *happening?*" Donovan's confused voice breaks through my spiral. "This isn't her at *all*."

I feel his heavy presence in front of me as I stare silently down at my hands. He nudges Deo and Jonah aside, though Hideo leaves a comforting hand on my shoulder, and I look up at him.

"Hey... *hey...*" Donovan modulates his voice – having started brusquely, but something in my face softened his tone. "What the hell is happening?"

"She doesn't do well on public transport. Especially the morning commute," Hideo explains succinctly.

"This is all because she took the fucking bus?"

Misery bone deep washes over me again. It *was* because I took the bus. I can't even be normal enough for long enough to take a freaking bus.

Burying my face in my hands, I run my fingers up into my hair and fist my hands, face tight, trying to block them all out.

Donovan's pushed roughly to the side as Smith crouches in front of me. He places his hands on my knees and squeezes lightly.

"Okay, Kai," he says, deep voice smooth and dark. "Name five things you can see."

Opening my eyes, confused, I look at him as he repeats quietly, "Five things you can see."

"Uh... you, the table... my coffee...," my voice wobbles slightly, and I have to try twice to form the words, "the uh... the phone, the whiteboard."

"Good, good. Four things you can touch?"

My voice is still quiet, and scratchy, but I answer him more readily. "The chair, my jeans, Hideo's hand... you...." The last word barely makes it out, said on a breath more than anything, and Smith looks at me a beat too long before clearing his throat and continuing: "Three things you can hear?"

"The guys in the hall, the printer, Donovan's foot tapping..." the tapping ceases immediately, and I see the corner of Smith's mouth twitch up slightly.

"Two things you can smell?"

"Coffee and Coffee," I respond, finally feeling my self emerge from deep within me.

"And name one thing you're feeling," he says, now *almost* smiling at me.

"Grateful," I say very quietly, meeting his eyes, watching the smile drop off his face.

"We all need to be grounded sometimes, Kailani," Smith says softly, voice strangled with some dark emotion. "We all get lost in our heads. Or our hearts." He squeezes my legs again in his massive hands, flashes me a quick, gentle smile, and stands up.

"What..." Donovan begins, but Smith snaps at him immediately and shuts him down.

"Shut it, Walker."

Donovan looks mutinous as Smith walks back to the front of the room, and he leans over to me, face angry. I start to pull back when he reaches out his hand and grabs mine.

"If we're on a team, we all have to know how to do this shit. So *WHAT* do I have to do...," he says loudly, and pointedly, staring at Smith, "to help the next time this happens?"

Smith stops and looks back at Donovan, who meets his curious look with a hard glare. "Ooookay," Smith says, surprise lacing his voice. "Maybe Reed can walk us through a 101 on her later today."

I groan loudly. "Seriously? I have to teach you all the ways I'm a fuck-up?" Turning to Hideo, I bury my face in his shoulder, and I feel him stiffen slightly in surprise, before a careful arm wraps around me gently.

"I can walk you all through it," he says firmly. "There's no need for Kai to."

I pull back to smile gratefully at him, face still heavy with sadness, when I see Jonah's face behind Deo. He's stripped bare, face raw and helpless, and he moves to take a step forward before stepping back again. I only have a second to wonder what's wrong with him before Deo squeezes me slightly and says under his breath, "Do you want to hit the Tank and I'll fill them in on grounding techniques? Though it seems like Smith might already be familiar with them..."

I shrug. "Maybe just hang in my office for an hour or two?" Giving an embarrassed wave to the group, I head out of the room as I hear Deo's voice begin.

"Okay, so there are several situations where Kai can be overwhelmed..."

I've only been working for thirty minutes or so when a quiet, polite knock sounds on my office door. I'm growling at my computer rebooting, unprompted, for the fourth time in a row, and snap out, "Come in!" expecting Hideo or one of the guys. Instead, the smug, smarmy face of James Tennireef peers around the corner.

I frown. "Booking room is down the hall, Senator Tennireef. What'd you do this time?"

He smiles gently, looking for all the world like I've welcomed him with open arms. "Ms. Reed. Delighted to see you. Do you mind...?" He motions to the open seat on the opposite side of my desk.

I grimace. He occasionally slips into a faux-British turn of phrase, and while, from almost anyone else, it might be charming, from him it was oily and obnoxious. Still, he's a Senator, and I can't very well turn him away without reason. Jerking my head slightly, I say with a saccharine sweetness, "Of course, *Senator*. Be my guest."

His lips twitch with genuine amusement for a moment, and he shakes his head slightly as he moves to sit across from me.

"Please, Ms. Reed. James." He raises an eyebrow, waiting for reciprocation, but I'm Petty White here and raise both mine back in mock confusion. "Ah. Right. I feel, Ms. Reed–" he stresses my name slightly, the only sign that I've annoyed him in any way, "that we've gotten off on the wrong foot."

"Which time?" I ask snarkily. "When you were here for trafficking? For suspected dealing? When you were implicated by four different gang members as being involved in several, shall we say, *unsavory* dealings? Only to have all four men get off with minor infractions, and later be found dead execution style by a 'rival gang'?" I put the last in air quotes, and he stares at me, jaw flexed forward, lips tight.

We stay for a moment like that before he surprises me by flashing a devastating grin at me and shaking his head, running his hand through his hair. Rather than messing up his careful image, he has somehow managed to make himself look charmingly disheveled. Leaning forward, he rests his elbows on my desk, still trying his damnedest to level me with his smile.

"Yes," he replies simply. "Those times." I lean back cautiously, unsure where he's going with any of this. "I understand, of course I understand, how it must seem to you." He laughs slightly, disarmingly, and says with a self-deprecating shake of his head, "I don't blame you. Truly I don't. You're welcome to read me if you feel I'm being disingenuous in any way."

Flashing a feral grin at him, I say, "What makes you think I haven't been?"

Too schooled to show I've ruffled him at all, he tilts his head curiously, like an eager bird. "Because you play by the rules, Ms. Reed. Unless pushed, in most cases you follow procedure. And I happen to know that, contractually, you are not allowed to read any higher ups without their express permission, in order to maintain a pleasant working environment. And I, Ms. Reed, despite your vehement protests, am classified as a higher up. Mmmm?"

Gritting my teeth, I glare at him silently.

"That's what I thought. Now Kailani – I *may* call you Kailani, can't I? Kailani, I honestly do believe we could work together for the betterment of the city. Let's be frank. I understand that not all of my... extracurriculars... are to your liking. But please believe I'm not as foolish or as stupid as you seem to think. Go ahead and read me now, please."

I drop my shields instantly, pushing out and around his careful facade. He meets my eyes calmly and blankly runs down a list. "I have never killed someone." True, damnit, but with an edge, a flavor of something else. "I want the best for Seattle, and Washington for that matter." True. He believes that what he wants is best for Seattle, but for himself as well. "I believe we could work together to create something great." True. "I would harm someone *only* if I felt the overwhelming *need* to, in cases of personal safety or similar." True... true-ish, anyways. That wording was odd. Very specific, and yet...

"Have you ever raped someone, James?" I ask, smiling prettily.

Lust flares from him, tightening my stomach unpleasantly. It's confusing and part of the reason I've only ever had a single boyfriend. When someone else's lust presses in on you, it can affect your own desires. I don't want to feel the thrills running down my skin at his response. It makes me feel nauseous, and I slam my walls back into place before he can answer.

He watches me carefully, lips pressed tight like he's fighting a smile. "If what we are discussing here remains private, as I assume it will, I enjoy consensual non-consensual sex. Do you know what that is, Kailani?" He drops his voice, so it's on the edge of a sensual whisper, and licks his lips slightly, staring at me, unabashed. "It's when you've both agreed to a sort of role play. 'Agreed' being the key word. It's all planned out before, there's a safe word, a safe signal... and yes, to an outsider it may *appear* non-consensual, but I assure you, it is."

"And Riley Beckett?" I ask, lowering my shields again to read his answer.

His pupils dilate immediately, and his breathing picks up slightly. "I never laid a hand on Riley Beckett, in any form."

I frown deeply, feeling truth from him, but also an echo of that horrible pleasure I had read from him on the first day. "You're telling me you had nothing to do with what happened to Riley?"

He smirks quickly before pushing it down. "I promise you, on my life, that I never touched Riley Beckett. Not once."

The wording swirls through my mind again, fogged with a heavy, suffocating desire. The guy sitting calmly and genteelly in front of me felt like he was seconds from coming. I open my mouth to ask him a question when he interrupts with a proposition so unexpected that I lose my train of thought completely.

"Kailani, I'd like to take you out sometime. I know how you feel about me, and I have to say, without being arrogant, that it's a highly unusual experience for me. Most people find me at least somewhat palatable."

I raise my eyebrow skeptically. "I find it incredibly hard to believe that no one has told you that you're an insufferable ass before. Not that *I'm* saying that. Just that it surprises me no one else has."

A tightness flashes across his face again before he plasters on that megawatt smile once more. *Ooooo dude. You are so close to the edge. You're not nearly as good as you think you are.*

He shrugs carelessly. "I'm sure someone has, somewhere, Kailani. I'm not in the business of not making enemies. 'A man with no enemies is a man with no character', after all. But I'd like *us* not to be enemies. Possibly more, if the chance is there."

I scoff. "You *can't* be serious. Why in seven holy hells do you think we'd be even *slightly* compatible?"

"Why would you think we're not?"

"I mean, the list is a million fucking miles long, James."

He smiles that same happy smile at me that he's been flashing all morning. "Come on now, Kailani. What do you possibly have to lose? Worstcase scenario you pick up something nefarious on me. Best case, we become friends."

"I think you have those reversed," I mumble to myself. "And I'm not going to lie. Your game intrigues me."

"One can only hope that *all* my games will intrigue you,"

he murmurs quietly.

"Gross, dude. I mean... I just vomited slightly in my mouth and that's still a better taste than your emotional signature. But sure. What's the plan?"

He holds out a glossy white envelope to me, thick vellum paper, clearly hand cut, and I stare at it like it's a viper. Chuckling lightly, he nudges it across the desk towards me. "There's a fundraiser October 27th. It's to raise awareness of human trafficking in Washington State. The Gaia Foundation is a major beneficiary, as well as Hope House and The Children's Garden."

I grit my teeth. The Children's Garden is a passion project of mine. It was started on a single-acre plot of land downtown where a building had been demolished. The city had raised money to buy the plot and turned it into a food and flower garden, taken care of by the children of low-income families. Since it was first founded, three other plots had been purchased and developed, and I spent a couple of weekends a month volunteering at the various sites. Hideo often accompanied me, and the memories of those weekends are some of the happiest in my life.

I stare at the invitation in front of me. James' smooth, practiced voice breaks into my consciousness. "I'll make a small donation to the organization of your choice, in your name, if you come with me," he says luringly. "Children's Garden is $10,000.00 away from a new plot. We could make that happen."

"You've done your research, I'll give you that," I snark, "but you may want to go a little deeper than my favorite color. If you knew *anything* about me, you'd realize offering me a bribe is the quickest way to earn a trip to You're-a-Dickville. One-way ticket, population – you."

"Ah, Kailani. Nothing as nefarious as that," he says, voice still coaxing, but the sharp edge of annoyance betrays him. "It's standard practice in Washington. Not a bribe at all. Just friendly support in return for your friendly support.

I'm not asking you to do anything illegal. I just want you to be my date for the evening. If anything, it's a gift."

Completely perplexed, I frown at him. "What are you getting out of this, Tennireef? What's so desperate that you'd donate $10k to have me attend a fundraiser with you?"

He stares at me through cold blue eyes. "I think you'll find, Kailani, that when I want something, I will go to any lengths necessary to obtain it." Leaning forward toward me, he reaches across my desk and taps twice on the envelope. "I know how you see me, Kailani, and I *will* change that. I'm not used to being thwarted." He's unnervingly focused, and it takes everything in me not to back away from his intense gaze. "The money is a small price to pay if it results in the outcome of my liking."

The air in my small office is heavy, pressing in on me, and I feel like a child trapped in the mesmerizing gaze of a snake. Then, in an instant, it changes as he sits back and smiles again. "Plus, tax write off, and it looks good to the press, am I right? You *will* accompany me, won't you Kailani?"

Unsure of what game he's playing, but knowing I can't lose this opportunity to get an in, I nod once, more of an acknowledgement of his question than an agreement. but he grins. "Good. I'll have my driver pick you up, of course, and we'll meet there? It will be a true honor to have you on my arm."

Standing, he adjusts the chair back to its original position. "And now I'll leave you to it. Thank you for your time this morning, Kailani. I trust it's the first step to a truly beautiful friendship."

"Tennireef..." I say as he gets up. "No donation though. This is not a monetary transaction."

Giving a brief wave and a little wink, he mimes locking his lips with a key and throwing it away, then leaves my office, closing the door carefully behind him.

Well, fuuuuuuuuck.

◆ ◆ ◆

I head to the conference room immediately, still somewhat bemused by my interaction with Tennireef, but have a small smile on my face as a thought occurs to me.

"You are not going to *believe* the meeting I just had," I say as I enter the room, having done a quick check and only registered the guys before I entered.

"Do share, Kailani." Elizabeth's cool, amused voice surprises me, and I start, shaking my head at her.

"I will never get used to that." Glancing behind her I see Fallon huddled in the corner, and I frown briefly, reaching out again and immediately registering her emotional signature. *Weird. I could swear...* Still frowning I do a second sweep of the room and feel Maddox and then Hideo pulse in and out of my awareness.

"Something wrong, Kai?" Jonah asks, concern lacing his tone.

I tap my head. "Wires are crossed or something. I think I'm over tired. Things aren't working right."

Elizabeth looks carefully at me, worry creasing her forehead slightly. She picks up her phone and shoots off a quick text, then murmurs something to Fallon behind her, who quickly gets up and brings me over a glass of water.

"You shouldn't run yourself ragged, Kailani," she says, brisk and blunt as usual. "It does no one any good, and you don't know your limitations well enough to risk anything."

I raise my glass of water in mock salute. "Yes, Mom."

She grimaces. "Oh lord. Could you even imagine? Me as a mother?" A look of distaste flashes across her face before she laughs a little. "I love the idea of children, but my goodness. The reality of sticky hands touching my chinoiserie couches? No thank you."

I laugh, somewhat surprised at her obvious dislike of children, especially given her line of work, but then again, she is *all* logic, and being a mother, I imagine, is all emotion.

"In any case, Kailani, will you elaborate on your eventful morning?"

I shake my head wryly. "You'll never believe who showed up uninvited in my fucking office this morning. James freaking Tennireef."

Everyone at the table sits to sharp and sudden attention. It's like I have a string attached to all of them and yanked it.

"Why in the world would Tennireef come to your office?" Hideo asks thoughtfully.

"Well, here's the good news–" I look towards Elizabeth. "He asked me to go to that big fundraising gala in a couple weeks with him, so we don't need to keep looking for an in with him. I'll be his plus-one."

The guys look happy with the news, but Elizabeth purses her lips tightly.

"What's wrong?" I ask her, concerned with her response.

"James Tennireef is the worst type of fool," she responds. "Just the absolute worst type of fool."

I grin at her in agreement. "I know that. I'm wondering why *you* know that. Did you know him personally when he worked at Gaia?"

For the first time since I met her, Elizabeth looks completely discomforted. Awkwardly, with embarrassment radiating out from her strong enough that it ripples across my shields, she fiddles with the ring on her finger.

"Not exactly. I run a sizable foundation, and don't often know all of the worker bees, if you will."

I cock my head, confused, and she rubs her forehead in discomfort.

"Ah. Well. That is to say... James was a mistake. A *single* mistake, which I do *not* plan on repeating. He was, shall we say, an anomaly in my plan."

"Why Elizabeth, you low-down, dirty *dog* you!" I tease. She shoots me a *look*.

"He's very ambitious, Kailani. And smart, seemingly

funny, and well regarded. On paper he checks all of the boxes. And he has no black marks against him. He *seems*," she says acerbically, "like a good bet."

"He does," I agree, softening my voice at her obvious distress. "Until you read him and realize he's an ass-monkey of the highest level. And Elizabeth," I add hesitantly, "this isn't an *actual* date, you know. It's just a means to an end. I'd never, and I mean *never*, date someone whose emotional signature tastes like rotten carrion. Did you... uh... did the two of you... I mean..."

"Well... yes, in so many words. And I didn't have the benefit of your particular skillset, so... That's why I need you to defect from this place–" she waves her hand around to indicate the entire room, "and join me instead."

"I'd do that for the price of friendship, Elizabeth," I respond. "One of the perks when you're in my circle. Free 'red flag' checks."

She looks at me consideringly. "You sell yourself too cheaply, Kailani. You're worth more than friendship."

I tilt my head, taking her in. "Nothing's worth more than friendship, Elizabeth. Real ones are few and far between. I'd take those over a pay cheque any day." I can't help but flick my eyes toward Hideo, who is looking at me with a strange look on his face. "My loyalty can't be bought and paid for. It's unwavering and unquestionable."

She meets my eyes, about to respond, when there's a rapid knock on the door, and one of her assistants drops a coffee in front of me without speaking, then leaves. I look at her, confused, and she waves her phone. "I'm learning you, Kailani. Wires crossed–", she taps her forehead, "usually means you're running low on caffeine, no?"

I take a sip, oddly touched at the unexpected gesture. "Well, Elizabeth, you've just earned yourself one 'is he an asshole' check, free of charge. Cash in at your convenience." She flashes me one of her rare smiles, then gets back on topic.

"So you're going to the Fundraiser with James, then?"

I nod gleefully. "It will be a good chance to do a real read on him when he's not expecting it. We should be able to get a lot of information."

Smith speaks up for the first time since I entered the room. "Be careful with that, Reed. I know we want to nail him, but we have to do it the right way."

Donovan snarks under his breath, "You want to nail him? Christ, what is it about this guy?" and I burst out laughing, earning me a long-suffering look from Smith but a reluctant grin from Donovan.

Still laughing, I respond, "Nah, Smith. All bets are off. I can't read my higher ups by contract, yeah. But that's in a work capacity. Tennireef asked me out in a social capacity. He made it very clear that it's a date, not a work function. Thus, during the time we're out together, as long as I'm able to stand his presence, I'm in the clear with reading him. It'll be hard with that many people around, dropping my shields, but not impossible."

The guys all start to smile and begin writing up plans for micing and wiring me, and Elizabeth watches through thoughtful eyes. Seeing me glance at her, she shakes her head ruefully and says softly, "The worst type of fool."

LIONS AND TIGERS AND BEARS. OH MY!

Thursday, 18 October – Maela

T his week the men put me into psychic boot camp. They work out a schedule between them: in the mornings, Emlyn and I will work on refining my control; I'll have lunch with Jorge afterwards, so that he can monitor my emotional state fresh off any visions; and in the late afternoons I'll have yoga and meditation with Kavi. Emlyn also announces that I'll continue my afternoon walks, dropping the bombshell that the creepy feeling I got last week in Beckton may be a sign that I am developing precognitive abilities. He's pretty excited when he tells me, no doubt thinking about all the benefits to law enforcement. I'm a bit wigged out myself – if I start seeing the future, won't that rear-end my sense of reality? – until I realize that I might be able to see the winning numbers on a lottery ticket. So, every cloud, right? Emlyn also reassures me that Ratko probably wasn't reaching for me in the vision but was bending down to pick up Altan's severed fingers. I gag but do feel slightly better.

Until we work out how I can leave and enter visions at will, Emlyn decides that I should try to see Jorge and Kavi during our sessions. Focusing on Ratko, Magda, or Tennireef is just too dangerous while I lack control. I have no problem with that – any excuse to see the guys! – but, conversely, find that thinking about them is in and of itself distracting. My mind keeps going off on tangents. Kavi's told me that most people are always thinking about the future or the past, never the present, and that one of the goals of meditation is to learn to be in the moment; but, for the first few days, all I end up doing is lapsing into fantasies. Jorge hand-feeding me tapas in Zamarramala. Kavi and I strolling hand in hand through the old streets of Ayodhya. Jorge, Kavi, and I going clubbing in London, the two of them grinding on me from both sides. And, since I've actually had only one proper vision where I wasn't asleep, apart from flashes, I don't have a lot of practice. But Emlyn is patient. In fact, he's a little too patient. Since the weekend, he's been a bit more distant, more correct, more professional. I thought, in a roundabout way, that we were becoming friends, but he's pulled back. And it makes me fret.

This morning I'm supposed to focus on Kavi. I slept well last night, so I'm feeling bright eyed and bushy tailed, as my Dad likes to say. Emlyn takes me through a series of stretching and relaxation exercises. He's quiet, and he looks tired, face drawn and eyes slightly bruised. Last week I'd have asked if he was OK, but he's giving off a "no trespass" vibe. I wonder if he's found out anything further about the mysterious Rhea, but it'll have to wait. Once the warm-up is finished, I get comfortable in the chair and close my eyes, my hands resting loosely in my lap. I'm going to concentrate on my root chakra, in the hopes that it will help me feel more grounded and focused. I breathe calmly in and out, just like Kavi taught me, trying to feel connected with the earth, visualizing a red glow, imagining the Kundalini energy uncoiling and rising. And my concentration flows up the chakras, and I try to see the silver rope twisting above me. And all of a sudden, there it is, and I pull myself up, up, up, hand over hand, looking around for Kavi. And here he is, in the yoga studio. He must be in between classes, as he's all alone. He's going through a complicated routine, and, oh my, he's shirtless, and I can see the glorious expanse of a broad chest and a stomach roped with muscles. I always thought that was a cliché. I mean: does anyone in real life really have an eight-pack? But, nope, it's not. Entranced, I count each individual muscle, one, two, three. Yup, all present and correct, and below, the flat, hard wall of his lower abdomen. I glance up, my eyes lingering on his pecs and shoulders, then sliding down his arms, watching greedily as his muscles flex and strain. He's beautiful: brown skin sheened with a fine layer of perspiration. Now, he's in a plank, and a few strands of soft black hair have fallen forward over his face. I want to run my fingers through them. Then I want to run my hands all over his torso, smoothing my thumbs over flat, brown nipples and lower down, delving into every hollow. I sigh and bite my lip. I think I could gaze at him all day. Somewhere, a bell chimes, and I turn my head to look for it. Kavi doesn't seem to notice anything. He's now standing on one leg, perfectly balanced, a statue made flesh. The bell chimes again. Annoyed, I glance around, and the room starts to fade. I can feel myself falling slowly backwards and make a grab for the rope.

When I open my eyes, Emlyn is watching me, a strange look on his face. "Success?" He seems unhappy, and I don't know why. This is progress, surely?

I nod: "Yes, I saw him. He was in the studio, going through a routine. It's amazing what the human body can do. I wonder if I'll ever get that good? I mean: wow. Did you know you can do a hand-stand with only one hand? One hand! Probably takes years of work, though." I'm nervous, which is making me babble, but Emlyn's being weird.

"I thought so. There were certain... signs." He taps his pen on the desk, eyes shadowed almost to charcoal.

Signs? What signs? I didn't feel myself up, did I? Or – did I have an orgasm? Did I have an orgasm and not know it? Is that even possible? Or maybe, maybe just a gasp or two? As in: Jeepers that's jolly impressive! What skill!

"Signs?" I quaver. "Like, like breathing? Rapid eye movement?"

"Something like that. So, now that you can get yourself

into a vision, we'll need to work on maintaining your awareness so that you can leave at will. Wouldn't want you getting stuck, would we?" There's a faint hint of peevishness in that last remark, and I look at him in surprise. Emlyn's not... jealous, is he? Not really. He's back together with the beautiful but cruel Clarissa.

His cheeks color slightly, and he looks down at some papers on his desk. "Anyway, we'll try again tomorrow. Now, if you'll excuse me, I need to get on with some research."

Bemused, I nod: "Sure" and get to my feet. He probably just didn't get enough sleep last night. Cranky-pants. But I hope he's in a better mood tomorrow.

The vision stays with me all afternoon, which I spend in a state of subliminal arousal. And I must be giving off pheromones or something, because both Jorge and Kavi seem a little more alert, intense, giving me little touches: a tap on the nose, a finger trailed down my arm to correct my posture. By bedtime, I'm in a froth. There's only one thing for it. Tossing my pajamas on the floor, I slip naked under the sheets. My mind goes back to the vision, Kavi looking a figure out of Indian epic, a warrior prince in his prime. I slide my hands over my breasts, imagining it's Kavi cupping them, leaning over me, leaning forward to kiss me. One hand darts down between my legs, and I fantasize that it's Kavi's, those strong, clever fingers starting to work me. I sigh deeply, stroking, caressing, not quite touching my throbbing center, but circling around it, seeking to prolong the sensation. I think of Kavi kissing me, tongue entwining with mine, and I wonder if he would taste of the chai tea he loves, warm and intoxicating. I think of him kissing his way down my body, licking, nibbling, sucking, and finally reaching my throbbing core, slippery as silk. He flicks out his tongue, tasting me, and I come violently with a wail.

I'm curled around myself, heart thudding double time, when the phone rings a minute later. I look at the bedside clock: 11:30pm. Why are my parents calling at this time? They never call so late. It must be an emergency! Who's dead? I scramble out of bed for the phone.

"Hello?" I'm breathless, worried, and dazed all at once.

"Maela?" Familiar crystalline tones shiver over the line.

"Emlyn! Why are you calling?"

"I heard you groan and then cry out. Is everything OK?"

Oh bugger. The feckity fecking surveillance devices! Of course he'd put one in my bedroom. It's where I sleep! How to salvage this? How?

"Uh, yeah, just had a dream."

"A dream?" he asks sharply. "Of Ratko?"

"No, no. Just your normal, run-of-the-mill dream. Kind of fading now. Probably tigers chasing me. Or bears. Or lions. I saw a documentary earlier. On Africa. Must be that." Lie, lie, lie, but it's the best I can do.

"Bears in Africa?" His voice now sounds amused.

"Well, maybe not bears. Maybe a tiger." I tremble: Kavi's eyes are as luminous as a tiger's, and his skin looks just as invitingly strokeable.

"I didn't think there were tigers in Africa, either."

"A lion then! Something big anyway. But I really can't remember."

"Well, as long as you're OK."

"I *am*, but thanks for checking. So... I think I'll go back to bed now."

"Alright. Sleep tight, Maela." His voice is suddenly soft and coaxing.

"Will do! OK! You too! Byeee!"

Hanging up the phone, I fall back onto the bed. Oh. Dear. God.

I'm determined to brazen it out the next morning. So Emlyn caught me *in flagrante*. Big deal. No doubt he'd fapped many a time himself. And I had a just about believable cover story. People dreamed of being chased, just like they dreamed of flying, didn't they? Anyway, he was hardly one to cast stones.

"Ah, good morning, Maela." Emlyn's voice is cool, and his entire bearing seems remote. He reminds me of the pictures you see of secret-service men, all impassive faces, straight backs, and 100% focused on. the. job.

I chirrup back at him and flop down into the chair. Today, I've paired my faded blue jeans with a soft, chick-yellow top, because Orgasms make me Happy!

"I trust you slept well?" he inquires, trademark elegant eyebrow raising.

"Yup. Like a log."

"No more wildlife? Not an elephant, say, or a mongoose, or perhaps a black panther?"

I narrow my eyes at him. Is he messing with me? "Nope. Not even a cobra, Sir Hiss."

He gives a short nod. "Excellent. Now, I've been doing some further research, and I'd like you to try this." He slides a clear, faceted stone across the desk to me.

I pick it up. "Quartz?"

"It's reputed to amplify energy and open pathways. I want you to keep it in your hand and try to retain awareness of it. Try to take it with you when you see. Try to use it as an anchor to come back to yourself."

I look up at him. "Seriously?" Despite the fact that I am living proof that not all stories are make-believe, giving a stone powers seems farcical.

"Seriously. Maela, we'll try what we can. We're operating blind here, remember, and we need to keep an open mind.

I shrug. "You're the boss." For some reason, this makes him frown – guess he didn't get enough z's again – so I'm glad when we move to our warm-up. Today, I'm going to concentrate on my sacral chakra. Kavi told me about it in our lesson yesterday. It represents creativity, emotions, and sensual pleasure so, after last night, seems an appropriate choice. I try to focus on my lower belly, roundabout where my ovaries should be, and imagine a deep, warm, orange glow. My attention sometimes bobs down to my root chakra, but soon I've got a sort of vermilion fire going. Clasping the quartz firmly in my hand, I let my consciousness flow up and out, searching for Jorge in the numinous black. I turn my head, this way and that, anxious to see him. He's in a small, dingy office, sitting in profile to me on a shabby chair. There's someone with him, an older woman with years of hard living stamped on her face. She's talking softly, and Jorge's listening intently, his entire being focused on her. I look around the office. There's a computer on the desk, and a battered wooden bookcase against the far wall, with, I squint, a few detective novels. Jorge's made an effort: there are a few colorful posters on the walls and a spider plant on the desk, but money's obviously tight at the clinic. The woman raises her voice, and I turn back to her, alarmed. She's sneering and swears, almost spitting, but he's looking tenderly at her, as if he can see past the rage to the hurt. Then her face crumples, and she starts to cry. He reaches out to pat her hand, and all of a sudden, I don't want to be here. I shouldn't be intruding, listening to her most private thoughts. It's wrong, and I want to go. I close my eyes and squeeze the crystal in my hand, willing myself away. I look for the rope, by my feet, and try to slide down it, fireman-style. There's a tingle and a vibration, and then I'm back. Opening my eyes, I nod to Emlyn. "It worked."

"You saw him?" He's looking intently at me.

"Yes."

"You saw him, and when you wanted to leave, you did?"

I nod again. "Yes."

He exhales slowly and rubs his forehead. "So, it can be done. I'll tell Seef to let Maddox know. They'll want that

415

information."

There are those names again. "They?" I cock my head at him.

He starts, as if he's forgotten I'm there. "Colleagues, at the Babylon Project."

"And they know *all* about me?" I'm starting to feel a little uneasy. Emlyn said he told someone at MI6, who told someone at the CIA, so does that mean that there's a file on me on a computer now? How far does this go?

He smiles briefly at me, as if in reassurance. "Enough. Who do you think gave me the idea to try the quartz?"

"Huh." I scuff my toe into the carpet. "Well, good?" I don't mean to end on a question, but my voice rises in spite of myself.

"It's all classified, Maela. We pool information, but it's known only to a select few. Your identity won't get out. It's the last thing we'd want."

I bite my lip. "OK."

"So, do you feel ready to take the next step, to try to see Ratko again, or Magda? For the moment, I think they're our best bets."

My eyes bulge: "You mean, now?"

He smiles again, longer this time. "No, not now. That's enough for one day. But on Monday, I'd like to give it a go."

I nod dumbly, looking into his eyes. They're pewter now, with a hint of a sparkle. My success has obviously energized him, and all at once, I'm excited too. "Yeah. OK. Yes. Yes, I will." I'm back to the super-awesome secret-agent fantasy, being dame-d by the Queen. Only this time, Emlyn's beside me.

Emlyn flashes me a brief grin, and, oh, that dimple! "Excellent, Maela. Well, take the weekend off, rest, and we'll start the hunt on Monday."

I practically skip out of the office. Jorge's visiting his grandmother this weekend; Kavi's leading a retreat; and Emlyn's probably attending a ball with Clarissa at his parent's country estate, but I'm going to download a few karate videos and start learning self-defense. After all, we secret agents have to be prepared.

FLUFFY DUCKLING

Monday 22 October – Maela

So, karate's kind of flippin' difficult. I don't know why I thought it would be easier. Jackie Chan, after all, has trained for years and years to get that good. And, it turns out he's broken practically every single bone in his body, or close enough, so I need to take baby steps. It's just that I, oh, I don't know, I want to be a bit more kick-ass-y. I think I come across as a fluffy duckling, quacking and wobbling along, and I really want the men to be impressed with me. They're so strong, each in their own way. Emlyn maintains a stiff upper lip and gets on with the job, even though he's grieving the loss of his younger brother; Jorge bears the pain of others with a smile; and Kavi's not only physically powerful but radiates peace, as if he's faced and conquered all of his demons. I feel like a moppet: all "weah, weah, I can't take a few scary dreams". I want the men to see me as capable, confident, and desirable. I want to see myself that way.

Emlyn's changed our schedule for this week. I'm doing my walks in the morning and sessions with him in the afternoon. He wants to vary our routine to maximize the chance of me spotting Ratko or Magda. I ask if we should also meet at night and Emlyn says we might do that a couple of times over the next few weeks, but Ratko's just as likely to do something criminal during the day. In some ways, it's better for him. After all, a group of people gathering at night in some run-down area is more likely to rouse suspicion, if spotted, then a bunch of men pretending to be technicians at midday.

I didn't have lunch with Jorge today, as he's flying back

this evening. And Kavi can't give me a lesson, as he has a work evaluation, but he's promised to make it up to me by bringing over another Bollywood film and cooking me a curry tonight. Just as friends, he assures me, so tell Jorge not to get his knickers in a twist. It's on the tip of my tongue to say that, regrettably, there hasn't been any knick-erage twisting, of any sort, and that I'm starting to wonder if I've been friend-zoned, but then I remember something my mother once told me. *No one wants to eat at zee restaur-ant where zere are no cars, Maela.* So I hesitate, and then the moment has passed. Emlyn's still being distant, which is really starting to bother me. I don't know what I've done wrong. I wish he'd tell me, but I'm afraid to ask. What if he thinks I'm crossing a professional line by bringing up per-sonal issues and then our working relationship gets weird? It would be too awkward. So I say nothing.

We decide that I'll start by trying to see Magda, as she's less likely to be doing something violent. It's easier today to relax into the meditation. Maybe the crystal really does help. But it feels like no time at all before I'm standing in a pool of muted sunshine spilling past the curtains and onto the beechwood floor. We're back in her apartment, and she's sitting on the couch, tapping away at the keyboard on her lap. I mosey around to take a peek at the screen, and it looks like she's checking stock reports. Oh. Well, maybe she'll make a phone call and I can eavesdrop. I wait and watch as she works. And wait. And wait some more. Well, this is boring. Any mail or magazines with her address? I look around, but the woman is obviously a neatness freak. She's reading *Crazy Rich Asians*, but so is half the country, so that's no help. Magda's reading, her brow furrowed slightly in concentration, and I sigh in frustration: she doesn't look like she's going to be doing anything interesting any time soon. After a while, I give up. I've had more excitement waiting for the dentist. Firmly grasping the crystal, I will myself back to Emlyn's office.

"She's in her apartment, checking stock reports."

Emlyn frowns but just says, "OK. Let's try to see what Ratko's up to then."

I close my eyes again and concentrate on Ratko. Ratko, who likes carving people up and setting fires. Who traffics people and sells drugs and runs arms to terrorists. Ratko, who cuts out your tongue before starting on your fingers. I try to find the rope. I try to vibrate into the soft darkness, but the only thing I see is ordinary darkness and the only thing I hear, the harsh sound of my breathing. I open my eyes. "It's no good. I can't see him."

"Yes, you can. You've seen him before."

"Not today. It's not working!" I know I sound petulant, but I can't help it. I'm feeling frustrated and panicky for some reason.

Emlyn's face hardens. "Come on, Maela. You saw Magda, didn't you? You can see Ratko. Just concentrate."

"I *am* concentrating! If you think it's so easy, why don't you give it a go? You have fun watching Ratko chop people up and throw their fingers at you! You have fun thinking he's going to cut off your fingers and toes or set you on fire! Go on! Have at it!" I realize I've jumped out of the chair, and I look down and away, dangerously near to tears. There's a moment of silence, then I hear Emlyn getting up and coming around the desk.

"All right, Maela." His voice is gentle. "I understand. It's awful what I'm asking you to expose yourself to, but you're our only lead. People whom we suspect of having dealings with Ratko are just too scared to talk."

I glance up. He's standing in front of me, and his face is kind. The man of titanium from two minutes earlier is looking at me tenderly, his eyes gone a soft dove-grey.

I nod and bite my lip. "It's not that I don't want to help, Emlyn. It's just that..." My voice trails off. What am I going to say, that I'm a coward, a great big fraidy cat, a whiney whinger?

"I know. It's a tall order. But, Maela? You can do this. I know you can." He puts his hand on my shoulders, still holding my gaze, and for one wild moment, I think he's going to lean down and kiss me; but he just gives a little squeeze and lets go.

"If you say so," I shrug.

"I do. I have faith in you, Maela. Now, why don't we call it a day and grab a drink?"

"I'd love to, but," I hesitate.

"But?" He looks at me quizzically. "Better offer?"

"Hah. Umm, well, Kavi's coming over later, so it would have to be a quick one." I look at him anxiously, and my heart sinks. His face is shuttered and remote, the grey of his eyes chill.

"I see. Well, I wouldn't want to keep you." He turns away from me back towards his desk. "Have a good evening. I'll see you tomorrow."

"Emlyn?" I say desperately. "Rain check?" I fiddle with the straps of my bag so as not to stick my thumb in my mouth and start chewing on my nail.

"Of course." His voice is expressionless, and he's back behind his computer. "I'll see you tomorrow."

"OK. Tomorrow," I mumble disconsolately as I make my way towards the door. I feel like I've really messed things up, but what else could I have done?

I'm still fretting about it later when Kavi arrives. He's looking scrumptious. His hair's slightly tousled from the wind, and there's a faint flush to his warm brown cheeks, maybe because he's had to walk up three flights of stairs with his arms full of carrier bags.

"Maela! Hello!" He grins and bends forward to kiss my cheek, and my mood instantly lightens.

"Hey, Kavi! Let me take one of those."

"No, no. I've got it. Just show me the way to the kitchen where I will be your personal slave and chef for this evening."

I laugh. "OK. Right this way. But can I at least get you a drink? What'll you have? I've got white wine, red wine, and IPA."

"Beer, please." He sets the bags down onto the counter as I go to the fridge. "Good day? How was your session with Emlyn?"

My face falls. "Not so hot."

"Why? What happened?" He looks up from the bag he's unpacking.

"Couldn't see Ratko. No," I shake my head. "More like didn't want to see Ratko. Cuz I'm. Well, yeah." I bite my lip after that remarkably eloquent explanation and busy myself tracing the rim of my wine glass.

"Maela," he coaxes. "It's OK to be afraid." He leans back against the counter, those long, powerful legs encased in soft blue jeans, a reassuring presence.

I grimace. "I know. But I just…"

"Just?" Green eyes smile kindly at me.

"Well, I tried to learn karate this weekend. Did you know that?"

He quirks a bushy black brow at me. "How'd it go?"

"Badly. I strained a muscle. That's why I didn't mind you having to cancel our lesson today."

Kavi bursts out laughing, a rich, deep sound that rings out and wraps around me. It's infectious, and I start to chuckle. "Stop! It's not funny."

Still laughing, he tries to compose his face. "So, you think that because you can't do karate after one lesson–". "Two!" I interject. "Two lessons. Oh, excuse me. And because you don't want to watch a murderer, that you are a coward?"

"Yes," I nod. "And I want to be brave and all roughty toughty. Like you and Emlyn and Jorge."

"Maela, I cannot speak for the others, but I am often

afraid."

"Hmm." I'm unconvinced. What could this gentle giant be afraid of? He practically radiates calm confidence.

He sees my skepticism. "It's true. Do you know what I am most afraid of?" I shake my head, and he looks at me seriously. "Calling my parents. I speak to them every week, but I am always afraid when I pick up the phone."

"Really? Why?" I shouldn't pry, but I want to know. While I don't enjoy my mother's interrogation about my love life, or lack thereof, I usually have a nice time talking to my parents.

"Hearing the disappointment in their voices when I talk to them about my work and my life here. They try to hide it," he says wryly, "but I can tell." He takes a sip of lager.

"Why would they be disappointed?" I mean, I wondered how Kavi ended up in London but figured he was like me and wanted to see a bit of the world. And he's a really good teacher.

"Because they wanted their eldest son to be a doctor. They sent me to private school – oh, they're wealthy and they could afford it, but it was still an investment. And I chose to become a yoga teacher. Not very glamorous." He looks down. "The thing is, I thought I wanted to be a doctor too. It's a respected profession, well paid, and a way to help people, make a difference in their lives, but," he shrugs.

"But?" I prompt.

"I didn't enjoy the courses. Just... wasn't inspired. My heart wasn't in it. And," he takes another sip of ale, "... sight of blood."

"Huh?" He's mumbled that last bit.

Kavi sighs: "I can't stand the sight of blood."

I stare. He looks so shamefaced that I want to laugh, but I rein it in. "You don't like the sight of blood?"

"No. Still think I'm brave?"

"Yes," I nod vigorously. "I do. So, you don't like blood. Big deal. You're still helping people, just in a different way."

"That's what I told myself. Yoga, meditation, they started out as a hobby, but I realized I was good at them and not only that but good at explaining them to other people. It took me a year to get up the courage, but, finally, I told my parents: 'Sorry, Mummy. Papa. I'm not going to be a doctor. I'm going to teach yoga.' That was three years ago. They still haven't got over it." He looks down at his glass and sighs again.

"Is that why you came to London?" I ask sympathetically.

"In part. But mostly because I refused an arranged marriage."

My eyes bulge: "You? Married? Aren't you a little young?"

Kavi starts to laugh. "Maela, my younger brother and one of my younger sisters are married! My brother already has a son, and my sister is expecting. I'm twenty-seven. According to my parents, I should have two children of my own by now."

"Well," I mutter, "I don't think there's anything wrong with taking your time."

"Nor do I. I wasn't ready for marriage. I'd moved to Delhi and was working in a studio there. Last year, I was home for a visit, and my parents said they'd found me a wife, the daughter of a surgeon at the local hospital. Usually, I'd be consulted, asked what I thought of this girl or that one. We'd meet a few times at family gatherings, have the chance to talk and get to know each other before deciding. But, I think my parents wanted to present me with a done deal, get me back to Ayodhya, or at least Lucknow, and back into medical school. My mother had spoken to the girl's mother; matters had been arranged. I had nothing against the girl herself. I didn't even know her. But I wasn't ready and wanted to make up my own mind. When I refused the marriage, it caused an almighty row. I could have returned to Delhi, but I'd always wanted to visit London, so I thought 'why not?' I got a visa, and here I am." He shrugs again.

I want to give him a hug, chase the shadows from his

eyes, but I'm feeling terribly shy, so I just say softly, "Sorry, Kavi." I put all that I am feeling into those two words, and he smiles awkwardly. "It's not all bad. I really like living here."

I remember something from the day we met. "So, when you said that you owed Jorge, that he'd done you a big favor?"

He nods: "I was pretty cut up about things. He helped me work through them."

"That's good. You deserve to be happy, Kavi. For what it's worth, I think you're a brilliant teacher, and I'm really glad we met."

This time, the smile reaches his eyes. "Me too. Now, enough sadness. 'He who does not climb, will not fall either.' I'm hungry, and, judging by that rumbling, you are too."

He laughs when I smack him on the head. "Just for that," I say severely, "I'm not going to help peel even a single onion."

"I wouldn't dream of it," he replies meekly. "You put this on," he hands me a DVD, "while I cook."

I look at it: *Mughal-e-Azam*? Don't you want to watch it with me?"

"It's a classic. I've seen it about a hundred times. Turn up the volume, and who knows? I might even sing along."

"That I have to hear." I go into the lounge as he starts chopping. Soon, the air is filled with the enticing scent of onions, garlic, ginger, and cumin frying, and my stomach gives another growl. It's so loud that even the music can't cover it. Kavi pops his head round the door. "I heard that."

I point at him: "You. Back to work. Sharpish."

"Ma'am, yes, ma'am." I hear the rattle of a pan and soon after Kavi humming from the kitchen. When he starts to sing softly, I grin: Kavi is tone deaf! It's adorable. He obviously knows all of the words, but he probably should never ever sing in public. That beautiful deep voice of his, so rich, so melodious when he speaks, cracks and wobbles when he sings. It's all over the place. I start to giggle and stuff my hand in my mouth, glancing over at the kitchen every so often. My eyes are still shining when he brings out two gorgeous plates of food.

"You look happier. Enjoying the film?" He sits down with me on the couch and hands me a plate.

I nod. "It's really good, and, uh, I like the songs." I do, especially when Kavi sings them, terrible though he is.

"Thought you would. Ah, we're coming up to a good part." We settle down companionably and get stuck in.

Later that night, when I'm getting ready for bed – alone – I stop to think about how much my life has changed in just a few short weeks. I mean, when I came to London, I hadn't had a date in months, and now I've got three... friends? The situation with Emlyn is weird, but it feels like we're more than colleagues. Not much more, of course, because it looks like Clarissa is back on the scene, but... And Jorge and I, are we dating? We see each other almost every day, but we only had that one brief kiss. He's told me he wants to give me time and space, until work isn't so stressful; so does that mean something will happen, only later, or has he decided he really does just want to be friends? And I'm so comfortable with Kavi and would be happy for something to happen, but he hasn't made a move and it's clear he's not going to. When he left, he just gave me a hug, which was wonderful, but I wanted to feel those warm, amaranth lips on mine, instead of on my cheek. It's all very confusing.

LACE LANE

Tuesday, 23 October – Maela

I'm still confused when I walk into Emlyn's office the next afternoon. A quick lunch with Jorge – he had a backlog of work – was enough to remind me that I still fancy him like crazy. He was looking lusciously edible, lithely muscled under his thin shirt, dark hair tousled, stubble a little longer, and I just wanted to breathe in the scent of him and taste. And now Emlyn's looking all broody and intense, and I want to yank his head down to mine and demand that he take me there and then on his desk. I give myself a shake. Get a grip, Driscoll! Emlyn's frowning at the screen, and sex is clearly the last thing on his mind. But it appears to have the same effect on my abilities as the crystal, because I'm soon blinking in a dimly lit room.

Ratko is there, sitting on a lumpy couch, smoking a cigarette, and chatting on the phone. I look around. To me, it says "drug-den chic": scuffed wooden floor, a small television in one corner next to a mini-fridge, and beige curtains at the window. I shake my head. What is with villains today? Everything looks so ordinary. Ratko's got on jeans, a dark-blue sweater, and brown boots. Why isn't he wearing a red velvet smoking-jacket and stroking a white cat, saying "Ah, good afternoon, Mr. Bond"? Then I remember what he was doing the last time I saw him and shudder. Ordinary is good.

"So everything's set for tonight?" There's a pause, and then Ratko nods in satisfaction. "*Dobro.* Good. Be here at 8:00. I'll expect a report after. And Vlado? Don't screw this up." Ratko hangs up the phone and takes a few more drags on his cigarette. Then he tosses it to the floor and grinds it under foot. I follow him as he gets up off the couch and goes to a door on the far side of the room, which turns out to be the toilet. Ratko doesn't close the door – eww! – so I spin around and wait 'til he's done. I'm tempted to leave but know that Emlyn will want more details, so I don't squeeze the crystal. Ratko comes out humming, without washing his hands, which is just gross, and goes to the fridge to grab a beer. I'm worried that he's settling in, but he downs it and heads for another door, which turns out to lead into a corridor decorated with de rigueur graffiti. There's an elevator, but Ratko takes the stairs and is soon pushing open a frosted glass door onto the street. I look around, trying to take as much in as I can. It looks vaguely familiar: 1960's yellow-brick boxes, with a few scraggly trees trying valiantly to grow from dusty patches of grass set in the pavement. There's a betting shop opposite, next to a pawnbroker's and a mini-mart. And then I recognize where we are. I walked down it last week. Lace Lane, in Poplar. Another homage to developers' sense of irony. Ratko gets into a nondescript white car, a Ford, I think; and I try to see the license plate, but it's obscured. There doesn't seem to be much point in staying, so I concentrate firmly on the crystal and the rope, and then I feel myself tingling and take a moment to reorient myself in my skin.

I'm almost giddy when I open my eyes to tell Emlyn, "Tonight, at 8:00. The block of flats on Lace Lane, in Poplar. I didn't see a number on the door, but it's on the second floor, about halfway down the hall."

Answering excitement flares in Emlyn's eyes, and I see his whole body tense, like a coiled spring, as if the emotions running through him at that moment are so fierce that he needs to physically restrain himself. "Tell me. What did you see?" His voice is clipped, even hurried, but he listens closely as I recount my vision, taking down notes and asking questions. He agrees that it doesn't sound like Ratko will be there, but, he says, if they can catch Vlado in the act of doing something illegal, they might be able to turn him. It'll have to be a low-key operation. We don't know what Vlado will be doing tonight and with whom, if anyone. They'll set up a discreet surveillance, ready to pounce if anything happens.

"Great!" I'm feeling fired up, all Xena Warrior Princess. "What time shall I meet you here?" I want in: this is my moment, to show everyone what I'm made of.

Emlyn stares at me. "Maela, you're not coming."

"But," I crumple. "But–"

"Maela, you are a civilian, completely untrained. Taking you with me would be madness and expose you to unnecessary risks. We don't know what will go down tonight, and you are going to be sitting safely in your flat with a cup of cocoa, brandy-laced, if I know your preferences."

I pout. OK, I knew deep down that Emlyn would never agree, but I'm just so excited! This is the moment we've been working towards all these weeks, and I want to be there. "Can I sit in a squad car?"

Emlyn looks exasperated. "No. You are going to be parking that troublesome posterior on your couch and staying there."

It takes me a moment to work out what he's said. "But I'd be out of harm's way! OK, well, can I listen in on a walkie-talkie?"

I swear those beautiful grey eyes roll so far back in his head he can see the wall behind him. Wonder if that's a super-power? Rotate your pupils 180 degrees and see out the back of your skull!

"Maela, that is not how we operate. And no, you will not be listening in. I repeat: you will be watching television or, one can only hope, reading an improving book."

"Tchuh!" I cross my arms and throw myself back in the chair. "Fine! Be like that."

A smile plays about Emlyn's lips, which, though thinner,

429

are very nicely shaped and a sort of soft rose. "I'll give you a full report tomorrow. I promise."

"Tomorrow! Can't you call me tonight?" I don't think I can wait even that long.

"I have no idea how long the operation will last, and I'll have to fill in paperwork afterwards. Now, scoot. I've got to get ready." He makes to pick up the phone, the phone I'd earlier imagined him sweeping aside so that he could lay me on his desk, rip open my clothes, and roger me senseless.

"Did you just tell me to scoot?" Lust wars with indignation.

"I did. Now please scoot. You've done well, but I've got to make some calls. We don't have a lot of time to prepare." His eyes dance at me as I stand and gather my things.

"Fine," I say airily. "I shall expect a full report tomorrow."

"You have my word." I nod, regally I hope, and turn toward the door.

"Oh, and Maela?" I half turn towards him, questioningly.

"Thanks." He grins and gives me a wink, and, oh lord, my heart gives a little flutter, and it's all I can do not to swoon.

I spend the entire evening hopping about, biting my nails, unable to concentrate. I think about trying to "see" what's happening but remember my promise not to attempt unsupervised visions. I know Emlyn won't call, but I keep the phone by me all night anyway. How I eventually fall asleep I do not know, and I dream I'm back in college, giving a paper, when I look down and realize I have no clothes on but no one's noticed.

The next morning passes in an agony of suspense. I tell Jorge and Kavi about the operation, and they too are keen to find out what has happened. By the time I burst into Emlyn's office I'm on tenterhooks. He's at his desk, looking grey and drawn.

"Emlyn!"

He looks up. "It was a disaster," he says shortly. He rubs his forehead and exhales heavily. "We almost had him, but he got away."

"What? How?" I'm gaping, my mouth opening and closing like a fish. How could MI5 bungle an operation?

Emlyn tells me that he had a good team, but that, for reasons of jurisdictional courtesy, an officer from the local police division had to be included. The force sent a rookie, who turned out to be the nephew of a Metropolitan chief inspector. When Emlyn catches my dumbfounded look, he nods. "Yes, it happens." He tells me that he paired the rookie with an experienced agent and placed them on the first floor, where he thought they'd be out of the way but close enough to help, if necessary. Emlyn and another agent were on the second floor, in a vacant flat. They'd placed security cameras in the hallway. They waited from 7:30, but no one came, apart from an elderly couple carrying groceries. "We didn't think it was them," he says wryly. At 8:05, a gun went off on the first floor. The rookie had been clicking the safety on and off and accidentally discharged it into his partner's leg. At that, a door down the hallway burst open, and a man matching Vlado's description came running out, along with a few other residents from neighboring flats. When they saw two ordinary-looking men, one with a gun and the other on the ground, the residents ducked back inside to call the police; but Vlado fled down the hall towards the stairs. Rather than engaging him, the rookie, thoroughly panicked now, called for backup. Worse, he used Emlyn's name. "He was so loud, I thought he'd burst my eardrum," Emlyn grimaces. He and his own partner were running down from the second floor. His partner peeled off to help the injured agent, while Emlyn gave chase to Vlado. "He hadn't done anything for which I could arrest him, but I thought that I might be able to question him, under the pretense of witnessing the shooting," Emlyn says wearily. "He was gone by the time I got to the ground floor."

I start. *Ground floor. Ground floor, first floor, second – oh fuck.* "Emlyn," I ask tremulously, "when you say you were on the second floor, you mean…?"

"Yes, I was on the second floor, or, as you say in America, the third floor." He sounds utterly spent.

I bury my face in my hands. "I'm an idiot. I'm so, so, so, so sorry. I was so excited, I didn't think."

"Don't beat yourself up. Neither did I. And for the same reason. But I, unlike you, am supposed to be a professional and to know better."

"It's not your fault you were landed with an idiot." I want to comfort him, to wipe the infinite weariness and, below that, the self-contempt, from his face.

He laughs shortly. "No. I suppose not. God, what a mess." He sits silently for a moment then tells me about the aftermath. The two agents in the patrol car across the street had seen Vlado walk quickly but calmly out, talking on a mobile phone. They hadn't heard the gun go off and hadn't been given orders to intercept him, but they did note down the license plate of the car he got into. It later turned out to have been stolen. The agents also saw two men walking down the street from the opposite direction, who made as if to enter the building but passed on by as the ambulance pulled up. The department was reviewing the CCTV footage to see if they could make an identification. The injured agent would make a full recovery; the rookie had been placed on administrative leave. "And I'm going to make sure that he spends the rest of his life issuing parking tickets," adds Emlyn with a savage smile.

"So, did you find anything, anything usable?" I ask hesitantly.

"A well-worn copy of *Playboy*."

"Oh." There really isn't much more to say, and I bite my lip.

"Oh indeed. And I can't arrest someone for that." Emlyn

runs his hand over his eyes and then rolls his neck, as if trying to get a crick out.

"No." I pause, wanting to make things better. "Emlyn? It's OK. I'll have another vision. We'll get Ratko and the rest of them sooner or later."

He looks at me, consideringly, and for the first time a genuine, if faint, smile lights his face. "Bless you. You don't know how much I needed to hear something positive. I've been fending off bollockings all day."

I smile back at him. "Don't suppose you need a cup of tea?" I'm craving caffeine and something sweet.

"I could definitely use one. So, pot of Lapsang Souchong for two?"

I look at him, alarmed, as he gets up and pulls on his coat. "Uh. Well. Uh." And then I notice the twinkle in his eye, and I smack him lightly on the arm as he comes up to me. "Ha, ha, ha. Just for that, you're buying."

He's still chuckling as we walk out the door.

FIVE-TIERED CAKE

Wednesday, 24 October – Kailani

Smith comes back in from lunch break, face like thunder, like glass about to shatter. "Damnit!" he growls, low and angry, into the phone. "Shit, Seef! Nothing? Nothing...?" He sighs deeply and rubs his forehead. "But what good is she if you can't even... Christ, Seef. I'm not insulting... Seef. I'm not criticizing her; I'm saying she's no good if you can't even... I'm saying it's your mistake, not... He shot his fucking partner?" Smith collapses into his usual seat, face in his hands. "Seef, you have got to be fucking with me right now..." There's a long pause, and he looks up at me, frustration and hope at war on his chiseled face. "Naw. Friday's still on so... our girl can handle herself, Bro. No worries there."

I flush slightly, lips turning up in spite of myself. Smith sounds oddly proud, and while I don't want his opinion to mean that much to me, somehow it does. Over the past week things have finally hit a rhythm. We've started meshing as a team, having reached a truce, albeit an uneasy one. We're beginning to form those tiny, meaningless habits that draw us together as a unit. I'm still hesitant to train with Smith or Donovan, but Deo, Jonah, and I meet first thing every morning to work out together, Jonah adding in a necessary element of surprise. Hideo and I have gotten too comfortable predicting each other's moves, and Jonah's consistent hits on both of us prove that we have to up our game. Jonah took my words to heart and has been making a noticeable effort to stop treating me with kid gloves. At first he'd wince every time he'd land a hit on me, but that fell to the wayside as soon as I took him down hard a few times. It's hard to pull punches when the other person is going all out.

Smith joins us as often as possible just to watch, and his input and critiques have been invaluable, but he's been tired, sleeping at odd times, having to work both Pacific and London time. He's clearly trying though – buying coffee for the team in the morning after workouts, creating agent-specific physical training regimes, and giving me scheduled time in the afternoons to work on my shields.

Donovan hasn't been around much, but when he is here, he isn't openly dismissive, so that's a tiny step in the right direction.

Our morning meetings, briefings, and planning sessions have been solid. We catch up with intel coming in from the other Babylon units if there's anything new, then scramble to connect it back to the mountains of information we already have. Everyone is being heard equally, all ideas and hypotheses discussed with open minds. The real issue is that no Kronos member has broken. We have no "in" anywhere, no agents to turn, nothing. We're following leads that are a year, two years old... honestly, the British team is our best hope right now, as their girl is seeing things in real time. The problem is that it's like having all of the ingredients laid out in front of you to a five-tiered cake, and a finished cake *right next* to the ingredients, but no recipe. You know they somehow go together to form the finished product, but have no idea how, and if you just throw them in a bowl and hope it works out, you'll be shit out of luck.

We've been banking on an operation the Brits ran last night, but hearing Smith's part of the conversation, it doesn't sound promising. And I'm silently wincing, knowing I have to follow it up with more bad news.

Smith ends his conversation, and, face still in his hands, calls out to me. "Reed? Please tell me we're still good for Friday. Things in England went sideways, to put it mildly."

An almost apologetic look crosses my face, and when I don't answer immediately, Smith looks up at me. "What happened?"

"Tennireef called me this morning and left a voicemail." I put my phone on the table, turn the speaker on, and play his message.

"... Kailani." His voice sounds tight, almost angry, before he clears his throat and regains his smooth, politician tone, "... Kailani. I am so very sorry, but I have to cancel our plans for Friday night. I won't be able to attend the benefit due to a personal matter that has arisen." Around the table all of the men share similar looks of disbelief. Tennireef doesn't really *have* personal matters as far as any of us know. No family, no girlfriend – he's very open and very present in the press. The message continues, "While I deeply regret my inability to take you, please know that I will still donate the amount to Children's Garden, as discussed previously. I *do* hope you'll let me make it up to you sometime in the future. My people will be in touch to plan something."

"Well... fuuuuuuuuck." Smith groans and picks up his phone to redial a number. "Seef?" he says and walks out of the room.

The others all exchange glances, and I can feel the thundercloud on my face. "You need to check that donation. It can't be in my name or attached to me at all. He's trying to create a paper trail where my ethics can be called into question."

Deo nods, and makes a note, and sighs. "What else is on the list now?" he asks. "Does this change our plans?"

Surprisingly it's Donovan who takes the lead.

"Okay," he begins thoughtfully. "Let's work this out. First, is there still a reason to go if Tennireef won't be there."

Hideo starts to shake his head, but Jonah interrupts him.

"Yes. For sure."

Donovan motions for Jonah to elaborate, and he reaches to grab our web of suspected traffickers, those who have bought *or* sold. He points to several of the men, and two women. "I did some research on the guest list. The very 'best and brightest' are going to be at this fundraiser. Looking through the past seven major fundraisers held in Seattle or the surrounding areas for anything to do with women or children, there has been a noticeable spike in trafficking cases immediately following. The only two that *didn't* have that spike were for the Children's Hospital and the Scholarship Drive. These guests were the only difference in the guest lists – for the major donors anyways. The fundraisers for the battered women's shelter, the crisis center, the children's garden... these all saw a dramatic increase in cases in the two-week period following. All *also* had fairly massive 'donations' listed from these people."

I feel the blood drain from my face. "How has this never been noticed?"

Jonah shrugs. "You don't tend to look at the people who are 'helping' as suspects, right? I mean, other events for sure. The Super Bowl has the highest incidence of trafficking in the US, followed closely by political conventions. But a fundraiser *specifically* to *fight* trafficking? Who would look at that?"

"And you think..." I begin, feeling sick to my stomach.

"That the attendees are using it to make connections? And basically order off a menu? Yeah."

Donovan, Hideo, and I all sit back in silence.

"Jesus, Jonah," I say softly. "I would have missed that."

Donovan nods. "Good job, Shotridge," he says gruffly. "So we go anyway?"

"We go anyway," I agree.

"The question is, how do we get invites and not scare away any potential predators? And who goes?"

"Not me." Hideo says this reluctantly, but I know his line of thinking. He's too well known in the city and carries himself like a police officer. He's never been very good at undercover work.

Jonah shrugs uncomfortably. "I don't think I'm the best option either, to be honest," he says, looking a bit down. "I'm not black tie enough."

Looking him over with a critical eye, I try to picture him in a tux. I get lost for a minute, thinking of him dressed to the nines, hair back, and I shiver slightly. The dejected look slides off his face immediately, and a mischievous glint lights his eyes.

"Kai?" he asks softly, humor lacing his voice.

"I think you'd be fine in a tux," I reply in a slightly strangled tone, clearing my throat. "But if you're not comfortable, there are other options."

"Yeah, I wouldn't fit in, I think. I'm not sure those guys wear any of this stuff typically." He motions to his silver and turquoise jewelry, the beaded leather braided surreptitiously in his hair. I love it. He's a contradiction – such a California surfer boy most of the time, but he wears his hair braided sometimes with the leather and silver, and has a hooked bone necklace he rarely takes off. His tattoos, the little I've seen, are beautiful, sharply outlined totems... he's warm and familiar to me in so many ways, our ancestry like old friends, shadows of similarities making an unknown feel known, and like home. And then at times he's so different, and wild, like the cold wind blowing off the Pacific, and a thrill runs down my spine as his eyes darken when the silence between us grows.

Donovan waits as the silence lengthens, and I try, but I have trouble looking away from Jonah until Hideo's warm comfort presses against me, and I immediately look up at him. Jonah makes a small sound of protest, but Deo speaks over it.

"Let's focus on obtaining invitations first, and then move on from there."

"I can ask Elizabeth," I say thoughtfully. "Gaia's one of the beneficiaries of the fundraiser this time. Or I could reach out to my contact at The Children's Garden. But they've invited me before and I've always turned them down."

We all sit quietly for a moment, running through our options, when I pick up a faint signature I recognize and smile. "Never mind. Problem solved."

The guys look at me, perplexed, as I turn toward the door and call out, "Hey, Elizabeth!"

She enters without knocking, looking at me curiously. "You picked me up?"

I nod. "Faintly, very faintly, but I'm learning to find you."

She glances behind her at the ever-present Fallon, who makes a quick note on her tablet. "Good to know. If I go missing, you can find me."

It's always hard to tell if Elizabeth is joking, but I flash a quick smile at her, and ask what brings her in today.

"Agent Smith asked me to drop off some papers..." She motions to Fallon, who quickly sorts out a few thin folders from her hands and places them on the table. "Just basic information regarding Gaia's operations, and the contact list he's been hounding me for. Now, why are you all looking at me like I'm Santa Claus and have a present for you?"

We all laugh – her humor is usually so dry, it's a surprising joke from her.

"We need invites to the Benefit," Donovan explains succinctly.

Elizabeth raises a single, sculpted brow. "What happened to your Mr. Tennireef?"

I cringe. "How dare you? And also, how *dare* you? He's not *my* anything."

She smiles unexpectedly, saying in a sing-song voice, "Oh, no Kailani and James sitting in a tree?"

"If your aim is to make me sick, you've accomplished it twice over," I groan, shaking my head at her. "He canceled on me."

"And you're still interested in attending?"

I nod. "We have some serious concerns regarding the fundraiser and ties to human trafficking. Will you sit down?" I motion to the chair beside her, and she sits delicately on the edge.

Elizabeth looks ill, her already pale skin going almost parchment white, and she looks at me questioningly as Jonah puts the lists in front of her.

"There's reason to believe that the people on this list have been using the fundraisers as an opportunity to find victims and make connections."

Elizabeth looks the list over carefully, then looks up, her face tight, jaw clenched, eyes almost incandescent with fury.

"Are you leading me to believe," she almost hisses, "that these people have been putting everything I've built at risk by *using my Benefits to commit crimes?*" Her voice, usually modulated and careful, trembles with rage. "And they've left a paper trail of some sort?"

Jonah nods. "It's a pretty clear correlation, and I've only had time to go back over the last year. I'm confident if I track back even farther, I'll be able to create stronger ties."

Elizabeth stares at the paper in front of her, thin, elegant fingers pressed white against the table, then clenching into a sudden fist, crumpling the paper in her hand. She glances at Fallon, who is sitting at tense attention, the first time I've seen her break her mousy persona outside of the Gaia Foundation headquarters.

"This. Is. Not. To. Be. Tolerated," Elizabeth bites out, and Fallon nods, making frantic notes on her ever-present tablet. Elizabeth rises suddenly, carefully brushing her clothes into place, and visibly wrestles a calm expression onto her face. "Kailani, you will have your invitation. I assume you can guarantee there will be no further criminal activity that will take place?"

I shake my head. "I understand how you feel," I begin, the ripples of her outraged emotion pushing hard against me. Elizabeth is beyond angry – her fury is volcanic at the moment "– but I can't promise anything. I'll do all the reads I can, but it's difficult in a crowd that size. It was one thing when I'd be focusing just on Tennireef, but reading in crowds..." I shudder slightly. "It's exhausting. My shields need to be down almost constantly. It's just... I'll do my best."

She nods tightly, then points at Donovan. "You. I'll invite you, and Kailani can be your plus-one. You can be a potential hire for me. That's easily believable. And people there won't pay attention to you once you indicate you'll be a blue-collar hire."

He frowns, and she shrugs slightly. "It's the truth of the matter. The people who attend these events are interested in the appearance of helping without actually having to *mix* with those outside of their social stratosphere. Fallon will be there to show you around, make introductions." Fallon makes a small sound of protest, the first I've heard from her, and I glance at her, surprised.

Elizabeth levels her with an even look, waiting, and I suddenly feel a little bad for the ever-present Ms. Agnew.

"Ah, Ms. Cole, I have our other engagement to attend Friday..." she says quietly, crisp accent adding an extra layer of deference to her words.

"Cancel," Elizabeth snaps out, and when Fallon opens her mouth to say something in reply, Elizabeth repeats herself sharply. "*Cancel.*" she says again, and there is something tight in her tone that has Fallon curl back silently. Elizabeth turns back to us.

"Also, I'll have a few other potential hires there as well, so your presence won't make a difference." A small smirk flashes across her face. "Your Chief Cruise is unhappy with me. I'm sniping his Bleeder Program."

I look up sharply, questions plain on my face.

"I'm trying to steal a few people from the programs, Kailani. You, of course. Someone by the name of Daniels, who's shown fairly good results, I'm told. Another from the program in New York."

I waver slightly in my seat, and Hideo presses his foot against mine. Elizabeth's sharp eyes miss nothing.

"Kailani?"

I shrug slightly. "Personal disagreement."

She watches me through careful eyes. "Would you ever consent to come work for me should I end up hiring this man?"

Without pausing to think about it, I shake my head.

"Well," she says softly, "I can't rescind my invitation to the benefit at this point, but rest assured, if his presence causes you any undue distress, I'll have him removed. And his name..." she flicks her eyes briefly towards Fallon, who nods immediately, "... is, as of this moment, taken off our list of possible hires."

My eyes widen slightly. "I haven't agreed to work for you, Elizabeth. You're risking losing a talented Bleeder on a long shot. I don't like the guy, but he *is* talented."

She shrugs again, almost French in her manner, disdain lacing her features. "I've told you before, Kailani. I value my people. I won't put any of them at risk."

"But I'm not your people, Elizabeth."

She smiles at me, some of her lingering fury fading as those champagne bubbles of amusement come to the surface. "You *are* one of my people, Kailani. You just don't know it yet."

Smith comes in at that moment, looking around the room at us in confusion, then sits down with a heavy sigh.

"Alright," he says. "Fill me in. Clearly I've missed something."

And for the rest of the afternoon we discuss logistics, major players, and protocol, Elizabeth's words floating, almost comfortingly, in my mind.

SWEET-BITTER MEMORIES

Thursday, 25 October – Kailani

Waking up with a sharp pain in my neck, I blink blurry eyes, trying to figure out where I am for a moment, before remembering Gemma and I had decided on a marathon session of 80's movies last night. Groaning softly, I try to sit up and realize my purple-haired bestie is sprawled across me, half-on and half-off our old couch. Smiling to myself, I roll her over, before standing to stretch out my tight muscles. Gemma usually sleeps like the dead, so I don't have to be careful or quiet moving her around and am able to push her back onto the couch and cover her with a throw. Looking down at her, I thank all the gods above and below for giving me a friend like Gemms. More a sister than anything, really. The couch creaks as she burrows into it, and the sound shoves me into a memory.

Gemma erupted into the cabin. It was always that way. She never just entered a room like a normal human being. For someone so minute, she was like a Tasmanian Devil when she came home – a whirlwind of chaos and disaster, wrapped in a tiny purple package of pure energy.

"That is IT!" she announced, storming to the kitchen without looking my way. Grabbing two giant mugs, she poured us both buckets of coffee before making her way over to me. "I'm sorry, girl. I am. But get off your *freaking ass* and *shower* for the love of all the gods in the universe. I love you to pieces, but the couch has an actual imprint of your enormous ass in it and it's time to reclaim your inner goddess."

I buried my face in the pillow beside me. "My ass is not enormous," I mumbled.

There was a disbelieving snort behind me, and a moment later she grabbed a handful of my *slightly* more copious-than-usual derriere. "This. Ass. Needs. To. MOVE! Again, and let me stress, I love you. I do. And I'll eat all of the ice cream with you that you want, honestly babe. But if you don't shower soon Lachy is going to kick us out. Not for nothing, but your ex is an ass-wad of epic proportions, and I cannot believe you are letting him turn your bad bitch into this... this..." she waved her hands around, seemingly at a loss for words. "Enough is enough. It is time to. Get. Off. This. Couch." She used every muscle in her body to haul me up and off the couch. Despite me completely dead-weighting her she was able to grab my arms and dragged my unresisting body across the floor, grunting with effort. "Oh you lazy fucking bitch!" she muttered through ground teeth. "You... Jesus... move... you..."

I stubbornly kept my eyes closed. "I'm *sad*!" I moaned. "Can't I just be *sad?*"

Gemma stopped moving suddenly and crouched down beside me, pushing my hair back and holding my face gently. "Yes, babe. Yeah. You can be sad. Pandas are going extinct. The Cleveland Browns have never won a Super Bowl. People are still hunting whales. Deforestation is rampant. Ben and Jerry's may never make another pint of Crème Brulée. There are definitely things to be sad about. But you can't let it cripple you like this. And Kai," she said softly, "I don't think you loved him. I know it hurts like hell. Honestly I do. But did you love him? Really? Because if you did, I'll drag your ass right back to the couch and we can cry some more together. I promise."

I took a deep breath and let it out slowly, ignoring the way she winced slightly at my exhale. *Okay, maybe I did need to brush my teeth.* Looking up at her through swimming eyes,

I tried to explain. "I... I don't know, Gemms. I loved the thought of him. I loved the possibility of him. Of not being alone anymore. Of having someone see me." I shrugged helplessly. "And now that's gone. And somehow that's worse."

Gemma slumped to the floor next to me, stretching out and wrapping her arms around me. "I know, KaiKai. I know. But being lonely with someone who is supposed to love you is worse than being lonely by yourself. It's the worst kind of lonely there is. And he didn't see you. He saw a caricature of you – something you constructed for him out of the pieces of you that he found worth looking at. But he never saw the entire thing. And babe, the entire thing is beautiful. You just need to be patient."

I lay still, letting the feel of her hand stroking my hair take away some of my sorrow. Closing my eyes, I whispered softly, "Gemms, what if... what if the way I am means no one... what if this is it."

She knocked her fist on my forehead, surprising my eyes open. "Better a lifetime of being true to yourself and being alone than a lifetime of being in a prison of your own making, trapped inside your body and becoming a willing puppet for someone else. But I promise you, Kai. Happiness will come. I promise. Don't settle for something wearing a mask of happiness, though. The moment you scratch the surface it will all crumble. And," she added thoughtfully. "I think it might look different than you think. Like, not like the movies, you know? Maybe the thing you think will make you happy is a tiger or something, but what really makes you happy is a... I don't know. A hippo or something." Gemma's eyes glazed over, and I could see the wheels turning in her head. "A... hippo-tiger? What would that even look like..." she mumbled.

I shook my head and slowly sat up. "Okay. Okay. I'm going to get cleaned up."

"Thank. GOD!" she exclaimed, nudging me so I'd know

she was mostly joking. "And then I can tell you about Tristan! He's a Film Editor! We met yesterday and hit it off right away and went out to dinner!"

I paused on the way to the shower. "Gemma," I said warningly. "How did you meet him?"

"Not important, babe!"

"Gemm."

"Uh... on the bus... he forgot his wallet... I bought his ticket... Like a real meet-cute, right?"

"Mmmhmmm. And who paid for dinner?"

"Well, I mean, he didn't have his wallet, Kai!"

"And who suggested the restaurant?"

"Kai! Don't make this into something..."

"Gemm!"

"He did, okay? He knew about this really nice little Italian place..."

I groaned. "Oh gods, Gemm. Seriously? I'm showering and then we're discussing this."

I turned again and heard her mutter quietly as I left the room, "I liked you better on the couch."

For what felt like the first time in weeks, I smiled.

I got out of the shower feeling monumentally better and even threw on some makeup after combing out and rebraiding the mass of my hair. After getting dressed in real clothes – no pjs for the first time in a week – I felt a bit more like myself. Knowing Gemma was waiting for me, I walked out to the front room, pausing as I heard her voice whispering angrily.

"I *know*," she hissed in a tone I rarely heard from her. "But we've been through this... I don't *work* for you any..." A long pause, which she tried to speak during several times, and then she cried out angrily, "Oh *fuck you!*" before throwing her phone into the couch.

I hurried into the room, concerned.

"Gemma?"

She looked up sharply and let out a deep sigh. "Oh. Sorry, Kai. That place I used to work called, my old department head wants me to switch back there and they're being... just so fucking unreasonable!" Completely frustrated, she started shredding the papers in front of her, tearing them into minute pieces.

"Well, I'm back in the land of the living. Can I help? I mean, I'm not sure what I can do, but I'll do what I can!" I started shadow boxing in front of her. "Bring 'em on!"

She stood up suddenly and rushed over to me, throwing her arms around my neck. I hugged her back uncertainly, not sure what had brought on this rush of emotion. I considered dropping my shields briefly to read her but remembered our agreement. I'd never read her without her permission. It was intrusive and invasive and affected our friendship. I had to depend on her letting me in, which at the moment, was incredibly frustrating.

"I love you, Kai. I really do," she mumbled against my shoulder.

"Sisters," I said firmly, hugging her back.

She pulled back from me and gave me a watery smile. "Sisters."

Wiping her eyes, she shook herself like a duck shaking off water and dug up a smile. "I'm gonna make some dinner."

While she walked to the kitchen, I started cleaning up the random things that had been left around while I was incapacitated. Usually Gemma was pretty good about cleaning up after herself, but the past couple of weeks had obviously let things slide. I called out to her as I was cleaning, "Hey! You have a commission or something? There is paint stuff *every*where!"

She responded over her shoulder as she riffled through the cabinets, "Yeah girl! I was going to tell you! Four paintings for the City Hall. Micro-paintings really, nothing huge.

But for the entrance hall, which is pretty awesome. High visibility. I'm pretty excited actually!"

"Gemma! That's huge! I'm so proud of you! Have you sketched anything out?"

"Yeah – dig through the pile on the table. They're in there somewhere!"

I started looking through the massive mound of papers scattered on the front table. Laughing to myself, I found little sketches on the back of receipts, napkins, and an old coaster. Making neat stacks, I came across a flyer for a hiring fair at the Seattle Police Department, including an opening for a Child Welfare Officer.

"Gemma!!!!" I shouted excitedly.

"Girl! Jesus, I'm making dinner here. I could have cut... Oh." Her voice fell slightly as she saw what was in my hands.

I waved the piece of paper around excitedly. "Gemms! The Child Welfare Officer!!!"

She shrugged, oddly flat in her response. "Yeah... I saw that and grabbed it for you... but I'm not sure... I'm... I'm not trying to be mean, Kai. But do you think... with your... thing. Won't it be hard?"

I smiled at her. "You have no idea how much I appreciate the fact that you worry about me. It's... I just really appreciate it. But I can do this. I know I can. This is what I've been working for! And it's a hiring fair so I don't have to send in my resume, right? I can bring it and they can meet me and... oh my god, girl! This is on Friday! Holy hells. I need to get my shit together!"

Gemma forced a smile at my excitement. "If you're sure, Kailani. Of course. If you want to."

I ran into the kitchen and hugged her. "Thank you for finding this! I swear I scour the website weekly and haven't seen a single thing about it. You're amazing!!!" She still seemed quiet, and I wanted to get her good mood back. Nudging her gently, I said coaxingly, "Of course, I'll need some new clothes for the interview..." Gemma's ears perked up, her shoulders relaxing slightly. "Maybe even a couple of options... Maybe I'll head to Target after dinner..."

She straightened up suddenly. "The *hell* you will!" she exclaimed.

"I *love* Target, Gemma."

"*Everyone* loves Target, you freaking idiot. But you don't buy *Fashion* there. You buy clothes. Okay. We're going out. Now. Put on your boots. If you're doing this, I'm coming along."

"But dinner!" I whined.

"We'll eat out. Boots!"

I smiled, seeing my Gemma reappear. Things were finally looking up.

Pulling back from the memory, I rub my face tiredly. It was years ago at this point. Years. But certain things stay with you, no matter how badly you want to leave them behind. Sighing, I look at the clock and decide not to go back to sleep. It's too early to go to work, really, but too late to go back to bed, so I decide to go in and do an early workout instead.

The night mist is still heavy on the ground when I get into the city, the street lights forming cold, tight pockets of light, rather than pushing back the darkness, and I shiver a little, my bike leathers providing me little protection against the damp night. Nothing feels right today – it's too quiet. It feels more like the city is lying in wait than sleeping, and I urge my bike to go faster, faster, just outside the bounds of safety, wanting to get inside and away from the heavy darkness.

The night guard gives me a silent tip of his head, buzzing me in, the lights still on energy-saving mode, casting odd shadows in the hallways. I head straight to the gym and run for a little, trying to shake off the strange malaise of the day. After running I switch to the punching bag, music blaring in my headphones, focused enough that it takes me a minute to realize the heavy bag isn't swinging like it should, and I look up to meet the cautious gaze of Donovan, who is holding the bag for me.

I start back in surprise, and he holds his hands up in a silent apology for startling me. Ripping my earbuds out, I stare at him, hackles up, jaw clenched, and he sighs.

"Sorry, sorry..." he mumbles, rubbing his hand over his short hair in discomfort. "Christ, I never get it right, do I?'

Staring at him, body tense in a fight or flight feeling, I whisper, "What the hell, Donovan? You scared the shit out of me."

"I really didn't mean to," he says placatingly. "I thought you'd sense me or whatever."

Not sure how to answer him, I shrug, and he sighs again. "Can we talk, Kailani?" he asks softly, and I'm completely thrown by his manner and tone of voice.

"Uh, who are you and what have you done with Donovan?"

He motions at the heavy bag, and I move back to it as he leans into it, holding it for me. Clearly, he needs something to do while he talks to me, so I start a gentle series of hooks, jabs, and reverse punches, warming up my muscles in a steady rhythm.

"I may have misjudged you," he begins, reluctance heavy in his voice.

Scoffing, I stop my movements to stare at him challengingly, and he shrugs, dimple flashing briefly.

"Right. Right. I *definitely* misjudged you. I think." Shaking my head, I go back to my workout as he continues speaking. "I don't... I don't like... I don't have a good history with social workers. Or Child Welfare Officers."

I can feel my movements slowing down and force myself to continue, knowing instinctively that he's depending on me to not look at him. "I didn't have the best family life as a kid, and it was made worse by the people who were supposed to be helping." He swallows audibly but keeps going, voice steady. "I had some preconceived notions about you, and Tanaka, and they seem to have been... inaccurate."

Coming to a full stop again, I look at him, baffled. "I thought you didn't like me because of the empath thing!"

He shrugs, a fucking adorable grin flashing across his face briefly. "Well, that definitely doesn't help."

Throwing my hands up, I turn away from him, and he reaches out to touch my arm gently. It was a kind of "asking" movement – he didn't grab me and demand I stop, he asked, fingers light on my skin, and, despite my better judgement, I turn back to him. All traces of the smile are gone, and he meets my eyes seriously, his light-green gaze focused intently on me.

"I'm not saying we're going to be best friends, Reed. I fucked up, okay? And Smith called me to task for it yesterday, and made me take a long, hard look at myself and how I've been acting." He rubs his head again uncomfortably but keeps talking. "You and I have to work together, and I'm creating an 'unpleasant atmosphere'." He's clearly quoting Smith here, down to his mannerisms, and I can't help but smile a little. "I have real, long-term problems with the foster system, welfare officers, etc., and those aren't going to go away overnight. It's hard for people who grew up with families and shit to understand." I almost say something, *almost.* But he keeps talking before I can, and to be honest, I don't know if I even want to. "But you guys really seem to care about your kids... I keep waiting for the other shoe to drop, for you to show what you're really like. But I could tell that court date really fucked you up the other day."

"And to be honest," he continues, "it's probably going to take me awhile to get used to the whole 'feelings' thing. It's just weird, Reed. But I'm a better agent, and a better teammate, than I've been showing. So I'd like to move forward with me trying harder and you agreeing to give me a chance to correct some of the shit I've done."

I stare at him thoughtfully and nod slowly. "We have to work together, so... yeah. Okay," I reply. "Thanks, Donovan. I'm sure that wasn't easy for you."

He motions towards the ring. "Want a less static partner?"

Smiling slightly, I reply, "Sure."

We start working slowly, having never really trained together, but speed up pretty quickly. We have a kind of natural instinct for how the other moves, and for a few minutes it feels like I'm fighting Hideo. That is, until Donovan goes for a quick leg sweep – not a move Deo would normally dive in for. Laughing, I jump back out of the way and say tauntingly, "You've gotta be quicker than that, Old Man!" and all bets are off. It's fun. It's *so fun*, both of us laughing and talking shit to each other, and I feel the beginning, just the slight glimmer, of a possible friendship. Right up until I throw him and he takes me down with him, twisting so I land partially on top of him, back towards his face. His shirt is pulled up, and shorts slightly down, so his taut stomach muscles and hip bone are exposed. A small, badly inked tattoo of a heart is dotted onto his hip, prison style almost, with noticeable pools of ink under the skin.

Poking it lightly with my finger, I start to tease him about it when he bucks me off and rears back, terror on his face and eyes wild.

"Don't you fucking..." His breath is out of control, muscles tight and flexed, and I back up slowly, hands up, voice soothing.

"Sorry. I'm sorry. I didn't mean..."

He holds up a hand to stop me from speaking, clearly trying to get control of himself, trying to shake off whatever feeling has taken hold of him. It presses out into me, the panic and absolute fear overwhelming me, knocking down my walls. Almost against my will I start taking some of it away from him, trying to make it better, trying to dissipate the razored-edge cloud of blackness that covers him, tasting like blood. It's so strong though, so strong, and as soon as I bleed some off, the rest rushes into me like a river that has broken through a dam, bringing all of his memories with it.

The crushing, chaotic fear of a child's terror pours into me, the feeling of being pinned down, the panic of being unable to breathe. My mouth feels full, or covered, something preventing me from inhaling, and there's pain, pain, pain in my body, pushing out from my hip where needle-like pinpricks are echoing out. I bend forward, head in hands, as the now and then merge, cruel laughter ringing around me, and darkness... I can't see, I'm beside myself, blind hysteria taking over, and I want to die, I want to die, I want to die...

"What are you *doing?*" A deep, furious voice breaks into my consciousness, and I jerk my wide eyes up to meet Donovan's wild glare. "*What did you do?*" He's beyond angry, the edges of him rippling like torn fabric in the wind, blurry through my unfocused eyes as he advances on me.

"I'm sorry! I'm sorry!" I babble frantically. "I didn't mean to!" I'm almost crying with the surge of emotion, the sickening, horrifying, rotten taste of old fear coating my mouth.

"Give it back," he demands, voice low and rough, veins popping out in his throat like he's doing everything he can to keep from grabbing me. "It's not yours. *Give it back.*"

I stagger to my feet, unsure when I fell to the floor, breathing deeply and shoving the emotions I unintentionally stole into a tight, locked box inside of me. Struggling to meet his eyes, I jut my jaw forward and say, "No."

He looks stunned, like I've hit him, and steps back. "No," I repeat, voice wavering slightly. "It's... it's too much for any one person to hold. No."

Sudden exhaustion washes over him, his face collapsing, propped up by only the echoes of anger. "You can't just get rid of them. It's not your choice."

I nod slowly, head pounding, and point at the couch in the corner of the training room. "The guys won't be in for another couple of hours," I say. "I'll hold them, I promise, if you go sleep for a little while."

He stares at me, confusion and fury and sadness and tiredness at war on his face.

"*Please*, Walker," I say, voice cracking on the word, tears now streaming unchecked down my face. "*Please*. Just... just go sleep for once without having to carry all of this with you. I promise you on my life that I'll give it back when you wake up. *Please*."

His face still a storm of emotion, he's too tired to argue and staggers over to the couch and falls into it, asleep within moments. For the first time since I met him, he relaxes into a soft peace, full mouth gentle, forehead smooth. I sit by him for a full two hours, watching over him, and when he opens his eyes and sees me, a beautiful, truly happy smile breaks across his face before he remembers. Sitting up slowly, he doesn't look at me again, just motions to me with his hand, and I, piece by piece, return what I took, watching his shoulders curl under its weight. I give back almost everything... almost. But as the cracks appear again, I stop, leaving a small pool of darkness in me, unwilling to finish. I don't *think* he notices the slight difference in pain, but when he stands and stretches, he pauses for a long moment, back to me. I wait anxiously for him to demand the rest, and prepare to fight him over it, but a moment later, he starts moving and walks away from me, out the door, never looking back.

SING, LITTLE BIRD

Friday, 26 October – Maela

Thursday is low key. My session with Emlyn has had to be cancelled: it turns out that when an officer is shot, there's a lot of paperwork and meetings, followed by a lot more paperwork and meetings. I tell Jorge and Kavi what happened, and we agree that we'll just have to work towards refining my visions. Yoga's going well; Kavi's introduced me to the third chakra, in my solar plexus, which is all about confidence and self-esteem and, so, perfect for my current state of mind. I need all the self-belief I can get. I haven't told him, but I'm actually starting to enjoy meditation and yoga. My head is usually a confusing and frenetic place, and they're helping to introduce order and calm. Jorge's on a mission to educate me about Spanish food. He brought back a whole box of his sister's mantecados for me, and, wow, they're just as good as he said. I'm thinking about trying my hand at them this weekend.

I've only had one vision, which was sort of, kind of unauthorized, but I don't want to get rusty. I considered shadowing Tennireef or Ratko but chickened out. I thought of Magda instead and listened in on a phone call. So far, the woman's life seems to consist of working and bonking Ratko, and I have to admire her dedication. She was speaking with Rhea again, telling her that another batch was almost ready, a few days at most. I'm desperate to know what it is – drugs, I'd guess – and I have visions of Magda cooking meths, *Breaking Bad* style. But that's probably what Ratko's for. Maybe he dopes the poor women he traffics into Britain so that they're compliant when they end up in

455

brothels. Towards the end of the conversation, Rhea must be asking questions, because Magda laughs and says, "Don't worry. I'm not like the boy wonder. It's all under control… Yes, alright." She then says that damn phrase again. It's not "enema" – it can't be. Maybe "enemy"? That would make sense. I'll ask Emlyn when I see him.

We have another session this afternoon. It's a nice day, and I take a moment to enjoy the sunshine as I exit Westminster station. I'm soon lost in my own little world as I drift along down the street towards Thames House. There's a song running through my head, which for some reason makes me think of Emlyn: "Un petit peu de toi me pousse me ramène / Au plus profond de moi je sens ton réveil." *A little bit of you pushes me, brings me back / In my deepest being, I sense your awakening.* Someone jostles me and apologizes. "Un petit peu de toi m'entoure me rappelle / Au plus profond de moi je sens ton réveil." *A little bit of you surrounds me, reminds me / In my deepest being, I sense your awakening.* Another person brushes past me, making me stumble, but then someone takes my arm from behind, steadying me. And they say chivalry is dead! I'm turning to say thanks to my rescuer when I feel a sharp pinch. Ow! I want to reassure my Galahad, who's no doubt ninety-seven and is clearly having trouble maintaining a grip, that I'm in no danger of falling and he can let go, but I start to feel woozy. I shake my head. I'm… falling? The sidewalk rushes up towards my face, but, no, I'm leaning on someone. And here's a van. The door's open. Someone's inside, but I'm having trouble focusing. And now someone's half-pushing, half-lifting me, and the other someone's reaching out for me, but it's all going blurry. So tired. Sleep. Just a moment.

Feck, my head hurts! I will never drink again. Bad Maela. Shameful Maela. Bad boozy Maela. I open my eyes and blink. Everything's fuzzy. And where am I? I peer blearily at the room. Dingy white walls. Dingy floor. Bare lightbulb.

"Good. You're awake," a voice says beside me. I turn my head – at least I try to. It sort of flops forward and rolls. There's a man sitting in a plastic chair, looking at me. Narrow face, dark hair, dark eyes, pockmarked skin. *'mye in a clinic? Where's white coat? Stetha– stetho– thingy. Clinic?* I want to cry. I've gone and gotten blotto, haven't I? I went and drank so much that I passed out on the street, like a common tramp, and now the police have had to scrape me up off the pavement and take me to a clinic to dry out. I will never ever live this down. A tear rolls down my cheek.

The man's face twists into a semblance of a smile. "No, you're not in a clinic." His English is heavily accented, and I feel like I've seen him before. Where? Tired. So tired. Just a little sleep. My eyes slide closed, and, all of a sudden, pain explodes across my cheek.

"Wake up!" The man backhands me across the other cheek, and my head rocks. I stare at him, uncomprehending. Fear crawls in my stomach, an insidious cold that slithers up my throat and chokes me. What! Why? I try to scramble away but can't move my arms and legs.

"The effects will wear off in a minute. And then you and I are going to have a little talk." He scratches his crotch, and my eyes lock on it, horrified. He laughs: "No, not that, you little slut. Unless, of course, you're a very good girl."

My head's starting to clear, but I still don't understand. Who is he? And where am I? What does he want with me? I swallow, trying to wet my throat, and realize I'm trembling. "Who? Who are you?"

"I'm your new best friend, Maela. I can call you 'Maela', can't I?" His voice caresses me, as if with a blade, sending icy shivers down my spine.

"How do you–"

"Know your name? Oh, we know who you are. What we want to know is: how do you know who *we* are?"

457

I shake my head, and the movement makes me groan. "I don't, I don't *know* you. I've never seen you before."

"Was it the Turks? Did those whoresons tell you? Were they hoping to take us out?"

He's not making any sense. I try again: "You've made a mistake! I don't know what you're talking about!" I look around the room, as if I can somehow escape. There's a metal table against one wall and a bucket in one corner. Apart from that, the room is bare.

"You're right. We've made a mistake somewhere. And you are going to tell us, little bird. You will sing, oh so sweetly, for us." He lifts his hand to stroke my cheek, and I flinch. "No? Well then. Let me show you how I can persuade you." He turns away towards the table, and I try again to get up, but I can't. I look down. My arms and legs are bound to the chair with cable ties. Scarface turns back to me, and he's holding a leather case filled with what look to be surgical instruments. I know it's no use, but I yank my hands and feet violently against the cables, whimpering. They hold.

He selects a thin, curved blade. It gleams in the harsh light, and I stare at it, transfixed, as he brings it to my face. I whimper again as the cold metal touches me, and he runs the dull edge across my temple, whispering: "Tell me, *kurva*." It's too much. My breath comes faster and faster as my eyes plead with his. I can't, can't get enough air, and it's too hot. My chest hurts, and my fingers and toes are going numb. A harsh sound leaves my throat. I can't breathe, can't – I faint.

Scarface is staring at me when I open my eyes. He's moved his chair, so that he's sitting directly opposite me. I want to go home. The crystal! Where's the crystal? I envision the rope, shining silver, and stare at my feet, waiting for it to appear. I will slide down the rope and out of this vision, and when I open my eyes again, I will be in my bed.

"So, you are awake again. Let us continue. How did you find out?" I look at the floor. The rope. I must concentrate. Emlyn said so. I hear a sigh, and then he slaps me. Once, twice, three times. My cheeks are burning, and there's blood in my mouth, hot and metallic.

"Who told you?" I don't know how to answer. I literally have no idea what he's talking about.

"Who?" He grabs my hair and yanks my head up, forcing me to look at him. His eyes are wild, like a wolf's, I think. "Inside the snow wind, the wolf's eye." The fragment floats up unbidden through my wretched brain. "Ratko only told me and Vlado. Was it Vlado? Or was it the Turks?" At Ratko's name, I give a slight start, and he notices. "So, we are getting somewhere." His grip on my hair tightens. "Tell me, *kuja!*" I don't say anything. What is there to say? He releases my hair, so violently that my head snaps back, and gets to his feet. "You won't talk? Well, perhaps you need some time to think. You remember my tools, yes?" He takes the leather case and leaves it open on the chair. "I will leave you alone with them for a little while. And then we will talk. Friend to friend."

As soon as he's out of the room, I try again to free myself, pulling, twisting, yanking until my wrists are bloody. It's no use. All I succeed in doing is tiring myself out. Along with the weariness, though, comes an unexpected burst of anger. Who the *fuck* does this *bastard* think he is? Yanking me off the street. Threatening me. The violence of the emotion catches me off guard, so much so that when Scarface comes back into the room after fifteen minutes and says "Ready to talk, bitch?" I don't think, just spit out, "I'm not telling you anything, *connard!*"

He loses it. There's a burst of invective, and then he's slapping and punching me, raining down blows on my arms, my head, my back. I hunch over, like a turtle, trying to protect myself as best as I can. My ears are ringing, and at one point my arm goes numb, and I think he might have broken a bone, but along with the pain I feel a small spark of pride. "To strive, to seek, to find, and not to yield." ... "Do not go gentle into that good night. / Rage, rage against the dying of the light." ... *Don't let the filthy fuckwit get you down!* I chuckle at my translation, which makes Scarface even more enraged, and he starts to shout, wailing on me even more.

Then there's the sound of the door opening and a sharp command, and the blows suddenly cease. I hear a brief exchange in a foreign language and footsteps coming towards me. There's a moment of silence, and my breaths are loud in the stillness. I know before raising my head that Ratko is standing in front of me. He smiles at me when I finally look up, and that chills me even more than all of Scarface's threats. For a moment, I pass beyond fear, and then I'm back in my all too aching body.

Ratko sits down opposite me and shakes his head. "You must forgive Bojan, Ms. Driscoll. He takes his duties very seriously and can sometimes be over-zealous. Now, let's see if we can make you more comfortable." He slides a flick-knife out of his pocket, and I start to hyperventilate again as he brings the blade towards me, but he only cuts through the ties. My hands are free and then my feet, but I don't move. I feel like a mouse caught in an open field, who thinks that it can escape the hawk circling overhead if only it stays perfectly still.

"So, Ms. Driscoll. You know who I am, and I know who you are. An intern, yes? And with MI5? Most impressive." Ratko's eyes bore into mine. They're so dark they're almost black, the eyes of an Egyptian cobra, and just as mesmerizing. I can only look dumbly at him. How did he find out? My question must have shown on my face, because he adds, "How fortunate that Bojan must have his afternoon coffee." Huh? Coffee. MI5. Intern. And then I remember. Damn Dean Fernsby and his booming voice! He'd practically shouted it all over the café the other day that I was working at MI5. And Bojan must have been there. I've got to try to salvage this.

"Thanks. But it's not really. I just do archival work." I try to shrug, and I wince: my shoulders hurt.

"Hmm. I think not. Codes, isn't it? Is that how you were able to crack the encryption on my phone?"

"Honestly, I don't know what you mean," I say desperately, and I don't. Encryption? I couldn't do a math problem if my life depended on it. "I study English literature. The librarian at MI5 is writing a history. He found a nineteenth-century poem, written in code, he thinks, and asked me to try to decipher it. I'm a postdoc at Queen's College and thought it would be fun."

Ratko strokes his beard thoughtfully. "It seems Mr. Ryder is a man of many talents: librarian by day, agent by night."

My eyes bug. "Mr.... Ryder? Sorry, I don't know a Mr. Ryder." What else did Dean Fernsby say? Furiously, I try to remember. He didn't mention Emlyn, did he?

"Really? When he asked for you specifically? And you see him every day, don't you?"

The fu–! Again, Ratko reads the question on my face. "Oh, the receptionist was happy to help when Bojan followed her to a bar on Wednesday and begged for your information. He'd met you at a café, you see, and you'd given him your number, but he'd lost it. He knew you worked with Mr. Ryder at MI5 and was desperate to see you again. She wouldn't give him your number or your address, but she did let slip that you go to the office every day."

Miss Moneypenny? Miss Moneypenny sold me out?

Ratko tosses the flick-knife. "Of course, you mustn't blame her. Bojan did add a little something to her drink. She was a bit... confused. And he is very good at asking questions." Ratko looks at me and smiles again. "Imagine how surprised we were when Vlado told us that an Agent Ryder had come with some friends to our party the other night. But how did he know the time and place? I'm afraid he spoiled it. My other friends didn't feel welcome. I'm a bit... upset. I'd worked so hard on it, you see."

What to say? What can I possibly, possibly say? But if he thinks I'm going to sell out Emlyn, he's got another think coming.

Ratko continues: "Of course, when Bojan heard the name, he remembered. A pretty, red-haired girl, with a pretty, pretty name, who works with a Mr. Ryder at MI5. Bojan's very good at remembering. It's why I pay him the big bucks, eh?" He laughs. "And he was sitting quite close to you. Such an interesting conversation."

I am a dead woman. Even if I were willing, even if pain managed to break me, there's really nothing I can tell him that he'll believe. I stay silent, and Ratko heaves an exaggerated sigh. "Come now, Ms. Driscoll. Unlike Bojan, I don't like to hurt women." Remembering the photo of Benny's mother, I choke back a sob. But I say nothing.

Ratko gazes at me. "So. Well, let's get that blood off you. I like to work with a clean canvass." He brings the bucket over. I look at it, my eyes following the swirling water, and Ratko looks at me, expectant. Am I supposed to splash off?

"No?" Ratko smiles: "OK." I'm still trying to work out what he wants when all of a sudden, he grabs my hair, and then my head is under water, and I'm on my knees, and I can't breathe, and I flail, but it's no use, and I can't breathe.

There's a yank, and, oh, blessed air, and I cough and gulp it in.

"Tell me about Mr. Ryder. How did you and he find out?" I've just enough time to shake my head, trying to make sense of things, before I'm drowning again.

"Was it the Turks?" Cough. Gasp. Gulp.

"Tell me." On and on. In and out of the bucket, trying to breathe while my tears mingle with the water. Throughout, Ratko's voice remains calm, as if we're having a pleasant chat about the weather. Then it's over, and he's helping me back to the chair.

"There, there. Hush now, *mila*." Tenderly, he brushes my hair back from my face. "You are loyal. That is good. I understand."

I blink at him. A drop of water slides lazily down my forehead, but I don't move to wipe it away. I just sit quietly, watching him.

He smiles at me again and takes my hand, twining his fingers with mine. At that, I do try to pull away, but his grip tightens. "You have a pretty face, Maela. It would be such a shame to spoil it." I start to shake. I don't want to, don't want to show any weakness, but I can't help it.

Ratko cocks his head at me, a travesty of Jorge's familiar gesture. Oh Jorge! Just a few hours ago, he was making me laugh, dueling fork to fork over who got the last bite of our shared dessert; and now...

"Perhaps I can persuade you another way." His thumb strokes the back of my hand. "Such soft skin you have, like the flower of an orchid. You are good and stay out of the sun, yes? And drink your – how much is it? Eight glasses of water a day?" My eyes go involuntarily to the bucket, and Ratko laughs. "You are welcome!"

There's a knock at the door, and Rako looks annoyed. "Excuse me, please." He goes to the door, and there's a short, low-voiced conversation. I can only make out snatches. "What! Here? Tell – Not now!" He sounds aggravated, but when he turns back, he's smiling. "Now, where were we?" He crosses the room to stand behind me, and I think about making a run for it, but I'm frozen in place. I can only wait and hope for – what, I don't know.

Ratko settles his hands on my shoulders. For one awful moment, I think he's going to snap my neck, but he only starts to rub, gently at first and then harder. It's painful: my shoulders are sore, and Ratko's digging into bruised muscles, but I say nothing. Kavi was right: it's OK to be afraid. "So, sweetheart. What can I do to loosen your

463

tongue, hmm?" His hands slide up my neck and down again. I want to protect myself, cross my arms over my chest, make myself a smaller target, but I stare fixedly straight ahead. "No?" His hands still, and then his voice is by my ear, whispering. "I think you'd find I can be generous." He runs his hands through my hair. "Come on, Maela. Why make this unpleasant?" There's a pause, and then his hands tighten. "Treat me well." He forces my head back, into his crotch. "And I'll treat you well."

Something snaps, the fear vanishing in a wave of disgust. "Take your hands off me, you sick bastard!" I yank away from him, and Ratko snickers. The sound sends me over the edge, and I hiss, unthinkingly, "Go to Magda if you want a fuck!" There's a gasp at the door, and Ratko's eyes narrow, all amusement gone from his face. "How do you–"

"Ratko!" A high-pitched voice snaps out angrily.

Ratko swivels to the door. "*Za'cepi!*" But he stalks out of the room, leaving me alone at last. I sink into the chair and try to take stock. My options are limited. Ratko's out there, and Bojan. And I'm not sure how far I'd get. Everything hurts. I'm eying up the bucket, wondering if I can somehow use it to bash Ratko over the head, when he comes back into the room. He's scowling, and he's holding a syringe. My skin shrinks.

"Time to say good-bye, *kuja!*" He flicks the bottom of the syringe, and terror drives me to my feet and darting towards the door. I don't get far, of course. Ratko catches me and knocks me against the wall. Then the needle's in my arm, and I'm slumping to the floor. As the darkness rolls in, I think I hear scattered words – *crazy, worth, find.* Then it's lights out and my mind goes blank.

JAMES BOND IS REALLY AMERICAN

Friday, 26 October – Kailani

S taring at the ceiling, counting tiles, I wait for the rest of the team to return. Walker sits next to me, silent as he watches me consideringly. Tired of the scrutiny, I turn to snap at him but see something in his eyes that holds my tongue. I look back at him, at first challengingly, then, once I see no fire in his eyes, more thoughtfully.

The rest of yesterday and most of today were... uncomfortable. Donovan was faultlessly polite, which set my teeth on edge. The rest of the team looked back and forth between the two of us so often it was like being at a tennis match, but they didn't ask any questions. We reviewed the players, the questions, and the plans over and over again. We knew all of the exits, where to be and when... everything was going like clockwork, no fights or faults or explosions. And yet, the odd silence made everything flat, and I was very worried I'd broken something in Donovan or put things back incorrectly. All of a sudden he surges to his feet and stands in front of me, staring down at me.

Walker isn't that much taller than me, maybe 5'11 to my 5'8. He's all muscle, not an ounce of fat on him, but not huge like Maddox. He's not quite as lean as Hideo though – somewhere between the two, like a Middleweight UFC fighter. Now, hovering over me in his long, grey peacoat and his crisp white shirt and black tie, he's the image of an old-time movie star, darkly handsome. He's like an American James Bond – lethal elegance, his deadliness concealed beneath dimples and flashing white teeth. His muscles strain against the tailored suit, just the hint of power visible in the way he moves... graceful, like a fighter, or dancer. He smiles at me suddenly – a flat line that doesn't reach his eyes.

"Well?" he asks, waving his hand over him. "Do I pass muster?"

His jaw is tense, green eyes hooded. I think back to the day before, when we were boxing, and Walker smiled, really smiled, at something I'd said. It's funny – Walker's features at rest are beautiful and intimidating – slightly heavy brow, thick, full lips, straight nose, square jaw. He's a coiled viper, ready to strike, muscles always tight like he's moments from unleashing. But yesterday, laughing with me for that brief moment before everything went to hell, his features changed. His smile is uneven – it's wider on one side than the other, and he has one slightly crooked tooth. His cheeks bunch up when he's really happy, deep dimples on either side of his face – and all of that cool perfection changes into something unexpected and wonderful.

I realize I've been staring too long as his small smirk falls away, and he raises a single eyebrow. "Reed?"

Trying to recover, I mutter, "Yeah. You'll do."

"Not half bad yourself," he returns, almost begrudgingly.

I smirk at him, batting my lashes in a poor imitation of some silver-screen siren. "What, this old thing?" I say disparagingly, while secretly loving the compliment. I hadn't wanted to go shopping for a dress for the fundraiser, thinking it would be a waste of time, but as soon as Gemms had heard, she insisted on accompanying me and helping me choose. Well, choosing for me. The result was a deceptively simple dress – thin straps, and a draped neck, skimming just over my curves 'til it hit the floor in a deep red pool. The back was magnificent though – a deep, deep drape, hitting just below the curve of my back, then falling heavily to the floor. She'd put my hair up loosely, almost messily, with curls escaping and trailing down my back. Together, Donovan and I looked like we were heading to a red-carpet event. At least on the surface.

Underneath, that was something else. I didn't necessarily agree with his attitude, but we are on a team now, and we have to find a way to work together. We have no reason to trust each other, have nothing built between us to make us count on each other, and I want to change that.

"Donovan?" I start hesitantly.

"Think you should probably call me Walker tonight. Might be a little suspect if we're on a date to this thing and we keep calling each other by our last names. And I think you need to fill me in a little on this Dustin guy. I get that he's an ex, but he works with the department, and he's going to be there tonight. If this cover is going to hold, we need it solid. Is he likely to make trouble of any sort?"

I make a small sound of agreement and try to find the courage to start again. He looks at me knowingly. "Whatever you want to say, Kai, you might as well say." Checking his watch, he sighs. "You have twenty minutes 'til the team returns, so spit it out."

Gearing myself up, I force an apology out. "I'm sorry for reading too deep yesterday." His face shuts instantly, going from tolerant friendliness to a cool professionalism.

"I don't know what you're talking about," he shrugs dismissively.

"You do," I insist. "No one else is here, man. Come on."

"It's all bullshit anyways," he snaps back, even the cool professionalism dropping away and revealing something darker, angrier. "Probably read some fucking brief on me or something. Can we just drop it please? Jesus. This night." He mumbles the last, rubbing a hand briefly over his face before turning away.

I sit carefully at the table and stare at my hands, now tightly folded together in front of me. My knuckles are white, and I swallow back sickness at the thought of what I'm going to tell this guy. It's all public knowledge, more or less, but having to feel the words inside my mouth, having to expose myself to someone who, on the surface, is so dismissive – it seems like a bad idea. Still, that vibrant pain that sits inside him that I reminded him of when I told him to think of something he loves... he didn't realize, I think, or he'd never have invited me in.

Taking a deep breath, I try to find the right words. "I was abandoned by my parents when I was six," I say conversationally. "Well, like, um, two, two and a half weeks before my birthday."

I can see him turn slowly to face me out of the corner of my eye. "Reed..."

Still staring at the table, I clear my throat and start again. "I'm trying, Walker. Okay? Just... Jesus. I can only go through this once, yeah? You and I can't be at odds all the time. It's exhausting. And I get it. I read something I shouldn't have, but I didn't mean to. And we need to fix this. So this is me trying to fix it, okay?" Running a hand over my eyes, I start speaking softly. "So. Yeah... they dropped me off at the police station..."

I guess the thing is, everything is simple until it's not. And sometimes the thing you want the most can be your greatest downfall. Those two statements describe most of my life. My parents really wanted a child. I mean, they REALLY wanted a child. I wasn't a result of a one-night stand, or a forgotten pill, or any number of mistakes. I was planned and desired and wished for for years. They wanted a child so badly they went down every route, and finally, right as they were giving up, discovered that Mom was pregnant. Finally. After years of trying. And because it had taken so long, I was their one chance. They were both getting too old to safely conceive again, and the problems that had plagued them the whole way along were only getting worse with age. They didn't even tell anyone until Mom was almost thirty weeks along. They had lost several pregnancies previously and didn't think they could withstand another public loss. Family and friends were hesitant to ask anything about Mom's slowly rounding frame, and, as she never really put on much weight, it really didn't become very clear until really far along in the pregnancy. At forty weeks plus a day, after a shockingly short and easy labor, I was born, and from the moment I took my first breath, the weight of their hope settled on me like a leaden shroud. I should say: I think they tried to be as good parents as they possibly could be. The years of empty expectation had taken its toll on them, though, and I grew up in the shadows cast by the plans they had woven together to weather the tumultuous rounds of "maybe next time". Finally, next time had arrived, and every second of every minute of every day pushed in upon me like a vice, seeing the confused disappointment in their eyes when what they finally had in reality didn't live up to the fervent dreams that had solidified into near-reality before I arrived. I was a demi-god of mediocrity in their house, and it was the great sadness of their lives that their one wish had finally and irrevocably come true.

They made it six very long years with me until their hopes became burdens too great for any of us to bear. Six years of ABCs, of first steps, of first foods, and first doctors' appointments. Of sideways glances, shared looks of concern, of trying, always trying, and failing. I remember them with as much love as I was able to find for them, but also canyons of hurt, and betrayal, and, at the bottom, buried deep, confusion. Because, without warning, one beautiful Saturday morning in early October, when the leaves were golden clusters on the trees and the promise of Halloween lay around the corner, they took me to our town's small police station. We'd just returned home from a brief overnight trip. They sat me on a small wooden bench outside the door with my little blue and white flowered suitcase full of my favorite toys, smiled at me, and asked me to wait just a minute, with the promise of ice cream to come for "being a good girl". They leaned over and kissed me and said they would be right back. And then, they left.

An hour passed, and another, and as the cold of the season began to set into my small body, I broke away from the bench at the risk of losing my ice-cream reward and went inside to ask for some help. Sgt Jeffers was on that day, one of five policemen in our little village. He was my favorite by far, big and jolly like I imagined Santa Claus, and surprisingly gentle with children. I explained to him what had happened and that I was getting worried that my parents had forgotten me, or gotten hurt, or something equally as terrible which kept them away from me. Sgt Jeffers looked immediately concerned – he knew Dale and Lela well, had gone to high school with Lela, and he put me in his patrol car to drive to our home on the outskirts of town. I remember what an enormous high I had felt, the lights flashing and siren going, people looking as the car sped by, and I wanted to yell out to them, "It's me! Kailani! I'm saving my parents!" I felt brave and invincible, riding with Sgt Jeffers, safe in the knowledge that we were going to take action. When we finally reached the long driveway leading up to my home, Sgt Jeffers slowed inexplicably, a crease of concern folding his brow. "KaiKai", he said, in his gentle way, with his booming voice quieted in a way that put me on edge. "Kai, are you... Did your parents mention to you anything about... about moving somewhere else?" I shook my head frantically, vibrating with an unknown emotion. "No Sir", I said softly but firmly. "No Sir. Mama and Daddy and I live here." He nodded, made a soft call into his radio that I couldn't quite hear, and drove the rest of the way up to our small farmhouse.

I had loved that home with everything I had in my little six-year-old body. It was old, paint peeling, boards on the wraparound porch warped and bending, but it was warm and comforting and safe. Its fireplaces and kitchen were enormous, and its wooden floors slick and worn. Sgt Jeffers peered at the house without getting out of the car, and everything on him fell for just a moment as he exhaled a long, slow breath. His face suddenly looked so much older, and I reached out a small hand to pat his cheek softly. "It's okay, Sgt Jeffers! It's okay! We're here now and we can go find Mama and Daddy!" He looked at me with tired, tired eyes and asked me to stay in the car while he went and looked around.

I watched as he got out of the car, paused for a moment with his hand on his holster, and then walked up to our front door. It stood cracked open slightly. "Dale?" called Sgt Jeffers loudly. "Lela?" He pushed the door open gently, and it creaked wide open. From the car I could see straight down the entrance hall into the great room. It took me a few minutes to understand what was wrong with the picture I was seeing through the door frame. When it hit me, though, it took away my breath as though I had tripped and fallen full force to the ground. The hall and the great room were inexplicably empty. No nicked wooden coat stand which I had ridden into on my trike, causing chaos. No long butler's table in the hallway. No overstuffed couch large enough to fit our family all together. Nothing. Sgt Jeffers glanced back at me and continued inside the house, still calling for my parents, the noise bouncing off blank walls and echoing through empty rooms. You could tell just by the unmuffled sound of his footsteps that there was no family left in the home to absorb his noise, to fold his voice into an existing cacophony of preparing dinner and watching cartoons and looking for missing pieces.

I was out of the car and running up to the front porch before I knew it. "Sgt Jeffers? Where... What's going on? Where's my Mama? Where's my Daddy?" He turned and looked at me with unspeakable sadness, and the feeling washed over me before settling in my throat, choking me with the bitter mix of pity and anger. These were grown-up emotions, and I didn't know how to process them at six. Their weight knocked me off my feet. My knees just gave way completely, and I collapsed down. "Why are you feeling this way? What's happening? Why do you feel like this?" I almost screamed. Sgt Jeffers looked at me with caution now, and opened his mouth to say something, when, from my position on the floor, I looked past him into the front closet and saw piles of framed photos. I made a small noise and crawled the few feet to the closet door. Every picture that had hung on our walls, every photo of my parents and me, all the moments that had been woven together to make us a family, lay there, discarded, glass cracked, frames broken. My first missing tooth, the most recent photo, discarded on top of the rest. I made eye contact with a different version of myself – a happier one, separate from me by only a few weeks. I remembered the moment my mama took the photo, how excited and proud I was, and then my eyes slid from my beaming face to my daddy's face in the background. I hadn't even noticed he was in the picture before, but now the look on his face struck me. My mama had just caught the corner of his face, barely anything, but he was looking at me with an expression so grim it was hard to understand that it was my daddy at all.

Sgt Jeffers cleared his throat softly and murmured my name. "Kailani? Honey? I think I need to take you back to the station with me for a little bit. Okay honey? Mrs. Miriam is gonna meet us there with some hot chocolate and some cookies. Won't that be nice? And we'll get this all figured out. Let's just head on back and get this all figured out, okay Kai?" I looked up at him slowly, eyes swimming, and said in a thick voice, "I don't feel so good." And then, mercifully, everything fell silent for a long, long time.

◆ ◆ ◆

"... So, uh... yeah. I went into the foster system for two years, was adopted at eight, by a couple named Lucien and Marian Price. Stayed with them for a year, but they, uh...

anyways, and then was put up for something called "Second Chance Adoption". Swallowing hard, bitterness fills my voice and hardens it as I force myself to continue. "I'm sure you could guess, but once a kid's been adopted and returned, they don't rank high on anyone's 'must-have' list. So I stayed in the foster system 'til I aged out. Almost aged out anyways. I graduated high school a little early, at 17, and the family I was with at the time wasn't super interested in keeping me longer, so I moved out."

A soft sigh sounds from behind me, and I startle like a frightened rabbit. Deo is there and reaches out immediately and places a gentle hand on my back. He knows better than to hug me here, where I would fall apart at his touch. His face is concerned, and confused, and I look beyond him to see Smith and Jonah there as well.

"Well, fuck..." I breathe out quietly.

He quirks an eyebrow at me, and I shake my head tiredly. "I was trying to right a wrong," I try to explain.

Nodding, he helps me to my feet. Smith's brow is burrowed deep, and his eyes are dark, while Jonah is desperately trying to hide his pity and sympathy behind a blank face, which I appreciate. Donovan is just staring at me, and I refuse to drop my shields to read him – I don't want to feel his pity, or disgust, or whatever the hell he's feeling. I hadn't meant to tell him so much at all, just even the playing field a little since I knew so much about him, but I'd gotten lost in the story like always. Nudging Deo, I whisper under my breath, "How long?"

He winces slightly and says, "The whole thing, KaiKai."

Groaning, I put on my big girl pants and turn to face the team. "This wasn't meant to be a group bonding session," I snap out. "It's the *polite* thing to do when you enter a room to let the people fucking *know*."

Smith and Jonah have the grace to look abashed, and Deo rubs my back gently. "To their credit, Kai, they thought you heard them come in. I was surprised you were telling the story, but didn't want to interrupt you because I know how hard it is for you to get through."

I answer his unvoiced question. "I was trying to explain the whole Dustin thing."

His face turns thunderous, like it does every time Dustin's name comes up. "Fucking Dustin."

The corners of my mouth quirk up into a small smile. "I love when you swear. It sounds extra dirty when you say it for some reason."

He meets my eyes with a small smirk of his own. "*Really now...*" he says thoughtfully. "*Do you?*"

His slightly flirtatious tone sets my pulse racing, and everything else that's happened falls away as I get lost in the sweet, milk-chocolate tones of his voice. We stare at each other for a long moment, before Jonah moves between us and Smith and Donovan.

"Uh, hey guys," he says softly. "Just gonna stand here and block you from some eyes until you look a little less like you're going to get naked with each other. Not that that's a problem to me, but Smith has a stick up his ass, sooo..." He stares studiously ahead of him at the wall, not looking directly at either of us, and I can't help but shoot a small grin at him. He feels my gaze on him and smiles back at me. "Aaaaawkward!" he sings under his breath, and my small grin turns into a full-blown smile.

Smith's voice resonates through the room as he calls a loud time check. "Five minutes 'til we need to head out. Are you two ready? Cole is meeting you by the silent bidding table so she can introduce you around."

Donovan pushes through Hideo and Jonah to be by my side. "Ready, Reed?"

I nod. "Better call me Kai."

"Roger."

"No. Not Roger. Kai. K-a-i."

He rolls his eyes at me, but for the first time I get a hint of a real smile from him, flashing quickly before he can stop it.

"Let's do this." He takes my arm, much more elegantly than I'd anticipated, and we leave the room.

◆ ◆ ◆

Several hours later the benefit is in full swing, and I'm exhausted. We've met a truckload of people, many of whom were pretentious assholes with more money than sense, whose presence even without reading them made my teeth hurt. Walker was getting really good at learning my signals and would gently steer me away from conversations where I was moments away from breaking noses. Cole introduced Walker to several major players as a potential hire for Gaia's security team, then left us to oversee the festivities.

The event is surprisingly raucous for a benefit. I can see Elizabeth in the distance, face tight, as she makes her way around the room, Fallon scurrying behind her. She is clearly focusing on a certain group, laughing uproariously in the center of the bar area. There are several women in *close* to inappropriate dresses, straps slipping carelessly off their shoulders, all surrounding a charismatic man who keeps shouting for more drinks. The barkeep is having a difficult time keeping up with the small crowd's demands, filling glass after glass only to have them replaced almost immediately.

The man, who is clearly the sun in the center of the orbiting chaos, is tall and slender, with an artfully dishevelled mop of brown hair. He has a squared-off jaw, and full, almost feminine lips, under dark eyes framed by eyelashes most women would kill for. His tailored suit is clearly expensive, but rumpled, and his tie is loose and open over his slightly unbuttoned shirt. His arm is slung around the shoulders of an equally unkempt, slightly younger man, who is looking at his friend in a way that makes me think all the women around them are wasting their time.

Elizabeth is watching them closely and visibly sighs

when *another* round of drinks is called for. She says something to Fallon, who scuttles off to the security by the door and relays a message. Before the guards have a chance to respond to whatever Fallon is saying, there's an appreciative shout from the bar, a rumble, a crack – all the sounds that are usually precursors to a brawl. As the bouncers move quickly over to the group, two of the women start yelling at each other, the crowd surrounding them torn between amusement and disgust. This is not the type of behavior Old Money likes to witness – at least, not this early in the evening.

I'm watching the events with a sort of sick fascination – this level of wealth is so foreign to me. It's amazing what money can buy – and what it obviously can't – when Donovan interrupts my thoughts.

"So," he began quietly, speaking under his breath. "You never filled me in about this Dustin guy."

I could feel the polite smile I had plastered on my face become strained. "Oh, you know. First love and all. Stupid young girl trusting the wrong guy. A million movies have been written about the exact same thing."

He listens carefully, then shakes his head slightly. "Naw. I saw your reaction to him, and Tanaka's, and I'm pretty sure he wouldn't respond like that just to a normal asshole."

"Lots of sharing already today, Walker."

He reaches out and takes my hand, studying my fingers. "I get that. I do. And it's up to you, but if you feel it's mission critical, I need to know about it."

Sighing, I look around the surrounding tables. Most of the seats are empty at the moment, the women making a group trip to "freshen up their makeup", and the men refilling double pours at the open bar. Only two gentlemen, and I use that word loosely, are left, on the far side of our table, and they're very obviously checking out the young waitress walking by. I make a mental note to do a little digging into their backgrounds later. But the sounds from the bar are still loud enough to make quiet conversation difficult.

"Who is that guy?" I ask, trying to change the subject, watching the leader of the drunken revelers try to bribe the guards with drinks and stacks of cash, smiling in an almost lascivious way at the clearly frustrated security.

"Cooper Firth. The only son of a *very* wealthy investment banker and a southern debutante mother. Guy's got more money than sense. He's in the news *all* the time. Crashed his Lotus last week, putting a friend in the hospital, and was laughing the entire ambulance ride."

"TMZ much?" I say, laughing a little, and Walker turns red.

"I read the news, Kai. Stop trying to distract me."

Sighing, I jerk my head towards an alcove on the edge of the room. He follows me over, and we sit, too close together, untouched drinks in hand, as I try to think about what to say.

"The only thing mission critical, really, is that he can play with resonance, which not a lot of people can do."

I can tell by his expression that Walker hasn't heard the term and inhale deeply, letting out a long slow breath.

"Oh. I thought maybe you'd... okay... Resonance is what's left when a Bleeder pulls a lot of emotion at once, or a little emotion over a long period of time. It dissipates, yes, but not always immediately. So sometimes once a Bleeder has pulled a large amount of emotion, a kind of cloud of that is left until it spreads out and disappears. Like if someone's smoking you can get faint traces of it for a while after. It's the same. Or if someone does a low-level constant drain, it doesn't give all of the emotion a chance to fade, so it just lingers. Barely there tastes of it, but it's there. You feel it differently second hand though. Like the difference between your favorite character in a book dying and your favorite relative dying. It's an echoed emotion, and really hard to pin down where it comes from. So it usually makes you really uneasy even if it's a positive emotion."

Looking at a point somewhere over Walker's shoulder I try to think of how to explain Dustin without making myself sound like a pathetic doormat. Here's the thing. I should have known. I mean, I really should have known. His name was Dustin Daniels. How, HOW did I end up romantically entangled with a guy named Dustin Daniels? His parents must have had some inkling when he was born, like, "yeah, this kid is going to be a fucking smug-faced bastard. We'd better warn people. What should we call him? Oh, I know, how about fucking Dustin? Dustin Fucking Daniels? Enough of a complete twat-waffle name? Great. It should warn off any sane human." But I wasn't sane, not then, and I wasn't even sure I was human at the time. And here's the worst part. I thought it was charming. When he first came up to me at a bar, smirked his smirkiest face at me, and said, "Hey. I'm Dustin. Daniels. I'm Dustin Daniels, and I know it's terrible, and I've said my name twice in less than a minute, but can I buy you a drink anyways? And if you need to you can call me something else?" I let out a short and totally unexpected bark of laughter, and he ordered me a Slim Shady, and we got drunk on cheap booze with bad jukebox tunes playing in the background, and for the first time in my entire adult life I thought: "This is it. This is happiness".

Nothing lasts forever though, right? That's one of the first things you learn, isn't it. Popsicles melt, Christmas is only a day, Halloween candy runs out. Nothing lasts forever. Nothing good anyways. The bad shit seems to outlive the good by light years. We were together for just over six months when I first told him about my ability. I shielded almost the entire time before that. I explained to him what I did, and he accepted it remarkably easily. At the time I wasn't sure he even really believed me, or got it, and I wasn't working at the Depot yet, so it wasn't something he really witnessed. He just thought I was closed off and that eventually he could break through the walls. He'd just say over and over, "Let me in. Trust me. I'm here. Let me in." And slowly, slowly I began to. He'd fall asleep, and I'd drop my shields for five minutes. It felt like peeling off a wetsuit after diving. Having shielded for so long, it was almost impossible to drop my barriers around another person, and that scared me enough that I tried more often. I didn't want to have the shields atrophy and be buried alive in my own body. So it would creep up to ten, fifteen, eventually an hour or more. And then. And then.

God, it makes me so *sick* to think of it now. I just didn't know. I hadn't ever met someone like me. I didn't even know they existed. We met in January, not too long after I met Gemma for the first time. We didn't really *date* exactly, not at first, but we... we were *something.* More than something, to me. By the time Gemma and I moved in together, Dustin and I were almost a couple. I hadn't ever dated before, so the progression seemed normal to me. Gemms would raise her eyebrow skeptically, but not say anything.

I knew Gemm didn't like him much, but she didn't have to see him as we never hung out together as a group, and once we moved, he refused to come out to the island. We'd meet up in the city and stay at his place, which was a closet that he shared with two frat-boy roommates who were constantly and boisterously drunk but gave us solitude. We never went out with his work friends – he said he saw them enough during the week and they were all assholes anyways. He was vague about his work, just saying he worked as a consultant for the city government. It's all so fucking obvious now, but at the time, I'd never *had* someone. I was always careful around him – so, *so* careful, because sometimes when I read him he was happy and loved being with me, and he'd make me laugh and we'd go up on the apartment rooftop and dance to the tinny music on his phone. But sometimes he seemed almost disgusted with me. If I was at all unhappy, he would feel impatient and annoyed. My job wasn't impressive. He didn't under-

stand why I couldn't handle things more easily. He'd get
so, so frustrated with me, so angry – beneath the surface.
But he'd never *say* any of that. He'd always smile and speak
in his mellow, easy way about the Universe being one and
how we're all connected. It was so *confusing.* He'd never,
never show what he was feeling, and if I asked him about it,
he'd act completely befuddled why I'd think that about him.
Why I'd doubt him. Why I was so insecure. I started doubting myself, my abilities. He'd say, so completely sincerely,
"You're amazing. I love being with you. I promise you. The
Universe brought you to me," but the feeling underneath
that was irritation, annoyance, dismissiveness.

It took me way too long to catch on to things. I'd always be happy, or close to happy, when I was at home with
Gemma, when I was out with her and her friends. But then
I'd go to his place, and as I'd tell him about my night, the
happiness would fade, and things that had seemed funny
now seemed stupid. Stories that were hilarious were banal.
And that sense of joy I'd felt would fade, but it was okay,
because being with Dustin made me happy. I'd curl up with
him, and a low hum of happiness would coat me. I never
questioned it. I'd tell him about things I liked doing and the
pleasure would fade from them, so I stopped doing them.
The few times we went out with people from the diner or to
school functions we'd leave early because I felt so miserable.
So I'd just stop going. And I'd spend all of my time with him,
the two of us at a bar, laughing at his stories, feeling happy
just being near him.

It's so embarrassing, actually, how I figured it all out.
So. Freaking. Embarrassing. We spent most of our time
in his tiny room in the already tiny apartment. His two
roommates were usually home with their Friday night con-
quests, who became Saturday morning regrets. And for
whatever reason, sex was always *so* much better whenever
all the guys were in their respective rooms. It wasn't great
usually – not bad, just not great, but he was my first so I had

nothing to compare it to. But Fridays after the bar scene – whoa. He'd tease me slyly about being an exhibitionist – not in a way that made me comfortable. I'd never been bothered by sex – very pro-kink and freedom of the modern woman and all that. And honestly, Gemma was a walking Adult Store by herself, so any hang-ups I may have had quickly went the way of the Dodo as she regaled me with stories about her rotating love life. You can only watch a tiny, purple-haired girl imitate a variety of sex acts so many times before throwing up your hands and jumping down the rabbit hole with her, so to speak.

But the way Dustin would say it, it was so... wrong. Accusatory, or slick, like he took pleasure in making me uncomfortable. He'd say something like that, or ask me if I was trying to be loud so his roommates would hear, or call me names "in the heat of passion", but not in a sexy way – in a derogatory way. It was always followed by an insane rush of pleasure though – a confounding, crazy haze of pleasure that faded quickly and made me sick to my stomach but was definitely there. And it fucked me up so badly. I tried to talk to Gemma about it, but I was too ashamed, too confused.

Then one morning, one fucked-up, fateful morning, I woke up to make us coffee, still feeling off from the night before. He was still asleep, and I was used to solitude in the early hours. That day, though, one of his roommates stumbled out, looking distinctly put out.

"You okay?" I remember asking, concerned. Jake usually had some sort of smile for me, even if we weren't great friends.

"You're a girl, right?" he had said, making me smile a little and nod. He pointed towards his room. "I don't know what's wrong with me, Kailani. I have a girl in there I am seriously into. And we're going to it last night, and it's getting good, you know? And then just... nothing. Just nothing at all. We kind of looked at each other and fell asleep. And it's happened before, but I thought it was because I didn't like the girls I was bringing home. And maybe it would be better with someone I actually *like*. But nothing." He gripped the side of his head with his hands and muttered, "I feel like I'm going crazy, man. I need to talk to someone."

It hit me like a punch in my gut. I almost threw up, hearing him. Dustin was doing that. I don't know how I knew, but shit, I *knew*. I sat at the table waiting for him to wake up, and when he came in, he met my eyes with a concerned, amused expression. "Uh-oh. Someone woke up on the wrong side of the bed."

"Can you do what I do?" I asked.

"I don't know what you mean, Kailani. Are you okay, babe?"

I stood up and screamed at him: *"Can you do what I can do?"*

"Shit babe! What the hell?" he said, backing up and bringing his hands up to cover his ears.

"Just tell me, D," I said tiredly. I could feel his emotions pulsing off him, the overriding feeling of which was amusement. Fucking *amusement*. I was coming apart at the seams, and he was laughing his ass off underneath his concerned expression. I could actually *feel* him trying to decide how much effort he felt like putting into the charade, how much he felt like trying before he had coffee.

"Never mind, you colossal bag of *dicks!*" I screamed, grabbing my bag and keys.

Jake stuck his head out of his door, looking worried. "Kailani, you okay?" he asked, and I didn't miss the fact that he didn't ask about his roommate.

I pointed towards Dustin with my middle finger, which I promptly turned upright at Dustin. "That fucker is why you can't come, Jake."

"Aw babe. Come on now. I did it to help you loosen up a little. No guy wants to fuck an icicle," he replied sneeringly. And that was it.

482

It was all terrible. Fucking terrible. And the worst part is, I don't know if any of it was real at all. I don't know if the first time I met him, with his awful pickup line and terrible taste in music and alcohol, I don't know if that was real or resonance. The first time I felt truly happy and wanted, the first time I felt like I had value, had a person, and it was all a Potemkin's Village. It was nothing. And it fucked me up for a long, long time. But I learned from it. Shit did I learn. It showed my shields had flaws. They worked against ambient noise, but nothing super low level like long-term resonance, or super high level, like "pushed" emotions. Not that Dustin could push. He just was really, *really* good with resonance.

"And now resonance doesn't touch me. So that's something. And unless I open myself to it, pushing emotions usually doesn't work on me. I'm fucking Fort Knox now," I say to Walker, pulling myself back to the present and smiling brightly at him. "I'm Willy Wonka's chocolate factory – no feelings ever get in; no feelings ever get out. I just can't have... I can't drop my shields. Ever. But it's important to know if he's around. He's been on probation more times than I can count. He loves to fuck with people – gets a little buzz on the taste of their pleasure before it fades. Just a waste of space really. It's a fucking shame he's talented."

He smiles at me slightly, but more like he's humoring me than that he finds me funny.

"Do you read your friends now?"

I shake my head. "Never. I... No. I have Lachy, Gemma, and Deo. And I've promised them I won't ever read them. I try not to read people unless it's required. It's not really fair to know people's feelings like that. I don't... I need to believe what they tell me."

His eyes widen when I mention Hideo's name, and I laugh a little. "Oh come on, Walker. Like you and Smith aren't buddies outside the office?"

He shrugs and does that funny half smile again. "Do you

want to read me? How I feel about our partnership?" he offers quietly.

I shake my head again. "I'd really rather not," I say tightly.

"Kai–"

"I'd *really. Rather. Not,*" I repeat.

He looks away, scanning the room, before returning his attention to me.

"Well," he says quietly. "Offer's on the table. You don't need to ask."

I don't know how to reply but am saved by the call to dinner, and, as the rest of the members of our table return, I begin to eat quietly, trying to shake the feeling that I exposed too much.

After dinner we make our way around the ballroom countless times, joining different groups and chatting with various guests.

Donovan is, surprisingly, an excellent date. He's courteous and conscientious, making sure I don't get left out of conversations by self-important businessmen, filling my glass without being asked, pulling out chairs. He catches at me looking at him once and goes on alert.

"What is it?" he asks tensely. "What do you see?"

I laugh a little. "Nothing. Sorry. You're just unexpected tonight."

He raises an eyebrow at me. "You think I can't behave myself on assignment, Reed?" he asks softly.

"No... I was just thinking that you'd make some girl a good boyfriend, actually. You're really almost pleasant when you try. Almost."

Throwing his head back, the most surprising, musical burst of laughter pours off him. I drink it up, feeling cleansed after the preceding hours of simpering and sucking up.

"Almost, hmmm, Kai?" Eyes are on us, mostly envious women, and he spins me in a sudden circle before moving me onto the dance floor. "Almost I can work with."

It's another hour before I finally give up.

"I need a break, Walker. Can we just head out for a few minutes?" He checks his watch against the schedule and nods.

"It's near eleven. Bidding closes in about five minutes. I'm watching a couple of potential marks who are floating around the Mexico trip." He looks discomforted for a moment. "I don't like splitting up. Can you wait a few?"

I shake my head. "I really need to get out. Things are starting to spill over into me. I just need a few minutes away."

He nods shortly. "Balcony A –" he says, pointing towards the nearby exit onto a wide, beautiful patio. "There are benches. I'll be out in less than five minutes. Just... just don't go finding trouble."

I waggle my eyes at him like Groucho Marx and try to do an old timey voice. "I don't go finding trouble, kid, Trouble finds me!"

His lopsided smile takes over his face, and he shakes his head reluctantly. "God, you're annoying. GO."

As soon as I get outside, I start feeling better. The night is cold – too cold, really, to be out without a coat on – and the sharp bite of the air helps clear my mind. Taking advantage of the silence, I try to build and fortify my shields until I feel completely alone, only the subtle, steady hum of mass emotions disturbing the peace. After a few minutes, just as I'm beginning to really *feel* the cold, but still reluctant to go inside again, a warm jacket is draped over my shoulders.

"Thanks, babe!" I say jokingly as I turn, only to meet the smarmy, self-important gaze of fucking Dustin.

"Babe, hey?" he says. "I've missed that."

Shrugging his coat off and letting it fall to the ground, I back up, purposefully stepping on it. "Oops." I say blandly.

"Come on now, Kailani. You don't need to be like that. We're on the same team here. It's all peace and love, right?"

Oh fuck a duck. I'd forgotten his tendency to "new-age" speak. If he's already talking about peace and love, that means...

"It's all zen, baby. Right? We're all surfers on the wave of life."

Oh my gods. Oh my sweet, holy gods of above and below I'm going to fucking lose it...

A low, unintelligible noise vibrates from my chest, and *just* before I go to throat-punch him into the next universe, a deep, disdainful chuckle breaks through my anger haze.

"Kai, did this guy just say that we're all *surfers* on the *wave* of *life?*" Walker's eyes meet mine questioningly. "You okay, Hellcat?"

I shrug and, pointing towards the wannabe Instagram In-fluencer in front of me, say, "Dustin."

"Oh you have *got* to be shitting me," Walker blurts out. "Dustin Dustin?"

"Hey man. I see you've heard of me," Dustin replies in his unctuous manner.

"Have I heard of you? Yeah, cum-stain. I've heard of you."

Dustin's eyes fly open in shock. He's completely not used to people treating him like this. Most people *love* him when they first meet him. They fall for his easy good looks, his smooth charm, his lazy vibe. He made friends easily, at least initially, and I could see him do a rapid reassessment of the situation. Standing a bit straighter from his normal semi-slouch, he puffs his chest a little and holds out his hand, which Walker ignores.

Turning to focus solely on me, Walker stares in my eyes, purposefully ignoring Dustin, who is still standing, hand half extended, beside us.

486

"You okay?" Walker asks again, this time more softly, with some unexpectedly gentle emotion woven in his words.

I nod as he lifts a hand to cup my cheek. "Is he bothering you?"

"He bothers me by existing," I reply, smiling slightly to make it a joke, but Walker's eyes tighten imperceptibly. Never lifting his hand from my skin, he slides his fingers down my cheek and along the edges of my face until his hand is wrapped lightly around the edges of my jaw. I can feel every thrum of my pulse under his fingers as he tips my chin up by squeezing ever so slightly, and I meet his dark stare, eyes wide, and he rests his head against mine gently.

Moving back, he holds my gaze until I give a little nod, and his lips meet mine, full and warm against my own. My eyes close as he pulls me into him. He kisses me slowly at first, just enough to make a point. And I think that's all he meant to do. But the feel of his mouth is surprisingly irresistible, and I move against him. The moment I come to life beneath him, he deepens the kiss, exploring my mouth like the world isn't burning around us, like he has every second 'til eternity to learn the feel of me. It's a masterclass in sensuality – nothing is touching between us but his hand on my jaw and our mouths together, and I can feel the icy pinpricks of wind ripple along my skin, chased by some fire he's creating in my blood.

His teeth nip unexpectedly at my lower lip, sucking it in slightly between his own, and I whimper and wrap my arms around him tightly, knees weak. The feel of him burns away the heaviness of the night, replacing it with a blazing heat of desire. He holds me to him with one arm, hitching me up against him so I'm almost tiptoe from leaning into him, as he memorizes the way we fit together. His warm, calloused hand is spread on the bare skin of my back, burning it like a brand, as his other hand rotates from the column of my throat to the back of my neck, then cradles my head against him, fingers laced through my hair. Everything, *everything* is silent but the beating of my heart and the low, almost feral growl that comes from Walker's throat.

Abruptly, and out of nowhere, he drops me and spins on his heel, launching a massive fist into Dustin's face with the full power of a trained MMA fighter. Dustin goes down like a paper doll, collapsing to the ground, holding his face and crying out. Walker stands over him like an avenging angel, face dark with a righteous fury, voice trembling with rage. "Don't you *ever* Bleed me without permission, you sick fuck!"

Drawing back a leg, he kicks Dustin in the stomach before I have time to react. "You're fucking *done*, you hear me? You are DONE!"

I grab Walker's arm, yanking him back. "Walker. Walker! You can't!"

He points a shaking finger at Dustin, who is crying and curled up in the fetal position on the ground. "That asshole bled me, Kai. Just now. I could feel it. It all just drained away."

Leaning over Dustin, I drop my shields. Dustin was feeling smug as fuck, though in serious pain, because he ruined the moment between Walker and me. He's also pissed off, and scared, and buzzing a little off the arousal he drained from Walker. I feel sick all over again that I ever let this snake touch me.

"Come on, Walker," I say tiredly. "Let's just go."

Walker moves towards me, then stops, and stares down at Dustin again. "You may have taken that moment, but I have a hundred thousand of them left with her, just like that. A hundred thousand moments where my hands get to touch her, where my skin is against hers, where my breath is her breath. You feel like a big man 'cause you took a single moment? You're nothing. And less than nothing, because you had someone like her, fucking didn't deserve a moment of her, but you had her..." Walker shakes his head and pulls me to him as Dustin flinches. Softly and carefully, Walker kisses me again, standing over the bleeding, beaten body of my ex. He kisses me for long enough that I forget to breathe, then takes my arm to help me step over Dustin and walk back to the party.

ILLEGITIMI NON CARBORUNDUM

Saturday, 27 October – Maela

There's a little bird singing somewhere, sweetly welcoming in the new day. It's going to be a cold one. I shiver in the chill air and try to snuggle deeper into the – ow! I open my eyes. There's frost on the grass, shimmering in pale beams of sunlight streaming through the bare branches of trees. Jesus, it's cold! I touch my hair, wincing, and wonder why it's damp. Then everything comes flooding back to me. Walking down Millbank, ready to cross the roundabout by Lambeth Bridge, in sight of Thames House. Bojan. I'm not telling you anything, connard! Ratko. Eight glasses of water a day. You're welcome. One pissed-off woman. Time to say good-bye.

I'm not dead, then. I sit up, all of my muscles protesting and half-wish I were. Everything from the waist up feels puffy, and it's all I can do to stay upright. I look down – I'm on a bench – and around – in a park. Oh, there's a playground. That's nice. *Focus, Maela!* I need to get up. Carefully, I push myself to my feet, both arms loudly protesting, and take a moment to get my balance. Right, must get help. I head towards the playground. I can see a road beyond it – is there an entrance? Yes! But, oh God, stairs. Right, take this slow. Careful, careful. Halfway down, my knees give way, and I fall, painfully, adding a bruised hip to my collection. I want to cry, and so I do, letting the tears slide down my cheeks. Everything. Hurts. Then I swallow the lump in my throat and half-crawl, half-slither my way to the bottom. I

490

take a moment to rest, leaning against the stone column, and, grunting, clamber to my feet. One step. Two steps. My vision's fading, and I'm crumpling to my knees again, going, going, gone.

I'm lying on a cloud, soft as spun silk. Soft and comfy and – Wait. No, it's not. There's a lump. A lump in my beautiful, special cloud, and... Wait. What? My eyes pop open.

I'm in hospital, I think. If so, it's the nicest hospital I've ever been in. The walls of the – private? – room are a sort of pale yellow, and there's a vase of autumnal flowers by the window. I hear a soft sound to my right and turn my head. Emlyn's sitting in the chair, dozing, his head fallen to one side. Even in sleep, he looks awful. His skin is dull, and there are deep lines carved into his face around his eyes, nose, and mouth. I gaze at him, studying his fine features, that square jaw, now with a hint of stubble, those soft-rose lips. The oak-brown hair is mussed, and his suit is crumpled, as if he hasn't showered or changed in days.

As if he can feel my eyes on him, he awakens. For a moment, worry clouds his gaze, then relief suffuses his face as he comes to fully. "Maela!"

"Hi Emlyn," I say softly. I try to smile, but the movement hurts, and I end up grimacing.

He stares back at me, his eyes bleak. "I thought I'd lost you. Dear God, I thought I'd lost you!" His voice is ragged and breaks on the last, and he passes a hand over his face. "I thought I'd lost you," he repeats and takes a deep breath.

My heart twists, and I want to reassure him. "I'm here," I whisper. "Just about." The rawness of the moment, this glimpse into Emlyn's unguarded soul, is, perversely, making me feel exposed, and I retreat into a joke.

He looks up at me, fury now stamped on his face. "What did those bastards do to you?" He looks so foreboding I shrink back into the pillows slightly. "Maela, tell me. It was Ratko, wasn't it? It was that foul, murdering piece of filth!" His hands, with those long, elegant fingers, flex, and I can see he's envisioning wrapping them around Ratko's neck and squeezing the life out of him.

I open my mouth and then close it. If I tell Emlyn, yes, it was Ratko and his gang, then Emlyn will blame himself. Right now, he's veering between relief and rage, but with one word, he will remember to add guilt to the mix. I know him. And then he will try to drop me from the investigation, thinking to protect me. I don't want either outcome. I'm a grown woman, and this case has just gotten extremely personal.

"I'm going to track him down," Emlyn seethes. "I'm going to find him, and then I'm going to dismember him, one joint at a time. But before I do, I'm going to beat him, just as you were beaten. And when I cut out his tongue, he'll be screaming your name."

Now, I'm the one to stare. His eyes are alight, and his face is glowing, as if he's just accepted a divine mission. An archangel with a flaming sword, ready to drive the snake out of my Eden. Passion sparks, catches, flares within me. The power is heady: all that will, all that intense masculinity, laid at my feet like an offering. I read Ratko's death in his eyes and feel an intense burst of satisfaction.

The door opens quietly, distracting me, and Kavi and Jorge come into the room, carrying three teas. My heart leaps up in welcome.

"Maela!"

"*Querida!*"

"How are you?"

As the two surge forward, smiles of relief on their faces, I see Jorge check and then glance sharply at Emlyn. Jorge says nothing but places a hand briefly on Emlyn's shoulder as he passes him a tea.

"Maela, tea?"

"No, thanks, Kavi. But, um, I wouldn't say no to a glass of Chardonnay." I mean it. So I'm in hospital. Big deal. So the last time I checked it was dawn. I've *earned* it. Tea is all very well and good when you have a sniffle, but I've been *roughed up* by *gangsters*.

Kavi looks at Emlyn, whose lips twitch. "I think that can be arranged. But for God's sake don't tell the nurse. You're on painkillers." He goes to the door and has a quiet conversation, then sits down again by my side.

"While we're waiting for the guard to come back, why don't you tell us what happened." Three faces look expectantly at me, and I can tell I'm not getting out of this. So I spill. About stumbling and feeling a prick in my arm. The van. Waking up to find Bojan next to me. I make it through telling them about the slaps, but when I remember the knives, my voice wobbles and I have to look down at the bedclothes. Kavi takes my hand comfortingly in his, and his warmth steadies me. I smile gratefully at him and sneak a glance at the others. Jorge's face is thunderous, and he's clenching his fists. Emlyn looks like the wrath of God personified: judge, jury, and executioner combined.

I continue, telling them about Bojan and Ratko's questions, how Vlado had heard Emlyn's name in the raid and Bojan remembered it from the café. At that, Emlyn swears under his breath. How they must have been watching for me. When I get to the part where Ratko forced my head into the bucket, the room erupts in curses. "I'll kill him!" "*Lo mataré!*" "*Me use maar daalooga!*" Kavi's hand spasms on mine, and I'm all of a sudden aware of his physical presence. My gentle giant normally radiates such good will that I tend to overlook his strength.

"Maela, honey. Why didn't you tell him? Nothing's worth your safety!" Emlyn's eyes are stormy, and I can see the creeping tendrils of guilt. Jorge's cloaked in an anguished fury.

"Tell them what? That I have visions? Anyway, I got

Ratko in trouble so, you know: all's well that ends well." I shrug, and Jorge looks darkly at me. "What? Too soon? So, tell me. What's the damage? Will I live?"

Emlyn answers: "You're bruised to buggery, but you'll feel better in a few days, thank God."

"So, my arm's not brok– Uh, you know what? Never mind." Seeing how tense they are, best not to mention I thought that was a possibility.

"*Querida.* How did you escape?"

I tell them the rest of it, how Ratko knocked me out after speaking to some woman, and I woke up on a park bench. As I get to the end of the story, I sag. Now that it's over, now that they know, for some reason, I feel incredibly tired. Kavi strokes my hair tenderly, erasing Ratko's obscene gesture. There's a knock at the door, and Jorge comes back carrying a large glass of wine in a plastic cup. "He had to go to the pub down the road."

As I'm reaching out for it, Emlyn's phone buzzes. "Tsk, tsk," I admonish. "Aren't you supposed to turn those things off?"

He smiles reluctantly at me. "Not in here, copperhead. I'm afraid I've been summoned, but I'll be back as soon as I can." He looks at Kavi and Jorge: "Stay with her?"

"Goes without saying," Kavi says. Jorge nods.

Emlyn leans over to give me a quick kiss on the forehead. His lips are warm and gentle. "See you in a bit." I'm so astonished I say nothing as he leaves the room, just gape and then take a sip of wine to cover my confusion. Jorge settles in the chair next to me, and a brief, companionable silence reigns.

Kavi stirs: "You scared him, *ladki.* You scared all of us." He takes a deep breath and lets it out slowly. Then he and Jorge tell me what happened. How Emlyn got worried when

I didn't show up to our appointment or answer my phone. How he went to my flat, knocked on the door, called me again, and heard the phone ringing inside. *Ah. Come to think of it, I'd been having fun checking out my horoscope and trying to work out what animal I was, and then there'd been a delivery from Ann Summers, and I'd been admiring my new cami set, sexy yet tasteful, I thought, black, polka-dot mesh with a cross-over detail at the neckline and sides of the shorts, and then I'd realized that I need to get a move on, and I must have left my phone on the couch.* How Emlyn called Jorge and Kavi, to see if I might be with them, and began to fear that I might be having an uncontrolled vision. How he'd knocked and called again and then made a decision to break down the door. I wince. *My poor door! I am so not getting the deposit back.* Fortunately, Jorge continues, giving me a stern look, *someone* never called the locksmith to have the lock replaced after the first time, so it was easy for Emlyn to get in. *Err. Well. Yes. My bad. But I have been very busy.* How Emlyn went through my flat and found my phone but not my bag. How he began to get a very, very bad feeling and called Kavi and Jorge again to ask them where they thought I might be. How they decided to divvy up Fitzrovia and each of them went round to my usual haunts, looking for me, and, eventually, found a barista at Goodge Street station who said he'd sold a latte to a "sweet but slightly ditzy redhead". I bristle. *Just because I'd been distracted by my new cami set was no reason for insults. Sheesh – cut me some slack! It's the most daring thing I've ever bought.* How Emlyn contacted the local police divisions to ask them to review their CCTV footage, and he himself began to review the footage from Thames House, while Kavi and Jorge searched the streets, this time around Westminster and Pimlico, not knowing which station I might have got off at – if I'd got off at all. But by now it was late, and most of the shops were closed. And, finally, how Emlyn caught me on security footage, walking past a group of people and then behind a van, and when the van pulled away, I was gone. The plates were obscured.

"We all felt sick to our stomachs then, but Emlyn?" Kavi shakes his head somberly.

"Eadric," Jorge says softly. "Emlyn feels that he failed to protect his baby brother and now he's failed to protect you. Emlyn was the one who found him."

I start: I didn't know that. God, poor Emlyn.

They were preparing to resume the search when a policeman found me at 6:00 that morning, just down the street from where I'd been taken, diagonally across the roundabout from Thames House, as a big F.U. to MI5.

I look at Kavi and Jorge, their faces weary and their eyes bruised, and my heart turns over. So many emotions are welling inside me. I feel humbled that they went to so much trouble and want to apologize, even though I know it's not my fault. I want to thank them, but mere words would seem trite. I want to make a joke and wipe away the fear that lingers in the lines around their mouths and in the tightness of their shoulders. I try all three.

"I'm sorry. Thanks, guys. Illegitimi non carborundum, right?" I try to give a reassuring little smile then, which ends up as a sort of horrible, jack o' lantern rictus, because what I really want to do is burst into tears. Fatigue, relief, fear, anger, guilt, pity, gratitude, tenderness – all spinning together, whirling and churning, dragging me along in their wake. I'm utterly spent.

Jorge looks at me, the hazel darkened to chestnut but no less beautiful. "We care about you, Maela," he says softly. "At the thought that you might be–" He shakes his head, a few dark-brown locks tumbling about his face. "I care about you," he repeats, almost to himself.

"We all do." Kavi's voice is deep and sonorous, a bell tolling in a quiet dawn. "We've become rather attached to you, Maela, so no more scares, eh, *ladki*?"

As my head gives a little bob, Jorge's gaze swings to Kavi, who looks back at him steadily. A moment passes, then two.

Then Jorge looks down, letting out a short, sharp breath, and his lips give a rueful twist. He looks questioningly again at Kavi, who gives an almost imperceptible nod, broad shoulders slightly flexing. Some wordless communication passes between them, which I don't have time to ponder, because I'm desperate to console them.

"Sorry," I whisper. "I... I care about you guys too." I swipe at my cheek; I don't know when, but I've started to cry. "I really do." And now the floodgates have opened. "And you came for me... when... when... and I'm sorry I scared you... and... and... I do," I sob.

"We know, *priya*." Kavi leans over to take the glass out of my hand, while Jorge tucks the covers gently around me and I fall back into the pillows, exhausted. "Sleep, *querida*. We'll be here." So I do.

YOU SEXY THING

Saturday, 27 October – Kailani

The funky, blaring guitar of Hot Chocolate's "You Sexy Thing" wakes me from a dark, heavy sleep, and I crack one bleary eye open, staring above me, completely confused, as my room comes into focus. There are... balloon dicks. Like, everywhere. Very colorful, very large, very sparkly... balloon dicks. I'm feeling like maybe I'm still asleep, and that is solidified in my mind when a feather-boa-wearing, gogo-dress-clad Gemma pops up in front of me, giant, purple, heart glasses covering half her face.

"WHERE YOU FROM!" she screeches at an uncomfortable pitch. "YOU SEXY THING!!!"

I'm reminded suddenly that Gemma's singing voice is like very loud nails on a very long chalkboard. She absolutely loves belting out tunes, though, and all of her friends have a pact to never let her know the... unique... qualities her voice possesses. We alternate monthly karaoke in an effort to keep our hearing intact, but to be honest, the sheer joy she gets from singing is 100% worth it. She lights up when she's singing, always putting an extra shimmy shake into her performances. When Gemma sings, she really *sings.* Several dogs may die from burst ear drums in the process, but she is a full-fledged diva performer.

"WHERE did you COME from BABY?!? HOW did you KNOW I NEEDED YOU?" Gemma was going full glam girl, yelling in my face as she leaned over from where she was standing on my mattress.

"What the... what's... what?" I mumble incoherently, still reeling from the wake-up, tired from the late night before.

She shakes her ass in response, reaching into her dress pockets and throwing something in the air.

"Aw fuck, Gemms! Glitter?" I groan, knowing from past experience how long it takes to get glitter out of just about *any*thing. Looking closer at the shiny cutouts covering me from head to toe, I realize it's not glitter at all, but sparkling, confetti...

"*MORE DICKS, GEMMA?*" I protest. She smiles widely, still singing, and dumps more confetti penises on my head.

"No more teeny Peeny for you, babe!" she screams at the bridge. "AHHHH! TOUCH ME! KISS ME DARLIN'!" Leaping off the bed, she grabs a small bag from the floor while still singing and begins throwing handfuls of gummy candy dicks up in the air like she's at a freaking wedding or something. "NO MORE TEENY PEENY! IT'S YOUR BIRTHDAY and we're getting you some GOOD DICK!"

Curling into a ball, I cover my head with my pillow. Yelling as loud as I can, voice slightly muffled, I try to make myself heard over the music. "It's TOO EARLY for so much PENIS, GEMMA!"

Too late I realize the song has ended, and the sound of my voice screaming "so much Penis" echoes through the tiny cabin. I hear faint laughter and freeze for a moment before Gemma surprises me, popping into the bed next to me, and pulls the covers overhead, cocooning us. Her smile lights up like a damn Christmas tree, and she bumps my head gently with hers as she whispers, "Happy Birthday, KaiKai! Time to get up! I have celebratory *things* planned!" Her face sobers for a moment, and she stares at me seriously. "Glad you were born, Sis. And I'm gonna celebrate the fuck out of you." Then, bouncing up with the force of a coked-up rabbit, she rips the covers off me and cackles like a freaking witch as she leaves the room with them, calling over her shoulder, "Get UP you lazy bitch! It's time to paaaaaarty!"

◆ ◆ ◆

Five minutes later, I stumble into the kitchen, only to be greeted by Lachy standing at the stove making cinnamon French toast like a boss. He glances over at me, then walks to me, grinning sweetly. "Happy Birthday, Suge!" he rumbles, reaching out one of his huge paws and gently pulling a shining piece of confetti from my hair. "Do you realize you're covered in penises? Peni? Not sure of the plural."

I flush all the way to my hairline. I'm wearing my favorite sleeping outfit, giant, ripped black sweats and a tank top, and I have crazy bed-head. Lachy, on the other hand, looks incredible – very mountain man-y, like a tough, rugged lumberjack, and he smells of woodsmoke. I have an uncontrollable urge to snuggle into him and get wrapped up in his huge arms for a minute. Evidently my brain hasn't fully woken up yet, because I realize that I'm just staring up at him and haven't replied to his question. Blinking slowly, I mumble, "what?"

He looks incredibly amused, which brings out a freaking adorable smile on his face. I can feel the edges of my mouth turning up in response as he leans over and kisses my cheek briefly, his beard scratching my face a little. "Go get dressed. Gemma has a day planned for you and I think it's best if you're prepared for battle." He pulls back and smiles down at me, saying "I'll have your birthday breakfast ready in a minute. Go ahead."

Thanking him, I take a quick shower, washing my hair and trying to get the rest of the freaking confetti out of my thick curls. Gemma peeks in as I'm braiding my hair into two thick ropes, hanging most of the way down to my waist. She looks at me critically, and I throw a towel at her.

"Christ, Gemms! Can I at least have a minute to get ready?"

She shakes her head primly and squinches up her face, replying, "No. I don't trust you to actually do yourself up."

I point towards my jeans and t-shirt laid out in my room, and she flits in, throwing them onto my overstuffed reading chair in the corner of the room, by my window.

"No."

"But they're–"

"NO! Kai, we are going OUT. And for once in your godforsaken life you are going to wear something pretty and colorful and sexy." She runs to her bathroom and comes back loaded down with her war paints, as she calls them. "Sit!" she snaps, pointing regally towards the chair she dragged into the room. "I'm going to work."

Almost one hour, and an entire Tom Jones album, later, she proclaims me done. She has mostly straightened my hair, leaving a gentle wave, and has smoothed it with some crazy serum that I swear is magic. With the amount of time she spent on my face, I was sure I'd end up looking like an 80's Valley Girl but somehow end up looking lovely. My skin is glowing and looks like I am slightly flushed, with pink cheeks. I don't know what she has done to my eyes – I can't really see any makeup, but they look about ten times their normal size, and she's left me with a really pretty nude lip. All in all, I still look like me, just like the very best version of me. I look, for lack of a better word, soft. It is uncomfortable in a way, how sweet she's made me look.

"Eh? Ehh?" she laughs, poking me with one of her makeup brushes. "Not too bad, right?"

"I concede defeat. Thanks, Gemms. I feel positively pretty right now."

She smiles at me and puts her hands together in a pleading gesture in front of her. "Okay, so you trusted me on that. Ride that wave and please, *please* wear the gift your bestest friend in the entire world looked so hard for, and had to sell three paintings to afford. And I can't return it."

"Gemma!" I say, shocked. "Please tell me you're kidding."

"No way, KaiKai. I want you to have the best birthday

ever. And everything lately has been... well, anyways. Let's just enjoy today, please. Wear it for me as my birthday gift."

"It's not your birthday!" I protest, laughing. "Why do I owe you a gift?"

She shrugs and replies, "Well, as my unbirthday gift then, okay?

I groan. "Let me see it first."

"No. Just promise first." She looks at me with her huge, pleading eyes like a flipping anime character, and I crack like I always do.

"Fine," I grumble. "Let me see it."

Gemma claps and runs to her room, bringing back a dress. It has a pinky-brown top, with a deep v neckline that hits a thickly banded empire waist. The skirt is long panels of the pinky-brown and a pale rose, and the entire thing is made of a very light, flowing material. There's the smallest ruffle along the deep neckline, and the banded waist has tiny white ruffles, white lines, pale rose lines, and some very small beading. The entire thing falls down to just below the knee, and Gemma has some pale rose ballet flats in her other hand. I try really, really hard not to like it – it's pink! It's a dress! Ballet flats! But I can't help picturing it on.

"Gemms!" I breathe. "It's gorgeous!"

She looks surprised for a minute, and then deeply suspicious like I'm teasing her or being sarcastic, but then realizes that I truly love it, and smiles.

"Right! Put it on and meet me in the kitchen for breakfast to review your itinerary."

"Aren't birthdays supposed to be relaxing?"

She shakes her head at me sorrowfully. "How long have we been friends? How long? And you still think you have a say in this? You wound me, Kai." Waving her hand vaguely at me, she commands, "Now get dressed," and walks out of the room.

I'm feeling almost shy when I leave my bedroom – an odd feeling that doesn't sit well on me. I walk into the kitchen quietly, and when Gemma looks up, her face looks incredibly smug and self-satisfied.

"Happy?" I snark at her, and she replies with a huge grin. "Very!"

Lachy turns around to see what we're talking about and goes completely still. Gemma, not noticing the change in his demeanor, starts chatting about the plans for the day. Neither Lachy nor myself have moved, and I feel my cheeks heating up under his careful inspection.

"... and then lunch at the pier, naps, spa, drinks, and naps again. And then tonight is the club, which, Lachs, are you sure you don't want to come? Lach..." she trails off, looking between us, then says slowly, "Oooooohkaaay... someone want to let me know what the heck is going on here?"

Lachy blinks slowly, like he's just waking up, and clears his throat before saying, "Happy birthday, Kailani. And no, Gemma, I don't want to go. You know clubs give me headaches. Who wants French toast?"

She looks back and forth between us suspiciously, like we're hiding something from her, but when I come into the room and sit down finally, she shrugs and continues. "Well, girl, we're talking about *that* later, but for now, look over the itinerary..."

I see the tips of Lachy's ears turn pink as he loads up the plates for breakfast, wondering when exactly he became so freaking adorable, before Gemma pokes me sharply with her fork. "I see what's going on here, woman. Focus for a minute on something other than Lachy's ass." I choke on my coffee; Gemma shrieks, "Don't ruin your dress!" and in the ensuing chaos I think she forgets about her comment. But I don't. And I'm pretty sure Lachy doesn't either.

As we're leaving to head into the city, my phone blares.

"No," says Gemma firmly. "No no no! It's your birthday *and* the weekend and we have *plans!!!* You have been working *non-stop* lately!"

I grimace slightly. "I'm sure it's nothing. Maybe Lachy? Maybe we forgot something?" But when I glance at the number and see "unknown" flashing, I groan. "Hello?" I answer cautiously.

Smith's voice barks out at me from the other end. "Reed. Are you okay? Are you with someone? You need to get to the office. Immediately."

"What the hell, Smith?" I answer, confused. "I'm with Gemma. We have plans for the day…"

Gemma reaches out and grabs the phone from me, veering slightly on the road, causing me to grab the dash. "Jesus, Gemms!"

She frowns at me and snaps into the phone, "She's not coming in…!"

I can hear the rumble of Smith's voice from the other end and watch the color drain from Gemma's already pale face. She's shaking slightly as she hangs up the phone and glances at the mirrors to see what's behind us several times.

"What the heck, Gemm?"

"Smith says you have to come in. There's reason to believe you're in some kind of danger. He didn't go into details, obviously. Just said I had to get you to the station, and not to leave you until someone comes out to walk you in."

She checks her mirrors again and reaches out to grab my hand. "No worries," she says, more to herself than anything. "I'm sure it's nothing."

But we sit in silence for the rest of the drive into the city.

Hideo walks out to get me once we arrive. He and Gemma greet each other coolly, like divorced parents at their kids'

pass-off, maintaining polite civility for the sake of the children.

"Gemma," he says shortly, more stating a fact than anything else.

"Hideo," she replies in the same tone. I frown, looking back and forth between them, but don't say anything. I tried for years to make peace between these two, but they rub each other the wrong way, for some reason. The first time we all got together was a disaster of epic proportions – stilted conversations with long pauses, and me, frantically and very confusedly trying to fill in the gaps. In a now historic attempt to get them to speak, still referenced by both of them at random times, I gave a very long, awkward summary of a lecture I had watched on the different types of mustard. I mean... it was bad. The only solidarity I saw from them all evening had been them exchanging confused glances, and Hideo saying to me gently, "Kai... are you okay?" followed by Gemma saying, "Dude, she's been talking about mustard for ten minutes. Pretty sure we broke her." The evening ended shortly after that, never to be repeated, and since then, when they've had to cross paths, they're carefully and painfully polite to each other, like they're incredibly worried I'll start babbling about condiments again. Neither will say *why* they don't get along – both just shrug it off. They just don't really get on. Which is strange and discomforting, but we've all learned to live with it.

I guess I stare at the two of them a little too long, because Gemma mutters under her breath, "Dijon isn't a protected food name..." and I *swear to god* that I see Deo's lips twitch minutely, like he's trying to fight off a smile, before he says, "Okay, Kai. Let's head in. Gemma, I assure you she'll be fine. It should only be an hour or two. She'll text you when she's done."

Gemma frowns and jerks her head in response, and I get out of the car to follow Deo in. He's walking ahead of me as Gemma pulls away and doesn't really look at me until he holds open the door to the station.

Deo's eyes darken as he takes me in, freezing at the door. He doesn't say anything, just watches me with a predatory gaze, like a panther stalking its prey. He's so still it's unnerving, and I walk towards him slowly, leaving space between us as I go to move through the door. Just as I pass him, one hand shoots out and he pulls me to him so suddenly I stumble slightly and fall against his chest. Wrapping both arms around me, he holds me against him, barely breathing. We stand like this, frozen in place, for so long the moment moves into uncertainty. Hideo's face is buried in my hair, his muscles flexed tight against me, and for a brief instant I wonder whether he's fighting to hold on or fighting to let go. I push against him slightly, and he moves back enough to look down at me, eyes almost black with some ferocity. We stay like this, a breath apart, and I question quietly, "Deo?"

He stares at me with an almost agonized expression before leaning his face against mine and whispering, "Happy birthday, Kai" against my lips. It's not a kiss, it couldn't be called a kiss, but his angular lips are surprisingly soft against my mouth, the warmth of his breath heating my skin. We pause there, lips barely touching, his words resting heavy in the little space between them. I murmur back, "Thank you, Hideo," more to feel his mouth move against mine again, even in this small way, than for any other reason. I don't know what would have happened had we stayed like that for even a moment longer, but the door's alarm begins to sound, as it does when someone leaves it open too long, and Hideo jerks back suddenly like he's been shocked. Shaking himself, he pushes away from me and motions me forward, not speaking.

When we walk into the conference room, Smith, Donovan, and Jonah are already there. Deo walks to the far side of the table to sit, a first, which elicits confused looks between the others. Smith is at the head of the table, speaking with a quiet intensity on the phone.

"She's okay? Walk me through it again, Seef... and you just *found* her? Mmmmhmmm... No one saw *anything?* The cameras should... yeah...."

As he's listening, his eyes keep darting between me and the computer screen in front of him. Every now and again he'll hear something that has him staring at me intently... flick *flick*... flick *flick*... it's making me nervous and jittery, that strange intensity in his face battering down my shields.

"How long's she due to be in the hospital?... How bad are the contusions?... Does she have water in her lungs? Any danger of pneumonia...?"

Flick *flick*... flick *flick*... His face tightens even more if that's possible. He looks like a stone carving, and his voice drops even lower.

"Did she say anything, Seef?... I *know* she's not a trained agent... Seef, I'm not accusing her of... I'm *absolutely sure* she did her best... goddamnit Seef! Just fucking listen! Jesus Christ! Did she *say* anything?" He waits a beat, then sighs in relief. "Good *girl!* Tough chick, Seef. Tough chick... that's the American in her...," he says, with a bit of a laugh in his voice, before it hardens again. "Right. Keep me updated. We'll have to put on extra security until we know." This time his eyes move to me and stay there, hard and determined, and not looking away. "Ours? She'll fight against it but... Ha. Yeah. Good luck with that. Later."

He hangs up the phone and knocks once on the table, drawing all of our attention to him.

"I'm sorry to have to call you in on the weekend," he begins seriously, looking at each of us in turn. "There have been some developments with the London branch that warrant our concern. Their contracted operative – the American studying overseas who has shown promising signs of being fairly powerful at telesthesia – was kidnapped off the street yesterday and was tortured for information. While she has limited knowledge of the American side of things, it's possible we have a breach in security somewhere and we're not sure how far reaching it is, or even where it originates. We're assuming Ratko and his crew found out about Driscoll by chance, and got further information from drugging an MI5 employee, but it could be a full MI5 breach, or MI6... hell, it's possible there's a leak in the CIA or FBI. Less likely that the leak is in Babylon itself, but there are so many cooks in the kitchen that the poison could be from almost anywhere."

Smith rubs his face, looking exhausted. "I'm afraid you'll have to be under surveillance until we get this mess straightened out, Reed."

I stare at him, trying to take it all in. "What level of surveillance are we talking about?" I ask cautiously.

"Round the clock, right now. We'll see as things progress."

I shake my head mutinously. "No way," I argue. "You're not even sure what information is out there. I'm not agreeing to being locked away somewhere when you don't even know what's going on. I promise not to fight you on it if more information comes to light, but no way."

Surprisingly, Donovan speaks up in my favor. "I think you're overreacting slightly, Smith," he interjects calmly.

I gape at him for a moment, then say hesitantly, "Yeah, listen to... Donovan?" It's so odd agreeing with him that the words come out as a question rather than a statement, and he grins at the tone in my voice, flashing his uneven smile without a hint of malice. *What the fuck is happening?*

Smith interrupts my thoughts, shaking his head definitively. "All, I understand that this isn't ideal, but we have to figure something out until we get clearer intel on the situation. Reed, and to a lesser extent, Shotridge, need to have coverage." He pauses, clearly thinking things through. "Shotridge, we should be able to work with an hourly check in. Voice only – *not* text. If I don't hear from you in person by five past each hour, that's immediate signal for search and rescue. If you trip a search and rescue because you fucked up..."

Smith trails off, and Jonah nods seriously, all traces of his usual cheerful self erased. "I'll set an alarm," he says, immediately grabbing his phone. Smith looks back at me thoughtfully, actually *seeing* me for the first time since I walked in the room.

"What, ah... what is...," he waves at me slightly awkwardly. "This is... you look nice?"

Deo rolls his eyes next to me, sighing. "It's Kai's birthday today. Speaking of..." Deo reaches into his bag, beside him on the floor, and slides over a small, beautifully wrapped present. I stare at it like it's going to bite me. Of course, Hideo has gotten me presents before, but they're usually like, Starbucks cards or something, kind of flung at me as I leave work. They're never exquisitely wrapped and passed to me openly, in front of other people.

He nudges it toward me, and I look at him questioningly. Sighing, he puts it in my bag and shakes his head. "It's a present, not a bomb, Reed." I can't help but grin at him, all squinched up, and he lets an answering, unchecked smile break across his face, like the first sunrise after a storm, sending shivers skittering across my skin. Smith and Donovan watch the exchange through careful eyes, but I can feel unhappiness pulse off Jonah in waves, and I turn to him, concerned.

"What's up?" I ask softly, and he frowns.

"I wish I had known it was your birthday," he answers quietly.

"Oh. Um. Why?"

He looks at me, browns drawn, and then, oddly, to Hideo.

Deo shrugs slightly and says, almost silently, "She's not used to people making a big deal of her birthday, man. She grew up thinking it wasn't important, and has really only started celebrating it in the past couple years. Well, she's kind of forced to celebrate it. Her roommate didn't even know when it was for the first couple years they lived together. So it's not a thing she thinks to tell people."

"*She* is right here," I say grumpily. "And *she* doesn't like her personal business laid out on the table like a party feast." Deo looks at me apologetically, and I shrug slightly, forgiving him. "Also, *she* doesn't *get* birthdays. Like – the point of them is weird. I was born? That's an accomplishment or something? Why are people going to go out of their way to celebrate that shit? It's weird asking people to celebrate you."

"You don't... *get* birthdays?" This from Donovan, sounding incredibly surprised, and a little sorry.

"Can we just... like isn't there some kind of emergency or something going on?" I shift uncomfortably, looking at Smith, who nods and gets us back on track.

"So Shotridge is calling on the hour. Reed, you'll need a protection detail."

I open my mouth to protest when there is a loud series of bangs from the hall, like tiny fireworks, little pops of sound. The change in Smith is startling. His entire body clenches, face draining of color. He doesn't move at all, but somehow he disappears a little, a private war being waged in his mind. I look around, confused, and see Deo and Jonah looking just as perplexed. Donovan's face is furious, though, but as he goes to stand, Smith reaches out to stop him.

"Walker?" I ask, concerned.

He looks at me curiously for a second, then answers. "There are two complete shits here who somehow found out Smith has some lingering issues with certain sounds, and they've been fucking with him. Nothing we can really do – it's hard to tell that it's specifically against Smith, since we've never actually met the fucks, and they're not actually breaking any rules, but it's clear they're targeting him."

I'm out of my seat so fast the chair falls over behind me, face incandescent with fury. "Markel and Posta?" I ask through clenched teeth. Walker nods cautiously in response. "Deo, get the file," I snap out and move toward the door, pushing past Jonah.

"Kai, we can't–" Hideo begins, and I turn to him, pointing with a shaking hand toward Smith.

"The *fuck* we can't. Get the fucking file!" I command and throw open the door to the conference room. Halfway down the hall now, Markel and Posta are laughing to themselves, little boxes of pop-its in their hands. They turn eagerly at the sound of the door opening, feral, twisted looks on their faces, and meet my eyes with surprise that changes quickly into an ugly hunger.

"Well, well, well," Markel says softly. "Look at what we have here. Off-duty Reed is fucking something, eh Posta?"

Posta nods in agreement, blatantly grabbing his crotch. "Looks like she took the stick out of her ass to make room for some pipe!" he chortles, a braying laugh overlaid with Markel's higher snicker. "She may not like it at first, but you hold her still and I'll teach her..."

Without breaking stride I stalk toward them and full out throat-punch Posta, taking him down in a single move. His eyes widen in surprise and pain as he makes a strange, thick gurgling sound, desperately trying to find a way to breathe. Markel backs up, cruel piggy eyes narrowing as he takes me in more carefully, ignoring his friend on the ground.

"Oooo, the pussy finally found some teeth?" He laughs softly. "Suck my dick to say sorry and we won't report you for this..." He motions to Posta, who isn't looking good, and I briefly wonder if I've crushed his larynx, before focusing back on Markel, who is entirely too confident after years of unchecked abusing me. I grin at him briefly, and discomfort flashes across his face, before I bring my knee up into his groin, then again into his nose as he collapses forward, hearing an incredibly satisfying crack as I crush it. Both men lie, crying and groaning, on the ground, and I hear Captain Cruise's furious voice echo down the hallway.

"Reed! What the *hell?*" he shouts, almost running toward

us. "I got a call from someone about these two flinging pop-its in the station, and come down to see you attacking them!"

I shake my head, slightly out of breath, and take a quick step back. *Fuck! Gemma will kill me if I got blood on this dress!* Doing a quick examination of the hemline, I let out a sigh of relief, then look at Captain Cruise. I can sense Hideo approaching from behind, and turn to grab the file from him, rolling my eyes at his disapproving face, knowing I'll have to apologize to him for making a unilateral decision without consulting him.

"Captain," I begin calmly, "Markel and Posta have been sexually harassing me since I started the Force. It's why I transferred from their teams. They were threatening me with rape and then tried to blackmail me for sexual favors. It was self-defense."

Cruise's eyebrows hit the ceiling. "Those are big accusations, Reed. You'd need to back those up with proof."

I push the meticulously kept file into his hands. "Everything is in here. Copies of wiped security footage before they were 'lost'. All my complaints to HR that were buried or paid off by these two. Witness statements, on tape or recorded and signed by witnesses. Emails, photographs of harassing messages left on my whiteboard then erased."

Cruise opens the folder, eyes widening at the number of pages. "Why didn't HR do anything about this," he asks incredulously. "Why didn't you come to me earlier?"

I look to Hideo, who responds quietly, "To be honest, Sir, we weren't sure whether you were on the take or not."

Cruise looks affronted, and Deo holds up his hands in apology. "They had two members of HR they were paying to ignore the complaints, and we weren't sure where you'd fall."

"So why now?" Cruise asks, still flipping through the pages.

I point behind me at the men who have followed us

into the hallway. "Witness statements from federal agents who are neutral third parties. They haven't met Markel or Posta, have had no personal interaction with them. And at least one of them is on the record with a federal agency as protesting my presence on the task force, so there's no favoritism here. He has said repeatedly that he would get rid of me if possible, and wrote a brief regarding my position weakening the team dynamic and requested my removal."

Donovan's eyes flare slightly in surprise that I know about his opinion about me, then his face settles into something between regret and determination. I don't have time to process it before turning back to Cruise.

"So this time," I say, smiling viciously, "you *have* to do something, even if you *are* on the take. Because it would cost you more to ignore it than these two are worth."

Posta glares up at me through the desperate, violent eyes of a wounded animal, and I meet his stare with an answering snarl of my own lips. Cruise sighs deeply and waits until I look at him. "I would have done something about this, Kailani," he says firmly. "This is unacceptable. I wouldn't stand for this occurring under my watch, and I'm sorry that you felt I would. Clearly I have some deep cleaning to do, and when you're able, I'd like to sit down with you to discuss this further." He looks up at the camera in the hallway and says, "I assume it's on film?"

I nod and check my watch. "You may want to get it before shift change though."

Markel makes a panicked sound of protest, saying weakly in a voice wet with blood, "You can't believe this shit, Chief! She's a fucking psychopath. She attacked us out of nowhere. Don't we get a say in this? We need medical attention for Christ' sake!"

Cruise pauses, and I point at the camera, then my watch. "That footage will go the way of the Dodo in the next half hour if you don't move now."

He looks down at the two officers on the floor, disgust

heavy on his face, and makes a quick call on his radio. Within a minute, two armed officers round the corner, pausing briefly as they see the scene in front of them. They exchange a quick look, then cuff Markel and Posta and take them to the holding room. Cruise watches the entire thing through careful eyes and shakes his head, face heavy with anger. "Deep, *deep* cleaning." He tilts his head at me, then motions with his jaw after the men walking away from us. I give a small nod, and he sighs.

"I'd check those cuffs, Cruise," I say quietly. "With officers you know you can trust. And get that footage. This is so much deeper than you know."

"Any suggestions," he replies, his voice bitter and full of rage. This is going to be a hard wake-up call for Cruise, who seems like a good man. His department is gangrenous with corruption, and it's been taking place openly on his watch. He's not going to take this lightly. The Force, as we know it, is about to come apart at the seams.

Deo speaks up from behind me. "Tyler, Jordan, Perry, Lee. All solid, all trustworthy. I'd start there."

Cruise nods and looks at the file again. "I assume you have a copy of this?"

I smile, cynical and acerbic, and say bitingly, "*You* have a copy of it. We have the original."

He nods shortly, then spins around, and leaves to deal with his demons.

I turn back to meet the faces of my team – Deo's tight with barely contained fury – and walk slowly back to the meeting room, shaking slightly with spent energy.

We all file in silently, taking our seats, before Smith calls on me. "Reed. What just happened?"

"What just happened," Hideo grinds out from between clenched teeth, "is Reed decided to blow maybe sixteen months of careful planning on a whim."

I glare at him. "I did not *blow* it on a whim," I snap back. "We knew we were going to push that out at some point,

Deo."

He responds immediately, voice growing louder until it's just under a yell. And Hideo *never* yells. "We've put up with months, *months*, of them pawing at you, baiting you, saying..." he chokes briefly before forcing himself to continue, desperately trying to reign in his temper, "... saying *untenable* things to you... things I... and I've been forced to sit there and do nothing, *nothing*, about it because of you convincing me to play the long game, Kai. I've dreamt of the ways I'm going to kill those two for what they've said and done to you, and you've made me bide my time, and for *what?*" His fingers flex, knuckles white.

Smith's deep voice breaks through Deo's anguished one. "*What* is going on?"

I lay a comforting hand on Hideo, who looks like he's about to come apart at the seams. "We've been watching Markel and Posta for months now... well, like a year and a half or so. There have been some issues on the force – shady dealing, cops on the take, things being changed and going missing. We know those two are involved, and we wanted to see how deep it went before we turned over evidence."

I exhale slowly, leaning against Hideo slightly, who is stiff and turns away from me. "I was their favorite victim, and Deo wanted to end it right away, but it was mostly just words, and I convinced him to sit on the sidelines while it was all happening, just film it or bear witness to it. They never did anything more than intimidation tactics... ugly words, that sort of thing..."

Deo growls out through a strangled voice, "They grabbed your ass, and tried to corner you. A *lot*. And it made you physically sick. I know it did."

I lean my head against him, sighing softly, "I didn't know you knew. I'm sorry, Deo. I didn't know it was so hard on you... you never said..."

He swallows convulsively, eyes pressed shut. "When I *think* about what I let happen so we could build that file..."

Startled, I grab his shoulders gently and turn him to me. "*I* let happen, Deo. We're equal partners, which is one of the things I love... I *appreciate* about our working together..." I scramble to cover the small slip in my words. "You trusted me to play my part. But I'm sorry I didn't take yours into deeper consideration."

The tension drains from him, slowly, but he softens toward me, turning back slightly, and I keep talking. "We tried a couple of times to pass info along, but it kept getting 'lost in the shuffle' or downplayed, and we realized pretty quickly how deep the corruption runs here."

"And you're sure Cruise can handle it?"

I shake my head. "He's definitely one of the good ones, but I was hoping to have a little more before we passed it off to him."

"Then why now?" Smith asks, confused. "Why now? If you weren't completely confident?"

I shrug evasively. "Ah. It seemed... I mean, we're focusing completely on the task force now, and we were kind of dropping the ball... it seemed like a good time to pass it off..."

Jonah frowns at me. "But they were harassing you under a month ago and you let it go. And you'd started the task force. Why not then? I witnessed it, so..."

Adjusting myself in my chair awkwardly, I flush deeply with all of the guys staring at me, until Donovan says quietly, "Christ. It's because of Smith, right?"

Pressing my face into my hands, I say, "No. It was just time."

Donovan shakes his head decisively. "No way, Kai. It's because they were attacking Smith."

Smith looks at me with a strange expression. "Kailani?"

"We had the info, Smith. It's no big deal."

"You let them harass you for months."

I shrug uncomfortably, feeling the weight of their eyes like a leaden blanket. And all the while, the image of Smith talking to his friend on the phone from weeks before, eyes full with exhaustion and hopelessness, flashes before me. How his jaw clenched and face went blank today at the sounds of the popping from the hallway. They'd been tormenting him since he got here, I realized. Causing repeated flashbacks, sleepless nights, endless internal battles, over and over. And he never said anything.

"Kai," Hideo asks, facing me and focusing on my face, "was it because they were attacking Smith?"

I press my lips together in a tight line, and he sighs, turning back to the rest of the team. "Reed's probably right," he says firmly. "We were holding on to that for too long. Selfishly, almost. We wanted the coffin nailed shut, but we have other things to focus on, and who knows what happens while we're not watching. It's better this way. Just took me by surprise. Anyway. We need a protective detail for Reed?" he asks, clearly changing the subject. The room is silent, Jonah, Donovan, and Smith clearly lost in their own thoughts.

"Smith?" Hideo prompts. "Reed? Protection?"

Smith snaps back into himself and focuses on the plans in front of him. "Right." He says and drops the other topic. Donovan, however, continues to study me carefully, and for the first time I can't feel Jonah's emotions press out against me.

It was another hour before I could call Gemma to come pick me up. The guys had talked over me about a bodyguard, though Hideo, surprisingly, had agreed with me that I'd be safe alone with Gemma and Lachy on the island, and going out with Gemma for my birthday tonight.

"Doll's smart, and aware of her surroundings," he'd said. "And they rarely, if ever, split up when they go out." With Hideo's backing, Smith had conceded, and we'd ended up on an arrangement that involved me always being with *some-*

one or calling one of the guys if I were on my own. It was cumbersome, but I was willing to give in on some points to avoid having a round-the-clock guard. My British counterpart had been grabbed off the street while walking alone, so it seemed a crime of planning and opportunity combined. Our goal was to avoid giving anyone the same opportunity.

After that had finally been settled, Walker and I took the chance to brief the others on last night's gala. We were fairly certain the Mexico trip that had been up on silent auction was a cover, the prices driven up by the same few buyers, and I'd had strong, telling emotional pulses from two others I wanted to look into. All in all it was a fairly successful night and gave us a few leads.

Hideo asked me at one point, "And no problems with Daniels?" To which Donovan replied with a satisfied smirk, "Naw. No problems." Deo looked at me, and I rolled my eyes, promising with a look to fill him in later. Smith forced me to run through Gemma's and my plans for the rest of the day three times, triple checking that I wouldn't deviate from them, that I'd call should anything seem off, that we'd stay together the entire time. He started on a fourth before Donovan broke in, "Jesus, *Mom*. Kai will be home by curfew!" Which caused me to Cheshire smile, and the wave of satisfaction that poured off him at the look on my face was incredibly confusing.

So finally, *finally*, after the chaotic morning, I was released to Gemma's care. She and Hideo repeated the pass-off from earlier, stilted and exceedingly polite, and he cautioned her about staying with me. Her face flared in a completely un-Gemma like look, and for a long moment she and Deo locked glares, until she ground out, "Kai can depend on me *completely*." Deo shrugged in an incredibly unconvinced way, and I pulled her to the car.

The two of us had a gorgeous lunch at a little bistro I'd been dying to try and had been saving up for, made all the more special by the fact that, when the bill came, it had already been taken care of. The maître d' dropped off a lovely little dessert plate with "Happy Birthday" written in chocolate script, and I looked at Gemma in surprise and gratitude. She returned the look of surprise and held her hands up, saying, "Wasn't me, kid!" The maître d' smiled at us and said, "Ladies, compliments of a Mr. Shotridge, who has taken care of your lunch today. And he asked me to pass along the message that he's 'incredibly lucky to get to celebrate knowing you'."

I flushed a deep, deep red, as Gemma cooed over the selection of cakes and chocolates. While she divided them up, I sent Jonah a quick text thanking him for his thoughtfulness and generosity. After we finished we headed to the hotel to check in, and all thoughts of the morning's worries fled in the excitement of the afternoon.

HAPPY BIRTHDAY

Saturday, 27 October – Kailani

The club is completely packed. It's a weird place. It's apparently owned by twin brothers – one who's totally into the hipster culture and one who's deep into underground rap, so it's a really eclectic vibe on all fronts. Urban Hipster is crazy popular though. The drinks are poured well, there are several floors of different music and style, and there are plenty of carefully crafted tucked-away places to hide.

Gemma has gotten us a VIP table on the electronic/pop floor. It separates the thudding bass of the downstairs rap and hard rock from the upstairs lounge with guitar music, coffee, and open-air balconies. We are currently guzzling water, out of breath from dancing and screaming. After we'd checked in at the hotel, which had a spa attached to it, we took full advantage, indulging in facials and massages, with some time in the sauna and hot tub. By the time we were done, around 4:30, we were both exhausted and crashed for a couple of hours once we got back to our room. Knowing we were going out clubbing that night, we ordered room service, and then Gemma spent what felt like *hours* getting us ready to go out.

She changed up my look completely for the evening out. Instead of sweet and soft, she went for dark and dangerous. She had completely straightened my hair, and it fell in a dark curtain to the small of my back. I had inherited my mother's Hawaiian hair and kept with our people's tradition of not cutting it. We believe that hair contains Mana, a kind of spiritual energy, and other than basic trimmings, I never fully cut it. My makeup was glittery and violent – Gemms had somehow painted a galaxy on my eyelids, sparkly purple and deep blacks, with subtly shimmering cheeks and some kind of lipstick magic that made it look like I had been kissing someone for hours. I had on black modern joggers that came in tightly at the bottom of my calves, high black heels with minute straps holding them on across my ankle and toe, and a simple, white, bralette top with my black motorcycle jacket over the top. I looked like I was ready to fight or fuck, and couldn't make up my mind which, and it was a freaking badass look.

Gemma once-overed me with a critical eye, then nodded her approval. She was a vicious pixie, vibrant hair and vivid make-up, snakebites glittering with some dark gemstones tonight. When we arrived at the club we skipped to the front of a considerable line – Gemma having some connection as she usually did, and the deep, bass thump of the club music changed the beat of my heart to match it. Tonight was a night for mayhem, for becoming someone else and losing the parts of myself, however briefly, that were weighing me down, and I welcomed it with open arms.

Gemma is glassy eyed and shining on the floor. She's lost to the music and is attracting a ton of admiring looks from the guys around us, but I see her end game as she glides in her fairy way to the heavy beats of the music. She's had just enough alcohol to keep her floating but not enough to impair her judgement – her sweet spot, she calls it. I never have to worry about Gemms drinking too much and ditching me or getting sick. When we're out together, we stick together. She thinks only crappy friends drink and ditch, or make their DD watch out for their ass, so she'll get right to the point of fuzzy and walk that tightrope all night.

Gemma always brings us here on our nights out. She

knows I don't drink often, but we both love dancing, and when everyone in the club is moving to the same music, I can let my walls drop a little and I get a silky, drunken buzz from the emotions in the club. It's why we avoid the other two floors – the rap and heavy metal bring out darker emotions in people, edges of anger and violence that I can't escape into. And the lounge upstairs is always mellow, but shadowed in sadness, and it brings me down. The Playground – what most people call the floor between Urban and Hipster, always starts with light, pop-y music before it moves into more trance electronic music. For some reason those beats zen everyone out, and I can lose myself in the crowd and their feelings.

Tonight is no different. It feels surreal, like we're in some other world away from everyday, and it's easy to lose yourself. The lights are flashing to look like we're dancing underwater, and some song called "The Egyptian Night Club" is thumping through the speakers. The crowd is moving in strange unison, rising and falling like waves, bodies sweaty and writhing, crowding the floor. Gemma and I are in the middle of the pack, having left our table almost an hour ago to dance. She's been locking eyes with a tall, slight man over by the bar off and on for the past twenty minutes. He's exactly her type – gauged ears, black hair covering his dark eyes, and simply but sharply dressed in skinny jeans and a black band shirt. His eyes are rimmed with heavy liner, and he looks like that gorgeous guy who played Hook on some TV show Gemma loves. She is *definitely* vibing on him, but I know she won't leave my side unless I push her. I've already told her to go over once, but she's determined to stay with me.

They lock eyes again, and honest to god, Gemma blushes. He turns to the bar and orders two drinks, Gemma watching the entire time. Then he pushes his way through the crowd to us and pauses. Turning to Gemma, he offers her a dark purple drink which matches her hair. She takes it hesitantly, looking at me, then to the bartender, Jade, whom we know pretty well by this point from our trips here. Jade's watching and gives Gemms a double thumbs up, and Gemma smiles. Then Hook turns to me and offers me a bottle of water, unopened. "I notice you weren't drinking," he yells over the music. Gemma's face falls slightly, and I get a pit in my stomach thinking that maybe we got this all wrong.

"I wanted to ask if it's okay if I ask your friend to dance, or if I'd be interrupting something special?" he yells again. "I don't want to break up the party if it's something important."

Gemma's eyes widen a little, and she looks like that heart-eyed emoji on my phone. I smile and reply, "You'll have to ask her!"

He nods seriously and says, "For sure. I just don't want to get in the way or anything."

I jerk my head towards Gemms, who's staring up at him like he hung the moon. He's playing with his lip ring nervously and half stutters, "You want to dance or something?"

Gemma looks unsurely between me and Hook, and I grin at her and wave her away. She grabs his hand to lead him out further onto the floor, and by the look on his face, I'm pretty sure he'd follow her anywhere if she asked him. I'm about to go to our table to take a break, when the music changes to "Bad Girls" by Pussy Riot, and a handsy guy from earlier that we'd waved off several times sees his chance and moves in towards me. I try doing the universal "small smile but hands up" move, and he's not having it. Pushing forward into me, he becomes a bit more aggressive, and I sigh, thinking I'm going to have to be a bit more forceful, when his eyes widen and he steps back. I feel a hard body pressing against me from behind. Rolling my eyes, I'm about to turn around and nicely brush the guy off when a heavily muscled arm wraps around my waist, and I catch my breath when I recognize the tattoos.

A deep voice asks, "Okay?" mouth pressed against my ear, sending cold shivers over my skin, sweat mixing with my own on my face. I nod slowly, and he drops his head to my shoulder, moving slowly to the music, letting my body get used to his. It takes a surprisingly little amount of time before we're moving in sync, bodies pressed against each other. His hand is splayed on my bare stomach, pulling me against him. My skin is lit up from where he's touching me, and I'm hyper aware of his massive body wrapped around mine, but by the time the song switches to "Boom", I've let the ramped-up emotions in the club blur me out a little, and I move to the music like I know I can.

The guy behind me is a surprisingly good dancer, but this club and this song are made for me. I slide sensually, swaying my hips slowly against him, then drop and turn, climbing back up his body 'til our eyes meet. Maddox's icy eyes lock on mine, and one huge hand wraps around the back of my neck, pulling my face to meet his, foreheads pressed together. The other is low on my back, resting on my bare skin lightly, like he's trying to learn the way my body is moving. His pale eyes catch the light briefly, and I can see how intensely they're focused on mine. The smoke of whiskey is in the air, and I can't tell how much he's been drinking, but the way he's moving and his touch indicate that, while he's had a few, he's not completely out of it.

Our faces are close enough that I can feel his breath brush over my skin, and I open my mouth to try to speak, but he presses his mouth to my ear again and whispers almost pleadingly, "Leave it. Just for tonight." I stand on tiptoe so he can hear me, and I feel his entire body react to my lips against his ear whispering, "Okay." He reaches up and grabs my hand off his shoulder and holds it pressed to his chest, locked between us, then wraps my other hand up and around his neck before putting his own on the curve at the small of my back.

Not 100% sure what I've agreed to, we keep dancing, the

lights in the club getting darker as the songs play on. We don't move from each other, despite the crowded dance floor and a single interruption. Another guy I had danced with earlier tries to muscle in, and Maddox straight up growls at him. The sound travels through my bones and rests low in my stomach, a deep vibration that sets my entire body on fire. Maddox feels me respond, and he shoots me a dark and dangerous grin, saying, "You wanna dance with this guy, Kai?"

I turn to the guy somewhat apologetically and thank him for the ask but say I'm good where I am. After about half an hour, I'm so on edge from the closeness of his body, and the heat from his skin, his forehead bent low to rest on my shoulder and his breath sending streaks of lightning along my neck and collarbone, that I need a break. I'm turned on and confused and slide my walls back up to get some focus. Pushing away from him, I yell over the music. "I have to go find Gemma and check on her!" I turn away and am surprised to feel his hand grab mine.

"I'll help you look for her!" he shouts back. "How are you going to find her in all this?"

I grin at him and waggle my fingers in the air like a magician, then lead him first to our table in the roped-off section. The table is empty, our stuff still on it, and there is a small piece of paper tucked under a water glass that says "1.2.3". I laugh to myself. *Dirty bird! Get some, Gemma!* Following our code, I move out of the main room into the side bar, where there are several alcoves and hidden nooks. I go to check the first one, by the window behind the bookcase, but don't even need to look to know the pornstar sounds coming from the dark corner are not my roommate.

Moving further into the room, I head towards the corner table. It's hard to get, a high back booth that faces away from the bar and looks out a large window over the city. Dropping my walls just slightly, I feel her familiar signature before slamming those shields right back up. She's clearly deep into... something... with someone, but enough time has gone by that I need to make sure she's okay.

I squinch my face up, closing my eyes dramatically as I round the corner, one hand waving in front of me, the other still held tightly by Maddox. "Gemma, you drunken harlot! Give me the all clear that you're okay and I'll leave you to it."

She snorts indelicately. "Open your eyes you sneaky bitch and introduce me to Sven Svenson here. Where the fuck did you find a Viking?"

"Right?!?!" I crack an eye open, don't see anything indecent, and open my eyes fully. "That's what *I* said when I met him too!"

"You did?" his bass voice rumbles. "I didn't know that."

"In my *head*," I say, exasperated, at the same time Gemma chimes in, "In her *head*!" Like he was a moron and it should have been obvious. The two men exchange a look, before holding out hands to shake.

"Maddox."

"Ryan."

"Sven," Gemma stage-whispers as I whisper back, "Hook," and we grin at each other. I waggle my eyebrows at her in a suggestive way and ask, "You good here? Need me to run interference?"

Hook, to his credit, smiles an absolutely cute as a button smile at Gemma and waits for her to answer. "I'm gooooood!" she chirps, giggling. "Meeting spot Three in..." she checks her watch, "forty-five minutes?"

"Roger that."

Hook honest to god raises his hand slightly, and I bite back a laugh. "I can take her home?"

She shakes her head. "Thank you so much, Ryan, but no. A) we never split up. We come together; we leave together. B) In approximately one hour we'll be so hungry we'd eat day-old dirt, so we need to get to The Curry House before that happens. And finally, *and* most importantly..."

I frantically try to get Gemma to stop talking, but she's

ignoring me. "*MOST* importantly," she continues, smacking my hand away, "it's KaiKai's birthday, so of any night, *tonight* isn't the night we'd separate."

Hook smiles up at me and half lifts his glass. "Happy birthday!" he says cheerfully.

Maddox's hand tightens on mine slightly, and he looks at me, some unknown emotion flashing across his face. All at once Gemma's head snaps around like she forgot something important, and she checks her watch again. "Shit!" she yells. "*Shit!*" Leaping up she leaves the table and runs to the bar, leaving the guys looking to me for answers, completely confused. "Who knows?" I shrug. "Pointless to ask sometimes. Just go along for the ride."

It's almost 1:15am at this point, which is the first of three "final calls" at Urban Hipster. The second is at 1:30, and the third at 1:45. The club shuts down officially at 2:00, but people linger until almost 3:00am on most weekends. Wondering if Gemma has gone to get refills, I poke my head around the booth, when the music suddenly cuts out and a spotlight appears on me. Instinctively I step back, and hit Maddox, whose hands come up to rest lightly on my hips. Ryan has gotten up and is standing next to us.

From the bar top a familiar shriek yells, "Happy birthday, Sex Bomb!" and Tom Jones' hit starts blaring over the speakers. Gemma is standing on the bar and really going for it, singing at the top of her lungs, waving a feather boa and throwing confetti penises everywhere. The drunken crowd is loving it, and by the chorus the entire bar is shouting along. "Sex bomb, sex bomb, you're a sex bomb!"

She jumps off the bar and comes over to me, dancing clearly choreographed moves around, and I laugh helplessly. I hate being the center of attention and am bright red, but she's so goofy and good natured it's hard to be mad. The bartender takes out what appears to be an enormous penis cake from behind the bar, and one of the waitresses brings over a huge handful of dick balloons. At the end of the song the entire bar cheers loudly, and she kisses me drunkenly on my cheek. "Love you, Kai! CAKE FOR EVERY-ONE!"

The whole bar cheers again, and I hide my face against Maddox's chest as Ryan stares at Gemma in what I hope is awe. The speakers start playing happy birthday, and I blow out some unfortunately placed candles before I'm able to slink away. I walk quickly down the hall to the old coat room, a large closet just inside the exit of the club. Gemma and I found it once when we were trying to leave and made a wrong turn. It's tucked away from the main hallway, which is probably why they stopped using it, and now it's mostly a storage room with a couple of old chairs and a broken couch.

It's where we always meet before we leave the club. If we get separated, or I need a break from the press of bodies, I hide away here, and Gemma finds me. Or if I'm lost in the music and she's drifting into a planned painting, she sometimes comes here for quiet. Looking over the room, I'm debating sitting on the couch, when the door opens again behind me, and the unmistakable warmth of Maddox fills the room. He closes the door quietly behind him, then pauses.

The dim light of a single bulb illuminates the shadows more than the actual area. My back is still to Maddox as I frantically try to get my breathing under control. I sense him moving towards me, then cool air runs up my back as he sweeps the curtain of my hair over one of my shoulders. I'm still frozen in place as he runs his nose up the back of my neck, barely touching my skin, and ripples shiver over me. He can hear my breath catch, and I feel the curve of a smile on his face, as he whispers against me, lips on my skin. "This is probably a bad idea."

I nod in agreement, unable to get my voice working. He wraps his hand lightly around the column of my throat, dragging his fingers gently down and across my collarbone to my shoulder, then traces down my arm, all with just his fingertips. I'm swaying slightly where I stand, fighting my body's desire to turn around and fling myself at him. He nudges my neck again with his nose, then rubs his lips gently on the bare skin. "It's your birthday, Kailani..."

I nod again, feeling ridiculous that I can't even get out a single word. "Can I kiss the birthday girl?"

Turning around finally, I lock eyes with him. His pupils are blown in the dark room, making them more onyx than ice, and his skin is lightly flushed. He drops both of his hands at his side, waiting. I stare at him with wide eyes, thinking of how much he reminds me of a caged tiger, muscles taut with barely restrained violence, coiled and ready to spring. He's waiting for me to make a decision, not moving until I let him, and the tension grows to an almost unbearable point.

"Stop thinking so hard, Kailani," he whispers. "Just for tonight. Or just for this moment." The moment I incline my head, he moves forward, not in the rush and fury as I expected, but in a slow, dangerous movement, sinuous and mesmerizing. He leans his head down, moving slowly towards me, and brushes his lips lightly across mine. Nothing else on us is touching; he's just kissing me lightly, waiting for me.

The instant I kiss him back, he unleashes. Grabbing my wrists, he slams me back into the wall behind me with frantic need. I'm just as frantic, writhing beneath him. He doesn't let up for a moment, completely overwhelming me as electric currents race up and down my spine. My hands are pressed over my head in his tight grip, and his body is pressed against mine, no space between us. Growling deep in his throat, he drops my hands and picks me up, wrapping my legs around him, back against the wall. His lips taste like whiskey, and I can barely breath, don't even want to if it means I have to stop kissing Maddox.

Supporting me with one arm, he brings the other hand

up to run lightly down the column of my throat before resting gently on the skin exposed below my collarbone. His hand is massive, like the rest of him, and I'm pretty sure I'm going to hyperventilate as he pulls the heel of his hand away, leaving only his fingertips dragging down to pause between my breasts. He lifts his head to search my face with heavy-lidded eyes, and all of the sudden I'm rethinking how much he's had to drink tonight.

"Maddox?" I ask tentatively, as he stares at me.

Leaning forward, he rests our heads together, frozen in the moment. "Jesus, Kailani. You could kill a man," he whispers raggedly.

We stay like that, until he turns his head to me and kisses me again, slowly and languorously, changing from quick flashing steel to slow, molten lava, somehow more dangerous than before. It's like he's trying to imprint himself on my soul the way he's kissing me – not the uncontrollable chaos from moments before, but a purposeful, deliberate branding. He leans into me, hand drifting lower and lower, and my breath audibly catches in my throat, and it seems like everything in the entire universe goes completely still, waiting to see what happens in the next moment.

A loud crash echoes through the empty hallway, shattering the silence. Maddox startles back from me, setting me down quickly and turning into a fighting stance as he faces the door. I reach out and gently touch his back, and he shakes my hand off, then pushes me back behind him. I realize I'm seeing something private, some response that he would normally keep deeply hidden, and I try again.

"Maddox? Maddox!" I say firmly. "It's just drunken Gemma and her pirate friend. I can feel her signature."

He doesn't move, and I quietly move in front of his face. "Maddox. It's Gemma." I see him come back to himself as he relaxes his stance and focuses on my face. He looks startled, and wary, and, worst of all, sorry. He straightens up and runs a hand through his hair, glancing around the room and shaking himself slightly. By the time he meets my eyes again, he's all professionalism, and the hints of Maddox have disappeared into the persona of Agent Smith.

"Reed," he begins, obviously searching for the right words.

I wave him off, affecting disinterest. "Too much to drink on a weird night. Let's just forget it."

He tries again, saying, "I think that you're..."

"Jesus, Maddox," I interrupt. "We kissed. For, like, five seconds. We were drinking, we danced... it's not a thing." I shrug. "Please don't make this uncomfortable." Privately I'm yelling inside for Gemma to come and interrupt this mess. I feel strange, like I want to cry and go to sleep, and I don't know why. Maddox is staring at me, and I flush under his steady gaze.

"Reed."

Someone crashes into the door, and I thank god under my breath as I wrench it open to see Gemma lying prostrate on the floor, laughing her ass off as Hook tries to help her back to her feet. He looks at me apologetically. "It was a Purple Dragon Martini... I didn't know..."

I groan. "Tequila?"

"I didn't know that this," he waves his free hand towards Gemma, "would happen."

Gemma laughs up at me and stage-whispers, "Kai! Kyyy-yyy... Kaaaaaaaiiiii! KAI! I think I'm drunk!"

I crouch down beside her, grinning, and whisper back, "I think so too!"

All at once, her bottom lip sticks out and starts to tremble. Still laughing, I look up at Hook and say, "Brace yourself!"

He looks wary, then incredibly worried when Gemma starts crying big, silent tears. "I'm sorry!" she says, reaching up to me. "I had *tequila*."

"I know, babe. Come on now. Let's get you home."

"No curry?" she asks sadly.

"No curry," I confirm.

Hook, to his credit, picks her up to help me get her to a cab. I look behind me to say something to Maddox, but he's already gone, having silently slipped by me without my notice. I sigh deeply, then turn to my friend and head home.

GRAB A CUP OF JOE,
AGENT DRISCOLL

Sunday, 28 October – Maela

When I wake up, there's bright sunshine streaming through the window. Emlyn's sitting in the chair next to me again, quietly tapping away on a laptop. He's showered and in a fresh suit. I glance down. I'm in – ugh – hospital pajamas, and my scalp prickles, telling me that my hair could use a wash.

Sensing movement, Emlyn looks up. "Ah, Maela. You're awake. How are you feeling?"

I think about it, giving a cautious wiggle. "Better," I decide. But I'm worried by the expression on his face. He looks serious and slightly remote, the passionate man of yesterday walled in behind the professional façade of impassive government agent.

"Good. I'm glad to hear it. Kavi and Jorge wanted to stay, but I sent them home. They needed to rest, and you and I need to talk."

Oh dear. This doesn't sound promising. "Yeees?" I say warily. "Do we need to do a proper debrief?" That's the word, isn't it? Debrief, as in *Grab a cup of joe, Agent Driscoll, it's time for your debrief. Tell us how things went down. You'll be up for a commendation, of course.*

"No. You've given us more than enough. In fact, I think we can take things from here. We've got warrants out for Ratko's and Bojan's arrests for kidnapping and assault, and Vlado's for suspected membership of an organized criminal group. As soon as we unearth them, we'll bring them in for

533

questioning. It'll be your word against theirs, and they've undoubtedly already manufactured an alibi, but I might be able to get one of them to break. We'll need you to testify if we can take things to trial, but it's time for you to go back to Queen's College and your book."

The fu–? He's kicking me loose? I take a deep breath, look up at him, and say flatly, "No."

"Maela–"

"No," I repeat. "We're a team, and teams stick together. And even if you round up Ratko, Bojan, and Vlado, Magda and Rhea and Tennireef are still out there. And you still don't have anything on them."

"Maela, you were grabbed off the street and tortured for information. They know you're working with me. It's not safe to continue our association." Emlyn's jaw is set, and he has a look in his eyes that says he means business. Big deal. My parents were right: I am a scrappy, demanding, *leetle cheftainess*, and two can play at this game.

I cross my arms and gaze at him calmly. "I'll take precautions. Now that I know that they know about me, I'll stay alert and vary my movements, shake off any watchers. It'll be fine." I'm quite entranced with the idea of jumping on and off the underground and busses, zipping around corners, dodging a tail. Finally, *finally*, being a calm, cool, and competent woman. Hah! Though I'll have to start up with the karate videos in earnest.

Emlyn exhales strongly through his nose and presses his fingers hard against the smooth skin between his eyes, as if I've given him a sudden headache. "Maela, it's a certainty that they know where you live. You had your bag and wallet with you, and it's safe to assume that Ratko looked through them. They might even have had time to make copies of your keys. Not only are you going to stop working for us, you're going to have to move into a safe house until this is all over."

The double whammy leaves me gasping like a hooked

fish. Leave my little flat in lovely Fitzrovia? OK, the flat's no great shakes, but it's right by Mary-Poppins-ville. And, in the few short months I've been here, it's come to feel like home. "Not just no, but heck no!"

"The matter is not up for discussion." Emlyn's voice is more clipped than usual, the lord of the manor dictating to a lowly serf.

"That's what you think! Have you thought that they let me go for a reason and that we could use that? If they'd wanted to kill me, they would have!"

Emlyn's eyes flash at me, grey frost in winter sunlight, and I realize that that may not have been the most judicious thing to say. "I am not using you as bait!"

"Emlyn," I plead, "don't take this away from me. We've got to keep going!" I'm feeling panicky. I didn't know how much this whole thing meant to me – training, learning, working for MI5, knowing that I was a part of something bigger, trying to make the world a better place – until now, when I'm on the verge of losing it.

His face softens, and for a moment, I think I've persuaded him, but he shakes his head. "I'm sorry, Maela. We just can't take the chance."

I fling myself back into the pillows. I'm so furious I can't speak, so I settle for glaring at him. He's unperturbed. "Now, can I get you something? You must be hungry. I'll see what they can rustle up, shall I? There's a guard outside the door, so you'll be quite safe."

I shrug and give a half-grimace half-grunt at him, as if to say "suit yourself". He nods. "OK. I can see you're upset, so I'll give you a few minutes." He puts down the laptop and goes to the door, opening and closing it quietly while I continue to fume.

He is not cutting me loose. I won't let him! I'm the one who saw Ratko and Magda and Tennireef. I'm the one who saw Vlado and the preparations for the meet on Lace Lane. OK, so I freaked out when I thought I was going to be burned to death in the warehouse fire, and then when Tennireef abused and murdered that poor woman, and, OK, when Altan got his fingers cut off, but any normal person would have. But now that I know what I'm doing and what to expect, I can handle things. I've got much better control, so Emlyn can suck it. I'm the one with the visions. My eyes narrow: *I'm the one* with the visions, and there's nothing Emlyn can do to stop me if I want to have one. I force myself to take deep breaths, in and out, and to relax, tuning my body to the vibrations, visualizing the rope, up, up, hand over hand, swirling darkness, seeking, seeking...

Magda's on the phone in her penthouse. Again. She's got the curtains drawn, and she's pacing in a bathrobe – short and silky, of course – in front of the windows.

"That's the question. How?" Magda stops to listen, those plush lips pursed. "Of course I'm sure... Yes, you may be right. If so, I'll find out... I think it's time. You agree? Good... Mmm-hmm... I'll let you know. Alright." I'm waiting for an enema-ooey, but she just hangs up. She stares for a moment into the distance, tapping a nail against the phone, then dials a number. "It's me... We need to talk... No, I'll come to you... Because," she purrs down the line, "you know how I like to slum it. You know what it does to me, seeing you in your natural element. Dirty and rough." A throaty laugh, and I think: Holy hell, woman! It's half past eight in the morning. I mean: I've nothing against morning sex, but she's all cigarettes and whiskey and leather in a bondage club. It's not decent at this hour. Another throaty laugh. "See you then." Magda hangs up the phone, and all traces of sensuality slide off her face. Her lips twist into that "not nice" smile, and she heads past me down the hall, disappearing behind a door on one side. A moment later, I hear bathwater running, so I shrug and look down at my feet for the rope.

When I open my eyes, Emlyn's glaring down at me. "I see," he says, in a voice that could slice steel. I'm unrepentant. His lips are set in a thin line, and his jaw is tight. There's a slight vein pulsing in his temple. I take the opportunity to smile sweetly up at him.

"Well?" he demands.

"Well what?" I say airily.

"What did you see?"

"Oh, that. Well, as I'm not working for MI5 anymore, I don't have to tell you. Ooh, toast and marmalade! Thanks."

His hands clench, and I can tell he's itching to give me a good spanking. Call me kinky, but it turns me on. I take a bite and make a show of moaning. "God that's good," I sigh.

Aaand, there's that tic under his eye. "Maela," he says warningly.

"Nothing to do with me. I'm just a civilian. There's nothing I could add to your super-duper operation." A swig of coffee to wash down the toast, then I flutter my eyes innocently up at him.

Emlyn sits down heavily, hands clasped loosely as he leans forward. "Maela, I'm trying to protect you."

"And I'm trying to help you, but we don't always get what we want, do we?" I sing.

He leans back and looks at me consideringly, one finger tapping on his knee. "You're going to have visions with or without me, aren't you?"

"Yup," I take another bite of toast.

There's a short silence, and then he sighs. "Alright."

My eyes gleam in triumph. "You mean it?"

"Against my better judgement, yes."

"And I can stay in my flat?" I rush on before he can answer. "Come on, Emlyn. It's a good idea. And you can set up security cameras or something."

But he's shaking his head. "No." I'm opening my mouth to have another go, and he holds up a hand. "No. Don't push me, Maela. I'm not going to bend on this. Now, you're going to stay here until we can arrange alternative accommodation. Don't worry, I've brought some clean clothes for you."

He nods to a duffel bag on the floor.

I'm momentarily distracted. Clean clothes! We can discuss my housing arrangements later. And then I think: oh my God, was Emlyn rooting about in my underwear drawer? Please tell me he picked the scratchy but sexy lace numbers and not the manky, mismatched tee-shirt bras and hip-hugger panties I usually wear. And did he grab my boring pajamas or my new cami set? I nod: "Thanks. OK, well, I should probably have a shower, so..."

"Of course. I've got to get back to the office, but, as I said, there's a guard outside the door. And I'll come back this afternoon." Emlyn heads toward the door, and I give a little wave.

As soon as he's out of the room, I dive for the duffle bag, and, oh, for feck's sake, the white, sateen pajamas.

That afternoon, Kavi and Jorge come by with chocolate, balloons, and a large, black and white teddy bear. "To keep you company when we can't be here," Kavi says. I love it: it's cheesy but cute and brings a silly smile to my face. Jorge's also brought a chess set. I'm terrible at chess, but Kavi says he'll help me, so I think I've got a fair shot at winning. Jorge, as it turns out, is rather good and takes the game seriously, which means that there are long, endless pauses while he considers his next move. At first, I try to maintain a respectful silence, so he can concentrate, but I soon give in to the urge to chatter. I tell them about my conversation with Emlyn that morning and how he's determined that I should move. "Which," I huff, "is just totally ridiculous, because if Emlyn were thinking like an *agent*, he'd see that this is a *golden* opportunity to draw Ratko out! I mean, as I told Emlyn, they let me go for a reason, and we need to figure out what that is. Why let me go, once I'd seen their faces? It doesn't make sense." I'm feeling much braver, now that I'm flanked by Kavi and Jorge, with Mr. Millefeuille at the foot of the bed. "I don't want to move. I like my linoleum."

I'm nibbling on a nail and sense rather than see Jorge and Kavi exchange a look. "What?" I demand, glancing up. "Do you think I should move into a safe house too? What if it's outside of London, have you thought of that? How will we–" I cut myself off. I'm not ready to go there, when I haven't even admitted it to myself.

Kavi gives the slightest of nods, and Jorge, a faint smile. Some message has passed between them, and I'm frustrated because I can't work out what it is. That, and my pain meds are wearing off. "You do, don't you? You agree with Emlyn that I should be packed away in cotton wool while the big, strong men save the day. Well, I'm an agent too. OK, not officially, but that's beside the point. I mean: I'm sure there are cameras we could put up, and we've already got the monitor, and if I carry a can of pepper spray with me or something, then." I stop, floundering. I don't know why I'm making such a fuss. Yes, Fitzrovia is nice, but my flat is pretty rank. I can't explain; I just feel as if everything has swirled out of my control over the past seven weeks and I need to make a stand.

"*Querida*," Jorge replies mildly, "don't fuss. We'll sort it out together. Checkmate."

I look at the board and try to move a piece. "Eh, eh, eh," Jorge shakes his head. "Bishops can only move diagonally."

I look again. If my king moves... No. Well, how about... No. I stare up at Kavi accusingly. "You were supposed to be helping me!" I hiss.

He bites his bottom lip, trying not to smile. "Maela," he begins. I raise my eyebrows. "I'm terrible at chess," he finishes. At that, Jorge throws back his head, laughing. Kavi soon joins in, a deep, resonant chuckle that feels like sunshine and spice washing over me.

"Not fair," I protest. "Did you know he was useless?" I ask, turning to Jorge, whose cheeks are flushed a warm bronze.

He's laughing too hard to respond, just nods his head. "Set up!" I cry dramatically. "Just for that, I'm not sharing any of my chocolates."

"Ah now, *ladki*, that's just mean. I did try. It's just that I really am terrible. One chocolate. One. Come on, have a heart." Kavi puts on a mournful face, but his eyes are dancing at me, and I melt.

"Fine," I sigh, reaching for the box. "As a consolation prize. Milk or dark?"

"Milk, please." He waits patiently, like a little puppy dog, as I look the selection over.

I pick out what I hope is a strawberry cream – I'm nice, but I'm not that nice, and fruit-flavored chocolate is just wrong – and hold it up. I'm expecting him to reach out a hand, but he leans forward and, looking up at me, closes his mouth around the chocolate. For a moment, the tips of my fingers are between his warm lips and on his tongue, then he slowly draws back, swallowing. I can't breathe, just stare at him, transfixed.

There's a whisper of sound, and now Jorge's leaning forward, smiling. I look at him, my breath quickening, eyes wide. "And for the winner?" I know without asking that he prefers dark chocolate, so, wordlessly, I take a piece and hold it out. He bends over, taking it delicately between his teeth, just grazing my fingers, his hair falling forward onto my wrist, and I shiver.

I honestly don't know what's going to happen next, when there's a knock at the door, and Emlyn's strolling in. He seems to take in the situation at a glance, and his eyes darken to fathomless pools; but then his jaw sets, and he's asking: "Maela, feeling better?"

I'm still in a daze; there's a throbbing pulse between my legs and my nipples are no doubt pearled to kingdom come; somehow, I manage to squeak out a "Fine, fine! Uh, meet Mr. Millefeuille," gesturing to the teddy. Emlyn ignores it, his attention fixed on me and the way Kavi and Jorge have curved their bodies towards mine.

"Maela tells us you want her to move," Jorge remarks.

Emlyn shoots him a hard glance: "Yes." His voice is clipped, tight.

"We might have an idea about that," Kavi joins in, earning him the same cool appraisal from Emlyn.

They do? OK, this is weird. Why are they all being so calm when I feel like I could cut the tension with a knife? What's going on? Maybe my brain got joggled when Bojan was wailing on me, because the world seems to have tilted on its axis.

"And I've said, I like my linoleum, so that's that." All three of them turn to look at me. "What? It could come back into style. Anyway, Maela makes her own decisions, and she's decided she should stay in her flat, so we can figure out why Ratko let her go and what the bigger picture is." There's that sense of the world sliding on its axis again, and now the three of them are a team and I'm on the other side of the interview table.

Another knock at the door, and happily the nurse is coming in with my dinner, because I'm really not sure where the conversation would have gone from there. I can stand up for myself one on one, but one against three?

As the nurse is putting down the tray and the men are leaving, I hear Emlyn say, "We should have a talk. Pub?" Kavi and Jorge follow him out, and I'm left alone with the nurse. She wants to know if I need another pill, but right at that moment, I'm too surprised to feel anything. What is going on?

STARING AT THE STARS

Sunday, 28 October – Kailani

I wake up slowly with a slightly green Gemma curled up into me. She cracks a single, bleary eye at me, and I smile at her.

"Girl," she whispers, both eyes tightly closed again. "I'm so, so sorry. I'm an asshole."

I pat her head, saying cheerfully but quietly, "It's okay, Gemms. You didn't know it had tequila; he didn't know your reaction to tequila."

"I was supposed to stay with you," she replies sadly, eyes still tightly shut, and I poke her until she looks at me.

"We're good. Promise."

She tries to nod, but groans instead, and says, "I hate to have to ask you, but…"

"Orange juice and coffee?" I guess, and she smiles at me beatifically. As I leave, I hear her call out weakly, "Don't think I'm letting you off the hook with Sven from last night! I need deets, lady!" and I shout back, "I want to hear about Hook first!"

We spend the rest of the morning giggling and rehashing the entire night, watching bad movies, and eating hangover food. It's awesome, and a perfect way to spend a gloomy Sunday. The sky outside is a cold, dark grey that makes you crave hot chocolate and a fireplace, and we burrow together beneath this giant Sherpa blanket thing she had bought for us when we moved in. The fire is roaring, and we're about to begin another movie, when there is a tentative knock on the door.

All traces of Gemma's headache disappear as she sits up

sharply and pushes me behind her. Her entire body is tense, like a cheetah the moment before it breaks into a sprint, and she's shaking slightly but won't move.

"If it's someone bad," she says softly, "go out the back and run up to Lachy's. I'll do what I can..."

Her voice is a bit wobbly, but filled with determination, and I can tell she means every word. Throwing my arms around her, I give her a giant squeeze before moving past her with a smile.

"Gemms. I love you to infinity. And I don't *think* it's someone bad, but you let me know if you don't want him here and I'll tell him to leave."

She looks concerned, then blushes bright red, at first with pleasure, then with dawning embarrassment as she realizes what she's wearing, as I open the door and reveal Hook from last night standing there.

"Hey, uh, hey Kailani. I hope it's not a problem that I came by. I, uh, I remembered your address and wanted to make sure Gemma is feeling okay today. I don't have to come in. Just brought by some soup and stuff." He motions awkwardly with his hands towards a bag and small bouquet of flowers he's carrying, and then he rolls his eyes endearingly. "I feel like a fucking idiot, man. Or a stalker or something. I never do shit like this."

Grinning at him, I'm about to say something, when Gemma's sweet, somewhat hopeful voice chirps from behind me, "Hook? I mean, Ryan?"

He looks around me, over my shoulder, and smiles at her. "Hey, Pixie. I brought you by some stuff."

They both pause, looking googly-eyed at each other, and the longer it goes on the more I feel like a very big, very noticeable third wheel. I run a quick check on Hook, and all he's giving off are super hopeful, super embarrassed vibes, so I do a quick glance at Gemma, who gives me a not-so-subtle wink.

"Right!" I say in an oddly loud voice, "I'm going... I have

to... Christ. I'm just going to Lachy's so you two can have some privacy, right? Gemma, scream if you need me."

She flashes a huge, ridiculously happy smile at me, and I head up the hill to Lachy's, a bittersweet pang of jealousy washing over me. I'm so happy for Gemma – this guy is a good one, and obviously into her, and not afraid to show it, and I wonder for a moment what that would feel like.

It's not in the cards for you, kid, I have to remind myself firmly. *That's not for you.*

Frowning slightly, I knock on Lachy's door but don't see his truck out front and can't feel him at all. Taking him at his word, I unlock his house, shouting his name just in case he's there, and, when I don't get an answer, I go to his library and curl up on my chair. All I want in the world in this moment is to see Lachy, and I can't think of where he'd be in the middle of a Sunday. It's normally our time, his and mine. I wander over in the afternoon, leaving Gemma to her painting, and Lach and I go on a hike together or out on his little Boston Whaler. We sometimes run to the market together, getting ingredients to try a new recipe, or we hang in his studio and I watch him while he works, how he reveals the creatures hiding in plain blocks of wood. It's unofficially become a standing date, and while neither of us ever says anything about it, he's usually here opening the door for me, waiting as I walk up the hill from the smaller cabin.

Needing the comfort and warmth Lachy provides, I grab a shirt he has hanging on the back of his chair and wrap up in it, surrounding myself in the scent of smoke and pine, rubbing my cheek gently against the soft flannel. Glancing at the place where I last saw the photo of him and me, I notice it's gone and am filled with a vague sense of unease. Nothing else in the room has changed, and, looking at the clock, I realize I'm an hour or so earlier than normal, so I decide to listen to a little music and wait for him. I must fall asleep though, because what feels like hours later but is probably just like forty-five minutes or so, I wake up to the shrill ring of my phone.

"Hello?" I answer sleepily.

"Reed?" Maddox's deep voice startles me awake completely, and I sit up to attention as though he is in the room with me.

"Maddox?" I ask, completely confused.

I can hear him sigh through the phone, and listen, suddenly on edge.

"Reed. We need to talk," he begins firmly. "First, I want to apologize about last night. I know you didn't officially want any guards, but I was concerned about a team member being out alone, so I let Walker and the guys know I'd follow you, but from a distance."

Shoulders tense now, I hunch over, curling around the phone. "Mmhm..." I respond indistinctly, as he seems to be waiting for a reply.

"I saw that guy approach you several times, and each time get slightly more aggressive with you, and I was worried it was a play to make a move. Walker told me how he diffused the situation between you and Daniels, and it seemed to be the easiest way to handle things without causing a fight."

"Wait, what?" I say in a strangled voice. "Walker, what?"

"When he and I were reviewing potential problems or security risks. He detailed how Daniels was harassing you, and how broadcasting that you were potentially in a... non-professional... relationship... seemed to dial down the situation. Of course it was a cover, but a good one."

"He... he did?" I ask, voice quiet.

"It's not a problem, Reed," Maddox hurries to reassure me. "It was the smart play. As long as you were both on board with it, and recognized that it was obviously a move specifically to throw Daniels off, it's not an issue. Having said that, you and I hadn't discussed a cover in a similar fashion to you and Walker, and I made that decision without your consent."

I open my mouth to respond but end up just gaping like a fish. *... The FUCK?* I think, completely blindsided.

"Reed?" Maddox's careful voice sounds slightly concerned. "You there? Did I lose you?"

"Walker..." I begin, then restart as he sighs again. *"Smith,"* I snap out. "We didn't *need* a cover story because *you weren't supposed to be there* last night. It wasn't *work*! You can't dictate how I spend my time off!"

His voice is annoyed now as he answers me. "Reed. That guy posed a security threat, and with everything going on with the British team and the risks..."

"The fuck he did!" I talk over the top of Maddox's mumbled explanation. "He didn't pose any more security threat to me than he did to any of the 200 other girls in the club last night. That's how drunken assholes *behave*. Women literally have to deal with that shit every day... what gives you the right to..."

"You are my subordinate on this task force, Reed," he snaps back, anger clear in his words. "It is literally my job description to keep you safe. There is an active and credible threat, and that walking piece of diseased meat was grabbing at you like you were a fucking Christmas present! I should have pounded his fucking face in!" By the end of his sentence he's practically shouting, and I can hear him breathing heavily, trying to calm himself down.

"That aside," he says tightly, voice tense with the effort to control his tone, "although I feel the cover worked, it's always best to be on the same page. I realize that you're not as comfortable with me as you are, say, with Tanaka or Shotridge. And in the future I will try to make sure that they are in the position to..."

"No one should be in that position," I reply with a leaden voice. "If we don't need to do that with anyone else on the team, we don't need it with me."

"We actively watch out for everyone," he begins, but I interrupt.

"Ah, so you'd kiss Donovan if some girl was coming on to him?"

There's a long silence before Maddox speaks again, and when he does, his words are quiet. "Fair point, Reed. We'll adjust our strategy in the future." He pauses, clearly trying to find the words, "Kailani, you know there can't be anything... we're – you, me, Donovan – this is a job... I hope... I mean, you knew it wasn't..."

I don't reply, and the line stays empty, a thousand words hovering in the air, unsaid, between us, until he breaks the quiet with a faux-jocular voice, sounding awful and fake, like a carnival barker.

"In any case, tomorrow we're bringing in three of the men from the benefit for questioning, and we'd like you to sit in. Donovan, Tanaka, and I will lead the interrogations, leaving you open to do your thing."

I nod, before remembering he can't see me. "Right. I'll be there."

Another pause, another silence. "Kai..." he says, voice hesitant, and I cut him off sharply.

"We good, Smith?" I ask. "We done here?"

"We are, but..."

"Okay!" I force out with fake cheerfulness. "Cool. I'll see you tomorrow!"

I hang up the phone and stare at it for a long moment before my eyes start to well up. Rubbing angrily at them, I mentally shout at myself. *Christ, Kai. You knew it wasn't a thing. You knew the Walker thing wasn't a thing either. And even if they wanted it, which they don't, it wouldn't work. You don't work.*

Jumping to my feet I head back to the cabin, which is suspiciously quiet, other than faint murmurs from Gemma's room. Getting dressed as fast as possible, I change to my workout clothes and head out for a run, leaving a note for Gemma. I know I'm not supposed to be alone, that it's a stupid choice, but I have to get some of this energy out.

Starting off on the dirt path past the homes, I push myself, running faster and faster until I can barely breath. Muscles screaming, I run until black spots appear before my eyes, and I collapse on the side of the road in the tree line. Because no matter how fast and how far I run, I can't escape myself and what I am, and with the silence of the forest pressing in around me, alone in the woods, I cry and cry until I'm empty.

The rest of the day is dull around the edges. By the time I get back to the cabin, Gemma and Hook are gone. Lachy sees me pass his house, and looks out with a concerned face, but doesn't stop me. I fill the afternoon with menial tasks – paying bills, writing grocery lists, laundry... and by the time I finish dinner, I'm exhausted. I decide to walk down to the Sound and sit for a while on the edge of the water on our small wooden dock. Night is settling in around me, the quiet of twilight dissolving into the soft hum of true darkness. This dock may be my favorite place in the world. Not very big at all – maybe six feet long at the most, and six feet wide – it's tremendously uncomfortable. The boards are coming loose, and nails stick up all over the place. I get a splinter *every* time I come here. It lists ever so slightly to one side, and I get the feeling that if I were to sit down too heavily the whole thing would upend into the water. But... when I bring a huge, heavy blanket, and a pillow, and lie down on it with the sky stretched above me, reaching for infinity, I can *feel* silence, pressing in around me.

The little dock stretches off a tiny, rocky strand on the shore. Heavy trees wrap around the little cove, and if Gemma isn't home, I can leave the lights of the cabin off and see nothing but stars for miles. The curve of land shelters us from other homes in the area, and it gives the illusion of complete privacy from the rest of the world. Lying back, staring at the stars, I relax into the peace of the evening, lulled by the lapping water and the quiet calling of the night's insects. Inexplicably I feel my eyes fill with tears again as the week catches up to me.

What am I doing? What am I doing?

Misery, bone deep, sinks into a hard pit in my stomach. My chest hurts it's so tight, and I close my eyes, trying to push through the unexpected crash of feeling. Just as the stars begin to swim overhead, blurred bursts of light swimming through my vision, I hear a quiet tread of footsteps from behind me and feel a familiar energy signature push its way into my consciousness. The tight knot in my chest eases inexplicably as Lachy makes his way to lie beside me, not saying anything, just resting near me. We stay that way for several long minutes, staring above us, not speaking. His scent swirls around me, smoky pine and coldness... it's hard to describe really. But Lachy smells like the forest and the lake and a campfire, all at the same time. And all of those together feel like *home* to me, whatever home is. It's the magic of Lachy, really.

I glance over at him through lowered eyes, and if he notices, he doesn't say anything. His head is lying on his two massive hands, and without thinking I roll over and curl against him, resting my head in the slight hollow where his shoulder meets his chest. Lachy doesn't move, just closes his eyes briefly, waiting for me to get comfortable. I bury my face in his chest, still suffocated with sadness, still tired and drained, and unwanted tears form again as I breathe in his comforting smell. The arm I'm lying on slowly curls down and around me, and I feel him shift as he gently kisses my head.

Almost hesitatingly, he rubs my back softly like you would a small child. A low, rumbling sound echoes quietly from his chest, and it's oddly soothing, somewhere between a cat's purr and a distant roll of thunder. Slowly, slowly, I feel the tension of the week drain from me, curled up against my friend, finally feeling safe after the onslaught of the past few days.

Eventually, after who knows how long, I pull away from Lachy and sit up, surreptitiously wiping my face. I've only fallen apart in front of Lachy three or four times, and each time I'm hideously embarrassed afterwards. I think he knows that and generally gives me a couple of days without having to see him, to let me pretend like nothing had ever happened. I feel him shift beside me, sitting up, and then making a move to stand, and all of a sudden I can't think of him leaving, of being without him again, alone on the dock in the dark. If he goes, I know with a certainty that he will take all of the quiet peace and comfort away with him, and I panic at the thought.

I reach out blindly and grab his hand. "Don't go. Please," I whisper into the darkness.

He startles slightly and sits back down. "I don't want to intrude, Suge," he responds softly. "I didn't mean to... I just saw you walk down as I was coming to drop off some wood for you, and I got concerned." He frowns slightly, shaking his head, and pats the wooden dock beside him. "I know you love this old thing, but I need to replace it. I don't think it's safe... I honestly don't know how it hasn't collapsed into the water yet."

I lean into his side, our legs dangling together off the edge of the dock, and don't reply. He tries again, clearly feeling like he's imposing.

"If you want to be down here alone, Suge, I can head back up. I was just worried about you... I didn't see you today." His voice is so quiet that the sound almost gets swallowed by the blackness around us. I wouldn't have heard him if I hadn't been right next to him.

I shake my head again, staring out over the still, dark water. "I'm sorry. I was early, and decided to go for a run while I was waiting, and lost track of time. Please stay, Lach. I feel... you... I just feel better when you're with me. All the time. Any time. I feel safe with you. You feel..." The darkness makes me bold, exposing raw truths that I didn't know existed until the words were already spoken. "You feel like home. In all the world, you're the only person who I can just sit and *be* with. I never worry if I'm enough with you. You *make* me feel like I'm enough, and I just..." I get lost in my words, the last few fading away on a breath, and I feel my face heat up as I blush furiously, thanking all the gods for the cover of night.

Lachy doesn't move, frozen beside me, and for a moment I'm terribly worried that I've somehow ruined everything. But then his fingers tighten around mine, and he lets out a deep breath. He moves as though to say something, pauses, and reaches up to rub his face instead, then winces slightly when his hand touches his cheek. I look at him sharply.

"What's wrong?"

"Nothing to worry about, Suge. This ol' dock of yours bit me, I think."

I lean in, concerned, and try to see his face in the dark. "Turn to me! Let me see what happened!"

He looks towards me obligingly, and I flip on the dim flashlight on my phone.

"Ooo. It did bite you. You've got a splinter in your cheek," I say, wincing slightly.

He reaches up to feel it and shrugs. "I'll get it later. It's alright."

I shake my head stubbornly. "No, I can get it now. I don't want it to get infected or anything." Trying to shift my body enough to get a good angle on his face, I lean out over the edge and am just able to brush the splinter out with my hand, when I wobble precariously and start to fall awkwardly kind of sideways towards the water. Lachy's arms shoot out quickly and wrap around me, pulling me up and into him. I end up straddling his lap with his arms wrapped around me.

"Whoa, Suge! No night time swimming!" he says with his

rumbling chuckle.

I laugh breathlessly, shaking slightly from the near miss, and look to Lachy to thank him. In this position, our faces are inches apart, and all humor falls from them as we stare at each other. I swallow audibly and take an unsteady breath. Lachy closes his eyes, looking almost pained, and rests his forehead gently against mine. His hands are soft on my hips, and I stare at the familiar lines of his face.

"You okay, Kai?" he says on a whisper, and I nod, which ends up rubbing our foreheads and noses lightly together. We sit like this for a moment, before he takes a deep breath, like he's steeling himself to do something, and I feel his arms tense as though he's about to move me. He pushes away from me slightly, and without thinking, I wrap my legs around his waist to keep him with me. His eyes flare wide as he meets mine in the darkness. With our gazes still locked, I reach a hand up and rest my fingers lightly on his lips. He doesn't move for what feels like forever, and there must be something in my eyes as I look at him, because as my fingers curl slowly back into my hand and away from his mouth, he lifts one of his hands and wraps it around mine, thumb opening my fingers back up, and he presses a long kiss into my palm.

Shivering slightly from the warmth of his mouth on me, I pull my hand back, and as he raises his head to look at me in a slow, almost drugged-like way, I lean forward and press my lips against his. This time there is no hesitation, and he leans into the kiss like he is trying to reach into my soul. One huge hand wraps around my waist and pulls every inch of me against him, and the other tangles itself in my hair, pulling it slightly so my mouth opens for him. Fire races down my spine, and I feel lit up, like a comet in the darkness, flaring to life. The constant worry of the past few days falls away, and all that exists is Lachy, the dock, the water, and this moment. The night surrounds us and hides us from the rest of the world, and just for this moment, silent and secret, everything in me is at peace.

What feels like hours later, mouths swollen from kissing, we lie next to each other, the earlier promise of coolness solidifying into a sharp and biting wind. Lachy's warmth wraps around me, and he pulls me to him tightly as he tucks the blanket in around the two of us. Neither of us has spoken, as though a word could shatter the fragile *something* that was born in the darkness between us. In the distance, on the water, the bobbing light of a ship hypnotizes me, along with the gentle stroking of Lachy's hands. Eyes heavy, I give in to the warmth surrounding me and drift to sleep in the safety of Lachy's arms.

The next morning I wake up alone, tucked in my bed. I open my eyes slowly, a smile on my lips before my mind is fully alive. And there, resting on the pillow beside me, is a black leather bracelet, intricately woven, somehow dangerous and delicate at the same time. Attached to it is a small, hand-carved charm – a gleaming black wooden star in the center of a compass. And written in strong, slanted cursive, the message on the small piece of paper next to it reads, "*so you can always find your way home*".

POETIC JUSTICE

Monday, 29 October – Maela

I'm watching a repeat of some house-hunting program the next morning when there's a knock at the door, which opens a moment later. Warm, brown eyes smile at me out of a lightly freckled face framed by long, dark hair. She's got a broad brow, a button nose, and rosy cheeks over a square chin and looks to be about my age.

"Hello! I'm Amy, one of the orderlies," she says cheerfully as she comes in, pushing a trolley before her. "Care for a cup of tea?"

"Yes, please! Dash of milk, no sugar." I struggle to sit up in bed, wincing a little. I'm still really sore.

"Here, let me help." Amy comes over and presses a button somewhere, lifting the backrest, and leans over to plump up my pillows. "There you are. Better?"

I nod. "Thanks. Oh, is that shortbread?"

"Nothing but the best for our patients." She hands me a cup of tea and two packs of shortbread, winking. "So, Maela. How are you feeling today?"

"A bit sore, but better." I take a sip of tea and sigh; it's hot and strong and bracing. I can literally feel it putting hairs on my chest, so to speak. Not that I'd want any.

"You're going to be stiff for a while, I'm afraid. You took one hell of a beating."

I raise startled eyes. "You know about it?"

"I was here when they brought you in. Terrible, just terrible. You want to talk about it?"

I shake my head, concentrating on opening the pack of shortbread. "Not really. I'd rather try to forget about it."

"Yeah, I understand. The things I see sometimes." Amy looks off into the distance, as if remembering, then seems to recollect herself. "Well, if you ever need a sympathetic ear. It's not good to keep things bottled up. Although," she grins at me, "you seem to have a very nice pair already."

"Huh?" I pause, shortbread lifted halfway to my mouth.

"Your visitor this morning? Mr. Hot from the planet of Hotness? Tall, toned, handsome. Ring a bell?"

I color. Emlyn had come by this morning to check up on me before going to work. "He's a colleague. Nothing more."

"Uh huh." She sits down, lively as a wren. "Sooo, how did you two meet?"

"Honestly," I protest with a laugh, "he's a colleague. We work together. That's it."

"Well," she cocks her head at me, "if I were you, I'd snap him up before somebody else does, because, wow."

All of a sudden, the shortbread tastes like sand, and I need to take a big swig of tea to wash it down. Emlyn dating. Someone else. Is he back with Clarissa? I haven't seen her round Thames House for a while. But what was she calling him about, and why *wouldn't* he want to date her? She might be a personality vacuum, but she's also strikingly beautiful, sophisticated, and moneyed. So why not Clarissa, or someone like her, but with character? Like this irritatingly nice orderly with her stupid doe eyes and candy-apple cheeks. I can see the two of them, cooking a no-doubt gourmet meal together, cuddling up on a leather couch, taking long walks in a sun-dappled park, jetting off for holidays in the Maldives, and I feel a sharp burn in my chest.

"Yeah," I try to shrug, "well." I can't think of anything to say so take refuge in the second shortbread packet.

"Although," she continues, "he obviously thinks of you as more than a colleague. He got you a room here, and let me tell you they don't come cheap. Most of the patients have gold-plated health insurance and doctors on Harley Street."

"Probably work," I mumble, then realize I sound churlish.

Maybe Emlyn is paying for this. Is he? Would MI5 fork out on a private room in a private hospital for an employee? "It's nicer than the last hospital I was in."

"Yeah? Where was that? Oh, more tea?" She gets up to pour me another cup.

"St Cosmas. I wasn't a patient, though, just took part in a clinical trial." Oops. Should I have said that? It's not classified information, is it? I'm just so distracted – could Emlyn possibly *like* me?

"Oh, I know St Cosmas." She hands me the cup. "That was really good of you. Wish there were more people willing to help out. Well," she sighs, "I'd better get on. I'd rather stay and hear more about your 'colleague'," here she gives me a wry look and makes air quotes. "But Matron will be on my case if I don't finish my round on time."

"Nice chatting with you." I fall back into the pillows as she goes out the door, narrowly avoiding spilling tea on myself. Does Emlyn like me? That way? Does he? *Does* he?

I'm still puzzling things over when I turn out the lights that night. I know it's greedy, but I can't help hoping that Emlyn really does fancy me. Call me selfish, but I want him *and* Jorge *and* Kavi. My libido, it appears, runneth over. But how would that work out? I can't see any guy being thrilled to be part of a foursome. Would we set up a schedule: Emlyn, Monday and Tuesday; Jorge, Wednesday and Thursday; Kavi, Friday and Saturday; and Sunday for rest? Yeah, what man wouldn't go for *that*? I wrinkle my nose. Well, if I can't sort out my love life, I can still keep honing my skills. Ratko wanted to know how I knew what I knew? Danger be damned, I'm going to find out what *he* knows. He wanted to scare me? I'm going to scare *him*. He's going to be in a world of pain. He's going to regret ever messing with me. He's... lying on his back, groaning. Magda's straddling him. She's groaning too, snapping her hips rhythmically, circling, rising, grinding down on him, seeking release. They're close, and I don't feel a thing except annoyance. Jeez, get on with it! Finish up, so I can find out what you're planning and *destroy* you. As if on cue, Magda throws back her head and cries out, her body stiffening. The white, silk shirt she's wearing, already half undone, slips off her shoulders and down her back, and I can see she's got a tattoo between her shoulder blades. I'm rolling my eyes at the performance when I do a double take: can it possibly be? Ratko keeps thrusting into her as she straightens, shivering, and I'm trying to get a better look when she reaches down, leans forward, and slits his throat.

Suddenly, I'm back in my body. Holy. Fuck. I mean: holy, flying, fuck! Did that just happen? I'm so shocked I lie still for several seconds, trying to get my head around what I saw. Magda's just killed Ratko. She just... I've got to tell Emlyn. Quickly, I grab my phone and hit speed-dial. He sounds groggy when he answers, and I have a brief vision of him, warm and sleep-tousled, and I realize I've gotten him out of bed. But he comes awake sharply when he hears my news. I don't think he can believe it at first; like me, he's in shock, and he asks me if I'm sure and makes me go over what happened step by step. There's not much to tell: they had sex; she killed him. I don't know where they were; presumably not the penthouse, as she wanted to slum it. I can hear Emlyn getting dressed as we talk, and I know that he's heading back into the office, but I'm not sure what he can do. Maybe start searches of all Ratko's known haunts? Emlyn tells me he'll stop by tomorrow, and after he hangs up, I stare into the darkness, my mind whirling. Why? Why did Magda kill Ratko? And did I see the tattoo I thought I saw? Thoughts and suppositions skitter through my brain, but I have no answers. And then I remember Emlyn, and my heart clenches. How does he feel to know that the man who murdered his brother is dead? Is he relieved? Glad? Does he feel cheated? Is he reliving the moment he found Eadric? I worry for him and want to call again, but I know that I need to let him get on with the job. Sleep is a long time coming.

Emlyn looks tired when he comes in. It's clear he hasn't slept since I woke him up last night; he's got a light layer of stubble, and his suit is rumpled. At the same time, though, there's an indefinable easing of tension, as if a weight he's been carrying for a long time has now been put down.

"Well?" I've been trying to distract myself all morning with a new novel but am desperate to know what he's found.

He nods, leaning against the door jamb, then comes forward to take a seat. "Ratko, Bojan, and Vlado were discovered dead in a warehouse this morning. It was made to look like a gangland hit."

I blow out through my mouth. "Fuuuuck." I mean: I know I saw it, but all three, dead? At Magda's hand. "How're you feeling?"

He takes a moment to consider: "Satisfied, I think. There's a poetic justice in knowing that Ratko was killed the same way he killed my brother and so many others, and not just that but by a woman he trusted. Maybe I'm callous, but that last bit makes me happy."

"She didn't even let him have an orgasm."

He's startled into a bark of laughter. "Really? She *must* have been angry with him."

"Why, though? Why kill him and the others?"

"I think," Emlyn says slowly, "that he'd become a liability. By taking you, he overstepped his authority and challenged Magda's. It was a rash move, motivated by anger that his deal, whatever it was, went wrong, maybe also fear. This is a group that likes to operate in the shadows, using threats and intimidation to keep people in line. When they do call attention to themselves, it's deliberate, like the warehouse fire, meant to act as a distraction. Ratko was too hot-headed, too much the thug, useful for a while but easily replaced. Bojan and Vlado could presumably identify Magda, so she took them out too. You say you heard a woman's voice when you were held. I'm guessing that was Magda."

It makes sense. Magda struck me as an intelligent woman, coolly rational and in control. Whatever she did, she did it for a good reason. Ratko underestimated her, probably thought he was the one calling the shots and using sex to manipulate her, when really it was the other way around.

"So, what happens now? Will you be able to track down the other members of the gang?"

Emlyn nods again, a lock of hair sliding over his forehead. "Without Ratko and his henchmen to keep them in line, they'll scatter and should be easy enough to pick up. Someone will undoubtedly try to take his place – there's always one – but it will take time for a new boss to establish his authority. We should be able to dismantle the network, at least in England. It's unlikely the remaining members have any useful information, though, about the bigger picture."

I'm quiet for a moment. It's all happened so fast. After weeks of trying to take down Ratko, Magda's done the job for us.

"So, we now focus on Magda and Tennireef?"

"We now focus on Magda and Tennireef. Despite my personal feelings, Ratko was only useful to Babylon as a way into the Kronos leadership." He rolls his neck, trying to work some of the kinks out, and I look at him and feel a surge of tenderness. I'd like to press soft kisses to his temples, his brow, the little hollow at the base of his throat, his mouth.

"I suppose I should have another go with the sketch artist. My first attempt wasn't very successful."

"I'll set it up." He yawns, covering his mouth. "Sorry."

"Don't be. It's been a long night. Shall I ring the nurse for coffee?"

"You might. God knows I could use a treble espresso. If you're feeling generous, I'll take some toast too."

I make the call – private hospitals are awesome – then try to sit up. I'm feeling much better, but there's one sore area on my back, and Emlyn catches my grimace.

"Hold on. I'll give you a hand." He comes over, taking me gently by the shoulders to help me sit upright, and I just breathe him in. The limes are faint today; the clean and cool notes that are Emlyn coming to the fore. He's adjusting my pillows and raising the back-rest when he stiffens. I look questioningly at him and open my mouth, and he holds up a finger to his lips.

"Better?" His voice is matter-of-fact, but his face is set in grim lines.

"Uh, yeah, thanks." What's gotten into him?

"So, Maela," he says, changing tack, "I'm sure you'll be glad to know that the doctors say you can go home today."

"Really? I thought–" and he shakes his head. "That it would be a few more days. So, they think I'm healing pretty well, then?"

"Yes, they were worried at first, but now that the swelling's going down, it's clear that there's no serious damage. You'll be sore for a bit and need to take some anti-inflammatories, but you should be back to normal in a few weeks. So, I'll pick you up and take you back to your flat this afternoon. With Ratko dead, you don't need to worry about another assault."

I nod, bemused. "That's great. Give me time to shower and get a prescription from the doctor, and I'll be ready."

There's a knock at the door, and a nurse pops her head round the corner. "Hello! Coffee and toast!"

"Ah, thank you, nurse. Right on time."

"You're welcome. So, anything else I can get for you?"

I shake my head. "No, we're good." I wait until she leaves

the room before saying to Emlyn, "You going back to the office, then? More paperwork?"

"Reams and reams. Everything needs to be filled out in triplicate. But I should be done in a couple of hours. That give you enough time?"

"Yeah, thanks." I'm running out of innocuous things to say. Emlyn clearly doesn't want to discuss the case further, and now that I need it, my usual propensity to babble has deserted me. I try again. "Do you think, on the way to my flat, we could stock up on some groceries? Milk, bread, eggs, pasta, chocolate…"

Emlyn's eyes gleam as if in approval. "Of course. And wine. We wouldn't want to forget that. Well, I'm off." He stands up, tossing back the last of his coffee. "See you in a couple of hours."

"Bye-ee!" When he leaves, I turn up the TV and decide to take a nice, long shower to pass the time. Does he think the room's been bugged?

I'm surprised to see Jorge and Kavi with Emlyn that afternoon. Shouldn't they be at work? I know that they've been putting in extra hours, to make up for the time they've been spending with me, but at this rate, they're going to lose their jobs. I don't say anything, though, just grab Mr. Millefeuille and the balloons and follow them out the door. Emlyn's picked up my duffle bag.

In the car, I'm bursting with questions, but Emlyn just says, "We'll discuss everything when we've got you settled in." I pass the time staring out the window, watching the scenery flash past. It's only when we pass Buckingham Palace that I realize we're going in the opposite direction to my flat.

"Uh, Emlyn? We're going the wrong way."

"No, we're not. We're going to a safe house."

"But," I sputter. "I thought you said... What about all my things?"

"Were moved this morning. I'll explain everything when we get there."

Wordlessly, I turn to Jorge, who gives my hand a squeeze. "It's all sorted, *querida*. Don't worry." I open and close my mouth, then turn back to staring out of the window.

Soon, we're pulling up outside a gorgeous white-stone townhouse on a quiet residential street in Chelsea. There's a wrought-iron fence edging the pavement, and square pillars frame a sedate blue door. I look up. There are one, two, three, four stories, a balcony with a balustrade and twiddly bits over the windows on the second – no, first – floor, consoles under the square windows on the floors above, and a cornice running under the roof.

"This," I say in a strangled voice, "*this* is the safe house?"

"Home sweet home," Emlyn replies, turning off the car.

"Are you *kidding* me?" My eyes are on stalks.

"Don't dawdle. Come on inside, and I'll give you the tour." He opens the door and gets out, looking at me expectantly. Kavi joins him, hands in his jeans, a faint smile on his face.

I haven't moved. "There's *no way* that this is an MI5 safe house. I've seen the films. Witnesses are usually placed in a dingy motel somewhere, right before they're murdered by the bad guys before they can testify."

"It isn't," Emlyn says. "It belongs to my parents. But it's roomy and central. They're not using it, so they said I could."

Jorge squeezes my hand again, looking at me reassuringly. "Come on, Maela. We'll explain inside."

I shake my head but follow him out and to the front door, which Emlyn opens. "Ladies first." I get a few steps inside before I have to stop, mouth falling open. There's a foyer, a foyer, for god's sake. Not a tiddly little hallway but a foyer with a marble floor patterned in black and white checkers, pale-grey walls, and a chandelier under which a table with a delicate flower arrangement has been artfully placed. To my left, a broad, balustraded staircase sweeps gracefully up; to my right are two doorways surmounted by pediments, and, at the end of the foyer, another two doors. The whole space is filled with light.

"I can't stay here," I whisper. "I'll break something."

Emlyn gives me a little push. "Get a move on, Driscoll."

I stand awkwardly by the table as the others file in behind me.

"Right," says Emlyn, "drawing room, library, conservatory, and kitchen," pointing to doors one, two, three, and four. "On the lower ground-floor: wine cellar, store rooms, bedroom and bathroom for the nanny; salon and private terrace on the first floor; master bedroom and bathroom on the second floor, two bedrooms and a bathroom on the third floor, bedroom, bathroom, and lounge on the fourth floor; garden and roof terrace on the top. Maela, I thought you might like the master bedroom."

My head's spinning. A salon? Who has a salon? "Um, Emlyn? Isn't this a little big? I'd be fine in a studio flat, really."

He shakes his head: "That won't do. So, shall I show you the master bedroom?"

"How about the nanny's room? That sounds more my speed."

"Can't. It's taken."

"Taken? By who?"

"Whom," Emlyn corrects me, eyes twinkling. "Why don't we go sit down in the conservatory, and I'll explain all."

Bemused, I follow him dutifully to a lovely, glass-sheathed room at the back. Greenery is twining up the walls from glazed pots placed at intervals along the biscuit-colored marble floor. There's a polished wooden dining table and striped, upholstered chairs in the center.

"Ooh," I breathe. I'm afraid to sit down, but Emlyn quirks an eyebrow at me, so I perch gingerly on the nearest chair.

Kavi and Jorge take a seat on either side, and Emlyn lounges gracefully opposite. I wait, wondering, scarcely daring to breathe. Why have Emlyn's parents given me the use of their townhouse? Who am I sharing it with? And the rent – holy hell, the rent! There's no way I could afford even a cupboard here.

"So, Maela," Emlyn smiles at me. "Welcome to your new home. Don't worry: the fee for early termination of the lease on your old flat has been paid off, and, as I said, all of your things have been brought here. I know you wanted to stay in your old place, but I'm afraid that I discovered something this morning that's made that impossible, even with Ratko out of the picture."

I blink at him; I'm feeling a bit groggy from the painkillers, and things are moving way too fast to keep up. What I'd really like is a cup of tea and a lie-down, although not here. I might get something dirty. "You discovered something."

"Somebody put a bug in your room, by your bed. It wasn't particularly well-hidden, so whoever it was had to have done it quickly. Can you tell me who came into your room at the hospital?"

"My *room* was bugged? You're joking! Aren't you? Wha–" I shake my head. "OK, umm, all of you, the nurse, Amy..."

"Amy? Who's Amy?" Emlyn asks sharply.

"One of the orderlies. She brought me tea and shortbread yesterday. She was really nice, and she thought you–" I stop, coloring. "Uh, yeah, she mentioned she saw you yesterday morning and that she was there when I came in."

"Did she come near the bed?"

"Mm-hm, she adjusted the back-rest for me. You don't think she – but she was so nice!" I say plaintively. I can't believe it. She was so jolly and... and offered to be a sympathetic ear. She was prying for information, wasn't she, and I was too dim-witted to figure it out. Oh, Christ, what did I tell her?"

"I bet she was. What did you talk about?" Emlyn looks grim. I think back, remembering that she wanted to know how we'd met and mentioned how nice the hospital was and that I agreed and shared that the last one I'd been in was St Cosmas, for a clinical trial. I look down shamefacedly, and one ankle snakes around the chair leg.

Jorge leans over and rubs my arm. "Not your fault, *querida*." I glance up gratefully at him and then over to Emlyn, who's looking thoughtful. "So someone's still trying to find out about our association. At a guess I'd say it's Magda. She must be wondering how we found out about the Ratko's deal too, and now she knows we're going to be going after her. This could actually work in our favor. She'll be anxious, trying to work out how we found out about her and Ratko and more apt to make a mistake."

I let out a breath, and Kavi smiles encouragingly at me. OK. No harm no foul. And that's why I'm here, I guess, because Magda must have gotten my address from Ratko, and if she could have a hospital room bugged, then my flat wouldn't pose much of a problem. If Amy had shown up at my door, I'd probably have blithely let her in and offered a glass of wine and a good gossip.

Emlyn tells me I'll need to work with a sketch artist on Amy, too, while he speaks with the guard and canvasses the hospital staff. It's unlikely that she's actually employed there. She must have posed as a volunteer. I'm to take the next day off, to rest and recover, but on Thursday I'll be meeting his counterpart at MI6.

My head jerks up. "MI6! Like, James Bond MI6? One of your colleagues at the Babylon Project? The one who's been speaking with the Americans?"

"Seef Arend," Emlyn nods. "He handles research into the paranormal at MI6 and serves as the British liaison with foreign partners. The programs are small and highly classified but closely connected."

"Why now?" I wonder. "Why does he want to meet me

now? I mean, he's known about me, what, almost two months?"

"At first, with Ratko, we thought we were dealing with at most a European operation. While it's normal practice to share information on operatives, ongoing research, and new training methods with our American counterparts, it wasn't until the end of September that we realized he and Magda were part of something bigger, although it turned out that only she knew it. Even then, because of Eadric, Seef was happy for me to take the lead. Besides, you needed time to develop your ability. But you can enter and leave visions at will now, and with Ratko's murder, the situation has changed again. Magda's going to want to replace him. She's going to have to break cover, as it were, and she's clearly taken an interest in you. We knew that she must be fairly high up in Kronos, with direct access to Rhea, although their exact status is still unclear. But the tattoo clinches things. A figure-of-eight surrounded by a circle, yes?"

I nod: "It was only for a moment, and the lights were dim, but it looked awfully like a combination of the Kronos tattoos. I'm guessing it's an hourglass encircled by a snake eating its own tail, with a scythe underneath."

"That's what I think. We've seen the individual symbols on packets of drugs, on gang members, on some of their victims. All of them in combination would suggest that Magda is part of the leadership – perhaps second in command? There's still too much we don't know. As I said, things will be in a state of flux here, which provides us with an opportunity. We need to step up our efforts and coordinate more closely with the American team. We'll be concentrating on Magda; they'll be concentrating on Tennireef. I mentioned they have an empath? She's not only able to sense emotions, she can wield them as a weapon."

That sounds completely kick-ass to me, and for a moment I'm jealous. Then I remember what Jorge told me about his own experience growing up, and I wonder what this woman's abilities have demanded from her. I gaze back at Emlyn: "So we're going to be a transatlantic team now, all of us working together?"

"That's the plan. Between you and Kailani Reed, we may just have a chance of cracking Kronos open. It won't be easy, but we've got a shot."

"And will she and I be given a special rank, say, SPA, seeing as how we're key to the whole thing and all?"

Emlyn's forehead wrinkles in confusion, and he looks a little wary: "SPA?"

"Secret Psychic Agent. I'd like it printed on my business cards, please." I grin impishly at him, and he shakes his head. "And," I continue, "we'll need to discuss a better salary and benefits."

"Such as fine wine, champagne, chocolates, perhaps a weekly massage?" Emlyn's tone is dry, but his eyes are dancing. Jorge and Kavi are listening in with wide smiles on their faces.

I take a moment, pretending to think, then sigh: "OK. I'll do it. But only on those conditions. It *is* the work of a nation and *regnum defende* and all."

"And we'll be here for you, Maela," Kavi's deep voice rumbles.

"Literally," Jorge smiles, his hazel eyes warm. I cock my head at him: "Hmm?" He's got a look on his face I can't quite read.

"Meet your new housemates," Emlyn says. "I'm in the nanny's old room."

My head whips around so fast I can hear the muscles in my neck creak. "What!"

"It's a sensible solution. Here, we can keep an eye on you and watch out for any would-be intruders."

"We," I stutter. "Who's we?"

"Me, Jorge, and Kavi," Emlyn answers calmly. "It's all been arranged. We talked about it on Sunday, and that bug I found this morning made it imperative. You need their support; Seef and I need you. From the basement, I'll be able to hear anyone trying to break in, and Kavi and Jorge can help me if someone does."

"But I can't... I mean... Uh," I sputter. Live with Emlyn, Jorge, and Kavi? In the *same house*? *Together*? Part of me is squealing with delight at the thought of being around three such gorgeous men 24/7, while another part of me is horrified: I'm going to have to get showered and dressed every morning before breakfast, aren't I? Before *coffee*. And then I think about the implications and turn from Jorge to Kavi: "But what about your flats?"

Kavi shrugs: "We've given notice, and Emlyn says MI5 will take care of the expenses."

"It's alright, Maela," Jorge leans towards me, arms braced on the table. "We want to do this. We've been talking about it over the past couple of days, and Emlyn's right: it's a good solution."

They're giving up their *homes* for me? And what about Emlyn? Has he given up his flat too? This house doesn't have the feel of being lived in. Why are they doing this? I know we're friends, and I think we could be more than that, maybe – me and Jorge? me and Kavi? me and... well, one of them – but to give up their flats? I raise my eyes to Emlyn and give it one more go: "Emlyn, this house is lovely, but–"

"My parents volunteered it," Emlyn says softly. "When I told them you helped to catch Eadric's killer and needed a safe place."

I can't speak, can only swallow past the sudden lump in my throat, and nod. There's a moment of silence, and then Emlyn says, "Now, who wants a glass of champagne to toast our new home?" His eyes are sheened a little wetly, so I raise my hand, chirping "Me, me, me!" and am glad to see a smile break out on his face. We follow him next door to the kitchen, which is something out of a catalogue, and settle round a small table, while Emlyn masterfully opens the bottle and pours. I raise my glass, "cheers," and the others follow suit. The champagne is the nicest I've ever had, with touches of peaches, cream, and toasted almonds, and everybody seems to relax at the first sip. Good grief, I think to myself, what will my mother say when I tell her I've got three hunky male housemates? On second thought: bad idea. She'd be over like a shot, trying to matchmake and driving me mad by sharing baby photos. Like I need them to think of me as any more of a moppet than they already do. Good thing I have a cell, not a landline.

"So, Emlyn, what's Seef like? Will you two be training me together now?"

Emlyn pauses, considering: "Seef? He's ex-military. Dedicated, efficient, a good chap. And, yes, we'll be training you together. But not this week. I'll drop you off on Thursday, but then I've got to go to Thames House to give these two their induction." He nods towards Jorge and Kavi.

I choke, champagne going straight up my nose, and this time, I don't try to hide it. I'm too busy coughing. Kavi pounds me helpfully on the back, and Jorge shakes his head at Emlyn: "Told you we shouldn't spring it on her." Emlyn, the fiend, is grinning.

"What," I splutter, "did you just say?" It sounds like he said "induction", which would mean that Jorge and Kavi are now working for MI5, which is mental, because they already have jobs.

"I persuaded Kavi and Jorge to come work for MI5, or rather, the Babylon Project. It didn't escape my notice that your ability to meditate and far-see improved dramatically when Kavi started teaching you yoga. As soon as I can massage his security clearance, he's going to be working with other agents and setting up a wellness program – they've got one like it in Seattle."

Kavi stirs. "It was just a small amount for personal use."

"And," Emlyn continues, "Jorge, strong or not, is still an empath. I think he's more effective than he suspects, and he may be able to develop his ability. At the very least, he can help to read suspects when they're brought in for questioning, as well as keeping an eye on the emotional health of all of the agents. It's a stressful job, and he's a trained counsellor."

I take a sip of champagne, trying to corral all the thoughts ricocheting round my brain. So, the operation to infiltrate Kronos is moving into high gear; I'm now living in a palatial Chelsea town-house with three knicker-melting men; and, oh yes, we're all going to be working together. I take another sip. Said men are all looking terribly pleased with themselves. "OK," I say faintly. "That makes sense. Cheers." I raise my glass.

"It's a great opportunity," Jorge assures me. Kavi nods: "It is, Maela. We'll be able to help a lot of people and serve the public at the same time."

"And," I narrow my eyes at Emlyn, "you'll be able to help each other keep an eye out for me. Go with me to work, maybe? Take me home?"

He puts on his cherubic face. "I was merely thinking of the project. *Regnum defende*, you know."

"How convenient," I drawl.

He grins again, flashing his dimple at me. "Do you want to see your room before dinner?"

I know when I'm beaten, and I *do* want to see the room. It's lovely, of course, and my whole flat could fit inside it, or rather, inside it and the adjoining private bathroom. It's done up in shades of sky blue and silver, and the furniture is Louis XV, delicate and elegant. Emlyn's mother clearly had the last word on decoration. My exercise ball looks more than a little out of place. I clutch Mr. Millefeuille to my chest and stare.

"OK?" Emlyn asks, clearly at home in these surroundings. I just nod like a puppet; if I open my mouth, my tongue will fall out. "Right, we'll let you get settled in. Dinner in an hour? Kavi's cooking, and he's promised not to make it too spicy." He grins at Kavi, who smirks back at him, mouthing "lightweight". They all troop out of the room then, leaving me puzzled. Since when did they become such matey mates?

MONEY FOR NOTHING

Monday, 29 October – Kailani

The man across the table from me is heavyset and balding, in a slightly too-big, tailored suit, with a ridiculously long tie. His heavy cuffs stick out from the sleeves of his jacket, with thick, gold cufflinks clunking on the table. Guess money can't buy taste, I think, meeting his leering gaze and twisted, smirking lips. This is a man who isn't used to losing, who has won so often that he's created a false narrative for himself that he's untouchable, and his behavior in the interrogation room this morning reflects that. Hideo follows the guy's porcine stare and frowns.

"Mr. Bianchi. Answer the question please."

I can tell from the flex of Deo's jaw that he's reaching his limit. Bianchi has been nothing but trouble, ignoring questions, saying wildly inappropriate things, rolling his eyes, making gratuitous gestures – it's really quite remarkable how slime can be molded to so closely resemble a human being.

"Why don't the tits ask me?" He brays loudly, his version of a laugh, echoing through the small room.

Hideo slams his hands on the table, like a cop in an 80's movie. I have visions of him yelling, "I'm getting too old for this shit!" and fight laughter.

"Mr. Bianchi," Hideo snaps out. "At this point you're looking at charges for impeding an investigation. It's literally a 'yes' or 'no' question. I'd suggest answering it."

Bianchi leans back in his chair, gut straining against his shirt, face smug. "You can try, Tanaka, but my lawyer would have me out before you could file the paperwork on it."

He nods towards the thin, anxious man sitting beside him, sweat beading across his face. I've gotten nothing but smug, diseased confidence from Bianchi, but his lawyer, now, his lawyer is a different story. Swirls of anxiety, worry, the feeling of walking a tightrope, of being backed into a corner, all overlaid by the strong, screaming feeling of "help me, help me".

For the first time, I lean forward, tilting my head slightly, taking in the man before me. "Your lawyer?"

Bianchi twists his face. "You deaf?" He looks at the man, Johan Schaff, one of the city's preeminent legal minds, and laughs again. "I don't think so, doll."

Laughing, I exchange a look with Deo. "*Doll*," I say, under my breath in a funny voice. "Like a 1950's talkie, right? 'Hey doll, get the sandwiches, the boys and I are playin' cards.'"

Deo rolls his eyes slightly and says, "I assume you've got something, then?"

I nod, and a vague, almost uncomfortable sense of unease pushes out from Bianchi as he shifts slightly in his chair. I ignore him and address Schaff directly.

"So, Johan. We've gone ahead and placed your wife and children in protective custody. They've been assigned a permanent police detail, and you have the option for Witness Protection following the trial. We've picked up four..." pausing, I look at a message on my phone, then say, "my apologies, six of Mr. Bianchi's 'managers', three of whom are on the record already in exchange for shortened jail time. This is your chance, and your only chance."

Bianchi suddenly sits up, thrown off balance, and glares daggers at Schaff. He can't threaten Schaff in front of us, obviously, and his wattle of skin wobbles as he shakes with suppressed rage. A feeling of intense relief pours off Schaff, though his face, on the surface, doesn't change, and he pauses thoughtfully.

"I have a sister..." he begins.

"Sara? In Springton?"

He nods, a small widening of his eyes the only surprise he shows.

"She's safe. We contacted the local force there, and they've got her. Anyone else?"

Smiling for the first time, he shakes his head. "That's it. I assume I'm turning State's evidence?"

Bianchi erupts from beside him, face red and mottled, jumping to his feet. "The fuck you will, Joe!" he snaps out. "Lawyer–Client privilege, you tiny dicked fuck! And if you think I can't get to you or your family you're insane! I'll dig out your eyes if you try this shit."

Schaff smiles up at Bianchi, surprising me. "Sit *down*, Tony," he says firmly. "First, I'm bound not to disclose what has happened in the past, but I have a duty to report any future or probable harm to the police. Second, I can breach confidentiality if I discover you've used my services to commit a crime."

"You'll bury yourself if you bury me!" Bianchi grinds out, having completely lost the plot. "You'll lose your fucking license, be disbarred!"

Schaff shrugs elegantly, uncaring, relief evident on his face. "If I go witness protection, I won't be able to practice anyway, Tony."

Looking up at Deo and me, he sighs. "I'm ready to give a statement, provided I'm offered proof regarding the information about my family. And I'd like to discuss the terms of my compliance."

I'm about to reply when Bianchi flings himself towards Schaff, hands flexing white, and three officers burst into the room to subdue Bianchi. Schaff is remarkably unaffected and remains in his seat. Bianchi fights the guards slightly, then forces himself to calm down, looking at the officers who are wrestling him into cuffs.

"Who are these jerks?" he says mutinously.

"Ah. Yeah, we've been doing some house cleaning," I say, smiling, and for the first time, real worry creases his face.

As he's taken from the room, our lawyer comes in to talk with Schaff, and Deo and I excuse ourselves. We meet a tight-faced Smith in the hallway and walk to our de facto headquarters with him without speaking. As soon as the door is closed, he turns to us eagerly.

"Anything?" he asks, and I flop into a chair as Deo takes charge of the brief.

It's been a long day. We started early, the team meeting first to review the suspects that we'd decided to interview. I'd walked in to our morning meeting after having a stern talking to myself on the drive over. *I am a fully capable adult,* I'd said to myself, *able to separate my work and personal life. I am a professional. I don't date, in any case. The covers were good. Everything is fine. You are fine. You are a calm, collected, grown ass woman.*

All that went out the window when I swaggered into the meeting room and looked at the guys sitting around the table. God help me, and I go bright red if I think too hard on it, but I'd *high fived* Smith, who'd looked stunned as hell, and, and I mean, really, Jesus Christ, I'd *double gun pointed* at the rest, before sitting beside Hideo and Jonah. Deo gave me a strange look and had the good grace not to say anything, but Jonah started laughing and shaking his head, saying under his breath, "What the *fuuuuu...*", so I smacked him. All in all not my *most* effective and elegant way to begin the day, but oh well.

Between Jonah's investigations into the guests at the fundraisers and Walker's and my time checking people out in person, we'd come up with seven fairly solid suspected traffickers. We brought them in, one after the other, and have interviewed five of the seven suspects so far. Two cracked right away, but were small time – low-stakes drug sales to high-end buyers, frequenting escorts, etc. These were little kids playing big-kid games. The other two didn't even blink, just requested their lawyers be present and went home. But Bianchi, he was overly confident. He showed up *with* his lawyer, which was a pretty vital mistake as it turns out. Because not only did it give us an in on Bianchi, it gave me an idea for the others.

"Can we bring in someone with the suspects? Like from the start?" I interrupt Hideo without thinking, and he and Smith look at me surprised.

"What?" Smith replies, and I try to elaborate, though I'm tired and sluggish from the weekend as well as doing so many readings in one day.

"Bianchi's not going to crack. At least, I'd lay money that he won't. He's way too confident... he's convinced he's safe. And the second he gets booked, he'll make bail for sure. We should have someone on him the minute he walks. But his people aren't as confident, because Bianchi will sell them out to cover his ass. And he's threatened a lot of them, so they're emotionally more chaotic and read better, especially in his presence. I'm thinking we can cut down on our time with this if we let them bring someone with them. They'll feel more confident, like we're kowtowing to them, and confident people are careless people."

I look to Hideo, who nods approvingly. "Good idea, Kai. Good idea. We can work that." He pauses and looks at me carefully. "You okay? You can do two more?"

I shrug, barely a movement at all, and rest my chin in my hands, breaking my jaw with a yawn. "I'll get through it. But a break would be nice."

Donovan stands up from the table and stretches, then reaches a hand out to me. Everyone falls silent looking at his hand hovering in front of me, and I look up at him, surprised. Determination lines every inch of his face, even though his cheeks have a light blush on them, and he ignores Smith, who clears his throat once, as though to get Donovan's attention.

"Kai? Do you want to grab a coffee, or maybe something to eat, before the rest of the interviews? Or if you want to take a break in the tank, I can watch the door for you."

"I... uh..." I know I look gob-smacked, but I honestly have no idea how to reply, and he waits patiently in front of me, hand steady, giving me time to make up my mind. My own hand starts to float up of its own accord, acting separately from my brain, and I have just enough time to see a very masculine flare of satisfaction in his eyes before we're interrupted by Cruise entering the room. It's such an unusual thing – I don't think Cruise has *ever* come in – that we all jerk to attention.

"Hey team," he begins tiredly. "Sorry to interrupt. Schaff is giving some information as a 'good faith' gesture, and he let us know Bianchi has a small 'shipment' planned for this afternoon. We're going to intercept, obviously, but need some safe places for the women until things are straightened out. You work with Elizabeth Cole, correct? Any chance you can contact her on this?"

I nod and grab my phone to make a quick call, putting my phone on speaker.

"Cole." Her voice is cool and distracted on the other end of the phone, and I know she didn't look at the number before she answered.

"Elizabeth? You're on speaker."

Her voice warms immediately, and I can tell I have her attention. "Ah, Kailani. How can I be of assistance?"

"Everything okay?" I ask, and she laughs.

"Just busy busy. But only a few people have my personal cell number, so when it rings, I answer, no matter what I'm doing. Now, what can I do for you?"

"We have some credible intel that we're going to be acting on shortly, and it will result in the need for housing and possible medical care for some women."

Her voice hardens. "*Trafficked* women, I assume?"

I don't answer, letting the silence speak for me, and there's a long pause before she speaks.

"I'll have something in place. If you can give me an approximate number before arrival, I'd appreciate it. Kailani, is this tied to the work you're doing with the team?"

I can tell she's trying to be circumspect, given the topic. "No," I reply. "We initially thought it did, but it seems to be a side-ring, rather than a subordinate ring. They're too careless, too open, about it. This doesn't appear to have any ties whatsoever. Other than the fact that they're using the fundraisers as opportunities to make connections."

"I can't keep having them at my events, Kailani. They're putting people at risk. They're putting my organization at risk."

I nod, even though she can't see me. "I know."

"Can I have a list of the suspects in order to blackball them from future events?"

I look at Smith, who shakes his head thoughtfully, and replies, his deep voice reluctant, "Hello, Ms. Cole. Agent Smith speaking. I'm not comfortable at this point giving you any potential names. I'm sorry." She makes a brief sound of protest before he continues. "However, as criminal charges are public record, and we've already had reporters here regarding our latest suspect, being booked as we speak, I *can* let you know Anthony Bianchi is being charged with multiple crimes."

"I don't know an Anthony Bianchi," she says slowly. "He was at one of my events? As a guest?"

Smith flips through the paperwork in front of him. "No event that was specifically hosted by or solely for Gaia. Only more broad-based fundraisers, like the last one."

"Hmmm. Thank you for the information, Agent Smith. I'll make sure our Fundraising Staff knows anyone associated with Mr. Bianchi is stricken from future events. And our lower Seattle shelter will be prepped and ready to receive anyone who may need care. That will take a little work, as we're fairly full at the moment, so unless there is anything else, I'll get to it."

"Thank you for your help on this, Ms. Cole."

"Of course," she replies. "Oh! And, Kailani?"

"Yes?"

"Happy belated birthday. I've taken the liberty of getting your motorcycle detailed and tuned as a gift. If that's acceptable to you, the mechanic can come over immediately and do the work while it's there at the station."

My eyes widen in surprise. "Elizabeth, that's completely unnecessary!"

Her dry, amused voice comes over the line. "What have I told you about my people, Kai?"

"Well, thank you. Sincerely. That's an incredibly thoughtful gift."

"We'll talk later today. I'll send them over now, but I wanted your permission first."

And with that, she hangs up the phone.

GAME OF DEATH

Tuesday, 30 October – Kailani

The rest of Monday was a blur of sorts. I sat in on the remaining two interviews, neither quite as productive as Bianchi's, but all at least slightly helpful. By the end of the day, I was exhausted, though; and when I walked to the garage, before I was able to get on my bike, Hideo and Jonah were there, shaking their heads.

"Not today, Kai," Jonah said gently. "I'm going to give you a ride to the ferry, and Hideo is going to call your friend to pick you up on the other end. It's just not safe to drive."

I wanted to argue, but surprised both of us by giving him a hug instead, and then turned to hug Hideo as well. Gemma picked me up from the ferry, and I was asleep before we got home.

Waking up today is like wading through mud. My mind is just groggy, and I can tell I need a break but force myself to get up. Stumbling into the kitchen, I flip on the news as I start making breakfast for Gemms and me, and the lead story sends a jolt of electricity through me, zapping the fog from my brain.

"... Breaking news from this morning. Real-estate mogul and businessman Anthony Bianchi, famous in Seattle for the purchase and subsequent lawsuits over the Baker Business corridor along the waterfront, was killed in a drunk-driving accident last night. He was charged yesterday with crimes, including human trafficking, and was released on his own recognizance late yesterday evening. Bianchi was seen, by multiple sources, drinking heavily at the 18th Amendment in downtown Seattle. Security footage shows him waving off his driver after leaving the bar, and getting behind the wheel of his car by himself. Within minutes, Bianchi crashed at full speed into the median on the highway. It is assumed he died on impact. By the time police arrived on scene, the car had become engulfed in flames. Bianchi is survived by his wife and two sons. This is a developing story..."

Without thinking, I pick up the phone and call Smith. He answers on the first ring.

"Maddox..." I say distractedly, still watching the tv.

"Kai. You're watching the news, I assume?"

"Yeah."

"I want you in here as soon as possible. There's some shit going down with the British team, too. This is a mess. Can you get a ride? I can come pick you up. I don't want you taking public. Or being alone."

"I think Gemma can take me... I'll check. If not, I can have Hideo meet me on the other end of the ferry."

"I can come get you, Kailani."

"It's okay. I'll see you soon, Smith."

There's a long silence, and I can practically hear his frown over the phone, before he hangs up. Deciding to skip a full breakfast, I go to bounce on Gemma and bribe her with mochas and croissants to take me to work. Sneaking into her room, I fling myself on her bed, flopping on top of her, which is, to be fair, our usual way of waking each other. Except the body beneath the covers feels different, and I don't have time to register the fact before Hook's sleepy face looks out at me.

"AUGH!" I scream, which causes Gemma to rocket from the bed like a Tasmanian Devil, also screaming.

"Sorry! Sorry sorry!" I babble. Gemma calms down, looks around her, and collapses in laughter on her bed. Hook, to his credit, is smiling at me. "Ack! Jesus, Gemms. Sorry! Hook! Sorry!"

Gemma's still laughing, thank god, and says in a shaky

voice, "I forgot to sock the door. Or lock the door. Which would work better?"

I cover my eyes with one hand, waving the other wildly in front of me, trying not to trip. "When did Hook *get* here?" I ask plaintively.

"Well, when you fell asleep at 8:30 at night, kid. Relax, we're both dressed. I invited him over to watch some Great British Bake Off, and we fell asleep."

Removing my hand from my eyes, I look at her accusingly. "You *didn't*," I say, voice heavy with betrayal.

"Chill, KaiKai. He's never seen it. We're starting at the beginning."

Turning, I look at Hook suspiciously, who raises his hands in defense. "It's the truth. We're watching someone called Jasminder or something?"

"Hmmm. Gemms, I was going to ask for a ride into town... I had to leave my bike at the station last night."

"Sure, babe. No problem." She looks to Hook, and he nods. "We were headed into town in like, half an hour anyways? Oh, and Lachy's down with one of his headaches."

I frown and say, "I'll be ready in half an hour." Throwing on some clothes, I swing back to the kitchen and grab a bag, then raid our fridge and cupboards. When headaches hit Lachy, they really hit him, and I'm sure he's locked up in his room and not taking care of himself. I grab some stew I'd made a couple nights ago, some cookies, some fruit, and a loaf of bread I'd made on the weekend and run it up to his house, dropping it in his kitchen with a note.

As I leave, I glance at his "family" wall, a place where he has an assortment of photos of his adorable nieces and nephews, his sister and brother, and his parents. I'd only met them a few times, but Lachy changes out the photos every so often with new ones, and I've heard so many stories about them I feel like I know them. He'd grown up in a Walton kind of household, where they all still talk to each other weekly and text all the time. His parents know about me and Gemms and send us Christmas presents every year. It's a strange situation for someone who'd really never experienced a normal family, and it had taken me awhile to get used to it.

Noticing he'd put up a couple new ones, I take a second to look at them – the girls are both missing teeth and have pumpkin grins, and I can't help but smile back at them – when I see the missing photo from his office, here, on his family wall. For some reason it knocks the breath out of me. This wall in his house has been reserved for just his immediate family for as long as I've known him... not even cousins make it up. He looks at it all the time – I know he misses them daily. In addition to the one of me in his office, he's added a couple of Gemma and me baking, covered with flour, and of all three of us by the fire one night. Reaching out, I touch the frames lightly, before I hear Gemma calling me, and I leave.

Jonah and I are the first two to the conference room today, and he flashes his megawatt smile at me. I smile back helplessly – his energy is always so warm and happy it's like swimming in the ocean in Bora Bora. Perfection, really.

"So Kai," he says. "Halloween!"

I raise my eyebrows questioningly at him, and he waves tickets in front of me.

"What would you say to a late-night showing of Rocky Horror Picture Show? A TOAST! I know you're probably not down for a theatre experience... this one is a modified drive in. It's open specifically for Halloween. I mean, they do Christmas movies and stuff too... It's in the park and they have a huge blow-up screen and speakers. You just kind of find a patch of grass. I can pack a picnic? And we can be far enough away that you have space. But it's a fun time and fun movie, so you shouldn't get much bad juju or whatever..." Jonah's speaking faster than normal, his usual smooth, smoky tone edged with nervous energy.

I'm surprised, and touched actually, that he thought of the fact that a theatre might be hard for me and that he remembers what I'd said about happy gatherings. "Um... sure?"

He beams. "Cool. Should I pick you up or...? And do you have your own stuff?"

"I can just meet you there. It would be pointless for you to take the ferry over and back. And what stuff? I've never seen it."

His eyes widen, and his grin gets even bigger, if possible. "I'll meet you at the ferry, and holy shit, you're in for a surprise."

I mock-frown at him, and he starts laughing. "Jonah – what have I signed up for?"

"You'll have to wait and see!" he says, still laughing, as the others walk in.

"Wait and see what?" Donovan asks curiously.

"I'm taking Kai on a date to see Rocky Horror tomorrow night," Jonah responds casually, and Donovan's brow furrows as my eyes widen in surprise. I hadn't realized it was a date, exactly. More just friends hanging out. But I can't help but smile a little at the thought that he's packing a picnic dinner for us, and a swirl of happiness starts in my stomach. Deo's cool presence touches my mind, and I turn to smile at him, but it slips away at the serious look on his face, mirrored by the one on Smith's.

"It's a no-go, guys. I'm sorry." Smith couldn't sound less sorry if he tried, and I narrow my eyes at him. Breaking my usual rule, I drop my shields slightly, and the weird maelstrom of emotion coming off him causes me to slam them right back up. *Bad Kai,* I think. *Stop it.*

Jonah looks mutinous and says in a slightly bullish tone, "Smith, we agreed that it's fine if Kai is out in public as long as one of us is with her."

"As long as one of *us* is with her," Smith answers, motioning to himself, Donovan, and Hideo. Jonah's face darkens to a thundercloud, eyes narrowed, waves of anger pouring off him like a storm.

"What is that supposed to imply?" he asks quietly, voice heavy with an unspoken threat. It's a side of Jonah I'm not used to seeing, and I take careful note of how still his body has become. Smith's own gaze turns predatory, like a lion sizing up its potential prey, coiled and ready to spring, and when he speaks, it's with a lethal edge.

"It's not *implying* anything. It's flat out *saying* that as long as she's with one of us, we know she'll be protected."

He's on the ground before he finishes speaking. *Holy shit, holy shit, holy shit!* I think. Smith is staring up at Jonah with an expression of complete surprise. Hideo, Walker, and I hadn't even had time to move out of our seats, Jonah moved so quickly. He took down Smith before Smith had time to get his arms up, moving like an eagle attacking its prey. None of us move as Jonah stands over Smith, staring down at him, foot on his chest, eyes lit with repressed fury.

"Don't ever, and I mean *ever*, think that I would put Kai at risk by being unprepared, or unable to do my job." Smith opens his mouth to speak, but Jonah presses harder on his chest, and Smith falls silent. "I was top of my class at the Academy. I train extensively in my time off, and grew up learning how to protect myself. You look down at me like I'm the class clown, like I don't have value or a place on this team, but trust me when I say I have the skills to handle my business."

Smith nods once, and Jonah releases the pressure on his chest, holding out a hand to help him up. He pulls Smith to his feet, and then they do some sort of weird bro-hug with a closed-fist double tap, before Jonah comes back to sit by me, and everyone relaxes. Smith looks at Jonah apologetically and says, "Shotridge, I've had word from the British team that there have been some issues. I'd like to run through them, but I'm not comfortable with that open of an environment this soon to the abduction."

"Okay. Cool man. No prob." Jonah shrugs and smiles at me, the last few moments seemingly forgotten.

I will never understand men. Never.

"So what's happening with the Brits that's so pressing?" I ask curiously.

"Maela, their American," my lips quirk up at the way Smith identifies their Viewer, like her most important defining characteristic is that she's American, "was hospitalized after the attack, as you know. Somehow her room was bugged – they think a member of the hospital staff, because her room was under constant surveillance by their team. The ease with which they were able to access her, despite her medical records being locked and private, and that she was entered at the hospital under a false name, is a problem. The reach of Kronos, or what we suspect is Kronos, is becoming more and more worrisome. They have operatives in places they shouldn't, and we don't know how they're anticipating the moves."

Walker looks thoughtful. "Was there a choice of hospitals? Like, did she go in an ambulance, or did someone take her?"

"The police found her. Sent her in an ambulance for care."

"So possible weak points are the police, the ambulance drivers, orderlies, intake staff, nurses… Christ. It's a mess."

Smith nods and continues. "She also had a remote viewing of their main lead into Kronos getting his throat slit. And by main lead, I mean the guy who was confirmed to have taken her and tortured her for information."

"Not a possible trauma response?" Deo asks curiously.

Smith shakes his head. "No. Their team is pretty convinced it was a true viewing. A guy named Ratko was separated from his head by an as-of-yet unidentified woman named Magda."

"Does their American have a description of Magda?"

"No," says Smith. "She's apparently having trouble remembering her facial features once she's out of her view. Anyway, based on the bugging at the hospital and the murder, they've decided to have their entire team move into a safehouse together."

I start shaking my head immediately. "Not happening."

"Not required. Yet," Smith answers.

"Not happening, ever," I shoot back. "I wouldn't survive like that. You guys are too much already. I can't leave the island. It's my home. Lachy's there. Gemma's there."

"If there is a credible threat of danger, you're out there alone in the woods…"

"I'm fully capable, Smith. And Lachy's there."

He growls under his breath. "What the fuck even is a 'Lachy'? Has anyone even run a check on this guy?"

I open my mouth to protest, when Walker says, quite matter-of-factly, "Lachlainn Baird. Age 33. Mother Scottish, and I mean *Scottish*; Father from New Orleans. Two sisters, one brother. Went to school for chemical engineering, graduated from Stanford Magna Cum Laude. Attended MIT for graduate work in the same field."

"What the FUCK?" I almost yell, before Hideo talks over me.

"He moved to Vashon right after grad school. Developed a patent for storing highly unstable chemicals and medications. Made quite a lot of money. Retired from his field for some reason and did a journeyman apprenticeship in carpentry, which is what he does now. Very successfully too, I have to add. His work is requested in showrooms nationwide."

Smith's eyes narrow. "Chemical engineering? Is this a guy we have to watch?"

I fly to my feet, vibrating in anger. "No one," I spit out venomously, "and I mean *no one*, is to say a single bad word about Lach. He is above suspicion, and he is *not* part of this."

587

"Kailani," Walker begins soothingly, but I slam my hands down on the table.

"You will leave Lachy the *fuck alone!*" I'm shaking I'm so upset. "He's not part of this, and if you test me on this, I will be out that door before you can finish speaking. Lachy is my home, and *none* of you are welcome in my home."

There is silence around the table. I'm almost panting my breath is coming so fast, and I see tiny flashes of black spots at the edge of my vision, panic riding up on me like fire.

"Kai," Hideo says quietly, touching my hand lightly, but I shake him off and stare at Smith.

"Your word, Smith."

Smith looks at me for a long time, too long, and my nostrils flare with the effort of keeping the panic at bay.

"*Your word. Maddox.*"

He nods and says quietly, "Okay, Kailani. He's not part of this."

Still shaking, I sit down, trying to concentrate on the papers in front of me. Hideo sits beside me, pressing into me, but I move away from him, feeling a brief flare of hurt from him before it fades. Moving from him pushes me closer to Jonah, whose calm, soothing presence washes over me, smothering the panic and helping me ground myself.

"Okay," Walker says bracingly, clearly trying to get the attention off me, a small and surprising kindness that I'm grateful for, "Where are we with Bianchi?"

There's a flurry of papers being shuffled, of movement in preparation for the seemingly endless plotting and planning, the frantic feeling of always trying to catch up, always being a step behind, but I can't move. My body is vibrating from the tidal bore of anger from moments before, and the sudden and overwhelming knowledge that things have spiraled out of my control. Something about them looking into Lachy, into my very small slice of something private and separate from...from *this*...has shaken me to my core. I feel like my worlds are being forced together, little gossamer strands of webbing thickening and hardening into something stronger and more interconnected, against my will.

I have few things that are mine, few things that I can call my own. Even my emotions don't fully belong to me – they're constantly battered by the storms existing in other people, the lightning and thunder of others' crashing through my shields and cracking the walls around my heart and mind daily. But Lachy, and Gemma, the Island and the Sound, those are mine, totally and completely. My home and my safety. My self and my sanity. And I'm filled with sudden unease that the distance that seemed so great before now seems just on the other side of a thin veil. Worry swirls through me, a grey mist filling my lungs, and this time, when Deo reaches for my hand, hearing my breath catch or sensing my rising panic, I take his like a lifeline, gripping it in both of my own.

He turns to me, a question on his face, but, seeing my own expression, simply pulls me closer to him, so I'm pressed against his side at the table, and the bedrock that is *him* steadies me, as always. His peace and presence wrap around me, curling like a cat, warm and comforting, reminding me that he is here, that Hideo, too, is a constant. As Lachy and Gemma are my respite, Deo is my strength, shouldering me up, supporting me, buttressing me against the constant press of emotion from others. Hideo is where I can breathe, where, if even for a moment, I can borrow his oxygen to fill my own lungs. And he gives what he can, ceaselessly, unerringly, and without question.

I can tell when he feels my shoulders finally drop. His own lower at the same time, a release of tension I didn't know he was holding, and he traces small circles on the back of my hand with his thumb for a moment, before squeezing it tightly and letting it go. It's amazing how empty my hand feels without Hideo's in it, but he places a fresh cup of coffee into my open fingers with a small smile, and my lips curl up in return. The room drifts away from us for the space of a breath, for the blink of an eye, and it is just me, and just Deo, and I am reminded that that is enough. That I am safe here, with him, and that he won't let me be torn to pieces by the wolves in the dark.

Smith starts talking, pulling us out of the moment, and I scramble for my paperwork to follow along. Jonah pushes the correct papers surreptitiously into my view, and I turn to thank him, only to meet a wave of his sweetness, his sunlight and starshine, his eager happiness washing across my chaos with bright abandon. And, as always, I have to smile in return, because Jonah... Jonah just makes me *happy*. There's no room for anything else when I'm with Jonah. It's a Disneyland of emotion with him, all blazing color and the noise of laughter in his smile. He nudges me gently with his elbow, and I realize out of nowhere that, at some point without me noticing, my heart has cracked open a tiny, tiny amount, and Jonah has quietly slipped into its shadows.

There's a pause in Smith's briefing, and I look up, like a student caught passing notes in class, blushing slightly. Smith shakes his head and opens his mouth to speak when Walker interrupts, voice staccato with stuttering thought. Clearly he's unsure of what to say, but is trying to find the right words to stumble through.

"Kai..." he begins, then stops, and starts again. "We... I... we should have asked. Okay? We were just doing due diligence, but... *I'll* try to at least warn you next time. Or we'll... I don't know. We'll come to you first or something. Okay?" His tone holds an unspoken apology, a contrite look sitting uncomfortably on his normally taciturn face, his brow furrowed, and I nod in return.

"Okay, Walker."

"Noice." His dimples flash briefly in reply, and Smith sighs.

"Fine. No more digging, although I feel it was pertinent to your safety in this instance and won't apologize for it." He's stoic, as always, icy eyes surveying the table, before continuing in a low voice. "I acknowledge that we may have overstepped slightly, but Reed, you're out there, alone, and I need to know you're...that the members of this team are safe. You're...*all*...my responsibility. Can you at least give me that? I just need to know."

I jerk my head once in response, less a nod and more just an acknowledgement of his statement. His face falls, a glacial shift more than a collapse, and I cock my head, realizing that, for some reason, he really means what he said. *He* needs to know. Not Babylon, but *Smith* needed assurance that we are...that *I* am safe.

"Just *ask* next time, Maddox," I say quietly, "I'll give you what I can if you *ask*, but I don't like when people force their way in."

"Heard." Smith lets out a deep breath that I didn't even realize he was holding, and with it, some of the tension in the room drains away. "Okay, team. Let's look at Bianchi's contact list and see where there's any crossover..."

Life has always been a series of tightly packed boxes for me, of carefully delineated lines. The last two months have been earthquakes of emotion, creating canyons and chaos in me that weren't there before. All of my safety nets and separations are failing, coming apart at the seams, torn to pieces as the men surrounding me at the table have pushed and pulled their ways into my circle of... if not *friends*, then at least... people who have become important to me, doubling that list in the space of what feels like a few short weeks. It's overwhelming, and frightening, even paralyzing, but... maybe... maybe growth can come from this turbulence. Maybe opening my worlds, just a little, can make me stronger. Or safer. Or... *happier*. I would never have done it myself, would never have let anyone else in, but... The emotion in my throat is unfamiliar, a heart-fluttering, almost painful thing. It's barely there at all, a butterfly caught in my veins, but now that I've felt it, I can't ignore it. I can *sense* the boundaries of my country expanding to encompass the men around me, and as battered as I feel at the moment, a little candle of happiness flickers in my heart. A little, dancing light of unknown hope. It's enough to chase away the clouds in my mind, letting me focus on the tasks at hand. And the rest of the day we spend discussing the interviews from the previous day, the almost unbelievable coincidence of Bianchi's death, and the next move in what is fast becoming a game of death.

EPILOGUE

I am the one who watches in the shadows. The others underestimate me, think I'm frivolous as sea foam. But an inch of water can drown a man. My half-sister knows. She knows my dark nature, my need for vengeance, that I can slay as easily as I smile. One by one I made them pay, all those who had wronged me. But their blood called to my blood, and it boiled in my veins. I found I had a gift for death, great and small. They are the same, you know? The choice. The chase. Stalking and circling, coming ever closer and pulling away. Coaxing. Yearning. Enticing. Intoxicating. The exquisite anticipation that leaves you trembling and weak yet vibrantly alive. A building excitement, coiling outward from your center. And then, the triumph of completion and the peace of transcendence. I grew indiscriminate, and my hubris almost brought me down. She came and offered me a purpose.

She thinks to rule, to command me as she does her offspring, offering power to one, wealth to another, an outlet for their perversions. For now, our goals are aligned. She is clever, my older sister. Clever and patient. Her scheme is working, and the golden age is at hand. The devouring eye to come which will remake the world anew. But she is jealous – she knows I can do what she cannot – a gift from our father. How ironic. She was the little princess, and I was the bastard child. Like severed seagrass, I drifted on the waves. But I have come home, and soon, with my sister's help, I will rise into my own. And who, then, will stop me? For all her brilliance, she can be curiously blind. Arrogance breeds complacency. She cannot see that the others are growing restless and will one day seek to take her crown. Will I let them? No. The crown must stay in the family. But, in the struggle, she may fall.

And I will shine.

ABOUT THE AUTHORS

Kate Fry is a midwestern-born Britophile who lives in a cottage in Scotland (or, as she and Elise like to say, "Jamie Fraserville") with her deliciously English husband and their adorably stripy kitten. She loves animals of all kinds, except maybe mosquitos and midges, which is good given that a flock of sheep recently charged through her yard. She has wistful aspirations of creating a beautiful garden – both flower and vegetable – turning her home into a stylishly chic haven complete with homemade wall hangings, learning how to do the tree pose in yoga, and getting her highlights done. She is lucky enough to be able to work from home and spends her weekends writing, reading romance and crime novels, and occasionally vacuuming.

Elise Fry is ALSO a Midwestern-born Anglo and Hibernophile, and currently lives in SoCal with her smokeshow of a husband, three amazing kiddos, crazy dog, placid tortoise, and surprisingly troublesome fish. She moves on a regular basis, and has been lucky enough to live all over the world, which is good, because she gets itchy feet staying in one place too long. Elise is a hot mess of chaos, because she loves creating things, but gets distracted easily, so is constantly surrounded by half-finished projects. She works from home, and spends her free time drinking coffee, going to the beach, reading, and trucking kids around to various activities.

Find us on Facebook at
www.facebook.com/elise.fry.author

Join our happy band of merrymakers in The Tower Room
www.facebook.com/groups/thetowerroom/

Look for us on Instagram at
https://www.instagram.com/elisefryauthor/

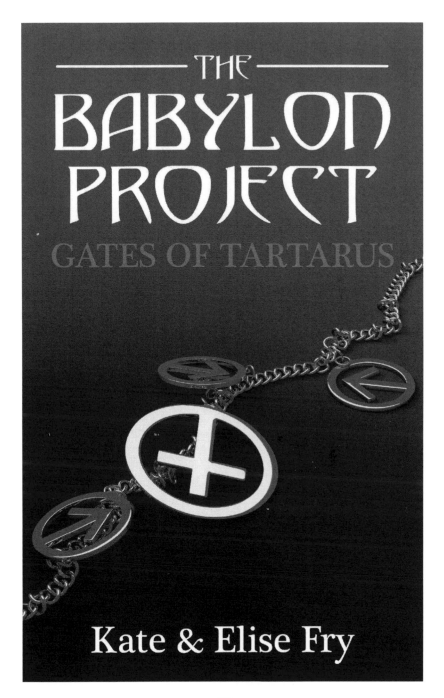

Printed in Great Britain
by Amazon

35970869R00342